ZACHARY GOLDMAN PRIVATE INVESTIGATOR

ZACHARY GOLDMAN PRIVATE INVESTIGATOR

CASES 8-10

P.D. WORKMAN

ISBN: 9781774681053 (Kindle)

ISBN: 9781774681060 (ePub)

ISBN: 9781774681428 (KDP Print)

ISBN: 9781774681435 (IS Paperback)

ISBN: 9781774681442 (IS Hardcover)

pdworkman

ALSO BY P.D. WORKMAN

Zachary Goldman Mysteries

She Wore Mourning

His Hands Were Quiet

She Was Dying Anyway

He Was Walking Alone

They Thought He was Safe

He Was Not There

Her Work Was Everything

She Told a Lie

He Never Forgot

She Was At Risk

Kenzie Kirsch Medical Thrillers

Unlawful Harvest

Doctored Death (Coming soon)

Dosed to Death (Coming soon)

Gentle Angel (Coming soon)

Reg Rawlins, Psychic Detective

What the Cat Knew

A Psychic with Catitude

A Catastrophic Theft

Night of Nine Tails

Telepathy of Gardens

Delusions of the Past

Fairy Blade Unmade

Web of Nightmares

A Whisker's Breadth

Skunk Man Swamp (Coming Soon)

Magic Ain't A Game (Coming Soon)

Without Foresight (Coming Soon)

Auntie Clem's Bakery

Gluten-Free Murder

Dairy-Free Death

Allergen-Free Assignation

Witch-Free Halloween (Halloween Short)

Dog-Free Dinner (Christmas Short)

Stirring Up Murder

Brewing Death

Coup de Glace

Sour Cherry Turnover

Apple-achian Treasure

Vegan Baked Alaska

Muffins Masks Murder

Tai Chi and Chai Tea

Santa Shortbread

Cold as Ice Cream

Changing Fortune Cookies (Coming soon)

Hot on the Trail Mix (Coming soon)

Recipes from Auntie Clem's Bakery

AND MORE AT PDWORKMAN.COM

SHE TOLD A LIE

ZACHARY GOLDMAN MYSTERIES #8

God bless the rescuers,
even when they are doomed to fail.

1

Zachary tried to stay in the zone he was in, just on the border between sleeping and waking, for as long as he could. He felt warm and safe and at peace, and it was such a good feeling he wanted to remain there as long as he could before the anxieties of consciousness started pouring in.

The warm body alongside his shifted and Zachary snuggled in, trying not to leave the cozy pocket of blankets he was in.

Kenzie murmured something that ended in 'some space' and wriggled away from him again. Zachary let her go. She needed her sleep, and if he smothered her, she wouldn't be quick to invite him back.

Kenzie. He was back together with Kenzie and he had stayed the night at her house. It was the first time he'd gone there instead of her joining him in his apartment, which was currently not safe for them to sleep at because the police had busted the door in. It would have to be fixed before he could sleep there.

Kenzie lived in a little house that was a hundred times better than Zachary's apartment, which wasn't difficult since he had started from scratch after the fire that burned down his last apartment. While he was earning more as a private investigator than he ever had before, thanks to a few high profile murder cases, he wasn't going to sink a lot of money into the apartment until he had built up a strong enough reserve to get him through several months of low income.

Zachary had been surprised by some of the high-priced items he had seen around Kenzie's home the night before. He supposed he shouldn't have been surprised, given the cherry-red convertible she drove, but he'd always assumed she was saddled with significant debts from medical school and that she would not be able to afford luxuries.

Maybe that was the reason that she had never invited him into her territory before. She didn't want him to see the huge gap in their financial statuses.

Once Zachary's brain started working, reviewing the night before and considering Kenzie's circumstances as compared to his, he couldn't shut it back off and return to that comfortable, happy place he had been just before waking. His brain was grinding away, assessing how worried he should be. Did any of it change their relationship? Did it mean that Kenzie looked down on him? Considered him inferior? She had never treated him that way, but did she think it, deep down inside?

Once he left her house, would he ever be invited back? He had only been there under exceptional circumstances and, while he hoped that it was a sign that Kenzie was willing to reconcile and work on their relationship again—as long as he was—he was afraid that it might just have been one moment of weakness. One that she would regret when she woke up and had a chance to reconsider.

With his brain cranking away at the problem and finding new things to worry about, Zachary couldn't stay in bed. He shifted around a few times, trying to find a position that was comfortable enough that he would just drift back to sleep, but he knew that it was impossible. His body was restless and would not return to sleep again so easily.

He slid out of the bed and squinted, trying to remember the layout of the room and any obstacles. The sky was just starting to lighten, forcing a little gray light around the edges of Kenzie's blinds and curtains. Enough to see dark shapes around him, but not enough to be confident he wouldn't trip over something. Zachary felt for the remainder of his clothes and clutched them to him as he cautiously made his way to the bedroom door and out into the hallway.

He shut the door silently behind him so that he wouldn't wake Kenzie up. There was an orange glow emanating from the bathroom, so he found his way there without knocking over any priceless decor. He shut the door and turned on the main light. It was blinding after the night-light. Zachary squeezed his eyes shut and waited for them to adjust to the light that penetrated his eyelids, and then gradually opened them to look around.

Everything was clean and tidy and smelled fresh. Definitely a woman's domain rather than a bachelor pad like Zachary's. He needed to upgrade if he expected her to spend any time at his apartment. He'd used her ensuite the night before rather than the main bath and, even though it was more cluttered with her makeup and hair and bath products, it was also cleaner and brighter than Zachary's apartment bathroom.

He spent a couple of minutes with his morning routine, splashing water on his face and running a comb over his dark buzz-cut before making his way to the living room, where he'd left his overnight bag when he and Kenzie had adjourned for the night. He pulled out his laptop and set it on the couch while it booted up, wandering into the kitchen and sorting out her single-cup coffee dispenser to make himself breakfast.

2

It was some time before he heard Kenzie stirring in the bedroom and, eventually, she made her way out to the living room. She had an oriental-style dressing gown wrapped around her. She rubbed her eyes, hair mussed from sleep.

Kenzie yawned. "Good morning."

"Hi." Zachary gave her a smile that he hoped expressed the warmth and gratitude he felt toward her for letting him back into her life, even if it was only for one night. "How was your sleep?"

"Good." Kenzie covered another yawn. "How about you? Did you actually get any sleep?"

"I slept great." Zachary wasn't lying. He didn't usually sleep well away from home. For that matter, he didn't sleep that well at home either. But after facing off with Lauren's killer and dealing with the police, he had been exhausted, and the comfort he had found in Kenzie's arms and the luxurious sheets in her bed had quickly lulled him to sleep. There was a slight dip in the middle of her mattress, testifying to the fact that she normally slept alone, and that had made it natural for them to gravitate toward each other during the night. It had been reassuring to have someone else in bed with him after what seemed like an eon of lonely nights.

It was the best night's sleep he'd had in a long time.

"You couldn't have slept for more than three or four hours," Kenzie countered.

"Yes… but it was still a really good sleep."

"Well, good." She bent down to kiss him on the forehead.

Zachary felt a rush of warmth and goosebumps at the same time. She didn't appear to regret having allowed him to stay over. "Do you want coffee? I figured out the machine."

"Turn it on when you hear me get out of the shower. That should be about right."

"Do you want anything else? Bread in the toaster?"

"The full breakfast treatment? I could get used to this. Yes, a couple of slices of toast would be nice."

Zachary nodded. "Coffee and toast it is," he agreed.

He saw her speculative look, wondering whether he would actually remember or whether he would be distracted by something else.

"I'll do my best," Zachary promised. "But it better be a short shower, because if it's one of those two-hour-long ones, I might forget."

"I have to get to work today, so it had better be a quick one."

He did manage to remember to start both the coffee and the toast when she got out of the shower, and even heard the toast pop and remembered to butter it while it was hot. He had it on the table for Kenzie when she walked in, buttoning up her blouse.

"Nice!" Kenzie approved.

"Do you want jam?"

"There's some marmalade in the fridge."

Zachary retrieved the jar and made a mental note that he should get marmalade the next time he was shopping for groceries. If that were her preferred condiment, then he should make an effort to have it for her when she came to his apartment. He tried to always get things for her when he was shopping because, as Bridget put it, he ate like a Neanderthal. Not one of those fad caveman diets, but like someone who had never learned how to cook even the simplest foods. Most of his food was either ready to eat or just needed to be microwaved for a couple of minutes.

Or he could order in. He could use a phone even if he couldn't use a stove.

"So, your big case is solved," Kenzie said. "What are your plans for the day?"

"I still need to report to the client and issue my bill. Then I've got a bunch of smaller projects I should catch up on, now that I'll have some more time. And I need to get my door fixed. I wouldn't want to impose on you for too long."

Kenzie spread her marmalade carefully to the edge of the toast. "It was nice last night. I'm glad you called."

Zachary's face got warm. All they had done was to talk and cuddle, but he had needed that so badly. He had been concerned that she would be disappointed things had gone no further, so he was reassured that she had enjoyed the quiet time together too. Their relationship had been badly derailed by the abuse Zachary had suffered at Archuro's hands, which had also brought up a lot of buried memories of his time in foster care. However much he wanted to be with Kenzie, he couldn't help his own visceral reaction when things got too intimate.

"Hey," Kenzie said softly, breaking into his thoughts. "Don't do that. Come back."

Zachary tried to refocus his attention on her, to keep himself anchored to the present and not the attack.

"Five things?" Kenzie suggested, prompting Zachary to use one of the exercises his therapist had given him to help him with dissociation.

Zachary took a slow breath. "I smell… the coffee. The toast." He breathed. "Your shampoo. The marmalade. I… don't know what else."

His own sweat. He should have showered and dressed before Kenzie got up. Greeted her smelling freshly-scrubbed instead of assaulting her with the rank odor of a homeless person.

Kenzie smiled. "Better?" She studied his face for any tells.

Zachary nodded. "Yeah. Sorry."

"It's okay. It's not your fault."

He still felt completely inadequate. He should be able to have a pleasant morning conversation with his girlfriend without dissociating or getting mired in flashbacks. It shouldn't be that hard.

"Are you going to have something to eat? There's enough bread for you to have toast too," Kenzie teased.

"No, not ready yet."

"Well, don't forget. You still need to get your weight back up."

Zachary nodded. "I'll have something in a while."

———

He still hadn't eaten when he left Kenzie's. She was on her way into work, and he didn't want her to feel like she had to let him stay there in her domain while she was gone so, by the time she was ready for work, he had repacked his overnight bag and was ready to leave as well. She didn't make any comment or offer him the house while she was gone.

"Well, good luck with your report to Lauren's sister today. I know that part of the job is never fun."

Zachary nodded. "Yeah. And then collecting on the bill. Sorry your sister was murdered, but could you please pay me now?" He rolled his eyes.

Kenzie shook her head. "At least I don't have to ask for payment when I give people autopsy results."

They paused outside the door. Zachary didn't know what to say to Kenzie or how to tell her goodbye.

"Call me later," Kenzie advised. "Let me know whether you got your door fixed or not."

Zachary exhaled, relieved. She wasn't regretting having invited him in. She would put up with him for another night if he needed her.

"Thanks, I will."

Kenzie armed the burglar alarm on the keypad next to the door and shut it. Zachary heard the bolt automatically slide into place.

"See you," Kenzie said breezily. She pulled him closer by his coat lapel and gave him a brief peck on the lips. "Have a good day."

Zachary nodded, his face flushing and a lump in his throat preventing him from saying anything. Kenzie opened the garage door. Zachary turned and walked down the sidewalk to his car. He tried hard not to be needy, not to turn around and watch as she backed the car out onto the street, checking to see whether she were still watching him and would give him one more wave before she left. But he couldn't help himself.

She waved in his direction and pulled onto the street.

———

Late in the afternoon, Zachary headed back to his apartment, hoping to find when he got there that the door had been repaired and he could feel safe there once more. Of course, if the door had been fixed, he would need another reason to go back to Kenzie's. Or he could invite her to join him and they could go back to their usual routines. Just because she had allowed him over to her house once, that didn't mean she would be comfortable with him being there all the time.

But he could see the splintered doorframe as he walked down the hall approaching his apartment. The building manager had promised to make it a priority, but it looked like whatever subcontractor he had called hadn't yet made it there. Zachary pushed the door open and looked around.

Nothing appeared to have been rifled or taken in his absence. Of course, he didn't have much of value. He'd taken all of his electronics with him and didn't exactly have jewelry or wads of cash lying around. Anyone desperate enough to rifle his drawers and steal his shirts probably needed them worse than he did.

Though he hadn't thought about the meds in the cabinet. There were a few things in there that might have some street value.

Zachary started to walk toward the bedroom, but stopped when he heard a noise. He froze and listened, trying to zero in on it. It was probably just a neighbor moving around. Or a pigeon landing on the ledge outside his window. They spooked him sometimes with the loud flapping of their wings when they took off.

He waited, ears pricked, for the sound to be repeated.

Could it have been a person? There in his apartment?

The last time he'd thought that someone was rifling his apartment and had called the police, it had been Bridget. She'd still had a key to the old apartment. She'd checked in on him at Christmas, knowing that it was a bad time for him, and had cleaned out his medicine cabinet to ensure that he didn't overdose.

It wouldn't be Bridget this time.

She didn't have a key to the new apartment, though he would have been happy to give her one if she had wanted it. Bridget was no longer part of his life and he needed to keep his distance from her, both to avoid getting slapped with a restraining order and because he was with Kenzie, and he needed to be fair to her. There was no going back to his ex-wife. She had a new partner and was pregnant. She didn't want anything to do with him.

There was another rustle. He was pretty sure it was someone in his bedroom. But it didn't sound like they were doing anything. Just moving quietly around.

Waiting for him?

He hated to call the police and have it be a false alarm. But he also didn't want to end up with a bullet in his chest because he walked in on a burglary in progress.

Unlike private investigators on TV, Zachary didn't carry a gun. He didn't even own one. With his history of depression and self-harm, it had always been too big a risk.

Zachary eased his phone out of his pocket, moving very slowly, trying to be completely silent. He wasn't sure what he was going to do when he got it out. If he called emergency, he would have to talk to them to let them know what was going on. They wouldn't be able to triangulate his signal to a single apartment.

Just as he looked down at the screen and moved his thumb over the unlock button, it gave a loud squeal and an alert popped up on the screen. Zachary jumped so badly that it flew out of his hand, and he scrambled to catch it before it hit the floor. He wasn't well-coordinated, and he just ended up hitting it in the air and shooting it farther away from him, to smack into the wall and then land on the floor.

3

He froze. His brain seized up.

He didn't know whether to turn around and run out the door or stay where he was and hope that the burglar hadn't heard him. He could dart across the room and pick up the phone. If he didn't, he had no way to communicate with the outside world and with the police in particular.

He could hear footsteps crossing the bedroom, turning into the hallway and coming toward him.

He swore under his breath, still not sure of the best course of action, then finally staggered across the room like a drunken penguin and snatched up the phone.

The alert was still showing on his screen—a message from Rhys Salter. With the screen lock engaged, it wouldn't show what the actual message was. He had been in too many situations where a suspect seeing his incoming messages could have been disastrous.

He wondered fleetingly what Rhys had said, and if it would be the last communication that ever passed between them. He spun around, trying to press his thumb over the unlock button.

How long would it be before the cops could get there?

Assuming he could even manage to call them.

The burglar strode out of the hallway.

4

Zachary nearly collapsed with relief.

The loose-limbed black teen looked at him and raised his eyebrows questioningly. He spread his hands out in a 'what's up?' gesture.

Zachary fell back onto the couch, putting his hand over his pounding heart.

"You scared the heck out of me, Rhys! How did you get here?"

Rhys seemed unperturbed. He pointed at the broken doorframe. Then he indicated a student bus pass that hung around his neck.

"You could have told me you were coming over here. I thought you were some serial killer."

Rhys raised his own phone and turned his phone screen toward Zachary.

Zachary couldn't see what was on Rhys's screen from that distance, but he looked down at his own phone. Rhys had messaged him. He finally managed to unlock it and tapped on the notification to bring up the message that Rhys had sent to him.

An animated gif of Charlie Brown knocking on the roof of Snoopy's dog house. Rhys's way of letting Zachary know that he was there at his apartment.

Zachary shook his head. "Sheesh. You gave me a turn. Come sit down."

Rhys complied, sitting in the easy chair. He pointed again to the broken door and lifted his eyebrows.

"I had… well, it's a long story. The police broke in."

Rhys gave a short laugh.

"I wasn't doing anything," Zachary told him. "I mean, they weren't breaking in because of something I did. There was a guy here… a murderer, and he was… well…" Zachary shrugged helplessly. "He was going to kill me."

Rhys settled back in the chair, folding his arms and giving a little lift of his chin. *Oh, is that all.*

Zachary chuckled. "I was glad the police came. I didn't even care that they broke the door. Except that I couldn't stay here last night."

Rhys made a kissing noise. Zachary's face got hot. He tried to appear casual. "Yes, I stayed with Kenzie."

Rhys nodded, his eyes dancing. Clearly worth it to have his door broken down if it meant Zachary got to spend the night at Kenzie's. Zachary suspected Rhys had a crush on Kenzie. He never failed to ask about her.

Rhys leaned forward again. The amusement left his eyes. He tapped his phone screen, looking for something. Rhys had come to the apartment for a reason. He clearly hadn't told Vera, his grandmother, that he was going to see Zachary, or she would have driven him rather than his taking the bus. If she approved of his going to Zachary's, which she probably didn't. She preferred for the two of them to meet at her house rather than anywhere they might be seen together. People might misunderstand their relationship.

Zachary moved down the couch, closer to Rhys, and leaned in. Rhys tapped a picture and turned the phone around for Zachary to see.

She was a pretty girl. A teen around Rhys's age, cute, dark-haired, smiling at something off-screen. She didn't look like she had been aware that her picture was being taken. There was no attempt to ham for the camera. Most of the phone pictures of teenagers Zachary saw posted on social media had them posing, making faces, or had some popular filter or photobooth alteration.

Zachary nodded. "Is this your girlfriend?" he asked, and then made the kissing sound that Rhys used to designate Kenzie.

Rhys shook his head, serious. His mouth turned down naturally. He always looked sad, and Zachary knew that, like he did, Rhys struggled with depression and his traumatic past. There had been too much violence in the

Salter family, and it had left its mark on Rhys. He rarely spoke more than a word or two and, even when communicating using his phone, usually avoided even written language, falling back on memes and gifs that the recipient had to interpret.

"What is it?" Zachary asked.

Rhys looked at his phone again. He tapped and swiped to find another picture, then turned it to Zachary again.

This time, the girl was smiling at the camera, her lips bright red. She hung on the arm of a tall, blond boy. He was a little older than she was. Maybe still a teenager, maybe twenty. He wasn't looking at her or the camera, but off to the side, eyebrows down like he was worried or suspicious about something.

"Is this her boyfriend?" Zachary asked, though he already knew the answer.

Rhys nodded. He turned the phone back around to look at the picture himself and, for a while, just sat there, quiet and unmoving, contemplating the picture.

"Did something happen to her?"

Rhys nodded. His dark eyes were full of sorrow. Zachary reached out and touched Rhys's shoulder.

"What is it? What happened?"

Rhys made a 'blowing up' movement with his fingers, flicking them all outward. At the same time, he puffed up his cheeks and blew the air out in a 'poof.'

Zachary searched Rhys's face, wishing he could read the interpretation there. The gesture had not been violent, so he didn't think it was an explosion. More like a puff of smoke. A magician. Now you see it, now you don't.

Zachary considered, biting his lip. "She disappeared?" he asked finally.

Rhys pointed at Zachary, nodding.

"And the boy?"

Rhys continued to nod.

"You think he had something to do with her disappearance?"

Rhys's eyes closed and he nodded again. Zachary could feel Rhys's pain and anxiety over her disappearance like it was centered in his own chest.

"How long has she been missing?"

Rhys held up four fingers, then five, then made a wobbling motion with his hand. *Four or five days, more or less.* Long past the 'I was just at a friend's house' period.

"Have you asked what happened to her? Do you know?"

Rhys's lips pressed together into a thin line and he gave a slight head shake, brows drawn down. Zachary had broken a cardinal rule of their communication system. Never ask more than one question at a time.

"Sorry. Do you know what happened to her?"

Rhys shook his head slowly. The slowness of it and the tension in his expression told Zachary that he didn't know for sure, but he had his ideas.

"Did you talk to her family?" He had to bite his tongue to keep from asking more follow-up questions. There was an urgency to their conversation. He wanted to move it along faster. But communications with Rhys could not be rushed.

Rhys shook his head.

"Have the police been called? Is she a missing person?"

Rhys gave a wide shrug.

Zachary was impatient, but he waited, analyzing their conversation and thinking about the pictures and about Rhys being there, waiting for him.

"You want me to look into it?"

Rhys smiled, nodding emphatically.

Zachary nodded and sat back, thinking about it. There was certainly no problem with his making some initial inquiries. Maybe her parents could tell him what had happened to her. Hopefully, there was an easy explanation for her disappearance. Maybe she had gone to visit a sick relative or her parents had put her into a better school. There were lots of reasons a teenager might be at school one day, and then not show up again.

"Okay, yeah. Can you give me her name and anything you have about her? Contact details?"

Rhys tapped away at his phone and, in a moment, Zachary had her name, phone number, and a couple of social network names in his messaging app.

Madison Miller.

"Got it. And can you send me those pictures?"

Rhys nodded and sent them over as well.

"Do you have others?"

Rhys was still. He considered the question. Zachary furrowed his brows.

"If you want me to find out about her, then I need whatever you've got."

Rhys shook his head. He pushed his phone into his jeans pocket.

Zachary looked at him. "What's going on here, Rhys? What aren't you telling me?"

Rhys motioned to Zachary's phone. He had the information he needed. But Zachary knew, going into it, that he didn't have everything. Rhys was keeping something from him.

"Are you worried it would get her into trouble? With her parents or the police?"

Rhys shook his head. But his expression was still veiled. Zachary didn't know if he were telling the truth. There was definitely something that he wasn't prepared to reveal.

"Rhys… I understand that you're trying to protect her. But you know… sometimes not knowing what I'm walking into can be hazardous. I don't want to get hurt, and I don't want anyone else to get hurt because of what I don't know. You know that… I've had some dangerous cases lately."

Rhys shook his head and drew a straight horizontal line with his hand.

"Nothing unsafe?" Zachary asked, to be sure of Rhys's meaning. "I don't need to worry about what I might be getting into here?"

Rhys gave a single nod and pointed at Zachary. His sign for 'you got it.'

Zachary looked back down at Madison's information and sighed. "I'll do what I can," he promised. "Now… we'd better get you home. Your grandma doesn't know you're here, does she?"

Rhys's hand made a wobbly side-to-side shake. *Well…*

"Yeah. That's what I thought. Ask me to come to your place next time. She doesn't want you coming over here. If you call me, I'll come."

Rhys shrugged. Zachary was left wondering how much else he was trying to get away with behind Vera's back. It wasn't likely the first time that Rhys had hopped onto a bus and gone somewhere other than home or school.

5

Zachary believed that Rhys didn't think he was getting Zachary involved in anything dangerous to himself or to Madison. Still, he had enough experience as a private investigator to know that Rhys could very well be wrong. He hadn't given Rhys any particular timeline for the investigation. After he had dropped Rhys back at home, he went to a coffee shop and opened his computer to see what background he could find on Madison Miller.

Was she really missing? If she were, did anyone have any idea where she was? Was she just staying with friends somewhere, or had something happened to her? Vermont was not known as a high-crime area, but that didn't mean they had escaped the seamy underworld. There was still plenty of violent crime, drug trafficking, and street life. Even postcard-perfect Vermont couldn't escape that, as Zachary had personally experienced.

Madison Miller's social networks seemed pretty clean. Only the occasional posting, mostly selfies or memes shared with friends.

At least, her social accounts that Rhys had known about.

Facial recognition searches led Zachary to several other user accounts that Rhys had not known about, and which were not quite so squeaky-clean. Zachary scrolled through several racier pictures of Madison and her boyfriend. Nothing X-rated. No nudes. But maybe not pictures she had wanted her parents or casual friends to see.

There was ample evidence Madison was drinking. Zachary wasn't as sure about smoking or drug use. There were hints of it in Madison's posts, but sometimes kids bragged about things like that when they never would have even considered using.

Going back through her history, it looked like Madison and the boyfriend had started showing up together about two months previously. While there was nothing overtly wrong in the new accounts, something about them rang alarm bells for Zachary. He couldn't put his finger on anything specific. But something wasn't right.

Maybe it was because Rhys seemed so young. He didn't seem like the kind of kid who would be interested in the drug culture and had always denied any interest in having a girlfriend. Zachary didn't want to believe that he or any of the kids his age were old enough to get themselves into that kind of trouble. Rhys was clearly not telling his grandmother about his concerns or about going to visit Zachary to ask him to investigate Madison's disappearance.

How much else was going on that Vera wasn't aware of? She hadn't handled her daughters' rebellion or mental illness well. She had denied everything for as long as she could.

Zachary made notes about Madison's activities and user names as neatly as he could so he'd be able to read them when he went back over them later.

Zachary's door was not fixed that night, so he spent another night with Kenzie—which really didn't hurt his feelings at all. Not totally exhausted when he got there like he had been the previous night, he took a few minutes while Kenzie was making dinner to explore the house.

In addition to the master bedroom with the ensuite where Zachary had spent the night before, there was one room that appeared to be a cross between storage and a home office, and there was a third bedroom, neat as a pin, set up as a guest bedroom. Zachary glanced over it and shut the door quietly, grinning to himself. When he had called to ask Kenzie whether he could stay with her while his door was being fixed, she had denied having a guest room, using it as an excuse to invite him into her own bed. He was delighted to learn that it had been a lie. She could have put him up in the guest room as a friend, but had chosen not to. He didn't need to feel like he was imposing himself on her. He was right where she wanted him to be.

Zachary returned to the living room and sat down on the couch with his computer, glancing into the kitchen to make sure that his absence hadn't been noticed. Kenzie gave no sign that she realized he'd been anywhere but the bathroom.

"Do you need help with anything?" Zachary offered.

"Do you actually know how to cook?"

"Well… no. But I'm pretty good at putting plates on the table."

Kenzie laughed. "Okay. Set the table."

He got up and looked through the cupboards, working around her, to find the plates, glasses, and cutlery, which he laid out neatly on the table. He even grabbed a jug of juice from the fridge and put it on the table. Kenzie looked up from the bubbling pot of sauce on the stove.

"You actually know which side the fork goes on," she observed in a surprised tone.

Zachary tried to restrain a smile. "I did remember some of the lessons my foster moms tried to drill into me."

"Didn't any of your foster families try to teach you to cook?"

Zachary shrugged. "That required a bit more sustained focus than setting the table. It never went very well."

Kenzie nodded. "Well, it's never too late to learn."

Zachary looked down at the pots on the stove. "Pasta?" he guessed.

"Yes. And this is something that is certainly within your capabilities. It doesn't take much to boil pasta and warm up some bottled sauce, if you don't want to learn to make your own sauce."

"On a good day," Zachary said. "But you have to remember to take the pasta off before the pot boils dry."

Kenzie raised her brows, chuckling. "Well, yes, that's true."

"It makes a terrible stink when it starts to burn."

"Really. So you have tried."

"Once or twice. I'm better at the frozen stuff you can just stick in the microwave."

"As long as you remember to take it out," Kenzie teased.

Zachary nodded. He had warmed up meals and then forgotten them in the microwave more times than he would like to admit. His meds tended to suppress his appetite, if not make him nauseated, so eating meals was more of a chore for him than a pleasure. Something that was easier to forget or not get around to.

A timer buzzed, and Kenzie took the lid off of the pot of pasta and tested it. "What do you think? Look good?"

Zachary nodded. "Looks fine to me."

She shook her head. "I have a feeling you'd eat it whether it was over- or undercooked. What are you thinking about?"

Zachary realized he'd been staring off into middle distance, reviewing the information he had on Madison Miller. "Oh… just a new case. Maybe."

"What is it?"

"Missing girl. You haven't had any teenagers in the morgue in the last few days, have you?"

"No. It's been pretty quiet, thank goodness. Have you checked around? Jail? Hospital?"

"Not yet. Just started with some background today. See whether she was likely to be involved in anything criminal or being bullied."

"And?" Kenzie removed the pot from the burner and poured the pasta into a strainer sitting in the sink.

Zachary remembered trying to juggle a hot pot and get out a strainer at the same time. One of the problems with cooking was that the recipes didn't remind you to do things like that. Put a strainer in the sink before you start. Set a timer when the water starts to boil. How to coordinate everything so that the sauce and the pasta were both done at the same time. Kenzie seemed to flow through the meal preparations easily. Zachary's executive skills had never seemed to be quite up to snuff for the myriad individual steps required for cooking.

"She has some alternate profiles. Not quite so innocent as her standard ones. But still… I don't see anything criminal or really bad. I'll get in touch with her family tomorrow and find out what they know. Maybe she isn't even missing at all."

"Who's hiring you, if not the family?"

"A friend."

"Oh, okay." Kenzie nodded. "Well, I hope there's nothing wrong. A lot of times, kids are just staying over with friends and didn't bother to tell Mom and Dad. They had a fight and didn't feel like going home. Or things are too strict at home and they want more freedom."

Zachary didn't bother to point out that he was a private investigator and this wasn't his first gig.

He was fully aware of the reasons kids ran away from home. Or walked away.

He'd been one of those kids more than once. He'd normally stayed wherever social services had placed him, but there were times when it had been too much, and he had bolted. And times when he had just lost track of time and supervisors had called the police.

But Madison had been gone for too long. She hadn't just lost track of time.

"She is usually home by nine," Mrs. Miller said. "They close at eight, then she has to help with cleaning up, clearing the till, all of that. Then she comes straight home. That still gives her time to do homework after she gets home too. She doesn't go to bed until eleven."

"And weekends?"

"Nine-thirty until five."

"And then she comes home?"

"No, sometimes she has other things to do. Hang out with her friends. Maybe go out to eat, watch a movie. Sometimes she had a sleepover. But she'd still get into work the next day. I never heard any complaints about her missing. And they had my phone number in case there were any problems, I made sure of that."

"You knew the people she worked with? Did you ever stop by to drop off lunch or pick her up after work?"

"I met her manager, the girl who hired her. I don't go by there. You know, teenagers are *embarrassed* by their parents. They want to pretend they don't exist. Like all kids don't have parents too."

Zachary nodded.

"When did she disappear? Can you give me the timeline?"

"It was… Saturday or Sunday. She was sleeping over with friends Friday night and Saturday night. She said she would still get to work. I don't think she worked both days, maybe just Sunday. But she never came home. We couldn't reach her or her manager. I tried her friends… the ones whose phone numbers I could find. They didn't know where she was."

"Do you know who she slept over with?"

Mrs. Miller shook her head slowly. "She was always very responsible," she said guiltily. "She'd tell us when she was going out and when she would be back. She'd usually say whose house she was going to, but it was so routine that… I didn't always listen. I don't know if she told me who she would be with. I'm sure she did. But it didn't register and I didn't have any reason to be concerned. And if I was trying to reach her, all I had to do was call her cell phone. It wasn't like when we were kids, and you had to have the family's land line."

"You never found out who she was with those nights?"

"No. I don't know if the police found out. They were going to make inquiries. But they haven't told us anything. When we call and ask about it, they just say it is under investigation and that they'll let us know when they find anything significant."

"And you don't know if she was at work on Sunday?"

"I tried and tried to reach the manager, but I couldn't. I tried the store and they said it was the wrong number. The police…"

"Said they would follow up on that as well," Zachary supplied.

Mrs. Miller nodded. "It makes us sound like irresponsible parents, but I can assure you that we are not. We always kept track of what she was doing, made sure that everything was okay with her. She wasn't neglected or abused. She wasn't bullied at school. She had good marks and a good job, and kids like that don't just run away." Her voice cracked, and she dabbed at tears leaking out of the corners of her eyes.

Mr. Miller sat there stoically, not crying. But that didn't mean that he didn't feel the same way as his wife. He wore a stony expression that told Zachary that he was doing his best to suppress his own emotions and show his wife a strong, supportive front. His throat worked and he stared down at his hands.

"I don't think you're irresponsible parents," Zachary soothed. "This kind of thing could happen to anyone. I wonder if I could see Madison's bedroom?"

"The police wanted to look at it too, but they didn't find anything." Mrs. Miller stood to show him to Madison's room. "Of course she didn't leave her phone or her computer at home. She took those with her."

"Did she take anything else?"

"Well… she was supposed to be away for a couple of nights, so she took changes of clothing, her toothbrush and deodorant. All of the usual things a girl needs if she's going to be away overnight."

"Nothing that surprised you?"

"No."

She opened the door and motioned Zachary into the bedroom. It was a typical girl's bedroom. Pastel colors from when she'd been younger, with band posters and other memorabilia pinned or taped up. No more frilly princess bed. A plain blue bedspread, neatly made. A desk to study at. Shelves with a mixture of middle grade and reference books. A few prized dolls and stuffies still kept close to the bed. And a closet bursting with clothes.

Zachary looked around. He walked toward the closet. "Who made the bed?"

Mrs. Miller blushed. "It was me," she admitted. "I hate an unmade bed. And I knew the police would want to come in here."

"But she didn't sleep here Friday or Saturday. So it was unmade from Thursday night."

"Yes."

"Did she ever make it?"

Mrs. Miller raised her hands, palms up. "She was a teenager."

Zachary turned his attention to the closet. If she had taken two or three changes of clothing with her, it was not obvious from the contents of the closet. It was nicely appointed with a couple of hanging rods, a shoe rack, and boxes on the shelf, but it was jammed too full of clothing to remain neat and tidy.

"She liked her clothes."

"Yes. That's most of what she spent her money on. I told her she had to put half of her money into savings for school, but she could spend the rest on what she wanted. I'm not one of those parents who demands rent just because she started working."

Zachary nodded. "Was she putting money away?"

"Yes."

"You checked her bank account?"

"No. But she told me she was putting money away."

Zachary spun in a slow circle, looking around the room. "Did she have a boyfriend?"

"No. I told her she was too young for a boyfriend, and she agreed. She said that the girls at school who had boyfriends just ended up getting stressed and distracted, and she didn't want to have to deal with that. She was much better off waiting until after high school to start dating."

"She said that?"

"I said she was better off. She said that she didn't want a boyfriend while she was still in school."

"Didn't she go to dances? Movies? Places where she would be expected to have a partner?"

"A lot of kids her age don't date yet."

"No, that's true." Zachary certainly hadn't. Even if he had wanted to, he had moved from one school to another too often and was too shy or anxious to ask a girl out. Sometimes they flirted with him, started conversations with him, or even asked him out. Girls were sometimes attracted to the new boy, the shy boy, or one who was clearly the underdog. But he'd always been too awkward to follow through.

"You have the names and numbers of some of her friends?"

"Yes… I'll write them down for you."

7

In the car, Zachary made a few more notes for himself. He wasn't a fast writer and wanted to get down as many of the thoughts and questions that were floating around in his brain as he could, before they flitted away. He turned to a new page and used the car Bluetooth to place a call to his friend Mario Bowman.

"Police Department, Bowman here."

"Mario, it's Zachary."

"Oh," Mario's voice warmed. "How's it going, Zach? I should come by and see the new apartment, now that you've had time to settle in."

"Sure," Zachary agreed. "Except the door was broken in by the cops this week, so I'm not there until it gets fixed."

"Oh, heard about that. That woman who was killed."

Zachary nodded. "Yeah. So that case is all wrapped up, and I'm onto something new today..."

"What is it this time?"

"Missing girl. Madison Miller."

He could hear Mario's keyboard clicks and pictured him hunched over at his desk, pecking away with two fingers. Bowman had been a good friend to Zachary, letting him stay at his apartment for months after Zachary's apartment was burned down. Much longer than the few days that he had initially agreed to. And when he'd helped Zachary to move in at the new apartment, he'd provided him with all kinds of kitchenware, towels, and other bits and pieces that he would need starting from scratch.

He was Zachary's go-to guy in the department to let him know what was going on with any cases he was involved with. Who was on a file, how to encourage them to cooperate, all kinds of little things that smoothed Zachary's way.

"Madison Miller. You're in luck, Campbell's got that one."

Joshua Campbell had been good in the past about the cases Zachary was investigating. He wasn't like some of the cops who had it out for any private citizen who might conceivably interfere with their cases. Zachary was careful not to get in the way of the police department and kept them informed about what he was doing. Campbell had given him a couple of tips in the past and put up with Zachary's questions and requests.

"Great. Thanks, Mario. I'll give you a call once I'm back in my apartment and we'll watch a game."

Not that Zachary was that interested in professional sports. But he enjoyed hanging out with Mario occasionally. He hadn't had many friends growing up, and consequently didn't have a lot as an adult. He needed to make sure he nurtured the friendships he had.

"I'll hold you to it," Bowman returned. "Talk to you later."

Zachary disconnected and tried Campbell. There was a click as it was picked up, then a pause before Joshua Campbell spoke.

"Zachary Goldman," he greeted. "Private eye."

"Yes," Zachary agreed. "I'm calling to interfere with another of your cases."

Campbell snorted. "Nice when everyone is upfront about everything."

"I've been asked to look into a missing persons case. Mario said it's on your desk. Madison Miller."

"Madison. Yes. Not much there, I'm afraid."

"She is missing."

"Well, she's not at home with her parents. I'm not sure that she's missing or that any law has been broken."

"What have you found?"

"It's all pretty run-of-the-mill. No indication of foul play. Looks like she just took off with the boyfriend."

"So there *is* a boyfriend."

"Mom and Dad told you that there wasn't one, didn't they? I suspect they didn't know. Madison kept it on the quiet. Parents weren't involved enough to know any better."

"Did you identify him?"

"Name is Noah. No last name, unfortunately. He didn't go to school with her, so no one could tell us his full name or any contact info. But her friends are all on the same page. She had been seeing him for a few weeks or a couple months. Spending more time with him and less with them or at school. It looks like she decided to take off with him."

"You don't think he did anything to her?"

"Nothing we've been able to find. Her car is gone. Backpack, electronics, toiletries, and clothing. That looks voluntary to us."

"But she is a minor."

"She is. And the file remains open. But I don't think she's going to be found unless she wants to be found. Maybe if they get tired of each other after a while, she'll show up at her parents' home again. Until then… we'll keep our ears to the ground. But we can't do anything without any evidence."

"No one at her work knew anything? When was she last seen? Mrs. Miller wasn't sure whether she had worked Saturday or Sunday."

"There is no job."

Zachary raised his eyebrows and stared at the radio. "There is no job?"

"Nope. Madison pulled one over on Mom and Dad. She never worked at Pedal Pushers. They'd never even heard of her. No application, no paychecks."

"Mrs. Miller said that she met Madison's supervisor. Had her phone number."

"Yeah. It was all a setup. I don't know who Mrs. Miller met, but it wasn't Madison's supervisor at Pedal Pushers."

Zachary tried to marshal his thoughts. He scribbled on his notebook, trying to break something loose. "Then where did she work?"

"She didn't. Her friends said she didn't have a job."

"Where was she spending her time, then? With this Noah?"

"Yep."

"Where was she getting money for clothes?"

"Couldn't tell you. This was a girl with secrets. She did *not* want her parents to know that she had a boyfriend. She built up all kinds of stories to keep them from finding out. In the end, she probably saw that the house of cards was going to come tumbling down, so she decided to get out while the getting was good."

Zachary nodded. "Yeah. Did you look at her social networks? Was she into drugs?"

"According to her friends, she liked to party. They're pretty tight-lipped about what that meant. Drinking? Drugs? It pretty obviously meant spending time with this boy."

"Her social networks show her drinking."

"Not the ones I saw. They were squeaky clean."

"I managed to find some that her parents probably didn't know about."

Campbell blew out his breath. "Of course you did. You want to shoot those my way?"

"Sure." Zachary was happy to share whatever might help them to find Madison. "I'll email you. You didn't get any from her friends?"

"Certainly not. They probably figured they're doing her a favor, keeping her out of trouble. I'll have a little chat with them about obstructing the investigation."

"You want to hold off on that for a day or two? So I can talk to them first and see if I can get anything out of them? Sometimes kids are more likely to talk to someone… unofficial."

"I'll give you a day," Campbell said grudgingly. "But I can't be seen as letting this investigation slip. There's not much for us to go on, but if people think we're just letting it go cold, they get a little anxious."

"I'll try to catch them at school this afternoon."

"Be careful hanging around schools asking questions. People will think you're a pedo and we'll get calls…"

"I'll get the school's cooperation. Mr. and Mrs. Miller can confirm that I'm on the case."

"They hired you?"

"Uh… no."

Campbell waited for a further explanation.

"You remember the boy in the Salter case?"

"The mute. Sure."

"He goes to that school. He was friends with Madison. Or at least… had a crush on her."

"Ah. You're not making him dig into his college fund to pay you, are you?"

"No. Just a favor for a friend."

"Good for you. But don't take too many pro bono cases. Even you have to eat now and then."

Zachary had to chuckle at Campbell mothering him. He was not the motherly type. "Yes, sir."

Campbell laughed at himself. "Well, you've got the bones of the case. Anything else?"

"You'd tell me if there were some leads. Any indication of where she and Noah might have snuck off to?"

"No, probably not. We'd be following them ourselves."

"Yeah. Well, let me know if there's anything you think I should know."

"And you let me know if you make some headway. This is a police investigation."

"We have parallel investigations," Zachary corrected. "I will definitely tell you if there is anything you should know."

Campbell cleared his throat. It wasn't the first time the two of them had danced around the details of who was required to tell whom what.

"We'll be in touch, Zachary."

"I'll get you those social network profiles. Maybe you'll see something that I missed."

"Thanks. I'll be looking for them."

8

Zachary talked to Mrs. Miller and had her call the school to explain who Zachary was and to ask them to cooperate with his investigation. The school was well within their rights to refuse but, in Zachary's experience, they would usually do whatever they could when the health and safety of one of their students were at stake.

But he still knew that they might shut him down as soon as he got there. Then he would have to stay outside of the school boundaries and figure out how he was going to get in contact with Madison's friends to ask them questions. Maybe Rhys would be able to help him.

He parked in the public parking, went through the main doors, and headed directly for the office so that he wouldn't set off any alarm bells. The school was far more likely to be well-disposed toward him if he were completely upfront about what he was there for than if he snuck around and tried to get a look around or started asking questions before checking in with the main office.

The secretary at the front desk had apparently been warned about his visit and knew what Zachary was there for when he gave his name.

"The principal will see you in just a moment. Have a seat, please."

Zachary sat on one of the uncomfortable seats in the waiting area, mentally sliding back to the many times as a child and teen that he'd had to wait in the office for a principal or guidance counselor or school resource officer to talk to him. Or to meet his social worker or to explain to a foster parent why he was in trouble yet again. A lot of uncomfortable chairs in a lot of school administrative offices.

A young woman approached Zachary, and he stood to shake her hand and greet her, expecting her to introduce herself as a student teacher or aide. But she introduced herself as Principal Lakes, surprising him. She looked too young to be the principal.

Lakes led him into her office and offered him a seat. The more comfortable chairs. If anyone were ever comfortable sitting in front of a school principal. Zachary always felt like he was a kid again, trying to explain why he couldn't keep out of trouble. He wondered if other adults felt the same way. Normal adults who hadn't spent so much time in the office as kids.

Principal Lakes looked Zachary over carefully. She smiled and cocked her head slightly. "You don't know who I am, do you?"

Zachary was taken aback. He shook his head. "Uh… principal of the school. That's… that's all."

"My predecessor here was Principal Montgomery."

Zachary blanked on the name. He thought about it for a minute, trying to place who Montgomery was and why he or she was so significant.

Then he remembered Rancheros, the cowboy bar. Sitting and watching a blond, middle-aged principal connecting with her date, an underage student from her school. Zachary felt the blood drain from his face.

"Oh."

Lakes nodded. "Yeah. Her. I recognized your name when Mrs. Miller called. I am very happy to have the chance to meet you."

Zachary nodded as if he were greeting her for the first time. "I… I'm glad to meet you too."

"It has been an uphill battle getting parents and students to trust me, after what Principal Montgomery did."

"I can imagine. But you've stuck it out."

"I have. And I think that, generally speaking, I've succeeded in earning their trust."

"Good for you."

"So," Principal Lakes leaned back in her chair, twirling a pencil between her fingers. "You're looking into what's happened to Madison Miller."

Zachary nodded. "Did you know her?"

"I try to know all of my students by name. Some of them I know better than others."

Zachary's face warmed. He had a feeling she sensed he was one of those students she would have known pretty well. "So tell me about Madison."

"She was a good student. Bright. Good worker. Friendly. Not mean or cliquey."

"Did anything change in the last couple of months?"

"There were some concerns expressed by her teachers. Her marks were down. She wasn't handing in homework. Was distracted in class." Lakes shrugged one shoulder. "It's not all that unusual. Adolescence is a hard time. Shifting hormones. Peer pressure. The work can be very difficult. Often there are family problems that the teachers are unaware of. Kids have a lot of responsibilities on their shoulders."

"And in Madison's case?"

"We talked to her parents. They said she was having difficulty with the school work. They were arranging tutors."

"And then she didn't show up for school this week."

"Yeah. We had the police here before school even started, asking questions and asking to speak to Madison's teachers and friends. Anyone who might know where she was or have some insight."

"I'm going to want to talk to the same people."

Lakes shrugged. "We'll do what we can. But we can't compel anyone to talk to you. It will be up to them."

"Of course."

"Did the police talk to Rhys Salter?"

"Rhys? Why would they talk to him?"

"He knew Madison."

"He might have known of her. Lots of people knew who she was. But he wasn't… in her circles. And as far as talking to the police… I don't know how much you know about Rhys, but he isn't verbal."

Zachary nodded. "I know him. But he can communicate, even if he can't usually speak."

Lakes grimaced. Zachary got the feeling that she hadn't spent much time trying to communicate with Rhys. "At any rate, the police did not ask to speak to him, and we didn't give them his name. Like I say, he wasn't in her circles. He might have had some classes with her, but they weren't close friends."

"I understand. If you could get me a list, and I could maybe start seeing some of them this afternoon before school lets out…"

"We can't pull kids out of classes."

"Can't you? When one of your students may be in danger?"

"The police didn't think she was in any danger. There was no indication of foul play. I really didn't get the idea they could do much of anything."

"What did you think? Did you think it was in keeping with Madison's character to disappear like this?"

"I thought it was strange," Lakes admitted. "But like I say… things had been a little rocky lately. It wasn't the first thing that was out of character."

"What else?"

"Like I said, her marks. Being inattentive in class. She just seemed… her demeanor was different. I don't know how to describe it. More secretive. Agitated. Mmm…" Lakes squinted her eyes and pursed her lips, looking for a word. "More intense. Emotional."

"Did you consider drugs or alcohol?"

"It's one of the things we're trained to watch for, so of course we considered it. Asked her if she needed any assistance or counseling in dealing with substance abuse issues… That didn't go anywhere. We didn't have any evidence."

"Did you know she had a boyfriend?"

Lakes frowned. "In the school?"

"No. The police said he didn't go here."

"Then I really wouldn't have any way to be aware of it. Unless he came into the school."

"She was dating him during the period when her marks dropped and these other changes occurred."

Lakes gave a small smile. "Boyfriends can be distracting. And relationships can be so intense at that age. They can be all-consuming. And you can't tell a teenager that in a year she won't even care about him anymore, but her school performance is something that will impact her path for years to come…"

"But it's pretty hard to convince someone to give up a romantic relationship for the longer-term good," Zachary suggested.

"Or even just to cool it a bit. Yes. I've learned that you can't talk kids out of these first loves, even in cases where they are clearly incompatible or abusive."

"Did you think Madison's boyfriend was abusive?"

"I didn't know he existed, so no." Lakes considered the question. "I don't recall ever seeing Madison with bruises, or hearing any concerns about abuse from her teachers. But there are a lot of kids in the school, and we can miss the signs."

"Did you have any other concerns about her? Just her academic performance?"

"Yes, that was the only thing that had been expressed. Her disappearance took me completely by surprise. I didn't know of any problems she was having at home. But even the most together student can be masking serious problems. Sometimes they can be homeless for weeks before someone realizes there is a problem. Reputation is paramount to teens."

Zachary could remember the fear of being different, being bullied because he was in foster care or a group home, because his clothes were worn or out of date, having gone through several kids before he inherited them, of being on meds, having ADHD, PTSD, and learning disabilities. He would have given anything to be normal, whatever he thought that was. As an adult, he didn't worry as much about how he looked to others. But he also wasn't in close quarters with a few hundred critical peers every day.

"If you think of anything else, will you give me a call?" Zachary put one of his business cards on her desk.

"Of course."

The first interviewee was Madison's homeroom and English teacher, who happened to have a prep period when Zachary began his interviews. Mrs. Wright was an older teacher, gray hair pulled back from her face in a ponytail.

She studied Zachary intently, and he worried for a moment that she might have been one of his teachers decades ago. Then she relaxed.

"I've never met a private investigator before."

"Well… I'm just an ordinary guy. Like anyone else. In real life, private investigators aren't usually hard-boiled, gun-toting womanizers."

"You've ruined my fantasies."

Zachary smiled. "I know you've already talked to the police, but I was hoping you wouldn't mind going over some of the same ground again."

"I would like to help you find Madison and make sure she is okay."

"That's what it's all about. Had you noticed any changes in Madison lately? Did you have any concerns?"

"She was definitely going through changes… but I didn't have any reason to think that it was anything other than the usual adolescent stuff. Development is so rapid at this age. They're bouncing between childhood and becoming responsible adults, and that's a big gap. Add in hormones and increasing scholastic demands, and lots of kids lose it."

"Did you think Madison was losing it?"

"I knew she was having problems. Her marks had dropped quite drastically. She was not turning in her work. She was distracted in class."

"Her parents said that they would get her tutoring?"

"That was what they said."

"Did you think that was a good solution?"

Mrs. Wright considered the question. "No, I was not confident that was going to solve the problem. I didn't think it was just a matter of her not understanding the work and needing to be walked through the process."

"What did you think the problem was?"

"I thought she was… experimenting. Some kids go off the rails, rebelling and trying out the things that their parents have told them to stay away from. It can be a long journey back when they get too deeply into drugs or some other alternative lifestyle."

"You thought it was drugs?"

"That was just one possibility. There are many of them. Lots of ways to self-destruct." She narrowed her eyes at him. "I imagine you have explored some of them."

"A few," Zachary admitted. He'd made some fairly disastrous choices in his life.

"She was tired in the middle of the day. Sometimes dozing off, particularly after weekends. Mondays you might as well give up on trying to reach her."

"Could it have been her job? Working too much in addition to school?"

"Could have been. Her parents threatened to make her quit if she didn't straighten up. I got the feeling that there was an emotional aspect to it."

Zachary frowned. "What does that mean?"

"Hard to explain. It wasn't just that she was tired and not doing her homework. She was… emotionally labile. Anxious, angry, defiant… and then other times, silly and giggly. Showing off her latest fashion statement. It was more than just being overtired. If it was because of work… then I would wonder whether she was being bullied or harassed at work. She was so distracted and emotional."

That sounded about right for a teenager. Zachary had felt out of control all the time, unable to corral his brain or his emotions to be a calm, productive student like so many of his peers seemed to be. But then, he *had* been bullied and harassed almost constantly, both at school and in his various homes.

He made a few notes in his notebook, trying to capture the thoughts and questions that flitted around his brain. It gave him a chance to breathe and distance himself from the childhood memories.

"Madison didn't ever talk to you about what was wrong, or say anything that gave you a clue. Maybe you overheard her talking to a friend, but didn't hear the rest of the conversation. Just… some sense…"

"I'm afraid not. I wish she had come to me. I would have done whatever I could to help her. But I don't know what was wrong or why she disappeared. I'm sorry."

"You've been very helpful. Thanks for answering my questions. And let me know if you think of anything, or happen to hear anything. Keep your ear to the ground…"

"I'll do my best," Mrs. Wright promised, and gave him a brief smile. "Thank you for taking this on. I hope you're able to find her."

9

Madison's three best friends were apparently joined at the hip. They came together into the conference room that Zachary had been allowed to use, and wouldn't be divided.

"I'd really like to talk to you separately," Zachary told them. "I'm sure the police interviewed you separately, didn't they?"

"You're not the police," the redhead challenged him.

Zachary shook his head. "No. I'm a private investigator. It would be most helpful to me—and most beneficial to Madison—if you would talk to me one at a time. Sometimes there are little things that you remember differently, and they wouldn't come out if you all talk to me together, because your recollections color each other's memories. I don't get three individual stories; I get one blended-together story."

"We're meeting together," the tallest girl, a brunette, declared, and she put her arms around the waists of her two friends. They, in turn, threaded their arms around her, so that they were all holding on to one another. Zachary looked at them helplessly. He didn't have any authority over them. He couldn't force them to talk to him, much less to do it separately. He counted himself lucky that all three had agreed to meet with him at all. He had expected at least some pushback, with one of them saying that Madison deserved her privacy and if she wanted to run away, he should just stay out of it.

The girls looked satisfied that they had talked him into it, and each took a chair.

"What are your names?" Zachary asked with a sigh. He felt overwhelmed and outnumbered. Another reason he didn't interview witnesses together was that it was so distracting to have to watch three different people and their reactions at the same time. It was hard enough to keep his thoughts and questions straight when he was only talking to one person. Three felt a little like trying to hear all of the words of a three-part round at the same time.

"I'm Josette," the redhead offered.

Zachary wrote it down.

"I'm Leila," the taller brunette said.

"And I'm Katelyn." The smallest girl, another brunette.

"How long have you each known Madison?" Zachary puzzled over whether to assign each girl a page in his notebook and flip back and forth as they answered, or whether to make three columns, one for each of them, or just to try to tag each note and keep track as they went along.

Josette and Katelyn had known Madison the longest, since some time in the early elementary school grades. Leila had gone to a different elementary school and didn't know Madison until she graduated to middle school.

"So you know each other pretty well."

They all nodded their agreement. Zachary tried to peg their moods before getting deep into the interview. They were more cheerful than he would have expected. With Madison missing, he would have expected them to be sad, maybe tearful. They weren't laughing and smiling, but they didn't seem to think that anything bad had happened to Madison.

"What's been going on with Madison lately?"

They exchanged looks, questioning each other with their eyes. Zachary could feel the communications passing between them, even if he couldn't interpret each look.

"What do you mean?" Josette asked.

"Several people have said that Madison was having trouble lately. Schoolwork, inattentive, and now this… you didn't notice anything different about her?"

More looks, trying to decide what they should tell Zachary. They clearly knew plenty, but they weren't sure that they wanted to divulge anything to him. They were closing ranks on their friend, shielding her from the investigation. Did they know where she was? Had they been in communication with her or had she told them ahead of time that she was planning to leave?

"She was good," Katelyn said. "Really. Maybe she wasn't doing so good with her schoolwork, but who does? I mean, it's hard, and where is it going to get us? Does it really matter how we do now? No one is going to be looking at these marks when they're deciding whether we can get into college or be hired for a job. All they'll be looking for is a diploma. Maybe SAT scores for college. That's all. No one cares what you got in high school English."

"It would be a problem if she failed."

"She wasn't failing. She was still passing. And the final exam is half the mark, so you can totally coast during the semester, as long as you do well on the final."

"So you think she wasn't doing well just because she didn't care about marks? She figured she could just study for the final and be okay?"

Katelyn shrugged. "I don't know. It isn't like we talked about it. We didn't talk about marks and studying. Sometimes we worked on homework together, but most of the time when we were hanging out, it was to have a good time together, not to do work."

Zachary nodded encouragingly. "What did you like to do together?"

"Go to the mall and shop. Girl talk. Internet stuff. Chill out bingeing on TV series. Whatever. Normal stuff."

"Did you spend a lot of time outside of school together?"

"Yeah, sure." Katelyn looked at the other girls for their reactions, and they nodded to back her up.

"Sure," Josette agreed. "Every day. We were like the four musketeers."

"What about her job?"

A more significant shared look. They knew that Madison didn't really have a job. But they didn't know that Zachary knew.

"Yeah, we all have jobs. But we make it work. We're not working all the time. Our parents wouldn't let us. It's just a few hours. You have to leave enough time for homework and socializing."

"Where did Madison work?"

"Pedal Pushers," Leila said instantly. They didn't have to look at each other for that one. They had the story established already.

"Are you the one who pretended to be her supervisor at Pedal Pushers?"

"What?"

"When her mother met the supervisor and got her phone number. Was that you?"

Leila looked at Zachary with wide eyes. She didn't look at the others, realizing that he was already on to them and knew at least one of the secrets.

"I don't know what you're talking about," Leila said in a thready voice. She swallowed and swiped at her eyes like she was crying, but Zachary didn't see any tears.

"Madison didn't work at Pedal Pushers. That's just what she told her parents."

"She did!" Leila insisted.

Zachary shook his head. "She didn't. Even if I didn't figure that out, the police have already checked. There is no record of Madison working at Pedal Pushers. Or of the girl she said was her supervisor."

They all just sat there, looking at him. Zachary wrote down a few notes and cleared his throat. "Lying about it isn't going to help Madison. If she's in danger, I want to help her. If you think it's going to get her in trouble, then tell me that. I'm not stupid. I'm not going to tell her parents or the police something that's going to get her in trouble."

Leila's head was bowed as she looked down at her hands, but she raised her eyes to Josette to see what she thought.

"Fine," Josette said in an exasperated voice, like Zachary was the one being stubborn instead of them. "She didn't work at Pedal Pushers."

"One of you acted as the supervisor?"

"No. Mrs. Miller knows all of us. We got someone else to do it. Someone she hadn't met. And we're not turning her over to you. She didn't have anything to do with Mad disappearing."

"But you were all in on it. You all knew that it was just an act that Madison was putting on for her parents and schoolteachers."

"Yeah."

"Why did she do that?"

"So she could spend time with her friends."

Katelyn spoke up. "Parents think it's okay to spend twenty or thirty hours a week at a job, but they don't like you spending that much time with your friends. They start to complain that you're not putting in the effort. So Madison wanted to keep her parents off her back. Make them think that she was working hard, instead of hanging out with friends." Katelyn gave an unconcerned shrug.

"So you want me to think that she was hanging out with you," Zachary said. "With her girlfriends."

"Yeah. She was," Josette said challengingly, looking Zachary in the eye. Her eyes stayed steady, as if she weren't lying. But he knew better.

"She wasn't with you. She was with Noah."

That got all of them. Their eyes widened and they looked at each other for help again. They put their heads together and there were furious whispers between them. Arguing about who had told, who had given it away. Somebody must have, for Zachary to know.

"She didn't hide it that well," Zachary said. "She was with him quite a bit. The police know his first name, but not his last name." Zachary looked at each of them. "Do you know Noah's last name?"

There was no need for them to check in with each other for that answer. They all shook their heads independently.

"None of us know his last name," Josette asserted. "I don't know if Madison even knew it. He was sort of... an enigma." She liked the word. He saw her smile, enjoying the chance to use it.

"An enigma," Zachary repeated. "Is that what he called himself? Or was that Madison's word?"

"Madison's, I guess. I don't think he ever called himself that." Josette wrinkled her nose. "It's not the kind of thing you can call yourself, is it? It's like saying that you're the smartest one in the room. You don't get to choose what other people call you."

"And Madison said that Noah was an enigma."

Josette nodded. The other girls followed suit.

"He was so hot," Leila said, and giggled.

Josette and Katelyn elbowed her. "Leila!"

"Well, he was—don't tell me that you weren't both thinking it. He was so..." She shrugged, having difficulty expressing it. "He was older, and he was good looking, and no one knew where he had come from or why he hooked up with Madison. He just... no one had ever seen him before, and then suddenly, he was there, and he and Mad were getting really hot and heavy, but it was like they'd always known each other. He really loved her."

"You didn't know him before? None of you did?"

"No. None of us."

The others both confirmed.

"Where did they meet?"

"Just…" Leila looked at the others for help. "Just here, right?" she made a motion to encompass the school. "He was just, like… there one day. Outside the school, like he was waiting for her. He knew her name. Stopped her to talk to her…"

"He said that he'd seen her at a party," Josette offered, inserting her memory. "At a party or a football game; I don't remember. Just that he already knew who she was, because he'd seen her before, but none of us knew him. He was just there. Out of the blue."

"Like an angel who fell from heaven," Leila said in a dramatically dreamy voice, and then laughed. The others made motions for her to stop and settle down.

"Leila!" Katelyn said in a low, stern voice.

"You don't know where he had seen her before?" Zachary looked at them each in turn. Leila sobered, putting on a serious expression, and they each denied knowing where Noah had seen Madison before.

"So, he approached her. Just called her name. And then suddenly, they were boyfriend and girlfriend?"

"Well… pretty much," Katelyn admitted. "I don't remember where he took her the first day. Out for ice cream, I think. Something like that. Something nice and sweet. And he was. He was always treating her like she was something special. Opening doors for her and taking her out."

"And buying her things," Leila added. "He, like, was always giving her something."

"Clothes?" Zachary suggested. "Handbags? That stuff?"

The three girls nodded. If anything, they looked jealous. They wished they could have had a boyfriend like Noah. A sweet, handsome older guy who liked to buy them things. What girl wouldn't like that?

"How much older than Madison was he?"

"Mmm… I don't know." Katelyn looked at Josette. "Did she ever say? I don't think she knew. None of us did."

"But he was for sure?" Zachary checked.

"He didn't go to school here, and this is the only high school in the area. So he must have graduated."

"Or dropped out," Leila added.

"He didn't drop out," Katelyn said, rolling her eyes. "He was smart. And he had a job. He must have, right? Otherwise, how could he get her all of those presents? And it had to be a good job, because some of that stuff was really pricey. No high school guy can afford to spend that much on his girlfriend."

Zachary nodded and wrote down a few details. He had seen some of the labels on the clothing and, as a private investigator, he'd learned clothing brands and designers in order to be able to tell how much people were worth. Or if they were suddenly spending more than they should. The brands he had seen in Madison's closet had been big names. And those were the ones she had left behind.

10

"What did the two of them do together?" Zachary asked. "You said that they were getting pretty serious."

They avoided his gaze, each pretending to be looking at something else in the room. The light. The table. Her fingernails.

"How serious were they?" Zachary asked. "From the pictures I saw, I'm guessing they were spending a lot of… intimate time together."

"What pictures?" Josette demanded. Her eyes were blazing. "What pictures are you talking about?"

"Pictures that other people took of her. And pictures she took herself and posted on social media accounts." He paused. "Not the ones that her parents knew about."

Leila started to flush. She rubbed her forehead. She turned her face away from him, shielding it with her hand, as if she could keep Zachary from seeing she was blushing.

"Yeah, well, her parents wouldn't have wanted to see that, would they?" Josette said in a hard voice, like if Madison's parents thought they had anything to complain about, they should just get over themselves. "She had to keep it a secret."

"They were pretty heavily involved."

"They were together. A couple. That's what couples do."

"High school couples?"

"Sometimes, yeah. Why would they be any different than adults?"

"On the weekend, Madison had a sleepover Friday and Saturday nights," Zachary said.

"Yeah, so?"

"She wasn't sleeping over with one of you, was she?"

"The cops already asked that. And they would know, wouldn't they? They could look at her phone records or something. They'd know she hadn't been with one of us."

"Besides," Leila said. "Her mom already called everybody. None of us knew where she was. If she'd been with one of us, Mrs. Miller would have figured it out."

"Unless Madison told you not to let her mom know."

Leila shrugged.

"So she was with Noah," Zachary said.

None of them argued with him.

"How often did she stay overnight with Noah?"

They all looked down, silent. Not telling Madison's secrets.

"Every weekend?" Zachary suggested.

She was with him every day after school when she was supposed to be at work. Every weekend when she was supposed to be at work. All of those nights that her parents thought she was sleeping over with girlfriends. He had worked his way into her life so that she was spending every spare moment with him.

"How much time did she spend hanging out with you the last few months? The four musketeers?"

Katelyn was sniffling and wiping her nose. The first of them to show any emotion. "Not very much anymore," she admitted. "We were always telling her that she needed to spend some more time with her *sisters*. I mean, boys come and go, right? But your girlfriends. They're your real friends."

"It bothered you that she wouldn't spend time with you anymore?"

"No," Josette said. "We all would have done the same, if Noah had picked us. It's stupid to say that we wouldn't. If we wanted her to spend time with us, it was just because we were jealous and didn't like to see her with him all the time."

"No," Katelyn sniffled. "It wasn't just that."

Zachary let them sit and stew for a few moments. He scribbled in his notepad. Not because he had anything to write down, but because he wanted them to think about it for a bit. He didn't want to rush the questions. They would tell him more if they volunteered it.

"It wasn't just because we were jealous," Katelyn repeated. "She was... different."

"Yeah, because she had a boyfriend," Josette declared.

"No. It wasn't just that. I mean... she was..." Katelyn's forehead wrinkled. She tried to tease the emotion out. "She wasn't always happy. You know. If I was with a guy like Noah, I'd be over the moon. I'd be happy all the time. I'd be gloating to my girlfriends about how awesome the sex was and how great the clothes he bought me were. I'd be bragging to everyone about him."

"And Madison didn't?"

Katelyn shook her head. The other girls didn't disagree.

"Why do you think that was? Was it just her personality? Maybe she was shy about it?"

"No. Maybe. Who knows what's inside people's heads. Maybe she felt guilty for being with him. Because her parents wouldn't have liked it."

"Or...?" Zachary let the word hang, hoping one of them would take it and come up with some ideas. Because he had no idea how teenage girls talked with each other about their boyfriends. He thought it was unlikely that Madison would be happy all the time. She had trials and troubles just like any other teenager. Even with the perfect boyfriend, she still had to deal with school and homework and her parents. With parents who wanted her to straighten up and start working with a tutor to improve her marks, when all she wanted was to be with her boyfriend.

Both the principal and Mrs. Wright had said that Madison had an attitude. That she had mood swings. They thought that something was wrong. Not that she was spending too much time with her boyfriend. But that she was using drugs or was upset by something going on in her life.

"If it was me, with a boyfriend like that, I wouldn't be complaining," Josette said.

"What did she complain about?"

Josette considered. She rubbed the center of her forehead, frowning. "She'd say that she *had* to go out with Noah. Act like she didn't want to. If it was me, I'd want to. No one would have to convince me of it. And after a weekend together, she'd be, like, all crabby and tired. She'd say how exhausted she was, and we'd be like, *we know why you're so tired.* And she'd just… be all mad about it."

"Was he possessive of her? Forcing her to go with him?"

They looked at each other, shaking their heads. "He was always really soft-spoken in front of us," Katelyn said. "She never said that he was making her. But she was… sometimes she'd act like she was having the time of her life. There were the new clothes, and booze, and parties, and she'd be on top of the world. She'd post selfies all over and make everyone jealous. And then she'd be down in the dumps, complaining about how we didn't understand what it was like, and she just wanted to stay home for once, or hang out with us girls. But she *had* to go with Noah, because he was her boyfriend."

"She scared me sometimes," Leila said. "She'd get really dark moods, say that she was no good and her life was crap and that if her parents knew what was going on, they'd kill her. We all tried to get her to just chill. You know, who cares what parents think? In a couple of years, they won't be able to dictate any rules. They'll be calling us, begging us to come home and spend time with them. They'll forget all about anything we did soon enough."

"But she'd get really down," Katelyn agreed. "You couldn't talk her out of it. I thought…"

Zachary waited for her to finish, raising his eyebrows expectantly.

"I guess I thought it was the alcohol," Katelyn said. "Some people are really downers when they've had a lot to drink. Or maybe she was using something else, and felt bad when she came down off of it."

"Was she using drugs?"

None of them volunteered any knowledge of Madison's drug use.

"I figured she probably was when I saw some of the pictures on her social media," Zachary said. "She looked pretty out-of-it in some of those pictures. Glassy-eyed."

"I don't know." Katelyn shrugged. "She never said she'd tried any hard stuff with me. Just alcohol. Maybe some pot. Nothing much."

"None of you knew if she was taking anything else?" Zachary looked from one to the other, but couldn't detect any signs they were lying. "Okay. So we don't know. Maybe she was, maybe she wasn't."

He was silent, letting the minutes tick by. The girls were moving around restlessly, uncomfortable. No longer united on all points. Thinking their own thoughts and what they ought to tell.

"What do you think happened to Madison?" Zachary asked finally.

"I don't think anything happened to her," Josette said loudly. "I think she just decided not to go home. She'd had enough of being harassed by her parents and teachers, and just decided to stay with Noah. Why not? What could anyone else offer her? She had it good with Noah. Had everything she could possibly want. Why torture herself by going to school and putting up with her helicopter parents?"

Zachary didn't answer. He looked at the other girls, waiting for their responses. Would they just follow Josette's lead? Or would they venture opinions of their own?

"Yeah," Katelyn agreed, in her small, sniffly voice. "I don't think anything happened to her. I'm sure she's okay, wherever she is. She's just with Noah somewhere. She didn't want to come back. Like Josette said."

"Find Noah and you'll find her," Leila agreed.

But no one knew where to find Noah. No one even knew his last name.

11

Zachary talked to Madison's guidance counselor about the boy. He kept the rest to himself, but he wanted to hear what Mr. Carlton thought about Madison's romantic relationship.

"I never saw her around the school with any boy," Mr. Carlton declared, running a hand through the hair on top of his head to make sure that the thinning strands were all arranged with the maximum possible coverage. "I wouldn't have guessed that she had a boyfriend."

"Apparently, he was older. He didn't go to the school."

"Oh. Well, that explains it, then."

"But he picked her up here. And when he originally sought her out, it was after school, when she was just leaving here. He told her that he knew her from somewhere."

"Maybe he did," Carlton agreed with a shrug.

"You don't find it disturbing that he would hang around the school grounds looking for her? Don't you have security out there, keeping an eye on things, making sure that there aren't strangers loitering around eyeballing the kids?"

Carlton grimaced. "It isn't like it's an elementary school, with creepers coming around to try to snatch little kids. It's not like that at all. Our students are almost adults. They're old enough to look after themselves. And to tell us if there is anyone hanging around that they feel threatened by. We don't exactly have security or supervisors patrolling the school grounds, chasing off anyone who doesn't look like they belong."

So the answer was no. They didn't have any security protecting the students from predators who might be looking for a mark.

"But you said that she's been dating this guy for a couple of months," Carlton pointed out. "If he was some creep or she was getting a bad vibe from him, she wouldn't have kept going out with him for months. She would have told him to take a hike. Told the staff if he was hanging around here when she didn't want him to. Our kids get lots of instruction on being assertive, speaking up, not staying in an abusive relationship. We have whole courses of study on it."

Zachary didn't point out that, trained or not, a teenage girl was not necessarily mature enough to recognize red flags in a relationship and know how to get out safely if something didn't feel right. Children were socialized to do what they were told. Not to rock the boat. To get along and not hurt people's feelings. All of those lessons were deeply ingrained and at odds with whatever relationship training the school was trying to do once they thought the students were old enough to make some of their own life decisions.

By the time Madison realized that she wanted out of the relationship, she might have been in too deep to get herself out.

With Rhys's permission, Zachary filled Vera in on the fact of Madison's disappearance and his agreement to do some inquiries to see if he could find out what had happened to her. Rhys sat cross-legged near the fireplace, staring down and running his thumbnail through the nap of the carpet while Zachary and Vera sat on the couch.

Vera's eyes got wide as Zachary gave a broad outline of the case. "Is that what's been bothering him?" she murmured, looking at Rhys. Rhys could clearly hear them, but he gave no sign that he knew he was being talked about. Vera looked back at Zachary, shaking her head. "I knew something was on his mind, but there are so many things for teens to worry about. I just didn't know what it was."

Zachary nodded his agreement. Neither of them said the obvious—that it was that much harder with a teen who was mute. Even when he wanted to share something, it was an effort for him to get his point across. His grandmother understood him better than anyone, but there was still a communications gap.

"I wanted to talk to Rhys about it some more," Zachary told her. "Just the two of us… but I didn't want you to wonder what was going on. I thought maybe we could go out for pizza, but you don't like me taking him out…"

Vera was too worried about rumors getting started about Rhys. A white man who had been in the news too much recently taking out a vulnerable black teen would be an easy target for gossip.

"You can order pizza here," Vera suggested. "The two of you can hang out in the kitchen or wherever you want. I'll give you guys your space."

Zachary knew that was as good as he was going to get. And, all things considered, it was probably better than going out. In a pizza joint or arcade, there would be a lot of distractions, things that could interfere with the already tricky flow of information between the two of them. Rhys could feel safe and secure in his own territory. It wasn't the casual environment that Zachary had initially envisioned, but maybe it was better that way. Zachary's questions were going to be far beyond casual.

He nodded. "That would be great. Sound good, Rhys?"

Rhys nodded, not looking up.

Vera quizzed him on what kind of pizza he wanted, but Rhys waved off her questions and pulled out his phone. He waggled it at her questioningly.

"Fine, order it on your app," Vera agreed.

Rhys tapped away at the phone. He pointed to Vera and raised his eyebrows.

"I'll have some of whatever you get. I'm not picky."

He switched his gaze and his pointing finger to Zachary.

"Same here," Zachary said with a shrug. "I'll eat whatever you get."

Rhys held his gaze. He knew from past experience that Zachary wasn't likely to eat much.

"I promise I'll eat a slice of whatever kind of pizza you get."

Rhys held up two fingers. Vera chuckled.

"Okay, two slices," Zachary agreed. He hoped that it wasn't a huge pizza, where each slice was the size of a personal pizza. He'd be hard-pressed to get through one of those, let alone two. He was on meds that took away his appetite and left him nauseated much of the day, so trying to gain back the weight he had lost was a constant battle.

Rhys bounced his hand, emphasizing the two fingers.

"Yes, two slices," Zachary repeated.

Rhys went back to his phone, tapping in whatever information the app needed. Eventually, he got up and walked over to Vera, showing her the screen. She took the phone from him, adjusting the distance and squinting at it. She didn't take a long time to read before handing it back. "Yes, that looks fine, Rhys."

Rhys held it up for Zachary. He didn't want to take the time he would need to read through the long list of toppings densely listed on the screen. He glanced over it for anchovies or hot peppers, but it didn't really matter even if Rhys had added them. Zachary had grown up eating different foods at each home he went to, and had become an expert at forcing down what he didn't like. What was the point in fighting with a foster parent or supervisor when all he had to do to show compliance was swallow a bite or two of the meal?

"That looks great," he told Rhys, handing it back to him.

Rhys frowned, and Zachary knew that he had responded too quickly. Rhys knew he hadn't really read the list of toppings. He turned the phone back around, craning his neck to look at it and point out one word to Zachary. Zachary followed Rhys's finger. He smiled.

"Yes, I'm okay with pineapple on pizza."

Rhys turned the phone back toward himself, grinning. He tapped through the next few screens to place the order.

12

Zachary chatted with Vera while they waited for the pizza, with the occasional contribution by Rhys. Zachary was waiting until they had the pizza and Vera was out of the room to ask Rhys more questions about Madison.

When an extra-large, steaming, fragrant pizza arrived at the door, Rhys set it on the counter in the kitchen and got out a stack of paper plates.

"Oh, I can wash a few dishes," Vera protested, heading toward the cupboard.

Rhys shook his head, handed her a paper plate, and pointed her in the direction of the pizza. *No dishes. Your night off.*

Vera made a few further noises of protest, but they weren't genuine objections, and she helped herself to one of the large slices.

"I'm going to use a TV tray and put on a movie for myself," she informed Rhys. "A grandma movie that wouldn't interest you. You boys keep the food in here so I don't have to clean it out of the carpet or the bed. Put the leftovers in the fridge."

Rhys nodded obediently, giving her a little grin. After Vera left the room, he grabbed a couple of cans of soda out of the fridge and handed one to Zachary. They sat down at the table with their paper plates and Rhys took his first piece. Zachary tried to pick out the smallest piece of what remained. They were definitely too big for him to eat two full slices, but he would do his best. If he left part of the crust of the first and ate a few bites of a second piece, then he would make good on his promise to have two slices, even if he hadn't actually eaten more than one slice. He took his first slice of loaded pizza and had a bite.

"Mmm. Very good," he told Rhys. It was a privately-owned pizza restaurant rather than one of the big chains. "I can see why you picked them. Really good crust, too."

Rhys nodded. He mimed stirring and then tossing a pizza.

"Hand made?" Zachary guessed. "Made fresh?"

Rhys nodded and pointed at Zachary.

Zachary took another bite. He didn't pull his notepad out. If he did, he was sure to get food on the pages. But he didn't really need his notes to start the conversation with Rhys.

"So, I talked with some of Madison's teachers and friends today."

Rhys nodded. He'd obviously already been aware of that. Zachary had intentionally not interviewed Rhys at the school at the same time as he had conducted interviews with her other friends. From what he had seen and heard, Rhys and Madison had not been close friends, and certainly not boyfriend-girlfriend, and he didn't want to shine a light on Rhys and cause people to speculate as to what his relationship with the missing girl was.

"I'm getting a better picture of what was going on with her before she disappeared."

Rhys continued to eat. Zachary hadn't yet asked him a question, and he didn't have anything to agree or disagree with.

"You had concerns about Madison."

Rhys nodded.

"Before she went missing."

Rhys paused in his consumption of the pizza, then nodded again, slowly.

"What, specifically, were you concerned about?"

Rhys thought about it, chewing and taking another bite. Zachary didn't rush him. They had all the time they needed. Eventually, Rhys pulled out his phone. While he ate, he paged backward through photos. Zachary couldn't see any dates or anything that would tell him the timeline Rhys was browsing through. Eventually, Rhys found the picture he was looking for and brought it up on the screen. He slid it across the table to Zachary.

Zachary looked down at the picture. It was just Madison. No Noah in the picture. No laughing friends. Not a posed family picture. But it didn't look like a selfie, either. Rhys had probably taken it himself and, since Madison was not looking directly at the camera, it had probably been a candid shot that she was unaware of.

"Okay." Zachary slid it back across the table after studying it for a moment. The Madison in that picture looked like any other student. Calm, pleasant, just a student sitting at her desk on a regular day. She was wearing jeans and a simple peach blouse. Not one of the designer items that Noah had given her later.

Rhys flicked through the photo album again, moving forward this time. He found another picture and slid it in front of Zachary.

It was another picture of Madison at her desk, from the same angle. She and Rhys apparently attended a class together, and both shots were taken while they were in their assigned seats. In the second shot, Madison had her head down on the desk, sleeping.

There were other subtle differences.

She had on quite a bit of makeup. In the first picture, she'd had some on, but it had been understated. It was much more dramatic and noticeable in the second picture. Her clothing was different. The camera angle didn't make it easy to identify, but Zachary could tell by the stitching around the shoulder that it was a higher quality product. Not something produced in a factory in huge quantities. Designer. He remembered the pictures he had seen on her social networks. More daring outfits. Off the shoulder or strapless, short skirts or shorts, cleavage. Formal cocktail dresses and sporty shorts and halter-top sets.

She didn't have the same glow in the second picture as she'd had in the first. Maybe it was just because she was sleeping, her face slack, not much of it visible to the camera. He wouldn't call her gaunt, but it looked like she had lost weight. She looked worn. But maybe she was just tired from a weekend of partying.

Zachary nodded at Rhys. "Her teachers said that she was tired, particularly after weekends. She wasn't going home. Her parents thought she was sleeping over with her girlfriends, but she was with Noah. You think she was partying too much?"

Rhys shrugged. He took the phone back. He didn't look at Zachary as he fiddled with it some more. He eventually handed it back to Zachary.

The triangle in the center of the screen told Zachary that it was a video. He tapped it and watched. It was a noisy environment. School had let out, and there were kids everywhere, chattering and on the move. The camera centered on a female figure, and Zachary realized it was Madison. She was walking more slowly than the other girls she was with, hanging back from them slightly, looking tired and sore like she'd been working out. There was a part in the crowd and Madison's friends moved out of the way as Noah came onto the scene. Zachary saw Madison flinch when he reached out to her. He put his arm around her waist and, at first, she looked like she was going to pull away from him. He moved his arm up to her shoulder and pulled her closer, squeezing her against his side. Madison's arm went around his waist and they kissed.

Madison, looking over Noah's shoulder, saw Rhys. "Are you recording me?"

Noah turned around. His face got red. "What the...? You can't go around recording people! Put it away, retard!"

"Noah!" Madison reprimanded. "Don't call him that!"

He glared down at her. "We don't want that idiot recording us. Why does he always have to be around you? Tell him to take a hike. You already have a boyfriend."

Madison looked at Rhys, warning him with her eyes. But also apologetic. "You better go, Rhys."

The video ended.

Zachary dragged the time indicator back to the beginning of the video and watched it a couple more times. He looked up at Rhys. "Do you think he was abusive?"

Rhys spread his hands wide.

"Did you ever see her with bruises? Do you think he was hurting her?"

Rhys shook his head.

Zachary pondered this. "Is there anything else?"

Rhys considered. The fact that he didn't answer immediately told Zachary that Rhys still hadn't shared everything he knew or was concerned about. "If you want me to help Madison, you have to tell me what you know."

Rhys took a big bite of his pizza and chewed it. Zachary rolled his eyes.

"It's not like you can't talk with your mouth full," he pointed out.

Rhys grinned broadly and covered his mouth to keep from spitting any of the pizza back out. He touched his phone, not doing anything at first, just considering it. Then he picked it up. Zachary watched him quickly finding the app he wanted and looking through a list. Eventually, Rhys pushed it back toward him. Zachary saw the messaging app that Rhys often used to communicate with him. But it was Madison's name up at the top of the screen.

Zachary saw a cartoonish puppy—Rhys seemed to have a thing about dogs—with the words 'you okay?' scrawled across the bottom of the graphic. He scrolled down and saw Madison's answer on the left side of the screen.

Rhys, I can't talk to you. You need to stop messaging me.

There was a single word question from Rhys. *Safe?*

And Madison's reply. *I don't want you getting involved. Leave me alone.*

Zachary looked at the date stamp on the message. The Friday before Madison's disappearance. He slowly pushed the phone back to Rhys. "You haven't heard from her since?"

Rhys shook his head.

"Tell me what you think."

Rhys just pointed to his phone, raising his brows. He shook his head.

Zachary sighed. Rhys couldn't tell him what had happened to Madison. He'd done everything he could to keep track of what was going on with her and to try to help her, but she had turned him away. He was the only one who had reached out to her personally, but she had refused.

"I'll do my best. If you have any ideas of where she might be, I need to know. It's already been a few days… the police didn't find anything and the trail is cold."

Rhys picked up his phone and returned to the video of Madison and Noah together. He pointed to Noah.

"They'll be together," Zachary agreed. "But no one knows who Noah is. They don't even know his last name."

Rhys pointed at Zachary. He was the private investigator. He should be able to find Noah. Rhys was counting on it.

13

It had been a long day. Zachary was determined to spend the evening relaxing with Kenzie, not thinking about the case. He couldn't work twenty-four hours a day to find Madison. As much as he wanted to find her and make sure she was safe, he couldn't be expected to find her the first day. It was going to take some time, and he would be more likely to make the proper connections if he got the rest and regeneration he needed than if he ran himself into the ground.

Kenzie had texted him to let him know she was on her way home and he could come over any time. Zachary stopped in front of her house and waited a few minutes, breathing deeply and trying to put all of the squirrely thoughts trying to distract him to the side so that he could focus on his girlfriend. If he was going to repair the relationship with Kenzie, he needed to give her the time and attention. Ignoring her or piling all of his troubles onto her wouldn't help them.

When he got into the kitchen, Kenzie was making a sandwich. She smiled over at him.

"You should probably eat too. You can handle making a sandwich, can't you?"

"I already ate."

"Sure you did. I mean a real meal."

"I did. I had pizza with Rhys." Zachary put a hand over his aching stomach. "He forced me to eat way too much."

"He forced you, did he?"

"I'm not used to eating that much. You wouldn't believe the heartburn I've got."

"Well, it's probably a good thing. You need to get fattened up."

"Mmm. Not like this."

"Have a seat. I won't make you eat, but you do have to visit."

Zachary was happy to sit down at the table with her.

"How's the case going?" Kenzie asked.

"I probably shouldn't talk about it. Why don't you tell me about your day?"

She sat down and took a big bite of her sandwich. "Why shouldn't you talk about it? Confidentiality? You already told me who it was."

"I just think… I shouldn't just talk shop. We should spend time together, talking about something other than work."

Kenzie chewed, considering. "I've always enjoyed talking shop together. There aren't too many guys that you can discuss corpses with."

Zachary snorted. He covered his mouth and cleared his throat. "Is that the only reason you want me around? So you can talk about corpses?"

"Well, it's a definite draw."

"I don't have any to talk about yet. And hopefully… I won't on this case."

Kenzie sobered. "Yeah, I hope not. That would not be a good resolution."

"But you could tell me about your bodies if you want to."

"With how much you've eaten, that might not be a good idea."

Zachary touched the notepad in his pocket. After fiddling with it for a moment, he pulled it out and looked at it. "I haven't had a chance to gather all of my thoughts and process everything yet."

"Do you have any good leads?"

"I don't know yet. The boyfriend is definitely key. But no one knows his full name. He didn't go to the school. He just showed up one day and… picked her up."

"She must have met him sometime before that."

"He said that he recognized her from a party. But her friends had never seen him before, so how likely is that to be true? If she'd been at a party, they would have been with her. And she didn't remember him. If they'd hit it off at a party, wouldn't she have remembered?"

"Depends how drunk she was at the time."

"I don't think they'd met before."

"So, what…? You think that he was lying? Why?"

"I think it was just a line. He wanted to pick her up."

"Possible," Kenzie agreed. "But why? He had to have seen her somewhere before. Then we're back to where."

Zachary shook his head. "I don't know. That's one of the questions to be answered. Along with his name. And where they have disappeared to."

"Do you think it was foul play?"

"Rhys doesn't think that Noah was hurting her. So that leaves… either she went off with him of her own free will, or he kidnapped her. I talked to Campbell. They didn't come across anything in their investigation that suggests there was any coercion or violence. And I didn't find anything like that either. So that means she chose to go."

"Girls do. All the time."

"Her parents have been calling her. The police have been calling her. Why hasn't she answered her phone? Why haven't the police tracked the signal to figure out where she is? Did she ditch it?"

"How about Rhys? Has he tried to call her? Or her girlfriends. They must have at least tried to find out if she was okay and what they should tell her parents."

"She told Rhys not to contact her anymore. He'd apparently… stepped on some toes. Hers or Noah's, I'm not sure which."

"So he didn't try to get her when she didn't show up on Monday and the police said she was missing and started asking questions?"

"Not that he told me. I'm not sure that's the same as *no*."

Kenzie nodded her agreement. She had a drink of water and another bite of her sandwich. "Does he know more than he's telling you?"

"I think that's true of every teenager. And every client, for that matter. They almost always have something they are hiding. And even if they are not being deceptive… they still know something they don't realize they know." Zachary flipped to random pages in his notebook, not reading anything. "I think that he's told me everything he believes is relevant."

"So, what's your next step? Or do you know yet?"

"Not yet. I need to think about it. Sleep on it."

"We'll have to make sure you get some sleep tonight, then," she teased.

"We could go to bed now and get a head start."

"Let's not move too fast," Kenzie warned, putting the brakes on.

Zachary should have been happy about that. He was the one who had been feeling uncomfortable with too much intimacy and needing more time. He was the one who had held back and caused the separation in the first place. But he felt a twinge of anger and frustration at Kenzie's words. She *had* been ready for more. She was the one who had gone to Zachary's foster father, Mr. Peterson, to ask him personal questions about Zachary's previous relationships and the possibility of past abuse. She was the one who had gone to Zachary's ex-wife to ask her about how he'd been between the sheets—specifically, whether he had dissociated when they had been together.

And now she was putting on the brakes?

Even though he knew it was a good idea for them to go slowly and take things one tiny step at a time, it still made his already-sore stomach feel tighter and heavier.

He picked up his notepad and held it in front of his face to hide any change in his expression from her. She had become too proficient at reading him.

"I might be able to track some mutual friends. Madison mostly spent her time with Noah, but the girlfriends were invited to a couple of parties and remembered the names of a few other people who were there. I might be able to connect through a friend of a friend of a friend."

"Uh-huh."

"And I have a couple of pictures with his face. I'll run facial recognition and see if I can track down his social media. Even if he's using a pseudonym, that might give me his friends or followers list, and I can get closer."

"Yeah."

Zachary looked at Kenzie. She was watching him closely. Serious again. Zachary cleared his throat and closed the notepad. "So, that was my day. You get anywhere with the stiffs you work with?"

Kenzie gave a forced laugh, and launched into a description of her day and the various puzzles and problems that she had run into. Zachary watched her eyes and her mouth as she spoke, hearing very little of what she said.

14

While he had expected Kenzie to want to spend all evening together, she suggested that they take a break so that she could read her personal email and check a few things off of her list.

Zachary was very bad at keeping lists, but it had been a while since he had touched base with Lorne Peterson, an old foster father, so he decided to take the opportunity to see if he was at home. He didn't have the energy to deal with a Skype call, so he just dialed the number on his phone and stretched out on the couch, listening to the line ring.

It was only a few rings before Mr. Peterson—Zachary still had trouble thinking of him as Lorne—picked up. "Zachary! Good to hear from you," he greeted cheerfully.

"I know it's been a few days," Zachary admitted. "So I didn't want to let it go too much longer."

"How are you keeping? Everything good?" the older man asked tentatively.

"Actually… I'm calling from Kenzie's house."

"Kenzie's?" Lorne's voice was surprised. "Well, that's a surprise. The two of you decided to give it another try?"

Zachary shrugged, his face heating. He was glad no one could see his face. "Yes. I tried giving Kenzie a call when I needed a place to stay for the night, and she accepted…"

"Nothing like the direct route."

"I didn't know if she would say yes. She didn't want to talk about getting back together before. But..."

"But obviously you managed to talk her into it. So does that mean you're officially back to being a couple again...?"

"I don't know what it means... I guess so. We're giving it another try."

"Well, you don't know how glad it makes me to hear that. That's fabulous news."

"Yeah, I'm pretty pleased about it."

"The two of you make a good couple. You really seem like you're good for each other."

"I don't want to jinx anything, but I think... I don't know. I'm hoping."

"Now you make sure you talk," Mr. Peterson's voice took on a stern, fatherly tone. "You can't communicate and keep your relationship healthy if you don't talk to each other. Even when you don't feel like it. You know you tend to bottle things up and not talk when you need to."

"Yeah."

"You could try some family therapy. Get a good couples counselor. Or a group. Or just ask your regular psychologist. But someone else in the equation could help the two of you to connect better with each other. Figure out what things need to be brought out in the open."

"I don't know if Kenzie would want to do that."

"Do what?" another voice asked.

Zachary's eyes flew open. He hadn't realized that Kenzie was walking by while he was talking on the phone. He choked, looking at her, trying to figure out what story to tell her.

"I, just... I was just talking to..."

"Tell her the truth," Mr. Peterson said in Zachary's ear.

Zachary licked his lips, considering. There was only one way to find out whether Kenzie would object to couples counseling or not.

"Lorne said... we should do some... therapy together."

Kenzie nodded. "Not a bad idea," she agreed. She continued on her way into the kitchen. "Say 'hi' for me."

Zachary breathed out. His eyes burned with tears and there was a lump in his throat. He coughed, trying to maintain his composure. Kenzie really didn't need a man who burst into tears at the slightest provocation. He swallowed and tried to continue the conversation with Mr. Peterson.

"Yeah, she says she'd be okay with that. She says 'hi' to you and Pat."

"There, you see? All you had to do was ask. Pat...?" he called to his partner somewhere else in the house. "Kenzie and Zachary say hi."

There was an answer from far away, casual and faint. Then Zachary heard a clear 'wait a minute!' The next time Pat spoke, it was obvious he was right next to Mr. Peterson. "Kenzie and Zachary? Together?" His tone was eager and excited.

"Yes. Zachary is at Kenzie's house as we speak."

"Well, that's awesome! Congratulations, Zach!"

Zachary murmured his thanks, blushing even more than he had when he had told Mr. Peterson that he and Kenzie were back together. He listened to Pat and Mr. Peterson banter back and forth for a minute, and then Pat departed to go back to whatever project he was working on.

"As you can tell, we're both just tickled that the two of you are trying again," Mr. Peterson said. "That's really good news."

"No guarantees," Zachary warned. "I really want it to work, but I can't guarantee everything is going to work out like I want."

"I know, Zach. Trust me. I've been through my own relationship issues. When Lilith and I split... well, you know how hard that was. I knew that it wasn't going to work, that I was just lying by staying in the relationship. But it was so hard to admit it and leave a relationship that I'd been in for so many years."

Zachary remembered showing up on the Petersons' front steps to get some help developing his photographs—something Zachary was allowed to do even though it had been a long time since the Petersons had been his foster parents—and Mrs. Peterson informing him that Lorne no longer lived there. It had been a huge shock. He had known they weren't well-suited to each other but he'd never thought that they would get divorced.

None of it had made any sense until he had met Patrick Parker and realized that Mr. Peterson had, as he had said, been living a lie for all of those years.

But Lorne and Pat had now been together for over twenty years, and it was hard to believe that there had ever been a time when Zachary had thought that Lorne and Lilith Peterson had belonged together.

"I'm going to do my best to make it work," Zachary repeated.

"Good. How about the two of you come down for Sunday dinner this weekend? It seems like forever since we have seen you, and as for Kenzie, I'm not sure if we've seen her since Christmas."

"It hasn't been that long," Zachary protested. He thought back, trying to think of each time that he'd been down to visit Lorne and Pat. He was sure Kenzie had been there at least once since Christmas, but Mr. Peterson was right, it had been a long time since she'd taken the trip with him. "I'll ask her if she's free."

15

Noah was a ghost. Zachary did several image searches to find him on the internet or track down his social profiles, and couldn't find him. He tried the image alone and in combination with the name Noah, but probably Noah wasn't even his real name.

It seemed highly unlikely that a boy of his age would not have any social networking profiles. But of course, some parents refused to let their kids set up social network profiles while they still lived at home, and people advised that young people not use their own pictures for the profile pics. Gamers liked to use avatars. But Noah didn't strike Zachary as the gamer type. Gamers didn't generally show up at high schools to pick girls up. They were the ones at home, leveling up virtually rather than in real life.

Zachary switched to looking at photos on the school's website. Kids who had participated in special events, spectators at football games, everything he could find. Maybe he had been a student teacher, and they had misjudged his age. Anything was possible.

That led to another thought, a leap that Zachary hadn't taken before. He dialed up Campbell's number and lucked out when Campbell answered.

"Zachary. What's up? I wasn't expecting to hear anything from you so quickly. You haven't found our missing girl already, have you?"

"No. Working on it, but I'm not even close yet. I had a question, but I suspect it's one that you can't answer."

"Why don't you call someone who knows, then?"

"I think you know; I just don't think you can say."

Campbell laughed shortly. "Okay, exactly what does that mean?"

"I'm trying to track down Noah. Anything about him. But I'm not pulling anything up."

"Welcome to the club. We weren't able to get an ID on him either."

Zachary considered that for a moment. But Campbell wasn't necessarily telling the truth.

"It occurred to me that it's possible he's an undercover cop."

"A cop? No."

"Is that a real 'no,' or just an 'I can't tell you that' no?"

"It's a real no. As far as I am aware, Noah is not an undercover officer." There were a few seconds of silence from Campbell. "But it's not an avenue that we considered. I haven't contacted any feds about whether they have someone in the area. Could he be DEA or another branch? I have no idea. I can put out a query, but chances are, they won't answer me."

"Yeah." Zachary leaned back in his seat, a less-than-comfortable chair at a diner, stretching. "They aren't generally too forthcoming about that kind of thing."

"You giving up?"

"No. Just rethinking. I can't find a social profile. But he's out there somewhere. Someone has seen him. What about traffic cams or surveillance at the school? Did any of them capture him? His license plate?"

"It's on the list of things to check, but it takes a lot of man-hours to go through video logs, if they caught anything, and if they were kept. We can't check every license plate of every car spotted in the area. We have to see one of the two of them getting into the car or driving it."

"I have the phone numbers of a couple of her friends. I can see if any of them can tell me what kind of a car he drove."

"I think I have that in here somewhere. Hang on a moment."

Zachary could hear Campbell rifling through papers and a few key clicks as he looked for the information. It was a few minutes before he came back on.

"Yeah. White late model Subaru is what I've got."

"So you wouldn't have to look for any car, just the white Subarus."

"Or anything that looks like a Subaru. Because witnesses honestly are not that good with cars. And there's always a possibility that he changed what he is driving, too. If they planned to disappear, he might very well have swapped for something else to lead us in the wrong direction."

"True," Zachary admitted. "But it wouldn't hurt to check the white Subarus."

"We will if we have the time and manpower. Until then, it's going to have to wait."

"If he took her, or if she went with him, then his address is the best place to look for her. Unless you've got some good leads in another direction. Without his name or identity, the best bet is to find his license plate."

"We'll get to it when we can," Campbell repeated.

"But you don't think there's anything to worry about. You think she's just shacked up with this guy somewhere."

"There's no law against disappearing."

"There is for sheltering a runaway."

Campbell grunted. "Not worth our while."

Zachary cast around for some other way to find Madison. "How do the phone logs look? She must have called this guy a lot over the last couple of months. So you must know his cell number."

"Looks like he's changed it a couple of times. My guess is that he's buying burners and not refilling the minutes. Use one up, switch to a new one."

"Are they registered?"

"Fake info. No joy there."

"What about location? Can you see where his phone was most of the time? You must be able to narrow down the location he lived and worked in by where the phone is most often."

"Need a warrant to get that kind of information from the phone company. And who knows how long it takes them to get it to us. Or how useful it will be once we get it. It's not like we live in a big city. It's not going to narrow the search radius much."

Zachary sighed. "Well, I'll keep up the search the best I can."

The only concrete information Zachary had on Noah was what he looked like. He had pictures of the boy's face. An internet search had not turned up anything, but that didn't mean it was a dead end. Zachary messaged Rhys to send him all of the pictures he had of Madison and of Noah.

Of course, Rhys wouldn't send him everything. Judging from what Zachary had seen so far, Rhys had a lot of pictures of Madison. He'd been watching her for a while, maybe for months before Noah showed up on the scene. Since the school year had started, if not before that. As far as Zachary could tell, Rhys had a crush on Madison and had demonstrated some borderline stalkerish behavior in taking candid pictures and videos of her.

Zachary could understand it. He'd had problems of his own with letting Bridget go after they had broken up. And with having to keep tabs on where Kenzie was and what she was doing when they had first started to go out together. Since he had gone back to therapy and had some med changes, he'd been able to curb most of those impulses.

Most of the time.

So he knew that Rhys wasn't going to send him everything, but Zachary needed as many pictures as he could get.

Rather than trying to send them all individually, Rhys set up an online album and shared it with Zachary, which allowed him to browse through them and pick out the ones that would work best for his purposes. Armed with several different shots of Noah and Madison, he started his search near the school, working in an outward spiral.

He approached everyone on the street or in the commercial establishments that he could, showing a couple of pictures of Noah and asking whether they knew him or had seen him around.

There were plenty of 'no's,' people who avoided him, and those who wouldn't look at the pictures. But he did get a few who looked at the pictures and thought that they had seen Noah around, or who identified other people in the pictures that they knew or had seen around. Zachary noted the information in his notepad, along with a list of addresses where people had recognized him. He would plot them all when he got back to his computer and, hopefully, there would be some clusters that would help him to nail down where Noah lived or worked or hung out. People had to know him.

If the police had thought that there was foul play, then they would have at least published Noah's picture to ask for information on him as a person of interest. But they didn't think that Madison was really missing. Putting Noah's picture in the paper, under those circumstances, could be considered inflammatory. It could ruin the reputation of a young man who was innocent of any crime.

At a bodega half a mile from the school, the elderly man at the counter frowned at the picture Zachary showed him and used his fingers to zoom in on Noah's face, and then on Madison's and each of the other people in the background of a party shot. Hopefully, people Noah and Madison hung out with on a regular basis. Eventually, the man put the phone down on the counter. He jabbed a finger at Noah's face.

"I know this boy. He comes from the neighborhood. Been here a few years. The girl, I don't know her. Not one of the ones I have seen him with."

Zachary was a little surprised by that. "You've seen him with other girls?"

"He's been here a few years," the man repeated. "He has one girlfriend all that time?"

"No," Zachary agreed that wasn't likely. Noah had only been with Madison for a couple of months. If he'd been there for a number of years, then of course he'd gone through a string of other relationships. "No, just the last little while."

"I have not seen him for a long time. Maybe a year. Used to be here all the time, when he was younger. Some of these other boys," he poked his finger at some of the other faces in the party crowd. "Some of them, I know. Seen them here. Not *in here*," he clarified, indicating his store, "out there… other places. On the street, in cars, in bars. Not a good crowd."

A knot tightened in Zachary's stomach. He nodded his understanding. "Do you know where any of them live? Any idea, even if it's not a particular building, just the area…?"

"Him… used to live with his grandma. Red brick building a few blocks down." He gestured in the direction of the building Noah had lived in with his grandmother. "But no more."

"Does she still live there? His grandmother?"

"No. She died. Then he was gone, not living here anymore. But then I started seeing him again. Maybe he was back for a while."

"With these guys?" Zachary suggested, indicating the other young men in the picture.

The old man scratched his bristly chin, thinking about it. "Yes, maybe. Them or other boys like them. Trouble."

"What kind of trouble?"

He shrugged. "Can't say. I'm not looking for any trouble."

"What are they? A gang? Friends? Organized crime?"

He shrugged his shoulders. "I keep my head down. Don't make waves. But that doesn't mean I don't have eyes. These boys are trouble. If he is in with them now…" He looked down at the picture. "Looks like he is. That means he's trouble too."

"Okay. I appreciate it. You know where any of the others live?"

"Don't know. Come back at night, check out the bars and clubs, maybe you see some of them. But you be careful. They hear you're asking questions…" He trailed off and grimaced. "I don't think you want to be on the wrong side of that crowd."

Zachary nodded. "Thanks. I'll be careful." He hesitated. "The girl, though, you've never seen her?"

"I don't remember. Not a good idea to stare at girls you don't know."

16

Kenzie wouldn't like the idea of Zachary going back to bars and clubs at night to find known troublemakers related to the missing persons case, so he didn't tell her. He said only that he had to go out to do some interviews.

If she knew, she would have told him it was stupid to go into a dangerous situation without a gun or some kind of weapon to protect himself. But Zachary would never carry a gun, and he knew that whatever weapon he took into a situation could potentially be used against him. There wasn't any point in trying to explain that to Kenzie. She already knew, but that wouldn't stop her arguing about it.

His guts were in knots as he got out of his car to check out a few of the hot spots. He could have taken a tranquilizer, and it would have helped to settle him down, but he didn't. There were some situations in which hyper-vigilance and his ADHD distractibility were advantages rather than disabilities. He needed to be aware of everything going on around him. He needed to key in on everything that was off by the slightest bit. Every detail could be significant. Any change in the environment, every person approaching him, could be a danger. And he would be aware of it all.

He took a few deep breaths before going into the first club. His chest and abs were tight with tension. He tried to look casual and relaxed, to smile and slouch and mask the anxiety. He circulated for a few minutes before going up to the counter. Took the temperature of the room, walked to the men's room in the back in order to scout out any extra security, any private areas in the back. He wasn't part of the club scene and, even if he had been, he probably would have avoided the area.

There weren't any obvious hazards. It might be a slightly tougher crowd than he was accustomed to, but there weren't obvious weapons or illegal activities going on. Any drugs were below the tables. Any illicit business being conducted there was quiet, not out in the open. After checking out the bathroom, Zachary wandered out to the bar. He ordered a beer because ordering a soft drink when he was there by himself might be suspect. He wouldn't do much more than wet his lips; it was only a prop.

He turned on his stool as he raised the glass, looking around. He had a good memory for faces, so he didn't need to refresh his memory looking at the pictures he'd already looked at a hundred times that day as he canvassed. He scanned faces, not meeting anyone's eyes or looking in any one direction for very long.

He saw one young man he recognized from a picture of Noah partying. Just one, but that was a good start, especially when it was the first place he had entered. He sipped the beer and put it down on the bar. There was a mirror on the wall behind the bar, and he used it to spy on the boy without looking directly at him.

He was loud. His manner confident, almost bullying. But not quite. He behaved pleasantly toward the small party he was in and toward the wait staff. Brash and full of smart comments and stories. Enjoying himself. Unconcerned with anyone outside of his bubble.

He downed several drinks before having anything to eat. Zachary suspected he was already high on something. Loud and talkative, having a great time.

There were mostly men in the group. A lower percentage of women, not a one-to-one ratio like there would be if they were all couples. The women with them were young, dressed well, showing plenty of skin and acting happy and eager to please. They all had drinks.

It wasn't easy to nurse his one beer for long enough to keep an eye on the party. Zachary ordered wings and fries and a coke as well, eating slowly, pretending he was using social apps on his phone and enjoying himself.

The girls weren't paired with specific men, but slowly circulated among them. They danced several times, different songs with different men. They sat in different seats, carrying on conversations with different members of the group. They walked down the hallway that led down to the bathrooms in the back at different times, in various combinations.

Zachary sighed, eating a few more fries. Something was going on and, as the old man at the bodega had pointed out, if he got into the middle of it and started asking questions, he was going to get in trouble.

It was late when Zachary got home. He counted himself lucky that his door had been fixed and he was back at his own apartment instead of Kenzie's house, and therefore wouldn't have to explain where he had been all night.

Until he got to his door and saw a sticky note on his door, Kenzie's way of warning him that she was there, so he didn't have a heart attack or call the police when he realized someone else was in the apartment. He smiled at the little heart that she had drawn on the note, and tried to pretend that her presence there hadn't just added additional weight to the already heavy burden he was carrying. Which felt like it was right in the center of his chest and stomach instead of on his shoulders, where people normally talked about responsibility or emotional burdens. He felt more like a heavily pregnant woman looking like she was about to burst with all of the additional weight he was packing. The stomach cramps only added to the mental image.

Zachary shook his head, trying to shake the distracting thought of Bridget and her pregnancy out of his mind. He didn't need that interfering with his life too.

He tried to be very quiet so he wouldn't wake Kenzie up. They hadn't talked about getting together. He had thought that she would be happy to have her space back to herself after a couple of nights with him.

Apparently, she wasn't looking for space.

He didn't turn any lights on, feeling his way around and occasionally using his phone screen for a bit of light if he needed it. He got ready for bed, plugged his phone in on the bedside table, and slid into the bed as quietly as possible. Kenzie tended to sprawl right in the middle when she was asleep, but this time she was keeping to her own side of the bed.

"I didn't expect you to be so late," Kenzie whispered. She turned over to face him.

Zachary's heart thumped. He didn't want to have to explain all that he'd been doing that night to her. As far as she knew, he could have ended up doing surveillance for the night. He didn't always come home.

"Oh, hey. You didn't stay awake all night, did you? Have you had some sleep?"

"Yes, a little. Pretty restless, though. I was worried about you."

"You don't need to be worried. Everything is fine."

She reached out in the darkness, feeling for his body, and put one arm gently around him, cuddling up to his chest. Zachary relaxed, letting go of the tension. He put one protective arm around her and sighed. He loved when she snuggled up to him like that. He breathed in the scent of her body and her shampoo, resting his face against her head.

"I do worry. I know you said that you were going to be out doing some interviews tonight, but I thought… that would just be during the evening. Unless you're interviewing someone on night shift."

"Some interviewing. Some investigating. Watching people, trying to sort out what's going on."

"Mmm-hm." Her voice was sleepy. "Did you figure anything out?"

"I think so. But I'm still not sure where to go from here. I will have to think about it."

"Sleep on it," Kenzie murmured.

"Yeah." Zachary kissed her hair. "That's what I need to do."

He listened to her breathing, long and regular. She was soft and relaxed in his arms, slipping quickly back into sleep.

But for him, sleep was always elusive, even when it was late and he was tired. Rather than clouding and slowing down when he got tired, his brain seemed determined to jump into a higher gear, worrying over everything that was on his mind; the case, his relationship with Kenzie, anything he had said or done during the day, whether he had made any mistakes, if he had failed to do something he was supposed to. If he was a good enough human being.

Some days, just the part about being a human being was hard enough.

He lay there holding her and tried to slow his breathing down to match hers and join her in sleep.

17

Despite how late he had been getting home, Zachary was up in the morning before Kenzie. He was having his second cup of coffee and poring over pictures of Madison and Noah when she got up. Kenzie rubbed her eyes, yawning.

"Don't you ever sleep in?" she complained.

Of course, she already knew the answer to the question, and they had discussed it many times before. Zachary did go through periods of depression when his body and brain wanted to nothing but sleep, or when a stressful situation became too much and he just shut down, but the rest of the time… sleep was elusive, and didn't stay for long.

But Kenzie wasn't actually looking for an answer.

"What time did you get in last night?" she asked after pouring herself a mug of coffee from the carafe sitting on the burner. "I know it was late, but I didn't look at the clock."

"I'm not sure. Maybe two."

"Too late. At least I got back to sleep after that. Sometimes when I wake up at night, my body decides it's time to get up, and I have trouble settling in again."

"Mmm-hm."

"What about you? You must have been exhausted. Did you fall right asleep?"

She probably already knew the answer to that one too.

"No. Took a while."

"You should have stayed in bed a while longer."

"Wouldn't have been able to get back to sleep. I would have just kept you awake tossing and turning."

"Maybe I could have helped you relax and get back to sleep." She put an arm around his shoulders, bending down to brush his cheek with a kiss. Zachary turned his head to kiss her on the lips, which tasted like morning breath and coffee. He closed his eyes and savored her closeness.

"I wasn't expecting you to be here."

"Well, my place felt so empty after you left. I decided I didn't want to knock around there alone."

"So you ended up knocking around here alone instead."

"I wasn't expecting that, but it was okay. When I'm here, I can still… feel you around me. Because this is where your stuff is, you kind of… leave an imprint here. But at my house, there isn't enough of you there to feel that."

Zachary considered the comment. Did that mean she wanted him at her house more often? That she wanted him to leave some of his things in her closet, drawers, and bathroom? That she wanted him to move in?

He tried to cut off the train of thoughts. He didn't want to push the relationship too fast. They would just end up derailing again.

Kenzie sat down on the couch and pulled a blanket throw around herself. "Did you make some progress last night, then? Was this on your missing persons case, or something else?"

"The missing person. I… have some thoughts about it. Spotted a couple of people that she or her boyfriend partied with. Watched them for a while."

Kenzie nodded. "Did you ask them if they had seen her? I suppose you would have started with that if they had said so."

"I didn't approach them. Just watched."

Kenzie raised an eyebrow. "You can't get very far if you don't ask. You didn't think it would be productive?"

"I was warned—and I could see—that they were not the kind of people who would want to share anything with a private investigator or the police. You have to be careful who you talk to."

"Yes, you do," Kenzie agreed, with a direct gaze that reminded him he had done just that when trying to track down Jose. He had not been as careful as he should have been. He had walked into it as if none of the people he was talking to might actually be dangerous.

Lesson learned.

He ducked his head, trying to suppress the red flush he knew was spreading across his face. As if he could prevent it just by trying.

"I'm glad you're being careful," Kenzie said. "I don't want you to get hurt."

Zachary nodded.

Kenzie leaned forward, looking at Zachary's screen. "Is this her? Do you mind if I look?"

Zachary considered, then decided it was okay. Kenzie helped him out with other cases. They were used to bouncing ideas off of each other. He got up from his desk chair, disconnected his laptop, and took it over with him to sit beside her on the couch.

"I'm looking at the pictures of her and her boyfriend, looking for people who reoccur across several pictures, and also looking for clues in the pictures as to where they were. The more information I can get about where they were spending their time, the more easily I'll be able to find where they are now. Chances are, they will have gone to places convenient to her house, the school, or his place. There should be two or three clusters of locations."

"And whichever one is not close to her house or the school should center on his place."

Zachary nodded. "Unless he is also close to the school. It sounds like he grew up close to there, but I don't know if he still lives in the area. And Madison doesn't live far from the school. So I might just end up with one big cluster."

"Nothing is ever for sure," Kenzie agreed.

"Yeah."

Zachary swiped to the next picture in the gallery. They both studied the faces and any location clues. Kenzie pointed to a window, through which a two-color neon sign was visible.

"That looks like it's close to Old Joe's Steakhouse."

Zachary closed his eyes, picturing the street and everything he could construct around it. Kenzie was right. There was a bar on the same street with a similar two-color neon sign. He wrote down the photo number and a notation next to it. "I'll check that out."

Kenzie had her phone with her. She tapped at it, zooming in on the steakhouse on a map until she got down to street view. She panned around, looking for the neon sign and for what was across the street from it.

"If it's that sign, then that was taken in something called Union Public House."

Zachary added this to his note. "Never been there. Have you?"

"No. Kind of a seedy place, if I remember right. Not the kind of place I'd hang out with the girls."

Zachary nodded. The bits of the interior caught in the pictures were not fancy. Dim lights, black and white photos on the wall, not a trendy place you might expect young adults to go. "They seem to show up in a wide variety of places. Some of them higher-class, and some of them… cesspools."

Kenzie laughed. "I guess young people are always trying out new places, experimenting, seeing where they are comfortable. Playing different roles. Trying to find out where they feel comfortable. What fits."

"Yeah."

Zachary swiped to the next picture. In each one, they looked for clues about the location.

"These aren't all pictures you got from Rhys, are they?" Kenzie asked, frowning.

Zachary immediately understood her concern. Rhys was especially vulnerable. And too young to be attending at bars and clubs.

"No. I pulled a bunch of them from Madison's social networks. Selfies that she or her friends took. She shouldn't have been there either… must have false ID."

Kenzie nodded. "I'm just glad Rhys wasn't."

By the end of the day, Zachary had identified as many locations as he could from the pictures. Some of them helpfully had geographical locations in the metadata, but most of the ones that Madison had taken did not. She or someone else had been smart enough to shut off geolocating on her phone.

He reviewed the different locations, trying to identify clusters that would help him to track her down. The pins were scattered much more broadly across the city than he would have expected. It was only a small city, not a big metropolis like in other states, but he still hadn't expected Madison to have had the run of the whole city.

There were also a few people who he had spotted in a number of pictures. There were, of course, several with the friends that he had interviewed at school. But there were also a handful of men Noah's age or older who made repeat appearances at different parties or clubs. Zachary tagged the various subjects. He'd try finding all of their social networks and then comparing friends lists. "Probably time to put those away," Kenzie commented when she saw Zachary rubbing his eyes. "You remember how late you worked last night. You need to give your body and brain a rest tonight."

"Every day that I let pass without finding her…"

Kenzie's lips pressed together. She nodded. "I know. I don't like thinking of her out there alone. But remember… the police don't think she was kidnapped. If she's just somewhere with this boy… then it's not like when Bridget was missing, or when you were… you know."

"But we don't know that."

"I know. But at least you've made progress."

Zachary nodded. He wasn't going to be able to go on another bar crawl looking for Noah and the other men and girls that appeared in the pictures. If he didn't get enough rest, his brain would let him down. He wouldn't be alert enough to spot danger or clues. He wouldn't be able to make the split-second decisions that might be needed to save his own life or Madison's.

18

Zachary knew that it was probably too early in the day for Madison and Noah to be out and about. If they were spending a lot of time partying, they probably slept until noon or later. But that didn't mean he couldn't look around and ask questions at some of the locations around the clusters he had identified. If he were lucky, maybe he'd be able to get a line on them before they even woke up.

People were not nearly as willing to help him as they had been when he had canvassed around the school. He met with a lot of blank stares and clenched jaws, and more than one person told him to get lost. Though not that politely.

He was glad he was there in the morning instead of at night. Experience told him that this was probably not a neighborhood he wanted to be wandering after dark. Not without a posse of his own.

He approached a woman sweeping the sidewalk in front of her store. "Excuse me, ma'am? I'm looking for a missing girl..."

She rested, leaning on the broom, looking at him. Zachary approached with his phone held low, so she wouldn't think he was trying to make some kind of move on her. Both hands visible, no weapons. Nothing threatening. He was glad in such situations that he was so short and slight; it would have been a lot harder to portray a nonthreatening appearance if he were six feet tall and two hundred and fifty pounds.

She studied his face for a moment before looking down at the phone, still wary, but willing to look.

"She's been missing almost a week," Zachary explained. "There have been some sightings in the neighborhood; I'm trying to find out where she might be staying."

"Staying? If you think she's just staying somewhere, why are you looking for her?"

"She might be in danger. I don't know whether she is being held against her will. If she is… I want to help her."

"And if she isn't?"

"Then I'll just talk to her. I'm not here to cause trouble, just to give her a hand, get her reunited with her family if she wants."

The woman studied Madison's picture. "I don't know. She looks like a lot of girls. They come and go."

Zachary nodded understandingly. "Is there someplace they tend to live? Maybe an apartment where a few of them share the rent, different girls rotating in and out?"

She started to sweep again, moving slowly, the movements of the broom short. Away from his feet, but Zachary still felt like she was trying to shoo him away.

"Who knows where they go, or why?"

"Right. So you don't know? Maybe a building you've seen girls at before? Young girls like this?"

She had been with other girls in the pictures. New friends, not the girls from school. Drinking buddies. Party girls. A new lifestyle. One that didn't fit with her home life.

"I didn't tell you anything," the woman muttered.

Zachary looked at her in confusion for a moment. "Okay," he agreed. "You didn't tell me anything. Send me on my way."

She nodded. Her eyes flicked down the street. "The brick apartment building down there. That's where they go. That's where I see them."

Zachary didn't turn his head. He looked out the corner of his eye. "I'm just asking!" he said in a louder voice, one meant to be overheard by any watchers.

The woman batted at his shins with the broom. "Just get out of here. I don't know anything."

He withdrew, not looking her in the face again, muttering under his breath about crazy old bats and striding across the street, shaking his head.

He stopped there, taking a deep breath. He pulled a water bottle out of the courier bag over his shoulder and took a drink, taking a glance down the street at the building she had referred to.

Was the woman overly cautious about reporting anything that went on in the neighborhood? Or were they being watched? Was she aware of something going on with the girls in that building and didn't want to be seen tipping him off?

There were plenty of old women who were just paranoid or delusional. She might be one of them. But she was not that old. And she had seemed to have it together. She hadn't been warning him about squirrels or unicorns or Martians trying to monitor their brainwaves.

Zachary took a few more swallows of his water, looking around for anyone who might be paying attention to him. He didn't see any watchers. But that didn't mean that there weren't any. They could be inside the buildings, watching through cracks in the blinds. They could be out of sight, listening and monitoring everything going on in the neighborhood. Zachary put his water bottle back away and walked down the street. He stopped to tie his shoelace, looking around from another angle. He went into a convenience store and bought a chocolate bar. He didn't ask the man at the counter about Madison. He didn't announce himself as a private investigator. He was just a guy having a chocolate bar for breakfast.

The owner or manager of the store didn't say anything to him. Watched him, but didn't comment on him being new to the neighborhood or warn him to stay out of business that had nothing to do with him. Just another guy, slaving away in a convenience store, making sure that he didn't get ripped off by a shoplifter or armed robber.

Zachary wandered back out to the sidewalk, unwrapping the chocolate bar slowly and eating it. He watched the birds, the clouds scudding across the sky, the few people who were out on the sidewalk waiting for buses or going about their own private business, heads down, paying no attention to anyone else.

As far as he could tell.

After consuming the chocolate bar, he proceeded down the street, still alert for anyone who might be following or watching him. Everything seemed peaceful and nonthreatening. The woman had just been a crazy old woman. Playing cloak and dagger with him. A little excitement to spice up her day. Something to tell her husband when they saw each other at the end of the day. Something to laugh about.

He crossed the street again when he reached the building she had indicated. Red brick. Old. Not exactly dilapidated, but not quite middle class, either. The type of place Zachary might have moved into. Something cheap, without a lot of amenities, that fell within his budget. And if there were several kids living together, they could split up the rent into something that was manageable for entry-level, minimum-wage workers.

He entered the front door alcove. The same as any apartment building entryway. A little glassed-in area with a button panel on the wall, some of them with names scribbled on labels or tape beside the buttons. Room numbers, last names, crossed-out previous occupants.

The easiest approach in an apartment building was just to press all the buttons. Most people would ignore it, or would answer in irritation, or sleep through it. If no one answered the first time, he would try again. Eventually, someone would just give up and press the door release because they didn't want to be bothered anymore.

He looked at the handwritten labels as he pressed each button in sequence. He didn't see a Madison, Miller, or Noah. But he didn't know Noah's last name and probably neither of them would want their name on a button. Did they have friends who came to see them? Or was it just a place to crash? There was no guarantee that it was Madison's building. In fact, the odds were against it.

Zachary continued to press buttons and ignore the irritated answers, until he heard the buzz of the door release. He pushed through it and started down the hall. The building was pretty quiet. It was too early for night-dwellers, and those who had stores to open or nine-to-five office jobs were gone.

A man opened one of the doors into the hallway, looking out blearily. He had an unkempt beard and long hair. He was shirtless, but at least had boxers and a dingy robe wrapped messily around him, showing plenty of curly dark chest hair. He had dark skin and very dark eyes. They looked completely black in the dim wattage of the hallway.

"Who are you?" he demanded. He scratched under his arm. "You don't belong here."

"Where is she?" Zachary returned, as aggressively as he could manage.

He pointed his phone screen at the man, closing in way too fast on his head so that he was forced to rear back before he could see it. “Dumb broad stiffed me! She stiffed me! I’ll teach her she can’t do that!”

The man seemed to be having problems focusing his eyes. He looked at the screen, blinking, moving in and out to get it at the right distance. He raised his eyebrows and shot a glance farther down the hallway, and up. Like he was looking at a room on the second floor.

“How do I know?” he protested. “Hasn’t got anything to do with me, man!”

“You think it’s good business to go around cheating people out of their money? I paid cold, hard cash. I should call the police. I should teach her a lesson she won’t forget!”

“Hey, chill, man,” the man said, his voice low and warning. “Look, if you weren’t satisfied, then take it up with her manager. Don’t go causing trouble. You’ll get the wrong end of that stick.”

“Her manager? She wasn’t with anyone. Just by herself. She thought I wouldn’t be able to find her. Well, I have my ways! I knew where to find her!”

“You’ve got the wrong place,” the man said, shaking his head. Even so, he couldn’t help looking up again. “There’s no one here like that. I’ve never seen her before. You’ve got the wrong place.”

“You said she was here. You said talk to her manager. Who is her manager?”

“I don’t know. I misspoke. I thought you were talking about a girl at the bar down there,” he motioned vaguely down the street in the other direction. “This girl? In the picture? No. She’s not around here.”

“You’re lying.”

“No, man. Seriously. Everything is cool here. No one like that around here. I don’t know who told you she was here.” He tried to close the door.

Zachary stuck his toe in the door, which momentarily prevented its closure.

“Is she in there with you? I’ll call the cops. They’ll come in there and take all your dope and they’ll put her behind bars. You can’t go around defrauding people like that!”

“There’s no one else here.” The man kicked at Zachary’s shoe with his bare foot. Ugly, yellowing toenails. Dark, hairy legs.

Zachary withdrew his foot and let the man close the door. He waited for a moment, watching for other people to open their doors to see what the ruckus was all about. Or to quietly shut the doors that had been opened a crack to allow for better acoustics. There was no sound. Everyone was still, waiting to see what he would do.

Zachary muttered a few times about crazy chicks and being ripped off, retreating toward the front door.

He stopped at the stairway that led up from the tiny lobby area. No elevators. Nothing that was going to break down and need regular maintenance. People who couldn't make it up the stairs need not apply.

Zachary stuck his head into the stairway first, listening for any movement.

Manager the man had said. That threw a whole different light on Madison's situation. Maybe the crazy woman with the broom hadn't been so paranoid after all. Maybe someone asking about girls in the neighborhood was putting himself in a dangerous situation. Maybe Madison wasn't just a girl staying with her boyfriend or renting with a group of girls. A manager? That meant an organization. Probably a criminal enterprise.

So he was cautious. If the man on the main floor knew that she was upstairs, then her location was well known. And possibly guarded. If Madison were being held against her will, Zachary needed to be very careful in his approach.

He listened at the stairway for a long time. Until he heard someone coming down the stairs at a slow, heavy plod. A man with bloodshot eyes dressed in a long, dark coat came down the stairs. He looked at Zachary, wondering what he was doing hanging around in the stairwell. Zachary stepped forward to the first stair, acting casual, like he hadn't been there waiting, but was just getting home like any other day. The man's eyes flicked to him curiously, then he kept going.

Someone who lived there? Or a client? His red eyes could indicate that he was a drug user. Or that he had been up late. He could be completely innocent, nothing to do with the girls. But he didn't appear to be armed or there to guard anyone—just a guy walking down the stairs.

Zachary only went up two stairs, then turned sideways to give the man plenty of room to get by him. Polite and respectful. Actually, he just didn't want to get too far up and be knocked down the stairs by the man if he had misjudged the situation. Much easier to fall down two steps than a full flight. Less chance of breaking a bone or being put out of commission.

The man gave a polite nod of acknowledgment and walked past Zachary. He didn't pause or look back, just kept going out the door.

Zachary climbed the stairs slowly, still listening for anyone else, either coming down the stairs or waiting farther up in the stairwell guarding against intruders. He went slowly so he wouldn't be out of breath and distracted when he got up the stairs, but would be alert to any dangers.

There wasn't anyone at the top of the first flight of stairs. As far as Zachary could tell, the stairwell was empty.

He was assuming that the man had been looking up toward the second floor, and not to a higher floor. He hadn't looked way up, just at a bit of an angle, like he was looking down the hall at his own ceiling.

Just one floor up.

Zachary hoped.

19

He walked down the hall.

It was quiet, like the first floor.

He could hear voices. A discussion, not a fight. Other than that, silence. No one walking around, slamming doors, or conducting business. Night people sleeping. Morning people already gone.

Zachary didn't see any signs of trouble. No guards. No threats. He looked at the ceiling. No surveillance cameras. There could be peephole cameras, but he didn't see any that were obvious. The building smelled musty and of leftover cooking smells. Not a high-class place, but not a rat's nest, either. Low class respectable.

After walking down the hall and back, he tried to decide on the best approach. Friendly like with the woman on the street? Aggressive like with the man downstairs? Waiting until the door opened to decide on an approach?

He decided to start at the apartment the voices were coming from. Might as well start where people were awake, rather than waking people up. They would be in better moods. And if the occupants could quietly point Zachary in the right direction, he wouldn't need to wake up any enforcers. They could sleep, and he could decide whether to call the police.

He went to the closed door and listened for a moment, but he couldn't make out any words. It was a woman's voice. Muted. He still didn't think it was an argument.

Zachary raised his hand and knocked on the door. Quietly, like a private caller, not like the police, hammering on the door and ready to break it down if the occupants did not comply with the initial demand.

The voices stopped. Zachary waited, listening carefully. He didn't think that he would have to run, but he needed to be ready, just in case. Not that running was his best skill. He'd never been particularly athletic and, since the car accident, he had done physiotherapy to get him walking again, but running was problematic.

There were footsteps, and then the door opened. Cautiously. Not all the way. A face looked out at him through a gap of several inches. Zachary blinked. He had not expected to see a face that he knew.

"Noah."

The boy eyed him warily. "I don't know you."

"Is Madison there?"

He looked back over his shoulder, a reflex reaction. So Madison was there. "Who are you?"

"My name is Zachary Goldman. I'm a friend of Rhys Salter's."

"Rhys." Noah shook his head, frowning, then remembered. "That re— handicapped boy? What does he have to do with it? What are you doing here?"

"Madison has been reported missing. Her parents and a lot of people are worried about her."

"Madison doesn't want to talk to anyone." Noah tried to close the door.

As with the man downstairs, Zachary already had his foot in the gap, preventing it from closing. "I'll leave if I can talk to Madison. See she's okay."

"She doesn't want to talk to anyone."

Zachary raised his brows. "She needs to talk to me so I can reassure her parents that she's okay. She's a missing person. She needs to let people know she is all right."

"She's fine. You can tell them that."

"No I can't, I haven't seen her. She could be hurt. Chained up. It could be someone else in there. I need to see her or I don't know."

Noah looked over his shoulder again, reluctant. Weighing his options.

"What's going on?" the female voice asked.

"It's some guy… friend of your buddy Rhys. I don't know how he found this place." Noah rubbed his whiskers, frowning.

"Rhys?"

There was movement behind Noah. Zachary couldn't see her yet, but she was there. Not being tortured. Not chained up. Just shacking up with her boyfriend.

Noah opened the door farther so that Zachary had a better view of him and of the room behind him. A small kitchen. A girl clad only in a long t-shirt, her hair still rumpled from sleep. Madison.

"Madison. Hi. My name is Zachary Goldman. You know your parents are looking for you?"

Of course she knew that. Did she think she could leave home and they wouldn't look for her? That they would just shrug it off? *Oh well.*

Madison bit her lip. She looked at Noah, then at Zachary, not sure what to say. "I just… tell them I'm okay."

"Why don't you call them? Let them know that yourself."

"I don't want to talk to them. They'll try to make me go home. I don't want to go home. I'm fine here. Just tell them that. But… don't tell them where. Tell them I want to be left alone."

She looked at Noah again. Careful. Not wanting to say anything that would upset him? Was he abusive? Was he holding her there against her will, and she was afraid to tell Zachary?

There were a lot of ways to detain someone. Ropes and chains were not the only way to keep someone captive. Zachary studied Madison's eyes. She avoided his gaze. Was she being drugged? Abused? Threatened? He wasn't sure.

"Your family wants to hear from you. They're not going to take my word that you're okay. Whatever you're running away from, it's best if you confront it head-on. If it's a problem with your family, it can be dealt with. If it's something else…" Zachary shook his head. "They want to help you, Madison. Just talk to them."

Madison shook her head. She put her hand on Noah's back. Reassuring? Stabilizing? "No. Tell them I'm fine, but I'm not going back. I'm staying here. With Noah."

Zachary looked for something that might convince her. But she was firm. And if he pushed too hard or made threats, they might run. It wouldn't be so easy to find them a second time. He reached in his pocket and brought out one of his business cards. "Call me if you change your mind. Or if you need anything."

He reached out to hand it to Madison, but Noah snagged the card out of Zachary's hand and skimmed it onto the floor of the hallway.

"Out," Noah said firmly.

Zachary withdrew his foot. He didn't want to push Noah into physical violence, either against himself or against Madison. He had already stirred the pot enough.

The door shut quietly. Not slammed. A bolt and a chain slid across.

Zachary took a couple of deep breaths, standing there and hoping that his heart rate would slow down, now that he was no longer face-to-face with Noah. There was no danger. He had communicated with Madison. He'd been told to leave. He'd withdrawn. Whatever was going on with Madison, Zachary was safe.

He picked up the business card from the worn carpet, considering it for a moment. He slid it under the crack of the door into Madison's apartment. Maybe she or Noah would just throw it away. But maybe Madison would pick it up and pocket it, and reach out to Zachary when she was not under Noah's supervision.

When he reached the sidewalk outside the building, he again stopped to breathe and relax. He had another drink to wet his parched mouth before taking his phone out. He dialed Campbell's number.

"I found her."

20

Zachary had hoped that the resolution of the case would be a big celebration. He would find Madison, bring her home, and she and her family would be overjoyed. Everything would be resolved. Rhys would be happy. Zachary could go on with his other work, knowing that he had made a difference in one family's life.

But knowing where Madison was and that she refused to go home was disheartening.

Campbell sent a couple of officers over to talk to her before they could ditch the apartment and find something else. The cops confirmed what she had told Zachary. She said she was there of her own free will. She wanted to stay. She didn't want to talk to her parents.

And there was no law against leaving. She was a runaway, but she was old enough that the cops knew there was no point in taking her home. She would just leave again. There was nothing to resolve with her parents. There hadn't been a fight. She had just decided to move in with her boyfriend. Maybe in a few weeks or months, they would have a fight and break up, and maybe then Madison would decide to go home again. Until then, there wasn't much that anyone could do.

Kenzie had agreed to Sunday dinner with Mr. Peterson and Pat. There was always a discussion over who would drive. Both liked to make the drive for different reasons. Zachary because he found it reassuring and meditative. Highway driving was one of the only times that his brain slowed down and he experienced being 'in the zone,' which he imagined was what it was like in most people's brains most of the time. Able to focus on just one thing at a time, his restless brain watching the horizon and taking care of navigation, leaving the remainder of his brain to think things through.

Kenzie, on the other hand, loved her little red sports car. Zachary had to admit that it was a sweet ride and, in the summer when they could ride around town with the top down, it was an exhilarating experience. But highway driving with the top down just made the wind roar around his ears, and it was still too cold for even driving around town, unless it was an exceptionally nice, unseasonably warm day.

"How about I drive this time," Zachary suggested. "And next time we go, you can take your car. When it's warmer."

"We could go down in separate cars," she teased. "Then both of us can drive."

Zachary opened his mouth, trying to corral the one argument that would convince her that was a silly idea. If they arrived in separate vehicles, Lorne and Pat would think that they were fighting. Or that something was wrong. It would use up twice the gas. And they wouldn't have the pleasure of each other's company on the way. It just didn't make any sense.

Kenzie grinned at him. "We're not going to go in separate cars," she assured him.

"Okay, good."

"You can drive this time. But just because you seem sort of bummed out. And because next time it will be warmer, so it will be nicer in the convertible."

Zachary nodded. "Good. Thanks. Next time you get to drive for sure."

It was a couple of hours, and mostly they didn't talk, but just listened to the music on the radio and enjoyed the smooth highway under the tires. The pavement was dry, so there were no worries about having to slow down for ice. Zachary drove a little above the speed limit. Still low enough that he didn't think any cop would bother to pull him over and Kenzie wouldn't complain that he was being reckless. He was very good at driving at high speeds. It was one of the few TV-private-eye skills that he actually had. But he didn't want Kenzie to think that her life was in danger. And he didn't want a ticket or to be delayed for dinner.

Mr. Peterson greeted them at the door, giving both of them warm hugs and Kenzie a peck on the cheek. He ushered them into the house. Zachary was surprised to see Tyrrell and Heather sitting in the living room. Mr. Peterson hadn't mentioned that they would be there. But Zachary was happy to see them. It was amazing to be able to see his siblings after decades of being separated. He still couldn't quite believe that it was true. Heather's husband was also there, sitting beside her, with his arm around her. And another woman was sitting next to Tyrrell.

Zachary hadn't expected Tyrrell to bring a girl with him. He hadn't told Zachary that he was going out with anyone.

"Uh, hi," he greeted, a little awkward. He didn't know how to address her.

Tyrrell smiled, putting his hand on the woman's arm. "Zach, this is Jocelyn."

Zachary stared at her for a minute, trying to process this. Jocelyn was the name of their older sister. Tyrrell was dating a woman with the same name as their sister?

Tyrrell kept looking at Zachary, and the woman looked up at him, both of them waiting for his response.

"Jocelyn?" Zachary repeated.

She kept staring at his face. "Joss," she said.

Everything finally connected, and Zachary's jaw dropped. "Joss?" He gasped for breath, finding that all of the oxygen had suddenly been sucked from the room. "Oh my—Joss?"

When he had met Tyrrell, they had hugged each other, both eager and excited. With Heather, she'd been less certain. A reserved handshake. She'd been dealing with her own troubles, trying to figure out how to ask Zachary for help and wondering whether he could do anything for her.

With Joss, it was like there was a wall between them. She didn't look inviting. She didn't stand up to hug him or reach out her hand to take his. She just sat there, waiting.

Zachary swallowed. "It's so good to see you, Joss. How are you?"

She nodded, a strained smile. "I'm good. Nice for the four of us to see each other again."

Zachary nodded. "Yeah. I didn't know you were going to be here. I'm sorry if I seem a little… I'm just surprised. I didn't know it was you."

He'd had practice in trying to recognize the faces of his siblings. Tyrrell's eyes had given him away, even if nothing else about him had seemed familiar. Heather looked very different, and he had trouble seeing anything of the little girl she had been. But every now and then he caught a glimpse of that little girl. One of the little mothers who had tried to look after him and keep him out of trouble before they had gone into foster care.

And Joss had been the other.

As a child, her hair had been blond, but it had darkened over time. Not the almost-black hair that Zachary and Tyrrell sported, but darker than Heather's. They were all sitting, so he could see that she was a little shorter than Heather. She looked older. The two of them were only a year apart, but she looked a decade older than Heather, at least. Her mouth was pinched, wrinkles and frown lines around it and her eyes. She looked like she'd lived a hard life. Probably a smoker. That aged the face and skin. Although she was smiling at Zachary, she didn't look even remotely happy to see him. She smile was just a mask. A social convention.

Zachary turned slightly toward Mr. Peterson, hoping for some help. Mr. Peterson was socially adept, he got along with almost everyone, and he was good at drawing people out. Zachary had no idea how to talk to Joss or what to say to her.

"They wanted it to be a surprise," Mr. Peterson said, his round face wreathed with smiles. "We know how much you can worry over things, and didn't want you to spend the last few days and your whole ride here wondering about how things were going to go. Jocelyn said she would like to meet you, so we just went ahead and set it up."

Zachary nodded as if it all made perfect sense to him. He looked for somewhere to sit down, and Kenzie steered him toward the seat on the couch next to Jocelyn. Kenzie herself picked the easy chair close by that Mr. Peterson usually sat in. Zachary wanted to move everyone around to more comfortable places. His three siblings on the couch together. He and Kenzie on the adjoining love seat. Mr. Peterson in the chair he belonged in. Everybody in the right, most comforting places. He didn't want to sit next to Jocelyn, with her fixed smile.

He swallowed, trying to think of something to talk to Jocelyn about. He should ask her about herself. How her life was now. He couldn't mention their childhood, how Zachary had destroyed the family, the abuse and hard life that each of them had suffered through as a result.

"So… really nice to see you," Zachary said, though he thought he might have said it already. "What are you doing with yourself? How are things? Are you… I don't know where you live."

"I'm on my own," Joss said, in a clipped tone. "No current spouse or partner. No kids that would claim me. Just looking after myself."

Zachary nodded. "Uh-huh. That's great. I'm… I guess you already know I'm a private investigator. Do you… have a job? Or…" he trailed off, unsure how to end that question. Was she just a bum? Living on the street or in some halfway house? Trying to get her life together? Where did he think he was going with that question?

"I have a job," Jocelyn said defensively. "I work at a restaurant."

"Oh, great. Anywhere I would know?"

"By the looks of you," she cast an eye over his narrow frame, "you don't eat out much."

"Well… now and then. Just not… very much at a time. It's my meds… they suppress appetite…"

She told him where she worked. It wasn't anywhere that Zachary knew. He shrugged. "Sounds like a nice place."

She rolled her eyes.

Zachary looked at Heather and Tyrrell for help.

21

"What have you been working on lately?" Tyrrell asked.

Zachary cleared his throat and swallowed, considering how much he wanted to share—or not to share. As long as he kept names out of it, he wasn't breaking any confidences. "I, uh, just finished up with a missing persons case."

"You should tell them about it," Kenzie encouraged.

"If you finished with it, does that mean that you found him?" Tyrrell asked.

"Her. Yes, I did."

"It wasn't—not like that other case?" Heather said tentatively. "You mean that you found her and…"

"She was fine," Zachary hurried to assure her. Not like Jose. He flashed for a minute on Dimitri's bloated corpse. He hadn't seen Jose after his death, but he'd seen Dimitri. Zachary wouldn't want to bring up Jose in front of Mr. Peterson or Pat. He had searched for Jose at Pat's request, and the results had not been good. He didn't want to risk setting Pat back on the progress he had made in recovering from his friend's death. "She was voluntary—that means she had disappeared because she wanted to, not because someone had kidnapped her."

"I think we all know what voluntary means," Jocelyn said dryly. "I may have dropped out of high school, but I still know basic vocabulary."

"Sorry… I didn't mean it to sound like I was putting anyone down."

"So why did she want to leave?" Tyrrell asked. "Was this like a battered spouse, or a runaway kid, or what?"

"A teenager. Ran away to be with her boyfriend."

"Figures," Joss said. "Waste of your time."

"I guess," Zachary said. "But she could have been in danger. I'm still glad that I took the case and could make sure that she was okay. Even if she did choose to stay with her boyfriend, at least her parents and friends know that she's safe. They know that nothing happened to her."

Jocelyn snorted.

They all looked at her. Zachary wasn't the only one who didn't understand why she was being so scornful.

"Wouldn't you rather know where your daughter was?" Kenzie asked.

"Just because they know where she is, that doesn't mean that they know what's happening to her. Most parents haven't got a clue what's going on right under their own noses."

"I saw her," Zachary said slowly. "She told me right to my face that she wanted to stay there with her boyfriend."

"And you can't see what's right under your own nose, either. I thought you'd at least have some sense, after being in foster care."

"What does foster care have to do with it?"

"Lots of kids are trafficked in foster care."

Zachary stared at her. He didn't argue the point. He'd been too worried about Madison and what might have happened to her. He remembered the man in the bathrobe downstairs saying that he would have to talk to Madison's manager. Not her boyfriend, but her manager.

Madison hadn't been bruised. Her body language hadn't said that she was afraid. But Zachary had still been worried. He'd sent the police there, despite her saying that she wanted to stay of her own free will, because he wanted to make sure. If she were being trafficked for sex, he wanted to make sure that she could get out. The police wouldn't let her stay there if she were being victimized. Campbell said that his officers confirmed back that she was voluntary. She had confirmed to them, even with Noah out of the room and out of hearing, that she wanted to stay there and that she wasn't being harmed or coerced. The police had dealt with situations like that before. They had their tricks. They could arrest the girl on some pretext to get her out of there, and her pimp wouldn't know what had happened. They would think she had just been arrested. People were arrested every day in that business.

So he didn't repeat 'trafficked' like he didn't know what Joss was talking about. And he didn't say that Madison couldn't be. He just looked at her, wondering how Jocelyn had focused in on trafficking with the little he had said.

"She wasn't being trafficked." It was Kenzie who objected, not Zachary. "She had just run away with her boyfriend."

"Not her boyfriend," Jocelyn said, "her Romeo."

Kenzie frowned. "What's the difference?"

"A Romeo isn't a boyfriend. She might think he is, but he's just there to get her into the business. Romance her and make her think that they're in love, so he can get her to trick for him."

Zachary thought about this. He pictured Madison and Noah together. They had seemed like a genuine couple. But they would, wouldn't they? If that's what she was supposed to think, then that was what her body language would say. And if he had set out to play her, then he would have the act down pat.

"But they've been together for months," he said. "He wouldn't take that long to turn her out, would he? That's too long."

Joss's expression changed ever so slightly. Zachary couldn't identify what it was that changed but, for the first time, she seemed to be viewing him with some respect. Not just the tolerant older sister, there to put on an appearance and make nice. Realizing, maybe for the first time, that he was no longer the little boy who had accidentally set the house on fire. No longer the bratty little brother who didn't know anything and was always getting everyone in trouble.

"Yes, he would have turned her out by now. But she might not realize what's going on."

"How could she not know what's going on?" Kenzie demanded. She looked over at Zachary, reading his warning look. "I'm sorry. I don't mean to sound like I doubt you, I just mean I don't understand it. Please explain it to me."

Zachary hoped that was a humble enough apology for Joss to decide to forgive Kenzie's question. As he remembered it, Joss could hold a grudge. She was scary that way. She'd been in charge of all of the kids when they were away from their parents, and she could be mean. Zachary had felt the sharp side of her tongue many times, and she'd been bigger and stronger than he was too. She hadn't been abusive like their mom and dad, but she'd done everything she could to keep their little gang in line.

Jocelyn studied Kenzie for a minute, glanced aside at Zachary, then focused again on Kenzie, since she was the one who had asked the question.

"There's no way for someone like you to know what it's like to be trafficked," she said coolly. "Someone like you doesn't have any idea what it's like on the other side of the street. None at all."

Zachary expected a protest from Kenzie. Saying that she wasn't that privileged. That she knew what things were like in the real world, even if that wasn't one of the things she had experienced herself. But Kenzie just kept her mouth clamped shut and let Jocelyn speak.

Jocelyn turned her attention back to Zachary. The familiar one. It had been decades since they had seen each other, but they had some shared background. She knew how he had started out life, and it hadn't been with a silver spoon in his mouth. She had been in contact with Tyrrell or Heather, so she probably had the broad strokes of Zachary's life since then. Not privileged. Far from it.

"He'll ask her to do it as a favor. Just once. Because he's in dire straits and some leg breaker is going to come after him. Just once, and he'll be able to pay off his debt and they'll be okay. He loves her and he doesn't want to ask her to do it and he'll understand if she says no, but… it's the only way he can see out. So she does it once. Nothing kinky. Something safe and vanilla. It's over quick, and he gets a wad of cash to pay off his debts, and they're okay. He loves her for what she did for him. It's proof of just how much she really loves him. And maybe there's enough left over for a fancy new dress. And for them to go out to dinner together. He makes it nice for her. Sets up all of those reward centers in the brain to feel good. So that when she tricks for him, she feels valued and appreciated and like she's really helping out someone she loves."

Zachary swallowed and nodded. "And that's the first time."

"The first time is the biggest barrier. After that, it's easier. Could she just help him out this once? They're getting evicted and they need a new place. They need to get out of that rat hole. If she could just do a couple of guys for him, then everything would be okay. And he's nice and loving and appreciative…"

Zachary sighed.

"And pretty soon," Jocelyn said, "he'll be sure to get her hooked on something too. Maybe heroin. Maybe meth. If she ever resists him, he holds back the drugs. It doesn't take long before she's desperate, and she'll do whatever he tells her to. Doesn't matter if she's not protected anymore, if she's seeing five or ten guys a night, if she's doing stuff she never would have considered before. She needs the drugs. She craves the love and attention he showers her with when she does what she's told. She likes the fancy dresses and purses and all of the proof that she's having a good time."

"And then it's too late," Kenzie said.

Jocelyn shrugged. "It was too late the minute she met him. These guys know what they're doing. He's got a boss above him who tells him how to do everything. Who to target, how to get her to fall for him. How to keep her on a string and to turn her out. He's given step-by-step instructions, and if he makes a mistake or she falls out of line, there's a consequence for him."

"So he's a victim too," Tyrrell said.

Jocelyn shrugged her shoulders. "There are layers and layers of predators and victims in every organization. If you've been there for a few months, you'd better be looking at who you're going to bring in. They don't want the money to dry up. It's like a pyramid scheme. The more people you can bring in, the more you get out of it. You get higher and higher in the organization. More money and power. More perks."

"What makes you think that she's trafficked and not just a runaway?" Zachary asked.

"Show me a runaway who's not being trafficked."

The knot in Zachary's stomach tightened. He didn't want to be worrying about Madison. He wanted to relax and have a nice time with his family and not to have to think about Madison again. He had finished what he had set out to do. Rhys had asked him to find Madison, and he had done so. It wasn't his fault that she didn't want to go back to her family.

"If she's being forced into these gigs, then why wouldn't she want to go back to her family? Wouldn't she get out at the first opportunity?" Kenzie asked.

"She thinks she's in love with Romeo. She wants to help him and protect him. And maybe she's addicted. And proud of her new clothes and position. And maybe someone at home is abusive, which is why she left there in the first place."

"I didn't see any sign of it," Zachary put in. "Seemed like she had a pretty good life. Parents were friendly and worried about her. I didn't get a bad vibe from them."

"But you don't know. People can put on the best show in the world for you. You would never guess what kind of creeps they are when the door is shut and they're alone with each other or their daughter. You have no idea what goes on behind closed doors. No idea. Trust me."

Zachary nodded. He'd seen how different people could be once the authorities had gone home. He'd had to live with people like that.

He still didn't think the Millers were like that. But Joss was right. You never could tell.

22

"So, are you a social worker?" Kenzie asked Joss as they dished up their meals.

Pat moved back and forth between the table and the kitchen, bussing platters and deep dishes of all sorts of rich foods. It was a wonder he still looked so strong and athletic at his age. He obviously did not eat very much of his own cooking.

Tyrrell and Heather spoke a little to each other, voices lowered. It was amazing how close they had become. Zachary was between Heather and Tyrrell in age, and he thought that he should be the one with a closer relationship with Tyrrell, but since Heather had made contact with them, they had become very close. He tried not to be jealous of their relationship and paranoid about what they were whispering to each other.

"I said I work at a restaurant," Joss snapped. "You were sitting right there."

"Well… yeah, I guess you did. But you sounded like you knew a lot about trafficking, and I thought maybe you were a social worker. Before. You could be a social worker and not be working as one right now. I'm sure they get hit by the economy just like anyone else. Or get burned out and decide they can't keep doing it. I thought maybe you were a professional."

"No," Jocelyn said curtly.

Kenzie looked at Zachary and raised an eyebrow. *Just what's eating her?*

Zachary shook his head. He would have to talk to her about it later. It was obvious to him where Jocelyn's knowledge had come from. Lots of foster kids got trafficked, she had said. And she'd been a foster kid. She knew how the organizations worked from the inside out. Who knew how many years she had been caught in that life. He wasn't about to ask her. Not over the dinner table.

"It's so nice to see you again, Kenzie," Pat said, finally sitting down. "It's been too long. How have you been keeping since you were here last? Any interesting cases?"

"You should know better than to ask Kenzie about interesting cases," Zachary warned. "Most people don't like autopsy talk at the table..."

"I promise no autopsy talk," Kenzie agreed with a laugh. "How about zombies? I have some new jokes..."

"Are you okay?" Kenzie asked when they got into the car.

Zachary didn't process her words immediately. He heard the silence, and then looked at her, then ran the tape in his head back and replayed it.

"Um, yeah. I'm fine."

He started the car and drove out of Mr. Peterson's neighborhood and out to the highway. He noticed Kenzie's silence again after a while and glanced over at her.

"What? Did you say something?"

"No."

"I'm okay." He repeated the assurance. "Why? I'm just fine."

"You didn't seem yourself at dinner today. I thought you would have a good time with so much of your family there. But you hardly even talked to anyone. Half the time, I don't think you had any idea what the conversation was about."

Zachary felt the tightness across his forehead and tried to smooth out his frown. To look bland and unworried. Nothing for Kenzie to be worried about.

"No, sorry. I think... it was just too many people for me. I'm okay with a small group, but once it goes past a certain level... I just get distracted. Overstimulated. Sorry about that. I didn't mean to make anyone uncomfortable."

"What have you been thinking about?"

"Just… the usual. Old memories. The family. Cases still waiting for me when I get back home. What I need to work on tomorrow."

"You told Rhys that you found Madison?"

Zachary broke into a cold sweat. He had told the police. They had informed Madison's parents. He hadn't immediately messaged Rhys with the good news.

Maybe because it wasn't good news.

Rhys wanted to see her again. He didn't want Zachary just to find her and assure him that everything was fine. He wanted to see her. Talk to her. Know for sure that she was okay.

And Zachary couldn't tell him that. He couldn't tell Rhys that everything was fine with Madison and she had just chosen to move away and to go somewhere else.

Maybe because he still had his doubts. Jocelyn's words had not reassured him. He knew that what she said was true. For a good part of dinner, he had not been thinking about Madison. Instead, he had been thinking about Joss.

He had always been a little scared of her as a kid. She'd been almost an adult in his eyes, and she'd ruled them with an iron fist. As much as a thirteen-year-old could rule with an iron fist.

And he was still scared of her. She was a hard woman. It was obvious that she too had been through a lot both in foster care and after she had aged out. She hadn't had an easy time. He hated the thought that she had been victimized just as much as he had. Just as much as Heather.

Maybe even more.

"Do you think she'll be okay?" he asked Kenzie.

"Madison?"

"Joss. I meant Joss, but I guess Madison too. If she's being trafficked by Noah like Joss said she is… I don't know how to get her out. I already tried to get her out, and the police tried. What else am I supposed to do?"

"I don't know, Zachary. I think you have to leave it to the police. There's not much you can do, especially about a criminal organization. If you were just trying to talk her out of staying with her boyfriend, of making contact with her parents, that's one thing. But trying to get her out of there if she's part of an organization… they won't take very kindly to people who try to take their assets."

Zachary shook his head. He pressed his foot to the gas pedal, whizzing by several slow-moving vehicles on the highway. Kenzie looked at him. Zachary eased off, letting the needle of the speedometer settle at a lower number.

"Why are you worried about Joss?" Kenzie asked. "She struck me as a person who can look after herself."

"She's always had to be grown up… but I don't think that means she can always look after herself. I think a lot of it is bluff. Trying to make other people think she's tough and in charge."

"Well, you would know better than I would, but she didn't seem like she was having any problems communicating her thoughts to me."

"That's not what I meant."

They covered the next few miles in silence.

"What did you mean?" Kenzie asked. "Why are you worried about Joss?"

"She's been through so much, and it sounds like she's just barely holding things together with her job at the restaurant. I'm just worried… things are going to go downhill."

"You guys barely even talked to each other. What do you mean about her being through so much? You mean when you were kids?"

"No. I mean what she was talking about. Sex trafficking. Being caught in that kind of business… and addicted to drugs. She can't be making very much waitressing at a restaurant, and if she relapses… it's just one step to get back into prostitution and get enough money for drugs."

"I don't think she ever said that she was being trafficked."

"She didn't have to."

"You think so? You think she was talking about herself when she was talking about what might have happened to Madison?"

"Yeah."

"Well… I suppose. There's nothing to say that she wasn't. I just figured, if she was talking from experience, she would have said so."

"When you asked her if she was a social worker?"

"Yeah. That would have been a good opportunity."

"People don't talk about that so openly. It's… it's just not done. People are ashamed. When they come out about being abused or trafficked… society doesn't treat them very well. They get bullied. People tell them that they're lying or imply that it's their own fault. They get re-victimized."

"Our society has moved forward quite a bit in the last few years. I think that with the latest developments, it's a lot more acceptable to talk about your experiences with being abused. Maybe not for men, still, but women… are allowed to be more open now. More supported."

Zachary shook his head. "No. Not really."

"You have to admit that we treat rape victims a lot better than we did back in the eighties, when Heather was a victim."

"I hope so." The photos he had seen of Heather in her cold case file were burned into his memory. He would never forget what she had looked like after the assault. And the police had still treated her like she must have asked for it. It was her own fault for dressing so immodestly and walking through the park, which was out of bounds for the school kids for a reason. "But I don't know. There are still a lot of jerks out there. Older people. Religious bullies. People who… just like to hurt others. They feel so insecure, they'll attack the weakest person in the room. Someone like Joss… she's learned to present herself as someone strong and independent, to keep people at a distance. Keep them from attacking."

Kenzie nodded slowly. Zachary was sure she had seen and heard enough examples to understand that they were still in the dark ages as far as treating victims went.

"Are you going to keep in touch, then? Let Joss know that you're available if she wants to talk about it? Sometimes, just having someone who is open to talking things through is helpful to someone… on the edge."

For some reason, her words made Zachary remember his agreement to do couples therapy with Kenzie. To somehow do something to help them to stay together and work through the difficult times. Zachary blamed himself for all of the intimacy speed bumps, but he didn't know how to get over them.

"Hey, umm…"

Kenzie looked at him, her eyes wary.

"So… I don't know if I ever said… when Bridget and I were together, we talked once or twice about doing some couples therapy. To see if we could work things out."

"Yes… good suggestion," Kenzie agreed. She sounded intensely uncomfortable. While she had been amused by Bridget at the beginning of their relationship, she had discovered over time just how twisted up over her Zachary was. How hard it was for him to separate himself from what they had been as a couple. How he was still in love with her even though he didn't want to be.

He wanted to move on and be totally devoted to Kenzie and not distracted by Bridget and her pregnancy with her current partner—after she had refused to even consider having children with Zachary.

"Sorry. I shouldn't bring it up."

"No, finish what you started. Where are you going with this?"

"Bridget… she wouldn't agree to any kind of therapy. She didn't need anything. I was the one who was broken, not her."

"And that worked out real well, didn't it?" Kenzie said with a sneer. "How can you expect to have a healthy relationship with someone if you refuse to put the effort into it?"

Zachary breathed slowly in and out. He knew that Kenzie was right, but his immediate reaction was to defend Bridget. She *wasn't* the one who was broken. She had put plenty of effort into the relationship, just not into therapy. She thought that Zachary needed to work harder at fixing himself. That he could *choose* to be healthier if he just wanted it badly enough. If he wasn't getting better, then it wasn't her fault. It was his.

They drove in silence for a while longer. It was dark, and Kenzie had her face turned away from Zachary, looking out the window into the blackness.

He watched the road and the taillights ahead of him. He knew the route; it was all automatic to him. Which lane to be in. Where the pot holes were. Where he could speed up on the straightaways, if he were driving alone.

"Zachary." Kenzie's hand was on his leg. A warm squeeze. "I think couples therapy is a good idea. I told you that when you were talking to Lorne. I should have suggested it before, instead of striking off on my own and… you know. Taking things into my own hands."

Zachary didn't nod or agree. He didn't think that would be very tactful. He didn't want to hurt her or to focus on what she had done wrong in the past. She had been trying to help him. She had been trying to find a way to make their relationship work. He had forgiven her, so he shouldn't bring it up again.

"I want us to get stronger," he said. "To grow together. Not to… end up going different directions from each other."

"I do too."

"Okay. So. I'll talk to Dr. Boyle about it. See if she'll do it, or if she recommends someone else." He looked over at her, gauging Kenzie's reaction, making sure he had understood her correctly. She thought it was a good idea. So she was prepared to go ahead with it?

Kenzie nodded. "You bet. Let me know, and we'll find a time that can work around my work schedule. I'll be there."

She would be there.

Zachary released a pent-up breath.

23

Zachary was at the Salter house when Rhys got home from school. Rhys raised his eyebrows at finding Zachary in his living room. He looked around for his grandmother, but Vera had left them alone for the conversation.

Zachary stood up to shake hands with Rhys, almost always a two-handed affair, with the non-shaking hand either patting Zachary on the shoulder or wrapping around him in a hug. Rhys was less effusive than usual, waiting for Zachary to fill him in on why he was there.

"I found Madison this weekend, Rhys," Zachary told him, not wanting to draw it out painfully.

Rhys squeezed Zachary's hand tighter.

"It's okay," Zachary assured him. "She's okay. She's alive, and she's not being held captive. She's just… with Noah."

Rhys sat down on the couch with a soft thump. He held his hand over his heart, breathing out a puff of air.

"Sorry. I wasn't trying to scare you. I knew you would assume that someone had kidnapped her and was holding her…" Zachary swallowed. "Like when Gloria took Bridget."

Both of them thought about Bridget's kidnapping. Rhys had been there, trying to help her and keep her alive. Zachary had been on their trail, and the timing had been very close. A few more hours, and she wouldn't have made it.

Rhys always asked Zachary about Kenzie, but never Bridget. He knew that Bridget was Zachary's ex. He had seen the reunion when Zachary found Bridget and knew that Zachary still had feelings for her. But he had never once asked after Bridget or teased Zachary about her. Only about Kenzie.

"I'm sorry. I wish I had better news for you," Zachary apologized, sitting on the ottoman to face Rhys on his level.

Would it have been better news if Madison had been kidnapped? If it meant that she was going back to her parents and back to school, back to her old friends and to Rhys? For that to happen, Madison first would have to go through the trauma of being kidnapped and held against her will for a week. Was that better than finding out that she was gone because she wanted to be? Because she chose one boy over everything else in her life?

Rhys shook his head and gave Zachary a thumbs-up, indicating that it was a good result. He slapped Zachary on the shoulder in congratulations and smiled at him encouragingly.

It was a good result. It was good to know that she hadn't been kidnapped and held against her will or, worse yet, killed.

But was it good? If she was only in love with Noah because he was romancing her to turn her out as a prostitute, how was that different from holding her captive?

Rhys got up off of the couch and went to the kitchen. He called over his shoulder, a single word directed at the rest of the house. "Gram?"

When Vera joined them in the kitchen, Rhys had his head and half his body in the fridge as he looked through it to see what goodies Vera had put away. He turned to look at her, and motioned to Zachary.

"Can Zachary stay over for supper?" Vera interpreted. "Of course he can. If he doesn't mind warmed-up leftovers. It's my night to volunteer at the old folks' home, so we always just have something quick from the fridge."

"Uh, sure," Zachary agreed. "I'm not picky."

It was funny to think of Vera volunteering at a seniors' home when, not that long ago, Zachary had thought that she was sliding into dementia herself. Once she got off of the meds that were causing her fogginess, that had changed completely. He was glad that Rhys had a family member who was able to look after him. He had grown up in his grandma's home and she understood him better than anyone else. She was protective of him after everything he had been through, but not a helicopter parent.

Rhys started pulling bowls out of the fridge and, in a few minutes, Zachary was warming up some leftover casserole while Rhys heaped food from several other dishes onto his plate. Zachary kept an eye on Rhys, wondering how he was feeling about the news about Madison.

"So, it's good news about your friend, isn't it?" Vera said to Rhys brightly, testing out the waters.

Rhys nodded without looking at her.

"Scary to have someone just disappear like that. You're lucky Zachary is such a good investigator."

Rhys looked over at Zachary as if waiting for him to say something. But Zachary didn't want to mention the possibility of sex trafficking in front of Vera. She had enough to worry about, without thinking about how vulnerable teens Rhys's age were to predators. Rhys himself was even more vulnerable due to his communication disabilities and the loss of his mother. If he had been targeted instead of Madison…

Zachary knew that there were plenty of boys being trafficked. They were not safe from predators either. As Joss had said, he'd seen enough in foster care to know about the possibilities.

"It's good that we at least know where she is," Zachary acknowledged Vera. "Though how long they'll—how long she'll stay there, I don't know. Girls will move around when there's too much attention from the police."

Vera had just a cold sandwich for herself, and left Rhys and Zachary alone again to eat their meal while she got ready for her night out.

Rhys took his heaping plate out of the microwave and set it on the table. He sat down and tapped on his phone for a minute. He slid it across the table to Zachary.

A video. Zachary tapped the triangle and watched the same video that Rhys had shown him before. Madison and Noah together. Telling Rhys to quit taping. Zachary opened his mouth to remind Rhys that he'd already seen the video. But there was a reason Rhys was showing it to him again. Rhys knew where Madison was now. Knew that she was with Noah and that she hadn't been kidnapped or murdered. And he still wanted Zachary to watch the video.

Zachary tapped it and watched it over. Madison, looking sore and tired.

Flinching and initially pulling away when Noah touched her. Noah's anger when he saw Rhys taping them.

With his elbows on the table, Zachary put his palms over his eyes, closing his eyes and reviewing the video and everything else he knew.

"I'm going out," Vera called out, as she walked by.

Zachary removed his hands from his eyes and saw her look in through the doorway. She stopped, head cocked to the side.

"Are you okay, Zachary?"

"Yeah. Just tired."

It was a good excuse, because he usually looked tired. He was chronically short on sleep. Vera nodded. "Don't keep him too late, Rhys. He needs to go home to bed."

Rhys nodded his agreement. Vera left the kitchen, and in a minute they heard her close the front door as she left the house.

Rhys motioned toward his phone, still beside Zachary's plate. Zachary pushed it slowly back toward him.

"She looks like… something could be wrong," Zachary said, not wanting to put ideas into Rhys's head if it weren't something he'd already thought of. He didn't want Rhys lying awake at night, thinking about what was happening to Madison.

Rhys nodded briefly. His eyes were on Zachary's, waiting for him to say more.

"You think this guy is taking advantage of her? That he's not… what he appears to be?"

Rhys nodded firmly. Yes. Of course. Why would he keep showing Zachary that video if he didn't think it told a story? Madison, tired and in pain from her recent activities. Flinching away from a man's touch. Pulling away from the one who was supposed to be her boyfriend. Noah's anger at Rhys catching them on video.

Did Rhys know? Did Noah and Madison realize that Rhys knew? Was that why Madison had to disappear?

Back at his apartment, Zachary scowled as he looked through the pictures he had of Madison once more, looking for signs that she was being coerced into trafficking for Noah. Or, if not coerced… encouraged. Pushed.

Emotionally blackmailed. Maybe, as Joss had said, she didn't even know that she was being trafficked. She didn't realize that's what it was. She thought that it was just her own choice to help out her boyfriend, not realizing that she was part of a larger criminal enterprise. Not understanding what would happen if she refused.

But the pictures were not a lot to go on. Rhys had seen her. He'd seen how she had changed and how she behaved around Noah. Something had struck him as being wrong, but he couldn't tell Zachary exactly what that was. He could keep showing him the same pictures and videos over and over again, but he couldn't explain what it was that he was seeing and feeling. And Zachary didn't think that was just his communication difficulties. Even if Rhys could put it all into spoken words, maybe he still wouldn't have been able to explain what it was he knew. But he knew.

He thought back to Rhys's response when Zachary had asked him, "What do you want me to do?"

Rhys had considered it for a few minutes, then he had pointed to Zachary, pointed to himself, and pointed to the video of Madison on his phone. *You and me go see Madison.*

Zachary had immediately shaken his head. He couldn't take Rhys there. He wouldn't do it. They would have to find another way to approach the problem.

He had thought that he was done with the case. He had told Kenzie that it was solved. He'd told his family that it was closed. But there he was, looking through the pictures and the notes he had written when he talked to Madison's family and the people at the school.

If Madison had been pushed into prostitution and drug addiction, then he was morally obligated to do what he could to help her. It wasn't just a matter of telling the police where she was and letting her family know that she didn't want to go back home. That didn't clear him of any obligation. It wasn't the end of the case, and he knew it.

Zachary rubbed his gritty eyes, looking for some other approach. He had talked to Madison and Noah. Of course, the next step was to approach her when she was alone. She might have a different response from what she had when Noah was there. Like in the video when she had told Rhys to stop recording and to leave her alone. That was what she had said out loud, but her eyes and facial expression had been apologetic. She didn't like the way

Noah had talked to Rhys. She hadn't wanted to tell Rhys to go away and leave her alone.

When Rhys had followed up with a message asking her if she were safe, she had told him that he shouldn't contact her again.

Noah could be controlling her use of her phone as well. He could be reading all of her messages and making sure she responded to them the way that he wanted her to. He could be controlling every aspect of her life, while she thought she was still in control.

So how was Zachary going to get her alone? That was what he needed to do. Maybe she hadn't wanted to talk to the cops even when she was alone with them. But Noah had been in the next room. He could have overheard. He could have the room bugged. If the cops had taken Madison out of there, he would have a pretty good idea that she had wanted to go. They didn't have any reason to arrest her unless she gave them a reason to.

24

Zachary shifted in his chair. He had not anticipated that he would be quite so uncomfortable in his session with Dr. Boyle. He had been seeing her for a while and, although he was sometimes nervous about telling her something or exploring his deepest feelings about a problem or an incident in his past, he had been forcing himself to see her regularly and not to cancel or reschedule any of his sessions. Not like after the assault, when he had avoided going to see her for weeks, when it was probably the time that he needed to see her the most. He hadn't been able to. He'd just shut down.

But having Kenzie in the room there with him changed things completely.

He wasn't afraid that Dr. Boyle was going to reveal anything to Kenzie or break any confidences. She had already promised him that. He still had his privacy. She wouldn't tell Kenzie anything Zachary didn't want to tell her.

And he wasn't afraid that Kenzie was going to tell Dr. Boyle anything that was shameful or embarrassing. It would be easier if Kenzie talked to Dr. Boyle directly about any concerns that she had than for Zachary to have to put them into words and bring them up himself.

But he'd never had anyone in sessions with him. Not since he was a kid and had been forced at several points to do family or group therapy. Bridget had never wanted to do couples therapy. It felt wrong to have Kenzie in the room with him.

He shifted again, looking over at Kenzie, who gave him a warm, reassuring smile.

Everyone had said everything right. They had all assured him that they would be respectful of his boundaries and his feelings. But it didn't feel that way.

Dr. Boyle's door opened and she walked in. "Sorry to keep you waiting, Zachary. I had an emergency call. That doesn't normally happen."

Zachary nodded and smiled tightly, saying nothing.

"And you must be Kenzie. It's nice to meet you." Dr. Boyle extended her hand to Kenzie, and the two women shook. They didn't make small talk about how they had each heard of the other and were looking forward to the session. Both quietly professional.

Zachary shifted in his seat, looking for a comfortable position. Dr. Boyle's eyes went to him as she sat down.

"You're looking a little anxious there, my friend."

"Yeah," Zachary croaked. "Sorry."

"That's okay. This is a stressful situation. It's something new. It might feel intrusive, like Kenzie isn't supposed to be a part of this life."

Zachary nodded his agreement.

"It's okay," Kenzie said. "After we've done it once or twice, it will be natural."

Zachary tried to keep his face blank and emotionless like a mask. He didn't want the two of them reading him, discussing him with each other. He wasn't a monkey in a cage.

But he sure felt like one.

He didn't need to pound his chest like a gorilla; his heart was already doing that, pounding so hard it hurt. He knew it was just anxiety. He wasn't having a heart attack. At least, that was what they always told him. It might feel like he was going to die, but he wasn't. If he just rode it out, it would go away by itself.

Zachary wiped at the sweat trickling down his temple. He tried to meet Dr. Boyle's eyes. To look like he was calm and casual and ready to begin the session. Just like any other session. Just like any other patient she had. Totally onside and cooperative.

"Do you need a minute?" she asked.

"I'm..." Zachary swallowed. He couldn't find the right words to respond.

"Zachary, are you okay?" It seemed to be dawning on Kenzie for the first time that something was really wrong. Her voice was full of concern. Not like Bridget, who had grown to hate his panic attacks, acting like he could decide to turn them on or off.

Dr. Boyle looked at her watch. "I can give you some time, if you need it. I realize that I'm already running late, but that's not going to affect your session. I'm not rushing you into your first couples session. I want you to be ready. To be comfortable with what we're doing here. If you feel pressured, you're going to associate those feelings with our sessions, and we want this to be a safe, comfortable place for you. So take your time."

The sweat was still gathering on Zachary's temples and was running down his back in long, cold streams. He grabbed a couple of tissues from the box on Dr. Boyle's desk and mopped his face. He used his right hand, aware that his left was clenching a handful of his shirt tightly over his chest. It was like it wasn't even under his control.

"Maybe we should do some guided relaxation," Dr. Boyle suggested.

Despite all of his efforts to appear calm, Zachary started gasping for breath, unable to get enough oxygen. There were too many people in the room. Kenzie was stealing his air. His breaths were loud in the room, horrendous gasps.

"Zachary!" Kenzie moved her chair closer and grabbed his right arm to comfort him. She couldn't exactly hold his hand while it was full of soggy tissues. "Hey, it's okay. Breathe. You're all right."

Dr. Boyle stood up and hurried over to Zachary, pressing her cool fingers firmly over the pulse point on his left wrist.

"Nice long exhales," she prompted. "When people start to hyperventilate, they aren't getting rid of carbon dioxide. It isn't lack of oxygen, it's that you aren't getting rid of the carbon dioxide."

"Can't," Zachary gasped. "Can't breathe. My heart!"

"You've had panic attacks before," Dr. Boyle said calmly. "You've never had one here, but you have a history, don't you?"

Zachary nodded his agreement. The pain in his chest was like a knife. Heart tissue dying. They didn't know what it was like. He was going to die there right in front of them. While they watched. Because they thought it was just another panic attack.

"Hurts."

"I know it does," Dr. Boyle agreed. "Do you have your meds with you? Do you want to take something?"

Zachary panted. He looked at Kenzie, sweat running down his hairline, embarrassed for her to see him like that. She'd seen him have one before. But he'd been triggered by Bridget. Kenzie had been able to see that he had been provoked. It at least made sense.

For him to break down in his therapist's office because he had to do couples therapy with Kenzie would be an insult to her. She'd think that he was trying to get out of it.

"It's okay," Kenzie assured him. "You can relax. It's fine."

But he knew it wasn't fine. He wanted to get through it without taking a Xanax. He still wanted to go through with the session, and the combination of a panic attack and Xanax would knock him out. He'd be too tired to do the session. He would just want to crash and go to sleep.

"No," he told Dr. Boyle. "I'm… I'm okay."

He took a deeper breath at another stabbing pain to his heart. He held back tears, struggling mightily to keep from completely embarrassing himself.

"Can I get you a glass of water? Do you want to be alone? How can I help?"

Zachary shook his head.

Kenzie rubbed his back. Zachary could feel how his shirt was soaked through with sweat, but she didn't recoil. She acted like she didn't even notice, moving her hand in slow, firm circles. "I know it's not a flashback or dissociation, but would anchoring help?" she suggested.

Zachary shook his head. But he tried anyway. What could it hurt? "I see… blue sky outside." He tried to pick the things he saw that would normally make him feel good. "Your lipstick. B-birds. Dr. Boyle's pen." He took a shuddering breath. "Coffee cup."

"Good," Kenzie encouraged. "How about five things you hear?"

"My breathing." It was drowning everything else out. Zachary tried to hear something else. He breathed out as long as he could, getting rid of the carbon dioxide and trying to hear something other than his own rasping gasps. "My heart. There's… a phone ringing." He strained, holding his breath. "You… moving…" He swallowed. "The air."

"The air?" Kenzie repeated. "I think you're grasping. You can't hear the air."

Zachary managed a couple of longer breaths. He pressed his fist into his chest, trying to focus on slowing his heart down.

"I can," he insisted. "It's forced air heating. I can hear it."

He swallowed. His mouth was very dry from breathing so hard.

"Smell?" Kenzie suggested.

Zachary swallowed again and tried to focus his attention on his sense of smell. Dr. Boyle released his wrist and leaned back on her desk, watching him.

"Your shampoo." Despite the sopping tissues in his hand, Zachary put his hand alongside Kenzie's lowered face and pressed his face against hers, smelling not only her shampoo, but her skin and everything that was Kenzie. She didn't pull away from him, but turned her head slightly and brushed his cheek with her lips. Not quite a kiss, but close. Zachary was breathing more easily. He closed his eyes and took a couple of slow breaths, counting the intake and the exhale. The hand over his chest loosened a little. He rubbed the muscles, sore from holding himself so rigid.

"That's looking better," Dr. Boyle said.

Zachary nodded.

Kenzie sat back down, drawing away from him, but at the same time holding his hand with the balled up tissue inside her own.

"Sorry," Zachary told them both, embarrassed.

"You don't need to apologize," Dr. Boyle said. "If this was easy, you wouldn't need me. You come here together, looking for my help with your relationship, which is very important to you. You don't want to mess it up. It feels strange to have someone else here. You're venturing into the unknown."

Zachary gulped and rubbed at his face, trying to wipe all of the sweat away with his left hand this time, keeping the right in Kenzie's grasp.

"I'm nervous too," Kenzie offered. "I've never done anything like this before. I'm kind of worried about what it's going to be like. What if I make things worse? What if Dr. Boyle says we're incompatible and shouldn't be together? What if you decide you're better off without me? That it's too hard?"

Her fears reflected a lot of Zachary's.

"For what it's worth," Dr. Boyle said, "I'm not going to tell you that you should break up."

"How do you know?" Kenzie challenged. "Maybe you decide that we're not good for each other. That I'm damaging Zachary?"

"I don't think that's going to happen. If one of you is being abusive, then we'll talk about how to change the dynamic. I might recommend certain individual therapies, anger management, something like that. I don't think that any relationship is hopeless. Not when both partners come here to see me and are determined to do what it takes to make things work. You're already way ahead of the curve by coming here to learn how to deal with your differences."

"My differences," Zachary corrected.

Dr. Boyle shook her head, smiling slightly. "You are both different than each other. Yes, Zachary, you have a lot of challenges. More than the average person, for sure. But that doesn't mean that you are broken and Kenzie and I are here to fix you. And it doesn't mean that you can't ever have a healthy romantic relationship. This is the starting line, not the finish line. You've got lots of road ahead of you."

"I can't even do therapy without having a meltdown," Zachary said with disgust.

"Really? This is the first time I've seen you have a panic attack. Which means that you can do therapy without having a meltdown. When is the last time you had couples therapy?"

"Well… never."

"So would you say it's something new?"

"Yeah."

"There are a lot of people who feel anxiety over new situations. You need to give yourself a break."

Zachary rubbed at a spot on his jeans, nodding. He looked at the clock on Dr. Boyle's desk. How much of their time slot had he wasted with his breakdown?

"We can still get started today," Dr. Boyle said. "In fact, I think it's important that we still go ahead, so that you can feel like you have achieved something today. It will make it easier next time."

"You don't think I'll have a panic attack next time?" Zachary sniffled, still trying to get his emotions smoothed down and under his control.

"I don't know. Maybe you will, maybe you won't. But even if you do, we can still achieve something, can't we? We can still move ahead with couples counseling."

"Okay."

"Good." Dr. Boyle returned to her chair and sat back, looking at the two of them. "So. What would you say are the biggest obstacles in your relationship right now?"

Zachary snorted. "Me."

"That's not helpful, Zachary." Dr. Boyle looked at Kenzie. "How about you, Kenzie? What do you see as the roadblocks?"

Kenzie let go of Zachary's hand and rubbed her palms together, then wiped them on her pants.

"The big one right now is Zachary's dissociation. His PTSD or whatever it is that's making him check out whenever we start being physical."

Dr. Boyle nodded. "How do you feel about that, Zachary?"

"Helpless. It's not like I can stop it. I want to be close to Kenzie."

"Good. I think it's helpful to label your feelings about it and to affirm that you do want the physical intimacy."

"I didn't have that problem with Bridget. So it makes me even more frustrated… I love Kenzie." He looked at her and gave a little nod to emphasize his words. "So why can't I… show her that? Why do my body and my brain have to block me from feeling that?"

"And there's the other one," Kenzie said with a sigh. "Bridget. It's like having a third person in our relationship. Whatever we do, I know he's always comparing me to Bridget. Thinking about her and about how things were when they were together. He idealizes her. Idolizes her. When she's… you would think from the way that he talks about her that she was the perfect wife. But she's not a nice person. To put it kindly."

"That's just toward me," Zachary explained. "Because of… my failings. She had to put up with a lot, and in the end, it was just too much."

"It's not just toward you," Kenzie said. "She may act nice toward other people, but you know what she's like on the inside. You know what she's like behind closed doors. You can bet *that* person comes out whenever she's not on public display. You're not the only one she treats like that."

Zachary furrowed his brow and shook his head. "No. She has friends who are very loyal to her. She makes friends wherever she goes. She always had more friends than I did, even in places where I had been for years. In a few minutes, she would have everyone eating out of her hand, and even though I'd been around forever, it would be 'Zachary who?'"

Kenzie rolled her eyes and shook her head.

"How do you feel about that, Kenzie?" Dr. Boyle prodded.

"Like I said, he sees her as perfect. But she's not. That's not what she's like. Did you tell Dr. Boyle about the latest developments?" Kenzie raised her brows.

Zachary appreciated that she didn't just drop the bombshell. He shook his head. "No, I didn't… I didn't think it was relevant. It's nothing to do with me."

"Something you want to share?" Dr. Boyle asked.

Zachary motioned toward Kenzie. "Go ahead. I'd… I don't even know if I could say it."

Kenzie looked at him for a moment as if double-checking, making sure that he really wanted her to say something, before it was too late to take it back. Zachary just shrugged.

"It's fine."

Kenzie looked at Dr. Boyle. "Bridget is pregnant."

"That's a complication, isn't it?" Dr. Boyle observed neutrally.

"It's nothing to do with me," Zachary repeated.

"But that doesn't mean it doesn't affect you," Kenzie said. "It obviously does."

Zachary stayed silent. He looked down at the carpet. He hadn't expected to have to talk about Bridget's pregnancy and all of the issues that it brought up for him.

"How do you feel about it, Zachary?"

"She can get pregnant if she wants to. I'm happy for her."

Kenzie snorted.

Zachary grimaced. "Okay, maybe I'm not happy for her. But… it isn't any of my business."

"When they were together, Bridget said she didn't want children," Kenzie explained. "When they had a pregnancy scare, she said she was going to get an abortion. Didn't matter what Zachary wanted. It wasn't a mutual decision. It was Bridget saying that she wasn't going to have his baby."

"Ouch." Dr. Boyle nodded. "That makes it hard to see her pregnant in another relationship, without you."

"It had to be planned," Zachary told them. "Because of her radiation, the doctor said she should have her eggs frozen. In case she ever changed her mind about having children. So… she didn't just accidentally get pregnant, and decide to go ahead and have them. She had to have in vitro. It had to be planned, with the eggs she had harvested before her cancer treatment."

Kenzie was looking at Zachary. "I didn't know that part," she said softly.

Zachary nodded.

Dr. Boyle had caught Zachary's accidental revelation. "Them?"

"What?" Zachary pretended he didn't know what she was talking about.

"You said she decided to go ahead and have them. Does that mean she's having twins?"

"I… don't know. When Gordon was talking, he said 'the babies.' Not 'the baby.' So… I guess she's having multiples. Hopefully just twins."

"So, she refuses to have your baby, but with Gordon, she'll have two," Kenzie summarized. "On purpose."

Zachary nodded. He swallowed and stared out the window.

"And how do you feel about that?" Dr. Boyle asked.

25

In the car after the session, Kenzie suggested going out for ice cream. Zachary looked at her, frowning, wondering if he had misheard.

"Ice cream?"

"We deserve a treat, don't you think? Where do you want to go? If you prefer something else, I'm game."

"A treat for going to therapy?"

"Sure, why not? Didn't any of your foster parents ever reward you for going to the doctor or dentist without a fuss?"

Zachary shook his head.

"My mom always got us a treat when we went to the doctor," Kenzie said. "So I think it's time to go out for a treat. If you'd rather go for steak or Chinese, I'm game."

Zachary didn't feel like a heavy meal. He was feeling drained after his panic attack and the session, and just wanted to go home and zone out.

"Okay, ice cream," he agreed. He thought it was still a little cold out to be going for ice cream, but if that was what Kenzie wanted, he didn't see why she shouldn't have it.

"Good." Kenzie gave him a sunny smile. "I think you deserve a treat especially. I had a hard time going and not giving in to the temptation to cancel at the last minute. I know it was a lot harder for you, but look at how strong you were. I didn't even hear a word about you not going. And after your… episode… you didn't even suggest going home. You just went right into it."

"Dr. Boyle said it would be easier next time if I did."

"Yeah. But you still could have said no."

Zachary nodded, keeping his eyes on the road. "Where do you want to go for ice cream?"

There was really only one good ice cream shop in town, assuming Kenzie wanted to go for a cone or bowl of the fancy stuff, and not just stop at the grocery store for a pint. Mostly, Zachary just didn't want to keep talking about therapy.

"We have to go to the Fro Zone," Kenzie said. "No other choice."

"Okay." Zachary headed toward the ice cream shop. "What kind are you going to get?"

"I won't know until I get there. I don't know what their special is today. Or what new flavors they might have added since the last time I was there."

"Chocolate?"

"Well, something with chocolate usually wins out. But I don't know what kind of chocolate. And they could have something special in another flavor. Something really awesome, like…" Kenzie trailed off, trying to come up with an example.

"Like double chocolate with chocolate sauce?" Zachary suggested.

Kenzie giggled. "Yeah. Something like that."

Bridget would never have double chocolate ice cream with chocolate sauce. It would ruin her figure. She was meticulous about what she ate and how much so that she wouldn't put an extra ounce on her perfect figure.

Zachary wondered how she was managing the pregnancy and the extra weight that it entailed. She'd told him she was never going to ruin her body by having a baby.

Yet another thing she had told him that had turned out not to be true.

Jocelyn sounded surprised when Zachary called her. She had obviously not expected him to reach out to her after the awkward meeting at Mr. Peterson's.

"What's this about? I have to work, you know. I don't have loads of free time."

"I'll come to you," Zachary promised. He worked for himself, but that didn't mean he had loads of free time either. Especially not when he was doing the investigation for Rhys pro bono. No matter how much time he spent on it, it wasn't going to bring him in any money. "I just wanted to ask your opinion on some things."

"What kind of things?"

"On my case."

"Your case? The girl you already found?"

"Well, yes. I still have concerns. I'm not sure how to proceed."

"You proceed by leaving it alone. You did what you were asked to do, so go on to the next case."

"Could I talk to you about it?" Zachary persisted. "Could we meet?"

"Are you going to pay me for my time as a professional consultant?"

Zachary winced. He still had money in the bank due to a few of the bigger cases he had taken recently. Gordon Drake had even kicked in some money on the Lauren Barclay case—though that had felt more like hush money than payment for services rendered.

"I could give you a small stipend," he said. "I'm not making anything on this case, but I do value your time."

She thought about that for a minute. "Fine," she agreed finally. "Can't we just discuss it over the phone? Do we need to get together? You'll have to travel on top of everything else."

"I don't mind driving. And I would like to see you again. I have some pictures and videos that you could look at, give me your opinion, some insight. Things that I wouldn't know because I'm not close enough to her situation."

"Why are you still pursuing it? You think you can talk her into going home?"

"I have to try. If she's not safe, I have to do everything I can to get her back."

"And if she won't?"

"If she won't, she won't. But I'm hoping that with your help, I might be able to convince her. It will at least give me a better shot than just approaching her without any understanding of her situation. Would you have left if some random guy just told you that you should?"

"Of course not."

"So I'm going to need something. Some way to at least have a chance."

"You know I'm not going to try to help you," Jocelyn warned. "I'm going to try to talk you out of it."

Zachary laughed. At least she was upfront about it. Did he want to waste his time trying to get answers from someone who thought that the whole thing was a mistake?

He actually did. He wouldn't be walking into it blind. If Jocelyn didn't manage to talk him out of it, then he would be ready. And if she did convince him to give it up, then there were obviously good reasons to do so.

"Fair enough," he agreed. "I guess I don't have to warn you that I'm stubborn and don't always make the smartest decisions."

Jocelyn's answering laugh was more natural. Much more relaxed and familiar to him than anything else she had said or done. Joss remembered what he was like, all right. And that made him feel closer to her.

26

He didn't mind another highway drive to meet with Jocelyn. It gave him a chance to try to sort out his thoughts and marshal his arguments before their conversation. Kenzie was working, so he was on his own and could drive a little faster if he felt like it.

The land surrounding the highway was turning green. The weather was still chilly, but things had started to come alive again after their long winter hibernation, and it cheered him to see it. Vermont was like a postcard in the winter, but he preferred the summer.

Would he ever consider moving somewhere that was warm all year? Somewhere people decorated palm trees or cactuses rather than evergreens for Christmas and there was no snow on the ground?

It was hard to say. He hated anything that reminded him of Christmas, but he wasn't ever going to be able to find somewhere there was no Christmas. Not in the United States.

He took the highway exit the GPS told him to, and followed its directions to the book store Jocelyn had directed him to. He thought that a book store was an odd place for a meeting, but they had a social area with a coffee shop and table and chairs, and it was clearly a popular hangout. Jocelyn didn't need to be worried about being alone with him, a man she barely knew.

She was there waiting for him, a book in hand. Zachary glanced at it but didn't recognize the cover or title. It was a thick book, and he wasn't a reader.

"Hi," Zachary greeted. He hesitated, not putting out his hand for a handshake or his arms for a hug. Jocelyn nodded and didn't offer either method of greeting, so he left it at that.

"Let's sit here." Jocelyn motioned to a table off to the side, by the window. "I ordered a couple of coffees. You drink coffee, right?"

"Sure."

"You never know these days. Health nuts, religious freaks, fair trade, blah, blah, blah. We're just talking about a cup of coffee, not a lifetime commitment."

Zachary smiled. He sat down. "If I could live on coffee, I probably would."

"Well, thank goodness for that. You really are a Goldman."

"Did you ever doubt it?"

Jocelyn shook her head. "No. You look just like I expected you to."

They waited. Zachary tried to make small talk with her and looked out the window at the people coming and going in the parking lot. Jocelyn waved to a barista who was looking around at the tables with two cups of coffee in her hands.

"Over here."

The woman saw Jocelyn's waving arm and approached them. "Jocelyn and Zachary?"

"Yes."

She put the cups down in front of them, and Zachary picked his up and took a sip, even though it was boiling hot.

"Thanks. Good stuff."

"Yeah. You bet."

Zachary sighed. He put his notepad on the table beside him. "So… you know that I'm trying to figure out how to get Madison back home."

"You should just stay out of it."

"She's only a kid. Don't you think it's best to get her out early? Before she gets in too deep?"

"No. I think you should leave her alone. It's her life, not yours. You don't have any right to tell her what to do."

"I know. I'm not trying to force her or tell her what to do, just to help her out. Wouldn't you have wanted someone to help you?"

"No. Plenty of people tried to interfere and get me to do what they thought I should be doing. And it didn't do anything but get me in grief. I just wanted everyone to stay out of it and let me live my own life the way I wanted to."

Zachary swirled the coffee cup. "But did you really know what you were getting into? Did you really understand what kind of life it was going to be? Or what kind of life you could have if you got out?"

"Life outside the business isn't all roses."

He thought about that. Zachary wasn't about to tell her that he knew better than she did. She had lived the life that Madison had been in, and she had gotten out. She was the one who had seen both sides.

"I don't know if anyone's life is all roses. Do you think things were better when you were..."

"In some ways, yes. I had drugs, and they helped me to feel better. As long as I was getting what I needed, I felt okay. I didn't have to think about whether it was right or wrong, or whether I could be doing something else or living another life. None of that came up while I was high. I could... be what I was, and no one cared. Least of all me."

"But that does things to your body. Makes you sick. Could kill you."

"But I didn't care. That's the magic of it. I knew I was living a crappy life and I wasn't going anywhere, but I didn't care. I knew drugs were destroying my body, but that didn't matter. When I almost died... that was the best high I ever had. I wished they hadn't brought me out of it. They should have just left me alone. Let me die."

"Did you think... no one would care? Or you didn't care if anyone did?"

"No one did," Jocelyn said flatly. She shook her head. "I didn't have anyone, Zachary. I didn't have any family or friends. I had my Romeo, and that was enough for me. He made me feel good, when I was doing what I was supposed to and keeping him happy. As long as I was bringing money in and keeping his clients satisfied, he would give me all the good strokes. Tell me that I was smart and funny and pretty. That he didn't want anything else in a girlfriend. He'd give me new clothes and tell me how nice I looked. He'd bring me drugs, and we'd get high together, and I would feel *so* good. Why would I want to get out of that?"

"But you did, eventually. What changed your mind?"

Jocelyn stared off into the distance. "There was bad stuff too. Of course.

There always is. Clients who weren't happy or who wanted to hurt someone just because they were sadists. So then I'd get in trouble with my boyfriend. And I was getting older. Not in as much demand. They were looking for younger girls, and they wanted me to help bring them up and turn them out. I could never agree with that. I never got on board with bringing someone else in. Seducing them, or punishing them and keeping them in line. It wasn't my thing." She took a long swallow from her cup. "I never liked to see Matt with other girls. I was jealous, but I couldn't show it. He didn't spend much time with me. Neglected me, didn't bring me drugs, left me to my own devices. While he was off partying with the little girls. Getting older isn't as bad for men. Older guys are still sexy. Look at Hollywood. But for women… we just get worn out, tired, ugly. Too fat and flabby or thin and bony. Our bodies change, so we don't look and feel like younger women anymore. Sure, there are some great looking old broads in Hollywood too, but they have plastic surgeons and personal trainers. They're not getting worn out by the constant demands of men and strung out on drugs all the time."

Zachary nodded, watching her face. It broke his heart to hear all that she had gone through. She was lucky to have survived as long as she had and to have been able to get out without being harmed. But she hadn't left that life behind. It had left its mark on her. And she would probably never recover from it.

But Madison? She was young. She'd only been in the business for a few weeks or months. If there was a chance that he could get her out of there and prevent her from living the life that Jocelyn had, year after year…

"You don't know what it's like, Zachary," Jocelyn said sharply. "You think you can just waltz in there and talk her out of it, and that's not the way it works. She doesn't have the choice to just walk away. It doesn't matter what you tell her; there's a lot more involved than that. Even if you could talk her out of it, she wouldn't get far. They would follow. Track her down. Snatch her if she wouldn't cooperate. They would take her away somewhere where no one knew her. Where she didn't have anyone to ask for help. And they would keep her chained up in some basement until she didn't have any more will to run away."

"Did that happen to you?"

"I seen it happen," Jocelyn snapped, not giving him the personal details. Had it been her, or had it been someone else? Or had there been so many of them that it was a ubiquitous experience? Maybe she didn't even remember anymore what had happened to her and what had happened to someone else.

Zachary resisted growling back at her. That wouldn't help anything. She was trying to tell him what it had been like. He didn't even have any right to know. She had agreed to do it, maybe to help someone else out and perhaps just to try to connect with him and let him know what she had been through.

"So if you were going to get someone out, how would you do it?"

"I wouldn't," Jocelyn said. She stared at him fiercely. "Don't you get it? You can't. There's nothing you can do. You're not a Navy SEAL. You're not some crusader of light rushing in and saving the day. You might think you're all of that, but you're not. These are guys who are not going to be trifled with. You've been lucky up until now, bumbling around and making headlines. That isn't what this is going to be like. Not at all."

"I haven't been… I don't see myself that way. I'm just trying to do what I've been hired to do in these cases. I'm not trying to get in the spotlight. Yes, some cases have made it into the media lately, but it's not about that. It's about helping people. About doing the things I've been hired to do."

"You haven't been hired. Being hired would mean you're being paid. I at least know that."

"Okay… so not hired in this case. Just asked for a favor. But I want to do everything I can for Rhys. And for Madison. I can't just walk away and pretend that she doesn't exist or that I don't know what she might be going through. Could you do that?"

"Of course I could! I do that every day of my life. Turn my face away from all of the other victims and remind myself that I got out. I did. And I can't live anyone else's life. That's up to them. I didn't get out alive just to rush back in there and upset the apple cart. I don't want to bring the whole organization down on top of me."

"I can't do that." Zachary thought about Annie, the girl who had died when he was in Bonnie Brown. He had kept quiet. He had been too afraid of the guards and what would happen to him if he talked, so he had kept quiet. For years he had been silent about what had happened to her. He pretended that he didn't know. He blocked it out. He walled off that part of himself and made himself forget.

Until he had walked through the doors at Summit. And then her ghost had been resurrected and he wasn't able to walk away again without acknowledging her. Maybe someday Jocelyn would have to face her own ghosts and either justify herself or give them a voice.

"I can't do that. It isn't in my makeup to be able to turn my back on Madison and pretend that there was nothing I could do."

"No one is going to care about this one. You make big news because you solve the murder of the child of a public figure. Because you manage to identify a serial killer. Whatever else." She made a brushing-off motion with her fingers as if none of it mattered. "But no one is going to care about one girl being trafficked. *No one cares.*" She said each word as if it were a separate sentence.

"I'm not trying to make the news. And people do care. Her parents care. Rhys cares. I care. Even if no one else does, that's enough. I can't leave her there."

Remembering Summit and thinking about Madison being trafficked and no one caring about it made Zachary think of Tyrza. She had been nothing like Madison. Young, yes. But black. Autistic. Not able to tell the police what had happened to her.

But her mother had cared. She had made sure that everyone knew she wasn't going to give up until she found her daughter. She was going to make a big, loud, noisy stink. And rather than let her do that, they had let Tyrza go. They had released her. Left her wandering by the side of the road. She had been saved by a mother who hadn't been afraid to be loud and ruffle some feathers.

"Dammit, I can see the gleam in your eyes, Zachy," Jocelyn said in a harsh voice. "I know what that means!"

27

Zachary turned away from Joss and looked out the window. It was too late. She already knew exactly what he was thinking and had seen the resolution in his eyes. If he had wanted to hide that from her, then he should have turned away from her earlier.

"You can't read my mind," he told her. Like the ten-year-old brat he had been. Like the bratty little brother she had tried to care for and protect. And he'd just continued to break the rules and get into trouble and go the wrong way.

Until he'd gone and sent everything he cared about up in flames. Literally.

"I can too," Jocelyn returned, in that knowing-older-sister voice that was familiar to him even though it was decades later. "I can see exactly what you're thinking. Why did you even come here today, if you'd already decided what you're going to do? Why not just stay home and jump right into hot water like you always do?"

"I wanted to learn what I could from you. I thought you could help me to figure things out. Figure out the best way to get her out of there."

"There is no best way. There is no way. Unless you're going to kidnap her. And then you'd have to get her out of the state, get her a fake name, hide her away until they don't care about her anymore."

Zachary nodded seriously. "You think that even if she agreed to go home, they would come back after her."

"Of course they would. She's an investment. She's theirs. Anyone who gets in their way, they don't care. They'll just cut down everything in their path and get her back."

"Her parents, you mean?"

"Anyone who stood up to them. If they went to the police and started making trouble? If you got in their way or tracked her down again? They'd cut you down. They would make sure that you never interfered with their business again."

Zachary thought of the business card he had left behind. That had been stupid. He should have known better than to give them his name and to leave his contact details behind. It was a criminal enterprise. Did he think that they wouldn't care about a private investigator nosing around? What if he had to leave town too? He'd made a life for himself there. He had friends. People he cared about. How was he going to feel if he had to leave everything behind and start over?

Joss nodded, feeling like he was finally getting it. "You can't mess with these guys. Just go home and stay out of it. Pick up a new case. Lose yourself in something else. Go to bed with Kenzie and stay there for a week. Just stay out of it."

Zachary sighed. He took a sip of his coffee, which was starting to cool down. It was rich and bitter and he tried to focus on the aroma and flavor and nothing else. He had to face reality. He wasn't a blow-em-all-up private eye from the silver screen. He was just one guy trying to make a living. Trying to help out a few people along the way.

Madison just couldn't be one of them.

The rest of the visit with Jocelyn had focused more on the business aspect of the trafficking world. He knew very little about how it all worked, and Jocelyn, of course, knew all about it. She might have been a naive teen when she had started out, who didn't know anything about anything. But she had learned the business from the ground up. From the way that the Romeos targeted and attracted girls to the way that they got them addicted to drugs and the party lifestyle and designer dresses and handbags. The way that they kept them under control with addiction, coercion, blackmail, and love for the boyfriend who had started it all in the first place.

By the time she understood what trafficking was, Jocelyn was in way too deep to get herself out or even to want to. There was only one way to maintain her lifestyle and that was by turning tricks and doing whatever she was told whenever she was told. Only then would she be rewarded.

She knew all of the ways that girls were advertised on Backpage and classified sites and the dark web. Sometimes out in the open, using code words that only regular clients would understand. If a girl was lucky, she'd have a place like Madison had with Noah. If she was unlucky, her lot would be much worse. If Madison could keep Noah and his bosses happy, that was the best that she could hope for.

Madison could continue the fantasy of being in love with her Romeo and lie to herself about what was really happening. And that was the only way she could be happy.

Zachary begged off of doing anything with Kenzie that night. He needed time to make notes of the things that Jocelyn had said and to process everything. He told her he was tired. He hadn't slept well after their couples therapy and he needed another night to try to catch up.

Kenzie said that she had some work to catch up on and that she was okay with a night on her own. He listened closely to her words and inflection, but she didn't sound upset. Maybe, like he did, she needed some space to herself now and then. She probably had some things to think of after their couples therapy too. Like whether he was the kind of guy that she wanted to spend time with long term. Maybe she should cut it off while she could and Zachary had Dr. Boyle to fall back on and to guide him through the breakup.

"But let me know if you change your mind," Kenzie said. "Or if you want to chat later on. Okay? I'm flexible."

"Okay, thanks. I'll let you know."

He hung up the phone and put some music on in the background, and fought hard to focus on his notes and to remember everything Jocelyn had said, refusing to let it pull him back down into unwelcome memories.

28

The next day, he worked on catching up on other cases. Paperwork, invoices, collection, passing on information, looking at his schedule to figure out surveillance time blocks. He had plenty of work to keep him busy. He didn't need to be wasting time on cases that didn't pay anything.

Unfortunately, you couldn't save everyone—especially those who didn't want to be saved.

It was evening, and he was watching the clock, wondering if he should call Kenzie or whether she would drop by the apartment. He didn't want to leave it too long between talking to her. He didn't want to make that mistake again and to fall back to where they had been before.

His phone buzzed.

Zachary picked it up, expecting to see a text from Kenzie. Maybe a suggestion that they go out for dinner, or just a note that she was on her way.

But it wasn't. It was a message from Rhys. Zachary tapped it and a gif popped up. An old *I Love Lucy* shot, with "Honey, I'm home," printed across it.

Zachary frowned, looking at it.

Rhys was at home. Was he grounded? Did he just want Zachary to call him? To stop by the house for a visit? They hadn't talked since Zachary had broken the news to him about having found Madison, but that she had refused to return home.

He tapped the phone icon to see if Rhys or Vera would answer the phone. But before it could connect, there was a knock on the door.

Zachary looked at the door. He ended the phone call.

He walked over to the door, but he already knew who he was going to see through the wide-angle peephole.

Honey, I'm home.

Zachary opened the door for Rhys. He looked back over his shoulder at the living room window, which was dark. He didn't like Rhys being out on his own so late. Vera wouldn't like it either. She would ban Rhys from seeing Zachary if he kept taking off to see Zachary on his own. Zachary shut the door.

"What's going on? You shouldn't be here so late. Grandma will be worrying."

Rhys ignored the question. He tapped his phone busily and turned it around for Zachary to read it.

A message from Madison's account. *Please help me.*

29

Zachary drew in his breath sharply. Madison had reached out to Rhys?

Maybe Jocelyn had been wrong. Maybe Madison was ready to get out of the business. Maybe she wanted to get back to Rhys and her friends and school and all of the normal teenage stuff instead of earning drugs and nice clothes through prostitution.

Rhys looked at Zachary, his eyes wide. He gestured to the screen insistently. *What do you think?*

"Do you know where she is?" Zachary asked. "Is she still in the same place or did they—or did she move somewhere else?"

Rhys shrugged. He used his finger to pull the message up and down, demonstrating that was the only thing Madison had sent to him. Just those three words.

Please help me.

And she could change her mind at any time. They needed to get to her while she still wanted out. Before Noah could return or talk her out of it. Zachary chewed on his lip. He needed to think it through.

But he had already made his decision without weighing any risks. Like Joss had said he did.

"I'll go see if she's still in the same place," he told Rhys. "If she's there,

I'll get her to come with me. If she's not… well, I'll scout it out and see what I can find out."

Rhys nodded eagerly.

"You can't come. It's too dangerous. I can't watch my own back and yours at the same time. I can't take a teenager into a situation that might be dangerous."

Rhys looked affronted. He pointed to himself. He pointed to the phone screen. *I got the message. She asked me.*

"And you came to me. Because you know it's too dangerous to go on your own."

Rhys pointed from his shoulder to Zachary and back again. *Both of us together.*

"No. I'll take you as far as her street. You can stay in the car and keep lookout. But you can't come up. And if something happens, if I don't come back out or you think something has gone wrong, then you call 9-1-1 and get help. You don't come up."

Rhys considered this, frowning.

"That's my only offer," Zachary said. "I shouldn't even be doing that. I should take you back home and you can wait there until I have news."

Rhys shook his head violently.

"I don't want you to get hurt. I can't risk that."

Rhys held both hands up in a stop position. He pointed to himself then made a steering wheel motion. *I'll stay in the car.*

"You have to do what I say," Zachary insisted. "If you think anything is wrong, you call the police. You don't come looking for me under any circumstances."

Rhys nodded his agreement.

Zachary got ready to go, his mind racing a mile a minute. He tried to think through all of the possibilities of what he might be facing. His ADHD brain was good at that. Coming up with all of the possible permutations and hazards and presenting them to him in rapid succession. Slowing down and thinking of just one course of action, that was a lot harder.

Rhys watched him, his eyes still wide. He looked at his phone every minute or two, watching for any further messages from Madison. Zachary noted that he didn't write anything back. He didn't send any gifs or emojis. Just kept checking to see whether she had sent anything else.

"Okay." Zachary blew his breath out in a long stream. It was time to stop preparing and go. Either it would work out, or it wouldn't. He would keep Rhys safe and he would do his best to get Madison out of there. If he didn't succeed, at least Rhys would be safe.

30

They got to Madison's apartment as quickly as they could, but it was already dark. Zachary looked up and down the street, regretting his agreement to bring Rhys with him. And regretting that they had gone over so late in the day. It wasn't that great a neighborhood. And wouldn't evening be the time that Madison started working? That didn't seem like an ideal time to show up.

But she had asked for help. What if she knew that Noah was going to move her? What if she'd been hurt after Zachary had left? Putting it off might endanger her.

"Okay. You stay here," he told Rhys.

Rhys looked out the window and back at Zachary, his eyes wide. He pointed at Zachary and raised his eyebrows. *You okay? You sure?*

Zachary opened his door and got out. "Keep the doors locked."

He left Rhys there without looking back. He didn't want anything to stop him. He couldn't show Rhys how nervous he was about trying to rescue Madison.

He wondered as he went up the stairs toward the apartment whether he should have called the police. They had already been there to try to talk her into leaving with them. And who knew what kind of consequences there would be if they came back. She wouldn't go with them. And then the things that Jocelyn predicted would happen. She would be taken away and hidden. Locked up and assaulted.

The police would be too obvious and attract too much attention.

No one would notice one lone private investigator walking into the building. He had been there once before and he didn't look anything like a cop. The guy who had seen him downstairs would think he was Madison's client. Other people, looking at his gaunt face and bloodshot eyes, would assume that he was an addict. He frequently went without shaving, knowing that people would discount him as a homeless person or druggie. Someone that they didn't want to look at or acknowledge, in case he asked them for money or targeted them some other way.

He could slip in, talk to Madison, and get back out quickly, unobtrusively. No one would even know he had been there.

He reached the top of the flight of stairs and stopped and listened for a moment. Making sure that there was no one else in the stairway, breathing and watching for his approach. He couldn't hear anything but his own heart pounding in his ears.

Zachary pushed the door open and slipped into the hallway, still on high alert, looking and listening for anything out of place. It could be a setup. But if it was, then it was Rhys that they were setting up, not Zachary. It was Rhys who had gotten the distress signal.

If they were watching for a young black boy, they weren't going to find him. Zachary could walk right by them and they wouldn't know who he was.

He padded down the carpeted hall, his light shoes making no noise. The only noise he made was the brushing together of his pants as he moved and his breathing, which sounded loud in his ears, but he knew logically it was not.

He stopped outside of Madison's door and listened. He couldn't hear anything going on inside this time. No argument or discussion going on. Maybe a TV way in the background, or maybe that was from one of the neighboring apartments. The walls were not built to be soundproof. There might not even be anyone home, though there was a light under the door. They could have left the lights on. Not everyone was diligent about shutting their lights off, especially kids who had never been responsible for paying electrical bills. Or it might have been left on to make it look inhabited so that it didn't become a target for burglars.

Zachary considered his approach. Send a text message to Madison to let her know he was there? Knock on the door? Which would be safer for her?

He stood there for several long seconds, considering, biting his knuckle anxiously. In the end, he decided it was better that he draw any negative reaction to himself, rather than alerting Noah or whoever might be with her that she was communicating covertly with someone. If Zachary showed up out of the blue, she had plausible deniability. She hadn't called him. There was no evidence that she'd ever reached out to him, because she hadn't. She'd messaged Rhys. And if she were smart, she had then deleted the message from her phone. Rhys hadn't messaged her back. So she was clean. No sign that she had contacted anyone.

Zachary raised his hand and knocked lightly on the door.

Maybe not loudly enough to be heard over the TV, or through a closed bedroom door. But if Noah were the one watching TV, that was probably for the best. It was better if Madison were the only one who heard him.

He waited. The sound of the TV kept going. No one shut it off or muted it, listening for him to knock again. There were no footsteps.

Zachary felt like the acid in his stomach was eating a hole right through it. He wanted something to happen, and he didn't want anything to happen. It took all of his self-will to raise his hand and knock again, a little more loudly.

He didn't hear the footsteps before the chain on the door clinked and the bolt slid open.

Madison opened the door and looked out at him.

Several emotions crossed her face as she recognized him. Relief, curiosity, confusion. Fear and anger.

"What are you doing here?" she whispered.

"Rhys got your message. I'm here to help you."

Her face was blank.

"To help you get out," Zachary said, waiting for the confirmation on her face. "You sent a message to Rhys."

Madison shook her head.

Zachary swore to himself.

Someone else had picked up Madison's phone and sent that message.

Or she might be lying. She might have messaged Rhys and then chickened out. She might be worried that someone would overhear them. She might not trust him. She had sent the message to Rhys, so why had Zachary shown up?

Or it might have been someone targeting Rhys. As Zachary had noted to himself before, Rhys was vulnerable. There were plenty of boys being trafficked too. Some for sex and some for slave labor. Rhys was young and part of a minority population, which made him more desirable. And he was selectively mute, using only a word or two in a day. He couldn't call for help.

"You did," he told Madison firmly, as if he knew she was the one who had sent the message. "You asked him for help." He tried to use his most reassuring voice, soothing Madison like she was a scared puppy. "I'm here to help you, Madison."

Madison shook her head again, stepping back slightly from the door. Distancing herself. Preparing to shut the door. She glanced nervously over her shoulder.

But it was too late, Noah had heard her, and he stepped into the kitchen.

31

Zachary's mind spun through a hundred reactions and scenarios at once. Reach inside and grab Madison by the wrist. Pull her out of the room and trust that she would run with him once she was out the door. But Noah could be armed. He was undoubtedly faster than Zachary, and probably faster than Madison. They couldn't escape with superior speed. And Noah was in his own territory. He wouldn't hesitate to go after them, to pull a weapon if he needed it. Who was going to report him? One of his neighbors? Someone who had to live with him in the building when he made bail and returned home?

Zachary didn't carry a gun. He might be able to hold Noah off for a minute if he didn't have one, but not for long.

Madison hadn't sent the message to Rhys. Therefore, Noah was the one who had sent the message. He knew that Madison hadn't betrayed him. He had been trying to set Rhys up. Rhys was safe, in the car with the doors locked. Noah's ploy had failed. He had no way of knowing that Rhys was close by. He could see that Zachary had come in his place. As long as Zachary didn't force the issue, he should be able to back out of the situation without endangering himself or Madison. A good guy, but a coward. Someone who fled at the appearance of danger. Not someone that Noah needed to worry about.

"Uh, hi. Sorry, I guess I got my wires crossed somehow. I thought

Madison had sent a message saying that she needed help. But she says it didn't come from her. She's fine, and no one needs my help, so I'll get out of here. My wife will be wondering where I am."

Noah continued to approach the door. He nudged Madison back, out of the way, so that Zachary was face-to-face with him, without a target or shield in between them. Zachary was glad that there was no chance of Madison getting caught in any crossfire. He wanted to keep her safe. Or as safe as he possibly could.

"I sent that message," Noah said, staring into Zachary's face, his expression blank, eyes deep dark pools.

Zachary tried to regulate his breathing, hoping that Noah wouldn't be able to hear how hard he was straining for breath or how fast and hard his heart was pumping.

"You sent it?"

Noah nodded. Zachary breathed through his mouth, waiting for Noah to explain. Noah would gloat, tell him that it was all a set-up and Zachary had fallen for it. Maybe it had been Zachary that Noah was hoping would come. Maybe his bosses wanted Zachary out of the way. Noah was hoping to please them by getting an obstacle out of the way.

Noah looked over at Madison. Zachary tried to analyze his expression. Not a threat. Not angry. He didn't see anything but Madison's own fear reflected back in Noah's face. Noah reached over and touched Madison on the arm. Reassuring.

Noah opened the door farther. "Come in. Out of sight."

32

Zachary's body was telling him to retreat.

Pull back and get away from the danger. Don't march right into the spider's parlor. Get away.

But his brain was at odds with his body. The fear on Noah's face. Madison's confusion. The strange interplay between them that Zachary couldn't figure out. Something didn't make sense. But if he stayed for longer, he could figure it out. He was good at sorting out body language and human behavior.

He stepped into the tiny kitchen. Noah shut the door and bolted and chained it.

The floor was a little sticky. Like the linoleum had softened too much over the years and turned tacky. The kitchen was too small for all three of them to be in there comfortably. Noah motioned for Madison to leave the kitchen first, and she walked into a living room that was almost as small. But there were places to sit. Dark, stained furniture that looked like it had been pulled from the dump. Maybe picked up from a curbside or garage sale. Madison sat down on a rusty-colored, flowery couch with dark wood accents. Seventies? Eighties? It looked like something that Zachary's family might have had in the house that had burned down.

Noah motioned Zachary to a chair and sat down beside Madison. He didn't cuddle up to her, but he took her hand and held it in another gesture of reassurance.

What was going on?

"You sent that message to Rhys? Asking for help?" Zachary asked. His mouth was as dry as cotton. Some of his meds gave him a dry mouth, but it was so bone dry he could barely talk or work up a drop of spittle. His tongue stuck to the roof of his mouth and felt like it belonged to someone else.

Noah nodded. He glanced aside at Madison and then looked at Zachary again. "You came here to get Madison. Because of Rhys."

Zachary nodded. It wasn't like there was any question of that fact. Why else would he be there? That was why he had come before, and that was why he had come this time.

Madison put her free hand on Noah's back. Like she was comforting him. She shook her head slightly. "Why?"

"You don't belong here. You should get out. You should go with him."

"I can't."

"You have to."

Madison shook her head more definitely. She looked at Zachary, as if expecting him to explain it to Noah. "If I leave, they'll go after him. They'll beat him up. Torture him."

She loved him. She wouldn't do anything that might put him in danger. Even if he was the one who had pulled her into the situation, acted the part of the Romeo and seduced her into something that she would never have thought she would agree to. Now she was stuck, and she wouldn't leave because of the danger to him.

"I hope they kill me," Noah said. "At least then, I wouldn't have to do this anymore. I'd be out of this life."

"No." Madison squeezed Noah's hand more tightly. "No, I won't let anything happen to you."

Zachary looked helplessly at the two of them. "Maybe… why don't you start at the beginning. Noah… I guess I'm being stupid here, but I don't understand. If you want out of the life, then get out. And if you want Madison out… then let her go. Help her to get away. You're the one holding her here."

"I'm not. I already told her to go. I told her she should have gone with you or the cops. If she stays around here… it's just going to get worse and worse."

Zachary could see the same pain in Noah's eyes that he'd seen in Jocelyn's. It felt like a stab to his chest, thinking about how scared and hopeless Jocelyn must have felt for all of those years, feeling trapped and too afraid to even try to get out. Until she was all worn out and no one wanted her anymore. Until she nearly died, and no one had cared.

"How is it going to get worse?" Zachary asked. If they were going to get Madison out, she needed to hear it. She needed to hear all of the gritty, sordid details and to understand what she had gotten herself into and how she needed to get out now, not to wait until she reached the end of the line like Jocelyn had.

Noah swallowed. He looked down at his hands, his elbows leaning on his knees and Madison's hand held between his. How old was he? Studying his face close up, Zachary wondered if he was even nineteen. He'd looked older. He'd acted older. But in the dim light of a yellow lamp, he looked very young. He didn't have any stubble on his face. His skin was smooth as a child's.

"You don't want to be in this kind of life," he told Madison without looking at her. "I've told you that. But I haven't… I haven't told you everything."

"What is it? Tell me now."

Noah looked up, across the room, across the kitchen, to the locked front door. Reassuring himself that he was safe from intruders, that there was no one else there to hear his confession.

Zachary's phone vibrated in his pocket. He suddenly remembered Rhys, sitting out there in the dark, cold car, waiting for Zachary to return. He pulled it out and glanced at the single character on the screen. A question mark.

"Give me a second," he said. He quickly tapped out a message to Rhys that he was okay and would get down as soon as he could. But Rhys was to sit tight for now. Then he slid the phone back away and looked at Noah. "I'm sorry. Just a check-in to make sure everything is okay."

Noah nodded.

33

"I was thirteen when I started," Noah said. "I don't know. Maybe twelve. I don't remember exactly when the first time I saw him was."

"Him?" Madison repeated.

"Connor." Noah's voice cracked. "The one who recruited me."

He didn't look at Madison. She stared at him, trying to understand what he was talking about.

"Connor said I was special. He said… I had a beautiful face. I'd never… I'd never been with anyone. Never had anyone give me attention like that. Never had anyone say a kind word to me."

Madison made a little noise of protest.

"I was living with my grandma. No one wanted me. My parents died. But they'd never wanted me around anyway. I bounced back and forth between them and different steps or uncles or whatever. And my grandma. She was the only one who ever gave me any kind of stable home. A place where I could sleep and not be afraid of who might show up in the middle of the night, or what kind of a mood people might be in. She was good to me, but she was old, and her health wasn't good, and it didn't help to have everyone always messing with her, disrupting things and dumping me there without a word of warning."

"And she died," Zachary filled in, remembering what the man at the bodega had said.

"Yeah," Noah agreed. "And… I was lost. I didn't know what to do with myself. Where to go or how to feel better. I drank, I did pot, I hung out with guys who broke all of the rules. Because I didn't have anyone else to go to. At least they put up with having me around. And then Connor…"

Zachary shook his head, his stomach flipping.

"He said he loved me," Noah said, eyes glistening. "He said he would help me. Take care of me. But it was just a sham. Just like they would teach me to do later, to bring other kids in. Other boys. And girls."

He looked at Madison. Her eyes were wide. Maybe it wasn't until then that she realized that she'd been intentionally targeted. Like Jocelyn had suggested, Noah would tell her that he just needed her to do something for him to help keep the leg-breakers off of him. Just one favor. And just another. And someday, when they had paid off all of the debts and had enough money, they would live an idyllic life with the two of them sharing a little house somewhere, safe and comfortable and able to put the hard days behind them.

She thought that he really did love her. That he was her boyfriend. She'd caught his eye, and he had been drawn toward her. It had been fate. Cupid's arrow. Not an act coldly crafted to draw her in and seduce her until she was willing to do whatever he asked her to.

"But… no." Madison breathed. "No. That's not what it was like."

Noah let go of her hand and put his hands over his eyes. "Yes. That's exactly what it was like. I found your social profiles online. That's how we identify who we're going to target. See where you go to school. What your schedule is. How much time your parents are away or doing their own thing. What you're posting online. We work up a profile. What kind of a person you are and what we'll use—what I'll use—to lure you."

Madison's breath rasped loudly. She stared at Noah, shocked and distressed, still not believing that what he was telling her was true. Despite everything she had done, she had thought she was doing it for him. To help him. Keep him safe. To get his love and approval and all of the good feelings that went with doing what he wanted her to. He was supposed to love her. Zachary had no doubt that Noah had told her that he loved her. And she had believed it with all her heart. She would do anything for him. Just like he felt about Bridget.

"You're not the first one." Noah's voice was strangled. "I turn out a couple new kids every year. You don't know what kind of... what a piece of crap I am."

"But..." Madison shook her head, tears starting to run down her face. "Why? Why would you do that?"

"Because I have to do the same thing as you... to keep my boss happy. And it's not enough to just turn tricks. That only earns so much money. I need to keep bringing in fresh meat. And each of them, eventually, will have to do the same. You move up in the organization, or you don't survive."

"And your boss is... Connor?"

Noah took a deep breath. "No. No... Connor died years ago. He had someone over him, and they had someone over them, and on up. When he was gone, then the person over him took over his stable."

In reading up on trafficking to verify what Jocelyn had told him, Zachary had come across an article that said that each person being trafficked earned their pimp in the neighborhood of three hundred thousand dollars per year. If Noah was turning tricks and bringing in two new kids each year, then he was bringing in almost a million dollars a year for his boss. And if each of those two new kids stayed in the business and also started targeting a couple of new girls—or boys—each year... it was no wonder traffickers were bringing in billions of dollars across the country every year.

And no wonder they didn't want to lose any of the victims to do-gooders like Zachary or police stings and would fight to get them back, forcing them to keep earning money until they were worn out and useless.

Or dead.

"Who's over you?" Madison asked. "Is it someone I've met?"

Noah nodded.

"Who is he?"

"She," Noah corrected. "Peggy Ann."

Madison's jaw dropped. Her eyes could not get any wider. She shuddered. "I knew... she was scary. I thought... I don't know what I thought. Just that she was... not someone to cross, I guess."

Noah nodded. His right hand went to his opposite shoulder, rubbing his bicep. Madison pushed the sleeve of his t-shirt up, revealing puckered burn marks. She smoothed them gently with her finger.

"Did she do that? Peggy Ann?"

Noah's eyes were far away. "I don't remember."

"You don't remember? How can you not remember who did that to you?"

Noah looked down at the scars. "There have been a lot of people. A lot of punishments. It's best… not to think about it."

Madison leaned into him, resting her forehead against his shoulder. Noah rested his cheek on the top of her head and he stroked her back gently.

"You do care," Madison said, slightly accusing.

"Of course I care," he murmured. "That's why I get in trouble. That's why he's here." Noah nodded to Zachary.

"So you want me to… take Madison away. Is that it?"

"Yes. Take her away. Make her parents go away with her. And if they won't go away, then she has to go by herself. She can't stay around here."

"My sis—my friend says that she'll have to change her name and move out of state to keep them from finding her."

"Yes. Do that." He held the back of Madison's head, pressing her against himself. "Get far away from here so Gordo can't find you."

Madison sniffled. "Who is Gordo?"

"He's… the top boss around here. I don't know if there's anyone above him, but I don't think so. I think everything goes back to Gordo. All of the money flows up to him. And… all of the information."

"You need to get out too," Zachary pointed out. "If you don't, they'll just come after you. Peggy Ann and Gordo and all of their enforcers. You'll be killed."

Noah nodded tiredly. "Yes."

"So you need to get out," Zachary repeated. "You can't just stay here and wait for them to find out."

"It won't take them long." Letting go of Madison, Noah rubbed his eyes and then pulled out his phone to look at it. "You need to get her out of here. Before they come looking."

Zachary's heart started pounding faster again. He had settled down, listening to Noah and realizing that he wasn't the enemy. He wasn't there to shoot Zachary or kidnap Rhys. He wanted Madison to be safe. After all of the boys and girls that he had turned out in the past five or six years, he couldn't do it again, and he wanted Zachary to take Madison somewhere safe.

But the fact that Noah wanted to help didn't mean that the danger was gone. It had just transformed into a different shape. Into Peggy Ann, who Zachary pictured as a tall, Amazon-like redhead, and Gordo, an enormous Mexican man, both of whom would do whatever they had to in order to keep their hooks in Madison, and would torture and kill Noah for letting her escape.

They were both out there, getting closer. Maybe looking in through the windows of Zachary's car, parked down on the dark street, seeing Rhys there waiting.

Zachary stood up, shaking off the inertia. They had to move. Sitting there talking about it wasn't going to do anyone any good.

"Come with me. Both of you."

Madison looked at Noah, waiting for him to agree. Noah shook his head.

"Yes," Zachary said firmly. He gestured for Madison to get up. A snappy, brisk command. She got to her feet. Zachary reached for Noah's arm and gave it a little tug. "Come on. You're coming with us."

"No. I don't want to. You go ahead."

"We're not leaving you here."

"I'm tired. I just want it all to be over."

Zachary pulled harder. "I know what it's like to be depressed," he said. "I know what it's like not to want to put in the effort to survive."

Noah nodded. "Then leave me alone."

"No. Other people pulled me through. Just because you can't see the light at the end of the tunnel, or imagine ever having enough energy to live again, that doesn't mean it's the end. Things can change. Now come on."

One more insistent pull. Madison grabbed Noah's other arm and, between the two of them, they got him to his feet.

Zachary juggled his phone out and messaged Rhys. *Coming now.*

He and Madison walked Noah to the door. Once they got him moving, the momentum seemed to keep him going. They didn't have to force him, but both still held on, guiding him, unwilling to release him and take the chance that they wouldn't be able to get him moving again. He wasn't big or heavily-built, but Zachary suspected that he and Madison did not have the strength it would take to move him if he were a dead weight.

Out of the apartment. They shut the door, but no one bothered to lock it. Down the hall. To the stairs. Zachary felt his phone vibrate. They coaxed Noah down the stairs. Zachary's heart was pounding.

When they reached the bottom, he pulled his phone out again. It was a stupid thing to do. He needed to get Madison and Noah out to the car without being distracted by whatever else happened to be going on.

Rhys, of course. Zachary stopped in his tracks.

A gif of a rotating red light.

Madison looked at him, still pulling Noah forward, but now Zachary was anchoring him on one side instead of helping to direct him and keep him moving. "What is it?"

Zachary turned the phone around to show her.

Madison scowled. "Dammit, Rhys, use words!"

Zachary felt the same way. Clearly, Rhys meant there was an emergency. But did he mean that the police were there? That someone was hurt? That the bad guys were there? Zachary didn't know whether to keep going, to hide, or to go back up the stairs.

34

When he looked at the stairs, he knew that wasn't going to happen. There was no way that he and Madison would be able to get Noah back up the stairs again. And it was probably the worst thing they could do. Going back up to the apartment would just mean that they were cornered. Unless they went up farther, to another floor, in the hopes that whoever was coming after them wouldn't expect them to be higher up in the apartment building.

But they couldn't make it.

Zachary looked out the narrow window in the door between the stairway and the lobby. There were no flashing lights out on the street. No police out there, waiting for them. At least, not police with a car with its lights on.

"This way." He jerked his head, and he and Madison hustled Noah through to the hallway Zachary had taken the first day. The domain of the man with the bathrobe. Zachary hoped not to run into him again.

Anyone who saw them in the hallway would think that Noah was drunk. Maybe they were trying to take him home. Though anyone who lived in the building would know that they were on the wrong floor. Zachary tried to think of a way to explain that, but couldn't come up with anything. Too many scenarios were running through his head and he couldn't find one that worked.

When they were on the other side of the lobby door, Zachary stopped and looked back. He stayed as far to the side as he could, so they wouldn't see his face blocking the window if they looked in his direction.

The lobby remained empty. He stayed there, watching, waiting for someone to enter the building. Maybe it was a false alarm. Maybe Rhys had been wrong. Worried by something that wasn't anything to do with Madison and Noah.

The inner lobby door opened, and a man and woman walked through. Zachary studied them. The woman was not the tall, well-built redhead that he had envisioned. She was rather petite, with dark hair, probably in her forties. Her face was not unattractive, but was hard. Sneering. She wore fashionable clothes with a red leather jacket.

Was she Peggy Ann? The woman who had scared Madison so badly? Who had burned Noah? Noah wasn't a big guy, and Zachary couldn't see the small woman being able to overcome him by physical force.

But maybe she hadn't needed to. There had been other threats, other ways to coerce him. And she didn't need to be strong to punish him for his failings.

The man was not big either. Nor fat. Probably not Gordo. Which made sense, because why would Gordo, the top boss in Vermont, or maybe in all of New England, be there to see Madison and Noah? Zachary backed away from the window. He looked at Madison and Noah.

"Is that her? Or someone looking for you?"

Noah didn't move. Madison moved in close to Zachary and peeked out. "That's Peggy Ann. I don't know who the guy is." She turned to look at Noah. "Is he one of your friends? I mean…" She had to shift her thinking, "One of your clients or bosses?"

Noah didn't move. Zachary took a step back so that they weren't all crowding around the door. Madison put her hand on Noah's arm to encourage him forward. Noah reluctantly looked through the window. He withdrew, pressing himself against the wall so he couldn't be seen through the door.

"Jorge," he said. "He's…" Noah hesitated, searching for a word. "A troubleshooter. He must have heard about you." His eyes met Zachary's. "Or about the police coming. He's come to… take care of things." Noah's eyes darted back and forth, worried. "Sort out any problems."

Goosebumps rose on Zachary's neck and arms. He looked through the narrow window, a quick peek to map the progress of the couple across the lobby to the stairs. As soon as they were on their way up the stairs, Zachary, Madison, and Noah would need to get across the lobby and outside. They could get to the car and get out of there before Peggy Ann and Jorge knew that Madison and Noah were missing. If they would even know there was something wrong. Maybe they would think that the two had just gone out for food or to see to a client.

Except that they'd left the door unlocked. Did they usually lock it when they left? They might not have a lot of money in the apartment, but Madison's clothes were pricey.

He waited a few more seconds, then took another peek through the window. They were disappearing through the door to the stairs. Zachary watched through the sliver of window, waiting for them to mount the stairs. That would be his signal to move. He didn't see them on the stairs, and wondered if he'd missed it. They might have been too far to one side and he just hadn't been able to see them. His heart was jumping all over the place, telling him that it was time to move, but he hesitated, wanting the confirmation that they were on their way up to the apartment. It wouldn't make more than a few seconds' difference one way or the other, but he wanted to be sure.

Still nothing.

Zachary put his hand on the doorknob, getting ready to lead the others into the lobby. Clearly, he had missed the couple climbing the stairs, and to wait any longer would be detrimental to their chances of making it out of there in one piece.

Then the door to the stairs opened. Zachary froze. Jorge, the troubleshooter, stood in the doorway. He looked around the lobby, eyes sharp. Zachary moved slowly to the side. Any sudden movement would attract attention, even if Jorge hadn't been specifically looking at the door to the ground floor apartments. He hoped that by fading gradually to the side, Jorge wouldn't see him, and they would avoid detection. He waited, frozen, not even able to breathe. He didn't hear footsteps walking toward them, and in a moment heard the *snick* of the other door closing again. He was afraid to look. Afraid that as soon as he put his face to the window again, he would see Jorge looking straight back at him, just waiting for him to make a mistake.

But if Jorge had gone on, they needed to get out. Zachary moved over again, very slowly, looking past the edge of the window with one eye, exposing no more of himself than absolutely necessary.

35

He did not see Jorge. There was no one in the lobby. He didn't want to see them going up the stairs this time. He'd been hiding for too long. Either they would go up or they would not, and Zachary believed that the last look around the lobby was Jorge's final look. He wouldn't stay down any longer after that.

"Let's go."

Madison stuck close to him. Noah was looking dazed. Zachary wondered for a moment if he were dissociating. Not even consciously with them any longer. He nudged Noah's shoulder, and the three of them moved through the lobby. Madison was dragging back, looking around, too worried that there might be someone hiding there. But if there were, it was too late. They were going to get caught. There was no way to avoid it once they were out of the hallway.

"Come on, keep moving. We need to get out of here."

"It's not going to work," Noah intoned. "We're never going to be able to get away from them together. You should go ahead. I'll stay back, try to convince them that I've moved Mad somewhere safe. I can keep them distracted, give you a chance to get away."

"You're coming with us," Zachary said firmly.

Madison looked at him, nodding her gratitude. She still had feelings for Noah, even if he had betrayed her. She hadn't had enough time to reconsider the impact of what he had told them. She kept operating on the same level, as if he were her boyfriend and she needed to protect him.

Zachary hit the release for the inner lobby door and hustled Madison and Noah through it. He followed them through and out the second door to the front of the building. They turned toward him, not sure which way to go.

"My car is down there," Zachary gestured toward it, in too much of a hurry to sort out his left from his right. They kept moving. They looked around the neighborhood with bright eyes, as if they had been released from a long prison term. The cold air and the darkness were startling after having been inside.

Zachary hurried, trying to press Madison and Noah forward faster. They still had time. Peggy Ann and Jorge wouldn't have figured out that they had run yet. They weren't yet in pursuit. But it wouldn't be much longer. They would arrive at the apartment and find the door open. They would look around, but it would be immediately obvious that Madison and Noah were not there. They wouldn't know how long it had been since they left, but they would run down the stairs anyway, they would look up and down the street trying to spot them.

"Come on. Come on."

Zachary could see, as they approached, that there was a cop standing beside his car. His heart sank.

Dealing with the police force was never quick. And if he didn't get out of there right away, Peggy Ann and Jorge were going to see them all together, and they would know who was behind Madison's and Noah's disappearance.

Madison and Noah stopped stock-still at the sight of the police officer. As if he might not see them if they didn't move and didn't get any closer. Maybe just because they didn't know what to do. Retreat? Run? Wait?

Zachary forced a friendly smile at the officer, getting closer and studying his face in the dim streetlight to see if it were someone he had worked with before. But it was just a beat cop or someone on traffic, not a detective that he had worked with. Not one of the administrative positions that Zachary might have had the opportunity to meet with and talk with before.

"Hi. Is there a problem, officer?"

The policeman looked Zachary over. He had a notepad and pen in his hand. Writing a ticket? It didn't look like a ticket clipboard to Zachary. Just a regular notepad.

"Is this your car, sir?"

"Yes." Zachary scanned the signs along the street for one that said he wasn't allowed to stop or park there. He didn't see any. The curb wasn't painted a different color. There was no fire hydrant close by. He couldn't see any reason the cop should be there making inquiries. Nothing that would have tipped him off that Zachary's car didn't belong to a resident. "Is there a problem?"

"Is this… your son?" The cop looked mildly uncomfortable asking the question. Zachary was clearly white and Rhys was not. Even darker in the shadows of the car. But there was no reason that a white man couldn't be the father of a black boy or responsible for him by some other relationship.

"No." Zachary gave Rhys a little wave, trying to look casual and unconcerned. So that Rhys wouldn't be anxious and the policeman would see that there was nothing wrong and would let Zachary drive away before Peggy Ann and Jorge came back out of the building. "Just a friend. I was just running inside to get the others." He indicated Madison and Noah. "I hope you weren't waiting long. You know how long kids can take to get ready sometimes." He smiled, inviting the cop to agree. To laugh about how long it took his kids to get ready. Though he didn't look old enough to have teenagers. Maybe he had younger siblings or cousins or could remember the days when he would take hours to get ready for a date or a dance or even just to go out to hang with other guys.

The cop didn't look too sure of this. He didn't laugh or give Zachary a knowing look. "I'd like you to open the car, sir."

"Of course." Zachary's key fob didn't always work, and he didn't want the car to flash its lights when he unlocked it, advertising his presence. So he walked around to his door and unlocked it manually. He hit the switch to unlock the rest of the doors.

"Would you ask your friend to get out of the car, please?"

"Sure," Zachary said agreeably. "But can I ask… if something is wrong? We have a thing that I'm supposed to be getting them to, and I didn't want to be late."

"I want to talk to him."

Zachary bent down to talk to Rhys, inside the car. "He wants to talk to you. It should just take a minute."

Rhys's eyes were wide and worried. He wanted to know what was going on. Wanted to know why Noah was there and what had taken Zachary so long. He knew enough to be worried about talking to the cop. He had grown up knowing that cops could stop him at any time, and they wouldn't like the fact that he was black and was refusing to talk to them.

As Rhys got out of the car, his hands raised to his shoulders to show that he was unarmed and wasn't planning to attack anyone, Zachary stepped back from the car, walking a couple of steps around the hood to have an unobstructed view of him. But he stopped there, not wanting the cop to think that he was being pincered between the two of them.

"You should know that Rhys is selectively mute," he explained calmly. "That means that he won't be able to talk to you out loud."

The cop didn't like this. He looked at Rhys suspiciously. As if he might be some kind of monster or predator and was trying to keep the cop from figuring it out. "How does he communicate, then? Does he use sign language?"

"He uses a combination of gestures and text or pictures on his phone. He's not going to cause you any trouble; you just need to know that it is going to take longer than usual to establish communication. And we do want to be getting on our way."

The cop ignored the last part of Zachary's statement, making no indication that he would move things along.

"Can we get into the car?" Madison asked. "It's kind of chilly out here."

She wasn't wearing a coat and the cop was. So was Zachary. The car would be warmer, and sheltered from the breeze. The cop looked at Madison, his hand at his hip. He looked her over, and his eyes spent even longer on Noah.

"You, I know," he said, looking at Noah.

Noah stared down at his feet, nodding.

"You pimping them out?" the cop demanded, eyes going back to Zachary. "I'm not going to put up with that on my watch."

"No. No sir. I'm trying to get them out of here. Away from all that. That's why we're here." Zachary looked back toward the apartment building. Peggy Ann and Jorge could be coming out the front door any time. "And why we need to get on our way. Soon."

"Turn out your pockets," the cop told Madison and Noah. "Put the contents on the car. Then put up your hands."

Noah obeyed. Madison didn't have any pockets. She looked at the cop for a moment, then slid a couple of fingers down into her bra and pulled out her phone. She put it on the car. They both raised their hands.

"Stay there," the cop told Rhys. He went over to the other two and felt their pockets and other key areas to satisfy himself that they weren't carrying any weapons. He opened the back car door and used his flashlight to check the back seats, footwells, and under the front seats. He ran one hand along the crack in the back of the bench seats. He finally nodded. "Fine. Get in. But if you cause me any trouble, believe me, you'll never get a break out of me again."

Madison and Noah got quickly into the car, bumping over each other and getting settled into place. The policeman looked at Rhys.

"Are you okay?"

Rhys nodded.

"Did he bring you here?"

Rhys hesitated, looking at Zachary, then nodded his head.

"Why did he bring you here?"

Rhys pointed at Madison.

"To get her?"

Rhys nodded again.

"Are you two turning tricks? Is he taking you to some party to make some money?"

Rhys shook his head violently, eyes wide.

"Why, then?"

Rhys frowned. He pointed at Madison, then he made a roof-and-house motion with both hands.

"To take her home?"

Rhys and Zachary nodded. Zachary was itching to explain the whole situation himself in a couple of brief sentences so that they could get into the car and get out of there before Peggy Ann and Jorge came looking for Madison and Noah. Madison and Noah were ducking down, making themselves as invisible as possible. Sheltering behind the seats where they wouldn't be as easy to see. Peggy Ann and Jorge would come out of the apartment building, and see the cop there with Rhys and Zachary. Maybe they wouldn't get close enough to see that Madison and Noah were there too. They wouldn't connect the two incidents.

But he knew that if he tried to help the conversation with Rhys along, the policeman would just view him as more suspicious. He couldn't speak for Rhys, but had to let him explain himself without interruption.

"How do you know her?"

Rhys considered. He pointed to his pocket and made a 'telephone' hand-shape beside his ear.

The cop nodded. "You can get out your phone."

Rhys nodded and lowered his hand slowly to take his phone out with two fingers. He held it up, making sure that the policeman could get a good look at it before changing his grip on it. Rhys tapped and swiped his phone to find a photo, then held it up for the cop. Madison sitting at her desk. One of the photos he had shown to Zachary.

The cop looked at it. "You know her from school."

Rhys nodded. He looked at the apartment building, and tapped his wrist where he would wear a watch. He looked back at the car where Madison and Noah were sitting. They were hunched down out of sight, which was good, but it would be better if they were out of there.

But the policeman wasn't sure he wanted to let them go yet. He wanted to be sure of what was going on before he let them take off. Better not to be the guy who had let a pimp operate right under his nose. That kind of thing never looked good when it hit the papers. People didn't understand that the police couldn't just arrest someone on a gut feeling.

"I want your name and contact information. ID if you have it."

Rhys nodded. He indicated the cop's pen and notepad. The officer handed them over. Rhys put the notepad on the car to write his information down. He handed them back when he was done and pulled his student bus pass lanyard out of his shirt. Turning it over, he displayed his student ID card. The policeman compared the information Rhys had written down with what was on his card.

"You can get back in the car."

Rhys got in. The cop went through the contents of Noah's pockets, which were still on top of the car. He wrote down detailed notes. Zachary was sweating with his anxiety over getting out of there. They had been there much too long. Peggy Ann and Jorge were probably watching the drama from inside the apartment building. Maybe making phone calls to have

Zachary followed or to call in hired guns. He knew the cop was just doing his job, but if it ended up with Madison and Noah being retrieved by their cartel and Zachary and Rhys in the crosshairs of some criminal intent on making sure that they didn't interfere again…

The officer handed Noah his possessions back, other than his phone, and didn't give Madison's phone back either. He left them side by side on the top of the car, face up, keeping an eye on them.

Then he turned his attention back to Zachary. "Now I want your information. And I want ID and your car registration and insurance."

Zachary nodded. He glanced along the street again for any signs saying he wasn't allowed to park there. He still didn't spot anything. If there was a sign, it was out of sight and he could challenge it in court. The cop wanted him for more than just a traffic violation, but if that were all he could get, Zachary was sure he would go for it. Then he would have an official record of who he had stopped. He would be able to show his superiors that he had done everything in his power to curtail any criminal activities.

36

Zachary slowly removed his wallet from his pocket and removed the items that the policeman wanted to see. His hands were shaking violently. The adrenaline was having an effect on him. Walking into the apartment not knowing what situation he was going to face, being confronted by Noah, trying to make a run for it and trying to avoid Peggy Ann and Jorge. Trying to deal with the cop when every fiber in his body was telling him to get out of there.

Closer to the cop, he could see his name bar. Burkholdt.

"Tell me how you got involved with this," Burkholdt said. "This is exactly the type of situation that we don't want civilians caught in the middle of. You shouldn't be here."

Zachary swallowed and looked down. That was probably true. He had considered whether to call the police before going to see Madison, but he had been afraid that she would just refuse to cooperate if he showed up with officials. And in retrospect, he was sure that instinct had been correct. He wouldn't have been able to make any kind of progress if he'd shown up there with the police, or if the police had gone there without him. Madison was not the one who had sent the message asking for help. She would have just looked blankly at them and refused to go. She would have denied knowing anything about that message. She would say that she hadn't sent it. Because she hadn't.

He told the cop about being a private investigator. About Rhys coming to him to help with finding Madison, and then returning for more help when he'd received her message asking for help. He left out the details about Madison not being the one who had sent the message or about Noah's involvement in the whole thing. He hoped that if he kept it simple, the policeman would finally agree to let them go.

"She was reported as a missing person?" Burkholdt asked.

"Yes."

"So if I called in asking for confirmation, I would be told that there was a report made?"

"Yes. Joshua Campbell was assigned to the case. I spoke to him."

"You did, did you?"

"Yes. I always let law enforcement know if I've been retained on a case that the police have had some involvement in. Or if they should know about it. I always cooperate with local law enforcement."

"Sure you do."

"You're welcome to call him. I have his numbers if you need them."

Burkholdt studied him closely, considering this. Eventually, he nodded. He wrote down all of Zachary's information.

"How is the other boy involved in it?"

"Noah?"

For a moment, the policeman looked blank. Then he shrugged. "Whatever name he gave you. He's been around here for a long time. I know him. Just how is he mixed up in this?"

"He was just... helping Madison out. Took her under his wing. Felt sorry for her, I guess."

"Figured he could turn her out, more likely. You can't trust him. If I was you, I wouldn't take him with me."

Zachary nodded. "I know... but I need to. I can't explain all of the details right now, but I think it's safer to have him with me than not."

"Don't count on it. He's more likely to call his pimp with her new location than he is to help her out. People like him don't change. He's not going to suddenly go from being a hooker to being the savior of a runaway. He's just looking for a higher paycheck. A way to move up in the organization. As soon as he knows where she's going, he'll tell them."

Zachary swallowed back the acid that rose in his throat at this suggestion. He had to admit that Burkholdt had a good point. What were the chances that Noah was really looking to help Madison out, after putting months into getting her established in the business? What were the chances that even if he had altruistic feelings toward Madison, or was feeling guilty for what he had done, that they would last?

Joss had talked about walling off her feelings. Compartmentalizing. So that she didn't have to think about the things she was doing. She could keep those parts of herself separate and not have to acknowledge them.

He was sure Noah would rather not admit what kind of person he was and the things that he had chosen to do to get the money or drugs that were dangled before him like a carrot. He would rather think of himself as a fair and compassionate person. The kind of guy who would help a teenager get back to her family. But when it came down to it, who was he more likely to be loyal to?

He started to regret having insisted that Noah come along. He had been affected by Noah's story and his tears. But Noah probably had a hundred different stories and could turn the tears on and off at will. He was playing them. Getting Zachary and Rhys right where he wanted them. Once he'd confirmed their intentions and found out everything he could about them and lulled them into a false sense of security, they would turn back to his supervisors. To Peggy Ann and the rest of them. That was what he had been trained to do for the past five years. If that part of his story was true.

The cop handed Zachary's ID back to him loose, leaving him to put everything back into his wallet. Zachary shivered with cold while at the same time, sweat dripped down his back.

"Listen to what I tell you," Burkholdt said again. "Leave the boy here. Don't take him with you and trust him not to report everything he sees."

"I can't leave him here."

Burkholdt looked into his face, lips tight. "You need to leave him here."

Zachary took a deep breath. "Are you arresting him?"

"I don't have any cause to arrest him. But I know this kid. I've arrested him before and I know what he does around here. You should listen to someone who knows."

Zachary nodded. He looked at the driver's seat of the car. "Thank you for your concern. Am I free to go now?"

The cop's jaw muscles stood out as he clenched his teeth. He nodded. "You're free to go." He handed Zachary the two phones.

Zachary's knees wobbled. He tried to keep himself together. Keeping tight control over his body, he managed to walk back around the car and to get into the driver's seat. He was looking around, charting his escape route, before he even got into the seat. The keys were still in the ignition. Before he even had his door shut or his seatbelt on, he was shifting into gear. He put it into reverse, backing up over the curb onto the sidewalk and then throwing it into drive and performing a tight U-turn to get them turned around and heading back in the direction they had come. The cop had jumped back out of the way when he had backed up onto the sidewalk. Madison gave a little shriek as they were thrown unexpectedly around the car. None of them had been braced for Zachary's maneuver. But he was desperate. His body was throwing up all kinds of signals that he was in danger and he wasn't going to ignore them. He wasn't going to sedately perform a three-point turn or drive forward until he came to an intersection where he could get himself turned around properly. If the cop jumped into his car and came after him, then Zachary would deal with it. But not until he had put some distance between him and the people who were after them.

Noah swore, hanging on to Rhys's seat in front of him and trying to stay upright. "Who taught you to drive? We're going to have that cop right back on our tail!"

"I'm getting us out of there," Zachary snapped. "I'm not staying around to see if they managed to get a tail on us while we were trying to get away from that cop. We were sitting there way too long."

He looked in his rear-view mirror, watching for any suspicious vehicles. He was going fast enough that they would have to make themselves pretty obvious if they were going to keep up with him. He was aiming to put as much space between him and any pursuers as possible.

When he got to a straight stretch of road, he opened and slammed his door to make sure that it latched properly, and pulled his seatbelt around himself and clicked it into place.

"You might want to put on your seatbelts too," he told his passengers.

Rhys was already pulling his out, grinning. Madison and Noah complained as they put theirs on.

"Do you want to get out of there safely, or not get out at all?" Zachary demanded.

He had a bad feeling. He'd missed something. He knew that there was a problem, but he couldn't think of what it was. Something had been off. His ever-vigilant PTSD brain had caught it but hadn't passed the message to his conscious brain.

"We need to go somewhere safe," he told his passengers.

He waited for the suggestions. First on the list, of course, was to Madison's parents. But he immediately discarded that idea. There were others in the organization who would know how to find Madison's family. They knew what school she went to. They knew her name. It would only take a few minutes to find out her address, if they didn't have it already. Her home was too dangerous. He was going to have to convince her parents to leave their home and make massive changes in their lives if they were going to be able to keep Madison alive and out of Peggy Ann's stable. He didn't know how he was going to approach that. How he was going to convince them of anything.

He needed to take Rhys home and to make sure that he was safe. Vera was sure to be wondering where he was and worrying over him. But he didn't want to take Noah to Rhys's house either. Though he supposed that Rhys's grandmother was just as easy to find as Madison's family. His only hope was that Noah and Madison hadn't told anyone who had come after Madison and how he knew about her. If they didn't know that Rhys had asked Zachary to look into it, then Rhys would be safe. If Peggy Ann and her crew knew who Zachary was, he was going to have to plant enough disinformation for them to believe that he had been hired by Madison's parents rather than by Rhys.

"We could stay with someone," Madison suggested. "What about Jeff? Or Roxanne?"

Noah shook his head. "Can't be anyone in the organization or known to it."

"But they're not part of… they're just friends."

"No."

"They're just people we hung out with. Friends."

"I don't have any friends, Mad. Anybody we've hung out with. Anyone we've partied with. They're all part of it. Or they're known. Clients or prospects."

Madison made a noise of protest. She looked at Noah, her face lined with anxiety and pain. "Noah… I don't understand this. I don't believe it. Tell me it's not true. You're just teasing. You just want me to go home."

"It's too late to go home. I want you to be safe, and you won't be safe there."

"This doesn't make sense. I love you, Noah."

"No, you don't. You've just been… conditioned. It's what we do. It's how we get people to do what we say." Noah cleared his throat, but his voice was still unsteady. "Praise and love when they do what they're supposed to. Consequences and punishment when they don't." He turned away from her to look out the window. "You think you're making your own choices, but you're not. You're doing what they want you to do. Whenever they want something, they tell me, and it's my job to get you to do it. Whatever it takes. If I can't, there's a consequence."

There was a long silence. Zachary glanced over at Rhys, who was playing with his phone, listening to the others.

"Where are we going to go, then?" Madison asked. "One of my friends from school? I know they're not mixed up in this."

"They'll look for you at the school. And if you're not with your parents, they'll start checking out your friends at school. You can't stay here, Mad. It has to be somewhere else."

"What do you mean, somewhere else? Where?"

Noah looked at Zachary in the rear-view mirror. "Did you have any kind of plan? Or were you just going to take her home?"

"We were still working that out. Your message took me by surprise."

"Where then?" Madison asked in frustration. "We can't just drive around all night."

"A hotel?" Zachary suggested. "Somewhere we can stop and regroup and figure it out? They're not going to find you if it isn't somewhere you have been connected with before."

"What hotel?" Noah grumbled. "We have people at hotels. They'll be on the lookout. She'll be seen."

"They can't have people at all of the hotels all of the time. We'll pick somewhere they're not watching."

Noah shook his head, but didn't argue it any further.

37

Zachary breathed a sigh of relief when they were all in the hotel room. He had watched carefully for a tail and was pretty sure that they couldn't have been followed. Every now and then, his ability to drive fast came in handy. He had a good eye for detail and noticed things in an instant.

The kids all seemed to be relieved too. Noah had been vigilant as they approached the hotel and looked around the lobby, watching for anyone that he knew or anyone that might be looking at them the wrong way. But he had gradually relaxed and, by the time they got into the room and closed the door, he was ready to crash. He went into the bathroom, and when he came back out, he lay down on one of the beds and buried his head.

Madison still hadn't been able to reconcile herself to the fact that Noah was not her boyfriend and had not necessarily had her welfare in mind for the past few months. She sat down and put her arm around him and, after rubbing his back for a few minutes, curled up against him and closed her eyes. Zachary wasn't sure whether either of them was asleep, so he tried to be careful what he said. He sat down on the one chair, beside the other bed where Rhys was sitting. Rhys slid closer to him. He pointed at Noah, raising his brows.

Zachary knew there was more to explain than he could manage there, especially right in front of Noah and Madison. He considered what to tell

Rhys. "I'll have to explain it all to you later," he said softly. "But… he was the one who messaged you. *He* was the one who wanted out."

Rhys's eyes widened and he raised his brows. He hadn't been expecting that. More likely, he had figured that Madison had refused to leave without her boyfriend and, rather than trying to fight it, Zachary had just agreed to bring him along.

Rhys looked at Noah, pondering this. He pointed at Noah, looking at Zachary again. *He did?*

Zachary nodded. "Yeah. He's got a good story. But… we can't trust him. Not yet." He was mindful of what the cop had said, warning Zachary not to take Noah with him.

Rhys nodded his agreement with the sentiment. Zachary still had Madison's and Noah's phones, and he took them out and laid them down on the desk. They were both locked, of course. He hadn't expected otherwise. He pressed the button to bring up the lock screen on Madison's. It was set for a four-digit numeric passcode. Zachary looked sideways at Rhys. "What do you think her unlock code is?"

Rhys rolled his eyes and pointed to Noah.

Zachary tapped in 6-6-2-4. The phone unlocked. Zachary chuckled. He wasn't bad at guessing passcodes, but he didn't usually get them the very first try.

He poked through a few screens, checking out Madison's call log and most recent messages and texts. She had a number of social networks set up on it, some of them with accounts that Zachary had been able to find, and others that he had not. The racier ones did not include her picture on the account summary or public feed. There were plenty of pictures on private feeds, but Zachary didn't have any desire to see them and quickly switched back out of them.

Rhys picked up Noah's phone and tried a couple of unlock codes on it before he put it back down again. He watched Zachary. After a few minutes, he tapped Zachary's knee.

Zachary looked up to see what he wanted. "Yeah?"

Rhys held up his phone, showing Zachary the gif he had sent earlier, the rotating police light.

Zachary nodded. "Yeah, thanks for the heads-up. We managed to avoid Peggy Ann and Jorge going into the building because of your warning."

Rhys raised his eyebrows and put his head forward. *Huh? Who?*

Zachary frowned. “Peggy Ann and Jorge. The people who were coming after Noah and Madison. To take care of things.”

Rhys shook his head. He pointed at the police light again.

Zachary realized all at once that Rhys hadn’t been warning him about the approach of Peggy Ann and Jorge at all, but had been telling him about the policeman standing outside the car, trying to talk to him. “Oh. Of course. You didn’t even know about them. You were just warning me about the cop.”

Rhys nodded. He raised his brows again, looking for more information.

“Your timing couldn’t have been better. Because you messaged me, I looked out in time to see Peggy Ann—that’s Noah’s boss—was coming into the building. And Jorge, some kind of enforcer. ‘Troubleshooter,’ Noah called him. So we ducked into another hallway so they wouldn’t see us and, once they were going up the stairs, we came out. I was trying to get away before they could come back down and see us. But the cop wouldn’t let me go.”

Rhys nodded slowly. He held up two fingers.

“Two? Two what?”

Rhys made a curvy shape with both hands.

“Two people. A woman and a man. Peggy Ann and Jorge.”

Rhys pinched a lock of hair between his fingers and showed it to Zachary. Then he pointed to his eyes. Then ran a finger over his skin.

“Hair, eyes—oh. What they looked like?”

Noah nodded.

Zachary did his best to describe the couple to Rhys. He had only seen them briefly, but he was observant and had trained himself to notice people and to be able to describe and remember them for later.

Rhys leaned back a little. He pointed at himself, then pointed two fingers at his eyes.

“You saw them? Before they went into the building?”

Rhys nodded.

It made sense that he had seen them. There were only two directions that Zachary would have expected them to approach from, so it was fifty-fifty that they would walk by Zachary’s car where Rhys could see them.

Rhys showed Zachary his phone again.

“The cop?”

Rhys nodded.

"What about the cop?"

Rhys held up two fingers again.

"Peggy Ann and Jorge."

Rhys made a duckbill motion with his hand, opening and closing it.

"Talking?"

Rhys held up the phone.

"The cop."

Rhys waited. Zachary put it together.

"Peggy Ann and Jorge were talking… *to* the cop?"

Rhys pointed at Zachary, nodding. *You got it.*

Zachary breathed out slowly, juggling the pieces in his mind. But he didn't have enough information yet. "They were talking to the cop… how? Did he confront them? He said that he recognized Noah. Did he recognize them as troublemakers? People he didn't want around his neighborhood?"

Rhys shook his head.

"Why was he talking to them? Was it just casual?"

He shook his head again, insistent.

Zachary didn't like where the conversation was going. He swallowed. "He was friendly with them? He knew them?"

Rhys nodded and pointed at Zachary.

The cop had known Peggy Ann and Jorge. Maybe that was why he had detained Zachary and his group. He had been waiting for them to come back down. To come out and see who he had cornered.

The last thing that he had done before Zachary left was to try to convince him to leave Noah behind. He had said that Noah would betray him, which was probably true, and that Zachary should leave him behind so he couldn't expose them.

But he was friends with Peggy Ann and Jorge. Maybe not friends, but he knew them and was on speaking terms with them. So he hadn't wanted Zachary to leave Noah there so that he wouldn't be able to tell them where Zachary took Madison.

He wanted Noah there to hand him over to Peggy Ann and Jorge. He wanted Noah to have to face his boss and the enforcer. To face the music. They could torture him, withhold his drugs, force him to tell them who had come for Madison and where to look for her.

Zachary swore under his breath. He looked at Noah and Madison, apparently asleep on the bed. On one hand, it was strange that they would be able to settle down and sleep when they were in so much danger. But Zachary had experienced the same phenomenon before, when his brain and his body would want to shut down in times of stress. Rather than melting down, like he had at Dr. Boyle's office when he had forced himself to stay and deal with his anxiety, he would just turn off. And there was nothing that he could do to stop it. Madison and Noah weren't sleeping because they felt safe to do so, but because they had been on high alert for too long and couldn't deal with it anymore. The body enforced rest sooner or later.

If they were really asleep, and not just watching and listening to see what he was planning.

There was no reason for Madison to turn on Zachary and Rhys. They had only done what they had to protect her, and she wouldn't turn them in to the organization.

Noah was another story. Despite the fact that the cop had been trying to mislead Zachary, what he had said was true, and Zachary had recognized it from the start. Once Noah was away from the criminals he was used to associating with, he would start to regret what he had done. He would realize that burning his bridges was a bad idea if he wanted to survive. He would remember he needed them. Like Madison, he had been conditioned to obey. He knew there would be consequences if he did not. He had suffered through their torture and punishments before. He knew that Peggy Ann and Jorge would not hesitate to hurt him or to hurt Madison. He would want drugs and easy money and, after five or six years, he had learned only one way to get it.

That's what Joss had tried to tell him. That it didn't matter what Zachary did and whether he managed to get Madison out or not. There would be people who would not stop at anything to get her back. Her friends would betray her, including her Romeo. That was Noah's job. To make sure Madison did whatever the bosses told him.

38

Zachary got up off of his chair and walked around the bed that Noah and Madison were lying on, so that he was standing behind Noah. The two were spooning. Zachary watched Noah's profile, the skin around his eyes and mouth, especially. He listened to the even inhalations and exhalations. If Noah was awake, he was a pretty good actor.

"Noah," Zachary said softly.

Noah didn't move.

"Noah."

The boy still didn't move. He looked very young, asleep there like that. Closer than ever to Madison's age. Tricking since he was twelve or thirteen? Under the control of a criminal enterprise for that long? He acted like an adult. He'd been forced to mature much faster than Rhys, who was still mostly boy rather than man. He had been on his own dealing with horrific people who put him through all kinds of abuse. Zachary's chest was tight. He felt for the boy.

He couldn't help it.

Ignoring the emotions, Zachary reached out and touched Noah's neck gently. He half expected Noah to stir or to strike out at him. Either pretending that he had been asleep, or actually startled out of sleep. But Noah didn't move. Zachary felt for his pulse, settling two fingers over the spot.

If Noah were awake, then his pulse would be racing, despite his pantomime of sleep. He could calm his outward body functions, making himself look relaxed and breathing slowly, but he couldn't control his heart. Not that well, anyway.

His pulse was slow, not fast. Like he was in a deep sleep.

Madison shifted. She didn't uncurl or get up, but Zachary thought that she might be awake. He kept his fingers over Noah's pulse, waiting for a burst of speed as Noah too woke up and remembered the situation he was in.

Madison turned over. She opened her eyes and looked at Zachary. A frown quickly replaced the relaxed, slightly parted lips. "What are you doing?"

"Checking on him."

Madison looked at Noah, then at Zachary's face. "Why?"

"I was surprised he was asleep. His pulse is very slow."

"He's sleeping," Madison said with a shrug.

"Why?"

"Because… neither of us has slept very much the past few days. With you coming around, and the cops, and dealing with everything else from his… well, from other people in the organization, I guess… it's been very stressful. Neither of us has slept very well."

"But he shouldn't be that much more deeply asleep than you. You're still worried about someone finding you, right? You're still feeling threatened. Like you need to be alert."

Madison rubbed her forehead, frowning. Eventually, she shrugged. "Yeah, I guess. But he's more tired."

"Why isn't he waking up with us talking over him?" Zachary gave Noah's shoulder a shake, then put his fingers back over Noah's pulse again. No increase in speed. Noah's heart still plodded away, too slow. Way too slow. "What did he take?"

Madison shook her head. "I don't know. How would I know if he took anything? I don't know that."

"Look at him. You know he did. And he's depressed. Giving up. Feeling people closing in behind him. What does he use?"

"Little of everything," Madison admitted. "It just depends. I don't know what he had on him. I don't know what he might have taken. I thought… he just needed to sleep. I need to sleep."

"I don't think you're going to get much sleep tonight. We're not here to sleep; we're here to talk strategy, somewhere we won't be seen."

Madison rubbed her eyes, smearing her mascara. "Come on. Just let us sleep tonight. We can figure it all out tomorrow."

"Tomorrow, you might change your mind. And he might be dead."

Madison's eyes widened in alarm. "Dead? What are you talking about?"

Zachary was looking at Noah's face. "His lips are getting blue. Do you know what that means?"

"He's not… Noah's always careful. He wouldn't overdose. He always knows how much he can take. He said…"

Zachary waited, brows up, for Madison to complete the thought. "What did he say?"

"He said you can always take more later, if you need it. That you can't take it back once you've taken it. There's no backing up."

"Do you have Narcan?"

"Umm…" Madison trailed off, shaking her head. "I don't need to. Noah always said, if you're careful, you don't need it."

"Then it wasn't an accident."

"No!" Madison shook her head. "He wouldn't do that. He was always careful. He told me what to do. He would never just… he would never just overdose like that on purpose."

"I think he did. Either way, it doesn't matter." Zachary pulled out his phone and started to dial emergency.

Rhys threw his school backpack down on the bed next to Noah. He unzipped one of the front pockets quickly, and handed Zachary a small black kit. Zachary opened it, knowing what he was going to find.

There wasn't time to ask Rhys why he was carrying Narcan. It was a nasal inhaler, and it was several doses. Maybe enough to keep Noah alive until the paramedics could get there. Zachary tossed his phone to Madison. "Get an ambulance here."

"But you've got the Narcan."

"It might not be enough. Get them."

Zachary positioned the inhaler inside one of Noah's nostrils and squeezed. He heard it puff, and waited for a reaction from Noah. He lay there still, breaths coming in very slowly. Lips dusky.

Zachary switched nostrils and tried another puff. Noah made a noise and pulled back. Zachary watched him, hoping that would be enough. But Noah remained still.

Madison babbled into the phone, trying to describe the situation and to tell the paramedics where they were. Rhys grabbed one of the keycard folders that they had been given on check-in and held it in front of Madison's face. She told them what hotel they were in, the address listed on the folder, and the room number handwritten in the blank. Her eyes on Noah's face, she sobbed and explained that they thought he might have overdosed. The dispatcher spoke to her reassuringly, and Madison nodded and answered the dispatcher's questions every now and then.

Zachary gave Noah another dose. And another. He shook the dispenser, but it was empty. Noah stirred and complained. Zachary felt his pulse. It had picked up a little bit and his face was pinker than it had been.

Rhys went to the hotel room door and opened it, looking down the hallway toward the elevator. Zachary could hear voices getting closer. Rhys stood with the door open and, in a few moments, he was stepping out of the way of the paramedics.

"Let's get some room here," one of them ordered. "Can the rest of you go sit on the other bed, please?"

Zachary slid off and caught Madison by the arm. "Come on."

She resisted, but eventually joined him, leaving Noah alone on the bed.

She sat with her face in her hands, sobbing. Zachary took his phone back from her. The other two phones still lay on the desk beside him.

"I gave him four doses," Zachary said, when one of the paramedics picked up the inhaler and looked at it.

"Okay. Good job. You kept him alive long enough for us to get here. That's the most you can do."

Zachary shook his head. There had to be something more that he could do. It was ridiculous that all he could do was sit there and give Noah four doses of Narcan, and it wasn't enough. He should be carrying the stuff himself, like Rhys. He should have it with him wherever he went, but especially when he was working on a case that involved young people and drug addicts. He should have known that and planned ahead.

He watched the paramedics working over Noah, giving him carefully measured shots. Noah grew more and more lucid with each dose, eventually blinking himself awake and pushing the paramedics away from him, complaining and telling them to go away.

"You need to go to the hospital, buddy," one of them told him. "You have an overdose and someone needs to keep an eye on you for a while. Your body could still be processing the opiates and you could lose consciousness again. You need to be under supervision."

"Just leave me alone," Noah growled. "I'm fine."

"You're not fine. Not with how many doses of Narcan you needed. Your condition is very serious."

Noah shook his head. "I'm fine. I'm not going to the hospital. You can't force me."

The paramedics looked at each other, then over at Zachary. But he didn't know how to convince Noah to go to the hospital. He was usually on the other end—trying to get out of the hospital when they didn't want to release him.

"Just give me the form to sign," Noah said, waving his hand at the paramedics. "I'm not going anywhere."

It took a few minutes to get everything straightened out. The paramedics continued to monitor Noah's vital signs for a few minutes but, eventually, they had to leave. Noah waited until the door was closed behind them, then looked at Zachary.

"So, what's your brilliant plan?"

39

Zachary's thoughts kept going in circles, but every time he thought he had a solution, he found a way to talk himself out of it. He needed some time to think it through, maybe to talk it over with someone who was not so closely involved with the situation.

At first, he had felt like they were moving too slowly, Noah and Madison sleeping and Zachary not able to get anywhere without their cooperation. But now that Noah was awake again, Zachary felt rushed, pressured to act without knowing for sure what to do. He needed to come up with a working solution.

"I need to make a call. I need to figure this out."

"Who's stopping you?" Noah asked. "Go ahead."

It would help if Zachary knew who he was supposed to call. He tapped his phone restlessly, trying to figure it out.

Rhys touched Zachary's arm. Zachary looked over at him. Rhys's lips pursed, and he gave a soft kissing sound.

"Kenzie? No dead bodies. Not really her area." Zachary exhaled, frustrated.

Noah was sitting on the bed. He leaned back against the wall and closed his eyes. "We gonna be here all night? If we are, I'm gonna go to sleep."

"I don't want you passing out again. I want to know you're okay. Keep him awake, Madison."

Madison held Noah's hand, looking into his face. With all that Noah had said and done, it was hard to believe that she was still so in love with him. It just went to show how well conditioning worked. It was going to take a long time to unwind all of the lies he had told her and to figure out what her true feelings were. Zachary was still trying to sort out his feelings for his parents, for Bridget, and for others who had harmed him under one guise or another.

Zachary unlocked his phone and looked at the recent calls list. He'd missed a couple of calls from Kenzie. Rhys said to call Kenzie. Maybe it was a sign. Zachary tapped her name. It rang a few times before Kenzie answered it.

"Zachary? Where are you? I thought you would be at home."

"Yeah, sorry. I thought I would be too, but I had to go out…"

"What happened?"

Zachary didn't want to say too much in front of Madison and Noah. "It's… the case I closed. Things… didn't turn out quite the way I expected."

"Are you okay?"

"Yes. Everyone is fine. Rhys says hi."

"Rhys is with you? Are you sure everything is okay?"

"Yeah. I want to get him back home, but I don't want to lead anyone there. Would you let Vera know he's fine and I'll get him back to her as soon as possible?"

"Sure. She's going to be scared, though."

"He's fine. So am I. I just need… I don't know what to do. I need to talk it through with someone who can help."

"The police? Have you called them?"

"No… there might be one of them involved on the wrong side, and I don't want to tip him off."

"A dirty cop?"

"Yeah. Maybe. No proof, just suspicions."

"Tell Campbell."

"I will. When I know more. Until then, I want to stay below the radar."

"You are not supposed to be doing stuff like this on your own."

"There's no danger right now. We're okay. I just have to figure out where to take them on a more permanent basis."

"Them?"

"Yeah, we kind of got a two for one deal."

"Another girl? One of Madison's friends."

"No."

"Not… oh. Not Noah…?"

"Yes."

"Sheesh. You can't trust him."

"No. I don't. But I still need to figure out what to do."

"Anywhere is better than where they've been."

"But it's like Joss said. The organization isn't going to let them go as easily as that. We've lost them for now, but they're going to be looking everywhere I can think of to take them."

"Where does Joss think they should go?"

"I haven't talked to her," Zachary explained. "Just before, when we had coffee. She said we need to get—her—out of the city and give her a new name and live that way. But how do you do that? Where do you take her and how do you set her up so that she's safe and independent?"

"And doesn't turn around and run back to them."

Zachary glanced over at Madison, still talking to Noah and holding his hand. Kenzie and Joss were right. If they weren't able to get through to her, Madison was going to go right back to them again.

"I imagine you have as many skills as anyone at getting her off the grid," Kenzie said.

"What do you mean?"

"I mean, you know how to find people. So you do the reverse. Make her unfindable."

Zachary thought about that. Could he hide her well enough that no one would be able to find her? Kenzie had a point.

"Why don't you call Joss and find out what she recommends?"

"She uh… may have told me to stay out of it. That was her recommendation."

Kenzie snorted. "Well, if she knew anything about you, she should have known that wouldn't work."

"Yeah, I think she had a pretty good idea."

"She's the one with the experience, so you might want to give her a call."

In the back of his mind, Zachary had known this, but he hadn't wanted to call Jocelyn again. Disregarding her advice and then expecting her to bail him out… he had a feeling she wouldn't appreciate that.

"I suppose."

"Do it. And then hurry up and get back to me. I don't want to be worrying about you all night."

"Okay. And you'll let Vera know?"

"I suppose."

Zachary said his goodbyes, and then hung up. Rhys looked at him, probably understanding a lot more of what was going on than he was meant to. He pointed at the phone and rolled his eyes about them having to call Vera.

"Well, you can't just disappear and not tell her anything," Zachary pointed out.

Rhys shook his head at Zachary's naivete. Zachary wondered what he had told Vera or how he had managed to sneak off without Vera knowing what was going on in the first place.

40

"Hi, Joss."

There was a huff of frustration from Jocelyn before Zachary could even tell her what was going on. "What did you do now?"

"I didn't do anything wrong," he protested, feeling again the like ten-year-old who was always in trouble for something. If all of the kids got in trouble, he could count on Jocelyn to blame him for it. She was the one who was in charge and supposed to keep them all in line, so he supposed she probably got the most severe punishment when she failed to do so. But he ended up getting it from her *and* from their parents, so he got punished twice when she only got punished once. And it wasn't always even his fault. Most of the time, maybe, but not all of the time, and it always stung the most when he was blamed when he hadn't done anything wrong.

"You're not just calling me for coffee again."

"Well, no."

"You got yourself into some kind of trouble. I told you that you were going to get into hot water, and you went ahead and did it anyway."

"I didn't. I let the case go." Zachary kept his voice low and turned away from the kids. They were talking to each other and had turned on the TV, so he had a measure of privacy.

"You let it go."

"Yes!"

"So you're calling me about something completely unrelated."

"Well, no."

"Then what happened?"

"She asked for help."

"She asked you for help."

"No, she asked her friend for help, and he's the one who came to me. So I had to—"

"You didn't have to. You're allowed to say no. And you should say no when it's something like this. I told you that you shouldn't have anything to do with it, and now you got yourself into some kind of trouble."

"I'm not in any trouble."

She was silent, waiting for him to explain why he was calling her if he wasn't in trouble.

"I'm not in trouble, but… I need to help them to find somewhere safe…"

"Them?"

"Well, yes." Zachary kept his voice low. He was turned away from them, but really didn't want them overhearing. He should probably have gone outside to talk. But he would have attracted attention pacing outside while talking on the phone. They were trying to keep a low profile and not give people any reason to notice them. "Madison and Noah."

"Who is Noah?" Joss groaned. "Oh, no! Tell me you didn't take her Romeo too!"

"Uh…"

"I warned you! I told you they're just going to get her back again. And especially if you're going to take one of them with you! You have to dump him." She swore angrily. "I'd tell you to slit his throat and leave him under a bridge somewhere, but you wouldn't do it, would you? How *could* you, Zachary!"

Zachary cupped his hand around his mouth and the phone receiver to try to keep his words from carrying. "It turned out that he was the one who sent the plea for help, not her. He was the one who wanted out. She does too, of course, but he wanted to get Madison out of there. And I need somewhere safe to take them. I can't take them back to my place."

"Obviously not. This guy's got you wrapped around his finger, Zachary. He's telling you stories. I know how it is. They get really, good at it. They could talk the socks off a kitten. But it's all lies. None of it is true. None of it."

"I know that he's probably telling me a bunch of stories. But I can tell how he feels. And I know that when he starts feeling better, he's going to panic and want to call back and turn them both in. I know. But right now, he needs somewhere to go, and I'm the only one who can help."

"You can tell how he feels?"

"I… yes. I can tell. He's depressed and suicidal, and I can't leave someone like that to his own devices."

"He's just reading you and reflecting your own feelings back. That's the best way to get someone on your side."

"He's already OD'd. I need to get him somewhere safe."

"He OD'd?"

"Yes. An intentional overdose. So I know… he's not just reflecting my mood. He got Madison out of there, and now he can't see the light at the end of the tunnel. He doesn't know where to go or what to do. He knows he's burned his bridges. They won't take him back now, after what he's done, and he doesn't have anywhere to go."

"You're some piece of work, Zachary."

"Is there any way you can help me? We're stuck here in a hotel and we can't stay here forever. I don't know how long it will take them to track us down. It's not exactly the big city. There are only so many places to look."

"Yeah," Jocelyn's voice was soft, as if she were suddenly afraid of being overheard.

Zachary looked at his watch. It was late, so she shouldn't be at work. She couldn't be worried about being overheard on the phone by a boss or coworker. But he hadn't asked her if it was a good time or if she were alone. He had no idea whether she had a boyfriend or was the type to seek out company when she was feeling down.

"Is someone else there?"

"What? No. Who else would be there?"

"Oh. Sorry. It just sounded like you were trying to avoid being heard. My mistake."

"I told you before, Zach, you gotta get her far away from there. She needs a new name and to stay away from anyone from her old life. Everyone she associated with before Romeo and everyone she's associated with since.

She can't talk to any of them, even if she doesn't think they have any connection to the syndicate. They can get to anyone."

Zachary opened his mouth to disagree and say that they couldn't get to *him*, that he would never put Madison at risk, but then he closed his mouth. He had called Jocelyn to ask her for her experienced opinion. How was arguing with that opinion going to get him anywhere?

"Okay. So… how far away to I need to get her?" He ran through different possibilities in his mind. "New Hampshire? That would be away from their territory, right?"

"It's not like they have to follow state borders."

"Noah said that he thought that Gordo was the head man over Vermont. So I assume that means that if we can get them out of Vermont…"

"Gordo?"

"Yeah."

"I can't believe you're dragging me into this." Joss's voice was suddenly angry and biting.

"I'm sorry. I didn't know who else to talk to. You're the one who has experience with this stuff. Kenzie said I should go to the police, but…"

"You already saw how the police handle this. They ask her if she needs help, and she says no, so they stay out of it. And you don't know how many people inside the police department might… be easily bought."

"Yeah. Actually, I might. Do you know this guy? This Gordo?"

"I know him." Joss was quiet for a minute. Zachary thought it best not to disturb her thoughts. She would have plenty to think through. "Would he know me? No. Maybe he would know my street name, but he doesn't know me as Jocelyn Goldman. I left that name behind years and years ago. I don't think he would know my face. I don't exactly look like I did when I was working for him."

"How… were you that high up in the organization? Do you mean you worked for him personally?"

"I've… I know him. He doesn't know me. I'm just another girl. He wouldn't take a second look at me. Not now."

Zachary shifted uncomfortably. He took a quick look at Madison and Noah, but they were still distracted, staring at the TV and talking to each other. Zachary hadn't expected Jocelyn to know Gordo's name. He supposed

Vermont was still a pretty small place. Jocelyn had been in the business for a lot of years and she would know a lot of the players.

"If I find someone in New Hampshire, do you think that would work? I might be able to make some connections there."

"You'd be better off sending her to Canada."

The Canadian border wasn't that far away but, in order to get Madison into Canada, they would have to smuggle her across. She wouldn't have the passport she needed to get over the border. Even if she did, she would be traceable. She needed to get somewhere without documents.

"We can start for the Canadian border," he suggested to Jocelyn. "And then circle around. Backtrack and go for New Hampshire. They would think we were going one way, when we were really going the other."

"Which would work especially well if you could dump Noah at the border. Especially if he's got more drugs on him. Throw him out and let the drug dogs get him."

She had a nasty imagination.

"I'm going to do it. Make a run toward the border, that is, not leaving Noah to the dogs. With any luck, they'll waste their time searching for data on who has crossed the border and not search in other directions until they've exhausted the possibilities."

"Okay. Whatever."

Zachary looked again at Noah. Noah saw the look and raised his brows. His lifted his hands palms-up. "What is it, bro? You got somewhere for us to go yet?"

"Maybe," Zachary told him.

Noah rolled his eyes and looked back at Madison, dramatizing his impatience. "This guy rolls in acting like he knows everything and is the big man, and he doesn't have a clue. I should never have called him."

Madison looked as if she might agree. She was looking tired and worn, her makeup smeared or rubbing off, her eyes tired and bloodshot. She hadn't, as far as Zachary could tell, had any drugs since they left the apartment and, if they had gotten her addicted to something, she was feeling it.

They were probably both thinking that they had made a mistake and should have just stayed with the organization.

"Get your stuff together," Zachary said. "We'll be leaving in a couple of minutes."

Everyone just looked at him. It wasn't like any of them had any luggage to pack. They had just run; they didn't have anything to get ready.

"Use the bathroom, splash water on your faces, whatever you need to do," Zachary said. "We're going to be in the car for a few hours and I don't want to have to make rest stops."

Noah got up. Zachary met Madison's eyes. "You'd better keep an eye on him."

"I can use the potty by myself," Noah growled.

"Last time you went in there you shot up. I don't want that happening again."

"I used up what I had."

"I don't know that. I'm supposed to believe you?"

"I don't have anything."

Zachary looked at Madison. "Unless you want a repeat, I'd keep an eye on him."

She looked ready to argue. Zachary turned away from her, focusing his attention back on the phone.

"You have a plan?" Jocelyn asked dryly. "*That's* your brilliant plan? You'll just start out toward Canada and then turn around for New Hampshire. And somehow, you'll know somewhere to drop them once you get there. It will all just magically turn out."

"I have more in mind than that. But I'm not going to tell *him* what it is."

"Well, that's something, anyway," Jocelyn conceded. "Do you really have somewhere to take them?"

"Well… we'll see," Zachary said. "I have an idea, but I need to think it over while I'm driving."

"It's pretty late to be driving. I don't want my baby brother falling asleep at the wheel."

"I won't fall asleep."

"That's what everyone says. Right before they fall asleep."

Zachary hung up the phone.

41

Before using the hotel bathroom to freshen up and prepare for the drive himself, Zachary told Madison and Noah about his plan to help them to escape over the Canadian border.

"You've gotta be kidding me," Noah protested. "We don't want to go there."

"It will be safe. Gordo's territory doesn't extend that far, right?"

"For good reason! It's freezing up there. Even worse than here. And there's nothing to do. It's all just igloos and dogsleds. They don't even have the real Netflix."

"You want to be safe or not?"

"How are you going to get us across the border?"

"I know a guy at Newport. I called him to see when he'll be on shift, and he'll be there if we leave now. He'll let me across without checking everyone's papers. For anyone following us, it will be like the two of you were ghosts. The trail will stop at the border."

"You know a guy."

"Yes."

"And how are you going to deal with all of the rest of the border guards? It's not just one person, you know. Everybody is going to see us crossing, and they're going to know something hinky is going on."

"Trust me. Madison trusts me, don't you?"

Madison looked back at Zachary, just as skeptical as Noah.

"And Rhys trusts me. Right Rhys?"

Rhys blinked at Zachary, then gave a nod and pointed at him, making a pulling-the-trigger motion. *You da man.*

"You see?" Zachary shrugged. "It's no problem. I know how to get things done. That's why Rhys came to me."

He went into the bathroom and gave them plenty of time to talk things over before returning.

"Great, everybody ready to go now?"

None of them seemed very excited. But Zachary was confident in his plan. It was going to work.

At least, he had some confidence in his plan.

It was a good plan.

It had at least some chance of working.

Zachary took a quick look around the hotel parking lot as he waited for Madison and Noah to get into the car. Rhys was quick, grabbing the shotgun seat, but Noah and Madison seemed to be moving very slowly, a lot of looks passing between them.

He had a bad feeling.

He'd been confident when he was still in the hotel room. Or at least, he'd had as much confidence as he could have in the half-baked plan, but as he stood there in the parking lot, he felt exposed and uncomfortable, sure someone was watching them.

He looked for security cameras. Shapes in parked cars. Cars that had too many antennae. But he couldn't see anything out of place. Not consciously. That didn't mean that his brain hadn't picked up on something, subconsciously. Something had alerted him to the fact that he was 'off.'

"Just get in," he told Madison and Noah, as they discussed which side each wanted to sit on.

They both looked at him, surprised at the sharpness that had crept into his voice.

"Get in," Zachary repeated. "I don't like being so exposed. Something… there's something wrong here. So get in and be quiet."

Noah gave Madison a 'he's cracking up' look, and then slid into the seat behind Zachary. Madison waited for him to move in and, when he didn't, she went around the car and climbed in on the other side, rolling her eyes at Zachary.

They could give him as much attitude as they liked, as long as they did what he said.

As Zachary got into the driver's seat and started the engine, there was a loud bang.

Everyone jumped. Rhys clutched his hand to his chest, gasping and laughing at himself. "Backfire."

But Zachary knew his car, and it was not a backfire. He looked all around, but couldn't spot any attackers.

"Get your heads down," he warned, still scanning for danger.

He hadn't turned the headlights on and, if it had been an old model car, he would have been able to roll out of the parking lot without lighting up, but it was a new car, and it had automatic lights. Drawing the eyes of anyone within a couple of blocks.

Zachary pulled his door shut as he put the car into drive and let it creep forward.

There was another bang and breaking glass.

Madison started to scream.

Rhys looked wildly over his shoulder into the back seat, the whites of his eyes glistening in the streetlights. He made a loud moaning noise, a panicked noise of alarm. Zachary reached over to touch him reassuringly on the leg, at the same time pressing the gas pedal to the floor. He withdrew his hand to grip the steering wheel and make a tight turn out of the parking lot, tires squealing all the way. The passengers were all thrown from side to side as he navigated quickly through the dark streets, turning this way and that, hoping to lose any pursuers in the maze.

He had a picture in his mind of the city streets. He didn't know every street in the city, but he had a pretty good mental map. He knew where he was relative to his apartment, the highways, and other familiar landmarks. He knew which direction was north and, after hopefully losing their tail, he pointed the nose of the car in the right direction on the highway and kept the gas pressed down.

"Everyone okay?" he asked, searching the rear-view mirror for any sign of a car that was following too close behind them. There hadn't been any headlights behind him for the last few turns, but that didn't mean they couldn't send cars in every direction to find him again. It was a big organization, if Noah and Jocelyn were right, and he didn't see any reason they would lie about it.

He patted Rhy's leg again.

"Rhys? Okay, bud?"

Rhys was still making a throbbing groan, checking anxiously behind them and looking all around for any other dangers.

"How about back there? You okay now, Madison?"

He spared a glance in the mirror at Madison. She was no longer screaming—that had only lasted for a moment—but she was definitely still scared. Probably regretting that she had ever let herself be talked into walking away from the organization that could either protect her or harm her. Better to do what she was told and to be protected.

"Noah?"

There was no answer from Noah. Zachary couldn't see him. He looked at Madison again.

"Is Noah okay?"

"He's hurt," Madison finally managed to get out. Zachary twisted around to see Noah. He could only take his eyes off of the road for a split-second, and then he was looking out the windshield again, part of his brain driving while the other part processed the image. One quick flash, and then his mind filled in the details as if he were developing a print from a negative.

Noah was slumped to the side like he had fallen asleep with his head against the window. Like a tired toddler who couldn't make it home. There was blood on his face. It was his window that had broken.

"Can you look at him, Madison? Turn him toward you and tell me whether it's broken glass or…?"

Madison sobbed. He could see, out the corner of his eye, that she was trying to do as he said, awkwardly moving in the confines of the back seat to turn Noah's body and head around so that she could get a better look at it.

"I don't know," she said in panic. "I can't tell. It's all bloody. He's bleeding so bad!"

"Head and face wounds bleed a lot. Lots of blood vessels close to the surface. It doesn't necessarily mean that it's a serious wound."

Zachary turned his face slightly toward Rhys, keeping his expression a calm, reassuring mask.

"Rhys, can you see? Can you tell whether he's been hit, or whether it is just the broken glass?"

There was a break in Rhys's moaning. He started to turn his head to look, but then stopped, as if he had encountered a wall. He seemed not to be able to turn his head past a certain angle. Had he been hurt? Maybe he got whiplash with Zachary's reckless driving. A fine thing if he ended up having to take Rhys back to Vera injured. She would never let him see the boy again.

Rhys moaned. He covered his face with his hands and hunched forward.

42

Zachary was holding back the panic.

He was usually pretty good in an emergency. His own inner thoughts and anxieties could turn him to a pile of mush, but confronting actual physical danger, his thoughts sped up and he processed everything at lightning speed.

That didn't always translate to being able to convince his body to react quickly. He often felt like he was moving in slow motion because his body just couldn't keep up with his revved-up brain.

Rhys was incoherent, but then Rhys was usually mute and unable to answer any questions out loud. It really wasn't that much of a change. But Zachary knew that this was far beyond Rhys's usual muteness.

Madison was crying and bordering on hysteria, but she seemed to be unhurt. The bullet must have come from the other side of the car, breaking the glass on Noah's side and lodging somewhere rather than hitting Madison or exiting through her window. Not a level shot, then, but something pointed down, maybe a sniper on a building. Zachary didn't think it could have come from a low angle. He would have seen or heard someone close to the ground.

"Madison. I need you to calm down."

"I can't!"

"I need you to calm down so that you can help Noah. I need to know if he's badly hurt. I can't stop in the middle of the highway."

"I don't know. I can't tell. There's so much blood, and it's dark out, all I can see is black."

Zachary had processed more than that in his one quick glance, but Madison was not a trained observer.

He remembered Dr. Boyle helping him, coaching him through his panic attack. "You need to calm down. Take a few deep breaths. Make sure that you're pushing all of the air out." He knew what Madison was going through. He knew how hard it was to stop when everything was falling apart in front of her eyes.

"Count your breaths. Ten seconds in. Ten seconds out. Just hold it for a moment. It will be okay, Madison."

He was looking for an emergency turn-out. He didn't want to stop; he wanted to keep moving so that whoever had been waiting for them in the parking lot or on top of one of the nearby buildings could not catch up with them. But he had a wounded child in the car. Maybe more than one. It would be irresponsible to keep going without evaluating them.

He found a place where the shoulder was wide enough to pull over and slowed the car, signaling, sliding over until they were rolling to a stop. He put the car into park and opened his door.

He had to be careful, because there was a lot of traffic zooming by, and there really wasn't a proper turn-out. Open his door or step out incautiously, and a passing vehicle might take him out. He watched the traffic and started to slide out of the car, looking back at Noah.

There was another crack like lightning striking, and Zachary jumped backward in alarm. He tried to spot the source. Where was the shooter?

"Call 9-1-1," he told Rhys.

But Rhys didn't move. Zachary strained back and forth, trying to see the shooter in the traffic behind them.

A car slowed as it approached them. Because it was the shooter, or just because someone was being cautious and didn't want to accidentally hit Zachary's car or an opening door?

The other phones were all with Zachary. He had hung on to them to make sure that Madison and Noah would not be able to call to warn anyone where they were going until he was ready for them to. Sooner or later, he would need to give Noah the opportunity to reach someone in the syndicate, to tell them that Zachary was headed for the border. But he hadn't expected a shooter to attack them right as they were leaving the hotel. He had thought that they would have plenty of time and not have to worry about a physical attack until they were much closer to the northern border.

Zachary shifted into drive and screeched into the driving lane without even shutting his door. The movement of the car slammed it shut.

Madison was shrieking and sobbing, all semblance of calm, reasonable thinking gone.

"Rhys. Your phone. Get it out."

Rhys kept his hands over his face and didn't move.

Zachary hit the car's Bluetooth button, but didn't get the answering tone that said it was listening to him. He pressed it again. He held it in, willing it to connect to his phone, but it didn't.

The other phones were in Zachary's pockets. He would have to drive, trying to avoid the pursuer, and get out one of the phones and place an emergency call, all at the same time. Maybe another driver who saw him driving recklessly or heard the gunfire would call it in. Maybe Zachary would be surrounded by police cars in a couple more minutes.

But he was not so lucky.

Zachary pulled one phone out and looked at it. Madison's. Using Noah as her unlock code. Not very secure. And Noah had sent Zachary a message from her phone, not his own, so he knew the password. He had probably given her the phone in the first place.

Both phones had probably come from the same source. The trafficking syndicate. So that they could reach their workers at any time, night or day.

Zachary swore. Even if Noah and Madison didn't answer any incoming calls or messages, the organization could still track their positions.

He transferred Madison's phone to his right hand, which was also holding the steering wheel steady, so that he could find the button to roll down the window with his other.

Tracking the phones. He should have thought about it earlier.

He had picked out a hotel where the traffickers didn't have anyone installed, but they didn't need anyone at the hotel to tell them where Zachary and his young charges had gone. All they needed to do was to follow the phone signals.

He should have thought about it. He knew better. He'd tracked phones and he'd had to outsmart others who were tracking them.

The technology was not new. It wasn't hard. It could be used by mothers to check on the location of their children, or professionals to track down their phones if they were lost or stolen. Certainly, a big organization like Gordo's trafficking ring would have plenty of resources for tracking employee cell phones on the fly.

With the window down, Zachary transferred Madison's phone back to his left hand, then tossed it out the window.

There were screeching tires behind him. Maybe he'd manage to hit the pursuing car with the cell phone. Two for the price of one. He looked into his rear-view mirror at the black van. Nice and anonymous. Invisible.

He knew what he was looking for this time. The next time, he wouldn't. That meant he had to lose his tail and not be caught again.

He worked another phone out of his pockets. This one was his, so he dropped it into the center console. He felt for the last phone. It took a while to locate which pocket he had shoved it into. He was always temporarily losing his phones. Kenzie told him if he always put it in the same pocket, he would always know where it was.

But she lost things in her purse, so who was she to tell him how not to lose his phone?

He transferred Noah's phone to his left hand and chucked it out the open window too. Then he rolled the window up.

"Now they can't track us," he told the others. "Watch out the back. Tell me if anyone else is following. I'm going to do my best to lose them."

Rhys was still holding his hands over his face. Madison turned her head to look out the rear window, but she was still crying and trying to tend to Noah, and Zachary didn't know if she would be any help.

He needed to lose the tail and keep them from picking him up again, and he wasn't going to have any help from the teens. He put on blinders, hyperfocusing on driving and escaping anyone following him.

He couldn't worry about Noah or Rhys or Madison. He would be no help to them if he didn't ditch the traffickers. So he shut it all out, focusing just on losing any tails. When he thought he had managed to lose anyone who was following him, he pulled over to the side under an overpass, getting out of the roadway. He took his foot off of the pedals and turned off the ignition. He sat there in the sudden quiet, heart pounding, watching every vehicle that went by. He watched for any of them to slow down, looking for him or for anyone taking notice of the car pulled over under the bridge. He watched any nondescript vans or SUVs. He looked for any windows that were open or broken. They sat there for what seemed like a long time, Madison still crying and Rhys moaning something under his breath.

As he watched, Zachary deliberated about what to do next. If he showed up at the emergency room with Noah, they were going to have a lot of questions. The police would get involved and word would get back to Burkholdt, the policeman who had stopped them at Madison's apartment building. He had written all of their information down. He would be watching for any reports that included their names.

Zachary turned around and craned his head around his seat to look at Noah. The boy was still unresponsive, even though Madison had been shaking him and trying to rouse him. It was too dark for Zachary to be able to see any details other than that his face was streaked with blood tracks.

Noah needed medical attention. And Zachary needed to make sure that everyone else was okay. Just because they didn't look like they'd been hit, that didn't mean that they hadn't been. Sometimes people didn't even know that they had been injured until the adrenaline burned off and they were out of danger.

Thinking about that, Zachary did a quick self-assessment, checking his hands, arms, and chest for any injuries. He quickly felt his head and his shoulders and back, as far as he could reach. He seemed to be uninjured by any of the flying glass or bullets. That was lucky.

"Rhys, are you okay?"

Rhys was murmuring something under his breath. Zachary had never heard him say more than a word or two at a time, and strained to make out what he was saying.

"Just stop it. Just stop it." Rhys kept repeating the words over and over again.

Zachary's heart gave a painful squeeze. He remembered Vera telling him about Rhys's traumatic reaction to his grandfather's murder. He had been in the house and had witnessed what had happened.

"Just stop it," Vera had said. "That's all Rhys would say for days after it happened. Just stop it. Just stop it. Any time anyone tried to ask him about it, that was all he would say."

"But eventually, he stopped saying that too," Gloria, Rhys's mother, added. After that, he had suffered a breakdown that had left him institutionalized for some time, and he had never regained the ability to speak or communicate in the usual way.

The gunshots had clearly thrown Rhys into a flashback of his grandfather's murder.

"Rhys. It's okay. You're safe. The shooting has stopped, and you're okay. Can you tell me what you can see and hear? What can you hear right now? The traffic driving by the car. The wind. Madison. Do you hear that? You're here, Rhys. In the car with Zachary. You're not back there."

He could see Rhys nod, his head bobbing up and down in the shadows. He reached toward Rhys.

"I'm going to touch you, okay? It's just me. You're safe."

He rested his hand gently on Rhys's shoulder. "It's okay now. Can you look around? Tell me what you see?"

At first, Rhys didn't uncover his face. He just hunched there, curled up into himself, like the little boy he had been when his grandfather had died.

"Look around, Rhys. I'm going to pull out soon, but I want you to see that you're safe. They're gone. Whoever was shooting at us, they're gone now. Look around."

Rhys slowly pulled his hands away from his face and raised his head slightly. He looked ahead of the car, then out Zachary's window, and his head swiveled to look out his own. He grasped at Zachary's fingers, still resting on his shoulder, squeezing them, holding himself anchored. He swallowed and nodded.

Then he turned his head and saw Noah in the back seat, and that was a mistake. Zachary should have anticipated it. Zachary's grandfather had been shot in the face, and Noah slumped in the back seat, face covered with blood. Rhys went rigid, letting go of Zachary's hand. He gave a squeal like a hurt animal and again buried his face, sobbing.

"Oh, Rhys…" Zachary squeezed Rhys's shoulder. But he couldn't delay any longer, hoping to be able to get Rhys into a better mental space. Noah's injuries might be critical. Zachary couldn't delay seeking treatment. He restarted the engine. "Okay. We're going to pull out now. Everybody be calm. We don't want to attract the attention of other drivers. Try to look natural."

Hopefully, no one would look into the car, because there was no way that any one of the three teens was going to act naturally. All he could do was to hope that no one would notice the broken window and the boy slumped over with blood running down his face.

"We're on the move now. Hang in there."

Rhys continued to sob, as did Madison. Zachary could feel everything spinning out of control. He tried to hang on and act like an adult who knew what he was doing. He pulled out from under the bridge, merging into the traffic, and tried to match the speed of the traffic around him. Nothing that would attract attention. There was nothing about his car that would attract attention, other than the broken window. Nothing that the bad guys would be able to see from far away. Hopefully, no police who had been called about the gunfire would notice it. It was just a detail on an otherwise nondescript car.

Picking up his phone, he held down the home button and told it to call Kenzie. Shutting off the engine seemed to have rebooted the Bluetooth, and he heard it ring over the car speakers.

"Zachary," Kenzie picked up after half a ring. "How did it go?"

He remembered he was supposed to have called her back after speaking with Jocelyn. But events had overtaken that resolution.

"Uh… things are getting complicated. Where are you?"

"I'm at your apartment."

"Can you go home?"

"You're not going to be back tonight?"

"I'll come to your house. Can you open the garage for me so I can drive in?"

"And where am I supposed to park my baby?"

"On the street. Just for a few minutes. I can't make it up to my apartment."

Even taking Noah into Kenzie's house was going to be complicated. Usually, he parked on the street and walked across the lot to get to the door.

"Are you okay, Zachary? What do you mean, you can't make it up to your apartment?"

"I'm okay. But… we have a casualty."

"A casualty? How bad? Go to the hospital."

"Too dangerous. They're going to be watching the emergency room. And the police will get called."

"And you think you've got a dirty cop."

"Yes."

"This is not a good idea, Zachary! I'm not qualified to be treating serious injuries. And if it's… something that has to be reported to the police, then I'm required to report it too."

"Can we just meet at your house? We can discuss it there."

"How bad is it? Are you putting lives in danger?"

Zachary looked in his rear-view mirror at the slumped, unmoving body. "No."

Kenzie let out a long breath, then grudgingly agreed. "Okay, I'll meet you at the house. But you'd better not be lying to me."

Zachary grimaced. She wasn't going to be happy when she saw Noah. But he had to do everything he could to protect the teenagers, and he didn't think he could do that by taking them to the emergency room. He needed to split them up. Kept in a group, he would just put all of them in danger.

"I'll see you there."

43

Neither Rhys nor Madison said anything to Zachary about lying to Kenzie on the phone. Neither seemed to be in any shape to talk.

He kept a close eye on the mirrors for any more gangsters or the police. A couple of other drivers gave him odd looks, but no one seemed to be paying too much attention to the little car with the broken window. Luckily, with the way that Madison had pulled Noah's face toward her, he was facing away from the broken window, hidden by shadows.

It seemed like it took much longer than it should have to get to Kenzie's house, like the timeline was stretching out, getting tight and thin as a rubber band. As promised, Kenzie had left her red convertible parked at the curb and the garage door open for Zachary. The interior lights were on. Zachary drove straight in and slammed the gearshift into park.

He jumped out of the car, ignoring the weakness in his knees, and walked past Noah's door in order to open it. Kenzie opened the door that connected to the house.

"Zachary?"

"Close the garage door."

"You said that you'd park by the curb."

"And I will. But for now, you need to close the door."

She looked like she would argue with him, but instead, she reached over and clicked a button beside the door. The motor ground and the chain clanked and the big door started to lower into position.

Zachary unbuckled Noah's seatbelt and retracted it, looking for any sign of a bullet hole or bleeding on Noah's torso. He turned Noah's head toward him and quickly evaluated his facial injuries in the light. It seemed to mostly be superficial cuts from the glass, but there was a long, straight, blackened line from his chin to his ear that Zachary thought was a bullet track. He gave the headrest a quick once-over for a bullet hole, but didn't see one.

"Times like this, I wish I'd done weight training," Zachary muttered. He tried to pull Noah out of the car and pick him up, like he'd seen done on hundreds of action movies on TV but, despite the teen's slight frame, he was a dead weight and Zachary couldn't get good leverage to lift him. "Rhys, can you come around here and help me?"

Rhys pulled his hands away from his face, but his expression was such a mask of grief and pain that Zachary knew he couldn't expect any help from him.

"Madison, can you shift him from your side? If you can push him up toward me, and I can get my arm underneath him…"

As he wrestled to get a proper purchase on Noah, he was aware of Kenzie coming around the car for a look, and braced himself for her objections and criticism.

"Oh, boy," Kenzie said from behind his shoulder. "Hold on a minute, just hold him there."

Zachary couldn't see what she was doing but, in a moment, heard something rolling across the concrete floor. She came around the car with a dolly; the kind that could be used as a vertical hand truck for a stack of three or four boxes and had a hinged section that could be pulled down to the horizontal to move several stacks of boxes at the same time. Kenzie wheeled it over to a wall of plastic storage boxes arranged in a grid and laid four boxes across the support rods of the horizontal section. Then she pushed it over to the car door.

"Okay, move out of the way."

Zachary frowned, confused. How exactly did she think Noah was going to get from the seat to the dolly unless Zachary pulled him out? Noah wasn't conscious; he wasn't going to crawl over there himself.

"Just do it," Kenzie insisted.

Zachary hesitated for a moment, then moved slowly back, keeping one hand on Noah to keep him from falling out. Kenzie moved into position beside him. She moved too quickly for him to anticipate what she was going to do. In a few seconds, she had rearranged Noah and somehow managed to pull him out of the car and lay him down on the layer of boxes.

She smiled at Zachary's stunned expression. "I help move bodies around all the time," she pointed out. "I know a thing or two about how to handle them."

Zachary shook his head and couldn't think of a clever comeback. He'd think of one in a day or two. In the meantime, he was just stunned at how effortless she had made it look.

Kenzie pushed the dolly over to the door, which luckily was level with the floor of the garage and not up several steps. She opened the door and pushed the dolly through it into the house. Zachary scrambled after her. Madison climbed out of her side of the car, wiping her eyes, and followed her boyfriend through the door.

Zachary stopped and opened Rhys's door. "Come on, bud. Come inside and we'll get this all sorted out. It will be okay."

With some encouragement, Rhys got out of the car. Zachary guided him into the house.

Despite all of his reassurances to the others, Zachary entered the house and followed Kenzie with a lead ball in his stomach. He was waiting for the recriminations from Kenzie. He had lied to her and he knew he should have taken Noah directly to the hospital. But he was too concerned about the safety of the other teens. They needed to be protected too.

Kenzie was in the kitchen bent over Noah, examining his face and torso, and then turning him on his side to look at his back. The boxes on the dolly were too low for her to work comfortably like she could over a gurney, but she made no complaint about the circumstances.

"How does he look?" Zachary asked anxiously.

"It all looks superficial. Lots of blood, but it always looks like more than it is, and facial wounds bleed like the dickens. He hasn't lost a significant amount, and I don't see any other injuries. Were you shot at?"

Zachary nodded. "Yeah. I think that one along his jaw is a bullet track."

"Looks like it. But it just skimmed the surface. Lucky for him." She continued to examine Noah. "There are cloths and towels in the linen closet at the end of the hallway. Bring me stacks of both, and fill a couple of bowls with warm water."

Zachary obeyed without asking more questions. He fetched the towels first, and then looked through the kitchen cupboards for large bowls.

"The most concerning thing is his loss of consciousness. A bullet certainly has enough force to knock a person out if it hits the right place. I don't see any entry point, so I don't think we have any internal trauma, but if the blow causes swelling to the brain, that is a dangerous situation."

Zachary nodded. Kenzie took a bowl of water from him and started to wipe blood from Noah's face. She worked in silence for a few minutes. She looked over at Madison and Rhys, huddled close by watching, both faces streaked with tears.

"Why don't you guys go wait in the living room. Zachary will make you some coffee."

Neither moved at first. Then Madison touched Rhys's arm and encouraged him to move out of the kitchen into the living room.

"Hot and sweet," Kenzie told Zachary. "Good for shock. Make enough for all of us. I don't think we need to worry about falling asleep tonight."

Zachary nodded. "Yeah. Sure."

He worked with the single-cup coffee machine on Kenzie's counter to produce one cup of coffee at a time and stirred copious amounts of sugar into them.

"He's so young," Kenzie murmured as she cleaned the blood off of Noah's face, revealing his smooth skin and rounded jaw.

"I know," Zachary agreed. "He says he's been doing this since he was twelve or thirteen. I don't know if it's true," he added quickly, anticipating her answer, "but I'd say he's been in the business for quite a while. He's pretty… skilled at what he does." Zachary's face heated as he realized how she might interpret that. "Managing Madison, I mean," he explained. "I don't have any experience with his *other* skills."

Kenzie looked up at Zachary briefly, laughing. "Oh, man, Zachary. I wasn't even thinking that!"

"Good."

Kenzie patted Noah's face with the towel, leaning close to see if the lacerations were continuing to bleed.

"So… he's okay?" Zachary asked. "I mean, as far as you can tell? Other than not knowing if he'll have a concussion?"

"I think you can count on him having a concussion. But his vital signs are all strong."

Zachary breathed a sigh of relief. He carried two cups of coffee into the living room and gave them to Rhys and Madison, then returned to the kitchen.

"Now," Kenzie said, "we need to figure out what to do next. What did Jocelyn say?"

44

At Kenzie's suggestion, Zachary hired an Uber driver to take him and Rhys to the Salters' house. Then his car could stay out of sight in the garage, and Rhys didn't have to be subjected to the sight of the bullet-damaged car again.

"Make sure Vera knows enough to understand that he's been through a trauma. That he's having flashbacks. She'll want to get him in to see a therapist right away. Probably keep him company tonight, rather than letting him go to bed by himself."

Zachary nodded.

"It's probably best if she doesn't know all of what happened," Kenzie said, looking toward Noah, "I don't want her worrying about these guys coming after them, but..."

Zachary sighed. "If everything works out, then we won't need to worry her about that, but..."

"Just get him home," Kenzie said, seeing the Uber car arrive in front of the house. "We'll worry about the rest later..."

Vera was waiting at the door when Zachary and Rhys arrived. Her face was drawn and tired. She looked Rhys over worriedly, reaching out to give him a hug to reassure herself that he was okay.

"What's wrong, Zachary? What happened? He was supposed to be at a friend's..."

"He came to me," Zachary said uncomfortably. "Let's go inside…"

She took Rhys into the house. Zachary stood outside for a moment, looking for anyone keeping surveillance on the house.

He joined them inside.

Zachary cleared his throat and tried to think of the best way to explain it all to Vera. Memories of all of the times he'd had to explain to foster parents or school officials what he'd done wrong came rushing back to him. He hated disappointing them. He hated explaining that he'd broken a rule or done something on impulse that, on reflection, he should have known was a bad idea. He waited while Vera and Rhys sat on the couch, then sat in the easy chair across from them.

The Rhys he knew was absent. Rhys was always present and engaged, focused intently on Zachary to be able to communicate with him. The boy sitting on the couch with Vera was a thousand miles away, sucked into the past, drowning in fear and confusion.

"Madison messaged Rhys asking for help. Rhys came to me."

"He should have come to me. We could have called the police." Vera looked at Rhys, frowning over his lost expression. "But what… why didn't you go to the police? What happened? Kenzie said that he was with you, but she didn't say what had happened."

"It's been a long night. We went to help Madison and her boyfriend Noah. But a lot of things happened. It was… Rhys had a bad flashback to when his grandfather was killed."

Vera rubbed Rhys's back. "What did he say? How do you know that? He never talks about…"

"He was saying 'just stop it, just stop it,'" Zachary explained. "You told me that's what he said after your husband was killed."

Vera's brows drew down. She nodded, eyes shining with tears. "Yes, that's right." She tried to look into Rhys's eyes. "Sweetheart… you want to tell me about it? Rhys?"

He didn't look at her.

"Kenzie said… you probably want to get him to a therapist right away. And stay with him tonight. So he's not alone."

"Of course," Vera agreed. "He was alone that night." She hugged Rhys close to her. "When we came home, he was in his bed, and Clarence was in the kitchen," she choked up, "dead. We thought at first that maybe Rhys had slept through it, but…"

But he hadn't. Zachary had a pretty good idea that he'd seen everything. And despite what Vera said, Rhys hadn't been alone with his grandfather that night.

"Just stay with him tonight," he repeated. "And get in to see his therapist. Whoever has been helping him."

Vera nodded. She ruffled Rhys's hair like he was a little boy. "And later, will you tell me more about what happened tonight?"

"I don't know how much I'll be able to tell you," he evaded. "You know, client confidentiality..."

"Oh. Of course. Do you... need anything? Some tea, or... is there anything I can do for you? I appreciate you taking care of Rhys and bringing him home."

"No. I've got to get back to Kenzie's. There's more work to be done tonight."

Vera nodded. "Okay. But call me. Tomorrow, if you can. Soon."

"I will. And I'll come back and see Rhys." Zachary looked down at his feet, unable to meet her gaze. "If you want me to."

"You're always welcome here," Vera said.

But he was sure it was just words. She was being polite and, once she'd had a chance to think about it and to see how badly he'd traumatized Rhys, she would have second thoughts.

Step one was taken care of. Rhys was back with Vera, safe and sound. Out of the way of any further retaliation by the trafficking syndicate if the rest of the steps went according to plan.

When Zachary returned to Kenzie's house, he found Madison asleep on the couch. Noah was still lying on the boxes on the dolly and, despite the hard, uneven surface, appeared to be resting comfortably. Kenzie had cleaned up the bloody towels and everything looked neat and tidy. Noah had a couple of adhesive strips pulling together cuts on his face, and Kenzie said he wouldn't need stitches. As long as she monitored him and he didn't have any unexpected brain swelling, he would make a good recovery. Concussions could cause long-term problems, but Kenzie hoped that he was young enough to bounce back from it quickly.

"You need to go take care of your car," she told Zachary. "There are some basic supplies on the tool bench beside the storage unit. Tape up some plastic over that broken window so you don't get pulled over by the police. Then you'd better get on your way." She looked at the clock on the wall. "It's getting late. Or early."

Zachary managed to find everything he needed in the garage and temporarily covered the window. He looked over the car and found several nicks and holes from bullets. It was going to need some body work when he was done. At least he had money in savings from a few recent cases.

Once the car was ready, he went back into the house and woke Madison up.

"We need to get you to the safe house," he told her. "Let's get moving."

Madison groaned and rubbed her eyes. "I don't want to go anywhere. Why can't I stay here?"

"It's not safe here. I don't want to put Kenzie in danger if anyone manages to track you this far. We need to get you out of here."

"Where's Noah?"

"He's still in the kitchen."

"Is he awake?"

"Not yet," Kenzie advised. "I'm still waiting for him to come around."

"Then we can't go yet."

"You're not going together," Zachary told her firmly. "We need to separate the two of you to make you harder to track. And to make sure that Noah can't turn you back in to Peggy Ann and Gordo."

"He wouldn't do that."

Zachary remembered how sure Jocelyn had been that he would do just that, sooner or later. "We can't be sure of that."

"He wouldn't!"

"We need to get you somewhere safe, Madison, and we need to do it right now, before Peggy Ann can find you. Do you want her to find you here?"

Madison's eyes widened. "No."

"Do you want them to target Kenzie, because she gave you safe shelter? You think that's a good way to repay her for what she's done for you and Noah?"

"No!"

"Then you need to get out of here before they can trace you. They were already tracking your phone. They know all of your friends and family, because Noah gave them all that information and they can look up anything they want to about your friends at school or on your social networks. I have a safe house for you, but you need to come with me and do what I say and not argue or ask questions."

Madison looked uncertain. Zachary stood there, looking as stern as possible, trying to channel all of those 'mom looks' he'd gotten from his various mother figures over the years. In charge and unmoving.

Madison nodded, dropping her eyes. "Yeah, okay," she agreed in a small voice.

"Go to the bathroom and let's get out of here."

"Okay."

He nodded and watched her retreat down the hallway to get ready to go. Kenzie smiled at Zachary. "I'm seeing a whole different side of you today!"

"Did I do okay? Do you think she'll listen?"

"No guarantees," Kenzie sighed. "I've heard that it's pretty hard to get these girls out of the lifestyle, once they're in. Their whole outlook is distorted. But all you can do is your best. Stick to the plan and hope that she can hang in there."

Zachary nodded. They waited a couple more minutes, and then Madison came out of the bathroom.

"Can I say goodbye to Noah?"

"Make it quick," Zachary said. If everything came together the way they had planned, then it would be the last time she saw him. They might as well give her one last moment with him.

Madison tiptoed into the kitchen and looked down at Noah. Her eyes shone with tears. Zachary wondered how much of it was true emotion and how much was being exhausted and coming down from the adrenaline and whatever drugs she might have taken earlier. She'd been through a lot, but her feelings toward Noah were strong. She'd been manipulated by an expert with plenty of experience.

She murmured a few words to him, promising him that she would see him again soon, and gave him a kiss. She looked at Zachary and Kenzie, awkward.

"You'll take good care of him, won't you? And he'll be okay?"

"I'll do my best," Kenzie agreed. "I'm just worried about his head. He really should have woken up before now."

Madison squeezed Noah's hand and reluctantly let go.

"All right," Zachary said. "Let's get on our way."

45

It seemed like it took a long time to get to their destination. Zachary was a little anxious about how it would all work out. He had only met the Creedys briefly before. That was one of the reasons they were a good choice for a safe house. His connection with them was very tenuous. It would be almost impossible for anyone to figure out where he had taken Madison.

He wasn't sure how they would respond to Madison or how long she would be able to stay there. Once she was settled, he would contact her parents and see if they were willing to pull up stakes and move away to start a new life with her. Even if they did, he wasn't sure it would work out. Madison had had a taste of independence, money, and drugs and, once most girls had been in that life, it was pretty hard to make a break from it and just go back to living at home with their parents and dealing with the normal responsibilities of teenagerhood.

Madison slept most of the way, so Zachary didn't have to worry about keeping a conversation going. Had she taken something, like Noah, while she was out of sight? Between being shot at and the coffee and his anxiety over Rhys's trauma and getting Madison somewhere safe, Zachary wasn't going to be able to sleep for some time. It might be days before he was able to calm down enough to get a good sleep.

Madison awoke as they entered the city, with the pink light of dawn peeking over the horizon and the abrupt stops and starts at traffic lights. She snorted, straightened, and rubbed her eyes, looking around.

"Are we there?"

"Almost."

"Where are we going?" She hadn't expressed much curiosity about his plans until then. "I'm not going to some kind of rehab or lockdown."

"No. It's just a couple that I know from another case. Not an institution."

"I don't need some kind of therapy or retraining."

Zachary shrugged. Opinions on that matter would vary. He knew there were a lot of people who would insist that the only way to keep Madison off of the streets and away from individuals who would harm her was to put her into a program of intensive behavioral therapy. He had been in enough institutions and programs to recognize that if the target of the therapy didn't buy into the program, there wasn't much point. She would pretend to be 'converted' and follow the program until she found a way to escape, and then she would run. If she were going to overcome the life she'd been lured into, that decision was going to have to come from her, just like Joss had said.

Madison sat there looking sullen for a few minutes, then apparently decided that it wasn't getting her anywhere, and relaxed her confrontational attitude. "What are they like, then? Who are they?"

"They're older than your parents. They lost a daughter a few years ago to a drunk driver. They have a set of twins. Grown. Empty-nesters."

"And they take in fosters, or what?"

"No. This isn't something they normally do. I just asked them for a favor. Be nice to them. They don't have any ulterior motives and aren't judging you; they don't know much about your situation. They're just giving you a place to stay for a few days while we sort things out."

"That's it?"

"That's it. An older couple doing a nice thing for you."

Madison stared out the window. She nodded. "Okay."

It didn't take long for Zachary to make his way across town to the Creedys'. He looked at Madison one more time.

"Be nice," he reminded her. "We want to keep you safe. That's why we're here. Not because anyone is trying to save you."

"Yeah, I hear you. I know."

They walked up to the house and Zachary rang the doorbell. It was Mrs. Creedy who answered the door. An attractive older woman with dark strawberry blond hair. Zachary didn't know if it were natural or dyed. He suspected it might be dye, but it was the same color as it had been the last time he had seen her.

"Mr. Goldman, come in." She gestured for them to enter and Zachary stepped up and into the house, with Madison behind him.

"It's Zachary. This is Madison, Mrs. Creedy. Thank you again for offering a roof over her head for a few days."

Mrs. Creedy studied Madison curiously. "Of course. I couldn't turn her down knowing that she wouldn't have anywhere safe to go. How are you, Madison; are you okay?" She touched Madison's arm, looking concerned.

Madison pulled away. "Yeah. I'm fine."

"You must be tired. It sounds like you've been up all night. I'll show you to your room."

Madison shook her head. She folded her arms, looking back and forth between Zachary and Mrs. Creedy. "This is really nice of you. I'm just… not sure about it all. I slept in the car, so I'm okay for now." She looked anxiously at Zachary. "Do you think you could call Kenzie? See how Noah is doing? I want to know…" She trailed off. She wanted to know what Noah would tell her to do, if Zachary guessed correctly. She was used to doing what he told her to and was adrift without him managing her life.

"Kenzie is going to call when she knows something. I don't want to interrupt her when she may be getting some sleep or be busy with Noah's care."

"Yeah… I guess…"

"Why don't you sit down, and you and Mrs. Creedy can get to know each other. You can tell her about school. What you like to do, your best subjects…"

Madison sat down, but she shrugged at Zachary's suggestion. School had not been her priority for a few months. Even though she had been attending up until her disappearance, she had been mentally absent. Sleeping through classes after spending her nights partying or servicing Noah's clients. Waiting for the end of the day when he would pick her up again. Her grades had been plummeting, and she had been completely disengaged.

Which was exactly why Zachary wanted her to talk to Mrs. Creedy about school. He wanted her to start thinking about school again. How important it was to her future. How normal it was for a girl of her age to be going to school, not hanging out with her boyfriend and turning tricks.

Madison scratched her ear, looking at Mrs. Creedy.

"I don't know. I'm not really into school."

"It can be hard for young people," Mrs. Creedy said generously. "I found it was a lot harder for my twins. Hope was different. She really loved school. Loved learning, and socializing with her friends. She got good marks, went on to college. I really thought she was going to turn out to be something great. A doctor or professor. Maybe something else. But…" Mrs. Creedy trailed off.

Madison looked sideways at Zachary. "Zachary said you had a daughter that died."

"Yes. She showed so much promise, and then… she was taken from us so suddenly. I don't know… how someone recovers from that. One day she was in our life, and the next, she was gone. I hope you're good to your parents. Don't ever think that you don't matter to them. Nothing matters like your children."

Madison pulled her feet up onto the couch, her bent knees in front of her chest. She looked pensive.

Zachary didn't speak up. It was what Madison needed to hear, and she needed to hear it from someone other than him. He would never say anything so absolute. He knew very well that children were not the most important thing to every parent. His biological parents hadn't wanted kids around. They had dumped their children when things got too hard. That freed them up to pursue their own lives, whatever it was they had wanted. Zachary had a hard time picturing what they had gone on to do after he and the other children were gone. He assumed that they had broken up. There were only two ways that his parents could have gone. Either they had separated and divorced, or one of them had killed the other. They hadn't gone on to live happily ever after, that much he knew.

And he'd had plenty of foster parents who hadn't given much thought to the children they were raising either. Sometimes they loved their own bio kids and treated them differently from the fosters. And sometimes there was no difference. They just treated them all like something unpleasant tracked in on their shoes.

But Madison's parents did care about her. Deeply. She needed to be reminded of that. Kids tended to think that their parents didn't love them because they had strict rules and expectations. Because the kids didn't want responsibility and their parents wanted them to grow up to be productive adults and, somewhere in between, they had to stand firm in order to shepherd their kids into the right path.

"I'll be talking to your parents," Zachary reminded Madison. "They're going to want to talk to you and to come and see you. But we have to be careful that they can't be tracked here. So it might take a few days to get everything arranged."

Of course, he was planning on Madison's parents agreeing to leave their lives behind in order to reunite with her and have her for a couple more years. That might not happen. Or it might not happen in the 'few days' that Zachary was promising. Zachary didn't know how long Mrs. Creedy would be agreeable to putting Madison up, or how long Madison would stay there before she got tired of it and ran.

He was hoping he'd be able to fit everything together like a puzzle and it would all come smoothly together. But that wasn't always the way that things worked out. His life had not turned out that way.

"Yeah, I know," Madison agreed. Maybe she had doubts that it would all be roses. After everything she had done to disrespect her parents and their rules, the way that she had broken their hearts by running off, maybe the reconciliation wouldn't be as easy as that. Maybe they wouldn't want Madison back.

"What do you like best about school?" Mrs. Creedy asked, returning to the topic that Zachary had introduced.

"I don't know. I like seeing my friends. I haven't seen any of them for a long time. But… I guess I won't be able to see them at all now."

"Oh, I'm sure you could still reach out to them," Mrs. Creedy assured her.

"No," Zachary said firmly. "Not in the near future. You don't want to be tracked through them. You're going to have to wait until you're safe. That's going to be a while."

He didn't want to suggest that it might be years before Madison would be able to see them or talk to them again. He didn't know how long it would be before the traffickers stopped looking for her and watching her friends.

Mrs. Creedy looked like Zachary had said something impolite. Her lips pressed together and she shook her head slightly. But Zachary had told her. He had explained that Madison was in danger if she tried to reach out to the people in her old life. Mrs. Creedy had to understand that. They both had to get it.

Zachary's phone rang, making him jump. He had left the ringer on, which he didn't usually do when he was with clients. He pulled it out and looked at the screen. Kenzie. He tapped the speaker button.

"Kenzie. Hey, how's it going? How's Noah?"

There was a pause before Kenzie answered. Long enough for Zachary to look at Madison and meet her eyes, and to see the worry there. Why did Kenzie hesitate? Noah had been doing well. She had said that his injuries were superficial. Teenagers were fast healers; he'd bounce back in no time.

"Zachary, can you take me off speaker?" Kenzie suggested.

Zachary pulled his eyes away from Madison's anxious gaze to tap off the speaker button on the screen. He put the phone up to his ear.

"Kenzie? What's going on? Is everything okay?"

"There have been some… unexpected developments."

Zachary stood up and looked around, trying to decide if he should leave the room. He took a couple of steps toward the door. He lowered his voice slightly.

"Unexpected developments? What does that mean?"

"Well, you know I was worried about brain swelling."

"Yes. Because of the way the bullet knocked him in the head. But he was doing pretty good when we left."

"He was… I wasn't expecting him to go downhill that fast."

"What happened?"

"I'm sorry, Zachary…"

Zachary looked at Madison, wondering how much she could hear of what Kenzie was saying. She would have to piece the rest together from his side of the conversation.

"Sorry… for what?"

"He turned so fast. He seemed like everything was just fine, and then his vitals went all to hell. I don't know if it was swelling in his brain or maybe he had an embolism… but it all happened so fast; there was nothing I could do."

"You had to take him to the hospital?" Zachary suggested.

"No, Zachary. I lost him. I know this makes things more complicated with Madison… I did everything I could. It was just too fast."

"No."

"I'm sorry."

Zachary looked at Madison. She was clearly following the conversation. She had gone completely white and stared at Zachary with wide eyes and a slack jaw.

"Madison," Zachary said, his voice rough.

"No! No, don't tell me! Don't tell me that!" Madison shrieked, going from calm a moment before to nearly hysterical with nothing in between. "Noah is okay! When we left, Kenzie said he would be okay. We just had to wait for him to wake up!"

"It was unexpected…"

"No! No, no, no!"

There were no tears yet. She was too shocked and horrified to work up any tears.

They would come later, when it all started to sink in.

46

"Oh, Madison." Mrs. Creedy moved over beside Madison on the couch. "It will be okay. I know it doesn't feel like it now, but you'll go on with life. It doesn't seem possible right now, but your life will go on."

She was speaking about her own life, of course. She had no way of knowing how Madison was going to take the news. She didn't know what Madison's choices would be. Maybe she would go back to confront Peggy Ann. Maybe she would have a breakdown. Maybe it was something that she'd never be able to get over and would stick with her for the rest of her life. Mrs. Creedy couldn't know how it would affect her.

Madison first pushed Mrs. Creedy away, and then fell against her, clutching her tightly and protesting in words that were so fast they were unintelligible.

But the words didn't matter. The fact that she was grieving and was accepting comfort from Mrs. Creedy mattered. She would bond to Mrs. Creedy, lean on her and depend on her to help her to make decisions. And maybe that meant she would be able to make the right decisions, ones that would lead her back to her family instead of farther away from them.

Zachary said a few more words to Kenzie that no one listened to, and then returned to sit on the chair he had been sitting on. He watched Madison. It hurt to see her so upset. His empathy and compassion for others was one of the things that drove him to do the things he did. Mr. Peterson had suggested to him a long time ago that maybe he could make some money with his photography by becoming a private investigator, but Zachary would never have done it if he hadn't cared about people and wanted to help them and to ease their pain. It was painful to see how upset Madison was. She had put her whole life into Noah's hands, and now he was gone. What was she going to do with herself now that he was gone from it?

Eventually, Zachary left the Creedys'. Mrs. Creedy had her hands full with Madison, but she seemed to take to the role eagerly. She'd lost one of her daughters, but here was a child who needed her. A way to exorcise her demons, to spend all of the compassion she had on someone else. She would take good care of Madison until Zachary could get her parents there, hopefully for the beginning of a new life.

He was exhausted and keyed up at the same time. He wanted to go home and go to bed, but he didn't know whether he would be able to sleep even after a few more hours of driving. He got into the car and started on his way back. He told his phone to call Mr. Peterson and listened to it ring a few times as he headed back onto the highway.

"Zachary," Mr. Peterson sounded cheerful, as always. Happy to hear from his former foster son. "How are you?"

"I'm okay. Just wanted to hear your voice."

"I'm happy to talk to you at any time. You sound tired."

"Tired… and not. Got a drive ahead of me still."

"Maybe you should take a break and catch some Z's. Not a good idea to drive tired."

"I'm not sleepy. Just… wrung out. It's been a difficult day."

"The sun is barely up. How has it been that tiring already?"

"I haven't slept. I meant… the last twenty-four hours. It was kind of crazy."

"Oh. You want to talk about it?"

"I don't know." Zachary watched the cars ahead of him, thinking about what he would tell Mr. Peterson if he shared the story. He couldn't tell him everything. And he didn't want to say anything that might be a breach of

Madison's privacy. "I was helping out some teens who… were in pretty bad circumstances. It's been tough."

"Do you think things will turn out all right? It can be hard with kids… sometimes no matter how much energy you put into it and how good your intentions are… you can't make things better for them." He might have been speaking of his own experiences with Zachary. He had been an important father figure in Zachary's life, despite the fact that he had not officially been one of his foster parents for more than a few weeks. He had stayed involved, and there had been plenty of times when he had given Zachary advice or tried to help him to get onto a better path. But Zachary had rarely listened to him. Or been able to follow through on the things that Mr. Peterson had suggested even when he knew the advice was good.

"Yeah. I don't know what she's going to decide, or if she'll be able to get herself onto a better path."

"It can take years. Sometimes there's a lot of damage and trauma to get through."

"Tell me about it," Zachary agreed.

Mr. Peterson gave a muffled laugh. "Longer for some kids than others."

"Yeah." Zachary made some quick lane changes and watched behind him for any tails. He was sure that no one had been able to follow him to New Hampshire. But he still needed to keep an eye out. If someone had managed to get a tracker on his car or his phone, it could wreck all of their plans. "How's Pat doing?"

"He's… on the way back," Mr. Peterson said finally. "I think he's stabilized on the antidepressants, and he likes the therapist that we've been working with."

"So you think…" Zachary wished that he'd had better results for Pat. If only he'd been able to find Jose alive… "You think he'll be okay."

"I know he'll be okay, Zachary. You don't need to worry about that. It's just taking him some time to work through the grief… and the guilt."

And Zachary felt guilty for Pat's guilt. He had made stupid decisions, and the consequences had been disastrous. As usual. Pat had felt guilty for involving Zachary in the first place. Guilt that he wouldn't have had to deal with if Zachary had been able to tamp down his impulsivity and act like the professional private investigator was supposed to be. Instead of still acting like the ten-year-old who ran into everything full-bore without considering the consequences.

"Well, say 'hi' to him for me."

"Sure will. How is your family?"

Zachary didn't answer immediately, trying to sort out an answer for himself. The problems with Jocelyn were not going to be resolved any time soon. She had a lot of trauma to work through herself, and a lot of that was also Zachary's fault. He didn't know if she could ever forgive him for the choices he'd made that had impacted the rest of her life. Or if she even should.

"How's Kenzie?" Mr. Peterson prompted. "Everything going okay there? It was so nice to see the two of you together again, but I understand that things don't always turn out the way you want them to, even when you're working on it as hard as you can."

"No, things with Kenzie are going good." Zachary was glad to be able to report this. "I think… we're closer now than ever. We went to our first couples session."

"Yeah? How did that go?"

"It was… horrible. And good."

His foster father laughed. "Oh yeah? Horrible and good?"

Zachary couldn't help chuckling at his own description. "I had… bad anxiety. Thought I was going to die. But… we stuck it out, and I'm glad. And we went for ice cream."

"Of course. Ice cream makes everything better."

"Well, if you ask Kenzie. And… I don't know if I can argue. It did feel pretty good."

"That's great. So you'll keep going?"

"Yeah. She'll kick my butt if I don't. So I know I have to. And that… we can get through it, even if it's hard."

"Sometimes the most important things are the hardest."

"If it will help me communicate with Kenzie, and work through… our issues… then it's worth it."

"Attaboy. I'm proud of you, Zachary. Good for you."

47

Despite Mr. Peterson's encouraging words, Zachary couldn't face Kenzie when he got back in town. He was just too worn out emotionally to deal with her feelings and his at the same time. He went back to his own building and shot her off a text to let her know that he was home before heading to bed. He sat in his car in the parking lot for some time, looking for any sign of trouble. As far as the traffickers knew, he had been headed for Canada. Even if Noah hadn't passed that message on to them, they knew he had been traveling north before they lost him. It would take them a long time to thoroughly check border crossings for any sign of the teens. They didn't have any reason to be surveilling his apartment, but it was still important to be careful. And if they were watching him to figure out where he had stashed Noah and Madison, he wasn't going to lead them back to Kenzie's house.

Zachary knew he couldn't sleep without help, and that sleep was the thing he needed most. So despite his resolution after the incident at Mr. Peterson's that he wouldn't take any more sleep aids, he went straight for the medicine cabinet. It was okay for him to take something, as long as he was careful not to mix his meds and to take the proper dosage. The mistake he had made then would not be repeated. He would stick to that part of his resolution.

He took the recommended dose and lay down in bed, closing his eyes and waiting for the pill to take effect.

Usually, while he was waiting for it to kick in, he would check his email or his social networks, or just play with his phone browsing popular videos until he started to feel drowsy. But he didn't even want that distraction. He wanted to think of nothing until he woke up again.

Thinking of nothing wasn't an option. The hamster that was his brain was running full-tilt on the hamster wheel, turning as fast as it could and getting nowhere. He second-guessed everything he had done in the past twenty-four hours. If he'd made better decisions, things might have turned out differently. But better, or worse? And which decisions would he have changed?

He pressed his fingers to his temples, trying to slow the hamster down and get rid of all of the worries pinging around in his brain.

It seemed like he would lie there awake forever.

He was feeling a lot better when he awoke a few hours later. He was still groggy from the meds and still short on sleep, but the deep emotional exhaustion had lifted, and the hamster-thoughts pinging around his brain had slowed down, back to a normal pace.

Time to move on to the next step of the plan. Zachary had a drink of water and wondered when he had last eaten. He munched a granola bar over the sink, then sat down at the table with his phone and dialed the number he knew by heart.

"Campbell here. Zachary?"

"Yeah. How is it going?"

"About usual. How about with you, Zach? Don't tell me you already have another case you need my input on."

"No, not exactly."

"What's up, then?"

"I'm wondering about getting a rumor started."

There was a long pause as Campbell considered this. Then he heard Campbell's chair squeak as he leaned far back at his desk. "Exactly what are you talking about?"

"I have a young lady who could be in some danger, and others who could be collateral damage. Unless we can convince some bad guys that she is out of the picture."

"Out of the picture how?"

Campbell would know who he was talking about, of course. Zachary had only talked to him about one young lady recently. "I've moved her out of state and she should disappear without a trace, if I've done my job. And if she doesn't rebel and decide to go back to the old life. But… I don't want certain people putting pressure on her family and friends to find out where she disappeared to."

"I'm not sure how I can help you with that."

"Let's say… there may be someone in your department who has a line of communication into certain quarters."

"An undercover agent?" Campbell jumped to the wrong conclusion.

Zachary considered it. What was the difference if Campbell thought that an undercover fed might be in position, rather than there being a dirty cop in his precinct? If the rumor were convincing enough, then it wouldn't matter which was true. Everyone involved would get the message, either way.

"Could be."

"Hmm. And what exactly is the rumor that you want spread around?"

"There were some reports of gunfire on the highway last night."

"Uh… yes, there were."

"After that incident, two teens that the police department was aware of dropped out of sight. There were reports that one or both teens were hit."

"Madison Miller and…?"

"A kid known as Noah. He probably has a number of different names on the street. He was involved in prostitution and in turning out new young girls and boys."

"Her pimp?"

"Yeah. Her boyfriend, as far as she was concerned. A Romeo, in the business."

"So Madison and this Noah might have been hit in this shooting last night," Campbell said, sounding concerned.

"Yeah. The police can't get confirmation of this, but word on the streets is, that's who was involved in the shootout, and both of them might have been hit."

"Might have been?"

"The *rumor* is that they were both killed. Again, the police are unable to verify any details. No bodies have turned up in the morgue. No injuries treated in emergency centers. But Vermont has a lot of wild, wooded areas, and the ground is soft enough to dig now."

Campbell snorted. "Can I just say that if you were ever discovered to be digging graves in the woods, I'm not going to be standing behind you?"

"You won't need to. So… do you think that rumor might get around?"

"I know a couple of people who like to share gossip around the water cooler. One would only need to plant a couple of details. Not even rumors, just… speculation."

Zachary nodded. "Exactly."

"And these rumors or speculations are not going to come back to bite us?"

"I've looked at it from all angles… I don't see how it could be a problem. But if the word leaks out to these bad actors, it might save the lives of anyone remotely connected with the former prostitute. They aren't going to be looking for someone who is dead. They'll just move on."

"No retaliation?"

"I don't see it. She was an asset, that's all. If she's gone, there is no point in wasting resources on retaliation. That won't bring in more money."

"No, that's true."

"I appreciate it. I don't want her family and friends to be harmed."

"I'll plant a little speculation, and we'll see what happens. I can't promise the results you're looking for, but it sounds like a reasonable plan."

"You're a lifesaver. Thanks again."

48

Zachary didn't know whether he should call Vera or just show up on the doorstep. If he called her, there was less chance of confrontation, and she could just tell him not to bother contacting them again.

But if he showed up on the doorstep, he was there, and it wouldn't be as easy for her just to shoo him away. Maybe he would get in to see Rhys one more time. Or she would concede that he couldn't have foreseen what would happen when Rhys had come to him for help.

Or she could punch him in the nose.

She was a kind, Christian lady, so that seemed like it was only an outside possibility, but still one that had to be considered.

In the end, he decided that despite the risk of confrontation, he had to chance it. He had to see Rhys one more time if he possibly could.

That didn't make it any easier to stand on the Salters' doorstep and force himself to press the doorbell.

Eventually, he was able to do it and, a few minutes later, Vera opened the door.

"Oh, Zachary!"

She stood there for a minute while they both considered how she would respond to his unannounced visit. Finally, she stepped back and let him into the house.

"Come sit down," she directed, pointing to the living room.

Zachary sat down in his accustomed seat. "Is he here? Or…?"

Zachary didn't want to hear that Rhys had been institutionalized again. But if that was the only way for them to help him, then it was the best place for him to be. Zachary scratched at the knee of his jeans, waiting for the accusations. Waiting for Vera to tell him that he had set Rhys back ten years and that chances were, he was never going to be able to recover again.

"He's sleeping right now." Vera looked at her watch. "He's been sleeping a lot lately. His therapist said that it's normal and not to push him too fast. Sleeping is apparently good. A way for his brain to try to process what happened and to start healing."

Zachary nodded. Some therapists subscribed to this theory. Others believed that it was best not to let patients sleep any longer than eight hours, but to get them out of bed on a strict schedule and get them to group therapy or whatever was the treatment of choice.

"I'm sorry," he said, shaking his head. "I didn't mean for anything to happen to him that night. I should have brought him straight back here. I should have been more responsible. Just called the police and let them deal with it…"

"When Rhys came to you begging for help?" Vera stared off into the distance, thinking about it. "I may spoil the boy, but I don't think I could deny him whatever help I could give him if he asked me for something."

Zachary shrugged, still looking down. "But I put him into unnecessary danger. That wouldn't have happened if I had just called the police and brought Rhys home."

"But would that have helped Madison?"

"Well… no, probably not. She wouldn't have accepted any help from the police. And it might have had a negative consequence for her, having the cops show up on her doorstep."

"Rhys really likes Madison. I know it's just puppy love; he isn't romantically attached to her, and she doesn't have those feelings for him, but he was… it felt like he was the only one who cared enough to help her. Even her parents, they weren't able to do anything to get her back."

"Yeah."

Zachary was silent, considering her reaction. "So… how is he?"

"I honestly don't know. It's so hard to tell with him, with the communication barriers. I was afraid when you brought him back… he was so distressed… and when you said that he'd had a flashback and been saying that… it took me back to how he was after Clarence died. And he just slipped away from us."

Zachary nodded. "I was worried that… he'd regressed all that way again."

"Me too. But he has been… he's still communicating. As much as can be expected. He's worried about Madison still, but I keep telling him that you would do everything you could for her. That he had to trust you to do what was best."

"Thanks… I don't know what she'll decide. So many of these girls just go right back to the life. All we could do was… give her a fighting chance."

Zachary finally looked up at Vera. She looked him straight in the eye, sharp and discerning.

"Can you tell me what happened? What it was that upset him so much? Made him go back to Clarence's death?"

She still had a hard time calling it murder. How could Rhys get better if she denied what had happened?

"I don't know… I don't think you'd be quite so kind to me if you knew what had happened. I had the best of intentions… I never meant for it to play out like it did. I didn't realize… I didn't think about them being able to track Madison's and Noah's cell phones. I should have known. It was stupid not to realize it. I know plenty about tracking technology. But…" Zachary shook his head. It was hard to believe that he had been so stupid. He could blame it on how complex the situation had been, on adrenaline, on trying to deal with three teens who wanted three different things. But he should still have realized that Peggy Ann and her crew would be able to track the phones they had given to Madison and Noah.

"All of that technology." Vera waved it away with one hand. "I would never have thought of it. I'm getting better at all of these gifs and emojis, because of Rhys, but I really haven't got a clue how it all works."

"I do, and I should have realized."

"Just tell me, Zachary. How can I help him if I don't know what happened? He can't tell me. If he tells his therapist, if he's able to, then the therapist still can't tell me. I think I need to know. Don't you?"

Zachary swallowed. He took a deep breath in and blew it back out.

What was the worst that could happen?

The worst was that Vera would tell him he could never again have anything to do with Rhys. And if he were going to make such huge blunders, then that was probably the best thing for Rhys. It might hurt Zachary, but he had to do what was best for the boy, not what felt best to him.

"Okay… we had gone to a hotel to hide and to work out a plan of action. Somewhere safe, where we wouldn't lead the guys who were after Madison back to you or to Kenzie or to Madison's family. We didn't want to bring other innocent parties into it."

Vera nodded. "And that's when you talked to Kenzie. And told her to call me to let me know that Rhys was okay."

"Right."

"That was the first I knew that anything was wrong."

"I'm sorry about that. I didn't want to worry you… but I didn't know if you already were…"

"It was the right thing to do."

"So… after we'd had a chance to rest and to put together a plan of action, we headed out again. And that was when… that's when they attacked. They must have had a sniper on the roof, and they had cars ready to tail us. It was a very dangerous situation. I should have seen it before we walked out there."

"How could you?"

"I should have known."

Vera dabbed her nose with a crushed tissue. "What happened?"

Vera had probably already guessed. He had, after all, said 'sniper.' What else did she think that meant?

"They tried to ambush us. I managed to get everyone in the car and to get out to the highway, but they were still following the cell signal, and they attacked again there. In the whole thing… Noah was hit. Mostly it was just flying glass. And he was knocked out. But you can imagine how it seemed to Rhys…"

Vera didn't say anything for a long time. Zachary waited.

"So they were shooting at you," Vera said finally.

"Yeah."

"And this Noah… he was okay?"

"He was knocked out. And he had blood on his face. So for Rhys…"

"It was just like when Clarence was shot. The sound of the gunfire. Hit in the face."

Zachary nodded. "I'm so sorry. I had no intention of putting him in any danger."

Vera shook her head. "That poor boy. That poor, poor boy."

Zachary stared down at his hands. It was probably time for him to leave. Vera wouldn't want him hanging around there. She shouldn't have to tell him it was time to leave. She was so polite, she would keep being nice to him even when she wanted him out of the house.

"I guess… I should…" He started to get up.

Vera shook her head. "No, no. Let me wake Rhys up. He'll want to see you. He'll want to know how everything went. He's been asking after you."

Zachary hadn't received any messages from Rhys and thought maybe Vera had forbidden it. He was relieved that Rhys was at least communicative enough to ask for him.

Vera got to her feet. "You just stay right here. It might take me a few minutes to convince him to get up."

———

Zachary waited, concentrating on breathing and trying to keep his anxiety at bay. It hadn't gone as badly as he had feared. Rhys hadn't completely regressed. Vera hadn't kicked Zachary out and told him not to return. Rhys still wanted to see him, and Vera was willing to let him. But he couldn't shake the anxiety that Rhys or Vera was going to blame him for everything that had happened and for re-traumatizing Rhys.

He could hear Vera talking in Rhys's room and, eventually, the two of them came out. Rhys went directly to Zachary and, as Zachary stood up, took him in a bear hug.

Zachary was startled. He froze, unsure what to do, and it took him several seconds to process Rhys's reaction and hug him back.

Rhys released him after a few more seconds and stepped back far enough to look him in the face. He gave Zachary a searching look.

"She's okay," Zachary said immediately. "I don't know if she'll stay with her parents. They're trying to work things out. But she's safe, and we've fed back false information to the organization that she was killed in the shoot-out. So they won't be looking for her."

Rhys nodded seriously.

"Rhys, I'm so sorry, I never meant anything like that to happen. I'm so sorry that… you were there, and you saw what you did, and that it made you flash back to when your grandpa was killed. I'm so sorry about that."

Rhys took Zachary's forearm in a strong handshake, squeezing tightly. He met Zachary's eyes and gave a slight nod.

Zachary let out his breath. He looked at Vera. She nodded.

"Well, why don't I put something in the oven for supper? You'll stay, Zachary?"

EPILOGUE

The visit with Rhys had turned out well, better than Zachary had dared hope, but he had a pretty good idea that his visit with Jocelyn wasn't going to go nearly as well. He had the highway drive to sort out his thoughts and prepare himself, but he still didn't feel mentally prepared for what was bound to be an awkward and possibly angry meeting.

This time, it wasn't at a coffee shop or other neutral location, but at Jocelyn's house. It was a tiny house, but picturesque and carefully-maintained. It wasn't a dirty, rat-infested apartment. It was probably better than anything she had lived in while she'd been in the trafficking business. Her own place.

He didn't have to force himself to press the doorbell. Jocelyn was watching for him and opened the door as he approached.

"Hey," Zachary greeted.

She nodded. "Hi, Zach. Come on in."

Zachary entered. He took a quick glance around and opened his mouth to compliment her on her home. But he didn't get the chance.

Noah emerged from the kitchen into the tiny living room.

He was looking much better than he had the last time Zachary had seen him. The cuts on his face were starting to heal. He had good color instead of being pasty white. The bullet track along his jaw was still ugly, but Zachary suspected he was probably proud of it. A sick-looking war wound.

"Noah. Wow. How are you doing?"

Noah shrugged. "I'm… doing okay. It's weird. I don't know what to do with myself."

Zachary nodded. Living in the tiny house with Joss instead of turning tricks in the city; that was a pretty big change. He suddenly had choices. And that might be pretty frightening.

"Sit down, you goons," Joss said irritably, motioning to the furniture. "That's what the furniture is here for."

The men meekly obeyed.

"Coffee?" Jocelyn asked sharply.

"Always," Zachary agreed.

She didn't wait for Noah's answer, but disappeared into the kitchen.

"Do you… know how Madison is doing?" Noah asked tentatively.

"Part of the deal is that you don't have anything to do with her."

"I know. And… I'm not going to try to contact her. I just wondered if she's okay."

"She's okay," Zachary said neutrally. He wasn't going to give Noah any details.

That was the deal.

Just like they weren't going to tell Madison that Noah had woken up with only minor concussion issues. The plan was to give her no reason to go back to the life. Noah wanted out of the business and he wanted Madison to be free to go back to a normal life. That meant completely severing their ties.

"That's good," Noah said contentedly, surprising Zachary by not pushing for more.

"She owes you a lot for getting her out of there."

"No, she doesn't. I'm the one to blame for her getting pulled in to start with. You're the one who got her out."

"Not without your help."

Jocelyn returned with a round of coffee. "Luke is in a rehab program," she informed Zachary without him asking anything. "Hopefully, he'll stick with it, and be able to get into some kind of training, get himself a good job."

Zachary nodded. "Luke?"

The boy shrugged. “New life, new name.” He sipped his coffee and stared out the window.

“That’s good. Is it… I just wondered if it is your real name. I know that Noah probably wasn’t.”

“It’s my real name now.”

Zachary shrugged. It didn’t matter what Noah’s name had been before he’d been trafficked.

All that mattered was what happened next.

HE NEVER FORGOT

ZACHARY GOLDMAN MYSTERIES #9

For those who remember
Even when it hurts

1

Zachary was on the highway driving home from Jocelyn's house, thinking over his visit with Joss and the young man she was helping out, now known as Luke. It was going to be a long recovery period for Luke, after being trapped in human trafficking—both servicing his own clients and forced to recruit and train new teens—for a number of years. Successfully separating himself from that life was going to be more challenging for him than rehabbing from years of drug abuse. But if there were anyone who could help him through the process, it was Jocelyn.

Joss had only recently come back into Zachary's life. Separated from his family when he was ten, he was gradually reuniting with his siblings. Joss was the oldest, and the hardest so far to reconcile with. He sensed that she blamed him for the hard life she'd led, and rightly so, since he *was* the one who had accidentally lit the fire, the straw that broke the camel's back. His parents had relinquished the children, severing all ties, and they had all been placed in foster care. So far, none of them had led particularly happy lives. Tyrrell seemed to have led the most normal life. Zachary hoped that the youngest children in the family would turn out to have had an easier time. They had been almost two and four when they had been put into foster care, and under-fives had the best chances of recovering from trauma and leading a happy life.

But despite their differences and Jocelyn's generally bitter attitude, when Zachary had freed Luke from the trafficking ring, she had agreed to take him in and help him out. Zachary had a feeling that they would be good for each other. Joss already seemed to be gentler and happier around him. She didn't have any children of her own—as far as Zachary knew—and she seemed to have taken Luke under her wing. He was legally an adult, but still needed her protection and direction, and it seemed to be working out so far.

He was enjoying the smooth highway drive, one of the only times that his restless brain would settle down and enter a more relaxed, meditative state, when his phone rang over the car's Bluetooth system.

Zachary hit the answer button without looking at the number, assuming it would be Kenzie. But the voice that answered his greeting was not Kenzie's.

"Mr. Goldman? Is this the right number?" an uncertain male voice inquired.

"Yeah, this is Zachary." Zachary looked at the number on the radio screen but didn't recognize it. "How can I help you?"

"Of Goldman Investigations?"

"Yes, sir." Zachary waited for an explanation, hoping it was a client and not the IRS or a reporter.

"Uh… my name is Ben Burton. I'm interested in retaining your services. That's how they say it, isn't it?"

"You don't have to use any special jargon. What is it you need to hire a private investigator for?"

"Well…" Burton still hesitated, unsure of himself. It wasn't an unusual reaction from a client hiring a private investigator for the first time, thinking of TV show PI's they had seen. Hard-drinking, gun-toting, brilliant investigators. Wondering if they could really hire someone for their own problem, or if it were just ridiculous. Knowing that TV was not reality, and not sure what to expect. "I'd like to discuss it face-to-face, if we could do that. It's really…" Burton groped for a word, drawing it out painfully long.

"Private?" Zachary suggested.

"No. Um. Unusual, I guess. I don't want you to just laugh it off as a prank call."

Zachary raised his brows as he navigated around a few slower-moving cars, intrigued. "I wouldn't laugh it off if you're serious."

"I'd rather not take that chance."

"Okay. Are you in town? Where do you want to meet?"

"I'm just visiting. I'm at the Best Western. I don't know the city; maybe you could suggest a place to meet."

"I could come to you there. If you don't want to meet in your room, they have meeting rooms and a restaurant and lounge."

"The lounge sounds good," Burton said, sounding relieved. "So, you will meet with me? You'll really come?"

"Yes, of course. I'm out of town right now, but I'm on my way back. When do you want to meet? How long are you in town?"

"However long it takes, I suppose. Hopefully… not too long."

"All right. I've got a supper date, but maybe after that? Seven or eight?"

"Yeah. I'll be around. Why don't you just call me when you're done and on your way over?"

"At this number?"

"Yes. Ben Burton," he offered nervously, and rattled off the phone number.

"I've got it. I'll give you a call tonight, then."

"Thanks. I really appreciate it. That's great."

Because Zachary had thought it was Kenzie calling him, he felt the need to connect with her. He told his Bluetooth system to call her, and the call started to ring through. She would still be at work, but she would answer if she could. He was getting more used to the idea that they were a couple and he was important enough for her to interrupt her routine work to answer the phone when he called. For a long time, he'd been worried about calling her during her work hours, unless it was about something to do with the medical examiner's office. He'd worried that she would chastise him, haul him over the coals like Bridget would have.

But that was Bridget. And as he was learning, he couldn't judge all other women by the way his ex-wife behaved. He had thought that she was just honest, that other women all thought the same way as she did but were just too polite to say so. But Kenzie wasn't like that.

"Zachary." She sounded relaxed and cheerful. A good day at the medical examiner's office. "How did things go with Joss?"

"I think it's better every time I go there. She's… less defensive. More relaxed."

"That's good. It seemed like there were… a lot of walls there. A lot to get through before anyone could see the real Jocelyn."

"Especially me."

"Maybe," she conceded. "She has her issues. I'm glad that you've stuck it out and didn't let her scare you off."

Zachary considered that. Joss was prickly. And he remembered how she had treated him when they were both young and she was in charge of him. He was always getting into trouble, and that would get her in trouble, so she was sometimes too harsh in her reactions to him when he was doing his best. But he still loved her. He'd loved her then, and it hadn't even occurred to him to walk away.

"Zachary?"

"Yeah, I guess," Zachary agreed. "I just… I've missed my family for so long. I'd never consider not having a relationship with her."

Kenzie laughed. "Well, you are unique, because most people wouldn't persist with someone who was so cold and put up so many barriers. But you've worn her down."

Zachary shrugged to himself. It was hard for him to take a compliment, even from Kenzie.

"I was calling to let you know that I have an appointment tonight. After dinner, though. It's not bumping our date."

"Oh, okay." She was probably disappointed that they wouldn't have the full evening together. Zachary was working hard on that relationship too, but he couldn't always meet her expectations. "That's fine. Is it a client?"

"Yes. A prospect, anyway."

"What kind of case?"

"He didn't want to tell me over the phone. Said I would think he was crazy. So… I don't know whether it is someone I will end up working for or not."

"Yeah. That's a little suspicious. Let me know what happens; it sounds intriguing. If he is crazy, I want to know all about it."

Zachary laughed. "Okay. We'll see how it goes."

2

Supper with Kenzie left him feeling pretty mellow, which was unusual for Zachary. He was happy to go with it. If he could step out of his stress and anxiety for a while, it would make his life a lot easier. After supper, he headed over to the Best Western lounge, giving Burton a call to let him know he was on his way. It was only a few minutes away.

"The bar is pretty empty," Burton informed him. "Why don't you just meet me there."

Zachary agreed. When he got there, he scanned the bar briefly. There were only a couple of men sitting on stools along the counter, and only one of them was watching the door anxiously. Zachary nodded at the man and approached.

Ben Burton was maybe a bit younger than Zachary, in his mid-thirties. He was pale, with black eyes and hair. What Zachary guessed was Italian or Greek heritage. Burton had a slightly receding hairline, ears that had probably earned him nicknames as a child, and thick arm hair that went all the way down the backs of his hands to his first knuckles. He held his hand out toward Zachary, looking as though he was going to pull it back again any second. Zachary took it and gave it a squeeze, trying to reassure Burton. Whatever he wanted investigated, it was stressing him out. A wandering wife? Child custody problem with an ex? Someone stalking and harassing him?

"Don't get up," Zachary said, as Burton shifted to slide off of his bar stool. Burton stayed perched there in an awkward position. Zachary sat down on the stool next to him. "Nice to meet you, Mr. Burton."

The bartender approached, eyebrows raised.

"Coke," Zachary requested.

The bartender nodded and filled a glass from the fountain. He placed it on a napkin in front of Zachary.

"Coke?" Burton demanded. "Don't you drink?"

Zachary glanced at the shot glass and half-full beer in front of Burton. A hard drinker, if Zachary didn't miss his guess.

"I generally avoid alcohol," he explained. "It interferes with my meds."

Burton rolled his eyes as if he'd heard this excuse a hundred times before, which wasn't how most people reacted to Zachary's explanation for not drinking alcohol. Usually, if people knew it was a medical thing, they would accept it and not harass him further to join them in their spirits.

"They're just covering their butts," Burton told him. "Most of the time, it doesn't have any negative effect at all."

He appeared to speak with the voice of experience. Zachary made a mental note of the fact but didn't pull out his notebook. He sipped his cola and waited for Burton to make the next move.

"So, I guess you want to know why I wanted to meet with you," Burton said finally.

"Whenever you're ready."

"Let's get a booth." Burton cast a suspicious look toward the bartender.

Zachary agreed, and let Burton pick one out. He did not, Zachary noted, pick a seat with a view of the doors. Not someone who was watching his back. So probably not worried about a stalker.

Zachary sat opposite Burton in the booth. He took his notepad out and laid it on the table beside his hand. "You don't mind if I need to make notes?"

Burton shifted back and forth, thinking about it, then nodded. Zachary started on a fresh page and put Burton's name at the top. He wrote the date carefully. Too many of his notes had dates that he had to guess at. A six or an eight? A one or a seven? He wanted to improve. Digitizing his notes meant that they would be in his cloud storage indefinitely. He wanted something he could read later on down the line.

Zachary looked at Burton, waiting.

"I don't know how to start this," Burton said.

"Just let me know why you want a private investigator. And don't worry about it, I've heard all kinds of stories."

Burton cleared his throat. He looked up into the corner of the ceiling of the lounge, fingering his glass. "I don't know. It's not like it's anything embarrassing. I just want to find the house I used to live in as a kid."

Zachary nodded. "Okay."

He waited to see if Burton would explain further. Burton remained silent and brooding.

"So you lived here in town when you were younger," Zachary suggested.

"I think so."

Zachary raised his brows.

"From what I can remember, I mean. I didn't grow up here, but I think *before*, I lived here."

"Your parents can't tell you?"

"I was adopted. I don't know anything about who my bio parents are. Or were. I don't know very much at all about my own history."

"Ah." Zachary nodded. "I grew up in foster homes and institutions, so I know a bit about what that's like."

"I'm not saying it was bad. It wasn't. I have great parents; they gave me everything I needed. I just… I need something else. I need to know where I came from. *Something* about my past."

"Sure."

Burton drank, not looking at Zachary.

There were physical similarities between the two of them. Zachary was also pale-skinned with dark hair. His was buzz-cut short so that he didn't need to do much to take care of it. He had enough to handle without having to worry about styling his hair too. He was shorter than Burton, shorter than most of the adults he knew. The result of poor nutrition before he was put into foster care and growth-stunting meds after.

Burton was clean-shaven. He kind of looked like an actor from a noir movie. That pale face and his dark eyes and eyebrows. Very dramatic and brooding.

"Maybe you could outline what you do know about your childhood. You came here, so you have reasons to believe this is where you came from."

"I don't know. Maybe it's something I just made up as a kid. Because I had to be from *somewhere*, you know? A lot of the things that I used to tell people about myself… I don't know how many of them are true and how many are just things I made up because I didn't have anything else to tell."

"And you told people you were from here. What else did you tell them?" Zachary wrote a couple of words on his notepad to help him remember everything later.

Burton studied him, his dark brows drawing down in a scowl. "What makes you believe me when no one else does?"

"Believe you? You said that you might be from here. I don't see anything particularly unbelievable in that statement."

"When I think about living here, when I try to picture the house that I came from… my heart speeds up, and I start to sweat, and I get this feeling in my chest. This… pressure."

Zachary nodded. "Because you can't remember, or because of something that happened in the past?"

"I don't know. I think that something happened, but I can't remember what it was."

"How did you end up with your adoptive parents? They didn't know your bio parents? You went to your adoptive family from…"

"I was in DCF custody. In a foster home, I guess. They didn't know much about the circumstances I had come from. Or they didn't tell my adoptive parents. Or Mom and Dad just couldn't remember the details anymore."

"Or didn't want to tell you about it."

Burton scowled again. "They wouldn't keep it from me."

"Social services would have to know something about what kind of home you came from. And they would need to fill your adoptive parents in with enough details to handle any problems."

"Why would there be problems?"

"Were you apprehended from your bio family? How old were you?"

"What difference does it make?"

"Because the older you were, the more likely it was you would have behavioral issues. And if you were coming from a home where you were abused or neglected, it would be that much worse."

Burton gulped down what remained of his beer and motioned to a waiter, pointing to his glass. "I was… five years old. And I didn't have any behavioral problems."

"So maybe you came from a stable home. And your bio parents were killed suddenly. Nowhere else to go, so DCF comes into the picture."

"Maybe," Burton agreed, giving a brief nod.

"Do you remember anything about your bio parents? Not necessarily anything concrete like their names or what they looked like, but... impressions. Two parents or one?"

"Two," Burton answered immediately, then looked thoughtful.

"What did you tell people you remembered about your home and family?"

"I lived here... in a house... My parents..." Burton frowned, trying to remember. "Two parents, I'm sure. A mom and dad."

Zachary nodded. "Any siblings?"

Burton rubbed his forehead. He looked around for the waiter with his beer. It was a few minutes before he got his beer, and then he looked at Zachary as if he'd just remembered he was there.

"Mom and Dad said I was very quiet, very well-behaved. I got good report cards at school when I started. I have copies of those. I wasn't a troublemaker."

"You can have a lot of different issues without being labeled a troublemaker." Although Zachary had always been labeled a troublemaker himself. Unfairly so. He hadn't been trouble. He'd just had problems. Problems dealing with his traumatic past, his abusive upbringing, his impulsivity. He'd been unable to control himself and never stayed in a home for very long.

So maybe he *had* been a troublemaker.

He'd always been singled out as one.

"Do you have any adoptive siblings?"

"No." This didn't seem to be as difficult a question for him. "Just me."

"Did you have imaginary friends?"

Burton puffed out his cheeks, his forehead creasing. "I don't know. Maybe. I don't remember much from when I was that young."

"Most people have a few memories from when they were five or six. Or maybe your parents had cute stories about you. What else have they told you about when you first joined the family?"

"Not a lot... they were really happy to get me. They wanted a kid and couldn't have their own, so they picked me out." Burton shook his head. "Is that right? Would they have been able to pick me? It's not like I was in an orphanage where you can go from bed to bed and pick out the kid you want."

"No, but most agencies have books of pictures you can look at. A little blurb about each child or family group. So they might have seen your picture in a 'waiting children' book."

Burton nodded. "Yeah, that must be it. I don't know. My mom just says how quiet and well-behaved I was. I didn't really… get my own voice until I was older. You know how teenagers are." A shrug.

Going from five to thirteen without having a voice of his own was a long time. Most kids would have explored their boundaries long before that.

"Were you in therapy?"

"For what?"

"When you first came to your parents. Were you in any kind of personal or family therapy to help you with the transition? Or to overcome any emotional issues."

"No. I didn't need any."

Zachary nodded and scratched a few words into his notepad. "What do you remember about the house you are looking for? Anything?"

"You'll take the case?"

Zachary nodded. "Sure, it sounds like an intriguing case. I think we'll be able to find something." Zachary reached into the satchel he had brought with him and pulled out an envelope. He handed Burton a one-page retainer agreement that set out his rates and usual terms. They discussed the various aspects for a few minutes, and Burton signed his name on the appropriate line.

"Do you take credit cards?"

"Yeah." Zachary turned his phone on and entered his payment app. He put the initial retainer amount in the field and handed it to Burton. "Go ahead and enter your credit card information."

Burton tapped in a long string of numbers without taking out his wallet. An impressive feat. He entered the expiry date and handed it back to Zachary. Zachary waited for the transaction to go through, then turned his phone back off.

"Great, that's all covered. So we're ready to get started."

Burton was gazing at Zachary's phone, his eyes glazing. How much had he already had to drink? It couldn't have been so much, or he wouldn't have been able to remember his credit card number.

"Mr. Burton. Are you ready to begin tonight? Or do you want to set up a time tomorrow?"

It was a minute before Burton blinked and looked at Zachary. "You can call me Ben. What did you say?"

"Let's set up a time to meet tomorrow. You look like you've had a long day. You should get some rest, and we'll talk tomorrow. See how much you can remember, so I have a place to start."

Burton rubbed the worry lines on his forehead and finally nodded. "Yeah, okay. Tomorrow I'll be fresh as a daisy."

"What time? Morning?"

Burton shook his head immediately. "I'm not an early riser. It takes me a few hours to get the motor running. Morning isn't a good time."

Which, if Zachary had him pegged right, meant that he would be too hungover in the morning to be any help. By noon, maybe he'd be feeling well enough to handle an interview.

"Fair enough. After lunch? One o'clock? Do you want to meet here?"

Burton looked around at his surroundings. "If they're open, yeah."

"I'll find out." Zachary didn't want to waste his time trying to flag down a waiter. They all seemed to be occupied, even though the lounge wasn't anywhere near full. They should have been past the dinner rush. Maybe they reduced their staff once the rush was over. Zachary went to the cash register at the bar.

"What time does the lounge open tomorrow?" He handed the bartender a bill to pay for his drink.

"Not until one o'clock."

"Great. That's fine." Zachary held up his hands when the bartender indicated the register. "No change. Thanks."

He went back to Burton, who, while no longer looking so anxious, was very somber. They finalized arrangements and parted company.

3

He went home to Kenzie's house rather than to his apartment. They were still splitting time between the two places, but Kenzie's was far nicer and better stocked with food and other necessities that Zachary tended to forget about until he really needed them. So most weekdays they spent there, going back to Zachary's for the weekend. Or sometimes they spent time apart. Each of them sometimes needed their own space. Zachary carefully monitored the amount of time he was away from Kenzie to make sure that he wasn't asking for more space than she was. He didn't want to be accused of being selfish or not invested in the relationship.

"So, did you take on the new client, and is he crazy?" Kenzie asked, after greeting him with a brief kiss.

They settled in the living room, close to each other on the couch. Kenzie shut her TV program off with the remote.

"I took the case. He didn't seem particularly crazy. Anxious, yes. But crazy?" Zachary shrugged. Was it crazy for a man to want to reconnect with his history and to visit his childhood home? Zachary didn't think it was that unusual.

He told Kenzie about the meeting, leaving out any names or identifying information. Kenzie wrinkled her brow.

"You don't think it's strange that he wants you to find this house that he can't even remember?"

"Well… no."

"I could understand it if he had fond memories of the place and wanted to revisit those feelings. But when he doesn't remember anything about it and, by everything he's said so far, it probably wasn't a good atmosphere for him, why would he want to find it again?"

"Because it's something that he's lost. It's something concrete that he can look at and touch, when he doesn't remember anything from that time."

Kenzie pursed her lips, considering it.

"Why do people research their family trees? Or have their DNA tested to see what their heritage is? People like to know… their stories. Their origins. Even if it isn't something that they can remember. Maybe… especially if they can't remember."

"Is that how you feel? Do you want to do your family tree and go back —" she stopped herself and didn't suggest that he might want to go back to his childhood home. "Go back to somewhere you used to live?"

"No. I was ten when I left there… I remember it all very clearly. I wouldn't want to go back there, even if it did still exist."

Kenzie nodded.

"But I do want to reconnect with my siblings," Zachary pointed out. "I haven't seen them for a long time, and the little ones wouldn't remember me at all. But I would hope… that they would still want to see me even though they don't remember me."

"Yes, of course. And would you want to see your parents again?"

Zachary caught his breath. He felt like he'd been kicked in the chest, suddenly unable to draw in any more oxygen. Would he ever want to see his parents again if he had the opportunity? He had pleaded to go back to his mother. He had begged his social worker to see if she had changed her mind and might take him and the others back again. For years, he had fantasized about going home again, escaping whatever situation he was in and living some happily-ever-after with his family.

"Zachary…" Kenzie rubbed his back. "Sorry, was that the wrong thing to say? I just wondered how you felt about it. I didn't mean to upset you."

Zachary tried to shake his head and draw another breath. The world felt like it had frozen around him. Or maybe that he'd frozen inside himself.

"It's okay. Think about the good things. Think about being here with me. About Tyrrell, and Heather, and Joss. You were so happy to meet them again. Think about how nice it's been to have contact with them again."

Zachary managed a tiny nod, but still couldn't breathe. Kenzie continued to rub his back, not trying to rush him back. Not like those who pinched or slapped him to try to 'get his attention' when he got lost in memories. Zachary forced a little air out, then breathed in shallowly. It was a few minutes before he felt the tension melting, the memories releasing him.

"Getting a drink," he told Kenzie, trying to rise.

"You just stay there. I'll get you a glass of water." Kenzie got up. "You need anything else?" She didn't ask him if he needed his Xanax. She would let him ask for it.

"No. Just… dry."

Kenzie had cold water in a filter jug in the fridge. She poured him a tall glass and handed it to him on her return. Zachary sipped the icy cold water. It was just what he needed.

"When I was a kid… I still wanted to go back to them. I thought I could make everything right again. Glue the family back together again. But by the time I was an adult…" He shook his head. "I knew that would never work and that… the kind of people they were… I wouldn't want to live with them again."

Kenzie looked into his eyes. "Things must have been pretty bad."

"When I was little, I didn't really know… it's just the way things were. I held on to times when things were better… kind of pretended that things were good most of the time. But as I got older, I realized… how bad they really were. And my mom…" Zachary took a deep breath, trying not to let the memories overwhelm him again. "I told you how she was when she decided to get rid of us. She was…" Zachary breathed in and out again, strangled. "I can't imagine anyone treating a child like that. I thought I was grown up and that I deserved it. For a long time. But now… when I look at Rhys, or other people's kids… I can't imagine it. Rhys is a teenager, and I would still never talk to him the way she did to me or hold him responsible for… making a mistake like that."

"Yeah. You have to realize… she was unreasonable."

"There were six of us, and I know I was in trouble a lot," Zachary started, jumping to his mother's defense even after pointing out himself how wrong she had been to treat him that way. "I get how she might feel overwhelmed… burned out…"

"That's no excuse for abandoning six kids. Or for calling you the names she did."

Zachary bit his lip and nodded. He took another sip of the water, welcoming the chill. "So… no. I think that even if one of them came looking for me… I don't think I would want to meet them. Never again."

Kenzie nodded. She put her hand over his, soothing him. "Anyway… I didn't mean to bring all that up. I just didn't understand why the house would be so important to your client."

Zachary chewed the inside of his cheek, thinking about it. While it had seemed natural to him, on a closer examination, he wasn't sure it was as logical as he had asserted. Why did Burton want to find his house instead of finding his parents? Did he come from a background like Zachary's? Had they been abusive or negligent? He might not even remember any of that. He could just be following a feeling. Drawn to the house, but not to his abusers.

"I don't know. If he was apprehended when he was five, he probably didn't have a great life. Or maybe his parents were killed. He might know that without remembering it, if it was traumatic."

Kenzie nodded. "Things to think about," she said lightly. "Follow the clues."

Zachary nodded. He deliberately leaned back into the soft upholstery of the couch, trying to relax all of his muscles. He didn't need to worry about his biological parents. They weren't going to show up out of the blue. He could just focus on the case without exploring the similarities to his own life. In the meantime, he was with Kenzie, and he should focus on her and their relationship.

"I wonder how Rhys is doing," Kenzie mused. "When is the last time you saw him?"

"Just after… everything happened." Zachary shrugged uncomfortably. "I don't want to get in the way. I'm not sure how Vera feels about me seeing him. She said it's okay, but I don't want to push my way in where I'm not wanted."

"It wasn't your fault that Rhys saw Noah—Luke—shot. You were trying to protect them."

"Yes. But maybe I could have made different choices than I did. His grandma has the right to be upset about it. It's one thing that he was there, in the middle of everything. That would be bad enough. But the fact that it triggered flashbacks to his grandfather being murdered…" Zachary sighed. "I don't know if she can forgive me for that."

"I think *you're* the one having problems forgiving yourself for that. From what you said before, it sounds like Vera was pretty good about it."

Kenzie was uncomfortably close to the truth. Zachary did blame himself for Rhys's increased emotional distress. He had been trying to help, but he should have been smarter. He should have known that the traffickers would be able to track Luke.

"You should message him," Kenzie said. "It can't hurt to just keep in touch, let him know you're thinking about him."

"If it makes him think about that night, and about Grandpa Clarence being shot, then it could hurt. It could make things worse when he is starting to recover."

"Then ask Vera what she thinks."

"Mmm." Zachary made a noncommittal noise. He'd have to think about it. Even though Vera had treated him with grace and kindness, he didn't relish having to call her up to ask for a progress report on Rhys. It felt like having to go to a neighbor to tell them that you ran over their cat. Even if they took it well, it still felt awful. "Maybe I'll just wait for Rhys to contact me."

4

Ben Burton wasn't looking quite up to snuff when Zachary found him in the lounge for the second day in a row. He was already nursing a drink, and his eyes were bloodshot and shadowed. He nodded as Zachary approached the booth, the same one they had sat in the evening before.

Zachary smiled. "How are you this afternoon?"

"Just fine." Burton's voice was gravelly. He rubbed his forehead and shrugged at Zachary, realizing that Zachary could see the condition he was in. "A few more drinks under my belt and I'll be better."

"Do you have a drinking problem?" Zachary asked baldly. There was no point in tiptoeing around it.

Burton rubbed a hand through his hair. "I drink," he said. "Some people have a problem with it. Do you?"

"Are you going to be able to hold it together? To answer my questions and to pay the bills?"

"It doesn't affect me. I can drink all day long. It doesn't make any difference."

Zachary doubted that was entirely true. He sat down across from Burton. "If you want me to work with you, you're going to need to be available. And coherent enough to give me the information I need from you."

"I told you it doesn't affect me. Do I sound drunk? I'm here like we arranged. I'm talking. I'm making sense. I could drive now if I had to. There isn't a problem."

Zachary shook his head but didn't bother trying to convince Burton otherwise. He knew how pointless it was to talk an alcoholic out of drinking. There had been a lot of people in his life who had drunk too much. It was nothing new. At least with a client, he could simply drop the case if Burton became abusive or wasn't able to give Zachary the information he needed to track down Burton's childhood home.

"You getting a drink?" Burton asked, his eyes sliding over to the bar.

Zachary nodded. If he was going to be talking, he would need something to combat the dry mouth that went along with his meds. He didn't order a Coke this time, but water. It arrived with ice and a wedge of lime on the glass. Burton eyed it dubiously.

"Don't know how you can drink the stuff."

"It isn't exactly hard."

"If it was hard, I'd drink it," Burton joked. "Don't know how anyone can go without ever drinking. At least last night, it was a Coke."

"I'm good with water for now." It wasn't like Zachary had to worry about the calories. His doctor was still on his case to put on more weight. But he didn't want to be drinking cola all afternoon, or however long it took to get what he needed from Burton.

"So, you've had a little bit of time to think about what impressions you have of when you were younger." He jumped right into the interview. "And to remember some of the stories that you told other people."

Burton nodded. He sipped his drink thoughtfully, staring out the window into the afternoon light. He turned his head away from it and rubbed his eyes. "So, I'm pretty sure it must have been here. I always felt like this was where I came from. I don't remember specifics, but this was where I felt like I belonged. I didn't belong *there*. And… the other kids knew that wasn't where I belonged either. You know how sometimes kids can just sense… that you're an outsider. You never quite get into any of the groups or develop those friendships that the other kids have." His mouth turned down in a frown.

Did Zachary know? He knew what it was like always to be the new kid. The outsider. But Burton had been adopted when he was five. Before any of them had started school. He'd been there for his entire school career. He wasn't a newcomer. But he'd still been an outsider. Why?

"I've been there. Did you feel good or bad about being from here?"

"I don't know. Just… like I didn't fit in. Like an alien from another planet. And that was why. Because I wasn't from around there."

"Do you remember some of the places that you went to when you were young? A park? Grocery store? Neighbor's house?"

"Yeah… I guess there must have been other places. I remember walking down the street. The sidewalk, I mean. I feel like I was by myself, but I must not have been if I was five or younger. There must have been someone with me. Maybe walking behind while I led the way."

"And what did you see when you looked around?"

Burton closed his eyes. "I don't know. A dog. Big German shepherd. I like dogs. I must have liked them back then too."

"Probably. Do you know who was walking the dog? Was it a neighbor, someone you knew?"

Burton shook his head slowly, eyes still closed while he tried to visualize it. "I don't think so. A man. Not someone I knew. Talked to me. Maybe… ruffled my hair and called me buddy. You know how people do. Men don't really know how to talk to kids."

"Did he talk to your mom or dad? Were they there with you?"

"I don't know. I don't remember anyone being with me."

"Did he let you pet the dog?"

A smile grew on Burton's face and he nodded. "Yeah. He let me pet it."

"Did he tell you its name?"

"That's asking a lot…" Burton shook his head. "Maybe. Maybe it was the dog who was named Buddy."

Zachary didn't press the point. He knew that every question he asked could alter Burton's memories. When people were asked to remember things that they couldn't or were told that something had happened to them when it hadn't, their brains built the missing memory to fill the gap. And people became convinced that the retrieved memories were real. A brain wasn't a bank vault. You couldn't take memories out, examine them, and put them back unchanged. Every time Burton told his story, his memories would shift slightly.

"What do you like to do?"

"What do I like to do?" Burton's eyes opened. "What do you mean?"

"You enjoy some activities and not others. What would you rather be doing right now?"

Burton grinned. "Drinking in my room."

"But you're drinking here. So what is it about your room that you miss?"

Burton's eyes flicked over to one of the wall-mounted TVs, thinking about it. If he liked to drink and watch sports, he could do that while he was sitting there talking to Zachary. If he preferred something else…

"When I was younger, I liked bugs," Burton offered abruptly. "That's something you can't say about everyone."

"No." Zachary could remember playing outside with his siblings, catching bugs, putting them in jars or racing them on the sidewalk. Or dousing anthills with water to watch all of the ants come swarming out. Other things that were not quite so nice. He couldn't say that he liked bugs, but he'd been interested in them when he was a kid with scraped knees. They were something to play with for a kid who didn't have the latest toys and games. "Did you want to become an entomologist?"

"A what? No, I didn't want to do it professionally. I just… was really interested in bugs. Got books about them. Read about them at the library or watched kid videos about them. Just… they were really interesting."

Zachary nodded. "So, where did you collect them or watch them?"

Burton rolled his shoulders. "Anywhere. In the back yard. In the park. When we went out for a walk. When I was in school, if the teacher screamed at a spider or something, I was the one who would put it outside. I wasn't ever scared of them or squeamish."

"Did you catch them in the back yard of your old house?"

He watched Burton's eyes, alive and glistening instead of looking dissolute as he had when Zachary had walked up. It was something that interested him, and maybe there was a flicker of recognition or memory there.

"I don't think… not in the back yard," Burton said slowly. "Maybe… in the basement? Sometimes bugs get into the house. Spiders, centipedes, ants. Lots of kinds of creepy crawlies can live in the dark corners of the basement."

"Yeah. Did you catch them or just watch them?"

Burton's hands made an involuntary movement. As if, just for a split-second, he was reaching out to catch something. "I'd catch them. Put them in jars. At my house in Colchester anyway. Maybe here. I don't know."

"That's okay. We're just going over things, seeing what pops into your mind. Did you have a friend that caught them with you?"

"No, none of my friends were ever interested in anything like that."

"Any siblings?"

Burton shook his head. "I told you I didn't have any siblings. I was an only child."

In his adoptive family. Zachary wasn't sure about in Burton's biological family.

5

What kind of car did you have?"

"When I was a kid? Let's see… mostly station wagons, probably. Maybe an SUV or van. I wasn't a big car guy. Not like some people who can tell you every vehicle they ever had since they were born. I don't know what my parents drove most of the time. Mom and dad vehicles. Nothing hot."

"Yeah." Zachary nodded, smiling. He'd ridden in a lot of mom vehicles. "And you always wore a seatbelt, right?"

Something flashed across Burton's features. He touched his shoulder. "Yeah. Of course."

"What was that?"

"What?"

"What did you think of when I asked if you always wore a seatbelt?"

"I don't know. Just… how uncomfortable they were to wear when I was a kid. I hated having my freedom restricted. I wanted to be able to move around. Lie down on the seats. Look out whichever side I wanted. But you can't, with seatbelts. You have to just… stay put."

Zachary nodded. He made a couple of notes in his notepad. Had Burton worn a seatbelt before he was adopted? Or was he allowed to do those things that he had mentioned? Had he ridden in a car that didn't have seatbelts or where wearing them was not enforced? An old car? Broken down? Parents who didn't care? Or just something that Burton had always hated to do?

"What did you see when you looked out your bedroom window?"

"Back yard. Grass, garden. Back fence. Nothing special."

"You grew up looking at that sight every day."

Burton nodded his agreement.

"Did you like it? Do you remember ever being interested or excited about it?"

"No." Burton's head wobbled back and forth. A negative head-shake, but something else too. Not just back and forth. There was too much up and down movement. The kind of 'tell' that some people had when they said something that wasn't the truth.

Zachary wrote a note about the bugs, waiting for Burton to think through the lie. Did he know he was lying, or was it something that his body knew, but his conscious brain would not release?

"I was… kind of scared of looking out my window when I was really little. Like… I might fall out of the window and land on my head." Burton rolled his eyes. "I got over it. Eventually. I'm not afraid of heights or anything."

"But you used to be?"

"I guess so. But kids are scared of a lot of things. And you grow out of them as an adult."

Sometimes. Certainly not all the time. And some people added fears and phobias as they grew up and gained experience. Especially when traumatized.

"What else were you afraid of?" Not bugs, clearly. Not dogs.

"I was afraid of a lot of things. A real mama's boy. But I grew out of them."

"What kind of things?"

"Things that might be too hot… fire, stoves, things like that…"

Zachary breathed, then took a few sips of his ice water, trying to anchor himself in the sensations and not to be drawn into a flashback to the fire.

"The dark. But all little kids are afraid of the dark. And things hiding under the bed or in the closet. You know how it is. Kids make things up to entertain themselves, and then get scared of them, like they were really true."

Zachary nodded. What kid hadn't spooked himself at one time or another?

"Uh… I don't know. Doors slamming. Sirens. Not *scared* scared, but… they get me here," Burton drilled a knuckled into the center of his chest, and Zachary could feel the heavy pain of anxiety and dread himself. He noted that Burton had used the present tense. He claimed to have outgrown his childhood fears, but he had just used the present tense. Things he was still afraid of.

"Do you take anything for anxiety?" The night before, Burton had said that drinking didn't really have much effect on meds.

"None of that stuff works. You want something to make you better…" Burton indicated the drink in front of him. "That's what makes you feel better."

"But it's a depressant. It will make you feel worse afterward. Make you swing lower."

"There's an easy fix for that." Burton leaned forward as if he were about to tell Zachary a secret. "Just don't stop drinking." He leaned back again and laughed loudly. He took a couple more gulps from his glass to demonstrate the point.

Just stay in a permanent state of drunkenness, and then you didn't have to worry about hangovers or crashing afterward.

"How old were you when you started drinking?"

"What does that have anything to do with? We were talking about when I was a little kid. When I lived here. Believe me, I didn't drink when I was five!"

"So how old were you when you started?"

Burton shook his head. "Who knows. A teenager. I don't remember when my first drink was."

"Were you copying someone else? Acting grown up?"

"Are you saying that my parents drank in front of me? They didn't. I knew they were against drinking alcohol, but that didn't make any difference. I didn't do it to act like a grown-up. I just…" He considered, a crease forming between his eyebrows. "I knew it would make me feel better. Even the most naive kid can't avoid seeing people laughing and drinking on TV. See how much better it makes them feel. Even if you don't know anyone who drinks, TV still tells you how much fun it is."

"And you drank to feel better, back when you were a teenager."

"Yeah. That's right. So what?"

"You told me you had everything you wanted growing up. Your parents provided for everything you needed. They were good. Not abusive. So why did you need something to make you feel better?"

"Because I had some trauma? Some child molester messing with me? There wasn't anything like that. Just… it's a chemical thing. A problem in the brain. That's all. It isn't the way that you were raised that makes you happy or anxious. It's just… the way your brain is wired."

Zachary had heard many different explanations for mental illness, and that was as good as any. "Sometimes, it's just the way you were born," he agreed. "In your DNA. But sometimes it is caused by trauma or abuse."

"And you think I must have gone through something awful before my mom and dad adopted me. But that's not the way it was. I don't have any memories of being abused before I was adopted." He took a drink and stared at Zachary. "And I would remember that. Trust me."

His certainty didn't convince Zachary. Quite the opposite, in fact. A lot of people would have been intrigued by the suggestion. They would have spoken softly and thought back, trying to put a thumb down on the shifting shadows of memory to test if it were true or not. But Burton was certain. He wouldn't even countenance thinking about it. That said something about him. And it wasn't that he had never been through trauma or abuse. The brain protected itself. It could wall away secrets for years. Decades. But that didn't necessarily mean they were gone forever.

The mind and the body still remembered.

6

Do you remember any of your birthdays?"

Burton nodded. "Sure. I've had some pretty good ones. Not like my parents are rich and always got the latest and greatest, I mean. But I had good birthdays. They put effort into making it nice for me."

Zachary nodded. "What was your best birthday present ever?"

"No question." Burton didn't have to think about it. "My ninth birthday. A dog. Just a mutt, nothing special. No breed in particular. A Bitsa, my dad used to say. Bitsa this and bitsa that."

"A dog. You must have been over the moon."

"Oh yeah." Burton looked nostalgic. A good memory. Lots of good times with that Bitsa dog.

"What was the worst birthday you ever had?"

"The worst? Hell, I don't know. Like I said, they always tried to make things nice for me."

"How about before you were adopted?"

Burton looked blank. He shook his head. "I don't know. Don't remember any before that."

"What do you think they were like?"

Still nothing. No changes to his facial expression, not even a twitch. "I have no idea. I probably didn't have any before I was adopted. Why have a birthday party when your kid is too young to know what's going on and won't ever remember it? You might as well put your resources into something else."

The best birthday present Zachary had ever received, and the first, had been a camera. Mr. Peterson, his first foster father and the only one Zachary kept in touch with, had given it to him for his eleventh birthday. His first birthday in foster care. Zachary had been elated to get a present. It was a second-hand camera, but Zachary had kept it for decades. It wasn't until the second fire, the one that burned his apartment around the time he had first met Kenzie, that he lost it. He'd lost all of his possessions. He had been able to replace the essentials, but he still mourned the loss of that old camera.

His birthdays before that hadn't been anything to remember. They barely even rated a mention.

"Most people still celebrate those early birthdays, even if the child isn't going to remember them."

Burton shrugged. "Well, we didn't."

It wasn't a tentative statement. He was certain that he hadn't celebrated birthdays. Not just that he didn't remember them.

"How about other celebrations?" Zachary inquired, bringing up his least-favorite holiday. "Christmas?"

"Nice times with my parents... but before that? I don't remember."

"Nothing? No tree? No lights or presents?"

"I don't remember any."

"Maybe your family wasn't Christian. What about... those Jewish candles?" Zachary's brain wouldn't produce the name, even though he knew it. "Or the songs or the..." Zachary made a spinning motion with his fingers, trying to remember the word for the toy top. "Uh... dreidel?"

"Nah," Burton scowled and shook his head. "I'm not Jewish. I wasn't anything like that. Jewish or Muslim or some other thing. I don't know if they were Christian or not. I don't really have a *faith*."

Zachary accepted this. People didn't need to be Christian to celebrate Christmas. But Burton was quite sure he wasn't something else. So probably not raised in some strange cult or sect. If his birth family didn't celebrate, it was probably the result of poverty rather than religious beliefs. Their search would, Zachary was pretty sure, lead them to the less affluent areas of town. Hopefully, that didn't mean that Burton's old house had been bulldozed to make room for another development or parking lot.

Zachary sipped his water and swished it around his mouth, trying to combat the dryness that came from his meds and from talking to someone in a stressful situation. He wasn't the one in the hot seat, but he still had memories of his own that he would rather not have to bring to light, and he was worried that any similarities in Burton's memories might bring them back. He turned his mind to what other things might trigger memories for Ben Burton.

"Some of the other things that tend to bring back feelings and emotions when we aren't sure of the memories they are attached to are food and music. Do you have any particular favorites? Or things you hate? Foods or songs that have strong emotions attached to them?"

"Can't stand fish," Burton offered, after due consideration. "And I'm probably the only kid ever who didn't like mac and cheese."

Zachary smiled. One of his favorites as a kid. "How could you not like mac and cheese? Next thing you'll be telling me you don't like French fries."

"French fries I like," Burton said, pointing at Zachary, a gesture that suddenly brought Rhys to mind. Mute though he was, Rhys had never learned American Sign Language, but made do with a mixture of gestures, facial expressions, texts, and pictures on his phone. It worked okay, but was always a challenge. He frequently pointed at Zachary when he got something right. *You got it.*

Zachary cleared his throat and tried to continue with the conversation without getting sidetracked.

"But not mac and cheese."

"Nope. Can't abide the stuff. Even the smell of the cheese sauce." He gagged and shook his head. "No way."

"Anything else?"

"I don't know. I'm not that picky."

"And how about music. Anything take you back? Or induce strong emotions?"

Burton stared off into space for a while, then shook his head. "No. I like loud music. I mean, I like it shaking the walls. Nothing quiet. If it's one of my favorite songs, it needs to be played at top volume."

"What do your parents like?"

A brief shadow, and then it was gone. The memories were there. But reaching them was going to be challenging.

"Have you talked to your parents about what they remember from when they first adopted you? Something that the social worker might have told them, or something that they thought just from your behavior?"

"I called them last night. They know that I'd like to know more about my history, but they don't think it's a good idea, and they don't know that I'm here looking for my house."

"Why don't they think it's a good idea?"

"I don't know. Just because… they don't want me to get upset, I guess. They don't think that it will lead to anything that will make me happy."

"So they don't think that you had a very good life before you went to them."

"Yeah, I guess," Burton agreed. He motioned for another drink. "But they don't *know*."

"Kids don't usually come up for adoption for happy reasons. Not five-year-olds."

"But it could just mean that my parents or whoever was taking care of me died. It doesn't mean that I had an unhappy childhood."

"Do you think you had a happy childhood?"

Burton waited until he had another glass in front of him. He took a few swallows. "Okay. So I probably didn't have a happy childhood. But I still want to know. I want to walk through that house. Or at least to see it again. I need—I just really would like to see it again."

"Do they think that you were neglected or abused?"

"My mom will say things now and then. Like how I used to not be able to sleep without a light on. Like it's significant. But lots of kids are afraid of the dark."

"It's only natural to be afraid of what we can't see."

"Exactly."

"What else did she say that she thought might be significant?"

"I don't know. I was skinny, but I ate a lot. I didn't fill out until I was older. But lots of five-year-olds are skinny. They have legs like sticks at that age. It's not unusual."

"Right."

"When I talked to her last night, she said that she didn't think the social worker wanted them to know about where I came from. That it was better if

I just started off fresh, like I hadn't lived anywhere else before that. So that's how they raised me. Like I'd always lived there and there was no history. But I *knew* that they weren't my natural parents, so what was the point of that?"

"Were they very different from your natural parents?"

Zachary again glimpsed something in Burton's eyes that was just out of his reach.

"They were…" Burton blew out his breath and slumped down. He took several long swallows, almost reaching the bottom of the glass. "I don't know. I have no idea. It's just not there."

"What do you like about your mom?"

"She's very loving. She… smells nice. She's soft and… she gives great hugs." Burton's pale face turned pink, and he laughed at himself. "So does that mean that those are the things about her that were like my birth mother? Or that those are the things that are different from her?"

"What do you think?"

Burton didn't answer the question, diverting. "They remembered the name of the social worker. I don't suppose she's still around anymore, and she wouldn't remember anything about my case, but it's a possible line of inquiry."

Zachary looked at him for a minute, then nodded. "Do you have her details?"

Burton gave him the name and the general description of the woman that his mother had been able to provide. Age, what she looked like. She was probably still alive, but would she remember anything about one case out of the hundreds she had probably dealt with during her career?

"What else?" Burton asked briskly. "There must be channels to go through. I filled out one of those online forms to request my adoption records, but they still protect the identity of the parents if you were born before 1986, unless they've signed a release, so they'll only give me non-identifying information."

"That might still produce something helpful. Sometimes there is actually trackable information included. Profession, ethnicity, other information that we can use to narrow things down. So if they release something to you, let me know."

"It was a few weeks ago. I don't know how long it will be before they send me a letter."

"It takes a while. But it might be getting close now. And there's a possibility that we can hurry things along if I can find someone who knows someone in the department."

"You can't do that."

"Not officially, no. But sometimes, just talking to the right people can move things along."

Burton nodded without enthusiasm and drained his glass. "Are we about done here?"

Zachary looked at his notepad, considering the information he had so far. Nothing that was going to provide the key to the search. But he could start brainstorming and come up with some suggestions as to where to go next.

"Soon. Have you spent any time driving around town?"

"Why?"

"In case you might recognize something. If you're that drawn to the city, you may recognize landmarks once you get out there. You might be able to find your house just by looking. I might be able to narrow down the neighborhoods to check out. It's not that big of a city."

Burton rotated his cup in a circle of condensation on the table. "I don't have a driver's license."

"It was revoked?"

Burton nodded.

"How did you get here?"

"That's really none of your business, is it?"

Zachary held up his hands. "Okay. No, it's not. We should schedule some time to go out driving together, then."

"Sure. But not today. I'm about done in today."

Zachary pressed the button on his phone to check the time. Burton had said that he wouldn't get up until noon, and he was done in after an hour with Zachary. Because of the emotional toll, or because there was something physically wrong with him? Did he have some illness pushing him to dig into the past before it was too late? Or was he just finished with talking with Zachary?

7

Zachary had carefully selected a few neighborhoods to take Burton to. He figured from the way that Burton had talked that he had grown up in one of the poorer neighborhoods. And it wasn't an apartment building, not if there had been a basement. Add to that the fact that Burton always referred to it as his old house, not his old home or apartment or just where he had lived. He had specified a house.

That didn't eliminate duplexes and fourplexes, unfortunately. There was nothing to indicate whether it had been a single-family dwelling or a larger building. Zachary pictured some of the areas of town, thinking of a young boy walking down the street with his mother trailing behind, of him meeting a man walking a dog, and maybe being allowed to pet the dog. Poor, but not crime-ridden. Somewhere it was safe enough to walk without fear of being shot in a drive-by or mugged on the way to the store or park. It was okay to stop and talk to a stranger or a neighbor who was also out for a walk.

There wasn't much else he could work out from what Burton had told him. Liking loud music and not quiet. Hating fish sticks. Was there a fish and chips shop close by? Or were they from a grocer or corner store? Mac and cheese could be sold almost anywhere, which was probably why Burton hated it. Food deserts existed even in Vermont. Neighborhoods where it was virtually impossible to get fresh food and the residents had to rely on highly processed foods for survival if they were not able to drive far enough away to find grocery stores and produce stands.

Burton's love of dogs and bugs didn't tell Zachary anything about where he had lived. Dogs and bugs were everywhere.

Burton was waiting in the parking lot of the Best Western smoking when Zachary arrived. He put the cigarette out and tossed it to the side. Zachary pulled in and unlocked the doors. Burton climbed in, reeking of cigarette smoke. Zachary cleared his throat a couple of times and nudged buttons to roll the windows down a crack, even though it was still chilly out. He turned the heat on, blowing toward Burton to clear as much of the smoke as possible. Burton didn't apologize, either not noticing or not caring that it bothered his host.

"How are you doing?" Zachary asked in a neutral tone.

"Didn't sleep. Couldn't sleep… thinking about things."

"What things?"

"What we were going to find today. If I'll ever know anything about who I am and where I came from. If coming here was just one big mistake. My parents can't understand why I would come back here. No one understands it."

Zachary cocked his head slightly as he drove. "Have you talked to any other adoptees? I think it's actually pretty common to want to know where you came from. People often search for their biological families. Even people who aren't adopted, but who don't know who their father was, or who grew up apart from siblings." He shrugged with one shoulder. "I don't think it's that hard to understand."

"Maybe it would make more sense if it wasn't about the house. Maybe they'd understand more if it was about finding my biological parents."

"But it isn't?"

Burton shook his head, staring out the window. "Maybe eventually, someday. I can't say I never want to see them again… not without knowing something about what happened. Why I was adopted in the first place. There's a big difference between a parent who put you up for adoption because they couldn't take care of you anymore, and being taken away from your family because you were… being hurt."

"Makes sense," Zachary agreed. "So you think that the house will lead to some clues about what happened? Whether they are… people you want to see again or not?"

"I guess."

Zachary glanced over at Burton following the unenthusiastic reply. He really didn't seem to have any goal beyond finding the house. Finding his family was secondary to seeing the house. Standing where it had all started. Something about the place drew Burton.

"If you had to say what direction it was now, which way would you say to go?"

Burton scowled. "I have no idea." He looked at the street signs and the intersections. "I don't know my way around here. None of this is familiar."

"But if you had to point in one direction, directly at your house, where would it be?"

Burton considered for a moment, then finally pointed ahead and to the right. Zachary projected the path of Burton's finger in his head, thinking of a map of the city and what Burton could be pointing at. He did have a neighborhood in that direction that he had been considering, so he would start with that one.

Did Burton know subconsciously which direction his old house was in? Would a five-year-old have absorbed that information? Could he have a picture of the city in his head and know the approximate placement of various landmarks, the most important of which would have been his home?

It was possible. If he had good visual-spatial memory. He thought he had remembered the name of the city. It was entirely possible that the details of where his house was were stored in his brain somewhere, even if he couldn't access them directly.

"We'll go to Eastside," Zachary suggested, watching Burton's face for any flicker of recognition.

Burton didn't appear to recognize the name of the neighborhood. Not like the name of the city. So maybe it wasn't where he was from. What were the chances that they would just be able to get into the car and find it on their first attempt? Not very good. More than likely, their driving around looking for a familiar neighborhood would be fruitless. Maybe there would be something in his adoption records that would be helpful.

They were both quiet. Zachary drove, watching the road and the traffic and pondering what else Burton might be able to remember, if Zachary only knew how to shake it loose. Everything was stored in there somewhere. Burton stared out the window, his eyes searching for some familiar landmark or feeling.

The landscape around them began to change. They got away from the commercial areas into residentially-zoned neighborhoods. Nice houses at first, but gradually getting down to older, more dilapidated houses. Burton's body language became more attentive. He sat forward and leaned toward his window, trying to catch sight of something that his brain wouldn't give up.

There were not a lot of people out for walks or other business, but there were a few. Zachary watched for someone walking a dog, wondering if it would unlock something for Burton. Anything around them could trigger him, could take him to a memory that would provide the information they needed.

Burton's nose was almost glued to the passenger side window. Like a dog who wanted out or a toddler flattening his face against the glass. Zachary touched the brake, slowing a little, giving Burton a long look at each house that they passed.

"Maybe," Burton muttered, studying them all. "Maybe, this could be the right area. I just… don't know."

"Don't force it," Zachary advised. "Don't try to remember. Just look at the houses, like you never saw them before. The harder you try…"

Burton nodded. He tried to relax in his seat, but that didn't happen. He touched the window with his fingertips, resting them on the glass as he searched.

"Turn up here," Burton said, pointing to the right at the intersection.

Zachary obeyed, but he took a scan around the intersection before turning to identify any marker that might have been familiar to Burton. What would a five-year-old have noticed in that intersection? There was a corner store, not one of the big chains, but a little neighborhood place. Had he gone there for candy? Had his dad picked up beer there? Did his mother buy his mac and cheese there? Zachary turned.

Burton's head swiveled back and forth. He hit his knuckles against the door in frustration. "No. This isn't it. This isn't right."

"What did you see? What was the feeling?"

"Nothing, it just seemed like… I might have been here before. But none of this makes any sense. It's not right."

"That's okay. We didn't expect to find it in ten minutes, did we? Let's just drive around, get a feel for the neighborhood. See what else might feel familiar. Don't worry if we don't find it today. We're just taking a chance."

Burton nodded, but his jaw rippled as he clenched and ground his teeth, clearly upset about it.

"This is going to take time," Zachary reassured him. "You don't have a lot of memories, so we don't have a lot to go on. But that doesn't mean we won't succeed."

"There's no way we're going to find one house in the whole city. Not without knowing anything about it."

"We might. And we'll figure more out along the way. Just keep watching. Notice when things are familiar. Take it slow."

Burton said nothing else for the next half hour. Zachary wound in and out through the residential streets. It didn't look like he had picked the right neighborhood on his first try. But there were others. He hadn't expected to be right the first time.

"Stop. Pull over!"

Zachary slowed, then guided his car into a parking space along the curb. Burton unlocked his door and was out the door before Zachary even came to a complete stop. Burton looked back the way they had come. He jogged back down the sidewalk, looking at the houses. He ran past one, then returned. He stepped out into the street and turned to look back at it from the same vantage point he'd had in the car. He stepped closer, and stopped on the sidewalk, studying it. Zachary let him look at it by himself for a minute and, when he didn't come back to the car, Zachary got out, locked up, and joined Burton on the sidewalk.

"Is that it?" He studied the bungalow. Dirty white with brown trim. Nondescript. Some shrubbery around it. The lawn not yet green.

Burton paced back and forth to the two front corners of the lot, looking at it, studying it from every angle. Zachary pulled out his phone and took a picture of the front of the house.

"Do you want to go around? Check the side and the back?" Zachary suggested.

Burton hesitated. "Do you think it's okay to go onto someone else's property?"

Interesting, Zachary thought, that he was so concerned about doing the right thing. His behavior up until that point suggested that he didn't care about social conventions. He didn't care if Zachary saw him as a drunk.

That was Zachary's problem. He wasn't concerned about getting into the car smelling of smoke, not even making weak excuses about how stressed he was. He slept halfway through the day. But he was worried about going onto someone else's property. Because the house looked like the one he had lived in? Or was he just a naturally law-abiding person and was concerned about trespass?

"If someone comes out, we can explain ourselves," Zachary said. "I don't think you need to worry about it."

"What if… *they're* here?"

"After this many years? I don't think you need to worry. People don't stay that long in one place, especially in an area like this. They come and go every year or two."

"So you don't think they're there?"

Zachary highly doubted it was even the house they were looking for. It had just happened to catch Burton's eye, to trigger some sort of memory. "No."

Burton stepped onto the lawn, then balked again.

"Do you want me to drive you around to the back?"

Burton nodded. "Yeah. Let's go around, instead of cutting through. More respectful."

Zachary led the way back to the car. Burton was hesitant to leave the front of the house, but eventually slid back into the passenger's seat and pulled his door closed.

Zachary had noted the house number in case it wasn't recognizable from the rear. He circled around to the alley and drove slowly down the alley until they reached the house. Zachary got out and Burton followed. The back yard was completely enclosed by a high fence. Too high for Zachary to see over comfortably. Easier for Burton. He peered over for a minute, then shook his head.

"This isn't it."

"That's okay," Zachary assured him.

Burton punched the fence, making Zachary wince. "I thought this was it!"

"What were you thinking and feeling, when you were looking at it?" Zachary made motions for Burton to get back into the car. Burton stayed there, staring at the back of the house.

"I thought… I don't know. I just thought I had succeeded."

"And how did you feel about that? Were you—" Zachary cut himself off before he could finish the question. He didn't want to suggest an emotion that might color Burton's answer. If Zachary suggested that he should be happy or excited, it might completely change Burton's analysis of what he had been feeling.

"I was…" Burton shook his head, a tiny movement, confused. "I felt anxious. Worried." He looked at Zachary, meeting his eyes for maybe the first time since they had met. "Why would I feel that way?"

"It's okay. You felt however you felt. Do you know what you felt anxious or worried about?"

Burton thought about it. "I'm not sure. That it was my house. That I was going to get caught there. I don't understand, though, why it would be a bad thing to find it. I want to find it. Don't I?"

"Consciously, yes. But sometimes we have mixed feelings." Zachary couldn't count all of the times that he had contradictory feelings about a person or situation. It would probably be stranger for him if he only had one feeling. It seemed like different parts of his brain and body were always fighting against each other. He felt a certain kinship with people with multiple personalities. It would feel like a relief to him to be able to assign each set of feelings a different name. To be able to say 'Tom feels like this and Joe feels like that' instead of trying to figure out which feeling was really him, which one won out in a situation.

"I didn't feel good," Burton mused. He looked at Zachary's car. "Are we going back now?"

"We don't have to. We can drive around some more. If you think that we've done all we can in this neighborhood, I have others that we can check out."

Burton nodded. "I think we've seen everything there is to see here. It obviously isn't the right area. Maybe we'll have better luck somewhere else."

Zachary didn't point out that it had been close enough that Burton had thought that he'd found the house. There were good reasons to think that it might still be the right area. They hadn't gone down all of the streets. But he understood Burton didn't want to stay there. They might have better luck somewhere else. Or Burton might just want to rid himself of the oppressive feelings that the 'wrong' house had brought him. They got back into the car. Before driving away, Zachary wrote down the address of the house they had stopped at.

Just in case.

8

There were a couple more houses that Burton had Zachary stop at. Zachary took pictures of each one and wrote down the addresses. It would be up to him to examine the houses and the neighborhoods to identify the similarities among them. Then he would have a better idea of what they were looking for. If Burton actually did remember something and wasn't just on a wild goose chase. Zachary believed from watching his changes in expression that Burton did have memories of his childhood and his childhood home, even if he couldn't access them on demand.

After stopping at one last house, Burton was too agitated and moody to carry on. Smoking and pacing around at the last house hadn't seemed to settle him at all. Zachary was getting anxious from his own client's behavior. It would be pushing his luck to stay with Burton much longer. He was winding himself up for something, and Zachary didn't want to be in the way when he decided to blow.

"I think we've done enough for the day. I'll drop you back at your hotel."

Burton shook his head in irritation. He looked around and pointed to a bar in a low, dark building with several restaurants and retail shops. "I'm going there."

Zachary didn't think that Burton was going there to make inquiries as to whether he had ever lived in the area. He had been several hours without a drink, and he wanted to remedy the fact.

"I'll drive you back to your hotel. You can drink there."

"I don't want to go back to my hotel. I want to drink here."

"Why? You'll be more comfortable at the hotel. And when you're done, you can just take the elevator up to your room and go to sleep."

"I'm not going back there," Burton growled. "I just told you that. I'm not going back there; I'm going to drink *here*."

"Does it have something to do with your memories?"

"What?"

"This place. Does it trigger something? Are you going in to have a look around or ask some questions?"

"No. I'm going in to have a drink. It's the closest place to drink, and I'm not waiting any longer."

"I can have you home in fifteen minutes. Better if you drink at the hotel."

Burton didn't argue any further; he just started walking toward the bar.

"How are you going to get back to the hotel?" Zachary reminded him.

"I can take a cab."

"That will cost money and you'll have to wait around. I can take you now."

Burton swore at him. Zachary didn't chase after him as he headed for the bar. He wasn't going to try to physically coerce Burton back into the car. He was bigger than Zachary and, if he wanted to drink in a bar, there was no reason he couldn't.

Zachary glanced at the lock screen of his phone. He still had a couple of hours before Kenzie would be getting home from the medical examiner's office. He had time to get a few things done before she got home and he would need to turn his attention away from the case and give her some face time. He flipped through his notepad and decided to see what Heather had found him on skip tracing the social worker.

He tapped her icon on his favorites list on the phone. Like Joss, Heather was one of his older sisters. But there were few similarities between the two. She had come back into his life after Tyrrell, looking for Zachary's help on finding the identity of the man who had raped her when she had been a teenager. A cold case that had not been easy to break since the police had destroyed the forensic exam kit collected after her assault.

One of the things that changed in Heather's life after the case was closed was that she needed something to do with her time. She no longer wanted to hide from the world and everything in it, living a quiet, isolated life. She wanted to work, to do something useful, but after decades of not having a job, finding something that would satisfy her was a challenge. So Zachary had taken the opportunity to train her in some of the basics of investigator work. Things that could be done from her computer at home or through discreet phone inquiries. Heather had taken to the job with an unexpected passion and was doing a lot of Zachary's routine investigative work while he pursued the bigger, riskier cases.

She answered the phone after the second ring. "Hey, little brother!"

"Hi, Feathers. I'm just checking to see if you had any luck tracing Aurelia Pace."

"Well, it's an unusual name. That makes it easier."

"If she signed up for services using her name and not just an initial."

"Yeah. Well, most of the time, I couldn't find an Aurelia. So either she used an initial, or she used a husband's name."

"Or a different last name. Got married or divorced."

"Right. All of the usual. But I did find a couple of good prospects."

"Great. Do you want to shoot them my way?"

"They should already be in your inbox. Mailed them to you a few minutes ago."

"Awesome. Thanks for your help, Heather."

"Thank you. I'm having a lot of fun with it."

"Good. Let me know if I push too much stuff onto you. Otherwise, I'm going to assume that you're okay with the amount I'm giving you, and I'm just going to keep giving you more."

"Load me up. I'm fine."

"Okay, remember you asked for it!"

"We should get together sometime soon."

Zachary thought of the last awkward dinner at Mr. Peterson's house, and wasn't sure he wanted a repeat. Lorne Peterson's house was one of the few places he felt welcome and calm, and he didn't want it to become a place he avoided going.

"Uh… yeah. Sometime soon."

"You okay, Zachy?"

Zachary cleared his throat. "Yeah, I'm fine. I'm just not sure that all of us together…"

"Not all of us. You and me. We don't always have to do everything together as a family. I find it easier… if it's just one-on-one. Having everyone in the room is exhausting. It's fine for holidays like Easter and Christmas, but I can't do it all the time."

Zachary breathed out a sigh of relief. "Me neither," he admitted. "Especially with Joss. She's pretty… intense."

"I thought the two of you were getting along together better."

"Better. But she's still… not easy to be around. And putting everyone together, there are just too many things to try to do at the same time."

"I know. Joss is kind of… an acquired taste. Small doses."

Zachary laughed. "Yeah. That's a good way of putting it. Okay. You and me can get together for coffee or a visit. You could come to my apartment if you want."

Heather was the first person he had actually invited there. Kenzie and Mario had taken it upon themselves to come see him and spend time with him at his home but, outside of them, it was the first time he had actually asked someone over. He held his breath for a moment, thinking about it and how it felt, and then released the air, letting it dribble out slowly.

"That would be nice, Zachary. Thanks. I'll see what Grant's schedule is like, and some day when he's busy with other things, I'll come for a visit."

"Okay," Zachary agreed. "That sounds good."

After the call with Heather, he clicked immediately on his inbox before he could be distracted by anything else. There were always so many things trying to pull him away from his work. He found Heather's email and focused in on it. He had set up his mail window so that he couldn't see the subject lines of the various emails, which helped him to avoid being pulled in by the promise of something more interesting or exciting.

Heather's work was neatly summarized and presented. Zachary looked at the time clock on the computer and decided there was still plenty of time to call Aurelia Pace. Hopefully, one of the numbers Heather had dug up would work.

He dialed the first, scripting the call in his head. He wanted to put Aurelia at ease, but still to be able to request information from her that she might not remember or be willing to part with. Adoptees had more rights than they had thirty years ago, but some of the restrictions that the government put on things still made things too difficult for adoptees to get the information they needed.

"Hello?" The phone was answered by a male voice. Maybe a bad sign. He pictured Aurelia Pace as a single woman. There was no reason to think that she couldn't be married, but he pictured her as either single, divorced, or widowed. Men tended to die before their wives. So even if she were married, chances were he had died before her.

"Yes, I'm looking for Aurelia Pace."

"Wrong number."

"Sorry, has there ever been an Aurelia at this number?"

"How would I know? Not a name I've ever heard."

"No one else has called this number looking for her?"

"No. Just you, buddy."

"And can I make sure I dialed properly? Is this…" Zachary recited the number.

"Yeah, that's the number you called. And there's no Aurelia here, okay?"

"Okay. Thanks for your time."

Zachary ended the call. He tried the next number.

"Hello?" A woman's voice this time. Older. Not shaky, but not a young woman's voice. Zachary breathed a sigh of relief. This would be her. This was the right one.

"Is this Aurelia Pace?"

"This is Aurie."

"Ms. Pace, are you the same Aurelia Pace who used to be a social worker?"

There was a pause before she answered. "I don't know of any other Aurelia Pace," she said cautiously.

"So you were a social worker."

"Yes. Who is this?"

"My name is Zachary Goldman. I'm a private investigator and I've been hired by a man you placed for adoption years ago. He's trying to track down some information about his past, and I was hoping that you would be able to fill in a few blanks."

"Information about adoptions is private."

"Yes. I will have you talk to Mr. Burton. He will confirm to you that I'm acting on his behalf. You can release information to him about his own history."

"Well, it isn't that simple. The law prevents me from releasing anything confidential."

"But there are some things that you would not be prevented from telling him. He knows nothing right now, so any information that you could provide to him would be greatly appreciated."

"Biological families have rights too. I can't share information about them."

"But you can share information about my client."

There was a long pause as she considered this. "Maybe," she said finally.

"If you want to set the parameters for the discussion, that's fine. And of course, if something is confidential, you can tell us that. We won't push you to provide information that you're not allowed to share."

"If I even remember anything about this client of yours. Why isn't he going through the proper channels? There's a form he can fill online. It's very easy."

"He has done that and is waiting for the reply. And that will, of course, be non-identifying information."

"Which is the only thing I can provide. I can't tell him anything that identifies who his parents were."

"You can talk about some of the circumstances."

Another pause as she considered this. "Some of them," she conceded finally. "If I can remember. It's been a long time since I was doing adoptive placements. A lot has happened since then, and I don't remember a lot of the cases very clearly."

"All you can do is your best."

She didn't voice any other objections, and Zachary waited for her to fill the silence. People didn't like it when there was too much time without anything being said. They liked to fill it, to have a back-and-forth discussion. Too much silence was uncomfortable.

"I suppose," Aurelia said eventually. "Where are you?"

9

When Kenzie got home from work, Zachary was examining the pictures he had printed off. Kenzie took a quick look at what he was doing.

"Looking at buying a house?" she teased.

"If I was, I think I could do better than these. I hope so."

"So, what are these?" Kenzie reached for one of the photos, pausing with her fingers an inch away, looking at him to see whether he would object. Zachary shrugged, and she picked it up.

"These are houses that provoked a response in my client. Houses that he initially thought might be his childhood home."

"Oh, how interesting." Kenzie lined the houses up in a grid, looking over them. "So you're trying to figure out what was the same between all of the houses. What it is that he sees that makes him think of home."

Zachary nodded. "But it might not be one thing the same between all of them. Some of them might have triggered a response because of… the colors, and others because of the windows. Or the porch or the fence. We don't know that it's one thing among all of them."

"Hmm." Kenzie looked at them, considering Zachary's words. "And we can probably assume that some of them have several things together that made him think of home. The right color and the right windows, but not the right porch."

"Yeah."

"Interesting. What have you got so far?"

Zachary laid his scratchpad down where Kenzie could read it, his face warming as he looked at his messy writing. If she could read any of it, she was doing better than most of his school teachers.

But Kenzie didn't complain about his writing. She looked over the list and then turned her attention back to the pictures, seeing if she could contribute anything to the puzzle's solution.

"Single-family homes. Mostly bungalows," she observed.

Zachary nodded. "I had a pretty good idea going into it that it wouldn't be apartments. He has possible memories of a basement."

Kenzie nodded. "And no duplexes."

Zachary closed his eyes for a moment, trying to center himself. He added this note to the list. He had been aware of it, but had not put it into words.

"What's wrong?" Kenzie asked.

"Nothing. I put it down."

"Yes… but I thought…" Kenzie trailed off.

She was very good at reading him. Too good, sometimes, so that it felt like she could get right into his brain. And there was danger in anyone being able to read his thoughts.

"Color schemes are all dull," Zachary said, pointing to one of the points on his list. "Mostly beiges and browns."

Kenzie looked at the pictures, then back at Zachary. He had been using the skills that he had developed in reading faces and body language to figure out what Burton remembered or was emotionally affected by, so why should it surprise him that Kenzie could do the same with him?

"It's nothing."

"If you don't want to talk about it, okay. But don't act like nothing happened," Kenzie said gently.

Zachary hesitated. He looked at the pictures of the houses. "With multiple-family dwellings, it can be harder to get away with abuse. Neighbors hear through the walls, report… what they might overhear."

Kenzie was still. "Oh. Yes. Hadn't thought about that."

She looked back at the pictures as well. Zachary waited for her to continue that line, to drill down to ask Zachary about his experiences, but she didn't. They were working a case, and maybe she recognized that it wasn't the right time to discuss his demons.

"You have the fences," Kenzie commented. "Lots of chain-link enclosed yards."

Zachary nodded. "Yes. More secure than a wooden fence. Strong, good visibility, easy to lock. There are not many plants. This place probably wasn't landscaped. A few shrubs, maybe, close to the house. But if you want good security, like the fence provides, then you don't want them close to the windows. You don't want people to be able to get access to windows while hidden by shrubbery."

"Just because it wasn't landscaped then, doesn't mean it isn't landscaped now," Kenzie pointed out. "It's been a lot of years since he lived there."

"Yes. Hopefully, that won't stop him from recognizing it when he sees it."

"You're going to need more than just his visual recognition, aren't you? Is that going to be good enough for him? He doesn't want proof that it was where he lived?"

Zachary hadn't thought that far ahead. "I don't know. If he feels an emotional connection, then maybe not. I don't know whether seeing the house is what he wants, or whether he needs to know what happened to him there. I don't think he knows. I don't think he will know until he sees it. He only has one goal right now."

"I guess if he sees it, then you can do a title history to see who has owned it."

"If his family owned it. But they might not have."

Kenzie conceded the point. "It's really interesting. I wonder how he's going to feel when he sees it."

"I asked him how he felt when he saw one of these houses that was close…"

Kenzie raised her eyebrows inquiringly.

"He was anxious and afraid."

"Hmm." Kenzie nodded. "So he's not chasing a happy feeling. Looking for a place where he felt peaceful and contented."

"No, I don't think so." Zachary considered how much to reveal to Kenzie about his client. He owed Burton some degree of confidentiality, of course, but as long as he didn't give Kenzie any identifying information about him, his privacy was assured. "He's not in the best shape emotionally.

Drinks a lot. He says that his adoptive family was very loving, gave him everything he needed, but he went badly off the rails."

"And you think that's because of what happened to him before he was adopted?"

"It's possible. Plenty of kids from loving homes still experiment and get dragged down by addiction, but he's quite a mess. He only has vague memories and feelings about what happened before he was adopted, but his facial expressions and body language… they don't lie. And they say that the memories are not happy ones."

Kenzie nodded, accepting his analysis. "What's your next step?"

"Tomorrow, we're going to meet with the social worker who placed him with his adoptive family. I haven't told him yet, but I've set up a time with her."

"You're meeting her without him?"

"No, I just haven't let him know yet. He's not doing anything while he's here, other than drinking and looking for this house, so he'll be available. But I don't want to tell him too much ahead of time. I don't want to make him any more anxious than he already is."

"You don't think you need to prepare him ahead of time?"

"I think it could send him on a binge, if he isn't already on one. Best not to chance it."

10

The pictures were cleared away. Their dishes from dinner were in the dishwasher. Zachary sat on the couch, staring at his phone screen, swiping at random.

"Everything okay?"

Zachary looked over at Kenzie. "I thought maybe I should touch base with Rhys."

She nodded. "I think it would be a good idea. He has to be wondering how you are, why you haven't been talking to him."

"Vera said she didn't think it would make him worse, if I called."

"How is he doing?"

"He's back to school, but his teachers say he is distracted. Not getting his classwork done. Vera said he's not telling his therapist much. He says everything is fine now."

Kenzie sighed. "Kids. Teenagers are not well-known for sharing their troubles with their parents or caregivers. And when you start with someone who is already non-verbal…"

"Non-speaking," Zachary corrected. "Or mostly."

She looked at him for a minute, then shrugged. "Does he usually talk to his therapist? Or have good communication with him?"

"Vera made it sound like it was less than usual. I didn't ask any details."

Kenzie nodded. "Well, pop him off a message. I don't see what harm it could do, especially if Vera said to go ahead."

Zachary looked back at his phone, shifting back and forth between screens with his thumb, as if he didn't know what to do. He was just concerned about Rhys and didn't want to make things any worse than they already were.

"Just bite the bullet," Kenzie suggested. "But it's up to you. I'm going to take a break. I have some things to catch up on."

She got up and left the room, leaving Zachary to himself. He suspected she didn't have anything to do that she couldn't do sitting beside him, but was leaving the room to give him privacy to work through his problems on his own.

And she was right. That was exactly what he needed. He opened his message app. It was at Rhys's name already. Zachary glanced through the last few words and pictures that he and Rhys had last exchanged. All before the shooting. Nothing since. Rhys had come to him for help, and Zachary had done his best, but had ended up scaring Rhys. Maybe permanently traumatizing him. Could he ever forgive himself for that?

Bite the bullet.

Zachary tapped out a brief message. *Just checking in to see how you are doing.*

He watched the screen for a reply. There was no guarantee that Rhys was looking at his phone or was able to answer him right away. He might be doing chores or be in therapy, though it was pretty late for that. He might be working on homework, unable to concentrate on his classwork during the day. He might have already gone to bed, overwhelmed by the anxiety he'd had since the incident.

Or maybe he didn't want to talk to Zachary. Or was unable to bring himself to reply. He'd had enough problems with communication before, usually choosing to use images and concepts rather than linear language. Ever since his grandfather had been shot.

Like Luke.

Although Luke's injury had been superficial and his grandfather's fatal, it had been similar enough to throw Rhys into flashbacks and cause ongoing issues.

Even though Zachary was staring at the phone screen, he had ceased to see it, and was surprised when the phone vibrated in his hand. He looked down and saw Rhys's reply.

It was a picture Zachary had seen before. The three women in the Salter family. Rhys's grandmother, aunt, and mother. All smiling at the camera. Rhys with them, looking solemn and unhappy.

Rhys usually smiled when he greeted Zachary, but the rest of the time, his face was naturally sad. Mouth turned down. A look of grief in his eyes. He had been through so much in his short lifetime, and it had left a permanent mark.

Zachary's chest hurt, looking at that picture. He knew now what he hadn't known when he'd seen it the first time. The secrets those three women and Rhys's silence had hidden. The ongoing pain and trauma that Rhys suffered as a result. They weren't the happy women he had taken them for the first time he saw that picture. The happy faces were just masks, hiding all of the ugliness underneath. Zachary touched his phone screen as if Rhys might feel it and be comforted.

I'm so sorry, Rhys. I never meant to hurt you.

He felt Rhys's hand around his forearm in the clasp Rhys had given him when he had visited last. Strong and forgiving. Rhys didn't hold it against him. But Zachary did.

Another message came through from Rhys. This time, a picture of Luke. Zachary immediately recognized it as a still taken from a video Rhys had made of Madison and Luke. Madison had been cropped out, only her shoulder still visible.

Zachary knew what Rhys was asking. He wanted to know how Luke—who Rhys knew as Noah—was doing. Had he recovered? What had happened to him?

Zachary wasn't sure how to respond.

Rhys would want to know that Luke was okay, that he hadn't died like Grandpa Clarence, but how would he feel about the fact that Luke was free? He hadn't been charged for his crimes and hadn't paid the price for what he had done to Madison.

The minutes ticked by as he thought about how to word his reply. Another message from Rhys bubbled up under the picture of Luke. A big cartoonish question mark. Zachary sighed.

He's okay. Recovered from the shooting with just a scar.

Rhys sent a thumbs-up.

Zachary breathed a sigh of relief. *How's school?*

Rhys sent back a gif of some celeb shaking his head slowly. Zachary wasn't sure who it was. He didn't watch a lot of TV that might be popular with the younger generation. But he understood the sentiment.

Any way I can help?

As he waited for Rhys's response, Zachary looked again at the picture of Rhys with his family and the picture of Luke. Even though Rhys had told his therapist that everything was fine, he was clearly still caught in the emotional vortex that the shooting had triggered. He was obsessing over what had happened, maybe remembering things that he hadn't been able to recall before. Zachary ran this thumb along the edge of the phone, trying to compose his thoughts in a way that would resonate with Rhys.

I know about flashbacks, he typed finally, though he knew that the language was awkward and someone else would have been able to be more eloquent than he was. *I still have a lot of them myself.*

Rhys posted a series of dots, which Zachary thought meant that he was trying to compose an answer. He waited, watching the screen for the next image or text to appear.

Eventually, a picture of Winnie the Pooh and Christopher Robin was added to the stream.

Even if we're apart, I'll always remember.

Zachary stiffened, alarmed. He quickly thumbed in a response. *Are you thinking about suicide?*

This time, Rhys's response came quickly. A red circle with a slash through it. Zachary took a deep lungful of air, strained.

If things are bad and you need help… it's okay. You remember when you told me to go to the hospital.

Yes.

But that wasn't what Rhys had meant. Zachary studied the picture of Pooh and the words written over it. He looked at the previous couple of exchanges, thinking. The picture wasn't about being apart or saying goodbye. It was the memories. *I'll always remember.* Rhys was thinking about Luke. About his dead grandfather. He couldn't get the images out of his head. Just like Zachary couldn't shake his flashbacks, even after so many years had passed.

It sucks, he typed, *having to remember things that you don't want to.*

Yes.

Have you talked to your therapist about them?

Another big red circle with a slash through it. Zachary had already known the answer when he asked.

He can't help you if you don't tell him.

:-L

Zachary had to look that one up. A quick internet search told him the emoticon signified frustration. A feeling he could understand and relate to. *Do you need a new therapist? Does he listen to you?*

:-L

Grandma would get you a new one if you need one. I can give her some names.

After a minute, Rhys sent a gif of a man raising and lowering opposite hands. *Maybe.*

I'll talk to her. You can still decide.

OK.

Zachary blew out a long breath. He didn't think he'd been holding it, but he felt like it was a long time since he had taken a full breath. He was worried about saying the wrong thing to Rhys and making him feel worse or decide to cut off communication.

Okay. If we find someone you can connect with, maybe he can help you feel better. Work through some of the memories.

There was no response from Rhys.

Sorry again, Zachary messaged. *Really sorry about Luke getting shot and bringing back those memories.*

Rhys sent back a picture of a baby with a scrunched-up expression and the name, *Luke?*

Oh. Noah. He's not going by that anymore.

:-O

Zachary smiled at the expression of surprise. *For the flashbacks, do you know how to anchor?*

Rhys sent a picture of an anchor.

It can help. You focus on your senses. Identify five things that you see, five things you hear, etc. Like I did with you in the car.

Helps U?

Yeah. Sometimes. I'm still working on it. My family tries to help me. Remind me to do it. Kenzie too.

Rhys sent back a picture of Kenzie with a red heart outlining her face.

When they were communicating face-to-face, Rhys always asked after Kenzie with a kissing sound. It never failed to make Zachary blush, however hard he tried not to react.

He turned his face toward Kenzie's bedroom and called out to her. "Kenz? Do you want to say something to Rhys?"

She returned to the living room and sat down, reaching out for Zachary's phone. "Of course. How's he doing?"

"Things are tough. But he's hanging in there."

"Good." Kenzie's eyes flicked up, seeing her picture in the message feed, but she didn't scroll up to see the rest of the conversation. Slouching down into the couch, she tapped out a message. She looked up from the phone after sending it and looked at Zachary. "So you're okay too? Wasn't so bad after all."

"Just had to bite the bullet, like you said. I was worried…" He trailed off. Kenzie already knew what he'd been worried about.

Kenzie looked back down at the phone as Rhys sent her a message back. They exchanged a few more messages, and then Kenzie handed Zachary his phone back. "Yeah, he seems a bit down, but okay."

Zachary nodded. "Sometimes people put on a false front and tell you they're okay when they're not. But Rhys… he's pretty good about not glossing over how he feels."

"Yeah. You know, I think part of it is his communication difficulties. He doesn't have the words to waste like we do. He'd better get the message out as succinctly as he can, because it's so hard for him."

"Yeah, you're probably right." Zachary looked down at the phone and said his goodbyes to Rhys, sensing that he was done with the conversation. *I'll talk to Grandma.*

A dog waved its paw at Zachary. He shut off the screen, turning his full attention back to Kenzie. "Okay. I'm done that. And done work. So I'm all yours."

She slid closer to him and put her arms around him. "Excellent. Just what I wanted."

11

Zachary tried several times to reach Burton, but there was no response to his calls and texts. Either Burton was still passed out, or he had decided he was finished with Zachary. Hopefully, he had made it back to his hotel. Zachary considered going over to check on him and have a talk, but decided that his attention probably wasn't wanted. Burton had made it clear that his alcohol consumption was no one's business but his own and that he would deal with Zachary on his own terms. So if he wanted to reach Zachary, he could be the one to make the next move. If Zachary had to cancel or reschedule the social worker, then he would.

After Kenzie headed off to work, Zachary had an appointment with his own therapist. He took a couple of minutes at the beginning of the session to tell Dr. Boyle about Rhys and to ask her for some recommendations for therapists who would take the time to learn how to communicate with Rhys, and not just assume that he either didn't want to communicate or was not able to.

"He sounds very interesting," Dr. Boyle observed. "He hasn't learned sign language or how to use a communications device? There are so many options; I would think that he would have succeeded in finding something that worked for him."

"He has… it's just kind of unconventional. His mutism seems like it's more than just a problem with speaking, but even putting language together in the usual way. His grandmother says that he does okay with multiple-choice or short-answer questions at school, but he doesn't write in full sentences and he couldn't write an essay or something like that. When he and I are talking, he doesn't type in sentences. It's all… concepts rather than structured sentences."

"Fascinating. I'd love to meet him myself, if you want to include me on the list of recommendations."

Zachary hesitated to add Dr. B's name. "How does that work, when you have two patients who know each other? I mean… with confidentiality and all."

"You would both have complete confidentiality. I wouldn't repeat anything that either of you said to the other."

"But what if… I had concerns about him or something he said, or vice versa. You'd have to bring it up, wouldn't you? Or take some kind of action."

"If you're not comfortable with me counseling both of you, that's fine, Zachary."

"It's just that… well, we both discuss personal stuff sometimes. Anxieties. Mental health stuff. Relationships."

"I don't want to do anything that would make it harder for you to talk with me. That's fine. You have a few names that you can give Rhys. Hopefully, one of them will work out."

Zachary nodded. "Yeah. If he goes all the way down the list and doesn't have any success, maybe then. Because I want him to get the treatment he needs too."

Dr. Boyle nodded. "You're a good man."

"Well," Zachary's face warmed. "I can see myself in him. I can feel his pain."

"Yes." Dr. Boyle gave a little frown. "I am a little concerned, though…"

Zachary's heart thumped harder. He didn't like Dr. Boyle's tone or that frown. "Uh… what?"

"It sounds like the two of you are very close."

"Well… friends, yes."

"You are discussing mental health issues and relationships. That's very intimate to be discussing with a teen."

"He doesn't really have anyone else who understands…"

"Yes, I get that. But you need to be very careful. This kind of situation can lead to inappropriate relationships. You're much older than him and you're discussing very personal issues. You don't want to end up…"

Zachary swallowed. "It isn't that kind of relationship. No. We're not talking about sex." His face grew hot just at the suggestion and he knew he was turning beet red. Would Dr. Boyle think that meant he was lying?

"Not now, maybe. But what would you do if he wanted advice? Or expressed an attraction or made an unexpected advance?"

"I wouldn't get into that kind of relationship with him. I wouldn't."

"Have you thought about how you would react? Because emotional closeness can cross boundaries. If you haven't made plans ahead of time, thought about how to handle it or made sure that you're never in a compromising situation, it can be difficult to make good decisions in the heat of the moment. You know your impulsivity is an issue that often works against you."

"His grandma makes sure that we only meet at the house. She's asked me not to take him out anywhere. For burgers or anything. We only meet when she is there."

Dr. Boyle smiled and nodded. "That's good. That's a good rule to have. I'm glad that she's already anticipated any possible issues."

Zachary nodded. His face was still burning and he didn't try to explain to her that Rhys didn't always follow his grandmother's rules and had shown up at his apartment by himself twice. Just the kind of situation that Vera and Dr. B would want him to avoid. And instead of sending Rhys immediately home, Zachary had made some less-than-optimal choices.

He wouldn't let that happen again. He'd told Rhys that he needed to follow his grandmother's rules. If Rhys ever did that again, Zachary would take him straight home. That was the only proper thing to do.

"All right. Let's move on with your session," Dr. Boyle said. "Our time is short now, but I'm glad to hear how you're helping Rhys out. You have a very compassionate heart."

Zachary shrugged and looked away.

"So, do you have something particular you want to bring up today? Or did you want to let me know how things are going with Kenzie?"

He and Kenzie had gone in for several couples sessions now, and it was getting easier for Zachary to talk about their relationship in front of Kenzie or to deconstruct how things were going when Zachary met with Dr. Boyle alone. Which was good, because the first time they'd done a couples session, the anxiety had been so brutal, he had thought he was going to have a heart attack and die.

"I guess... talking about things with Kenzie works. If you think I need to."

"What do you think?"

Zachary looked down at the carpet where Dr. Boyle's desk met the floor. Talking about their intimate relationship, he needed something to focus on other than Dr. Boyle herself.

"I think... things are pretty good. We're close. But... we still have problems. You know."

"With you dissociating?"

Zachary nodded. He was glad that his face was already red from their discussion about Rhys, so she couldn't see him coloring again. It didn't just embarrass him to talk about his physical relationship with Kenzie. He felt completely inadequate. He should be able to have intimate contact with her without either getting overwhelmed by flashbacks or losing himself and mentally floating away from his body, making Kenzie feel like she was in the room by herself.

Zachary had hoped that after a session or two with Dr. Boyle, things would be fixed. He would be able to go on and carry on a normal relationship with Kenzie. What was even more embarrassing to him was that he had not had problems with dissociation while he'd been married to Bridget. He didn't want Kenzie to think that it was her fault. It was Zachary's problem and had been triggered by an assault that had triggered the emergence of a whole slew of repressed memories.

"I know you're disappointed by that," Dr. Boyle observed.

"I wanted... I hoped that we'd be able to work through things, and I'd be... I'd be normal."

"These issues didn't just develop overnight. I know it seems a little like that, because you weren't having them with Bridget, but they were already there, they were just under the surface."

"Why couldn't they stay there? Or why can't I... repress them again?"

"Even though you want to, repressing them is not healthy. That was the only way you could deal with them when you were younger, but you've grown and developed since then. You have other tools in your toolbox, and you have the ability to work through them instead of just shoving them down."

"So you think it's good that I'm having problems."

"Well… not exactly. But yes, I think it's better for you to be able to talk about the issues and work through them in therapy than not to deal with them. Repressed memories just continue to fester and to pop up here and there as other kinds of problems."

Zachary stared at the carpet, thinking about this.

"Have you ever had an unexplained reaction to something?" Dr. Boyle asked. "You get really angry when someone puts their hand on your shoulder, or you hear a song or smell a scent and feel like something bad is going to happen?"

Zachary nodded. "Yeah. I've had that happen."

"That could be due to repressed memories. Your body and brain have a reason to react to a stimulus like that, but you have no idea what it is. You don't remember what happened to you and don't know why that trigger is there. You may learn to anticipate it, and avoid that trigger to avoid it happening again, but that doesn't mean you've dealt with the memories; you're just avoiding them."

"I have a client who is trying to find where he used to live. He can't remember a lot from that long ago, but I can see him reacting to things when I ask him a question or make a suggestion. I know he's not lying to me about not remembering. He just… can't reach it."

"Exactly. Sometimes things are locked away so tightly it can take years to identify them and work them out."

"So… you think it will take years for me to sort things out with Kenzie? Because I don't think she's going to wait that long."

"No, that's not what I meant. Your memories have surfaced, and that means that we can deal with them. While they were still locked away, we couldn't deal with them, could we?"

"Well, no. Not if I didn't even know they were there."

"And it may take a long time for your client to be able to access his memories. Or it may need… a big trigger to bring them to the surface."

"Like I had."

"Hopefully, not like you had."

"Yeah." Zachary wouldn't wish what he had gone through on anyone. Burton was better off drinking and not remembering. Better if he just went home and quit looking for his past.

12

It was nearly two o'clock before Zachary got a call from Ben Burton. Zachary determined not to ask Burton any questions about where he had been or how much he had drunk the night before. Zachary had enough issues of his own; he didn't need to take on Burton's too.

But he was grateful that he had never become addicted to alcohol. Unlike Tyrrell, who had been an alcoholic before he'd managed to pull himself out of the hole. Or their parents. Joss, too, had dealt with alcohol and drug addiction. Zachary was lucky to have avoided that particular issue. He mostly avoided it due to his meds, but he had remembered how ugly his parents had gotten when they drank, and he didn't want to be like that. Didn't want to be like that with his family, when he had still hoped to have a family of his own. He wouldn't ever want to treat his children the way his parents had treated him and his siblings.

But would he ever have children? It became less and less likely. First getting married to Bridget, who had insisted she never wanted to have children but was now pregnant with twins, and then getting into a relationship with Kenzie that he couldn't seem to stay in mentally. Yes, he could still perform physically, but what woman would want to have children with a man who checked out like that? And if he still had so many emotional problems, what were the chances that she would ever trust him around children?

What if one of them triggered an involuntary response? What if his impulsivity put one of them in danger?

What if he couldn't be a good father?

Burton called at two o'clock. "Driving around looking at houses isn't getting anywhere," he growled without preamble.

"I have an appointment set up with the social worker who placed you, if you can get yourself together for a three o'clock meeting. I was just about to cancel it."

"I'm up. I can get wherever you want."

"We're meeting at a coffee shop," Zachary told him. "She wanted something on neutral ground." In reality, he just didn't want Burton in the bar. He would probably bring a flask with him, but he would have far less alcohol available than he would if they met in the hotel lounge.

"Do you want to pick me up?"

"You can take a cab. Here's the address." Zachary gave it to him slowly, taking extra care to get the numbers in order. He didn't want Burton to have any obstacles in getting there. Zachary wouldn't have to put up with Burton getting into his car reeking of smoke. Hopefully, if Burton had to take some responsibility in getting himself there, he would be sober and more receptive to whatever the social worker might have to say.

Burton muttered something that Zachary didn't hear. Zachary could hear background noises; rubbing and banging and Burton cursing under his breath. Eventually, Burton's voice was in his ear again. "Okay, I've got a pen. Can you give that to me again?"

Zachary got to the coffee shop before the meeting time they had arranged. He looked around for anyone who appeared to be a retired social worker sipping a cup of coffee while waiting for him, and didn't see anyone who fit the bill. There were only a couple of people who were there by themselves, and they were intent on their phones. One had a phone in one hand and a notebook under the other, scribbling occasionally in the notebook. Too young to be the social worker. A student, maybe.

He ordered himself a coffee and sat down at a table where he could watch the door for the other arrivals. The social worker was the next to arrive. A tall woman, mature figure, long graying hair that had probably been done up in a bun when she had been on the job. Now softer around the edges. Someone who was no longer required to see the worst that society had to offer every day. Zachary waved a hand at her.

"Ms. Pace?"

She walked over to him and Zachary stood up to shake her hand. "Aurie. And you must be Mr. Goldman."

"Zachary."

She gave him an appraising look. He remembered the many social workers and other professionals who had dealt with him while he was in foster care. Many different faces, and yet all the same face. The same looks in their eyes as they examined him, coming to conclusions about what kind of a boy he was.

Mostly wrong.

Sometimes horribly accurate.

"Yes. Have a seat. I'm just waiting for my client."

She made a motion to the counter and went over to get herself a pastry and a cup of tea, and returned to sit with him.

They made small talk while waiting for Burton. Awkward, Zachary watching Aurelia Pace break the pastry into bite-sized pieces, getting flakes all over her napkin and the table, occasionally looking at her face, wondering what she must think of him. It was an unusual situation, a private investigator contacting a social worker to ask about one of her old cases. He hoped that they would be able to get something out of it. Something Pace said could lead them to the house or could provide Burton with part of his story.

It was quarter past three by the time Burton pushed through the door and made his way over to the table. He didn't bother to get a cup of coffee at the counter. He slid into one of the free chairs and looked Pace over with interest.

"You're the social worker?"

She put her hand out. "Aurie. Aurelia Pace."

"Aurie," he repeated. "I would have known you as Mrs. Pace? I don't remember you."

Pace withdrew her hand and continued to worry her pastry. "Why don't you tell me who you are?" she said. "We need to establish your identity before I say anything at all."

"Ben Burton. I don't know who I was when you knew me. What my name was before."

She just looked at him. Burton flushed. He reached into his back pocket and worked out a wallet. He removed his driver's license and tossed it across the table to her. "My parents are Elsie and Jack Burton. They live in Colchester. I was about five when I was adopted."

She checked his identification and slid it deliberately back to him. Zachary could see the beginnings of recognition on her face. Zachary remembered seeing Tyrrell for the first time when they had been reunited. Seeing his eyes and knowing him. No matter how he had changed, Zachary knew those eyes. They had been the same when Tyrrell was small. Everything that had happened since the fire had not extinguished that twinkle.

If Pace recognized Burton, then she remembered placing him. Remembered his case and what his history had been.

"Robert," she said finally. "That was your preadoption name."

Burton's jaw worked. His name. Somebody knew his name. Now he knew it too. "Robert what?"

"I told Mr. Goldman that I could only give non-identifying information. I gave you your first name. I can't give you your last."

Burton's eyes were angry, but he kept his temper and didn't even raise his voice. "And they lived here? *I* lived here? In town?"

She nodded.

He relaxed slightly. A confirmation that his memories—or the feelings he'd had—were correct. Confirmation that he wasn't crazy.

"What happened? How did I end up being adopted?"

"Are your parents still living? Your adoptive parents?"

"Yes."

"Then you already know the details from them. Your profile was shown to them. They had been waiting for some time and knew that it was unlikely they could get a child that was any younger unless he was severely handicapped. There were a couple of meetings before placement so they could see whether you all clicked, whether they thought you could all function as a family." She paused, looking at him. "Are they still together?"

Burton nodded. "Yeah. They are."

She smiled slightly. "So many couples end up divorcing. I hoped that it would work out. But you never know."

"Why? Because I was so difficult? My mom said that I was an easy child.

Quiet and well-behaved." He pulled a flask out of his pocket, unscrewed it, and took a few gulps. "I didn't start developing problem behaviors until later."

Burton was putting it all out there. Not pretending to be a mature, well-adjusted man. He was what he was, warts and all.

"Quiet and well-behaved doesn't necessarily mean well-adjusted," Pace said, taking it all in stride. She'd seen humanity at its very worst. She wasn't going to be shocked by a man drinking and being antagonistic. Zachary imagined that a lot of her former charges had ended up self-destructing. He'd seen that in foster care. While there were good homes and kids who managed to rise above their less-than-stellar beginnings, all too often, they just ended up crashing and burning—ending up on the street homeless, addicted, starting a brand-new cycle of abuse. Or obliterating themselves with a gun, razor blade, or some other method.

"But I want to know the other side," Burton said. "I want to know why I was in foster care in the first place. What happened?"

"Your biological parents were unable to take care of you."

"Why?"

She considered the question silently, swirling her tea. "You were apprehended for abuse and neglect," she said finally.

Just as Zachary had expected. But it wasn't much information to go on. No specifics.

"What were they like? My biological parents? Did you meet them?"

"I did not."

"But you knew about them. What did you know about them?"

"They had a dysfunctional relationship. They were unable to care for you."

"That's not telling me anything."

"As I said, I can't say anything that might identify them. They are accorded confidentiality under the law, even though you are an adult now."

"You must be able to tell me something about them. How old were they? What about professions? What part of town did we live in?"

Pace's eyes slid over to Zachary. "She was young. He was not. He worked in a variety of casual labor jobs. She didn't disclose how she earned money, if she did. Probably through illegal means."

Burton considered this information, his expression grim. "And where did they live?"

"Why does that matter?"

"Because I want to see the house. I want to go there."

She shook her head and waved this idea away. "It probably isn't even there anymore."

"Then it won't hurt anything to tell me where it was."

She considered this seriously. She looked at Burton, then looked at Zachary. "I'm sure it's not there anymore."

"Then…?"

She brushed her crumbs into a careful pile, and then off the table onto her napkin, which she laid back down on the table. She was chewing on her lip.

"Peach Tree," she said eventually. "Peach Tree Lane."

A lovely sounding name, but Zachary knew the area it was in. There were no peach trees. Not anymore. He didn't know if there ever had been. Burton's shoulders dipped down in relief. He knew something concrete. He knew a street. Not just the city anymore, but the street that his house had been on. Even if it had been bulldozed and replaced with a condo building or a gas station, at least he could go back there, stand where it had been, close his eyes and imagine himself there.

"What else can you tell us?" Zachary asked.

"There isn't much more to tell. That's it."

Burton shook his head at Zachary. He had what he'd come for. The street his house had been on. He didn't need anything else.

If it had been him, Zachary would have wanted more. Not the details of the abuse, maybe, but something. Something about what he had experienced in those first five years. What had made him the way that he was.

"Why didn't you meet his birth parents?"

Pace shook her head. "It wasn't in the cards."

That was a load of crap. If she'd said that Burton was already in foster care when she had first met him, Zachary might have believed it. But Pace's answer was too vague. Not the kind of thing that would have gone into an official report. There had been a reason she hadn't met his parents. A real reason.

"Why?" Zachary repeated.

"Mr. Goldman, I told you that there were things I would not be able to tell you. I'm sorry that I can't answer all of your questions or tell you the reasons that I can't answer. I'm doing the best I can."

"You were the one who took me to my parents?" Burton changed the subject, returning to an inquiry he already knew the answer to.

"Yes. I drove you to your new home. Handed you over to your parents. They seemed like lovely people. I hope I did not misjudge them."

"No. They were always good." Burton pondered for a moment. "Maybe not prepared to handle a rebellious teenager, but before that… they did everything right. I don't remember having anything to complain about."

She nodded, satisfied. She didn't ask Burton why, if his adoptive parents had been so great, he needed to dig into his past. She hopefully knew, after being in the business, that the one thing didn't necessarily have anything to do with the other.

"Well, I wish you the best of luck, Mr. Burton. I hope you find what you are looking for."

Burton summoned up a smile and nodded at this.

But Zachary was watching Pace's eyes, and he could see that she was holding something back.

She was lying when she said that she hoped he found what he was looking for.

What she really wanted was for him to forget it all and go home.

13

Peach Tree Lane," Burton said exultantly when they had said goodbye to Aurelia Pace. "Peach Tree Lane." He said it like he could taste the words, and they were just as sweet as the name. Did they resonate with him? Did he remember that was where he had lived as a child? Five was not too young to teach a child his address in case he was ever separated from his parents or something happened to one of them.

"Yes," Zachary agreed. He tried to picture it in his mind. He hadn't spent a lot of time in that area, but he knew the neighborhood generally. He frowned, trying to remember any areas that had been developed in the last few years. Despite what Pace had said, he couldn't remember any redevelopment.

That didn't mean that a house hadn't been bulldozed and replaced with a duplex or a fourplex. Just that there hadn't been any major revitalization. Pace knew more of the story than she was willing to admit, so she might know exactly what had happened to the house.

Zachary couldn't help being suspicious. Maybe it was just because he'd been lied to by social workers in the past. They had told him things, promised him things, just to keep him quiet.

"Today, we celebrate," Burton said cheerfully, pulling out his flask and downing the rest of the contents. "Come with me. Have a drink on me. You can do it just this once."

Zachary shook his head. He found it particularly unpleasant when people pressured him to drink. Burton was an alcoholic and naturally wanted to celebrate by drinking. He didn't mean it to be offensive. People who drank so much seemed to think that *not drinking* was somehow a slap in the face, a holier-than-thou attitude that they needed to fight back against.

Zachary didn't care if Burton wanted to drink. He could spend the night drinking yet again, and not wake up until noon or two o'clock. But Zachary had no interest in joining his binge.

"I have other work to do tonight," he said. "You'll have to do the celebrating on your own."

He was surprised that Burton didn't want to head over to the house immediately. He would have thought with how eager the man was to find his childhood home that he would want to waste no time in getting there. But he wanted to celebrate first, putting it off another day—what a waste of time.

"I'll drive you back to your hotel, and then I need to get back to work."

Burton waved his offer aside. "You don't need to do that. I'm not a cripple. I can get around."

"It's not a problem to drop you off."

"No. I'll see you tomorrow. We'll go to Peach Tree Lane together, right? You'll go with me?"

"Are you sure you don't want to see it by yourself? You want an outsider there?"

"I..." Burton rubbed his forehead, frowning. "I don't know if I could... go there myself. I mean, physically, sure, I can take a cab. But... I feel like you understand this quest, and how important it is for me. So... is that okay? Will you come?"

Zachary nodded. "Of course. Touch base tomorrow and let me know when."

Zachary looked around, unsure where he was. The walls around him seemed familiar, and yet not familiar at the same time. He stood up and walked around, looking at the hallways and decor, looking in classroom doors, walking down up the main stairs to the dorm rooms, before it finally occurred to him that he was at Bonnie Brown.

He'd spent a lot of time there while he was in foster care, so he didn't know why he hadn't recognized it immediately. He'd been in and out of Bonnie Brown regularly, especially every year around Christmas, when his anxiety and depression made it too difficult for any foster family to manage him. And there were other times when he had to be moved, but they didn't have a family lined up for him yet, and he'd find himself in Bonnie Brown again.

It was a pretty dismal place, especially to an outsider but, for Zachary, it had represented stability. A predictable routine, strict rules that he knew, and familiar halls never adorned with Christmas candles or lights or other fire hazards.

Zachary spun in a slow circle, looking around. It had been decades since he had been there, yet it looked exactly the same.

A matron walked toward him, two children with her. Zachary looked down at them curiously. Two boys. Dark hair and eyes and pale skin. They were twins. Younger than most of the kids at Bonnie Brown, but they did occasionally house younger children, especially if they were prone to violence or self-harm.

"You can only take one," the matron told him.

Zachary looked at the two boys, not understanding. Take one? "You can't separate them," he countered. "They're twins."

Though, of course, they had separated him from his siblings. And even though they had promised to keep them in sibling groups, they had broken up Joss and Heather within a year. Tyrell and the younger children had stayed together longer. But just because social services said they would try to keep brothers and sisters together, that didn't mean that they did.

Twins, though? They should let twins stay together.

"You can only save one of them," the matron said solemnly. She looked down at the two boys, a hand on the shoulder of each. Waiting for Zachary to make his choice.

"Save one? Why? Why can't they both be saved?"

"Which will it be? This one?" She raised one boy's face up with a finger under his chin. "Or this one?" She showed him the other.

"No, no. We have to keep them together."

"They cannot both survive."

Zachary tried to reach out to take both boys from her. He was there. He could help both of them. He didn't need to listen to her.

But he found himself grasping at empty air. He pushed his hands forward farther, trying to reach them, but he could no longer see them and couldn't feel them. He stretched his arms out and windmilled them around, looking for the lost boys.

"No! No, wait!"

"Zachary."

There was a hand on his arm, trying to hold him back. Zachary shook it loose, still trying to feel for the twin boys. He had screwed up. She had told him that he had to choose one of them, and then when he'd refused, he'd lost both of them. He could have saved one and he tried to take back his wrong choice.

"I will, I will, just let me!"

But he couldn't see them or feel them and he was no longer at Bonnie Brown. Zachary blinked, trying to see around him. He was enveloped by darkness. Had the power gone out? Where was he?

"Zachary." A light turned on suddenly, power apparently restored. Zachary covered his eyes. They teared up and he tried to blink to get them used to the brightness.

He looked around him in confusion. At first, he didn't recognize Kenzie's bedroom. Then he did, but it didn't make any sense. How had he gotten from Bonnie Brown to Kenzie's house? He continued to reach out, looking for the boys in the now-illuminated room. They weren't hiding in the shadows. They weren't under the blankets or pillows.

He suddenly felt bereft, as he had when he had first been taken away from his family. Longing to hold his brothers and sisters in his arms. To comfort and be comforted. To cuddle them close and hum a lullaby until they all felt safe again.

"Zachary." Kenzie's hand was on his arm again, and this time Zachary didn't shake it off. He covered his face, eyes welling up with tears.

Why hadn't he saved them? Why hadn't he been able to save one of the children?

Even as he gradually understood that it had been a dream, Zachary's heart still ached. It was as if he had lost everyone all over again. He turned toward Kenzie and hugged her close.

"No," he murmured. "No, no, no."

"It's okay. It was just a dream. You're okay."

"It was... but it wasn't..." Zachary sniffled. "Why couldn't I save them?"

"It was just a dream. You didn't do anything wrong. It's not real."

"No. My family... everyone... why couldn't I save them?"

"You did." She squeezed him and rubbed his back. "You did, you saved all of them."

"No."

"Yes. You did. They're all okay. Nobody else got hurt. Okay? You're okay. They're okay. It was just a dream."

"They're okay," Zachary breathed.

"It was just a dream. I know it can feel real. But it was just a dream."

Zachary dragged in a couple of deep breaths, trying to calm himself. He kept repeating Kenzie's words. It had just been a nightmare. A disturbing dream, but just a dream. The feelings were not real.

"I tried," he murmured.

"They're okay, Zachary." Kenzie nuzzled his neck and kissed him. "You're okay. It's all over."

Zachary shuddered. He remembered the eyes of the twins, though the clarity of the dream was starting to leave him now. The deep, dark, sad eyes. He had wanted to save them. He had thought that he could save them both. And they had slipped away from his fingers.

"Do you think it would be okay...?"

"What?"

Zachary breathed in through his nose and blew his breath out in a long stream between pursed lips. "Do you think it would be okay if I called Tyrrell?"

"It's the middle of the night, Zachary. Call him in the morning."

Zachary closed his eyes. He could just go back to sleep. He would fall asleep for a couple more hours, and then when it was a decent hour, he would call Tyrrell just to chat and make sure he was okay.

He leaned back. Kenzie lay back down with him, cuddling up close to him, kissing him on the forehead and cheek and stroking his hair. "Better? Okay now?"

Zachary breathed slowly. "You can shut the light off."

She moved away from him for a moment to switch off the lamp, then lay against him, holding him. In a few minutes, her breath had lengthened out and he knew she was asleep once more.

He tried to match his breathing with hers, convinced that if he could mimic a calm, sleeping rhythm, he would be able to fall back asleep just like she had. But he knew better. He'd tried that trick a hundred times, and it had never worked.

He waited a few more minutes, making sure that Kenzie was deep asleep, and then he slid out of bed.

"Hello? Zachary?"

"Hi, T."

"Is everything okay? What time is it?"

He could hear Tyrrell moving around, sitting up and checking the time.

"Sorry. Kenzie said I shouldn't call."

"No, it's okay, Zach. Of course you can call, any time. I've told you that before. Day or night, it's okay."

"I couldn't get back to sleep."

"Yeah? What happened?"

"Nothing. Just a dream."

"What about?"

Tyrrell knew not to ask whether the nightmare had been about the fire. They both still dreamt about it, but Tyrrell bringing it up might trigger a flashback for Zachary.

"About… I don't know. I was at Bonnie Brown."

"Yeah?"

"And there was… there were twin boys, and they told me I could only save one of them."

"Save them from what?"

"I don't know. I just know I had to choose."

"What did you do?"

"I tried to save them both."

Tyrrell chuckled. "Of course you did."

Zachary had to laugh at it himself. It was, after all, typical Zachary. Immediately looking for a way out when he faced a rule he didn't want to follow.

"Then you couldn't get back to sleep."

"Yeah. Kenzie's gone back to sleep and I don't want to wake her up again tossing and turning."

"So does that mean you're up for the day? Or are you going to try the couch?"

"Probably up for the day."

"You're crazy, man. I would die without sleep."

"Not just one night. And I did sleep a couple of hours."

"But I know you don't sleep the rest of the time either. There's a disease where a person can't sleep, and it eventually kills you. You should be dead ten times over by now."

"I usually sleep. A couple hours, anyway."

"Not enough for me."

"I guess I should let you go back to sleep again. I just wanted to hear your voice."

"Hang out with me for a couple more minutes. I want to make sure you're okay."

"I am."

"So, dreaming about these boys, is that because of a case you're working on right now?"

Zachary considered. "Yeah, maybe," he said. "I don't really know if that's what triggered it. I have a client who's looking for the house he grew up in. No twin brother, though."

"Looking for his house?"

"Yeah. He was adopted, and he remembered that this is where he used to live. He wants to see his house again."

"Huh. Well, why not?"

"Would you go back? If you could?"

"I don't know. I did my best to put that behind me."

Zachary wondered why he never had. He had suppressed other things. Why did he have to keep reliving the fire?

"Tell me about your kids," Zachary suggested.

Tyrrell's voice was warm as he talked about his kids for a few minutes, telling Zachary about the last time they had visited and what they were each doing in their lives.

"You miss them," Zachary said.

"Of course I do. I see them whenever I can."

Zachary didn't say anything. He couldn't ask Tyrrell if he would ever choose between his children.

It had just been a dream.

It wasn't about Tyrrell, or his kids, or Burton. It hadn't been about Zachary missing his siblings or growing up without them. It wasn't about returning to Bonnie Brown.

It was just a dream.

"Good thing none of us were twins," Tyrrell commented.

Zachary thought about how difficult it had been for his mother, having so many children so close together. She had never dealt with it well. Zachary could remember the newborns. Tyrrell, Vinny, Mindy. How amazing it had been to look at the new lives that his parents had brought into the world. The overwhelming feeling of potential and of his love for them.

Maybe they, as kids, had tried to make up for the lack of love that their parents showed.

For his mother, another baby was just another problem. More trouble. More tears. Another mouth to feed. She would be in bed for the first few weeks. Zachary had thought this normal, and it wasn't until he was an adult that he realized it wasn't. Mothers didn't just hand over their newborns and take to their beds for weeks after birth. But it had been normal in his family, and Zachary and the older girls had taken the babies and cared for them the best they could, rotating through the duties of feeding and changing and trying to keep the little ones quiet so that their mother could sleep, until she finally got out of bed and started to see to her responsibilities again.

And there was something else niggling at the back of his mind, but he couldn't think of what it was. He couldn't quite seem to reach it. Like an itch in the middle of his back.

"Tyrrell?"

There was no response on the other end of the phone. Zachary sat down on the couch. He readjusted the pillows and pulled a blanket over him and lay partly reclined, listening to Tyrrell breathing.

14

Kenzie rubbed her eyes and ran her fingers through her mussy hair, looking at Zachary.

"Where were you? I woke up and you were gone."

"Just here. I didn't want to keep you awake."

"You should stay. You don't have to leave if you're having trouble sleeping."

"You're working today. You needed to get your sleep."

"Well, so do you."

"Not as much. And if I need to stop and take a nap in the middle of the day, I can."

"And when is the last time you did that?"

Zachary didn't answer. If Kenzie thought about it, she knew the answer to the question. He had done little but sleep after the assault. He would get up late in the morning, try to do some work, and fall asleep in the middle of it. His brain just shut down, not letting him function. It had taken some pretty intense work with Dr. Boyle before he'd been able to start to regulate his sleep schedule again. As regular as it could be.

He preferred not being able to sleep to sleeping all the time.

"Do you want coffee, or are you going to shower first?" he asked Kenzie.

Kenzie yawned and considered. "I think I'd better have the coffee first, or I'm going to fall asleep in the shower. You want one?"

Zachary passed her his mug. "Yes, please."

"How many have you had?"

Zachary looked at the mug in her hand, considering. "I think… two."

"You need something other than coffee for breakfast."

"A granola bar?" Zachary suggested.

He knew the sugary granola bars weren't the healthiest choice. But he was usually too nauseated to eat in the morning. Kenzie had tried enough different breakfast possibilities on him to come up with a limited list of acceptable choices, one of which was chocolate chip granola bars.

So she nodded without arguing about it and went into the kitchen.

"Are you feeling okay this morning?" she asked when she returned and they were both sitting down with their mugs. "That nightmare really seemed to bother you."

"Yeah." The horror and grief of the nightmare had faded over the hours that he'd been up, puttering away at the pile of computer work and billings that were always piling up. "It's fine now. I'm not sure why it bothered me so much."

"It wasn't… a dream about Archuro this time?"

"No." Zachary described the dream to her. She listened with a frown.

"Huh. I wonder what triggered that."

"Current case, I think, but I don't know about the part about choosing between twins."

"Oh." Kenzie took a sip of her coffee.

Zachary frowned. "What?"

"Twins. I can only think of one reason you'd be thinking about twins right now."

Zachary analyzed the expression on her face. She wasn't happy about it. Few things would put that expression on her face other than Bridget.

Bridget was expecting twins. Or at least, that was what Zachary assumed from Gordon's mention of "the babies" rather than "the baby." Hopefully, "the babies" only meant twins, and not triplets or more. He couldn't imagine Bridget, who had steadfastly refused to consider having children when she and Zachary were married, agreeing to carry more than two babies to term. It must have taken some convincing for Gordon to persuade her to keep twins.

"I hadn't even made that connection," he told Kenzie.

"Are you worrying about her having twins?"

"Yes. I didn't think it was keeping me up at nights, but... it's hard to get it out of my mind."

"You think she can't handle it?"

Zachary shook his head, trying to put it into words. "Well... what do you think?"

"She's not exactly the most stable person."

"Kenzie..." he protested.

"She's fixated on you. She says she wants you to leave her alone, blows up if she even happens to see you somewhere, and pops back into your life acting like she's concerned about you or because she wants a favor."

"She's just... we were together for a long time and it was a very emotional relationship. And I made a lot of mistakes; she's right about that." It wasn't a new argument. And it was something probably best left for their next session with Dr. Boyle.

"Well, maybe having twins will take her focus off of you. She'll be distracted by other things."

Zachary nodded. "Yeah. Maybe it will be good for her."

But he still worried. How was Bridget going to manage it? He couldn't help returning to his thoughts the night before of how his mother had been after she gave birth, and how impossible it would have been for her to handle twins. Bridget had sophisticated tastes. She liked the company of adults, attending events and going to museums and fundraisers. She didn't even like children, as far as Zachary could tell. He'd been the one in the relationship who was baby hungry, who'd been happy when she had a positive pregnancy test.

Only the test had been wrong.

And that had been the beginning of the end of their marriage. Not just the revelation that she had cancer, but the fact that he had been happy about the possibility of a baby, and she had unilaterally made the decision to terminate.

"Gordon has money," Kenzie said, her eyes on Zachary's face. "They can afford all of the nannies and maids they need."

"Yeah." Zachary crumbled the granola bar into the bowl that Kenzie had given it to him in. "She'll have lots of help."

15

Burton was up earlier than usual, surprising Zachary by calling him before noon.

"Are you free? What time could we go to see the house?" he demanded.

"I'm pretty open today. But remember, Ms. Pace said that it might not be there. She thought it might have been redeveloped."

Burton snorted. "That was just so I wouldn't go look. I don't know why she didn't want me to go. I don't care what anyone says about it, I'm going to go back."

"Okay. You could be ready in an hour?"

"Yeah. I'm ready any time."

"All right. I'll give you a call when I get there."

But as it turned out, he didn't need to call Burton when he got to the hotel. Burton was already outside the Best Western in the parking lot, chain-smoking. He tossed his cigarette aside when he saw Zachary, and climbed into the car, immediately filling it with the smell of cigarette smoke. Zachary rolled the windows down farther than he had on the previous occasion, glad that he was wearing a jacket and that it was warmer than it had been recently. Burton made no comment about the windows and made no apology for the cloud of smoke that clung to him.

Zachary had checked to make sure he knew where Peach Tree Lane was before leaving his apartment, and also had his phone in its dash mount with the maps app on display in case he had any trouble finding it.

"I can't believe I'm finally going to see it," Burton said, sitting forward in his seat and staring out the window like it might come into sight at any minute. "You must think I'm crazy for being so attached to a place I can't even remember. But… I have to see it. That's all I can say. I really, really need to."

Zachary nodded. "I actually don't think it's that strange. Why do people build monuments? Some places are important in our lives. Sometimes, we just need to stand where our ancestors stood. Or where we came from."

Burton nodded. For a while, he just watched out the window. He broke his gaze to look over at Zachary. "Thanks for agreeing to come with me. I know I could have just taken a cab, but I… could use your support. I didn't want to do this alone."

It was too bad that he hadn't brought his parents or a friend along with him. Zachary felt like a poor substitute for the emotional support that Burton needed. But maybe he had burned too many bridges with his previous behavior.

"We're getting close now," Zachary said, pulling off of the main road into the development. He glanced around. "You might start to recognize some of the landmarks in this area. I don't know what they looked like twenty or thirty years ago, but a lot of these places look like they've been standing for a good while."

Burton nodded. He didn't say what he recognized, if anything. His face was very pale, a stark contrast to his hair and eyes.

Zachary slowed, looking at the street signs and at the crossroads marked on the GPS map. Two more blocks. They seemed interminably long. Much longer, he was sure, for Burton, who was sitting so far forward on his seat that Zachary worried what would happen to him if they were in an accident.

"Just coming up to it now," he warned.

At the next intersection, he turned onto Peach Tree Lane. Burton rolled his window down all the way and hung out the window like a dog, looking at each of the houses with ravenous eyes.

Zachary slowed the car to a crawl. He didn't want to be responsible for Burton getting hurt if he suddenly decided to jump out of the car, or be unable to stop the instant Burton saw what he was looking for.

"Is this it? Is this it?" Burton called out, gesturing.

Zachary hit the brakes. Burton jumped out. He looked at the house they had stopped at.

Chain-link fence. Bungalow. It hadn't been replaced with a duplex. Nor had it been knocked down and replaced with a new single-family dwelling. The structure was clearly more than thirty years old.

It was run down. Faint blue paint, cracked and peeling. A couple of windowpanes broken and taped over with cardboard. The front lawn was brown and probably wouldn't grow unless it were reseeded. There were no peach trees ready to bloom. In the front yard, there were a couple of old, rusted tricycles. A family lived there. Or had lived there at some point.

Burton stood on the sidewalk outside the yard, looking in.

"Is this it?" Zachary asked.

Burton didn't answer. Zachary took a picture of the house, then took a couple of pictures of the corners of the yard.

"Do you want to look at the back or ask if you can go inside?"

Burton looked back at him with wide eyes. Zachary gave him time to think it through. He knew it had to be pretty difficult for Burton to work through. If Zachary had been able to go back to his home, or had even gone back to the lot where it had once stood, it would have been impossible for him to talk about it or do anything. Not for a long time.

Zachary looked around the neighborhood. It was the type of area he had envisioned. Low income, an older area. Not quite a slum. There were people in yards or on the sidewalk. Not behind closed doors, afraid of gangs.

People were watching them. Neighbors watching to see what was going on. Curious about the strangers staring at a random house along the street. Debt collectors? Cops? Salesmen? Missionaries? They didn't quite fit any of the usual scenarios.

Eventually, a man came along the sidewalk to talk to them. Taller than Zachary but shorter than Burton. Lots of tattoos, piercings, and a straggly beard. He was heavyset. Someone who sat in front of the TV a lot, or maybe on a motorbike or driving a truck or bus.

"Help you, guys?" he challenged.

Zachary gave Burton a few seconds to explain and, when he didn't, but kept staring at the house, Zachary filled the biker dude in.

"My friend used to live here. He wanted to see it again. He just needs... some time to process it."

The man's eyes narrowed, thinking about this. He shook his head. "Lived here when? What's the problem?"

"When he was a child. Very young. He's been trying to find it for some time. To reconnect with his heritage."

The biker looked around, his bushy brows pushed together. "Reconnect with his heritage? What kind of crap is that? What's the point in that? Seeing the house he lived in? It's not like a foreign country or different culture. It's white trash growing up in a white trash neighborhood."

"No, this isn't what I grew up in," Burton said. He looked around him, taking in the rest of the neighborhood for the first time. "This is nothing like what I grew up in."

The man gave a short laugh. "Well, good news for you. Congratulations. Don't know why anyone would want to come back to a trash place like this."

Burton put his hand down on the chain-link fence and looked at it, like his hand was something alien. Did he remember the fence from another perspective? How tall it had been when he had been four or five years old? Was he remembering his little-boy hand grasping the links of the fence, trapped like an animal behind it? Burton stared, mesmerized.

"You guys should move along," the biker advised. "You've seen what you came for. So get out of here. Go back to your fancy houses and leave us alone."

Zachary bit back a sharp retort. It wasn't like they were hurting anything, standing there looking at the house. But he'd dealt with guys like this before. It would be very easy to trigger a negative reaction, and Zachary had no desire to end up in some kind of physical altercation with the stranger. He was the one who was off of his own turf. The police would not be sympathetic to someone who had trespassed on the hospitality of another neighborhood and stirred up trouble.

"If you could give him just a few more minutes," Zachary said. "I know it doesn't seem like much, but this is the only piece of his past that he has. He just needs a few minutes."

"Well… wrap it up quick. I don't want to have to warn you again." The biker gave a curt nod, and left them alone again.

Zachary breathed out slowly. He studied Burton, wondering how long it would be before he could suggest moving on.

"Do you want me to take a picture of you here?" he suggested.

Burton looked at him, eyes hollow. "What do you think happened?" he asked.

Zachary raised his brows. "I don't know what happened. Do you… remember something? Have an idea?"

"No," Burton growled, as if Zachary had been pestering him about it. "I don't remember."

"You have… a bad feeling about it?"

Burton nodded jerkily.

"Do you want to go around the back? Talk to the owner?"

"They don't live here anymore. Tell me they don't live here anymore."

"I wouldn't expect so. People in neighborhoods like this… they don't stay for decades. A year or two maybe. I'm sure your birth parents don't still live here. Do you want me to make inquiries? We shouldn't stay too long; I don't want to cause any trouble."

"What would you say?"

"What do you want me to say? Do you want me to tell them who you are and to see if you can go inside? Or do you want me just to get some general background? How long they've been here, and if they know who owned it before they did?"

"I don't know."

"Do you want to go in?"

"No. I don't think so."

"Okay. Why don't you just wait here, then, and I'll go see if there is anybody home?"

Burton nodded jerkily.

Zachary breathed slowly and evenly. While Burton's reaction made him anxious, it wasn't like it was his own house. It wasn't part of his past. He could do what he had set out to do, helping Burton to find what he needed —just inquiring for a client. He pushed back the catch for the gate and let himself into the yard. He closed the gate behind him and made sure the latch caught. If they had a dog or a child, they wouldn't be thanking him for letting it out of the yard.

He walked up the broken sidewalk blocks to the door and knocked politely. A woman opened the door. She had dark hair and eyes and was around Zachary's age, some fine lines on her face, especially around the eyes. She hunched her shoulders, looking at him fiercely.

"Who are you? What do you want here?"

"I'm just helping out a friend, ma'am." It wasn't the time to be announcing that he was a private investigator. "He used to live in this house a long time ago."

Her eyes went to Burton, still standing outside of the yard, then back to Zachary. "So what? Why do I care about that?"

"I just wondered how long you've lived here. If you know any of the history of the house?"

"The history?" She shook her head, scowling. "What would I know about the history of a place like this? I live here. My son lives here. His children. We don't know anything about the house."

"I understand. Have you lived here long?"

"What does it matter? A few years, that's all."

"Do you know who lived here before you did? The previous owners?"

"Same owners, probably," she told him. "I don't own this pile of sticks. I just rent."

"Oh, of course. Sorry. And the owners haven't changed?"

"I told you I don't know. I only live here. I rent. I don't ask anyone questions."

Zachary nodded.

The woman looked past him again. Zachary heard a squeak and, turning around, he saw Burton coming in through the gate. He left it ajar and walked up to join Zachary.

"I told him, I don't know anything," the woman said to Burton, raising her voice. "You call the owners."

"Could I see inside?" Burton asked, his voice gravelly like he was hung over again. "Could I just take a minute or two to look around? Then we won't bother you anymore. I'm sorry about all of this. I just need to see it."

"You don't need to see anything." She motioned to him. "You've seen the outside. You don't need to hang around here and you don't need to see inside."

"Just for a minute," Burton begged. "Please."

"I don't know who you are. I'm going to call the police."

"We're not doing anything wrong," Zachary pointed out.

"I could pay you," Burton offered, taking another step forward, crowding so much that Zachary was forced to take a step back, away from the door.

He was going to tell Burton that they should go before the woman decided to make trouble for them, but the woman was looking at Burton, her eyes narrow and suspicious, and was no longer trying to shoo him away.

"How much money?"

Burton looked at Zachary. Zachary wasn't sure what to offer. What was an appropriate amount to pay someone for a look around the inside of their house? He'd never had the opportunity to ask before, despite all of his private investigation experience.

Burton pulled out his wallet and looked in it. He tweezed out a wad of bills between finger and thumb and held it toward the woman. She reached out eagerly to take it, but at the last moment, he pulled back, keeping it away from her. "Let me in first."

16

And just like that, they were into the house. No police were called. The woman allowed them both to enter and then closed the door behind them. The windows were covered with blinds and, with the door closed, the interior of the house was dim. The low wattage bulbs were not up to the task of lighting it properly. Many of them were still turned off or were burned out. Zachary could understand if it had been the middle of summer and they were trying to keep the house cool but, in the cool spring weather, it felt dismal and oppressive.

Burton looked around, his eyes wide. Zachary tried to imagine what he was feeling and thinking as he looked around. How similar did it look to what it had been thirty years ago? Probably a different paint color and carpet. Different furniture. But the bones of the house were still the same. Burton walked around the main floor, looking at the living room, kitchen, and bedrooms. He poked his head into the bathroom but didn't go inside.

"Do you remember which room was yours?" Zachary asked, when he walked around each of the smaller bedrooms.

Burton shook his head and brushed past Zachary like he was an irritating child.

Zachary followed him back out to the kitchen and to another door. The door to the mudroom and back door, Zachary assumed. And to the basement. Burton opened the door and stood at the top of the stairs, facing the back door. Zachary waited, thinking that he would probably step out into the backyard, where he had undoubtedly played when he was a child. Maybe there would be things back there that were familiar to him.

But Burton didn't step out the back door. He turned his body slowly and looked down the stairs.

It was a narrow stairway. Not well-lit. To a child, it had probably been scary. Though maybe his parents had installed brighter bulbs and the walls had been freshly painted an ivory or cream color instead of the odd beige and brown that decorated them now. Beige on the top and brown on the bottom like wainscoting.

Burton looked back at Zachary, wide-eyed like the child he would have been back then. *Would you go down with me?*

Zachary took a few steps into the back entryway so that he was close behind Burton.

"Thanks," Burton murmured.

They both stood there for a moment, looking down the stairs, while Burton worked up the courage to go down the dark stairway into the unknown.

Then he started walking like it was perfectly natural and there was nothing to be afraid of. Because of course, there wasn't. Even if it had been a frightening place full of imaginary monsters and too real spiders when he had been a small boy, there was nothing that posed any threat to him as an adult. Zachary followed him down.

Neither had to hold on to the handrail as a five-year-old boy might have done, clinging to it all the way down and taking one uncertain step at a time.

Zachary tried to shake off the feeling that there were ghosts there, specters of the past. Of course people had lived there, had come and had gone, Burton among them. But there was nothing sinister about that.

They got to the bottom of the stairs. There was a doorway right in front of them, one on the same wall as they turned into the basement hallway, and then a closed door at the end of the hall when they turned the corner. Burton paid little attention to the first two rooms. Zachary glanced in as they walked by. A combination bathroom and laundry room, followed by a storage room with shelves lining the walls and boxes stacked high.

They looked at the third door. Closed. Zachary waited for Burton to either decide he didn't feel like going any farther or to open the door. Eventually, Burton reached out and touched the door. Not the doorknob, just the door itself, as if he didn't quite believe that what he was seeing was real.

"Are you okay?" Zachary asked quietly, wondering if he was having flashbacks. Did he remember this place, or was he so tentative because he didn't? Maybe none of it seemed familiar and he was disappointed.

Burton turned his head slightly to look over his shoulder at Zachary. In the dim light of the basement hallway, his face looked skeletal. Zachary tried to look relaxed and confident. Like any normal adult would be. There wasn't any reason for him to have second thoughts about the basement. He was a grown-up and he had no history there. No bad memories. Whatever had happened to Burton there, the abuse and the neglect, it hadn't happened to Zachary. He had his own memories, some of them accessible, and some of them not.

Eventually, Burton lowered his hand and grasped the doorknob. He turned it.

"It's unlocked," he said, surprise in his voice.

"Do you want to go in?"

Burton pushed the door open and let it go. It was dark on the other side. He reached around the doorframe, grasping for a light switch.

He apparently found one, and in a moment a couple of bare bulbs in the beams above them came on, filling the space with more dim light.

Zachary looked around. It was furnished as a den or entertainment room. A ratty old couch that should have been taken to the city dump. A TV that had probably been expensive ten years before, but now looked small and old. An ancient videotape player was hooked up to it and some Disney VHS videos scattered nearby. The carpet on the floor was thin and Zachary could feel the cold concrete beneath it. No subfloor or underlay. It didn't even go all the way to the walls; it was just a big piece of carpet discarded from some other project that someone had laid down there on top of the concrete to make the room more comfortable. But it didn't do much to make the room cozy.

The walls were still bare concrete, and a chill poured off of them. The windows were covered with black garbage bags, eliminating any light or view of the outside.

Burton stood there looking around, searching for all of the details in his memory. He shook his head at Zachary. "It's not right. It's been changed."

"People do change things over the years. Replace things, renovate, try to make things more comfortable for themselves."

"It was… I don't know what you call it. Not a crawlspace, but…"

"Unfinished?" Zachary offered.

"Unfinished. But…" Burton shook his head. "There was no floor."

For an instant, Zachary had a vision of a bottomless pit in the basement. A dark, terrifying hole. But he shook his head, reframing it, understanding what Burton was saying.

"Just a dirt floor? The concrete hadn't been poured?"

Burton nodded slowly. "Yeah."

"Were there rooms, or was it all just one big area?" If there was no floor, then they wouldn't have developed the utility room or storeroom. They wouldn't put up studs for the dividing walls until there was a concrete floor, at least.

Burton looked around, his eyes uncertain. "Maybe. I don't know."

"Was there storage down here? Maybe it was just a cold room. A root cellar."

Burton sat abruptly. Zachary wasn't expecting it and reached to grab him and help him to the floor, thinking he had stumbled or fainted. Burton sat there on the thinly carpeted floor, looking around him with wide eyes.

"This is… this is not right," Burton whispered. He swallowed, looking up at the ceiling and the covered windows, down at the floor, around and around. "Where is… where is the furnace?"

Zachary glanced around and listened for the hum of the furnace. "Over here." He walked to a folding door that looked like it was a closet and opened it up. The large furnace was situated behind it, fan whirring loudly. Burton crawled along the floor on his hands and knees until he was at Zachary's side. He looked up at the furnace. On his knees, he probably had a similar perspective to that he'd had as a boy. Looking up at everything.

He pushed past Zachary, crawling past the ragged edge of the carpet onto bare concrete once more. He looked at the furnace, all around it, a prominent frown line between his eyebrows.

He reached and craned his neck around the furnace, trying to see around all sides of it. It was a few inches away from the wall, so there was a small space behind it. Burton touched the wall, touched the sides of the furnace, like a blind person trying to recognize his surroundings. He reached behind the furnace, into the space between the furnace and the outside wall, and Zachary heard something shift.

17

Burton's hands were big and clumsy compared to what they would have been when he had been a small boy of five. He knocked it down, then finally managed to get his fingers around it and pulled out a skinny glass jar. Something that might have previously held olives, pickled onions, or maraschino cherries. He held it close to his eyes, studying the dusty, cobwebby jar. He held it up to show Zachary.

"What is it?" Zachary asked, afraid at what he might see if he examined it too closely. What looked like pieces of brown, dried leaves filled the first inch of the jar.

Burton held it in front of his eyes again, then looked at Zachary.

"Bug jar."

"Oh!" Zachary laughed. "Of course. You said that you caught bugs in the basement." Looking around the room and picturing it the way that it had been when Burton had lived there, with only a dirt floor, he could believe that there had been plenty of centipedes, beetles, and earthworms for a young boy to catch, if he weren't squeamish.

Burton put his bug jar carefully to the side where it would not get knocked over, and looked back at the wall. He held his hands flat against the wall and held his nose just an inch or two away from it.

"Look," he breathed.

Zachary got closer, but he couldn't see anything on the wall and Burton was blocking him from getting any closer.

"What? I can't see."

Burton backed away until he was out of the little closet. He picked up his jar and motioned for Zachary to go into the closet and have a look for himself. Zachary was much smaller than Burton and it was easy for him to fit into the space. He looked back at Burton, unaccountably worried that Burton was going to close the door on him and imprison him in the small closet.

He hated closets.

He swallowed and crawled in on his knees, wanting to get in and out quickly. He pulled out his phone and turned on the flashlight utility. Shining it at the wall, he looked for what Burton had seen.

Then he saw it. A crayon scrawl across the concrete, almost hidden behind the furnace.

Bobby

Aurelia Pace had said that Burton's name had been Robert. Bobby. He had left his mark there thirty years before and it was still there.

Zachary's eyes slid down to the word beneath Bobby to read his last name.

A different crayon. Maybe it had been red at one point, before all of the dust and dirt had caked around it.

Allen.

18

Bobby Allen," Zachary said. "That was your name." He couldn't help the smile that spread across his face. Burton now knew his full name. Robert Allen.

They had set out to find the house, but Zachary knew that it had been more than just the house that Burton was looking for. Maybe Burton himself didn't know, but he was looking for his identity. Who he was. And now he had his name.

"Bobby Allen," Burton repeated softly, looking stunned. "My name was Bobby Allen?"

Zachary nodded. He watched Burton to see if he wanted anything else from the furnace closet and, when he didn't appear to need anything more, Zachary squeezed back out through the door and closed the folding door over the opening once more.

"It doesn't feel real," Burton said, sitting on the carpet, not looking like he had any intention of ever moving from the spot. "I was here. Me." He picked up the bug jar and held it in his hand like a treasured artifact, looking down at it with wide eyes. "I caught bugs here. I wrote my name on the wall. This was me. I was *here*."

"Yes."

He could see Burton *becoming*. Changing from the two broken pieces into one. Not one little boy who had lived in a different city and another little boy who had been adopted and raised by the Burtons, but one person who was both. Like Zachary's dream of the identical twins. Burton was suddenly more than he had been when he entered the house. His history went back further. Another five years. He was now whole instead of missing that piece.

Burton looked like he was going to sit on the floor for a long time. The woman who had let them in did not come down the stairs and shoo them away, and Zachary hoped she would not. If the strange men wanted to sit in a cold, dimly-lit basement, then let them sit there. Burton had paid well for the privilege. They were out of the way, not underfoot.

Zachary sat down on the end of the couch closest to Burton. He didn't want to sit on the hard floor.

"Do you remember more?" he asked. "Being here again, and looking around, and knowing your name, does that help unlock anything?"

Burton frowned. His eyes moved back and forth, searching. "There is more… but I can't quite reach it. It's closer, but I still can't quite grasp it."

"Maybe it will come over time, as you've had a chance to think about it. You might want to consider therapy. They can help you to remember and can help with… emotions it brings up. Because it does. It isn't like just reading a story in a book. All of the emotions come back."

Burton's eyes flicked over to Zachary curiously. He nodded. "Maybe. I've been in therapy before. Can't say it ever helped me very much."

"I know. But it can, if you put the effort into it and find the right therapist."

Burton waved this suggestion away. He reached into his pocket to pull out his flask, looked at it, and slid it back away again. He held the bug jar in both hands and looked around the room, eyes wide, drinking it all in.

"I am Bobby. Bobby Allen."

They stayed in the basement of the house for a long time. Zachary took pictures of everything he could think of. He had taken a few pictures upstairs, but Burton did not seem to be interested in the main floor. He was in his element. Downstairs, where he had hunted bugs and scrawled crayon on the walls. He didn't drink the whole time they were down there.

Eventually, they made their way back upstairs. The lady of the house looked at them with dark, puzzled eyes, and shook her head. "What were you doing down there for so long?"

Zachary shrugged. "Just taking some time, collecting memories. Thank you for your hospitality."

She frowned again and herded them to the front door.

"Did you want to see the back? Before we go?"

Burton shook his head. He followed Zachary out, moving slowly, somewhat reluctant to again leave behind the place where he had been a child.

"You won't forget it now," Zachary encouraged. "And you can have whatever pictures you want of it. Do you want me to take one of you standing in front of it?"

Burton considered, then nodded. It might seem a strange thing to do, but this was the only part of his pre-adoption history he had, so Zachary could understand him wanting to memorialize it in some way. It would help when he looked back later.

They got back into the car. Zachary could see the biker dude who had stopped them down the street, watching them go.

As they left the neighborhood, Burton's flask came out again and this time he gulped down several swallows as if he were dying of thirst. Zachary pressed his lips together and said nothing. Drinking wasn't going to solve anything. But who was Zachary to say anything about dysfunctional behavior? Burton was who he was, and he would have to work his way out of that trap himself.

"You want me to drop you back at your hotel?"

"Could you stay for a while? Have supper with me?"

Burton didn't say how he was feeling, and his face was an unreadable mask. His voice didn't quiver or sound vulnerable when he said it, but Zachary suspected he was probably feeling pretty unstable after finding what he had been looking for.

"Uh… yeah, I can manage that," he agreed after consideration. "I'll need to make a couple of phone calls. Then we can break bread."

Burton nodded. He let out a pent-up breath. "Thanks."

"Yeah, you bet. It's a bit of an emotional rollercoaster, huh?"

Burton didn't answer, staring out the side window.

Zachary explained to Kenzie about Burton needing someone to stay with him for a while after being in the house and, while he could hear tones of disbelief in Kenzie's reply, she didn't argue. They both worked hard, and sometimes that meant overtime, night surveillance, or having to break a date to take care of something urgent. While choosing not to stay with Burton wasn't likely to cause any harm, only Zachary could decide whether it was important enough to take time away from Kenzie.

"You're off tomorrow, right?" he asked. "We can spend some more time together tomorrow. Maybe go out to brunch together."

Kenzie liked her pancakes and eggs.

"No," she sighed. "I've been called in for tomorrow. Ernie is down with the flu."

"Oh, I'm sorry. I didn't know. Well… maybe I should come home, then. I'll tell my client—"

"No, go ahead and have dinner with him. The guy's been through a big, emotional thing. You and I will still see each other tonight. And we'll get some more time together over the weekend."

"Are you sure? You're not upset?"

"No. A little disappointed, but you aren't going to be that long. You don't anticipate it taking all night?"

"No. I'll make sure he knows that I have somewhere else to be once we're finished eating. Who knows if he'll even eat."

"Oh?" Her voice was curious.

"I haven't seen him eat yet. Only drink."

"Oooh." This time, she understood. "Well… be careful. Who knows what the guy could do if he goes on a real binge after an emotional experience like that."

"He says it doesn't affect him, and I haven't seen him act drunk, even with the amount he's consumed. So I think it will be fine."

"Still be careful. You never know. Even someone who is used to drinking a lot can get belligerent or violent."

"Yeah. You're right. I'll be careful."

"Okay. See you tonight."

19

Burton did, as it turned out, eat some of his calories in solid form. He ordered a burger and fries once he and Zachary had sat down together and had a chance to peruse the menu. Zachary ordered a small steak and a baked potato with sour cream. Burton looked surprised at that.

"You're such a skinny dude, I thought you'd order a salad."

Zachary shrugged. "I lost some weight recently. I'm trying to put it back on." He didn't have a lot of appetite due to some of his meds, but it was better later in the day when they started to wear off and he wasn't so nauseated. Small amounts of calorie-dense foods were his best bet to get back up to a healthy weight.

"Have you been sick?" Burton inquired.

"Sort of, yeah." Zachary didn't bother telling him it was mental health related. He had a feeling Burton would just scoff at that.

Burton nodded his understanding.

"So how are you feeling?" Zachary asked. "Now that you've had a little time to process."

"I don't know. I don't really want to talk about it. I just don't want to be alone."

"Fair enough. Did you call your parents? Are you going to tell them about it?"

"No. I suppose I'll tell them sometime, maybe. If it comes up. I'm not rushing to do it. Wouldn't make much sense right now anyway. I don't really know anything, just where I lived. They won't care about that."

Zachary nodded. They watched the games showing on the various TVs mounted around the lounge and didn't talk much. When their food arrived and they dug in, Zachary brought up his next question.

"Is that it, then? When you came to me, it was to find your house. Now we've found it. Are you satisfied? Ready to go home?"

Burton considered this. "I guess… yes. That's all I really wanted to do. We're not going to be able to find my biological parents. Social services won't give any identifying information."

"I could find more. We have your name and address. There is plenty I can do with that." He was, after all, a private investigator. That was what he did.

"Oh." Burton was quiet. He took several big bites of his burger, chewing slowly, thinking it through. It was a lot to take in at once. It had been a big step for him to see the place where he had once lived and to find out his name. He was still integrating that experience. Zachary didn't want to dump him if he were still interested in finding out more, but he didn't want to push Burton into anything either. They were emotional decisions, and he didn't want to be accused later of taking advantage of the situation.

"You think that's enough to find my biological parents, even though they don't live there anymore?"

"Yes. Enough to find out their identities. And I'm pretty good at finding people once I know who I'm looking for." Not everyone, of course. Sometimes people took great pains to hide from those who might be searching for them. But were Burton's biological parents hiding from him? Probably not. Had they been involved in something that would have required them to completely change their identities? Most people couldn't manage to leave their old lives and identities behind. Even people who went into WITSEC didn't always choose to stay there, finding it too difficult to be completely cut off from everyone and everything they had known.

He could find Burton's parents.

He was pretty sure.

Even Heather, with her brand new skip-tracing skills, would probably be able to find them. It wouldn't take that much skill. Just access to the right databases.

"You think I should find them?" Burton asked.

"I'm not going to tell you whether you should or not. It's totally up to you. The answer is going to be different for everyone. Depends on the circumstances. If you're happy with what you have and just want to walk away, then you can do that. There's no reason you have to go further. But if you want to, you can."

"When do I have to decide?"

"No particular time. You can come back to it in a few years, if you want to. The longer you wait, the greater the chances that they will be gone, but…"

"Gone?" Burton asked, frowning. "Gone where?"

"Sometimes when people go looking for their parents, they find out it's too late. They already passed on. Sometimes just a few months or a year before they started searching. If you wait for your adoptive parents to die before you take up a search, like some people do, then the chances are much higher that your biological parents could be dead as well."

"Oh. Well, my adoptive parents are still in pretty good shape. I think I've got a few years."

"Remember that they are wealthier and have better access to good health care. People who live in neighborhoods like the one you saw have shorter lifespans."

"Yeah, I guess."

"You can wait if you want to. You don't have to jump into anything."

Burton nodded. "I think I'll at least sleep on it. I don't think I'm going to look for them, though."

"Okay. No problem. Just wanted to make sure that I knew what your thoughts were."

Zachary kept an eye on the time so that he could get home to Kenzie.

"You look like you're falling asleep over there," Kenzie commented, digging her toes into Zachary's leg. She was sitting lengthwise on the couch reading a book with her feet against his leg, and he was sitting facing the TV, though he wasn't sure what was on it anymore. His mind had been wandering and his eyes slowly shutting.

"I'm awake."

"Not for long. And you only got a couple of hours of sleep last night. You want to head to bed?"

"Only if you're ready."

She hesitated.

"I can stay up for a while," Zachary assured her. "I'll at least watch the end of this show." He glanced at the TV to see what was on. "Uh..."

"Top Gear," Kenzie told him with a smile. "Are you into fancy cars now?"

Zachary cleared his throat. He looked at the time on his phone before saying that he just hadn't changed to the program that he wanted to watch yet. It was twenty minutes into the show. "Well..."

"Admit it. You were sleeping."

"Not actually asleep... but maybe... daydreaming a bit," he waffled. He looked at the TV screen, remembering one of the children he had met during his investigation at Summit Learning Center. What had his name been? It took Zachary a minute. Ray-Ray. He wondered how the little guy was doing. Hopefully, better now that he had been pulled from the abusive program. He smiled.

Kenzie kneaded his leg with her toes. "Just a few minutes longer then," she said. "I don't want to have to carry you to bed."

Zachary grinned at the mental image. But Kenzie did help with moving dead bodies around at the medical examiner's office and he had been surprised at how easily she had shifted Luke's weight when he had been unconscious. She probably could carry him a short distance. But he wasn't about to test the theory.

He looked down at his phone to take a look through his social networks. Maybe that would keep him alert until Kenzie was ready to put down her book.

It didn't work. He awoke with a start, his whole body going rigid, ready to defend himself or run for it. Kenzie laughed. She moved beside him, pulling her feet back and turning her body to put them on the floor.

"You okay?"

Zachary looked around, blinking, getting oriented. He tried to shake off the cobwebs. "Sorry. I guess... I did fall asleep."

"You dropped your phone. I think that's what woke you up."

Zachary looked down and found it on the floor at his feet. "Oh. Yeah." He picked it up, then rubbed his eyes. "Sorry. I'm awake, now."

"Well then, walk yourself to bed. I'm going to brush my teeth and then I'll be in."

"Okay."

She waited.

Zachary moved rustily. "Did something happen?"

"What do you mean? You just fell asleep."

He shook his head, unable to escape the feeling that something important had happened and he had missed or forgotten it. He must have been dreaming and, like the night before, the vestiges of the dream, the feelings it brought, had stayed with him.

He turned his phone on and looked down at the screen. Maybe it was something he'd been reading before he fell asleep and dropped it. Something had just stuck in his brain. But nothing in the feed on the screen was familiar. Probably it had reset when the screen powered off, or Zachary had drifted off while scrolling and hadn't seen what was next. He pressed his home button and saw that he had a message. Tapping it, he saw it was from Rhys.

It was a gif of Marge Simpson talking to her sleeping husband. "Homer, are you up?"

Zachary looked at Kenzie. "Go ahead. I'll just be a minute. It's Rhys."

"Get into bed first, in case you fall asleep again. Then all I have to do is pick your phone up."

Zachary agreed and shuffled to the bedroom, trying not to wake his body up too much, and yet to be alert enough to talk with Rhys for a minute before bed. He would probably fail at one of them, either waking himself up too much to go back to sleep, or unable to stay awake for the conversation with Rhys. More than likely, he would be unable to go back to sleep. He got comfortable and messaged Rhys back.

Up for a few more minutes. Are you okay?

Rhys sent a thumbs-up. Zachary waited to see if there was more. A few seconds later, Rhys sent a picture of Kenzie.

She's here. Just getting ready for bed.

Another delay while he waited to see what else Rhys wanted to talk about. Since he had initiated the conversation, Zachary had to assume that he had a reason to want to talk.

Then a picture of a black actor whose name Zachary couldn't remember, with the caption "I was just wondering..."

Zachary typed a question mark and waited for Rhys to say what he was wondering about. Zachary had given Vera the names of the therapists that Dr. Boyle had suggested, so Rhys wouldn't be wondering about that. Something else about his flashbacks? How to manage the emotional stress? Admitting that he needed more help and should probably be admitted to the hospital?

Rhys sent another picture, and Zachary found himself looking at Luke's face again. Clearly, Rhys was having difficulty moving beyond the shooting.

Luke is okay, he assured Rhys. *You don't need to worry about him. He has recovered.*

Rhys sent back an image of a dog nodding eagerly.

Yes. He's okay. It's true.

There was only silence from Rhys. Zachary watched the screen, waiting for something further. Finally he tapped out another message.

Are you okay, Rhys?

A large green checkmark appeared on the screen.

Zachary was still puzzling over the conversation when Kenzie returned from the bathroom and climbed into bed.

"How is he?" she asked.

"He says he is okay."

"You don't sound sure, though."

"Yeah. I'm not sure if I'm missing something. He sounded like he was concerned about Luke, but he... I don't know. The responses just don't sound right. Like I'm missing the point."

"Well, it's an easy thing to do, with the way that Rhys communicates. Do you want me to take a look at it and see if I can think of anything?"

Zachary considered. He scrolled back through the short conversation, but didn't see anything there that Rhys would be embarrassed about him sharing with Kenzie. He handed her the phone.

It only took a few seconds for Kenzie to scroll through it. She considered for a moment, looking up at the top of the opposite wall where it met the ceiling. After a few minutes of silent contemplation, she looked back at the phone. She scrolled back farther, which Zachary knew meant she was into the last conversation he—and she—had had with Rhys. She handed him the phone back, frowning slightly.

"You're not getting it either?" Zachary guessed.

Kenzie shook her head. "Well… I'm not sure. I have a thought, but it's a little out of left field."

Zachary shrugged. "If it might help…"

"I noticed he hasn't asked you about how Madison is. He only asks about Luke."

Zachary nodded. "Yes… that's true."

"He originally came to you about Madison, because he was concerned with her well-being, right?"

"Yes."

"Then why isn't he asking about her? Making sure that everything is okay with her and she hasn't gone back to the life or gone off the rails somehow?"

"I don't know. He's asking about Luke because he's the one who got shot. It was seeing him all bloodied up that triggered Rhys's flashbacks to Grandpa's shooting. So that's what's stuck in his mind, what he's constantly worried about."

"Unless that isn't what he's worried about. Or asking about."

"What, then? He's worried that Luke might get Madison away again? We engineered everything so that Luke would never know where Madison had gone, and that she didn't know he survived. Luke couldn't lure Madison away again."

"No, that wasn't what I was thinking."

"What, then?"

"I wonder if Rhys had a crush on him."

Zachary's mouth dropped open. "What?"

Kenzie shrugged. "It's a possibility."

"But Rhys isn't…"

"You don't know. He's at the age that people are figuring themselves out, deciding what they are attracted to. Just because he's never said anything to you to indicate he might like boys, that doesn't mean he doesn't."

Zachary stared down at the phone in his hand. That put a whole different perspective on things.

"What do you think?" Kenzie asked.

"Maybe."

She seemed surprised at his acquiescence. "Maybe?"

Zachary nodded slowly. "When we get together, sometimes I ask him whether he has a girlfriend. You know, he teases me about you, and I ask him about his love life. Just one of those things that guys do."

Kenzie nodded.

"And he's always been very adamant. No girlfriend." He imitated the X gesture that Rhys would use and shook his head. "It's never 'maybe' or anything to indicate that there's a girl that's caught his eye, even if he's too shy to pursue her. Until Madison."

"And that might not have been romantic interest. She was missing and he was concerned about her."

"And he'd been watching her with Noah—with Luke. Because he was interested in Madison, or because he was interested in Luke?"

Kenzie shrugged. "You can't tell unless you ask."

Zachary looked back at his phone, scrolling down to the bottom of the conversation. "I don't know if I want to do that. It's not any of my business. And I don't want to start a deep conversation right when we're going to bed."

"Then tell him you'll talk to him tomorrow. Or drop in on the weekend. Then you can ask him when it's a better time for you."

Zachary blew out his breath. "You don't think that would be rude?"

"Ruder to just ignore him. And you really do need to get to sleep. You'll just fall asleep mid-conversation if you try to pursue it tonight."

"Yeah, I guess."

Zachary tried to think of how to compose his message so that it sounded casual but not like he was disregarding Rhys's feelings or not wanting to talk to him.

Falling asleep, Rhys. Can we talk tomorrow? I'll check to see how Luke is and let you know.

He got a big smiley face back from Rhys, which made him feel better.

Okay. Goodnight.

Rhys sent him back a picture of a snoozing kitten. Zachary shut off his phone and put it on the nightstand.

Kenzie wanted some time to snuggle, which gave Zachary the opportunity to relax his body and to try to get back into the right frame of mind to go to sleep. His brain worked on the possibility that Rhys was interested in Luke, examining it from every angle. He couldn't find anything that would disprove Kenzie's theory, and Rhys's response to Zachary's promise that he would check on Luke in the morning had been… very large, yellow, and smiley.

He listened to Kenzie's deep breathing as she started to doze. He rested his face against her head, breathing in the smell of her shampoo.

20

The next morning, it was Kenzie who woke up first, which was very unusual. She wrapped her arms around Zachary and pulled herself closer to him.

"Hey. You're still in bed. What's wrong, are you sick?"

Zachary took a couple of long breaths, feeling relaxed and happy. It was rare for him to wake up in such a calm, focused mood. "That was a really good sleep."

"It must have been. You're never still asleep this late."

They cuddled for a few minutes, but Kenzie had work, so she eventually pulled back from him and rubbed her eyes. "I'd better get up and get ready, or I'm going to be late getting into the office."

"It's not like the bodies are going anywhere. They're already late, so what does it matter if you are?"

Kenzie laughed. "It's not the clients I'm worried about, it's the coworkers. And the boss. And they are, unfortunately, all very much alive."

Zachary turned and slid his feet off the bed. "You go ahead and get ready. I'll get breakfast ready."

"Sounds good."

Zachary picked up his phone and left the bedroom. He used the main bathroom so that Kenzie could have the ensuite to herself, and went to the kitchen to start getting the coffee and toast on. He noticed that his notification screen was full of messages. He focused in on them.

Burton.

Over and over again.

He tapped the message at the top of the screen, which was the most recent one. Burton was incoherent, rambling on about something that was obviously a continuation of all of the other messages that he had sent to Zachary. Zachary went to the app and scrolled up so he could read the messages in a logical sequence.

Burton must have had a lot to drink. In the middle of the night, he had started texting Zachary about how he had changed his mind and he needed to find out more about his past. The truth and not the lies that the social worker and his adoptive parents had told him. He needed to know what had really happened, who his parents were, and where they were now. He didn't necessarily want to meet them, but he wanted information. Where they were and what they had done with their lives.

Zachary read through the thread a couple of times. While there were parts of Burton's texts that he couldn't quite figure out, he got the gist of them.

He sent back a text of his own, telling Burton to let him know when he was up and they could talk.

A minute later, the phone started to ring. Burton. Zachary hadn't expected him to be awake already. Or still. He silenced the alarm and looked at the screen for a minute, trying to decide whether to talk to Burton or not. But Burton already knew that he was awake and using his phone, so it would be rude to just send him to voicemail because he hadn't been prepared to talk quite so soon. Zachary tapped the answer button and held the phone up to his ear.

"Ben. Hi. I wasn't expecting you to be up."

"I've been texting you all night," Burton told him with some pique. "Of course I'm up."

"You should probably get some sleep."

"I will. But I didn't want to miss your call."

"Sorry, I'm usually up a little earlier."

"Doesn't matter. Doesn't matter. What I need is for you to tell me that you're going to find them. You said last night that you could. I didn't think I wanted to, but it's been bugging me all night long. I couldn't go to sleep until you said you would find them."

"Sure. I'll look for them," Zachary agreed. "I told you I could if you wanted me to."

"I didn't want to. I didn't want to know who they were or what they were doing. But it won't leave me alone. I can't forget the basement. I want to know where they went. Where did they go?"

"I don't know. I'll look into it." Zachary tried to sound calm, hoping that it would settle Burton down. He'd clearly had plenty to drink in the time he'd been waiting for Zachary to wake up. And hopefully, that meant he'd go straight to sleep once he was satisfied, and he wouldn't keep calling Zachary throughout the day for an update. He'd had more than one client figure he had a monopoly on his time and that his was the only case Zachary had to work on.

"You're going to find them, right? You said you could."

"I can't promise I'll have that for you today, but I will get started on it today, okay? I'll track down their names first."

"Their names," Burton agreed. There was a bang, and Zachary winced, wondering what Burton had run into or dropped. "You'll get me their names, and then I'll know who they are. I'll know their very own names."

"Yes."

"Okay."

There was a pause. Zachary waited for Burton to say goodbye or hang up the phone.

"You know, Zachary…"

"What?" Zachary suspected he knew what was coming next.

"I love you, man." Burton's voice shook with emotion. "You're the best, you know that? You're the best private detective in the world. I mean it, man. I love you."

"You too," Zachary said with a laugh, and he ended the call.

He made himself a cup of coffee and went over to his computer, beside the couch where he'd been using it the night before. After a couple of sips of coffee, he put it on the side table where it was out of reach unless he leaned over for it, so that there was no danger of bumping it by accident and baptizing his computer or staining Kenzie's furniture or carpet. He started typing.

"Zachary?"

Zachary looked up from his computer at Kenzie, standing a few feet away from him, looking at him expectantly. She'd obviously asked a question, and he'd been too focused to even hear it.

"Uh, sorry, what?"

"You didn't make anything?"

"Uh..." Zachary looked at her, taking in her still-damp hair and work clothes. She was between him and the kitchen, and it was a minute before he realized she was asking him if he'd had any breakfast. "Just a coffee. I'll grab something a little later."

She nodded, still looking at him.

Zachary looked back down at his computer to follow the next lead.

"Zachary."

He looked back up at her, slightly irritated. She could see that he was focused on a case. "What?"

She rolled her eyes up at the ceiling, shook her head, and went into the kitchen. Zachary turned his eyes back to the screen. He could hear her, in the back of his consciousness, putting toast into the toaster and banging her mug down on the counter. It still took a while longer before he looked up from his computer, suddenly realizing what she was upset about. He put the computer to the side and hurried to the kitchen. Kenzie was sitting at the table with her toast and coffee, looking at a textbook.

"Kenzie, I'm sorry. I got distracted. I didn't even realize... I'm sorry. I told you I'd make breakfast and I got completely sidetracked! You should have said something."

"I thought I did."

"No, I'm sorry. It was all my fault. I should have finished making it before I left the kitchen, and I didn't. That was really inconsiderate."

"Being sorry doesn't get the breakfast made. I thought that I had a few extra minutes for my shower because you were getting it ready, and now I feel rushed."

It only took two minutes to make coffee and toast. But Zachary could have done that for her. He should have done it, like he'd promised.

"I really am sorry."

She shrugged irritably. "Go back to your work."

"Burton called, and I wanted to get started on his search, and I completely forgot I was supposed to be making you breakfast."

Kenzie took a deep breath. When she spoke, her words were perfectly enunciated and flat, and he recognized that she was using one of the communication patterns that Dr. Boyle had talked to them about. "When you get distracted by something like that, it makes me feel like I'm not important."

"You are. I didn't do it intentionally. I didn't mean to choose the work over you; I just got distracted."

"But obviously it was more important to you than getting breakfast for me."

"No. The call from Burton just pushed it out of my mind."

"You had enough presence of mind to still get yourself a cup of coffee."

Zachary looked down at his hands, which were empty. He looked around the kitchen, but didn't see the cup of coffee that he had made for himself. Kenzie sighed.

"It's in the living room. On the side table."

"Oh." Zachary went back to retrieve it, then sat down at the table with Kenzie, determined to make her his sole focus until she left for work. He sipped his coffee, but it was cold.

Kenzie shook her head, allowing a slight smile at his grimace.

"I forgot I made it," Zachary said.

"Well, that's something."

21

At his own apartment, Zachary continued to search through the published historical records for the five years that, as far as he knew, Burton had lived in the house on Peach Tree Lane. There was no listing for an Allen family on Peach Tree Lane. He couldn't account for every year, so maybe they had been there during the intervening year or two. But he could remember being there, and he had written his name on the wall, so he had to be older than two or three when he lived there. He should have been there during the time he was four or five. But during that time, there were no Allens listed at that address. Only a couple by the name of Weaver. And census records didn't indicate that any children had lived in the household.

Zachary sat back, rubbing his gritty eyes and trying to puzzle it out. Burton clearly remembered the house. He knew about the bug jar by the furnace, and that was proof enough for Zachary. Burton could have pretended all kinds of memories of that house, but he couldn't conjure a glass jar out of the air. Or his name on the wall. The social worker had said that his name was Robert, and Zachary had stood there and watched Burton find the name Bobby on the wall. He hadn't written it there himself and it was clear from the dirt and cobwebs on the wall that it hadn't been a recent addition. A child named Bobby had lived in the house.

He moved backward and forward through the records. Perhaps Burton had not been five when he had been adopted. Maybe that was only an estimated age for a child whose birth had not been registered. He could have been four or six. If he were very small for his age from neglect and malnourishment, like Zachary himself had been, then he might be seven and mistaken for a younger child. But Zachary couldn't see them being wrong by more than two years. If he had been eight years old, he would have been able to tell them that, and it would have been obvious from his maturity level even if it were at odds with his size. The doctors would be able to tell from his bone and tooth development. And similarly, he couldn't have been younger than four. A three-year-old did not look like a five-year-old, even if he were large for his age.

But even adjusting for a mistake in ages, he couldn't find any record of an Allen family. He couldn't find a record of any family with one young child who had lived in that house during the right period. It was possible they hadn't registered as voters, answered the door to census takers, or had driver's licenses. But he found it hard to believe that they hadn't been listed in any directory, consumer database, credit history, or social security registry.

He went into the kitchen and made himself a fresh cup of coffee, working through the possibilities.

If the Allen family didn't exist, and Burton wasn't some kind of scammer, then Allen could not have been his last name. It could have been his middle name. He might have been called by both, or he might have been intending to write his full name but got interrupted and never returned to the project. There were a number of possibilities, but Zachary was pretty sure by then that there was no Allen family.

He returned to his desk, sipping the coffee.

That left him with the Weavers. They had been living in the house at the right point in time. Not listing the fact that they had a young child on the census was not a huge oversight. People made mistakes filling out forms. The census taker didn't hear, forgot to check a box, or there was an interruption and the adult who was doing the interview had never finished answering the question in full.

Robert Allen Weaver. It was a nice, strong name.

Parents Elizabeth Weaver and Samuel Weaver.

Zachary noted them down. The census had a woman in her twenties and a man in his forties, which fit with the social worker's statement that

Burton's mother was young and his father was older. His profession was listed as a delivery driver. Elizabeth listed as unemployed, which the social worker had not believed.

Now that he had the names, he dug deeper.

There had been no further calls from Burton, and Zachary assumed that he would be sleeping for a good long while with the amount of alcohol he'd consumed. That was fine with Zachary. He needed some time away from the computer screens, and he knew just where to go.

He timed his visit for around the time Rhys should be getting home from school, and watched the house for a few minutes, not wanting to bother Vera before Rhys arrived. If Rhys were late, then Zachary being there waiting for him would just emphasize the fact for Vera and make her more anxious. Zachary didn't know if Rhys had any after-school activities. He didn't usually, but that didn't mean he didn't have a tutoring session or an appointment with his new therapist, or something else that Zachary hadn't thought of.

He kept an eye on the door while he checked his social networks and email inbox.

There was a tap on his window that made him jump, and he turned his head, expecting to see a cop or an irritated dog walker who wanted to know why he was sitting there in his car like some creepy stalker.

But it was Rhys. He spread his hands wide and raised his brows. *What are you doing here?*

Zachary opened his door. "Just waiting for you. I didn't want to bother Grandma."

Rhys waited while he climbed out and locked up, then walked with him up to the front door. The door was unlocked and Rhys let himself in.

Vera was in the living room reading a book. She looked up and smiled at them.

"Zachary. I didn't know you were coming."

"I didn't arrange anything ahead. I hope that's okay."

"Of course. You know you're welcome any time. How was school, Rhys?"

Rhys rocked his hand back and forth. *So-so.*

"Looks like you have plenty of homework to keep you busy."

Rhys shifted the loaded backpack, rolling his eyes.

"Okay, well, relax and have a visit with Zachary, and you can hit the books after supper."

Rhys nodded. He led the way, not to his bedroom, but to the kitchen. He motioned for Zachary to sit down and had his head in the fridge, on the hunt for something good to eat. With the fast metabolism of a teenager, Rhys ate at least twice as much as Zachary, and it was no surprise he got home from school hungry. Zachary watched while he assembled a sandwich, slathering the bread with mustard and mayo and stacking the fillings high. He sat down across from Zachary and grinned.

"Looks great."

Rhys pointed at Zachary and raised his eyebrows inquiringly.

"No, not for me. I… just ate."

Rhys jerked his head back, lifting his chin and giving a little shake. Clearly expressing his doubt about that fact.

Zachary shrugged uncomfortably. "Okay, maybe it's been a few hours, but I'm not hungry."

Rhys nodded and took a big bite from his sandwich.

Zachary took out his phone and laid it on the table in front of Rhys, with the picture of Luke on the screen.

Rhys nodded and looked at Zachary eagerly to see what he had found out. Zachary looked at his face, reading the signs there. Pupils dilating slightly. Leaning forward in attention. Breathing a bit louder and faster.

"You like Luke?" Zachary asked, pointing to the picture.

Rhys nodded.

"I mean, you *like* like him?" Zachary asked. His face warmed and he looked away, as if something else had distracted his attention. Just because Rhys was a teenager, that didn't mean Zachary needed to talk like one. There were probably better ways to ask Rhys what his feelings were. But nothing helpful had come to Zachary's mind.

Rhys nodded again.

"Oh!" Zachary rubbed the short whiskers on his chin. "Well, some detective I am!"

Rhys grinned and took another bite of his sandwich. As he chewed it, he made a motion back toward the living room, where Vera was still reading. He made a locking gesture at his lips.

"I'm not going to out you," Zachary promised. He'd known too many kids who had been kicked out when their parents had found out they were gay or something other than cis and straight. Things were improving, but Vera was the older generation and knew what it was like to be part of a minority. She had previously expressed to Zachary that she didn't want him to meet with Rhys in public because people might think the two of them were having a romantic relationship, when Zachary had been mistakenly identified in the media as being gay.

Zachary pursed his lips, thinking about that. Rhys cocked his head, looking at him questioningly.

"Are you sure she doesn't already know?"

Rhys's eyebrows went up even higher. He shook his head, frowning.

"Just… something she said once," Zachary said. He tried to remember what her words had been when she asked Zachary to only meet with Rhys at home from then on. But the words were elusive. It had been a very bad time for Zachary, and a lot of what had happened during that time was fractured and incomplete. He shrugged in irritation. "I don't remember exactly what she said. I just wonder… if she at least suspects."

Rhys shrugged as well. He made the locking-lips gesture again, and Zachary reaffirmed his agreement.

"I won't bring it up. I won't say anything."

Rhys nodded. He pushed Zachary's phone back toward him, tapping the screen, even though it had turned off and the picture of Luke was no longer visible.

"Luke is good. I talked to the woman who is helping him out today. Physically, he's healed up. Barely any marks left from where he got cut, though he'll have a scar from the bullet track," Zachary traced the length of his jaw, following the path the bullet had taken. "Kenzie had been concerned about how bad his concussion was because he was out for so long, but mentally he seems to be fine. Some headaches and dizzy spells, but when you consider the drug withdrawal…" Zachary gave a shrug. "All of that is to be expected and more."

Rhys gave him a thumbs-up. Zachary nodded his agreement.

"All good."

Rhys pointed at himself and then at his eyes. *Could I see him?*

"I don't know." Zachary took a deep breath and let it out. "Let's leave it for a while, anyway. I don't want to distract him from his recovery. We really don't know yet whether he's going to be successful in staying away from drugs and the trafficking business. And I don't want you anywhere near that."

Rhys's frown became more pronounced, but he didn't argue.

"I'm sure you don't want to derail him either. Let's give him some time to figure out where he's going… who he is. Remember, he hasn't really had a chance to be his own person since he was twelve or thirteen. He has lots of 'inner' work to do."

Rhys nodded slowly, and Zachary thought he was a little more understanding this time.

"I'm sorry for not understanding," Zachary said, his face warming again. "You must have thought I was being pretty dense."

Rhys laughed and gave a little nod.

Zachary laughed too, not having expected that answer. "Well, I'll try to be a little more discerning in the future."

22

Burton called as Zachary was leaving Rhys's house. Zachary looked at the time on his phone and started the car. He answered it once it connected with the Bluetooth system.

"Hello, Ben. How are you feeling?"

Burton groaned, not even bothering to put on a front that overindulging never bothered him. "When can we meet? Have you got anything?"

"I have some information for you. We're not quite there yet, but I can tell you what I've got when we meet. When are you going to be in shape to get together?"

"I'm going to head down to the bar now. I'll be fine by the time you get here."

Zachary pictured Burton staggering down to the lounge still with bedhead and a rumpled shirt, determined to drink until he was no longer feeling any pain. "Well, hold off on getting drunk until after we meet. I want you to be coherent."

"When have I not been coherent?" Burton demanded. "I've been just fine. I haven't caused you any trouble. I got us into the house, didn't I? Didn't just barge in there like a bull in a China shop and get us arrested."

"No. You did just fine. But I want you to be able to focus on what information I have."

"I will. Just get over here."

"I'll be there soon."

Regardless of whether Burton slowed down or not, it wouldn't take Zachary more than twenty minutes to get to the hotel; Burton couldn't have too many drinks in that length of time. With his level of tolerance, he would have to drink longer than that to be feeling the effects.

Zachary's mental picture of Burton hadn't been far off the mark. The bartender was already eyeing him, even though he'd only been there for a few minutes.

"Let's grab a booth," Zachary suggested, steering Burton toward the one they had sat at previously. It felt like home—his own place in the lounge.

Burton grabbed his glass and motioned to the bartender to bring him another at the table. They got settled in their usual seats. Zachary got out his notepad.

"So, what do you know?" Burton demanded.

"You're sure you want me to go ahead? You've been back and forth on this. If you want to wait…"

"I don't want to wait. I'm here now. I want it now."

"Okay. First off, Allen is not your surname."

Burton blinked at him, eyes narrowing. "Then who is Allen?"

"I'm thinking Allen is probably your middle name. Or maybe a double-barreled first name. Bobby Allen."

Burton shook his head. "No. What is my surname, then? That doesn't make any sense."

"Weaver. Unless I miss my guess, you were born Robert Allen Weaver. Known as Bobby or Bobby Allen."

Burton continued to shake his head, not believing it.

"There was no Allen family that lived in that home in the years that I checked," Zachary explained. "If you were five when you were adopted, there is only a very narrow window for me to check for your family to be living in that house. If that was your house when you were four or five, then your family name is Weaver."

"Weaver," Burton repeated. He frowned and had a drink, thinking about it.

"Does that sound at all familiar to you?"

"I don't know."

"You would have known your last name when you were five years old. Most five-year-olds have been taught their last name."

"No… I don't think I've ever heard that before. What are… their other names?"

"Elizabeth and Samuel."

"Elizabeth Weaver. Samuel Weaver." Burton considered the names as he continued to drink. He was downing the drinks quickly. Like someone who had just run a marathon without any water. Desperate. Trying to drown the memories even as Zachary was trying to tell him the details.

"Just think about them for a minute," Zachary suggested. "Stop everything else, close your eyes, and just repeat the names to yourself. Elizabeth Weaver. Samuel Weaver. Maybe they had nicknames. Lizzie. Sam. Maybe your mother still went by her maiden name; the authorities weren't very good at keeping track of that kind of thing back then. They just assumed that the wife would take the husband's name."

Burton stared at Zachary, his eyes bloodshot and his expression stony. Eventually, he pushed his glass away an inch, placed his folded arms on the table, and closed his eyes. He swayed a little with them shut, the alcohol affecting him even though he insisted it didn't.

"Lizzie Weaver. Sam Weaver."

Burton sat there, eyes closed, thinking about it. He breathed in and out and Zachary waited for his response. Were those names buried in his memory somewhere? All kids heard their parents' names from time to time. Even if he didn't know their last names, he would still have heard his parents speak to each other, occasionally using each other's names when they were calling across the house for help or reprimanding the other. Answering phones. Talking to salespeople at the door. *Yes, I'm Mrs. Weaver.* Answering census interviews.

Burton opened his eyes. He looked at Zachary.

"Who was Allen?"

23

Zachary let the words stand between them for what seemed like a long time. It couldn't have been that long, because nothing happened in the silence. No conversations between other patrons, people coming and going, the bartender serving drinks. Zachary thought about Burton's question.

Who was Allen?

Wasn't Allen Burton's middle name?

What if it wasn't? What if the two names were for two different boys? Two children. Daring each other to write their names on the wall behind the furnace. Making their mark on their territory, like lower-order animals.

Two different colors of crayon. The names one below the other, not in a straight line. Were they the names of two separate people?

"If Allen was not your second name, then you must have had a brother," Zachary said. "Or else a friend you were allowed to have over who played with you in the basement."

He couldn't imagine any mother letting her child go over to the Weaver house to play in the dark, dank basement with a dirt floor. But she wouldn't necessarily have known. If Allen never told her what went on over at the Weaver house, then how would she know?

Burton gazed at Zachary. "A brother?" he repeated. "I don't have a brother."

"Maybe he was just a friend, then. Did you have friends over?" He had been about to add 'to play,' but he was afraid of influencing Burton's memories too much. Taking them out and molding them into something different before putting them back on the shelf. He didn't want to be accused of planting false memories.

"No," Burton seemed sure of himself. As if it were a ridiculous question. Having friends over? Not something he ever would have considered. Or that would have been allowed.

"If you didn't have friends over..."

"Then who is Allen?" Burton repeated.

Unexpectedly, he slammed his open palm down on the table with a crack like a rifle. It shook Burton's glass, the condiment bottles, and everything else on the table. People looked over at them to see what was going on, eyes wide.

"Who is Allen?" Burton repeated in a loud, confrontational voice.

Zachary made calming gestures with his hands. Downward, soothing motions that there was nothing to be concerned about or to start swearing about. "It's okay. There's no need to yell or get upset."

Burton smacked the tabletop again. Not as hard, but still distracting and frightening to the other customers. He would get them kicked out of the lounge. And they probably wouldn't let him sit down at the bar again. He'd have to move to a new hotel.

"What's wrong?" he asked Burton reasonably. "If you think I'm full of crap, just fire me. I don't have to do anything else. You have some names you can look up, or you can do nothing with them. It's totally up to you."

"I want to know who he is." He didn't yell this time, but kept it in an undertone.

"Do you want me to find out if Allen Weaver was your brother? If he is still around?"

Burton sat there, morose, thinking about it. Zachary could see the bartender watching them, making a decision as to whether to kick them out or not. If Burton could keep himself calm, he would probably be allowed to stay, but one more outburst and they would be pushing him out the door.

"Allen Weaver."

"Yes. Does that sound familiar?" Zachary had a thought. "Maybe the social worker remembered the wrong name. Maybe she placed both of you, and she gave you the wrong name. Do you think *your* name is Allen Weaver?"

"No." Burton seemed sure of that. "No. I'm not Allen. But… where is he?"

"I don't know. I could look into it, if that's what you would like."

Burton nodded slightly. Not a definite answer, but his brain telling his body what it was he wanted, nudging him along.

"Okay. Let me look into it. I don't know how much I'll be able to find. If he was also adopted, he'll have a different name now. It's hard to track kids through adoption finalizations."

"I don't have a brother," Burton said, shaking his head slowly.

"Maybe. We can look and find out. Or maybe you'll remember who he was."

"No. Allen is…" Burton stalled. "I don't know what I was going to say. Allen is…" He reached for the words. "Not there? Allen is not there?"

Zachary listened, analyzing it. Had Burton remembered the phrase? Someone telling him that Allen was not there? Or was it just part of his drunken ramblings. He smelled strongly of drink. Possibly he still had alcohol from the night before in his system. And he'd had a jugful since waking up.

"Allen is not there," Zachary repeated, making it a statement rather than a question.

Burton stared at him, his mouth tightening in anger. "Why did you say that?"

"Allen is not there. Does that bother you? You don't like me saying that?"

"No. Don't say that. You don't know anything about it."

"No, I don't. I don't know anything about Allen."

"But you can find out?"

"I can try."

"There must be a birth certificate. You have the parents' names, so can't you look it up?"

"If he was not adopted. If he *was* adopted, then all traces of the original name are wiped out and replaced with the new information."

Burton picked up his glass, but it was empty. He looked toward the bartender. The man shook his head. Burton was already being disruptive; the bartender wasn't going to give him anything else.

"There's a minibar in the room," Burton said. "Costs an arm and a leg, but at least I can keep drinking. Let's go up."

"I think you've had enough to drink."

Burton shook his head. "I'm just getting started."

While he stayed with Burton for a couple more hours, Zachary didn't really get anything helpful out of him. Burton bounced from one topic to another, abandoning anything that got too intimate or led back to questions about his brother and what had happened to him.

"There were two tricycles," Burton told Zachary. "But there weren't two boys. I would remember if there were two boys."

"Those tricycles wouldn't have been yours. They were old, but thirty years old? I don't think they've been sitting in the yard for that long. They belonged to other children, not to you."

"No. Not me."

"Do you remember playing outside? You remember catching bugs in the basement. You must have caught them outside too."

"No… don't remember that. I just remember… I don't remember, I have impressions… I recognize things. But I don't remember."

"It's okay not to remember things very well. It was a long time ago and it might have been traumatic for you. That makes it harder to remember things properly. Some things get pushed to the front and you keep remembering them over and over again. And other things… you want to remember, but can't. They just never coalesced into a memory."

"I don't have them," Burton asserted.

"That's fine. That's the way it is sometimes."

Burton downed another tiny bottle, setting the empty down beside him on the floor with the rest. "I want to know who Allen is."

24

It might take a lot of alcohol to affect Burton, but he wasn't immune to it. Zachary left him sprawled across the bed in his hotel room, snoring away, and hoped that he would be okay after sleeping it off.

He headed for home. Or for Kenzie's home, where she would be waiting for him. He hesitated when he looked at his phone, trying to decide whether to tell her he was on his way or just to show up. He settled for calling her on the Bluetooth once he was on his way.

"Hi, Kenz. I'm on my way. Just running a little later than I expected to."

"Okay. Supper will hold for that long. Everything okay?"

"Yes, just fine. Just getting my client settled for the night."

"Are you offering a tuck-in service now?"

"You tuck your clients in, don't you?"

Kenzie laughed. "I suppose so. But I'm hoping your client hasn't entered that stage of sleep yet."

"No."

"See you when you get here."

After hanging up, Zachary turned the radio on and let his mind wander while he listened to the music. He needed to let his brain just go for a while; he'd been concentrating too hard most of the day and it was exhausting.

Sometimes, not thinking about a problem was the best way to come to a solution. Zachary would let his subconscious mind worry over whatever bits of his investigation it wanted to, and it tried to put the puzzle pieces together. Hopefully, the next day he would feel a better sense of direction as he tried to find out what had happened to the elusive Allen, if he was a second child. Zachary wasn't convinced that he was. The crayoned names had looked pretty similar; he hadn't thought when he saw them that they were written by a different hand. Maybe all kids had similar handwriting at that age, or anyone writing with crayon on the wall would end up looking similar. He wasn't a handwriting expert, though he'd studied the science a little in the course of his investigations.

He had parked his car and was most of the way up the sidewalk to the house when he realized that his body had been operating on autopilot and he didn't even remember most of the drive back. He paused at the door to try to rein in his brain again. He wanted to give Kenzie the attention she deserved, especially after his goof that morning forgetting that he was supposed to be making her breakfast.

He took a couple of deep breaths, and went in.

Kenzie was in the kitchen. At his arrival, she bent over to open the oven and pulled out a loaf of crusty garlic bread that set Zachary's mouth watering. He didn't care what else she had made to go with the bread. He just wanted the fragrant, yeasty bread on his plate.

"That smells absolutely heavenly!" he told her.

"Well, good thing you weren't too long in getting here, or it would have been dry or burned."

"It smells just right." He watched Kenzie carefully remove the foil and reveal the loaf, crust shiny with butter. She started to slice it, and each piece looked even and perfect.

"Quit slobbering and set the table."

"Set the table," Zachary repeated, and went to the cupboard. No way he was going to forget what he was supposed to be doing this time. He wouldn't even forget the cutlery, which he frequently did. Kenzie always rolled her eyes over his doing jobs only halfway, such as setting plates on the table, but nothing else. Or maybe cups and cutlery and no plates. But she didn't give up on getting him to do it properly and today he would get it right. He muttered to himself as he got out everything that needed to go on the table. He might sound crazy talking to himself, but it helped him to get all of the steps done if he could hear his own voice instead of trying to keep it straight in his head.

When Kenzie was finished cutting the bread and getting the rest of the dishes on the table, Zachary looked over the place settings, again listing off plates, cups, knife, fork, spoon, and cloth napkin—because their fingers were definitely going to be greasy with the delicious garlic bread.

He raised his eyes and looked at Kenzie, waiting for her approval or criticism. At least Kenzie wasn't Bridget, who would go up one side and down the other when he did something stupid. There was no way she would have trusted him to set the table. Not with all of the specialized silverware she liked to use, with special forks for salad, pickles, or caviar. He never knew what everything was for and, even though he tried to watch her and copy what she used everything for, he would still make a mistake, and she would rip into him.

"Zachary."

Zachary blinked, swallowed, and looked at Kenzie.

"Looks good," Kenzie said, sounding like she was repeating it for the second or third time. "Good job."

"Oh. Thanks." He sat down, and then wondered if he should have held her chair for her. They weren't usually so formal but, thinking about Bridget, he wondered if he should do more to try to make Kenzie feel special. She did the lion's share of the cooking and other jobs maintaining her house and many of the things in his apartment as well. He should be able to keep up better.

He smiled, hoping it didn't look too strained.

"Relax," Kenzie advised. "You seem really tense tonight." She sniffed, "Have you been drinking?"

"No." Zachary smelled his shirt. "Burton was, but I don't remember him spilling anything."

"You might have just absorbed the fumes." She took a couple of bites of her salad. "Not that you can't drink. I'm just surprised, because usually you don't."

"No. I didn't have anything tonight either. It was all Burton."

She nodded. "Everything went okay?"

"Well… no, not exactly. I mean, nothing went wrong, but he had a lot of problems with the information that I gave him."

"He didn't get violent?"

"Slapped the table and shouted. That was as bad as it got."

"What was he so upset about?"

Zachary thought about it, tearing his bread into smaller pieces as he ate it. "We think that maybe he had a brother named Allen. Initially, I thought that was his last name, but it turns out it wasn't. It could be a middle name, but he is quite certain that it was not, and that Allen is someone else. Best bet is that he was a brother."

Kenzie nodded. "And this upset him because…"

"I think mostly because it was just a shock. He hadn't realized before that he had a sibling. He wants to know where he is, what happened to him."

"That's going to be pretty hard, isn't it? Unless his brother starts looking for him, the same as he did. There are adoption registries."

"I told him I would do what I can. I'll start on it tomorrow."

"Sounds like a plan." Kenzie put a bite of roasted vegetables in her mouth. "Are you going to eat anything other than garlic bread?"

"Uh…" Zachary looked at the other dishes on the table. "Yeah, sure. I'll have a bit of chicken and vegetables."

"But mostly garlic bread."

Zachary put another piece of bread in his mouth and grinned.

25

Zachary went through the records that he had already compiled on the residents of Peach Tree Lane, looking for families that had lived there at the same time as Burton would have been there with his family. There wasn't anyone still living on the street from that time, which didn't surprise him. As he'd told Burton before, it wasn't the type of place people would live for more than a few years. Only as long as they had to. They would get kicked out or get enough money saved up to move somewhere else. Somewhere nicer.

But he was good at tracking people, and he was able to dig up phone numbers in order to contact a couple of them. A lot of people retained their landline numbers from the eighties into the new millennium, and only recently had started dumping them because they just didn't use them anymore. Even the grandmas and grandpas were using cell phones now.

He looked at the first name on his list. According to the census numbers, Elise Perry was around the same age as Burton's birth mother. With any luck, their kids had played together and she would remember the Weaver family, and maybe know something about what had happened to them. It was odd that Zachary hadn't been able to trace Burton's parents after he had been adopted. Unless, perhaps, they had died in an accident and that was why he had needed to be adopted. It was also possible that they had moved out of state, had changed their names, or a whole host of other possibilities. It should have been easy to track them by their SSNs and credit records, but sometimes people stayed under the radar intentionally.

He dialed Elise Perry's number and waited. It went a few rings before being picked up, and he imagined that it was in her purse as she shopped or drove. But eventually, she found the phone and answered it.

"Hello?" She sounded a little breathless.

"Is this Elise Perry?"

"Yes?"

"I'm a private investigator, Ms. Perry, and I'm trying to track down a family that used to live on Peach Tree Lane. Which is where you used to live."

"That was a long time ago, Mr.…"

"My name is Zachary. Goldman Investigations."

"It's been years since I lived in that part of town. I don't think I can help you."

"Did you happen to know the Weaver family?"

She didn't answer for a moment. Zachary had been hoping against hope for immediate name recognition, but if she did recognize it, she wasn't announcing it.

"I don't know. The name sounds sort of familiar, but it wasn't anyone I had anything to do with."

"They would have had kids. Did your kids play with them, maybe?"

"Weavers… I don't think… there was a couple called the Weavers, but I don't remember them having any kids. Maybe they were older than mine."

"Bobby Weaver was five when they left. I'm not sure whether Allen was older or younger."

"No, I don't think so. I don't remember any kids by those names."

"No Bobby?" Zachary was surprised. It was a common name. He thought there would have been a few of them around.

"No, not on the street. And I knew all of the kids that age."

"And no Allen?"

"I can't remember any Allens my son's age, not even at school."

"But Weaver sounds familiar."

"That's all I can tell you. I must not have known them very well, but maybe heard about them at Community Watch or something like that. You know how you can hear someone's name a few times, so they get familiar, even though you never actually met the person."

"Sure. So you don't think you even met them? Maybe a community lunch or breakfast? Canvassing for the Heart Foundation or Diabetes?"

"No, sorry. I'm not much help."

"Would your husband know, do you think?"

"I'm not in touch with him anymore. But I wouldn't think so. He was always working during the day. I'm the one who got to know people in the community. He would just get home from work and sit in front of the TV for the rest of the night. Like he'd earned his right to sit there and didn't have to be responsible for anything else."

Zachary grimaced. It was probably a good thing that the two were no longer together.

"Okay. Well, thank you for your time, Ms. Perry. Can I leave you my number in case something occurs to you later?"

"It's on my call log. I'll let you know if something comes up, but I don't expect it to. I just didn't know them. Our kids didn't play together and I don't remember what either one of them would have looked like."

———

Elise Perry hadn't remembered very much, but her call confirmed that Zachary was on the right track. Neighbors remembered things. Even that many years later. The names and faces came back to them—or they didn't. Her lack of memories of Bobby and Allen didn't mean that the boys hadn't lived there. Just that they hadn't played with the neighborhood children, which Burton had already told him.

He didn't have friends.

He didn't play outside.

They had kept to themselves. Maybe the parents had been religious nuts. Or paranoid about the coming apocalypse. Who knew?

The next mother on his list was May Richmond. Zachary tried the first number he had for her, and got a recording that it was out of service. He was not surprised, and it wasn't the only number he had found for her. And, of course, there might be several May Richmonds, but he was pretty confident in the information he had managed to dig up. He tried the next number on the list.

"Hello?" It was a male voice. Zachary looked down at his screen to see whether he had dialed correctly.

"Hello?" the man repeated.

"Sorry, sir. I'm looking for May Richmond. Is she at this number?"

"You can get her on her own cell."

"Is it…" Zachary slipped down to the next number on the list and read it off.

"No," the man answered, and dictated May's number to him. Zachary wrote it down.

"Thank you very much. You have a nice day, sir."

"You too."

Zachary tried May's cell phone, and she answered it quickly.

"Mrs. Richmond?"

"Yes, this is May."

Zachary again explained his dilemma, how he was trying to find people who might have known Burton's family all of those years ago. She gave a disbelieving laugh.

"I'm not in contact with anyone from that time anymore," she said. "Those were not my friends. We didn't keep in touch."

"I realize that, I'm just looking for a little bit of direction. If you don't remember anything, that's fine. I'm hoping someone will remember this family and be able to point me in the right direction. I lose their trail after Peach Tree Lane."

"I don't think I'll be able to help you, but go ahead."

"Do you remember the Weaver family at all?"

"The Weavers." Her voice held a note of disbelief. "Why would you be trying to find them?"

"I'm sorry, does that mean you know something about them?"

"I remember them," she said slowly. "They were not friends with anyone in the neighborhood. Kept to themselves. They were…" her tone was hesitant, "they were not the kind of people you wanted to be around."

"Oh?"

"They were… you know what they did, don't you?"

"No. What did they do? I thought Mr. Weaver was a trucker."

"I don't mean that. I mean… when we all heard what they'd done to that boy…"

"What boy? Bobby?"

"Yes! You must know, then."

"No. I know that he went into foster care and later went on to be adopted. But I don't know anything that happened before that."

"He was just like a skeleton when he got out of there. They say they'd abused him. Kept him locked up all the time. Didn't feed him. Beat him. It was horrible. We were all devastated that something like that could have gone on right under our own noses. You don't know. You just don't know what goes on behind closed doors."

Zachary could attest to that. A person could never assume that he knew what things were like for someone, what kind of a person they were behind closed doors. Or what kind of person they lived with behind those closed doors.

"What do you remember about it? How did anyone find out?"

"He got out one day. Escaped. Somebody didn't lock the door or pull it shut, something like that. So he ended up wandering down the street, this strange little boy that no one knew."

"And someone called the police."

"Yes. Exactly. By the time the police got there, we were all gathered around him, trying to figure out where he had come from, how he had gotten there. We thought… someone dumped him there. That he came from somewhere else and had just been abandoned there, where someone would find him. We didn't know that he'd lived right on our street. That he'd lived just a few doors down from where we found him."

Zachary nodded, fascinated with the story. "How did they trace him back to the Weavers, if no one knew him?"

"He was old enough to talk, to point out which house was his, who Mommy and Daddy were. They didn't do DNA testing back then. But when they came looking for him, the police were waiting."

"I guess that was a shock for them."

"They were not too happy about it, that's for sure."

"What happened to them? They went to prison?"

"We didn't hear much. It wasn't a story that got into the newspaper, and we didn't have internet back then. I heard rumor that they were both convicted, but I don't know what the sentences were. Less for her. She said it was all his fault, she had just been doing what she was told and she was afraid of him."

"I didn't come across any of this when I was searching. If they served prison time, that should have shown up on my searches."

"Weaver wasn't their real name. I don't remember what it was. And like I said, there was no internet and I don't think it ever made it into the papers. Maybe a line or two on a slow news day."

Zachary sat there with the phone, thinking about everything.

"That was Bobby?" he asked eventually. "The little boy who wandered off?"

"Bobby… yes it was something like that. Yes."

"And what about the other boy?"

"The other boy?"

"They had two children. Bobby and Allen."

"No. They only had one. Just Bobby."

Zachary tried to keep his breathing steady.

Then what had happened to Allen?

26

Zachary wasn't sure how to go back to his client with more bad news. Not only did he not have anyone who remembered Allen, but he didn't even know the right surname. After considering it for a while, he called Aurelia Pace.

"Aurie. It's Zachary Goldman. The private investigator."

"I remember who you are," she sighed.

"Then you probably know why I'm calling you back, too."

"You went back there, didn't you?"

"Yes, we went back to Peach Tree Lane. And Ben Burton went into the house."

She made a sympathetic noise. "Why did you let him do that? Why couldn't you let him think that the place had been knocked down and there was no point in going there?"

"I'm working for him, not for you."

"But you must know that wasn't good for him. He should never have gone back there."

"My job isn't to do what's best for my client. It's to do what I'm hired for."

She sighed. "How was it?"

"Initially... okay. He got to see the house, wander around, find a link to his past."

"And then?"

"And then… he found his name and Allen's written on the wall beside the furnace."

"Allen's?" Pace repeated in a blank tone.

"Allen. His brother."

"Bobby didn't have a brother."

"Then who else was down there with Bobby? Who else was it that wrote his name on the wall?"

There was only silence from Pace.

"You never had any clue that there was another child," Zachary said.

"No. Never. Bobby didn't say anything. His crapbag parents didn't say anything about another child."

Zachary snorted in surprise at Pace's choice of language.

"Well, they were," Pace asserted. "I don't sugarcoat it. They were evil people who should never have been allowed anywhere near children. Horrible people. It's the kind of existence that you wouldn't wish on your worst enemy."

"No," Zachary agreed. "I sure wouldn't."

Neither of them said anything for a few minutes.

"They had another child?" Pace said finally.

"Yes, apparently there was another boy."

"And no one knows what happened to him."

"No one knew he existed until now."

She swore.

Zachary thought about the dimly-lit basement. He thought about it back when Burton lived there, when there had been a dirt floor.

Zachary knew that Joshua Campbell was probably his best bet in the police department, but he was a busy man and might not have any time to see Zachary. So he decided to give Mario Bowman a call and see what he thought.

"Zach, my man," Mario greeted. "What's going on in your world today?"

"Well, I have a case that needs some police involvement."

"It wouldn't be the first time."

"No," Zachary agreed with a little laugh. He seemed to be attracting more and more of those lately.

"So what kind of case is this?" Mario asked. "Another serial killer? Breaking up a trafficking ring? What's on the menu today?"

"It's a cold case. A child who disappeared in the eighties."

"And you found him?"

"No… I think he met with foul play, and that I know where his remains might be found."

"Do you know for a fact that they are there? Is this something that you've seen and are calling the police in to 'stumble' across it themselves?"

"No. I haven't seen them. They're probably buried under concrete."

"And what makes you think so?"

"My client is his brother. The children were both imprisoned in the basement for most of their lives." Zachary hoped this wasn't stretching the truth too far. "My client managed to escape and was rescued, but his brother was never seen or heard from again. I think he died before Burton escaped, and the basement was unfinished with a dirt floor. Awfully convenient place to dispose of a body."

"Yes, but can your client corroborate that's what happened?"

"His memories are very vague. I would rather not ask him about that part. I don't want to suggest or taint anything. I'll leave that to the police. To question him properly, I mean."

Mario snickered. "So how do you know this, if your client hasn't told you?"

"He told me that the basement used to have a dirt floor. We found evidence of both children in the basement, which now has a concrete floor. I've talked to a neighbor who told the story of Burton escaping and the police coming to take the parents away. I've talked to the social worker who was involved, and she confirms that part of the story. She didn't ever know that there was a second child."

"That's not really a minor detail."

"Five-year-old traumatized child. Neglected, abused, malnourished. He probably saw his brother killed and buried. Would you confide in any grown-ups?"

"He must have had therapy. Why didn't it come out then?"

"Because kids who have been told not to tell, who have been threatened… they learn to keep their mouths shut."

Mario's computer keys tapped in the background. "You say that the parents were arrested?"

"Yes. I don't know their real last names, but they were Elizabeth and Sam Weaver when they were arrested, so there should at least be an alias in the system."

"If those records were digitized, which is touch-and-go, as you know. A lot of stuff was just shoved into boxes and stored away. Then it gets black mold into it and has to be destroyed."

"Give it a try anyway."

Mario typed away for a while. Zachary kept quiet and let him do his job. Mario knew what he was doing. If anyone could find any trace of the cold case, it was he.

"Yeah, there's a file connected with those names."

"What were they charged with?"

Mario read through whatever had appeared on his screen. "Sketchy details. Looks like only the summary was digitized. But you're right, child neglect and abuse. No mention of another child."

"Because they didn't know about him. But now we know about him, so…"

"You think we should tear up someone's basement just because you have a hunch?"

"Where would you look?"

"First, I would want to verify that this other kid even existed. Did it ever occur to you that your client might have an imaginary friend? Or even DID?"

Zachary was taken aback by that. "Like dual personalities?" He remembered how similar the writing of the two names had been. Because Ben Burton had written both? Two fractured personalities who didn't know that the other existed, or someone he had made up? "Uh… no, I hadn't thought about that."

"Do you know anything about this client's psychiatric history?"

"No."

"So he could be snowing you completely. You have no idea. He might not even be who he says he is. He might have just heard the story or read it in the paper and decided to play a part and see how far he can get with it."

"I don't think so."

"I don't either, but it's a possibility. Until you've verified his identity, you don't know who he is. And I think you need to get access to his medical records, if you can. Make him prove his case. Because he's going to have to before the PD is going to touch it. We can't just dig up someone's basement on some lunatic's tip."

"Right. Okay. He did verify his identity to the social worker, and she knew his names before and after adoption. But I'm not sure how much of this *can* be proven, though. Both children were kept a secret. No one on the street even knew they lived there. So no one but Burton or his parents could verify that there was a brother."

He could hear Burton asking over and over again. *Where is Allen? What happened to him?*

Did Burton know? Was it there, buried in his memories? Or was he shining Zachary on, enjoying playing a role?

And even if he believed it was true, was it? Were Bobby and Allen two different sides of the same person? From what Zachary understood of DID, it was usually caused by the kind of abuse Burton had been through. Horrific, ongoing child abuse. The inability to deal with reality as an integrated person. The need to dissociate to remove himself from it, just as Zachary found himself doing when something reminded him of the assault by Archuro.

"You need to find out what you can," Mario advised. "We'll need as much proof as possible before rushing into something like this."

27

Zachary knocked on Burton's hotel room door. He knew that Burton had consumed a huge amount of alcohol the day before, and who knew when he had finally stopped drinking and either passed out or gone to sleep.

"Do not disturb," Burton growled back from within. "Can't you read the sign?"

He had the door handle sign hung to keep the maid service from disturbing him.

"It's Zachary."

"I don't need any more towels."

"Ben. It's Zachary."

"What?"

"I need to talk to you. Are you decent?"

Burton started muttering to himself. Zachary assumed he was getting himself together and would let Zachary in when he was finished. It took some time, and there was a lot of muttering and walking back and forth in the hotel room before Burton finally opened the door.

He was looking pretty rough, but he was all in one piece. He motioned Zachary in, and Zachary took a few steps into the room before changing his mind. The room smelled rankly of alcohol, sweat, and vomit, and Zachary had no desire to sit in the fumes for a couple of hours.

"Let's open a window and let this place air out," he suggested, and proceeded to open one window a few inches without waiting for Burton's answer. "And we'll go somewhere else to talk." He considered. He wasn't going to go down to the lounge again, having to deal with Burton's constant drinking and possibly loud and threatening behavior. "We'll go back to my apartment." He hustled Burton out of the hotel room, grabbing the key card off of the dresser on his way out. "I don't usually have clients to my apartment, so—"

"We don't need to go to your apartment; we'll just go downstairs again."

"No, not this time. We need some privacy."

"Why?"

"Just come with me." Zachary motioned to the elevator down the hall, and Burton went along with him, dragging his feet the whole way.

Zachary managed to get him past the lounge with difficulty, and out to his car.

"At least let me stop for a smoke," Burton whined.

"I don't want the smoke in the car."

"I'll smoke it out here."

"You'll still smell like it. No."

"Sheesh, why are you being such a hard case all of a sudden? Knowing all of what I've had to go through, don't you think I have the right to drink and smoke a bit?"

"You've been through a lot of crap," Zachary agreed. "Worse than most people can even dream of. But that doesn't mean you need to drink and smoke constantly."

"Well… it kinda does."

"No. Just get in the car. We can stop and get something to eat if you want. Comfort food. Calm yourself down that way."

"Comfort food," Burton repeated dubiously. "What, like chocolate ice cream?"

"Chocolate ice cream works," Zachary remembered Kenzie insisting that they go out for ice cream after their first couples therapy appointment. It had become a tradition, and he had to admit, he looked forward to it, despite his usual lack of appetite. "Is that what you want?"

"No, I don't want ice cream. It's not my period," he sneered. "I want… a steak and a case of beer."

"Do you cook?"

"Not really."

"Well, we want to grab something you can take back to the apartment. Our steakhouses don't do takeout. So something you can get as takeout or at the grocery store and cook yourself."

Burton sniffed. He sat looking out the window while Zachary drove toward the apartment. He was behaving like a sullen teenager. But eventually, he decided that he'd better pick something or he was going to end up at Zachary's apartment with nothing to eat. Or having to choose between granola bars and frozen burritos.

"Burger and fries," he grumbled finally. "I suppose."

"Sure. Five Guys?"

Burton nodded. Zachary detoured to the nearest fast food place and they went through the drive-through.

"Aren't you getting anything?" Burton demanded after Zachary relayed his order to the crackling speaker.

"A milkshake. I've already eaten."

Not much, but he had eaten a little before going to pick Burton up.

"Milkshake," Burton repeated.

"You want one?"

"No."

In a few minutes, they were on the road again, and then back to Zachary's apartment. When he unlocked the door and let Burton in, his client looked around at the set-up. Zachary waited for the criticisms or teasing to begin. But Burton shrugged and headed over to the couch with his fast food. "I don't know what I was expecting. Jim Rockford worked out of his trailer, right?"

Zachary shrugged. He wasn't sure what Burton had been expecting either, but he was grateful not have to defend himself and his choice of where to live. Burton didn't know anything about the apartment fire where Zachary had lost everything he owned and nearly his own life. Burton didn't know about Zachary's history or the vagaries of the private investigator business. He indicated the table.

"Eat there. I don't want ketchup on the furniture."

"I wouldn't spill."

"Use the table."

After Burton sat down, growling grumpily, Zachary sat across from him. He took a few sips of his milkshake while Burton sat and got his food arranged on the table. Zachary wasn't surprised when, after drinking the first few inches of his cola, Burton lifted the lid to pour in the contents of his flask.

"So, why did we have to come back here for privacy?" Burton demanded. "Why not just meet at the lounge? That was good enough for you before."

"How much of last night do you remember?"

Burton didn't answer at first. He had said that drinking didn't affect him, so he was conflicted whether to admit that he couldn't remember everything that had happened or bluff his way through it. Zachary waited, seeing which he would choose.

"Fine," Burton said, "I might not have a clear recollection of everything that happened last night. What does that have to do with it?"

"I just think we should give the lounge and the bar a day or two to forget about it too. Give them a break. Otherwise, you might not find yourself able to drink there again."

Burton rolled his eyes. He worked quickly on his hamburger.

"Whatever. I don't see what difference it makes."

"So..." Zachary pulled out his notepad to make notes as he needed to. "I have talked to a few people today about you and Allen."

Burton froze and met Zachary's eyes. Then he reared back, moving farther away from Zachary and leaning back against his chair, when he'd previously been sitting forward. He was afraid of what was to come.

"Allen. What did you find out?"

"I found out more about you, but not very much about Allen."

"What?" Burton was cautious, not sure he wanted to hear. Zachary determined to take it slowly. He didn't want Burton to have a meltdown and to punch him in the face. Having a flashback and seeing him as one of his abusers.

"Do you remember telling me about walking outside one day? The day that you saw a dog?"

Burton nodded. The corners of his mouth lifted slightly at the memory of the dog. "His owner let me pet him."

"Was that the only time you had been out of the house?"

Burton's forehead creased. "The only time I'd been out? No, of course not."

"How often did you go out?"

"I don't know. How often do kids go out of the house?"

"I don't think you got out very often. But you remember what the outside of the house looked like, so maybe that wasn't the only time you'd ever gone out."

"No, of course not."

"When we were at the house, you weren't that interested in what was upstairs. Why was that?"

Burton shrugged. "I don't know. It just wasn't very interesting. Just a normal house, I've seen a hundred like that. Nothing remarkable about it."

"You barely even looked at the bedrooms. Usually, kids remember which bedroom was theirs."

Burton raised his eyebrows, looking at Zachary blankly. "Why would it matter which one was mine?"

"People care about things like that. They want to belong somewhere. To have a room that was theirs."

It was one of the things that had bothered Zachary about foster care. He never felt like he had a place of his own. Even though he was assigned a bedroom in every house he went to, it was never just his, and changing homes so often meant that he never felt like he put down roots and had ownership of a place.

"I know where my room is in the house I grew up in," Burton said, "With my adoptive parents. That was my room."

"And the room you wanted to see in the old house was the basement."

"Yeah…" Burton trailed off, apparently unsure as to where Zachary was going.

Zachary nodded. He sipped the milkshake, taking his time. Letting Burton think about it and get used to the idea before concluding, "Because that was where you lived. That's where they kept you."

Burton's face became a thundercloud. "No."

Zachary cocked his head and let Burton think about it. He needed time to go through his memories and sort it out. Did he have memories of the upstairs? Did he have memories of the basement? Where had his jar and his name been?

Burton shook his head again, definite. "No. They didn't keep me in the basement like an animal. That's wrong."

Zachary nodded. "Okay. Tell me about it, then. What else can you remember about your house? You've had some time to think about it. Maybe some more memories have come to you since we talked last."

Burton's anger abated slightly. He ate a few French fries. His forehead was still creased with worry lines. "That would be cruel," he said. "No one would keep their kids locked up in a place like that."

"People do. I'm sure you've seen in the news from time to time. Not very often, but it does happen. Sometimes just one child in the family, sometimes all of the children. Maybe the basement, maybe a locked bedroom or closet. Kids go to the bathroom in a bucket or a corner. Get fed now and then, not regular meals. Maybe they don't have any way to keep themselves clean or have clean clothes. It's horrible, I agree."

"Why would anyone do that? How bad would a kid have to be to be treated that way?"

Zachary studied the expression on Burton's face. Guilt. Dread. They had undoubtedly conditioned him. Made him feel like it was his own fault that he'd been locked up like that.

"A kid wouldn't have to be bad at all. Parents don't do it because they have bad kids. They do it because they are bad parents. Evil people. Normal people would never treat their kids like that. You know how your adoptive parents were. They loved and protected you. They would never do something like that."

Burton shook his head. "No. Never."

"And that's how normal parents are. But the people that you were born to… they were not like that. There was something wrong with them, not with you. It isn't your fault that they locked you in the basement. It isn't anything that you did."

"No," Burton repeated. But he didn't look convinced. Deep down inside, he still thought he was that naughty child. The child who was so bad that his parents had to lock him in the basement. The cold, dark, damp basement with a dirt floor.

"I'm sorry they treated you that way. They were wrong."

Burton swallowed. He had a long sip of his drink. Cola and whatever had been in his flask. Zachary was sure he wished they had stayed in the lounge, where he could have ordered drink after drink to satisfy his craving. Instead, all he had was the weak mixed drink, and only one cup. His eyes started to rove to Zachary's cupboards and fridge. But he wouldn't find any alcohol in the apartment. That was one of the reasons Zachary had taken him there. He couldn't deal with hours of Burton drinking again.

"They wouldn't do that," Burton said softly.

"Some people would. When you got out and went on your walk down the street, people recognized that you had been badly neglected, and they called the police. The police connected you with your parents, and they were arrested and went to jail."

Burton's eyes were wide and disconcertingly childlike. He had been holding those memories inside for decades. He had always kept that part of himself separate. That child had remained locked up in the darkest corner of his mind, just as he had been locked in the basement.

"Who found me?" he asked.

"I talked to a woman named Elise Perry. She remembers when you were found. When you went out for a walk and saw the dog, and the neighbors called the police. They thought someone had dumped you there, but then the police traced you back to the Weavers. Or the people calling themselves the Weavers."

"How?"

"You knew where you lived. You probably showed them. The police watched to see what happened. When your birth parents discovered you were missing and went out looking for you, that confirmed to the police that they were the ones who had been holding you. They arrested them, went into the house, and would have found the evidence in the basement showing that you had been kept there, neglected."

"It was still my home," Burton offered.

Zachary nodded. "Yeah. The only place you knew. It must have been very strange to be taken away from there. Put into foster care and then to your adoptive parents. Lots of disruption, strange new experiences."

"How could anyone do that, though?"

Zachary sucked on his straw, trying to focus on the cold, sweet, thick milkshake. If he could keep his focus on his senses and physical surroundings, he didn't need to go back into the past. Isolation cells at Bonnie Best when he 'acted up.' Being locked in a closet for 'cognitive time' when he'd broken rules or done something to irritate his supervisors at one of his group homes. He hadn't been forced to live in an unfinished basement, but he'd had enough experiences with isolation to empathize with Burton just a little too much.

He didn't offer Burton another explanation for why his biological family had treated him like that. It was inconceivable to most people. But some adults needed power. They needed absolute power over those who were under their control.

A child who wet his pants or wouldn't eat his peas simply couldn't be tolerated. Such defiance was a slap in the face and had to be crushed in the strongest possible way. They had to show who was boss and make sure that the child had no way to fight back.

No way to express any more defiance or independence.

28

What they did was unforgivable," Zachary said simply. "All that the state could do was to put them in prison. But that's not justice. That doesn't take away what happened to you or make you feel any better."

Burton shook his head in agreement.

"Do you remember Allen?" Zachary prompted after a period of silent contemplation.

Burton raised his eyes and looked at Zachary in confusion. "I lived down there with him? You're sure?"

"Someone wrote that name behind the furnace. Maybe you did. Maybe he did." Zachary didn't offer anything else, not wanting to plant any thoughts or false memories. Those things were indisputable facts.

"Maybe I wrote it," Burton said. "Maybe… Allen was an imaginary friend. Someone I made up to keep me company."

Zachary nodded. "Maybe you did."

Burton put his hand over his chest like it hurt. He shook his head. His eyes glistened with tears. Zachary waited. He hoped that Burton wasn't about to have a heart attack. That would put a definite crimp in the investigation. Burton was probably just feeling anxiety, like Zachary did when confronted with a truth he didn't want to face or a change that seemed insurmountable.

"Take deep breaths," he advised. "Nice and slow. Make sure you're breathing the air all the way out."

Burton's hand closed into a fist. The lines of his face hardened. Putting on a mask and trying not to let his emotion show.

"It's okay," Zachary assured him. "This is hard. Do you want to take a break?"

Burton looked around the kitchen and into the living room. "To do what?" he demanded. "There isn't exactly anything to do around here."

"You could stand up and walk around. Look out the window. Check your email. Just get grounded again."

Burton got up and left the table, left the rest of his food there and went to the big window in the living room. He looked down at the parking lot below. Zachary took out his phone and checked his mail, not wanting Burton to feel like he was under scrutiny. He clicked through a few of his emails. There wasn't a lot that he could respond to on his phone. The ones that weren't junk required some research or attachments. There was one from Lorne Peterson, his old foster father, and he made a mental note that he needed to call him. It had been too long since their last visit. Zachary needed to be more diligent about keeping up with him. He had little enough family; he needed to keep them close, let them know that they were appreciated. That Zachary didn't just reach out to them when he needed something.

"I didn't make him up," Burton said from the living room, not turning around, still staring out the window.

"Do you remember…?"

"Allen," Burton said, testing the name out. Rolling it around his mouth and considering the memories that saying it out loud brought back.

Zachary waited.

"He was… older," Burton said. "I think he was older than I was. He knew things I didn't. He was… my protector."

Zachary's own heart ached at the thought. The two little boys trapped down in the basement, Allen trying to protect five-year-old Burton. Allen probably wasn't much older than Burton, but he had put himself between his little brother and the adults who had all control over him. There was no way that he could protect himself or Burton against the abuse. But he'd been heroic. He had tried.

"He was my brother." It sounded more like a question than a statement.

Burton turned around to face Zachary, and Zachary saw the deep creases between his eyebrows smooth out. "My… big brother?"

Zachary did his best to look sympathetic, but not to nod or to feed Burton any more information. Burton needed to remember and work out what he could on his own.

"What can you remember about him?"

"It's so hard… it was so long ago."

"Yeah."

"He wrote the names. Do you think he wrote the names?"

"Is that what you think?"

"Yes. He must have written them. He was the one who could write. He knew… he knew things I didn't know."

"What things did he know?" Zachary wrote a few words in his notepad and waited for Burton to fill in the details.

"He was the one who knew about… dogs and cats. Other animals that he told me about."

"Because you hadn't ever seen them?"

Burton shook his head. "I don't know. I must have seen them before. What kid hasn't seen cats and dogs? I just… didn't know very much about them. We didn't have a dog."

"Most kids still see them on the street. Read about them in books. See them on TV."

"Must have," Burton mused. "I must have… I just remember the bugs. They were the creatures I knew best. What I could catch in my hands or my jar. We knew some of them… the spider that built its web in the corner. We would see it come out, watch it working on its web. Eating other bugs. The flies in the summer…" Burton's nose wrinkled. "There were so many flies in the summer, buzzing around us. Around…"

Zachary nodded. They would get a reprieve in the winter when the bugs were no longer flying outside the house and getting in through cracks in the windows or walls or through doors that stayed open too long. But during the summer, even in a cool basement, they would still be attracted by the smells of two little boys who were not properly cared for. Dirt, open sores, rotten food, excrement. Zachary could imagine how the flies would have plagued them.

"They get everywhere," he agreed.

Burton paced back and forth, rubbing his temples. He probably had a headache. All of the emotional work on top of being hung over and not having more to drink to numb it.

"What things do you remember about when you first went to your adoptive family?" Zachary asked. "Things that you were impressed with. Surprised by. Excited about."

Burton scowled. Maybe he was regretting that he had hired Zachary in the first place. It would be easier to just go home and not think about it anymore. Not to have to dig up and expose all of the old memories. "I don't remember a lot of specifics. I liked them. Mom and Dad. They were nice. I remember… they had lots of good things to eat. When I look at it now, they weren't anything special. But to me back then, it felt like… sort of like when you look at Christmas or Thanksgiving dinner. That there is just so much to choose from and everything looks, smells, and tastes so good. It felt like that. Like every day was another Christmas dinner. But when I think back to it now, it was just sandwiches. Oatmeal. Roast and potatoes. Not feasts. Not anything fancy. But it was all so good and made me feel… strong and healthy and like life was good because of it."

"You were very skinny when you got away. Malnourished."

"My mom says that's why my legs are a little bowed," Burton offered, looking embarrassed by the fact. "That it was from not having enough vitamins those first few years. But I thought… it just meant I didn't eat all of my vegetables. I didn't ever understand that I had… really been neglected."

"What else did you remember about living with your adoptive parents?"

"They had a nice house. Clean and sunny and everything neat and tidy. I had my own room. Nice soft bed with clean, white, fresh-smelling sheets. It wasn't even like I had special sheets with Batman or cars on them. I don't think they really had any idea about kids and what was popular. They were just clean, white sheets. And nice clothes. Whatever I wanted to eat."

Food again. It was probably hard for someone who had been so starved to think of anything else. That had been the most important priority in his life after his experience. Getting the calories that he needed. Filling his stomach. Food had been limited in Zachary's home, but he hadn't been as malnourished as Burton had been. Skinny and small, but he hadn't had rickets.

29

Zachary took a break from talking with Burton and called Aurelia Pace. He needed her input and confirmation before he could go back to the police department with any hopes of their getting a search warrant to look at the old house on Peach Tree Lane.

"Did you find him?" Pace asked immediately when she picked up the phone, and Zachary realized that she had been waiting for the call confirming that they had found the body of little Allen Weaver. He got a lump in his throat but tried to ignore it.

"No. We haven't gotten in yet. The police didn't have enough to go on. I've been interviewing Ben, and I have some more questions for you. I'm going to need your help if we're going to get them to look into it after all these years."

"I'll help however I can. What do you need?"

"I need some information on Ben after he was rescued and went into foster care."

"Yes?"

"Could he read and write?"

"What?"

"I want to know whether he already knew how to read and write when he went into foster care. Even a little bit."

"No… not that I remember. I would have to talk to his foster parents at the time, or maybe you could talk to his adoptive parents and find out whether he could read and write yet when he was placed with them. But I don't think so. He had been badly neglected. He didn't go to school. Would his parents have locked him down there and then taught him his lessons? Tutored him in his schoolwork? I can't see it."

"A lot of people choose to homeschool because they don't trust the state to do it. They may have felt like they had to teach him their beliefs and philosophies. That might have involved lessons in reading and writing."

"Maybe. Like I said, I would have to follow up to be sure, but I don't think so."

"Then he wasn't the one who wrote the names on the walls."

Pace was quiet for a minute as she thought about it.

"No. If he hadn't been taught to write his name, then he wasn't the one who wrote it."

That seemed obvious, and yet it had not occurred to her before.

"So someone else wrote it. That points to the possibility that another child did exist."

"Yes, I agree with that. I thought we had already established that there was another child at some point."

"You and I agreed… but the police say they need more. That maybe Allen is just a split personality or imaginary friend and never actually existed."

"Oh, I'm sure that's not the case."

"Still, we need a way to prove it."

"I suppose."

"It helps if we can say that Ben wasn't able to write his own name, and yet those names are written on the wall."

"I wish I had my file notes from back then, but I don't. If there were other things that he said or that we had concerns about, I would have written them down. But I can't remember now. Did he ever mention the name Allen? I wish I could say that he had. But he obviously never told me that he had a sibling, or I would have looked into it. It's very frustrating. It's horrible that this is only coming out now. If he'd only told us years ago, it could have been investigated at the time. We could have torn up the floor in that place."

"There's no guarantee it would have made a difference. Allen could be buried in the back yard. Or he could have been dumped in a dumpster or in the woods. There are a hundred different scenarios. There's no guarantee that we're going to find anything if we get a search warrant. And even if we find his remains… that is no guarantee that we'll be able to prove his cause of death or to charge his parents."

"I would like to be able to get justice for Ben. And for Allen."

"I don't know if either of us will ever be able to do that. There's nothing we can do to bring Allen back. Or to give Ben those first few years back. They were taken away from him forever."

Zachary dropped Burton off at the Best Western after another exhausting interview. While Burton's memories were getting closer to the surface, Zachary still wasn't sure they were going to find enough information to convince the police to issue a warrant to search the house and property for any sign of Allen's remains. All they had was Burton's memory and, as Mario had said, he could be trying to pull a scam. Trying to get attention.

But the emotions that Burton was going through, the reactions he'd had and the pain and grief in his eyes, those were all things that Zachary was sure were genuine.

He looked in the rearview and side mirrors as he pulled out to go to Kenzie's house for the evening. He was tired, but Kenzie would want to hear how things had gone, and he would sleep better if he spent time unwinding with her than he would if he went back to his own apartment and ping-ponged around it alone.

There was a motorcyclist stopped in the parking lot behind him but, as Zachary watched, he just sat there and didn't pull out. Maybe he had stopped to talk on his phone or to get something out of his packs, but he didn't seem to be going anywhere. Zachary pulled out and drove from the parking lot out to the main road. He turned the radio on to try to distract his busy brain from working on the problem of how to get a search warrant for the old Weaver home. He didn't want to go back to Kenzie with problems on his mind. He'd be distracted and she'd feel like he wasn't paying her any attention.

He resisted the urge to call anyone on the phone to discuss matters. Who would he talk to? He'd already talked to Pace and Burton. He didn't have anything new for Mario. He couldn't really discuss the case in any detail with anyone outside the case. There were confidentiality concerns, and he didn't have Burton's permission to share it with anyone else.

He glanced over his shoulder before changing lanes, then quickly corrected and slowed when he saw a motorcycle in his blind spot. The motorcycle shot past him, and he watched it weave through the traffic ahead of him. He checked the other lane, passed a stream of slower vehicles, and switched back again. The motorcycle was just ahead of him, holding its speed.

Zachary glanced at which exit he was at and noted the time. Ten minutes later, the motorcycle was still there, riding just behind him.

He was on a main thoroughfare. It was natural that other drivers would be going in the same direction as he was. But he had a bad feeling about the motorcycle.

He couldn't swear that it was the same one that he'd seen in the hotel parking lot. But if it was, it had been keeping just ahead of him way too long to be coincidental.

Zachary hit the brake, slowing a little. His distance from the bike should increase. Bikers liked to go above the speed limit.

But the space between him and the bike stayed the same. The bike had also slowed.

Zachary didn't like it. He sped up and blasted past the motorcycle and a few other vehicles, then settled behind a white van and watched the traffic behind him. Pretty soon, the motorcycle had also made its way past the cars that Zachary had. He didn't pull right in behind Zachary, but sat a lane over and just behind Zachary.

Who would be following him? His mind flashed immediately back to the members of the trafficking syndicate who had followed him and ended up shooting Luke. Zachary had neglected to spot that tail. They had used the cell phones that Luke and Madison had been using to track their positions. This time, they didn't have a cell signal to follow. Was it possible that one of them had spotted Zachary or had placed a tracker on his car sometime during the day and they were now moving in to deal with him?

He couldn't lead them back to Kenzie's house. Hopefully, they hadn't been following him for long and didn't already know about Kenzie and where she lived. He didn't think the motorcycle had been on his tail for that long, but there might be several other vehicles in the tail. Or motorcycle guy might have only been on Zachary's tail for one day, while someone else had been there previously. They wouldn't take that long to act, would they? They would strike fast, like they had before. They weren't patient enough to develop a longer-term plan.

Were they?

Zachary hit the Bluetooth button and called Kenzie. But what if they had put a tracker on his car and a bug inside where it could monitor his calls?

If they were that sophisticated, he was in trouble either way. They'd probably been on him for a while and listened to several other calls exchanged with Kenzie.

"Zachary. Running late?" Kenzie asked, upon picking up.

"Well, I wasn't, but I've run into some problems. I… might have a tail and I'm going to have to do something about it."

She didn't respond at first. "A tail?" she asked finally. "Who would be following you? I don't understand."

"I don't know. It could be related to an earlier case. I don't want to take any chances."

"You think it's the guys that shot Luke?" she discerned immediately. "Zachary, those guys are dangerous. I thought you said that they wouldn't be interested in you if they thought that both Madison and Luke were dead?"

"That was the plan."

"You don't think it's those guys, do you?"

"I can't think of who else would be following me now."

"You should be calling the police, not me."

"I don't think the police would do anything if I called them right now. They'd think it was a prank call or some crazy."

There was, again, a space of just too long before Kenzie responded again. Like she was considering whether he were paranoid, or whether what he said could really be true.

"Do you think they're tracking your phone?"

"No, I'm pretty careful about not opening any attachments or strange links. I don't see when they could have installed any kind of tracking on it. I'm sure it hasn't been hacked." Zachary thought some more about it, keeping an eye on the motorcycle, which so far was not taking any action, but was just sitting there, waiting for him to make the next move. "But why would they change tactics? Those guys know how to track people without being seen. They kept out of sight when they were tracking Madison and Luke. Why wouldn't they put a tracker on my car this time and stay out of sight?"

"Maybe they didn't have a chance. You surprised them."

"I'm not that hard to find. All they have to do is wait at my apartment building. Watch to see what vehicle I get out of, if they don't already know my license plate number."

"Your address isn't listed, is it?"

"No, but I know how easy it is to find someone."

"That's not exactly what I want to hear."

Zachary slowed his car, watching the motorcyclist for his reaction. He slowed and stayed behind Zachary.

"This guy is being pretty obvious," he said, relieved. "I don't think he's a professional."

"Then who is he?"

"I don't know."

Zachary watched him for a while longer. Where had he picked the motorcycle up? He had seen him at the hotel. Was it someone who knew Burton? Someone who was following him for some reason? It could just be something like a debt-collector. Zachary wouldn't be surprised if Burton had borrowed money from someone he shouldn't have or had gotten in deep with a bookie. He was the kind of guy who just dove into things that he knew he shouldn't be doing. Drinking, smoking, why not gambling? Maybe the guy on the motorcycle wanted to know who Zachary was and to see where he would go to find out if he had any money. If he could pay off Burton's debts, given the right incentive. It could be something like that.

"I'm going to see if I can lose him. I'll call you if I'm not going to be there within the hour."

Zachary hung up. He made sure that there was no one right behind him, then slowed abruptly and pulled up over the curb to sit in the grassy verge beside the road. The motorcyclist had to make a split-second decision as to whether to fall back and find out what Zachary was doing, or to keep going and hope to connect up with him again later. He could take the next exit, circle around, and come up on Zachary again from behind. See whether he was having car trouble or what was going on.

Either the motorcyclist didn't have fast enough reactions to pull over in time to stay with Zachary or he made the decision to go on so as not to look suspicious. Zachary watched him go on through the traffic, and kept an eye on him as far as possible. The motorcycle took the next exit ramp. Zachary pulled back onto the road and hit the gas, zipping down the thoroughfare as quickly as he dared. He wove in and out of traffic, took the exit after the one the motorcycle had taken, and took a few random turns that took him into a residential area. Once there, he pulled over to the side and watched for any sign of the motorcycle. If he showed up again, that meant that Zachary, his car, or something in the car was tagged with a tracking device.

He waited for half an hour without any sign of the motorcycle. He kept his ears pricked, and didn't hear any approaching.

He had lost the tail.

For now.

30

Hopefully, the fact that the motorcycle had been tailing him meant that the pursuer didn't know Zachary's name, where he lived, or anything about Kenzie. He would be safe going to her house.

Zachary waited for his heart to slow.

Eventually, he started the engine and worked his way through the quieter residential streets toward Kenzie's house. He didn't want to hit the main thoroughfare again, in case the motorcyclist was looking for him.

When he pulled to the curb in front of Kenzie's house, his phone rang. Zachary saw that it was Kenzie's number.

"Kenz?"

"I just wondered if maybe you wanted to pull into the garage. So your car is out of sight."

He considered for a moment, then shook his head. "No. I'm sure no one followed me here. And if they were following me, that means they didn't know I was coming here. You can keep your baby in the garage."

Kenzie's cherry-red convertible was her pride and joy, and he wouldn't want it on the street where it could be hit by a drunk driver. Or stolen. Kenzie might never forgive him if something happened to her baby.

"Are you sure? You could park in the alley."

"No. It's fine."

"Okay. See you inside."

She hung up the call. Zachary slid his phone away and removed his keys from the ignition. He locked the car once he was outside and checked the door. He looked at the house, looked up and down the street, and checked the handle again. He beeped it one final time to arm the alarm, and headed inside.

Zachary managed to get past the gatekeepers to reach Campbell about his case in the morning. Mario had clearly filled him in on the details that Zachary had previously provided.

"I understand your concern, Zachary, but I don't think there's enough for us to get a warrant."

"I've done a little more investigating, and I'm hoping we might be there."

"Okay." Campbell's chair squeaked as he tipped it back, and Zachary heard him take a noisy slurp of his morning coffee. "Tell me about it."

Zachary outlined what he knew, then waited for Campbell to think it through.

"I still don't know, Zachary. It's a stronger case, but I don't know if it is quite there."

"There was someone else in that basement with Burton," Zachary asserted.

"How can you be sure?"

"Because he couldn't write. So he is not the one who wrote those names on the wall. He was not able to read or write. Who do you think wrote them? The parents?"

"The social worker could be wrong. Maybe he could write his name. A lot of kids know that before they can read or write other things."

"I think she knew him pretty well. They would have had all kinds of examinations done to see what kind of shape he was in and what his IQ and educational levels were. They had to know all of that kind of thing to bring the parents to trial. They needed to know exactly how bad the damage was."

"Have you seen the tests that were done?"

"No. I would have to get in contact with the prosecutor and see if he still had all of the documentation on file and would let me look at it, and I haven't gotten the court documents yet to see who it was. You may have a lot of that information in the police file too, whatever investigations were done on your end. You could request them from storage and have a look."

"Yes, convenient for you, isn't it? Letting us do all of the work."

"I've put a lot of hours into it already. If you want me to look through the file, just let me know and I'll be at the police station the minute you want me."

"I know that," Campbell said, and Zachary could hear the smile in his voice. "I'm just teasing you." There was another sharp squeak from his chair. Zachary pictured him sitting up now, leaning over his desk, making some notes. "I'm going to have to think this through and see what we've got in the files. I wasn't around when this happened, obviously, so I don't have any background on the case. And I don't think we have anyone around who was here at that time."

"It was a long time ago, and the police department thought that they'd done everything that was required. They didn't know that there might have been another boy, or they would have looked into it then."

"Or maybe they did," Campbell pointed out. "I might open up that file and find that they already did a search at the time and didn't turn up any sign of the older boy."

"That's true." Zachary hadn't thought about that possibility. "You're right."

Maybe there wouldn't be any need for a search warrant at all. Maybe Campbell would call him back and say that the floor of the basement had already been dug up and there were no remains to be found.

"Have you looked for birth records for this other brother?" Campbell asked.

"Preliminary only, yes. I figured at the time that there was a possibility that the other boy had been adopted, so his name was changed, but the social worker said that they didn't have any idea there was another boy. He must have disappeared sometime before Burton was found."

"You don't think it means there wasn't another brother?"

"No. I think it means the births weren't recorded. The public records that I looked at never indicated that there were any children living with the Weavers. The census done during that time period states that there were only two adults living there. None of the neighbors knew that there were any children. I think the children were probably born at home and never attended to."

Campbell grunted. There were, of course, cases he was aware of where just that had happened. People didn't trust the government or wanted to stay off of the radar for some nefarious reason. Undocumented children. Ghosts who, as far as the government was concerned, never actually existed. They might be kept by the parents, as Ben and Allen had apparently been, or they might be trafficked or sold through black-market adoptions.

"I'll take a look from my end," Campbell promised. "It may take a few days to even get the files, so don't call me tomorrow looking for answers."

"Okay. You'll let me know what you find?"

"I'll let you know if I find anything actionable. No guarantee that I will. If we decide to investigate further or to get a warrant, I'll give you a heads-up. If not, I might not get back to you."

"I'll touch base next week, then," Zachary said. "Wednesday?"

Campbell grumbled. "I don't have time for this."

"That's why I'll call you. You have plenty else on your plate. You can give me an update then."

"Talk to you next week." Campbell hung up.

Zachary decided to spend the weekend with Lorne Peterson, his oldest friend and former foster father. He would have dinner with Lorne and Pat, his partner, and go see Joss and Luke, who lived closer to Lorne than Zachary did. Vermont was a small state, but it still took time to travel from one end to the other. However much Zachary enjoyed highway driving, he didn't have time to go back and forth twice over the weekend.

"Do you want to come?" he asked Kenzie. "Do you have the time, or are you busy over the weekend?"

"I've put in enough hours that I should be able to escape for the week-end. Unless someone calls in sick."

Zachary nodded. "I'll tell Pat that we'll both be there, then. If you end up not being able to go, he'll be disappointed, but it's not as inconvenient as showing up with another person who wasn't expected."

"I'm ninety percent sure I'll be able to go."

"Great." Zachary smiled at her. It was always nice to get away for a day or two, and they would enjoy a change of scene. As long as she didn't think he was planning a romantic getaway. He glanced back at her once just to be sure.

But they were still trying to work things out between them and Kenzie had promised not to push him into anything he wasn't ready for. As much as he wanted a close romantic relationship with her, his body and his PTSD brain set roadblocks in his way. He could push through them physically, but as he and Kenzie had discovered, that just resulted in his dissociating. Not being mentally present for the more intimate moments sort of defeated the purpose.

"It sounds nice," Kenzie said, catching his glance. He wasn't sure if she had picked up on his moment of anxiety or not. "It's always good to catch up with Lorne and Pat."

"Then, on Sunday, I'll be going over to see Joss and Luke. I'm sure it would be okay for you to go with me."

Kenzie drew in her breath and held it, thinking about the suggestion. She breathed out again. "I think I'll let you do that on your own for now. It's probably best for Luke if he doesn't have to worry about more people knowing where he is, and I'm not sure Joss would want me around."

"I don't know if she wants *me* around," Zachary pointed out. "I think she's prickly with everyone. It's certainly not just you."

"And then there's you."

Zachary opened his mouth, but didn't know what to say.

"I know it gets harder for you the more people who are there. It's pretty comfortable when it's just us and Lorne and Pat; they're laid back and you don't get too stressed out when it's just them. But with Joss… it's a lot more difficult to be around her. You're on edge, worried about doing or saying the wrong thing."

"Yes…"

"And then you add Luke in there. He's a whole different ball game. Lots of stress dealing with him too. Not personal, like with Joss, but worrying about all of the consequences of anything you say to him and what his future choices might be. And now knowing that Rhys is interested in him too…"

Zachary nodded more definitely. She understood him better than he gave her credit for. The combination of her experience with him and her intuition, and now the sessions with Dr. Boyle too… she really had a chance to get to know him more deeply than anyone in his life probably had before. Including Mr. Peterson. Including Bridget.

"So I think it's already stressful dealing with Joss and Luke, with all of the personal stuff and the potential repercussions. So maybe it's best if you don't have another person there to deal with as well."

"You don't stress me out."

"Not normally. But if you're trying to run interference between me and Joss or Luke… that's a different story. Or just having too many people in the room at once. I know it's not easy. You don't want to get overwhelmed."

Zachary nodded slowly. "Okay. Yeah. You're probably right. So you don't mind… staying at Lorne's while I go to Joss's?"

"Not at all. They always make me feel at home. And if they need some space, or I do, I can go over to the library or a coffee shop and get some personal time."

"Yeah. All right." Zachary considered the list of items that was starting to build up in his head. "I'll… I'll call Pat first, so I don't forget."

31

Spring came earlier in the southern portion of Vermont. It wasn't usually that noticeable, but things were definitely greener as they traveled south. When they arrived at the little white bungalow, Zachary saw Pat's tulips were coming up, splashing the yard with bright, welcoming color. He took a deep breath as he got out of the car, taking in the sweet smell of freshly-cut grass.

"It's so nice," Kenzie said. "I think we should stay here for a week or two until things catch up at home."

He looked at her quickly, then realized she was kidding. She might be able to get a couple of weeks of vacation since she had worked at the medical examiner's office for more than a year, but she would need to give them notice before just dropping off the map.

"It sure is nice," he agreed. "Sometimes, it seems like spring is never going to come."

They walked up the sidewalk together, Kenzie slightly ahead of Zachary, and Mr. Peterson had the door open by the time they got there.

"Kenzie, Zachary!" He pulled in each of them in turn for a hug, giving Kenzie a friendly kiss on the cheek. "Good to see you. Come in. Tell me how everything is."

Zachary always found himself examining Mr. Peterson for signs of aging and declining health. A fear that he could lose someone else in his life, one of the only people who had been there to support him over the years, almost since the fire. Lorne Peterson continued to age well. He was a little heavy around the belly, and his fringe of hair was completely white, but he still moved with vigor and always seemed happy and healthy. Zachary couldn't see any signs that he was declining.

They gathered in the living room to chat. Pat poked his head out of the kitchen, where he was cooking up something that made Zachary's mouth water, even with his suppressed appetite.

"Kenzie. Zach. How was the drive?"

"Great," Zachary answered, at the same time as Kenzie answered, "Pretty."

"Next time we'll be able to bring the convertible," Zachary said to Kenzie. Flying down the highway in a convertible with the top down was fun, but not pleasant if it were too cold. Kenzie was looking forward to when she could take it out again.

"Sounds good." Pat wiped his hands on the dishtowel he was holding, then flipped it over his shoulder. "Dinner will be on shortly."

———

Kenzie and Zachary each filled Lorne and Pat in a little on what they were working on. Kenzie was careful not to share too many details of her work, which was not generally acceptable for dinner conversation. When Zachary started to talk about Burton's case in general terms, Lorne laid down his fork and watched Zachary intently.

"I think I remember that case."

Zachary stared at him. "You do? But it happened upstate, and it wasn't even in the papers there."

"No. But we were still fostering then. That kind of thing goes through the fostering committee like lightning. Hearing that a child who has gone through that kind of thing is going into the system? Everyone follows it. Holds their breaths to see who gets him, wonders about what kind of problems he's going to have. Something like that… Well, to be honest, it's like what happened to you, Zachary. When the community hears about something so unusual or extreme, the whispers start. Even before the internet and texting, people would get on the phone and light up the lines."

Zachary nodded slowly. It made sense. It hadn't even occurred to him that Mr. Peterson would know anything about the case. He knew that foster parents weren't allowed to share confidential information about their charges with each other. But apparently, there was no such prohibition against sharing gossip and speculation about where such a child would go or what problems he might have. There would be no names or private information shared, but people who knew the circumstances might still spread it on a no-names basis.

And he hadn't thought about his own story being shared between foster parents before. He knew that the social worker would tell them what she thought they needed to know about the circumstances, but they also held things back, trying to make it so that a child sounded less damaged or needy than they were in order to get them into the right home.

He shifted uncomfortably. How much had the Petersons known about him before he was placed there? And later families and group homes?

"Did you hear anything about him after he was placed in foster care?" Kenzie asked.

It took Zachary a few moments to remember that she was talking about Burton, not him.

"Heard he was quiet, withdrawn. You never know, with a kid who's been through so much trauma, if he's going to be angry and destructive."

Like Zachary had been. He wasn't *actually* angry and destructive, but easily upset, impulsive, and making poor decisions. And foster parents and teachers had thought the worst of him. His social worker had been compassionate, but even she had dressed him down on more than one occasion, trying to get him to keep out of trouble. That had proved to be impossible.

"Do you know who got him? Did you know the family he went to?"

Lorne thought back, his forehead crinkling. "I think… oh, it was a long time ago… Marty and Kathy Anderson? I think… yes, I'm pretty sure they were the ones who got him. We had conferences that we attended in Burlington. Everyone in the state. So you got to know other foster parents, even if they weren't close by."

"You don't know what happened to them do you? If they stayed in the state? Still foster parents?"

"I didn't keep track of them. Maybe I could hire a private investigator to track them down." Mr. Peterson smiled and winked. "Sorry it's such a common name."

Zachary shrugged. "It makes it harder, but not impossible, if they stayed around. Helps if they stayed together too, but even if they didn't, I might still be able to find them."

"What would you ask them? They won't be able to share anything confidential."

"If I take Burton there, they can talk to him about his own case. Or he can sign a waiver allowing them to talk to me."

"Not sure of that. It's statute protected. They might need to get lawyers involved before they can say anything."

"If it's about a crime that was committed? Abuse and possible murder of another child? I think there's an exception."

Lorne nodded, conceding the point. "Probably. But they still might want to get a lawyer involved just to confirm the fact. People have to be careful these days. Such a litigious society."

"Yeah." Zachary nodded. He pulled out his notepad and wrote down the names before he could forget them, drilling Mr. Peterson to see what he remembered about where they lived, Marty Anderson's profession, and anything else he knew that might help Zachary identify and track them.

"Do you think they'll know anything that will help you with this case, though?" Kenzie asked. "They weren't involved until after Ben was taken out of the home. Social services probably didn't tell them all the details. And they couldn't share things they didn't know."

Zachary rolled his shoulders. "I don't know. They might know something. You never know what Burton might have said to them in the time he was there. Maybe he asked after his brother. Told them a few details. They wouldn't necessarily know that anything had happened to the brother. They might have thought that both boys were recovered and sent to different homes." Zachary looked at Mr. Peterson. "Did you know that it was just one boy? What would you have thought if one of your kids had started talking about a sibling you hadn't been told about?"

"I wouldn't have thought anything of it. Kids come from all kinds of diverse backgrounds. They might have step-siblings, half-siblings, foster siblings, kids that were raised in the same family, facility, compound, whatever. The native kids often refer to their cousins as brothers and sisters. I would have just assumed the other child was apprehended before him, or left and went to a different home with a different parent at some point."

Zachary looked back at Kenzie. "So he might have said something to them and they never even thought to report it."

"I guess so. Hopefully, you can find them and they'll remember something."

32

Dinner at Lorne and Pat's went well, as it almost always did. While it was sometimes awkward or overwhelming if there were too many people there, it was easy when it was just Kenzie, Pat, and Lorne. Zachary could relax around them and not feel like he was in the spotlight or had to put on a show all the time.

The next day was the visit with Joss and Luke, which wasn't nearly as comfortable. Zachary had to be careful of every word he said, worried that Joss would take it the wrong way and be angry or offended. He hoped that one day she would forgive him for his part in the family's breakup and the sequence of events that had happened to her, so he was always trying to make up for it and to play the part of the penitent, perfect brother. But it wasn't a role that he could fill.

He was more distracted this time by Luke and focused on him more than on Joss. Not just because he wanted to know how Luke was and how he was settling in, but how likely he was to reform and stay on the right side of the law, to recover completely from his addictions, and to possibly be someone who would be stable and a good example for Rhys.

It seemed like a long shot.

"Are you… making new friends here?" Zachary tried. He wasn't sure how to find out whether Luke was looking for a new partner and, if he were, whether he had found anyone who suited him. While Luke had been with Madison when Zachary met him, he knew that Luke had, in the past, had relationships with both boys and girls. He had no idea which Luke preferred, if he had a preference.

"Yeah, I'm meeting other people in AA and NA," Luke said casually. "I'm… pretty good at making people like me."

Zachary nodded uncomfortably. Luke's previous life had him luring young people of both sexes into the trafficking business. He was very charming and easy to talk to. He was handsome and had a way of appearing vulnerable and likable.

"Anyone in particular that you really click with?" Zachary still tried to keep the question casual, as if Luke's answer didn't mean anything to him. Just chit-chat. Small talk. Two people marginally connected with each other catching up with the other.

"No…" Luke stared off into space. "I don't know that I want to get involved with anyone at this point. I mean, a hookup, okay, hanging out together or calling when things get tough with the recovery. But someone special…? No. I don't really feel like I can trust anyone at this point. Maybe in the future… when people have had a chance to prove themselves. Right now. I don't really know anyone… *know* them. I don't want to get too close to anyone."

Zachary nodded. "You open yourself up… to being hurt, betrayed."

Luke clicked his tongue. "'Zactly. I'm not ready for anything… personal yet."

Joss cleared her throat. She rocked back in her easy chair, bringing her legs up to a crossed position in front of her. "So what are you doing in these parts? Checking up on us?"

"No… just came to see Lorne and Pat… thought it would be good to see everyone in one trip. Them. You guys. Catch up a bit."

"You didn't bring your girlfriend this time? Mackenzie?"

"Kenzie. I did, actually. She just stayed back at Petersons'. I thought… might be too much of a crowd here."

"How did she feel about that? I bet that went over well, you invite her along and then pawn her off on your friends."

"No, it was her idea, actually. I thought she would come all the way. But she knows me too well. Didn't want to make it more difficult by having to juggle…" Zachary motioned to Joss and Luke and made a third motion to where Kenzie would have been. "Dealing with everyone at once. She didn't want to be…" He couldn't think of the right word. Third wheel? Extra baggage? Nothing sounded respectful and appropriate. There wasn't anything negative about Kenzie being there with him. It might just have been too much for him to focus on, when he was trying so hard to heal his relationship with Jocelyn and evaluate how Luke was settling in and whether he was likely to maintain his new life or fall back into his old ways.

"She's smarter than she looks," Joss said coldly.

"Kenzie's very smart," Zachary told her, not sure how to take that. "She has a doctorate."

"Yeah, but that's book smarts. I'm talking about being people smart. I don't get the feeling she has a lot of experience in… dealing with people like us."

"Well… no. I guess you're right there. But she's trying. And she's been really good for me."

"You're lucky to have her."

"Yeah. I know. Trust me; I count my blessings every day she stays with me."

"Can't be easy for her. We're not exactly the easiest people to get along with."

"No." Zachary rolled his eyes. "She's had to put up with a lot of my crap. I try, but I don't always succeed in being… good relationship material."

Jocelyn blew out her breath. She made a noise in her throat and spoke to Luke. "You should have seen this guy when we were kids. He was always 'trying.' But man, did he like to screw up. There was always something. And it didn't matter what you did, how many times you told him not to do something, he'd always find another way to screw it up, or just plain disobey. Man, he gave me a lot of grief."

Zachary tried to swallow the lump in his throat. "I know, Joss."

"You were the most aggravating kid. You wouldn't believe that someone could want something so bad, and screw it up so royally."

Zachary nodded, unable to think of anything to say in his defense. She knew that he tried.

And he knew that he failed.

Every single time.

"You've been quiet since you got back," Kenzie observed.

They were on the highway again, back on their way home. Zachary was glad to be going home. And glad to be on the road, where he could zone out and not have to think about anything as he drove. It was one of the only times that he could reach what he thought of as a flow state. A time when his brain seemed to stay on track instead of running out of control, and he could stay focused and think things through more easily.

"Just thinking."

"About what? Joss and Luke or the case?"

"A bit of both. Burton's big brother. My big sister. The different ways our lives have taken us."

"Yeah. You lead very different lives. Imagine what yours would have been like if you had been adopted when you were five, and grew up in just one home."

Zachary thought of Burton's nonstop drinking and antisocial behaviors. Zachary had managed to avoid substance abuse. But he had gone off the rails in other areas where Burton seemed to be more secure. What would Zachary's life have been like if he'd been raised in a single stable home after age five, like Burton and Zachary's brother Tyrrell. Would it have helped him? Or would he have still had to deal with the same problems?

And what about if he had spent his first five years locked in a dark, lonely basement instead of growing up in the dysfunctional family he had? While he'd had to deal with violence and neglect in his own home, he'd had five siblings to play with. He'd had the great outdoors to stomp around in and run off his energy in. It had been a completely different start from Burton's.

"Different lives," he acknowledged Kenzie's comment. "I don't know if it would have been better to grow up in just one adoptive home, like he did."

Kenzie raised her eyebrows and looked at him. "Really?"

"I mean… I think that would have been better overall… but it would depend on what the parents were like… and the therapy and everything… I think Burton grew up in a pretty good home, but maybe that doesn't matter with the amount of damage that had already been done. To him. To me. Maybe once you reach a certain threshold… no amount of love and stability can fix you."

He stared at the road, thinking about it. He'd told Rhys that they were alike in that way, both broken inside. And so was Burton. Rhys had a good life with his grandmother, but she'd made her mistakes in the past, and what he'd had to live with the first fourteen years with his mother and his aunt and the loss of his grandfather… was her love and attention now enough to keep him on the right track? Zachary wanted to think that he would be okay. But he'd already seen warning signs. Rhys taking off on his own to go to Zachary's house in the evening, when he wouldn't be able to get back home before dark. Lying to Vera about where he was going and holding things back from Zachary. Now showing an interest in Luke, someone who was not just lost, but dangerous.

"Do you think it can make a difference? After the damage has been done, does anything make a difference?"

Kenzie sighed and looked out her window. "I don't know. I'd like to think so."

33

It wasn't as hard as Mr. Peterson had feared for Zachary to track down Marty and Kathy Anderson. Unfortunately, only Kathy Anderson was still alive. Her husband had died a few years earlier, and Zachary was still trying to figure out by her explanation that he'd been "taken suddenly" whether he had died of disease or accident. Not that it made any difference to his discussion with the widow.

They had introduced themselves at the door. Burton was quiet and more subdued than usual, not drinking openly or being difficult to get along with. All of the emotion he'd shown over Allen's name and what had happened to him was suppressed. He acted as if he remembered none of it. He introduced himself as Ben, one of Kathy's former foster children, and she hadn't shown any recognition at first. They'd fostered a lot of kids over the years. She had probably had others show up at her door in the past. She couldn't be expected to remember all of them.

They sat down in her tidy living room and made small talk for a while, Zachary saying more to Mrs. Anderson than Burton did. He asked about her home, how long they had fostered, and anything else he could think of that would make her comfortable and put her at ease before the more uncomfortable questions that would follow.

Eventually, there was no way to avoid it, and Zachary took the plunge.

"Ben's name when he was here as a foster child was Bobby Weaver. Do you remember that name?"

"We've had more than one Bobby," Kathy said thoughtfully, digging back deep into her memory. "Bobby Weaver…"

"He came to you after a very negligent home," Zachary went on. "He was quite thin and malnourished."

"He wouldn't be the only one." Kathy closed her eyes briefly. "Yes… Bobby. That was…" she looked at Burton for a moment, and then away, careful not to stare. "He'd—you'd—been kept in a basement."

Burton nodded.

"Oh, yes. I remember Bobby." Kathy Anderson's chin lifted as she thought back to it. What she had known at the time. Maybe other things she had learned since. It had been a big deal when he had been put into her home.

"I've heard that he was pretty quiet," Zachary said. "And he would only have been with you for a few months before he was placed with his adoptive parents."

"Yes. That's right. All of that is right."

"He wasn't disruptive?"

"Oh, no," Mrs. Anderson gave a short laugh and shook her head. "On the contrary. He had to be pushed into any new experience. Encouraged to try new things. To experiment. He was very quiet and would just sit there if you didn't get him doing something."

"And did he like… animals?" Zachary tried.

"Oh, yes. He was a bit scared. Especially with dogs that were loud or moved quickly. But gentler animals, yes, definitely. And his bugs!" Her eyes lit on Burton once more. "You probably don't remember how obsessed you were with bugs."

Burton gave an embarrassed grin. "Actually, yes. I do remember. They were… my whole world. Always trying to catch them, looking for something new."

She nodded agreement. "Yes. I never knew what I would find when I went into your room. You had jars, but sometimes there were escapees. Or sometimes, maybe, you didn't put them into jars in the first place."

Burton scratched the back of his neck, smiling. "Maybe." He admitted. "I didn't like them to be trapped."

They all sat and thought about that for a few moments. They all knew what Burton's experience with being trapped in on small room had been.

"Could Bobby read or write?" Zachary asked.

"No. He didn't have any reading readiness skills. We taught him the alphabet. Things like shapes and colors that he wasn't familiar with. Reading through books like *Richard Scarry's Cars and Trucks and Things that Go* to learn about things that were out there in the world that he had never experienced. And feeding therapy."

"Feeding therapy?"

Kathy looked at Burton, verifying with her gaze that it was okay for her to talk about it. Burton nodded.

"Normally, you start toddlers on soft, smooth foods, and then work your way up to different textures and learning to chew things properly. You expose them to a wide range of foods so that even picky kids have a lot of options to choose from and can stay healthy. Bobby had a lot of sensory defensiveness. He didn't like different textures or strong flavors. He had probably only been given pablum or oatmeal, or maybe some soups. So he would gag or spit food out a lot. We thought at first that he was sick, that there was something wrong with his stomach. But it was just that he wasn't used to eating what a normal child would."

Zachary made a couple of notes. Who could help but feel sorry for the little boy who had been so neglected he didn't even know how to eat properly?

"He was very quick to make up for lost time," Kathy said. "He was very curious about things and learned fast."

"So he couldn't write his own name?"

"No. Not when he came to us. It took a few days to teach him how, when he'd learned his alphabet and spent some time developing the fine motor skills for drawing and writing."

"Do you remember him ever talking about a brother?"

"A brother?" Kathy looked puzzled. "No. I don't think we knew about any brother."

"Allen," Burton said.

She looked at him, her brows drawn down. "Allen," she repeated.

They both waited for it to register, for her to access any memories she might have of the name. She shook her head slowly. Then, "Allen?" she said again.

Burton nodded.

"Let me think."

She got up from her seat and went over to a bookcase where there were volumes and volumes of large books. She ran a finger over them, looking at the spines. Then finally pulled one out. She sat back down next to Burton, and Zachary saw when she opened it that it was a book of photos.

"Do you want to see a picture of you when you came to us?"

Burton nodded wordlessly.

Kathy flipped pages until she found it, then pointed. Zachary didn't have a good vantage point, but he could see the small figure in the middle of the pictures. A little waif of a boy. All alone in the middle of the picture.

"This is the day you came."

Zachary looked at the pages of pictures, and the volumes of books on the shelf. "You took a picture of every child on the first day?"

"Once you've had a child run the day he's dropped off… yes. You don't ever again want to call the police and not have any pictures of the child you are trying to report missing."

Zachary nodded. Very practical. Kathy gazed down at the picture of little Ben. Except he'd been Bobby, then. Bobby Weaver, just rescued from where he'd been held in the cold, dark basement all of his life. Or at least, a good portion of it.

"Allen," she said again. "Allen was your brother?"

Burton cleared his throat. "I think… he was."

"But he wasn't with you when you… escaped that place. When the police went and arrested those… those horrible people."

"I don't know what happened to him. I'm trying to remember. To find out. And if I ever mentioned him to you… maybe the police will agree to look."

She gazed at him blankly. "Look? Look where?"

"In the basement."

"But they looked in the basement."

Burton looked at Zachary.

"We… would like them to see if there are any remains. If he was buried there."

"Buried in a basement?"

"There was a dirt floor."

"Oh." She shook her head sadly. "Oh, I hope not…"

Burton looked down at the picture of himself. So long ago. So small and forlorn.

"What do you remember about him?" Kathy asked.

"Not very much. He was there with me. He told me stories. Tried to protect me."

Burton touched the picture tentatively, as if doing so might help bring the memories back. Had they looked similar, as brothers often do? Maybe seeing his own face back then would help to trigger a memory, bring another fragment of it back.

"We know that he could write," Zachary said. "The boys' names were written on the wall. Bobby and Allen. If Bobby couldn't write them, then it must have been Allen."

"And he was older," Kathy discerned. "Because he had been taught how and Bobby hadn't. Maybe he even went to school at some point."

Zachary nodded. It was an avenue that he hadn't pursued, on the assumption that neither boy had ever seen the inside of a school. But who had taught Allen how to write? Their mother? A woman who didn't even seem to care about feeding her children properly? Why would she take the time to teach him his letters?

And if he had gone to school, what name would his records have been in?

"Do you know what their real name was?" he asked Kathy Anderson. "The name Ben went by was Bobby Weaver, but that wasn't their right name, was it? They were just trying to stay below the radar, taking on a pseudonym."

"Oh, yes. You're right. Bobby came into the system as Weaver, and we just left it at that. His birth hadn't been registered before then, and we didn't want there to be a connection between him and his parents. Particularly when he got into school. We didn't want any of the other children making that connection."

"Do you remember what their name was?"

"I might remember if you give me a few minutes." Kathy put her fingers to her temples and rubbed them, closing her eyes and concentrating. "Oh… O' something. It was so long ago, but of course we followed the story, because it impacted our family so directly."

Opening her eyes, she placed a tentative hand on Burton's shoulder. He swallowed and gave her a forced smile. Zachary wondered whether he remembered her at all. He had lived with her only a few months. Did he have good feelings about her, even if he didn't remember her clearly? Or had it been such a confusing, traumatic change that his feelings about that time had been negative?

There was no telling how the woman, despite her appearance of kindly compassion, had treated him in the time he had been there. She might have been gentle and encouraging, or she might have been a strict hard-liner. Or both. Sometimes the ones who flip-flopped were the most difficult of all.

"Dougherty," Kathy said suddenly. "That was it. Doughertys."

"Did you know their first names? Were they the same, or had they taken on different first names too?"

"I think they were the same. What were they?"

Zachary didn't answer immediately. "Do you want me to tell you? Or were you trying to remember?"

"Elizabeth. And Sam?"

"Then they kept the same names." That would, at least, mean that Zachary could look them up at the courthouse and see what had come out in the trials. And he could check to see if there were a birth certificate or any kind of announcement or social security claim for an Allen Dougherty. It was highly unlikely that he had survived and was still alive out there somewhere. It was always possible that he'd been pawned off on another family and ended up in the system, but the chances that Zachary would be able to find any records of him were slim to none. Chances were, Allen had never left that basement.

But Burton might have extended family out there who were decent people. Cousins, aunts and uncles, grandparents. Just because his parents had been pieces of crap, that didn't mean that everyone related to them was.

34

Zachary had worried that it would be hard to get Burton out of his old foster home. That he would be so happy to have some link to his old life that he wouldn't be able to leave Kathy Anderson behind.

But it had turned out not to be a problem. Even as Zachary was still asking Kathy more questions about what Burton had been like while he had been there and to ferret out any clues she might have that she didn't even know she had, Burton was making noises about wanting to go. He wanted a drink, Zachary knew. He wanted to wash everything away, to forget about his former life, foster mother included, and not to have to talk about it anymore. He was no longer the little boy in the picture.

Or maybe he was, and that was the problem.

He stood and motioned to the door, hurrying Zachary along.

Zachary rolled his eyes and followed him. "I'll call you if I need anything else," he told Kathy. Now that he had her information, he could circle back when he needed to. She had seen that Burton was fine with his information being shared with Zachary, and they could continue the conversation privately, without him shifting around and breathing noisily, like a six hundred pound gorilla in the middle of the room.

"Sure. Thank you for coming. It's always good to see one of our old kids again..."

Burton was hurrying out the door toward Zachary's car. He shrugged at Kathy. "Sorry. It's all been pretty difficult for him."

"Yes… I'm not surprised. We haven't had many that have come from such terrible situations."

Not many.

Just that phrase was shocking. It should have been 'he's the only one.'

But Zachary had heard of and read too many stories about children being the victims of such horrific neglect or abuse it was almost beyond belief. Some of them survived. Some did not. And of the ones who did survive, how many were too broken to ever fully recover?

Zachary followed Burton out to the car and clicked the key fob to unlock the door for him. Burton climbed in without a word and shut his door, isolating himself in a quiet bubble of space. Zachary took his time walking to the car and around to his door. Long enough for Burton to take a few breaths to steady himself.

Or, as Zachary saw when he opened the door and slid into his seat, a few belts from his flask. He didn't say anything.

"Don't act all judgy with me," Burton snapped. "You've got no idea what it's like."

Zachary knew how overwhelming his own issues were, how difficult it was for him to deal with flashbacks or to deal with reunions with his own family members. He didn't judge Burton for how he chose to handle it. That was his own business. Was spending most of his time drunk better or worse than having a complete meltdown? Or attempting suicide? There were just some things that were too harrowing for people with normal, unremarkable pasts to understand. There was no polite, conventional way to deal with the cruelties that Burton had survived.

———

Zachary was so deep into his investigations that he was barely aware that Kenzie was there. He should have put his computer aside and spent some quality time with her, but he'd felt like he couldn't leave what he was doing. He was startled when she sat down next to him and touched him on the arm. He looked at her, then looked at the system clock on his computer.

"Oh… sheesh, I'm sorry, Kenzie. I was… sort of focused on what I was doing."

"Sort of?" she teased.

"Uh… have I ignored you all night? Did we eat?"

"I ate." Kenzie looked to Zachary's side, and he saw a piece of pizza with a bite or two out of the tip congealing on a plate on the side table where he must have laid it down and promptly forgotten about it.

"Really. I'm sorry."

She slid her arm around him and snuggled in close. "When I was in school and we covered learning disabilities, I never really understood what they were talking about when they said that ADHD wasn't the inability to pay attention to something, but to regulate your attention in the usual way. It sounded like it was just semantics. They did say that people with ADHD sometimes hyperfocus. On things like video games or areas of particular interest. It sounded like an ADHD diagnosis was just an excuse for not doing your work, but playing games or doing what you liked instead."

Zachary nodded and rubbed his neck. He'd clearly been bent over his laptop in the wrong position for some time. He would probably have a stiff neck for days. "Hyperfocus," he agreed.

"You are the king of hyperfocus."

"I didn't mean to ignore you."

"It's a compliment. I know you're doing work, not just messing around on social networks. Your ability to dig in like that… that's what makes you such a good investigator. One of the things."

Zachary wasn't used to having his dysregulation complimented. If it had been Bridget he'd ignored all night… even for just ten minutes…

"So, have you made progress?" Kenzie asked. She reached around him to grab his plate and took a bite of his cold pizza. Then she handed it to him, and he knew he was supposed to finish it. He took a couple of bites. It was good; he just didn't feel like eating.

"I did find a birth certificate for Allen Dougherty. I think that, together with the fact that both the social worker and the foster mother agree that Burton could not have written the names Bobby and Allen on the wall, will be enough for the police to pursue a warrant."

"How much older was Allen?"

"Four years older than Bobby. Or Ben. He probably attended a year or two of school before… before whatever it was that happened that resulted in Bobby and Allen being imprisoned in the basement."

"You think there was a… trigger? An inciting event?"

"Maybe. Sometimes there's a specific incident that makes people start treating their children differently. They probably weren't great parents before that, but Allen knew how to read and write, and Bobby didn't. I think… maybe something happened in between."

"Maybe not. Maybe it was just a gradual descent into depression, abuse, addiction."

Zachary shrugged. "Maybe. I've ordered copies of the court transcripts, but I don't know how long it will take to get them. Maybe there will be something in there that will tell their story. They must have had something to say in their defense… some sob story. People like this don't take responsibility for their own behavior. They always blame it on someone else."

"Yeah, I've met people like that."

"I'm going to see if I can work out a family tree, too. If they have family in the area. Grandparents might speak up if they are asked now about Allen. Even if it's just to say that they don't know when he disappeared or what happened to him. They can at least verify that he existed. That they had seen him at some time."

"Are you going to be able to do that?"

"Dougherty is not a common name. Not uncommon, but if they have been in Vermont for a while, I might be able to find some obituaries or other information that will help me to build a family tree."

"How long did his parents serve?"

Zachary had been looking at his computer again, going through the information he had been able to collate on Allen and the parents. It wasn't much more than names and dates, but there were, at least, official records to back up the story that they had been trying to construct. He looked at Kenzie quickly.

"What?"

"How long did Ben's parents serve in prison? How much time?" When he didn't answer, she raised her brows. "What were their sentences?"

Zachary blinked. In his mind, anyone who did what Elizabeth and Sam Dougherty had done deserved to stay in prison for the rest of their lives. But he hadn't come across that detail yet. The news reports had been sparse to nonexistent, and neither the social worker nor Kathy had mentioned how long the Doughertys had been sentenced to serve, or even what they had been convicted of.

Murderers got out of prison. Not the worst ones, maybe, but plenty of people who had served time for murder got out after twenty years and continued their lives. Burton's parents had been convicted decades earlier. If they had killed Allen, no one had known it at the time, and at most they had been convicted of child abuse and negligence. Not likely to be life sentences.

He swore under his breath.

Kenzie sighed and nodded. "I doubt they're still in prison," she said gently.

"After all they did to that little boy? People knew what they had done and they wouldn't put them away for life? How could they be out when he is still suffering?"

"Yeah. It's not very fair, is it?"

"No." Zachary rubbed his fist against his forehead, fighting the impulse to beat it against his head. "No, no, no."

She put her arm around him and squeezed him to her. "I know."

Zachary leaned into her.

He knew that there was no justice for kids who were abused. While he blamed himself for the fire that had burned the family home down, and for all of the things he had done that had driven his mother to abandon them, he knew that his parents had been abusive. It took a lot of years in therapy to finally accept that the abuse had not been his fault. He had not brought that on himself. They had drunk too much, and they had hurt each other and their children.

The things that their mother had expected—for the older girls to look after the younger ones, for them to all stay out from underfoot, and for them to generally fend for themselves—had been unrealistic and unfair. Children didn't raise themselves. And yes, they made messes and got into mischief and had accidents. Even if Zachary had gotten into more than his fair share of trouble, that didn't justify beatings.

And not buying food or feeding the children much of the time hadn't just been a matter of poverty. There were programs available to help. But money had gone toward alcohol and other vices instead of food, food stamps had been bartered for other things, and if children were sent to bed hungry, they'd better not have the nerve to cry about it.

His parents had never gone to jail longer than overnight, usually for brawling so loudly that the neighbors had called the police. They'd never gone to prison for abuse or neglect. While Zachary and the others suffered through hardships in foster care, his parents had… done what? They hadn't stepped up to take responsibility.

Zachary had never investigated to see where they had gone after abandoning the children. Had they stayed together and eventually killed each other? Gone their separate ways and started two more families? He didn't imagine that they had reformed. That would not be consistent with the behavior he had observed as a child.

So he knew there was no justice for children like him and his siblings. The system had failed them. He only hoped that the youngest children had fared better. Tyrrell had gone through some tough times, but he said that he had been able to stay with the younger ones until he was a teenager, at least. He hadn't told Zachary much about Vince and Mindy, but he mentioned them now and then and Zachary knew they were still in touch through email. One day, maybe he'd meet them and find out their stories.

"They couldn't just let them out," he told Kenzie.

But he knew it wasn't true. He just wanted it to be true. He wanted to help Burton to recover, to be able to reconcile with his past, as horrific as it was. He wanted Allen to rest in peace, and maybe for Burton to be able to connect with extended family. The idea that the people who had forced him to live like an animal in a pen were walking around free was just too much.

"Maybe it's time to put all of this aside and relax for a while before bed," Kenzie suggested.

"Yeah. I'll clean up." But Zachary didn't move. He stayed leaning against Kenzie, taking comfort in her warm, soft body molded against his. He didn't want to move.

She rubbed his back in circles, not pushing him to tidy his things away or telling him he had to finish eating his pizza and put the plate in the dishwasher. He closed his eyes and just felt what it was like to be with her.

35

He didn't remember anything that happened after that. Probably not much actually happened. They just cuddled and talked quietly about things other than Burton and his abusive parents walking around free like they'd never done anything wrong. He must have cleaned up at some time and they had gone to bed, because that was where he found himself at two o'clock in the morning, wide awake after another nightmare.

"It's okay," Kenzie murmured sleepily, giving him a hug and a kiss on the cheek before falling back asleep with her head on his chest.

He stared into the darkness, trying to focus on the good things. On how nice it was to be there with her and have her comforting him. To lie there with her asleep on his chest, all warm and cozy. That he was in a better relationship now than he'd ever been in with Bridget, even in those early, honeymoon days.

He tried not to think about Bridget, when that was the subject that kept rising to the surface.

Kenzie had suggested before that when Zachary had dreamed about twins, it had been because of Bridget. Knowing that she was expecting multiples weighed heavily on his mind when he had wanted so desperately to have children with her himself. If he could change things around so that he was the one with Bridget and so that both Gordon and Kenzie had partners who made them happy and satisfied… and if the babies that Bridget was carrying were his and Bridget's, conceived in a loving, tender moment. Or in a lab after Bridget's fight with cancer, he didn't care.

He just couldn't let go of that dream.

He should have been thinking about his nightmare instead of the dreams he'd had with Bridget. Twin boys again, not four years apart like Allen and Bobby. Twin boys, both looking exactly like Bobby had in the picture that Kathy had taken. Except that they were dressed in clothes that hung off their bodies in rags. Like zombies in a B-movie. But they hadn't been zombies, they had been children. Children that Zachary had forgotten about, left alone and neglected when it was his responsibility to keep them fed.

He didn't know how anyone could do that. How had Elizabeth and Sam Dougherty consigned their children to the dungeon beneath their house while they walked around above, clothed and well-fed, free to come and go as they pleased, living out a perfectly normal life in a neighborhood that knew nothing about what was going on? How could they act like normal people when their children languished in the basement?

Had they ever felt that sickening guilt that Zachary had felt when he woke up, left over from the dream, still reaching out to help them before they dissolved from reality? Had they ever felt one twist of guilt and regret over what they had done? Or had they only felt like victims, sure that everybody else was out to get them, misjudging them, not understanding that it wasn't really their fault at all?

He shifted, trying to find a more comfortable position. Kenzie's head was grinding against his sternum, a bone that had been broken more than once before and was letting him know it with flares of pain. He loved having her against him; he just needed her to move a little bit to ease the pain radiating from his chest into his ribs.

"Are you okay?" Kenzie murmured. She hugged him, moving closer to his shoulder. Zachary breathed and rubbed his sternum tenderly.

"Yeah."

"Can't sleep?"

"No. But it's okay. Go back to sleep."

"I'm okay. I don't mind staying up with you for a bit."

"You need your sleep."

"So do you. You want to talk for a few minutes? Would it help?"

"No. I don't think so. I'm just… restless."

"You had a dream?"

"Yeah."

He wondered if he'd cried out in his sleep. He knew he could be pretty loud when he was fighting his demons.

"What about?"

"Nothing. The fire," he lied, not wanting to tell her it had been twins again, and to think that he was pining after Bridget. He was devoted to Kenzie. Bridget had her own life now. Another man in it. Another man's babies growing inside her.

He felt suddenly nauseated and lurched up to a sitting position.

"Zachary?"

Zachary knew it was too late to calm his body. After getting his feet free of the covers, he made a dash for the ensuite bathroom and reached the toilet just in time. He hit the floor on his knees. It was a long time before the vomiting and retching ceased and he was able to rest his head for a moment and try to catch his breath.

Kenzie waited until he had splashed water on his face and rinsed his mouth and blown his nose. Then she tapped on the door he had slammed behind him. "Are you okay? You got a bug?"

"I'm fine." Zachary wiped his mouth and nose with toilet paper, trying to eliminate all evidence of being sick. He rinsed his mouth with mouthwash. "Sorry, it's okay. Just go back to sleep."

"I'm worried about you. Is it something you ate?" She laughed at herself. "Of course it wasn't something you ate; you barely touched your dinner."

Zachary shut off the light before pushing the door open, so as not to blind her. Instead, he was nearly blind himself. Kenzie put a sympathetic hand on his arm.

"Probably just my meds."

"If they're making you sick, you should talk to the doctor about adjusting them. Lower the dosage or look at a different medication."

"Most of the time it's okay; I just get nauseated. Just this time…"

She stroked his arm and guided him back toward the bed.

And then the car alarm sounded.

36

Zachary froze for an instant. And then he was to the bedroom window, sure that it was his alarm sounding. Even as he took the few strides to the window, he knew he would get there and there would be no reason for his anxiety. It would be someone else's car, a proximity sensor that was too sensitive and had been set off by a tree blowing in the wind or an animal. Nothing to panic about.

But when he peered between the slats of the blinds, he saw that it was his car. The lights had come on as well as the siren blaring. And his alarm was not a proximity sensor. It was a break-in alarm that would only be set off by someone lifting the handle, putting a key in the lock without disarming it first, or breaking the glass.

There was a man standing beside the car. Zachary didn't recognize him. He was too far away to be sure of the details, but he seemed to be an older man. In his sixties or seventies, but the type who still looked vigorous and strong. A tough guy Zachary would not want to tangle with or come face to face with in a dark alley.

"Zachary?"

"Can you hand me my phone?"

He could hear Kenzie moving around behind him. She picked up his phone and handed it to him. "Is there someone there?"

The man was already moving away and, by the time Zachary got his phone turned on and switched into camera mode, there was not much to see but the man's retreating form. There was no point in calling 9-1-1; he would be long gone by the time the police managed to get there.

He lowered his phone and watched the man disappear from sight.

"Who was it, did you see?" Kenzie asked when he turned around. "What happened?"

"No one I recognized. A man. Trying to get into my car or messing with it. I need to go out and take a look."

"It could be dangerous."

"He's gone. It's fine."

"He could come back. He could have a partner."

Zachary turned and watched out the window for another minute. But he couldn't see any other sign of life. "I'll be careful."

"It's times like this that I wish you carried."

"A gun doesn't help in a situation like this. Like you said, he could have a partner, and they could be armed. Me walking out there with a gun would just escalate things. If I'm not armed, I'm less likely to be shot. Besides… well *you* know…" He couldn't vouch for his own safety with a gun in the house.

Kenzie sighed and didn't argue it any further. "You could at least take a baseball bat. A kitchen knife."

Zachary looked out the window one last time. "There's no one out there."

Before she could argue any further, he headed for the front door. Kenzie disarmed the burglar alarm. He slipped his shoes on without untying them and they flopped under his heels as he walked up to his car. He looked around him carefully, then examined the car. No glass was broken. So the man must have tried to open the doors or messed with it in some other way. Zachary clicked his fob to disarm the security system and unlock the doors, and had a quick look inside. Nothing appeared to have been touched.

It was too dark to see anything underneath the car; he'd have to take it to Jergens, his mechanic, for a quick look before he did any driving around. He brought up his bug sweeping app on his phone, but it didn't detect any radio transmissions or magnetic distortion. Other than the vehicle recovery module he'd installed himself. If the man had put a tracker on the car, it wasn't transmitting yet.

Zachary locked the car and rearmed the security system. He returned to the house. Kenzie had pulled on her robe and was waiting for him, arms crossed and looking anxious. Her phone was in her hand. Ready to place an emergency call if something went wrong.

"Everything is fine," he assured her. "I'm okay." He looked down at himself as he kicked off his shoes. It might have made sense to pull something on before going outside in his boxers. He cleared his throat, face warm.

"You think it was just a random thing? Someone checking for unlocked cars or something valuable left on a seat?"

"Probably." But Zachary's mind went back to the motorcyclist who had followed him. First a tail, and now someone trying to break into his car? It was probably just a coincidence, but he didn't like coincidences.

"It's not like you're hunting some serial killer." Kenzie gave a weak laugh. "Not this time."

"No. Burton is probably my biggest case right now, and that's something that happened decades ago. I can't see how I could have stirred anything up with my inquiries."

"And it isn't the guys who had Madison? It could be, couldn't it?"

"It's possible, but I can't see why they'd have any interest in me since Madison and Noah are both supposed to be dead. Or why they would come here and then not do anything. If it was those guys… there probably would have been bullets through the door."

Kenzie seemed reassured by this. "Yeah."

Zachary approached Kenzie and offered a hug. She cuddled into his arms, and he gave her a reassuring hug. She had tried to calm him earlier, and now it was his turn to make her feel better. "Let's get you back to bed."

"You too."

Zachary shook his head. "I'm going to… keep an eye on things."

"You said he won't come back."

"And he won't. But I won't be able to get back to sleep. I'll just keep you up. Better if I keep myself busy."

"I don't know if I'll be able to either."

"You will." He gave her a nudge in the direction of the bedroom, and they walked down the hall together.

Kenzie climbed into bed, and Zachary sat on the edge.

"Are you going to read me a bedtime story?" Kenzie teased.

"Shh. No more questions. It's time for sleep. Be a good girl."

Kenzie closed her eyes, holding his hand. "Reminds me of putting Amanda to bed," she murmured.

Zachary didn't say anything, waiting for sleep to take her.

37

Zachary made the decision to reach out to Elizabeth Dougherty's parents to see if they could be of any help. He figured that between the two parents, Elizabeth was the more sympathetic figure and her family would be more likely to help him if he showed some compassion toward her and claimed to want to hear her side of the story.

What he really wanted, of course, was information about Allen. Had they known about him? Had they seen him? Did they know what had happened to him? Hopefully, whatever they could provide, together with the little bit of information that Zachary had with Allen's birth certificate and the few details they knew would be enough to convince the police to try for a warrant to search the house, including breaking up the basement floor. They had x-rays or radar they could use to look through concrete, so they might be able to see whether there was anything down there before beginning.

Elizabeth Dougherty had been born Elizabeth Johnson. Her parents, Sylvester and Edith, were still alive, as far as Zachary could tell. He didn't call ahead, but went to their door and rang the doorbell. It was a pleasant little house. Not the best neighborhood, but not the worst, either. Better than the one Elizabeth had lived in with Sam, Allen, and Bobby. She had, presumably, grown up there or in a similar house.

A woman came to the door after a couple of doorbell rings, opening it slowly and peering out at Zachary. She was bent and white-haired, but her eyes seemed clear and alert. "Yes? Who are you?"

"Mrs. Johnson, my name is Zachary Goldman. I'm here to ask some questions about Elizabeth and her children."

Her face was immediately shuttered. She started to push the door closed. "No comment."

"I'm not a reporter." Zachary put his hand against the door. She could still shut it, but it did stall her for a split-second. "I know Bobby."

She stared at him. Eventually, she opened the door again and motioned for him to enter. Zachary was directed to the living room and sat down. He looked around. Books. Displays of china. Pretty furniture. A feminine, grandmotherly room. Little male influence, if any. Edith didn't say that her husband would be joining them or that he was lying down. The doors to the closet at the front door were closed, so he couldn't see if there were any men's clothing or shoes.

Edith sat down in an upholstered chair. "You know Bobby?"

"His name now is Ben. He came looking for the house he grew up in. He's been… unraveling his story, trying to remember what happened and to put it all together. I'm helping him with that, and I thought you might be able to answer some of his questions."

"I didn't have anything to do with any of that business. I don't know anything."

"What do you think it would be like, not to know the things that had happened to you when you were younger, in a different life? You would still react to things, but not have any idea why. You would have vague, shadowy memories, visceral reactions, but not know any of your origins. Your heritage."

"I can't help any of that."

"You can, because you can provide some of the pieces he is missing. Not everything, maybe, but you can still help him. He wants to know more about what happened. About the family he came from."

"Why would he want to know about anything that happened back then? It was horrible business. Nothing that anyone should have to hear, let alone go through. That poor boy. To have something like that in your family…" She shook her head, looking angry. "It's a black spot on our name."

"I know it is. Maybe we can start this from another direction, and that would make it easier. You haven't had any contact with Bobby, of course, with all that happened. Social Services never offered kinship care?"

"No. They never tried to contact us. Never tried to place him with family."

"I guess in a case like this… they wanted to make a clean break. Make sure that Elizabeth and Sam would never have any more contact with him."

Edith shrugged.

"What about Allen? Had you met him?"

Edith's eyes widened. "Allen?"

"Bobby's older brother. That was his name, wasn't it?"

She nodded automatically.

"Mrs. Johnson," Zachary leaned toward her slightly. "What happened to Allen? Do you know?"

She looked around the room, not meeting his eyes. Zachary waited. It was awful for him to expect her to answer questions like this about her own child and grandchild. To admit to what had happened and the fact that they had not been able to stop it.

"We kept expecting someone to talk about him. To say what had happened… but no one ever mentioned him. It was like he had disappeared off the face of the earth."

Zachary had been afraid she was going to relate some fiction about Allen being adopted by another family, maybe informally. She would claim he was still alive out there somewhere; they just weren't sure where he had ended up.

The clean break was better. They had known about him, and then he had disappeared and no one had ever mentioned him again.

"Did you ask Social Services about him? You must have been confused."

"We asked… once… but they looked at me like they didn't have any idea what I was talking about. I didn't mention it again. I hoped… I didn't want to know… I wanted it to be a happy ending. And if I asked them… then it wouldn't be."

"So you never asked the authorities again."

"No."

"What about Elizabeth?"

Edith's lips pressed together.

"Did you ask Elizabeth what had happened to Allen?"

She swallowed and looked down at the carpet, staring at it as if mesmerized. "No. I never did."

He didn't need to ask why. She wanted to believe to herself that her other little grandson was still out there, somewhere, healthy and strong, living a happy life.

Like Bobby.

Except that Burton's life wasn't happy either. It should have been. He'd had good parents after that initial five years. They had given him everything he had needed. They had been loving and kind and pleasant. They had, by all accounts, done everything right. But Burton needed more. He needed to know his past to become an integral person. He had to know the past to move into the present and to see past the bottle in his hand into the future.

"Did you meet Allen?"

She smiled, the sun bursting through the clouds. "Oh, yes. He was a lovely baby and little boy. Such a sweet little fellow."

"And… when did things change? When did you notice that something was wrong?"

"We had a falling-out… a series of fallings-out, really. Sam was… not well. He was making strange choices. Always paranoid. Like he really did think that people were after him, talking about him. He was sometimes violent. Elizabeth and Allen would have bruises. They never admitted that he hit them, but what other explanation is there? They came over less and less, and it didn't matter what we said to Elizabeth, we couldn't convince her to leave him, to go somewhere safe."

"It had to be her own choice."

"Yes. And she wasn't going to listen to her mother. She always was the rebellious sort, didn't like to be told what to do. She knew better than her mother. She was an adult and could live her own life."

Zachary nodded. Independent. Dysfunctional. Butting heads with her parents who didn't think she was safe staying with her boyfriend or husband. She knew him, they didn't. So she had let herself stay in a bad situation, thinking she could change Sam, help him or fix him, or that if she just made all of the right choices, he wouldn't blow up at her. If she could just get things right.

"So they disappeared from your life when Allen was…"

Edith shook her head. "It must have been around the time she got pregnant with Bobby. She wouldn't return calls. They moved and didn't let us know their new address. We couldn't contact her at all. She just disappeared."

"And you didn't hear anything about her until five or six years later?"

"I don't know." Edith avoided his eyes and shook her head. "Then we were hearing about this boy they had found, this boy in terrible condition, horribly neglected, held in a basement. They didn't have the names right. Sam had talked her into taking a different name. But as soon as we saw their pictures on TV, I knew it was her." Edith put her hands over her eyes, reliving the horror of it. "Oh, that poor, poor boy. I couldn't believe that she could do anything so cruel. I've never seen anything like that before."

She had undoubtedly seen pictures of starving children before, but always in other countries, other contexts, not where she'd been so personally connected with what had happened.

"Did you see Elizabeth after that? Or did you stay away?"

"It was a while before I saw her. She was in jail, then in prison."

"And did you talk to her about what she had done?"

"She said it wasn't so bad." Edith's voice grew lighter, apparently imitating Elizabeth's answers. "She said it had all been exaggerated. She hadn't done anything to hurt Bobby. He had food and shelter. All of his needs were taken care of. What business was it of anyone else what room he had slept in? What difference did that make?"

"He just… slept in the basement? That was her answer?"

"More or less. She said it was all just an exaggeration. People trying to make her bad so that the jury would send her to prison. I couldn't stomach it." Edith shook her head. "It made me physically sick. I couldn't bear her excuses."

Zachary remembered being sick the night before at the thought of Bridget's twins. They hadn't even been born yet and he was worried about them. Bridget didn't have a great track record for being a kind, loving person. She might be a wonderful mother toward them. But he was familiar with the sharp edge of her tongue. He'd been faced with it too many times.

"It must be pretty upsetting, knowing that your daughter could do something like that."

"Yes. I thought we would go to the trial to begin with. Show our support. Be there every day. But I couldn't listen to it. I couldn't keep going, knowing what she had done. And that she wasn't…" She bit her lip. "She wasn't innocent. She was not locked down there with him. Them. She never called for help or to take him away to somewhere safe. She was… a participant. Not just a woman who was abused and trying to avoid getting hurt again."

Zachary nodded. He could understand how hard it must be, even though he'd never been in that situation. He knew how hard it could be to believe that someone close to you was not what you thought they were. To have those buried layers revealed and exposed to the light of day.

"So if you didn't attend the trial, you don't know if they ever mentioned Allen?"

"They didn't. If they had, it would have been in the news. There would have been more charges, more police investigation. No one knew about little Allen."

And she hadn't stepped forward to tell about him. She had been willing to ignore what had happened to him to spare her daughter the additional charges and prison time. While Zachary knew it couldn't have been an easy decision, he had a hard time understanding how she could have made the one she did.

Because she loved her daughter.

Despite everything she had done.

"Now that Bobby knows about Allen… it may come out. You'll need to be prepared for that."

Edith stared at Zachary. "Why would you do that? You can't… it was so long ago. What would be the point of making it public now? Let Allen rest… wherever he is. What good would it do to say anything?"

"No one has had to pay for what happened to Allen."

"But no one knows what happened."

"Someone does. Several people do. And they think they got away with it."

She shook her head in disbelief. "You can't do that… just out of revenge. It has nothing to do with you."

"How long did Elizabeth end up serving? Do you know where she is now?"

Edith turned her head toward the hallway at the sound of running water. Her husband was apparently up from his nap or whatever he'd been doing when she answered the door. Zachary glanced at the time on his phone, trying to plan the next few things he would have to do to get the ball rolling with the police department.

There were footsteps in the hallway. Quiet, for a man.

"Mom? Is there someone here?"

38

A woman walked into the living room and looked at Zachary, her brows drawing down. Zachary got to his feet, shocked into action. He didn't know if Edith had more than one daughter, but she had looked toward the hallway when Zachary had asked where Elizabeth was. It had to be her.

"I was just on my way out," he told her. "Mrs. Johnson, it was nice to meet you. Thank you for your help."

Elizabeth was staring at him. She looked out the living room window at his car parked out on the street, then back to him again.

She was in her fifties. Younger than her husband. He was more the age of the man who Zachary had seen trying to break into his car the night before. Zachary took a few steps toward the door, feeling like his feet were on some kind of time delay. He always felt awkward when he had to change his pace or walk backward, ever since a spinal injury shortly after he had met Kenzie. After their first date, actually.

He was tripping over his feet to get to the door before Elizabeth could get through the thought process clearly taking place. He had no idea what her reaction to his presence there would be.

Nothing in his research had pointed to Elizabeth living at the same address as her parents. There had been a few possible addresses, all of them probably places she'd rented in the previous couple of years, moving from one place to another.

And now she was back to living with her mother.

And Sam? Where was he?

Zachary reached the door and twisted the doorknob.

"Hey!"

He ignored Elizabeth's shout and kept going.

"Who are you? What do you think you're doing here?"

He moved as quickly as he could, his toes hitting cracks in the sidewalk two strides in a row so that he was sure he was going to trip and fall flat on his face. But he managed to recover and keep his balance. He didn't know whether to watch the sidewalk in front of him to avoid any further cracks, or to focus on his car, his goal, all the way down the sidewalk and a few vehicles down the street.

Elizabeth didn't follow him, but stayed behind to talk to her mother. Until, apparently, Edith told her what Zachary had been there for, and then she let out a shriek.

Zachary couldn't run, but he did his best, bounding toward his car at his top pace.

He really needed to spend some time with a physiotherapist learning how to run again. He felt like an ungainly giraffe.

Elizabeth came out of the house. Zachary hit the buttons on his key fob to unlock the door, unable to look down at it to press the right one. He knew the layout of the fob, but he couldn't remember it or instinctively hit the right button in the heat of the moment. The lights of the car blinked. The horn beeped. The trunk clicked open.

Not quite the results he had been hoping for.

He got close enough to grab the handle of the driver's door and just about sprained his fingers lifting it up when the door didn't unlatch for him. Still locked. He pushed buttons on the key fob again, trying to do it more slowly now. Elizabeth was still coming after him.

The lights blinked and he saw the locks pop up. He wrenched the handle again and the door opened. He fell into his seat and pulled the door shut so quickly that he nearly shut his leg in the door. He hit the armrest button to lock the door, but nothing happened. He was trying to fit his key into the ignition at the same time.

He looked at the armrest to find the right button to lock the doors and managed to hit it just before Elizabeth reached the car. She banged into the side of the car and grabbed the door handle, but the door didn't open. She howled again and bashed her fist on the window.

He turned the key in the ignition and the car roared to life.

Thank you.

He stepped on the brake and shifted the car into drive. He didn't hit the gas right away, but took his foot off of the brake and let the car start to roll forward. He didn't want to run over Elizabeth, no matter what she had done to Ben and his brother or what she had intended to do to Zachary. He didn't need that on his conscience. She stepped back from the car slightly, still banging on the window and screaming at him that he'd better not ever come back again and that if she ever saw him again…

Needless to say, she didn't welcome his return. She didn't have any trouble thinking of creative ways she could hurt him if he happened to show his face again.

As the car pulled away from her, he put his foot gently on the gas and sped up. She ran after the car, but of course, she was no bionic woman and she couldn't keep up with it. He drove away, leaving her behind.

He drove directly to the police station. He hoped he hadn't royally screwed things up by going to Edith Johnson's house. He had not intended to confront either of Ben's parents. He had just meant to talk to his grandparents, to find out what he could about Allen. But now Elizabeth was in the know, and if she contacted Sam, he would be too. If he didn't already strongly suspect that Zachary was going to cause trouble for them.

Judging by the motorcycle that had tailed him and the man who had tried to break into his car the night before, Zachary suspected that Sam was already fully aware that Zachary was on the case and was determined to get him off of it as quickly as possible.

His heart was still hammering hard when he got to the police station. He sat in his car for a minute, breathing slowly, trying to bring his body back under control, but he didn't have much success.

At least he wasn't having an anxiety attack. Those always seemed to be caused by emotional issues rather than imminent physical danger. He might not make the best decisions when he was facing a challenge, but he at least didn't fold.

He'd kept it together. He was fine, and he had a job to do.

He got out of the car, testing out legs that were quivering like Jell-O. But they held his weight. He carefully locked the car, armed the security alarm, and walked from the parking lot into the police station.

"I don't know if he'll be free," he told the officer of the day, "but I'm looking for Joshua Campbell. It's Zachary Goldman, and it's… somewhat urgent. If you could tell him that there have been developments…"

The officer of the day took down the information and nodded. "If you'll have a seat, please, Mr. Goldman. You'll be called up when we have an answer for you."

"Thanks."

He wobbled over to the seating area and selected a seat that wasn't too close to anyone else. He was glad to get off of his feet so he could be sure that he wasn't going to topple over anytime soon. For the first few minutes, he just sat there, breathing, trying to calm himself down, and pretending that he wasn't watching the OD for any sign of whether he had been able to reach Campbell and whether Campbell was going to have anything to do with him.

He would probably end up getting shunted to someone junior. They would take his statement, roll their eyes, and tell Zachary that someone would get back to him.

Which they wouldn't.

Ever.

Probably.

He checked his email and answered a few quickie questions. He didn't want to deal with anything more complicated, so he switched over to his social networks to see what was happening. But all the time he was browsing through the mixture of friends' posts, memes, and fake news, his brain was working away on what Edith Johnson had said.

She had provided him with what he needed to get started. And Zachary knew where Elizabeth was. Or where she had been. There was no guarantee she would stay at her mother's house for any longer than it would take to pack a bag and get out the door.

But maybe she would have to wait for Sam, if they were still together. They had obviously been in communication, or she wouldn't have looked at

Zachary's car when she saw him, ascertaining whether he was the person that Sam had told her was investigating the old child neglect case, and who might be digging into something that could send them to prison once again.

Whether or not they were together, they were still communicating.

Somehow, their relationship had survived their prison terms. Elizabeth had probably been out for longer than Sam. Unless there had been clear evidence given that Elizabeth was the worse offender. People didn't like to give long sentences to young women, and she had been a young woman at the time. A young woman who, she could claim, had been abused and coerced into something that she hadn't wanted to do.

It wasn't her fault, of course. It was his.

"Mr. Goldman? Mr. Goldman!"

He looked up from his notepad. A young officer stood in front of him. Zachary straightened up. "Sorry. Far away thoughts."

The young officer looked at him, evaluating whether he was high or crazy.

"Just distracted," Zachary said. "Thinking through a case. Is Campbell available?"

The officer considered for a long moment, then nodded. "Yeah. This way."

Zachary pushed himself back to his feet. His legs were steadier, the chase fading from his mind and the adrenaline spike gone. He couldn't quite keep up with the pace that the officer set, but the man slowed down, realizing he was outstripping Zachary, and settled into an easier speed for him.

39

Campbell was sitting at his desk, chewing on a pen. He pointed to the visitor chair facing the desk. Zachary sat down. The young officer stood close by, not leaving as Zachary had expected him to.

"Well?" Campbell demanded. "What's happened?"

"I have more details for you, hopefully enough that you can get a warrant. But I also… ran into one of the suspects. Unintentionally."

"And he knew who you were?"

"She. Yes. Afraid I spooked her and she may be on the run already."

Campbell grunted and shook his head. "Nothing we can do about that. We can't go after her until we have the evidence that she committed a crime. Which we won't have until we get a warrant. Which we don't get until you give me the rest of the details you were able to find."

Zachary nodded. He settled back into his seat. Campbell was right, of course, there was nothing they could do to make sure that Elizabeth didn't run. They had to go through the proper channels and hope that they'd be able to catch up with her later.

"I have evidence from several sources that there was an older son named Allen," he told Campbell. He detailed the birth certificate and what Edith had said about Allen's existence—and subsequent disappearance.

"She didn't think it was important to tell someone at the time that there had been another child?" Campbell demanded, shaking his head.

"She knew that if she did, it would mean a longer sentence for Elizabeth and more notoriety for the family. She decided to avoid that."

"How the public expects the police force to do their job when they won't do their duty and report what they know, I'll never understand."

Zachary had to agree. "I guess… she loves her daughter and didn't want her to have to suffer the consequences of whatever she did."

"And she's letting the woman live with her now? Knowing what she did to her own children?"

"I don't know if she's living there or I just happened to catch her there, but yes, I think she is… it would appear that all is forgiven and Edith would prefer to forget about it."

"Do you think the father is living there too?"

"Probably. They must be in contact with each other." Zachary told him about the tail, the attempted car break-in, and Elizabeth immediately looking at the car and realizing who Zachary was.

"So they might both be on the run now."

"Possibly."

Campbell pulled a form out of one of the stacks of paper on his desk and filled in a few details. He reached toward the young officer who was still standing by. "Get that to Judge Wilkes ASAP. He's expecting it."

Zachary raised his brows. Campbell smiled.

"I knew you would eventually get the information we needed. We'll get the warrant and then see what we can find. How confident are you that the boy's remains are buried in that house?"

"Not one hundred percent. They could be buried somewhere else on the property, or taken out to the woods or dropped off a cliff or into a lake somewhere. But it feels to me like… the basement is the most likely place. That's where the boys were kept. No one in the neighborhood knew they even existed. It feels to me like… they would have kept him very close."

"You think that even with Bobby there, they buried Allen in the basement."

Zachary turned this over in his mind. Had it happened right in front of Burton? Had he watched his brother being buried? Wasn't that taking an unnecessary risk?

"I can't be sure, of course. But… I think so. They didn't expect Bobby to get out. They didn't expect to be discovered. They buried one boy there, and probably assumed they would bury the other there too. Maybe even used it as a deterrent for Bobby. 'If you don't do what we tell you to, the same thing will happen to you.'"

Campbell grimaced. He didn't argue with Zachary's assessment. "I've got the equipment lined up so we can visualize what's under the concrete floor without having to tear it all up. No guarantees, of course. Depends on how thick the cement is and how deep the bones are buried under that. We could be looking for something twelve feet deep. But I doubt it. These are not criminal masterminds. They didn't think anyone would be looking for him. And they were right, in the beginning."

Zachary imagined that the grave would be very shallow. Just deep enough to cover the boy's body. Elizabeth and Sam didn't strike him as the industrious sort.

———

Zachary had discouraged Burton from going back to the house for the search, telling him that it would probably take quite a long time and would be too upsetting for him. He'd already seen how Burton reacted to the empty basement and to talking about any of his memories or his family. It wouldn't be good for him.

He thought that Burton would agree and be happier staying at his hotel room drinking until Zachary got back to him with the results. Then he could be assured of getting the news at the earliest possible opportunity, but wouldn't have to see the remains or deal with the emotion of being at the house again. It was the best possible solution.

But Burton did not agree. As soon as he heard that they were heading over to the house and would begin the search the second they got word that they had the warrant, he wanted to be there. Nothing Zachary said dissuaded him, and eventually he agreed to pick Burton up so that he could stand outside the house until they got some word from the police. By the time they got to the house, the police were stringing yellow tape around the perimeter, even though they were still waiting on the warrant. They were staying off the property, stringing the tape on the outside of the fence.

Zachary found Campbell, but stayed back, knowing that he would be busy and wouldn't want Zachary getting in the way. Campbell noticed him after a couple of minutes and nodded to him as he continued to talk with his men and get things organized. There was a truck stopped in the street with equipment on it that Zachary assumed was the x-ray or radar or whatever the technology was to look through the concrete for the remains.

Campbell eventually approached Zachary, looking at his watch. "We should be able to start any time now. Is this…?" He looked at Burton questioningly.

"Yes, Sergeant Campbell, this is Ben Burton. Formerly Bobby Weaver. Ben, Sergeant Campbell."

Burton nodded. He held out a tentative hand. "Thank you for looking after this."

"I hope we can find something. Hate to drag everyone out and have it go belly-up. And it must be very stressful for you."

"Yeah." Burton ran one hand through his hair. "I just feel like… I left Allen behind here. Everybody left him behind. And we need… we need to find him. Lay him to rest."

"I hope we can do that. And that we can bring your parents to justice."

Burton frowned slightly at this. He looked at Campbell, then at Zachary. "But… they're already in prison, right?"

Zachary took a deep breath, looking at Campbell. Campbell did not jump in to give Burton the bad news.

"No," Zachary said gently. "They're out. I don't know what their original sentence was; I don't have the court documents yet." He looked at Campbell. "Unless you know?"

Campbell cleared his throat. "Father for two years. Mother for one."

Burton looked at him, wide-eyed. "One year? They only put her away for one year after what she did to us?"

"After what she did to you. Not for what she did to Allen. That will have to be considered once we know whether we have a body or not. And yes… I realize it's completely unfair. There's no way that they should have been able to get out so quickly. Unfortunately, that is the law." He shook his head. "I'm sorry. I'm just glad that she couldn't find you. If she had come after you, tried to get you back…"

"So that means… she's out?" Burton looked around him at the strangers gathering on the sidewalk and in the street. "She could be here. She could be anywhere. She's just out, walking free, as if nothing ever happened?"

"Yes."

"And Allen." Burton motioned to the house. "He's still in there. And me. I'm still trapped in there."

Zachary touched Burton tentatively on the back. "I'm sorry. If he's in there, the police will find him and get him out. And you… part of you will always be in this place, but the rest of you, you're walking around free too. More free than her, because you don't have the guilt for what happened."

"Oh, don't I?"

"Well… you may feel guilty," Zachary knew that he still carried around a lot of his childhood guilt. He blamed himself for a lot of the things that had happened to him and his siblings. Even though, as an adult, his logical brain told him that they were not his fault. It wasn't his choice as a ten-year-old to send himself and his siblings into foster care, where they would suffer more abuse and other terrible situations. "But you're not at fault in any way. It doesn't matter what you said or did as a kid; you did not deserve for this to happen to you. That was the choice of cruel, evil adults who had the responsibility to make better choices."

There was a shout from one of the officers gathered around a couple of squad cars. He straightened up and waved to Campbell. "We got it!"

"We got the warrant?" Campbell demanded, double-checking. There could be no ambiguity. Not *it*, but *the warrant.*

"We got the warrant," the officer confirmed.

Campbell nodded to the teams gathered around him. "Let's go, then. Time to get started."

He and a cadre of experts walked into the yard and up to the door. The householders had been watching everything from inside and opened the inside door to talk to them. Campbell explained that a warrant to search the house had been issued, and that they could let him in, or they could wait until the paper warrant got there so they could examine it.

"We don't own the house," the woman told him, her voice screechy. "We just rent. I don't know what you're looking for. We haven't done anything wrong. We haven't broken any law."

"We aren't looking for something that you did. We're looking for something that has been here for many years, long before you moved here. Do you have the owners' phone number?"

She read it to him through the door, and Campbell called the owner and had a discussion with him. There was a lot of back and forth, and, by the time he was granted access, another officer had arrived with the freshly-inked warrant. They displayed it to the residents as they entered but, by that time, no one was asking to see it. They had been told to let the police in and didn't have any argument to make.

"Why don't you go out for a while?" Campbell suggested. "Go out for dinner or a drink. We're going to be here a few hours, at least."

"What are you going to do? You can't go through all of my personal property!"

"We won't be pawing through your drawers, ma'am. We will be looking under the basement floor, in the backyard, maybe in closets or the attic. We will not be looking through your personal items."

She clearly did not believe him but, in the end, decided that she did not want to be on hand during the search. Zachary remembered what it was like to be trying to sell a house and having to vacate for people to look at it. He didn't like the feeling of someone invading his territory, but it was just something a person had to put up with. As a child, it hadn't been up to him to make that choice. Nor as a married man when Bridget wanted to upgrade to something nicer.

She'd upgraded now. Zachary had seen her home with Gordon, and it was like a showcase.

40

Then there was nothing to do but wait. They couldn't see what was going on in the house, though Zachary imagined it in vivid detail. The cops and experts going down the stairs to the basement. Turning on the dim lights and looking around the dismal little space. Getting out the equipment to be rolled across the rooms in narrow lines, back and forth and back and forth until they found something.

Burton paced. He drank. He spoke to Zachary in fits and starts. Phrases and sentences that seemed to come out of nowhere, without a cogent connection. Blurting bits of what came to his mind as he stewed in his fragmented memories.

Zachary saw the man who had stopped and talked to them the first day. The biker man. He was standing around in the crowd, curious like everyone else, wanting to know what they were looking for. People speculated on what the equipment that had come off of the truck was for, some of their guesses bizarre and some uncannily accurate.

Zachary watched the biker, thinking about the motorcycle that had followed him. Had that been the neighbor? Was he Sam Dougherty, or did he know Sam? Was he the one who had decided to tail Zachary to see where he took Burton and where he lived afterward?

Campbell was inside, and Zachary didn't know which of the officers outside would listen to him and take his claims seriously if he suggested that the biker might know something about what was going on or where to find Sam Dougherty. He kept an eye on the man, trying to decide what to do.

An hour later, his phone buzzed. Zachary took it out of his pocket. A text notification. He didn't have them display on his lock screen, just in case it were something confidential that he didn't want a client or interviewee to see. He unlocked it and touched the messaging app to see who the message was from. He tapped the bolded number and the message popped up. A photo. It was monochrome, lights and shadows. Like an x-ray or ultrasound.

He remembered being dragged along to one of his mother's ultrasound appointments. He had been on school suspension at the time and his mother had not wanted to leave him home alone in case he got into something.

The ultrasound screen had seemed mysterious and magical. He could actually see the baby that was inside his mother's belly. The ultrasound technician had pointed to a curved line of dots.

"They call it a string of pearls," she explained. "That's the baby's vertebrae. His spine."

Zachary had stared at it in amazement. He twisted his arm behind him, feeling the knobby bumps along his own back. He had a spine. And the baby, growing inside his mother, had a spine. And translucent little arms and legs that the technician traced on the screen. And a heartbeat, fluttering like a little bird.

But the string of pearls that Zachary saw on his phone screen did not come with a heartbeat. There were limbs angled off this way and that, and a small, round, skull, but no heartbeat.

Burton looked over Zachary's shoulder. He grabbed at Zachary's phone. "Is that it? What did they find? Did they find him?"

Zachary couldn't very well stop Burton. There was no point in telling him that they hadn't found anything. There was no way to spare Burton's feelings.

"It looks like he is," he said gently, holding on to the phone, but angling it so that Burton could see it better. "This here, what looks like a pearl necklace, that's his spine. And…" he pointed to the chicken wings. "His arms.

And his legs." Drawn up to his chest, as if he had curled up into the smallest ball possible, knowing that he was going into the womb of the earth. Back to the dust.

Burton sat down on the sidewalk. "Allen! Allen, oh Allen!" He drew his own knees up, rocking and sobbing. "They found you." He cursed softly. "They found you, Allen."

He broke down and wept openly. Zachary circled an arm around his shoulders and squeezed, trying to comfort him. How could he make Burton feel any better when he had just had it confirmed that his brother was dead? After three decades of repressing all that had happened to them there in the basement of the cursed house, he finally had his answer.

That was where he had lived, had been tortured, and where his brother had died. That was where he had been buried without ceremony or sanction. Buried where they hoped he would never come to light again.

41

Zachary tried to get Burton to move from the place he had collapsed to the sidewalk, but Burton wouldn't budge. Zachary wanted to get him into his car, away from prying eyes and ears. Somewhere he could have a little privacy and gather his thoughts.

But Burton didn't care what anyone saw or heard or thought of him. He wasn't moving from the spot. He was going to stay there forever, glued to that one place, the place he'd been when he found out that Allen had been murdered and buried just feet from him.

Eventually, Burton's tears and loud sobs and groans slowed. He leaned against the chain-link fence, hands over his eyes, body gradually relaxing. Zachary had ignored the men going past him with more equipment. Jackhammers and shovels and other heavy tools. He didn't want to draw Burton's attention to them. He was already going through enough without picturing them digging up his brother's bones.

Zachary rubbed Burton's back and brushed back his hair a couple of times. "How are you doing? This is terrible for you. Is there anything I can do? Anything I can get you? Do you want to talk to someone on the phone? Your mom and dad?"

He shook his head. "No, no one." He felt his pockets for his flask and eventually brought it out, but it was empty. He threw it away from himself, sending it clanking into the street.

Good riddance. Zachary hoped that Burton never went to get it back and that it got driven over by a truck, crushed flat in the street. He hoped that this one moment would sober Burton up enough to see that he was wasting his life crawling into a bottle, that it was time to start living. One of the Dougherty boys had survived, but his spirit was still stunted, like his body had been when they got him out of the basement. It had never been allowed to grow up. It was time for him to start living.

"He was my brother and I let him die." Burton's words were anguished.

"You were four or five. There was nothing you could have done to save him. You are not responsible for anything that happened."

"I should have been able to stop them. I should have helped him. He helped me. He protected me. And I didn't do anything. I just… stood there!" There was horror in Burton's voice as if he couldn't believe it. How helpless and paralyzed he had been. He didn't believe what Zachary had said. He saw himself as the cause of Allen's death.

"There was nothing else you could have done. You were too small. No matter how hard you'd tried to fight them, you couldn't have saved him. And they might have killed you too."

"They should have! They should have killed me too, and I wouldn't have to go through this. Why couldn't I be the one who died?"

Zachary continued to rub his back, trying to find some way to soothe him. "He wanted you to live. He was your big brother. He was trying to look after you."

Burton leaned forward and buried his face in Zachary's shoulder. "Allen, Allen…"

"He loved you. And your adoptive parents love you. You're not alone. You should call them."

"No." He choked the word out. Zachary wondered what his relationship with his adoptive parents was like. They had, by his account, done everything they could for him, and he had done everything self-destructive he could. He didn't share with them that he was looking for his house, didn't want to share the news about his brother. There was clearly a rift between them. He had, perhaps, been too old and too traumatized to bond with them properly. Those early years were vital for relationship development. Zachary wondered about his own ability to form normal relationships. He didn't have a lot to show for his efforts. An ex-wife, a struggling relationship with Kenzie, one foster father.

He did love his brothers and sisters. He'd developed those relationships early, like Burton. Before he was broken.

He couldn't think of anything else to say. He was quiet, staying close to Burton and trying to give him the moral support he needed, watching the curious watchers. The biker dude was still there. Pretending he was watching the house more than he was watching Zachary and Burton. Zachary saw him take out his phone to make a call. He quickly slid his own phone out and tapped a message back to Campbell, inside the house.

There is a man out here who confronted us when we were here before. I think maybe the one who followed me.

He didn't know whether Campbell would take out his phone and look at the message, or whether he would be too busy with what was going on inside. It would be loud and close and he might not even notice that he'd received a text.

Is it Sam Dougherty? Campbell fired back.

Don't know. Could be. Or a friend.

What's he doing?

Been watching us. Making a call now. Maybe to Sam?

There was no answering text from Campbell for a few seconds. No dots to tell Zachary that he was composing his message. Then his phone rang. He held it up to his ear. "Hello?"

"Officer Blau is going to come talk to you. I want you to point this guy out to him. Discreetly."

"Okay. Sure."

A heavyset officer approached. Belly straining over his duty belt. He rocked side to side as he lumbered toward them, looking like a bear or a Sasquatch. He looked at Burton, then Zachary. He leaned closer, talking to them with a voice that was raised instead of confidential.

"Everything okay here, sir?"

Zachary glared at him and spoke quietly. "You need to check on the guy behind you. By the red truck. Doo-rag on his head and tats down his arms."

"You should go home," Blau said loudly. "There's nothing to see here. Nothing is going to be happening here tonight. You're making a scene."

"The black and white doo-rag," Zachary insisted.

Blau straightened up, hitching up his belt. "See to it. You'd better be moving on your way soon, or I'll do what I have to to see you off the property. We don't want drunks and meth-heads hanging around here."

He wheeled around one hundred and eighty degrees and walked away again. Zachary tried to reconcile what had just happened with what Campbell had said on the phone. He knew what he was supposed to do, but Blau had appeared to be totally off-script. Like he thought he was there to protect the scene and see Burton and Zachary off rather than looking into the biker dude.

He watched Blau walk around the edges of the onlookers, eventually working himself into a position behind the biker, who had finished his phone call and was chatting to another neighbor while he kept his eyes glued on Zachary and Burton. Blau tapped him on the shoulder and he turned slowly, unconcerned, then froze when he realized that he had been flanked. He said something and looked like he was going to make a run for it. Blau grabbed his arm and stopped him cold. There was no struggle, but the biker dude suddenly had his arm twisted up behind his back and couldn't seem to move out of the hold.

Zachary turned to face Burton to prevent anyone seeing his grin. He had thought that Blau was stupid, but he'd been anything but.

Burton was wiping his face, looking at Zachary with his brows drawn down. He didn't understand what had just happened or why Zachary was smiling.

"I have a right to be here. No one is chasing me away."

"No. You're fine. It was just a distraction. He didn't mean it."

"He didn't mean it?"

"He just needed to know who I wanted him to talk to." Zachary glanced at Blau and the biker out the corner of his eye, not making it obvious he was looking at them again. "Him." He nodded sideways. "They need to talk to him."

"Why?"

"He knows something. He might know Sam."

"Who is Sam?"

"Sam is your birth father."

Burton's eyes went over to the biker. "That's not him, though. That's the guy that talked to us before. Last time."

"Yes. That's right. But… I think he followed me the other day after I dropped you at the hotel. And he's here again, watching us, calling someone on his phone."

"You think he's calling… my birth father?"

"He could be. Or I could be totally wrong. It's not like I haven't made mistakes before." Zachary rolled his eyes. "Plenty of times. But the way he was acting… I think he knows something, even if he says he doesn't."

"You don't think he was here back then? That he knew Sam when we lived here. In this house."

"He might have. People don't usually stay in this neighborhood that long, but he could be an exception. Or he might just know Sam and moved here coincidentally. You know 'Hey, Sam, would you believe that I just moved onto your old street?' That kind of thing does happen. But I don't like coincidences."

"When did he follow you? You didn't tell me anything about this."

"You have enough to worry about. I didn't want to bring it up. Nothing happened, and I thought… that it might have been connected with an old case, something that I'd already wound up. I didn't realize until later that it might be related to this case."

"Or not at all."

Zachary conceded. "Right."

Burton rubbed his eyes, which were red and swollen. He sniffled loudly and looked around. He seemed to have cried himself out. At least for the moment.

"What are they doing in there now? They found him, so… now what?"

"They'll declare it a crime scene. Take what evidence they need."

"How?"

Zachary didn't want to give too much to Burton. He didn't want Burton to see it in his head. "I don't know all of the details. They're going to need to remove… the remains. And they'll have lab work that needs to be done. There may be other pieces of evidence to examine. Maybe clothing or jewelry that survived."

"Allen didn't have any jewelry."

"No, of course not. But there could be things that would last longer than cloth. A belt buckle. A zipper. Pocket rivets or buttons. I don't know what else."

Burton nodded, sniffling and snorting some more. He rubbed at his eyes, which Zachary imagined didn't make them feel any better, just rubbing whatever grit was on his face and hands into his eyes.

"I can't… I can't believe they would do that to Allen. Just… bury him there. Leave him there. No one knew? No one knew anything?"

"Just them. I don't imagine they would have told anyone. Criminals can be stupid, but they had to know that if they told anyone, it would mean more charges against them. They had to keep it a secret."

"How could anyone not know?" Burton shook his head. "How could everyone just forget him?"

Zachary had the same questions. Elizabeth's mother had known about Allen, but she had kept quiet to spare her daughter. How many other people had known and not said anything? Sam's parents were still living too; wouldn't they have known Allen before Sam started 'acting funny' and being paranoid, eventually locking the boys up? What about neighbors? No one missed him? School teachers and friends? Had no one asked whatever had happened to the Dougherty's boy?

"I don't know. But now we found him. Now they'll have to pay."

"I can't believe that they weren't sent to prison for the rest of their lives. Wouldn't you? You wouldn't let someone like that just get out and go free in a year, would you? You know… that they can't be let out to just… do it all over again." He swallowed and looked at Zachary, thinking the same thing as Zachary had. "What if… they had other children? Does anyone know? Was anyone watching to make sure that they couldn't ever do it again?"

"Probably not. They might have had parole rules when they got out initially… but that was years ago now. They can't watch people forever. Eventually, they have to let people just go free and stop monitoring them."

"They monitor sex offenders."

"Yeah."

"Why wouldn't they monitor murderers? Do they seriously think that just because someone has done their time that they're not going to do it again? Sex offenders re-offend, but murderers don't? What kind of logic is that? Why don't we have monitoring for killers?"

42

The biker had been discreetly removed from the scene, maybe taken to the police station for questioning. Zachary and Burton waited for some word from inside. It was starting to get cooler, the sun beginning to sink toward the horizon. Most of the curious neighbors dispersed, deciding there was nothing to see.

There were still a few onlookers on the street and in nearby homes but, for the most part, Zachary and Burton and the officers who were watching the perimeter had it to themselves.

There was a buzz from Zachary's phone. He pulled it out. Another message from Campbell.

Prepare Burton. We're going to be coming out.

Zachary slid the phone away again. When he looked at Burton, his eyes were already on Zachary.

"They're getting ready to come out."

"Does that mean… they're finished?"

Zachary nodded. He didn't know whether the police would need more time at the scene, but the part that Burton was concerned with was done. They had recovered Allen's remains.

"What are they… what will happen?"

"They'll be bringing the remains out. They'll take them to the police lab.

They'll examine them, try to make an identification and determine cause of death."

"We already know his identification." Burton's voice was angry. "It isn't like there were any other children in the basement."

"I know. But they still need to confirm it scientifically, if they can. We all know who it is."

"I told you. I told you he was in there."

"And we managed to get them to look. They were able to recover him. You were right, and because of you, Allen will be laid to rest somewhere… more appropriate. Somewhere you can put a headstone and visit if you want."

"When?"

"I don't know how long it will take. A few days to a few weeks." Kenzie would know. She would be involved in checking the remains in, cataloging everything, maybe involved in the post-mortem with Dr. Wiltshire. "They'll get it done as soon as they can."

Burton looked toward the house, waiting. Zachary was cramped and cold sitting on the ground with Burton. He rose to his feet, and in a moment Burton followed suit, looking like a newborn horse or deer testing out its legs.

"You okay?" He touched Burton's arm to steady him.

"I'm fine."

Zachary withdrew his hand and let him be. "It won't be long, now."

The front door opened as if on cue. The officers started coming out. A couple of them with the x-ray and digging equipment first. Then behind them, several in a line, men carrying boxes. They were closed and sealed and marked as evidence. They didn't joke around and talk among themselves like police officers often did, but walked in a solemn procession. The officers who were standing around outside removed their caps and stood watching. The equipment was loaded onto the truck, and the evidence into a white van. Campbell joined Zachary and Burton.

"How are you holding up?" he asked Burton in a low, respectful tone.

Burton wiped at his eyes, leaking at the corners again as he watched them put the bones of his brother into the van. He shook his head. "I can't believe this is happening. It feels like I stepped into a nightmare. I keep waiting to wake up, but… I can't. I just keep getting deeper and deeper."

Campbell nodded. He slapped Burton on the shoulder. "I'm sorry about all of this. You shouldn't have to go through it."

"Why didn't they find him back then? How could they just leave him there? Pour concrete over top of him?"

"They didn't know. If they had known, they wouldn't have left him there. At least you remembered, when you came back here, what had happened."

Burton's eyes slid to the side. He looked at Zachary, and then back at Campbell.

"We'll set up a time to meet tomorrow," Campbell suggested. "I'll need to document everything you can remember."

"But… I don't know if I can do that."

"It was a long time ago, and your memories will be hazy. We'll take that into account. But we need your statement. You are the only witness, other than your parents. At least, I assume that is the case."

Burton tried to nod and shake his head at the same time. "I don't remember…"

"We'll have some experts available. They'll be able to help you to retrieve some of those memories. We have psychologists, hypnotists, other kinds of experts. You may not remember a lot, but every little thing will help."

Burton's arms wound around his stomach and he held himself like a child with a stomachache. He looked at Zachary again.

"You've done fine so far," Zachary told him. "You did remember things. Even though you thought you couldn't. You remembered the house, what it looked like, and where you had been. You found your bug jar and the names on the wall. You remembered Allen's name and you knew that we would find him here. That's a lot."

"But it's not enough." Burton's eyes were wide and worried. "That's not enough to put them back behind bars."

"You let us worry about building the case," Campbell said. "We'll get the evidence we need and pass it all on to the prosecutor. We'll have enough. We're not going to drop this."

"He was only a little boy." Burton wiped his face with one hand and went back to holding his stomach. "We were just little."

"Yeah. That's one of the horrible things about it. He was so young. He never had a chance. But we're going to do something about it." He squeezed

Burton's upper arm. "We don't forget innocents. We're not going to let them get away with it."

"How will you stop them? How will you even find them?"

Campbell glanced at Zachary. "We already have some leads on that. Don't worry about the police work. We know what we're doing. All you need to worry about is getting a good night's sleep tonight so that you'll be ready to give your statement tomorrow." He paused, weighing his words. "We'll expect you to be clear and sober."

Burton scowled. "Would *you* be?"

"This isn't a question of how I would be. I'm sure I would be an absolute wreck. This is about you and what you can do for your brother. You need to hold it together for his sake. You need to be alert and coherent. You don't want alcohol blurring things. You need to be able to give a legal statement, which you can't do if you're under the influence."

"I *can* stay sober," Burton growled. "I don't know what nonsense Zachary's told you. I'm perfectly capable. I can speak for myself. I don't walk around here letting everybody else speak for me. No matter how much I drink, I can still function just fine."

"I'm sure you can," Campbell said without any hint of sarcasm or criticism. "And tomorrow, you will need to be that person. Sober and ready to make your statement."

"I will be."

"Good man." Campbell gave a nod. "I'll see you tomorrow, then. First thing?"

Burton looked suddenly trapped. He looked at Zachary for rescue. "I might..."

"I don't think I can be there in the morning," Zachary said. "And I'd like to be there for moral support. Could you do early afternoon instead?"

Campbell gave him a disapproving look. "Suddenly this isn't the most important thing on your calendar?"

"I have a doctor's appointment in the morning. You know I can't miss those. Besides, it's been thirty years. A few more hours isn't going to make that much difference. Maybe in the afternoon, you'll have a preliminary report from the medical examiner. What they've found on gross examination of the remains."

"Fine. Afternoon, then," Campbell agreed. "I'll make time for you on my calendar. And I'll have the experts in, so if you don't show up, you're going to be wasting a lot of people's time."

"We'll be there." Zachary looked at Burton and raised his brows. "Right?"

Burton nodded. "We'll be there. Early afternoon. No problem."

"It better not be."

43

Campbell walked away from them once more to talk to his men as they took the last of the evidence out of the house and moved it safely to the van. The police started to take the yellow tape back down and, after a few minutes, Burton turned away, finally ready to go.

"That's it. That's all they're going to do."

"They'll still be doing more behind the scenes. There's lots to do in the lab, and they need to track down Elizabeth and Sam, which will be more difficult if they have bolted. They're done here, but there is still more to do."

Burton looked at the house one more time. Committing it to his long-term memory, Zachary thought. Making sure it was something that he would never forget again. Saying goodbye. Reconciling himself to the fact that he would need to go on with his life. He had found Allen, and now it was time to go on.

"Come on," Zachary invited. "Let's go."

He didn't grab Burton by the arm, but waited patiently for that last goodbye to be finished. Then Burton turned and followed him to the car.

"Thanks for…" Burton cleared his throat uncomfortably. "For talking to the cop, telling him it would have to be tomorrow afternoon."

"No problem. I actually do have a doctor's appointment tomorrow morning."

"Oh. What for?"

While he would normally have considered it an invasive question, a client stepping over the line and trying to become too involved with his life, Zachary felt like it was only right that after Burton had lain bare his soul that there should be some kind of reciprocation. Zachary knew everything personal and private about Burton's life, and Burton knew nothing about Zachary's.

"She's a therapist. I have a lot of… mental health issues to be resolved. She helps me work through them."

Burton buckled his seatbelt, thinking this through. "So, like, depression?" he asked. "What kinds of things?"

"It can be depression. I get very depressed before Christmas, but it can actually hit at any time of the year, and then it hits me all the harder because it is unexpected. I have anxiety issues, compulsions, PTSD. My girlfriend and I have started couples sessions so that she can help me to get better at relationships, at… overcoming some of the traumatic stuff I've had to deal with."

Burton motioned to his window, back toward the house as Zachary put the car into gear and started to pull out. "Traumatic stuff like this?"

Was it a competition to him? Pull out their respective traumas and compare them, see who had suffered the most? Who had bragging rights?

"That's private. But… yes, some pretty nasty stuff. I didn't see my brother killed in front of me… though sometimes I was afraid I would."

Burton closed his mouth and thought about that as they drove into the rapidly-falling darkness.

Zachary was glad that his appointment with Dr. Boyle was by himself, and not a couples session, as had originally been planned. Kenzie had a coworker call in sick, and she had been asked to help with the post-mortem of Allen's remains. Something that Zachary had encouraged her to do, both for his own sake and for Burton's. Though he had initiated the couples sessions, he found them much more difficult than individual sessions. After all of the emotion that he'd dealt with in helping Burton get through the previous day, he didn't think he could have managed a couples session.

"How are you doing today?" Dr. Boyle asked, smiling at him and giving him a chance to think about what had happened in the last few days since their last session. Zachary thought of the nightmares, about visiting with Joss and Luke, and about the events with Burton.

"It's been… a busy few days."

"Professionally? Personally? What's been going on?"

"A little of both. And I haven't been sleeping very well."

"Do we need to talk about a prescription sleep aid?"

"I've already got those… but I don't like to use them."

"It's important for your mental health for you to get enough sleep."

"Yeah. But… I had that episode before when I had a reaction to mixing them with a painkiller, and… I just don't think it's a good idea for me to take them."

"Well, ultimately, that's your choice, of course. But I think that having a blanket policy that you'll never take them, even if you need them, isn't the best idea."

"I still have them. And if I was going to go all night without sleep for a few days, I would take them. But just for the odd night having a hard time… I don't want to do that."

"So you only occasionally have restless nights? It isn't anything serious and it doesn't last?"

"Well… no. You know me, most nights are difficult. But things were going better. I was having better sleep. I think this is just temporary."

"Do you know why you're having a hard time? Can you tell me what kind of sleep trouble you're having? Do you have trouble getting to sleep, problems with waking up in the night? Nighttime restlessness? Waking up too early?"

"Well, any of those. But lately… nightmares. Ones where I wake up and I still *feel* the feelings that I had in the dream. Where I don't know when I wake up that it was a dream and that it's gone. I'm still looking for something or feeling panicked. Still almost in the dream."

Dr. Boyle nodded and made a notation on her notepad. A few words to remind her of this later. "Yes, I know what you mean. I've had dreams like that."

"Sure." Zachary nodded, feeling relieved. "I'm sure I'm not the only one."

"Is there anything similar between the dreams you've been having lately? Any one dream, or a recurring image or theme? Is it always the same feeling when you wake up?"

"Kenzie thinks it's because of Bridget. Her being pregnant."

"Oh? Why?"

Zachary realized that he'd skipped a step. "I've been… dreaming about twins. It's kind of been related to a case that I'm working, because there are two boys, brothers, and I've been helping him to find out what happened to his brother."

"But they were not twins."

"No. Four or five years apart."

"But in your dream, they're twins."

Zachary nodded.

"Sometimes dreams are like that," Dr. Boyle said. "Our minds flip a switch, change something up. It could be, like Kenzie suggested, because you're thinking about Bridget and her expecting twins. Or it could just be that you didn't have a good mental image of this brother, so you made him identical, to give him a concrete form that you recognized."

"Yeah, maybe that was it," Zachary agreed, nodding eagerly. He didn't want it to be about Bridget.

"Have you been thinking about Bridget a lot when you have been awake?"

Zachary looked at the questions from several different angles. He didn't want to answer it. Which in itself was an answer. Dr. Boyle wrote something else down. Zachary couldn't see, from where he sat, if it was 'thinks excessively about ex-wife' or something else. Maybe a note to herself not to forget to pick up milk at the grocery store.

She waited for him to answer.

44

Zachary shifted, trying to find a more comfortable position, and cleared his throat.

"I guess."

"You guess what?"

"That I've been thinking about Bridget a lot. Or about her babies a lot."

"Is it a package deal, or do you think about them separately?"

"It just feels so unfair. That she would refuse to have children with me, insist that she never wanted to have children of her own, and then to get pregnant with Gordon. And have two babies, or even more. It's just… so unfair. I wanted to have children with her. I always wanted to have children, even though she had said she didn't want them."

"It is unfair," Dr. Boyle agreed. "I can see that it would be tough to deal with that."

Zachary warmed to the topic. "Was it because of something that Gordon has that I don't? Or did she just change her mind? Suddenly became aware of her biological clock?"

"Hard to say without talking to her." Dr. Boyle held up a finger. "And I am not suggesting that you talk to her. In fact, I'm telling you not to."

Zachary nodded. He knew that if he tried to make contact with Bridget, followed her in his car, or just happened to be in the neighborhood, she would take out a restraining order. And he could go to jail because he'd been warned before.

"Instead, let's just unpack this a little further. Why do *you* think she agreed to have children with Gordon? It isn't possible that it was just an accident? And they decided to go with it?"

"No. She had her eggs frozen before she had radiation. She couldn't have had children without them planning it."

"Okay. So we can assume that it was planned. And that's the reason she's having multiples as well, because they fertilized more than one egg to give her a better chance of conceiving."

Zachary nodded.

"So why do you think she chose to have children now, if she was against it before?"

"Her new husband… he's a very persuasive guy. One of those guys who's really… dynamic. I guess, he just talked her into it."

"That's a possibility. So how does that make you feel?"

"Like… I should have tried harder, instead of just accepting it when she said she didn't want to have any children. Maybe I just needed to push harder, to come up with a better argument. Maybe she was waiting for me to say something that would convince her. To step up and insist… say that I wasn't going to stay with her unless she agreed to have kids."

"Do you think that's how Gordon convinced her to have children?"

"No." Zachary looked down at his pants and scratched at something that had spilled and hardened there. "I doubt he needed to make any threats."

"You don't think so?"

"He's… like I said, he's really persuasive. He would just talk to her, and she would agree. And maybe he didn't need to say very much. Because he's a better man than I ever was."

"In what way?"

"He's very wealthy. He owns an investment banking company. I mean… he could buy and sell any business in the city. And he's not arrogant and stuck up. He's a very nice guy. Always very respectful, not the kind who would call me names or make comments about me, even though Bridget gives him permission. He's always been really nice to me."

"Well, that sucks," Dr. Boyle said.

Zachary laughed and nodded. "Yeah, it really does. I wish he would at least be a villain! I wish I could hate the guy and pick away at all of his shortcomings, but I can't. He is a good guy. He's good to Bridget; patient, but he doesn't put up with a bunch of nonsense. He's firm, stands up for me if she starts to run me down."

Dr. Boyle called Gordon a name and Zachary snorted. Dr. Boyle was right. It really did gall him that Gordon was such a perfect guy for Bridget. The kind of guy that Zachary could never have been, even if he'd tried his whole life.

There was a tickle in the back of his brain. While he believed that what he said was true, he did have the tiniest of doubts about Gordon. He had worried that Gordon had been involved in the death of one of his employees, but had been proven wrong in that regard. And he didn't believe the claim that the victim's sister made that Gordon was a manipulative egomaniac.

At least, he didn't think so.

Bridget would not have gotten together with someone like that. She liked to be the one in control. She had married Zachary thinking that she would be able to control him, to fix him and make him behave the way she believed he should. She hadn't understood what a huge undertaking that would be, and that Zachary's behavior wasn't always a matter of choice. And being broken definitely wasn't. He would have changed. He would have been what she wanted him to be, but he couldn't.

"Zachary."

He blinked and focused back on Dr. Boyle again. She did not comment on his momentary mental vacation. "So do you think you are focusing too much of your time and energy on Bridget and her unborn twins?"

He sighed. "Yes. Of course. I shouldn't be thinking about it at all. It isn't anything to do with me. I've moved on. She's moved on. We're in different relationships, and what she chooses to do or not to do is her own business. It doesn't affect me at all."

"So what are strategies you can use to focus less on her and more on the things that are important in your life?"

"Spending time with Kenzie… telling myself to stop and having something else to distract me. Visualization." He shrugged. "I know what I *should* do."

"But it isn't always that easy, is it?" Dr. Boyle sounded sympathetic. "Have you examined the reasons that you should be focusing your attention on Kenzie and other things instead of Bridget? Look at your motivations and think about what you are getting out of obsessing over Bridget and what things you want in your life? I think it's important to be motivated, or you're not going to follow through on any of the things you know you *should* do."

Zachary shook his head slowly. "I don't have any reason to think about Bridget and the babies. I don't know why I do it. I don't get anything out of it, and if I was focusing on Kenzie or a case, or even just meeting my own needs, that would make a lot more sense than thinking about her."

"Why do you think you do, then? What benefit are you getting out of thinking about Bridget?"

He rubbed the center of his forehead and thought. He had never considered that he might be getting some kind of reward from thinking of her. It was just where his mind went. His mind wandered and he thought about her, about his regrets, worried about the babies, wished that he could get back together with her and try again. To make it work this time.

"Um… wow. I guess… part of it is fantasizing about the great life we could have if she would just take me back."

"Because you had such a great life when you were together?"

He knew that wasn't true.

"Well, in the beginning, it was really good. She complimented me, made me feel good. And she was so pretty and so popular, it was like… I was suddenly *that* guy. I was lucky. I had everything. All the good things that I'd never had before."

"But that didn't last long."

"No. Because… she started making little digs… trying to 'motivate' me. She was impatient that I wasn't the perfect date. That I wasn't making enough progress toward the mold she was trying to press me into."

"And those little digs escalated."

"Yeah. By the time we got married, she would go into full-blown banshee mode… screaming at me for what I thought was a little thing, or for something that I couldn't help."

"And why didn't you confront her about that? Why did you stay—and get married—when you saw this happening?"

"Because when she wasn't screaming at me, it was good. I felt good. She would be kind and empathetic. She wanted to hear about me, about my life, my worries and concerns…"

"And that made you feel good. Did you recognize it as the cycle of abuse?"

Zachary hesitated. "No."

"Do you recognize it now?"

"Maybe… but I have a hard time seeing it like that. I think… most of the time, things were good. She was kind and loving. But then I would screw something up, and she would lose it. And that wasn't her fault; she was doing the best she could dealing with my crap. It was my fault, because I couldn't toe the line. Couldn't do the things that she asked me to, even though they were perfectly reasonable."

"Were they? Give me an example."

Zachary tried to pull one thing out of the mess that had been his life with Bridget. "Uh… letting her know where I was going to be. When I was going to be late for dinner or a planned event."

"So she expected you to let her know ahead of time?"

"Yeah. And that's just being considerate, you know. People expect that. Especially if it's an event with other people and she's going to end up being there alone. People talk. They think that I'm just blowing it off, that I don't think she's important enough to make sure that I'm there."

"And did you try to let her know when you were going to be late for something?"

"Yes, of course. But… with my work, I don't always know if I am going to be out on a case a particular night. If a subject under surveillance was on the move, things were going down… sometimes I didn't know much ahead of time, but I just couldn't get away."

"Uh-huh."

"Or else…" He ducked his head, embarrassed even though she already knew all about his failings and foibles. "You know, with my ADHD, I'd forget I was supposed to be somewhere, or not give myself long enough to get there in time. That really drove her nuts." He thought about the other night, when he'd completely blocked out Kenzie, not even able to change his focus for long enough to eat dinner. If that had been Bridget, he would still be smarting from her verbal lances.

"Is that something you can control?" Dr. Boyle asked.

"Well… I try. But I get distracted by a case, or I hyperfocus on something… and everything else just falls by the wayside. It isn't intentional."

"Did Bridget know that?"

"I tried to explain it to her."

"And how did she take that?"

Zachary shook his head. "She didn't. She wouldn't accept… my ADHD as an excuse."

"So… going back to the question about the cycle of abuse. If she was verbally abusive because of something that you could not control, then is that your fault or her fault?"

Zachary shrugged. They both knew the answer, but he didn't want to voice it aloud. He didn't want to think or say that Bridget was an abuser. He had dealt with enough abusers in his life, and he liked to think that he had gotten himself out of that cycle.

Even though he hadn't.

Not with Bridget.

Kenzie was different. While he always expected her to go off like Bridget would have, she didn't. She'd been there for him. She'd been supportive. Exasperated sometimes, yes. Pulling out of the relationship when he wasn't able to handle it. But she hadn't yelled and screamed. She hadn't belittled him or hit him. She was different.

"Do you think that maybe with Bridget, you were seeking a familiar experience? The same kind of relationship as you had been in before. The way your mother treated you. The way that you were judged by school teachers and professionals as being obstinate instead of having challenges?"

"Yes." They had discussed this before. But he didn't like it, and it didn't stop him from thinking about Bridget when he should be thinking of other things.

"So one of the things that you got out of your relationship with Bridget was familiarity. Being in an environment that felt the same as your home environment."

"Yes, I guess."

"And you got her kind words and strokes when she was in a good mood."

"Yeah."

"And if you could go back to her and start over, what would you get?"

Zachary shrugged. "Nothing, I know that's just a fantasy."

"But when you think about her, you think of those good times. Your brain gets those same good feelings as when you were together and she was showing you love and attention."

"I guess, yeah. So you think that's why I think about her and worry about the babies so much?"

Dr. Boyle cocked her head.

Zachary replayed the question in his head, but didn't know what it was that had caught her interest. "What?"

"*Think* about Bridget, but *worry* about the babies."

Zachary furrowed his brows, thinking about that for a minute. The dreams he'd had hadn't been nice, soothing, happy dreams about newborn babies. They hadn't been happy, cuddly dreams. They were full of menace and danger, of the specter of death.

"Do you think… I'm worried about the babies because of what happened to Burton?"

She raised her brows. "I don't know what you're talking about. You'll need to give me context."

"Um—my client. I've been helping him to connect with his past. He was badly abused and neglected. Yesterday… we found the remains of his brother. He was killed thirty years ago, by one or both of his parents. And buried in the basement."

Dr. Boyle winced. "Yes, that could certainly cause nightmares. And concerns about how Bridget and Gordon are going to treat their children."

Zachary closed his eyes, letting the feelings wash over him. He'd been trying to suppress the emotions and to compartmentalize. Keep Burton and his brother in one box, and Bridget and the babies in another, and his own history in yet another. Now he let go and let them mix.

45

The image that bubbled up and rose into his mind was not Elizabeth Dougherty and Allen and Bobby, or Bridget and the babies.

It was his mother.

He again saw her after the births of the younger children. Too tired to get out of bed or show any interest in them. Easily angered if one—or more—of the children got in her way. Zachary and the older girls had done what they could to take care of the younger ones. He remembered carrying them with him, rocking, feeding, and changing them.

They were, in his mind, the best part of his day. He dragged himself off to school and dealt with schoolwork and teachers and bullies and distractions, but when he got home at the end of the school day, he didn't see taking one of the babies as a penalty, but as a reward.

What could be better than holding and playing with a baby? They sometimes cried, but they didn't hit him or scream and criticize him. They didn't steal his lunch, make fun of his stained clothes, or tell him to do his homework. They just loved him back.

He knew that his mother didn't see them that way. She complained about their demands. She didn't nurse and preferred to let one of the other children bottle feed them. She would, eventually, get out of bed and once again take up her responsibilities of making dinner and trying to keep the house in some kind of order. An impossible task with the number of children in the house.

She and their father drank and fought frequently. Joss and Heather and Zachary tried to keep the little ones out of their way and shelter them from the violence. Sometimes they were successful, and sometimes they were not. Like Burton, he was too small to stop an adult who was intent on violence. He could run and hide, but he did not have the strength to stop them.

"Do you want to share?" Dr. Boyle asked.

Zachary opened his eyes and just sat there for a moment, pondering. "Maybe I am worried about how Bridget will be able to care for them," he said cautiously. He certainly didn't want Dr. Boyle calling Social Services to say that Bridget needed to be investigated. The babies hadn't even been born yet. He was sure that she was getting all of the prenatal care she needed. That would not have been a problem for Bridget.

But when they were born? What then? He assumed that there would be a nanny. Bridget would not be responsible for all of their care. She had a maid and other employees to help around the house and grounds. She was bound to have someone to help with child care as well, especially with twins.

"If I married Bridget because she reminds me of my mother…"

"And you know how your mother treated you as a child."

"And the littler ones. I didn't care so much about how she treated me. I mean, I did, but I could try to be better and not to irritate her. But the babies couldn't do that. We had to… look after them."

"You personally?"

"Yes. Me and Heather and Jocelyn. We tried to take care of the little ones and make sure… nothing happened to them."

"You were not very old yourself."

"I was eight when Vince was born. And six when Mindy was born. That's old enough to help."

"To help… yes. But it sounds like you're talking about a little more than that."

Zachary nodded.

"I'm interested in hearing that you had that much responsibility. Usually, when you talk about your childhood, you're talking about the trouble you got into. And I don't think that the whole of your existence consisted of getting into trouble."

"Well…" Zachary cleared his throat. "Mostly. That's what I remember. Always being on edge, trying to avoid screwing anything else up."

"That's what I mean. You were trying to be responsible. You weren't just ignoring everything your parents or teachers told you and willfully getting into things. Seeing you as an adult… I don't think you spent very much time intentionally breaking the rules."

"No. But I got in plenty of trouble anyway. Ask my sisters. Joss says I was always getting into trouble, and," he swallowed, "getting her into trouble too, because she was supposed to be watching me and keeping me out of mischief. I don't remember that, but I do remember my mom saying that I was incorrigible and could never behave. And my dad… didn't talk so much as he took action."

"He punished you for your behavior, a lot of which wasn't your fault, but was the result of your ADHD and learning disabilities."

"But I still did stuff that I knew I shouldn't."

"So do all kids. How do you think you would treat a child who broke a rule? Or who got into some other mischief? How do you think Bridget will react?"

"I don't know." Zachary scratched the back of his neck. "She'll have help. And Gordon isn't like my father. He'll make sure she has someone to help with the babies."

"That's good. Does that make you feel better?"

"On the outside," Zachary said slowly. "I get it logically. But on the inside… I guess I'm still worried."

46

At the police station, Burton and Zachary didn't have to sit in the hard chairs of the lobby waiting area. The officer of the day had been told that they were coming and had another officer escort them to an interview room. It was a comfortable room, with soft boardroom chairs rather than the hard plastic tubular chairs that Zachary knew were in the interrogation rooms intended for criminals. It was more the type of room that a family would be invited to when they had bad news. Or where a couple of chiefs might meet to discuss their teams.

Burton looked around and fidgeted a lot. He wasn't looking good. He had probably not obeyed Campbell's advice and abstained from alcohol the night before, but he'd been up for long enough to have time to think about what he was being asked to do.

A woman joined them after a few minutes and introduced herself as a therapist who was experienced in meeting with victims and helping them to provide statements that would help the police to investigate crimes and could later be used for the prosecution. She didn't introduce herself as 'doctor,' but as Harriet Sonbaum, and invited Burton to call her by her first name.

"I don't really remember anything clearly," Burton said uncomfortably. "I don't have a picture in my head of what happened. Just... feelings and impressions."

"That's fine," Harriet assured him. "Let's start with that." She settled herself into a chair and pushed a strand of dark hair back behind her ear. It was obvious that it was not long enough to stay there and would swing free again as soon as she shifted. "You came here, if I understand correctly, looking for the house that you had lived in when you were young."

"Yes."

"What feelings did you have about that? You wanted to come home?"

Burton considered that.

"Well. No, I don't think that was it, no. I didn't want to move here, or to have some kind of reunion. I wanted… to see it again. To know where I came from."

"What did you know about the life you had before you were adopted?"

"Nothing, really. My parents only talked about my life after I was adopted. Before that… everything was kind of a blank. I don't know if they thought I remembered, or if they thought that if they didn't talk about it, I would forget, and that was better."

"Did you ask them about it as an adult?"

"No. I don't want to hurt them. I don't want to challenge them about it. I just… needed to have some kind of connection to… the *before*."

"And after Mr. Goldman helped you to find the house, how did you feel? When you first saw it and knew that it was the right place."

"I was… I don't know. Stunned. I didn't know how to feel. But I wanted to see inside. To walk through it. Looking at it from the outside-in was not what I was looking for."

"You probably hadn't seen it much from the outside as a child, from what I understand."

"I guess. I just… needed to be inside. Where I had been."

"Because it was familiar."

"Maybe. I don't know why. I just wanted to be there."

"Okay."

Burton looked at Zachary. He looked back at the therapist. "I don't know what else you want."

"Tell me about going into the basement. How did you feel? What were you thinking?"

"I wasn't thinking that my brother was buried there, if that's what you're asking," Burton growled.

"No. So what were you thinking?"

"I was thinking… that it wasn't the same. Too much had changed. It wasn't the same place as it had been before."

"What had changed?"

"I don't know. I guess the floor had been poured. That was the biggest thing that didn't seem right. When I was there before, it had been a dirt floor."

"Anything else?"

Burton shook his head. "Everything. It had been open before, no smaller rooms. No closet around the furnace. All just one open area."

Harriett nodded. "Yes?"

"And… you know, there were finished walls and floor and the carpet. And the lights weren't there before. Not like that."

"What kind of lights were there before?"

"I don't know. It was dark. All of the corners were dark. Black. So I guess they weren't very good lights. Low wattage. Maybe just… a couple of bare bulbs."

"What do you feel when you think back to the way it was before? When you lived there?"

"Nothing." He shook his head slightly. "I just lived there. That's all. It was… like my room. My house."

"You felt like you belonged there? Like it was your possession?"

"I don't know. If I was so little when they started to keep me down there… then I would never have known anything else, would I? So how would I judge it? I wouldn't know if it was a good or bad place; it was the only place I knew."

"That's true." Harriett let some silence pass. "How about the people? Do you remember your biological mother and father?"

"No, I don't think so. I don't… have a picture in my mind. It's just… nothingness."

Though he had been pretty sure that the motorcycle dude wasn't his father.

"How about Allen?"

Burton rubbed his chin. He looked around the room. He looked down at the table and his hands clenched into fists and then released again. "I don't remember him," he said finally. "It was just… too long ago. I can't help the police with anything that they're looking for."

"Don't worry about the police. Don't worry about helping anyone. Just relax and explore the basement in your mind. You knew that your bug jar was behind the furnace."

"I didn't know it was there."

Harriett didn't ask any questions, just waited for him to clarify.

"I knew… something was there. I knew the furnace was there, somewhere. I knew that. But that's not really anything special. Any house in the neighborhood has a furnace."

"Of course. But not everyone would be concerned about it and want to look at it. Unless they were, say, a furnace repairman."

"So I wanted to look at it for a reason."

"Your jar was there."

"Yeah. And the names."

"What did you think when you saw the names?"

"I don't know. I didn't think anything. Until Zachary said that was my name. Bobby Allen. I thought it really was." He pushed his chair back from the table slightly. "You see? I didn't know about Allen. If I knew about Allen, I would have known that wasn't my last name. That it was his name."

"Maybe." Harriett said. "And maybe you did."

"No," he shook his head with certainty, "I didn't."

Harriett let it go. She looked at the clipboard she had brought with her.

"When did you start to remember that Allen wasn't your last name, but was a separate person?"

"I didn't. Zachary did."

Zachary shook his head. "No… I told you it wasn't your last name. But that maybe it was your first and middle name. Or a double-barreled first name. You were the one who kept asking 'who is Allen?'"

Burton patted his pockets, then went still again. He scratched his head anxiously. "Allen was my brother," he said, answering his own question back across time. "My… big brother."

"Yes."

"He was the one who wrote the names on the wall. Not me. I didn't know how to write. Or to read the names. But he'd gone to school, so he knew."

Zachary listened, fascinated. They hadn't had any confirmation before that Allen had gone to school before being shut in the basement.

"He went to school?" Harriet asked.

"Yes. He must have."

"Did he got to school while you were at home in the basement?"

"No. No, I don't think so. It was… a long time ago. He told me stories, but he didn't go to school anymore…"

Harriett nodded. "What other stories did he tell you?"

Zachary remembered Burton saying that Allen had told him about animals. Nice, furry animals rather than the many-legged denizens of the basement. Dogs and cats and animals in other parts of the world. What had Burton thought when Allen told him about those things? Could he picture them? Did he think they were fantastical, like unicorns and dragons? Did he think that Allen had just made them up for entertainment?

"I don't know." Burton closed off immediately. Every advance was followed by a retreat. Fear kept him from moving forward.

"What did he tell you about school?"

"I don't know. It was where you went to learn. There were lots of other kids there. Teachers to tell you what to do. There were… slides and swings."

Burton said 'slides and swings' like they were something mystical. And to him, they must have been. He was attached to the ground. He didn't know about sliding from a high ladder. He didn't know about swinging way up above the ground, until the horizon seemed like it was at his feet.

"Yes," Harriett agreed with an appreciative laugh. "That must have been very puzzling for you. Like a rollercoaster or jet plane is to someone who has never even seen a picture of one. Did you want to go to school?"

"Of course. He did, so I did. He made it sound wonderful."

"Were you disappointed when you eventually went to school?"

Burton considered this for a few moments. "I was and I wasn't. It was not as grand as what I had imagined… and it was more. I just didn't have anything to base it on."

"Your experience was very limited."

"Yes."

"Do you remember," Harriett said slowly, "anyone coming down the stairs to see you?"

This time she hadn't suggested specific people like his mother and father. And she had added in a new trigger, something that had to be part of Burton's experience. People coming down the stairs.

They could not have fed him or taken care of any other physical needs without coming down the stairs. They could not have killed and buried Allen without coming down the stairs.

Burton shook his head at first, but no one said anything and he had some time to think about it. He must have also known that people had to have come down the stairs at some point. So he made himself remember. But was it really a memory, or was it something his brain created because it should logically have been there?

"I… didn't like it when people came down the stairs," he said slowly. "That scared me."

"Did it? But there must have been good things about someone coming down the stairs too. Food to eat or other new supplies."

Burton nodded. Zachary thought about the foods they had talked about before. How Burton hated mac and cheese and fish sticks. How when he had gone to the foster home, he had not been able to eat textured foods without gagging, and had to be taught to eat. He ate pablum and mush. A few soft things. His diet had been very restricted.

Had his mother fed him by hand like she must have done when he was a baby? Spooning food directly into his mouth? Playing 'airplane' to try to get him to eat it all up?

"There was food," Burton agreed. "I don't remember it being very good… about being hungry for it. I had to eat it when they brought it. That's all."

"How about Allen?"

Burton pushed back immediately. "I don't remember Allen!"

"Okay."

There was a period of silence. Burton rubbed his face and jaw and the back of his neck. He was holding it back. He didn't want to remember.

He didn't want to have to compare notes. He didn't want to say what his parents had or had not done. Logically, they must have come down the stairs at some point. But he didn't have to remember more than that.

"Let's skip ahead to when you were rescued," Harriett suggested after letting some minutes pass in silence. "What do you remember about that?"

"I don't exactly remember being rescued… but I told Zachary… I can remember walking down the sidewalk and seeing someone walking a dog. I wanted to pet the dog."

"That must have been a very big step for you. For someone who had never seen an animal before, a dog could be a big scary thing."

"I guess Allen never told me they could be scary. So I wasn't scared. I thought… that all dogs were friendly and nice."

"Ah. That makes sense. Still. Approaching a stranger and a strange beast that you'd never seen before seems like a really big step in your life."

Burton gazed off into the distance. He nodded.

"Did the man walking the dog call the police? Did other people come to help?"

"I guess. I just remember petting the dog."

Zachary could picture it. The thin little boy he had seen in the picture, stroking the big dog's silky fur. Just enamored with the dog and ignoring the rest of what was going on around him.

47

There was a knock at the door, and Campbell entered. He must have been watching the interview on a monitor somewhere, and he had decided it was time for him to take over. Zachary still thought that there was more that Burton could remember, but he clearly wasn't ready or willing to share it yet. Campbell hadn't wanted to unwittingly color any of Burton's memories prior to his working with Harriett, but probably felt that they had hit an impasse and it was time for him to move things forward with the information he had.

Burton eyed Campbell and the thick folder in his hands warily. Campbell reintroduced himself and sat down.

The file folder looked old. Like it had been in storage for many years. When Campbell opened it, it was filled not with perfect computer printouts and photocopies, but lots of handwritten notes, carbon copies, and copies made on machines that were precursors to the modern laser and inkjet technology. Lots of different shades of gray and purple.

Burton stared at the file, mesmerized.

"This was the initial police investigation after you were discovered," Campbell explained the obvious. "From the time that you appeared on that street, it was clear that something was wrong. You were alone, you were ragged and unkempt, and malnourished. The police were called and began their investigation."

Burton nodded.

"You were several houses down the street from the house we searched yesterday. You were able to point it out to the officers who talked to you, letting them know that was where you had come from. You were only five and your speech wasn't entirely clear—" Probably the result of the fact that he had been kept away from all human contact, "—but you were able to make yourself understood."

Campbell flipped through the dusty pages and lifted the edges of the top pages to show Burton fading photos of the house as it had been thirty years previously. Zachary looked at it curiously. It had not changed very much at all. The fence and the exterior of the home looked newer, but the shapes were still the same. There was not much vegetation. It was a summer picture, but there was no green grass, only brown, dusty, dead grass dotted with green weeds that had been able to force themselves up through the sod.

There were no tricycles in the yard. There were no outdoor toys at all like a family with children would normally have. There was nothing to show that the children lived there.

"The police investigated the owners—actually, the renters—of the home without making direct contact with them. They decided that there was enough to get a warrant to search the house. They had it under surveillance and, before they could get the warrant, the male subject was observed making his way down the street looking for something."

"Something?" Burton echoed.

"Or someone. He was calling quietly, looking into neighboring yards, checking under cars that were up on blocks, into side yards, various places that a small boy might have been able to crawl. He was detained."

Burton's eyes were wide. He again patted his pocket, but he'd thrown his flask away when they were out at the house. An action that he probably regretted now. He was used to anesthetizing his emotions, and now he couldn't. Confronted with the reality of what would happen, he had no buffer to keep it at a comfortable distance.

Campbell flipped through a few more pages, then displayed a photo to Burton of a man in his forties or fifties, in classic mugshot poses. Zachary studied the lines of the man's face and hair. The same man who, thirty years later, had tried to break into Zachary's car, but then made a run for it when the alarm had sounded? He hadn't been close enough to see his features clearly.

Burton's mouth opened and closed. His face turned gray. He stared at the monster who had kept him in the basement all of those years ago. Sam. His biological father. Zachary touched him on the back, trying to steady him.

"That's him!" Burton said in a choked voice.

Campbell nodded. It wasn't obvious whether Burton remembered him, or whether he was just shocked at seeing the man for the first time after so many years.

Campbell waited to see whether Burton would say anything further and, when he did not, Campbell continued. "As I said, the police were already in the process of getting a search warrant. They amended the application to add the new facts on the fly, and waited for it to be granted. It was not granted until the next morning when judges were back at their desks and in their courtrooms, but they had kept surveillance on the house to ensure that no one could escape before they had a chance to enter the premises."

Campbell showed a copy of the warrant that had been granted, but it didn't have any effect on Burton.

"At ten o'clock the next morning, police entered the house. Elizabeth Weaver, who was actually Elizabeth Dougherty, was still in the home. She had made an attempt to clean up any incriminating evidence but, as she had not had the opportunity to leave the house, everything was still on the property. Soiled rags, a bucket that had clearly been used for some time as a toilet, worn and ripped clothing. It was all logged into evidence."

Burton nodded mechanically. Zachary was expecting to see pictures of these items, but Campbell apparently thought that too cruel.

"And the basement?" Zachary inquired.

"The basement was a hole in the ground. Undeveloped. No floor. But a child had clearly been playing there. There were broken bits of plastic bottles or Corelle dishes that had been used as digging tools. Buttons and coins and other small objects that were toys."

And a bug jar behind the furnace that they hadn't identified as something of value to little Bobby Weaver.

And two names written on the wall out of sight, not just one.

"The female subject was Mirandized, questioned, and gave a preliminary statement. She was arrested and remanded."

Campbell looked at Burton's face, searching it. Burton gave a tiny nod, his eyes on the papers. Campbell released several pages so that the photo of Elizabeth Weaver fell into place.

Zachary probably wouldn't have recognized her. She bore little resemblance to the woman he had seen at Edith Johnson's house. Her face and body looked wasted, her long blond hair oily and bedraggled. She had obviously not been at her best, waiting for the police to arrive. She had to have known that they would be arriving sooner or later. She had a distant look. An addict, Zachary suspected. Addicted to what? Heroin? She was better now. Maybe she had gotten cleaned up in prison. Bobby's escape might have saved her life.

Burton covered his face with both hands. He choked back sob after sob, trying to stop them, releasing one choked gasp after another.

"It's okay," Zachary told him. "Do you need some time? Maybe a break…?" He looked at Campbell.

Campbell shifted to get up, but Burton shook his head. "No," he managed to gurgle out. "Get it done."

Campbell settled again. He looked at Zachary, then at the thick file before him. He waited for Burton to calm himself down.

Burton wiped his nose. Zachary looked around the room and found a tissue box and handed it to him. Burton blew and wiped and used several tissues to dab at his eyes, trying to slow the waterworks. He shook his head.

"Why would I cry? I don't care about her."

"No," Zachary said softly. "You care about Allen. About what happened to him."

"They buried him in the floor!" This brought a fresh stream of tears. Burton looked at Campbell for confirmation. "*He* did it. He dug a hole and put Allen in it!"

Campbell nodded wordlessly. Saying nothing that would change Burton's recollection of the events, if he did, in fact, remember what had happened so long ago. It had been so traumatic, Zachary wondered if he would ever remember it in any detail. And it was best for him, perhaps, if he didn't.

"I dug holes. I buried things." Burton wiped his eyes again and sucked back the mucus running down his nose and throat. "I wanted my Allen." His entire body shuddered. "If I dug too close, he beat me. Told me he'd cut off my fingers. And he would have."

Burton put down his head, sobbing wildly. Zachary rubbed his back, murmuring soothing words that meant absolutely nothing to Burton.

"So I just… sat down there. Sat and looked at where he was buried. Forever."

Zachary looked at Campbell, wondering if they had the medical examiner's report yet. Had the bones shown a clear cause of death?

Campbell correctly interpreted Zachary's look. He closed the file and watched Burton, waiting to see if he would calm down. If Campbell should or shouldn't discuss what they had discovered about Allen in the previous twenty-four hours.

Burton grabbed another handful of tissues and tried to stanch the flow of tears and snot.

"Do you know how Allen died?" Campbell asked quietly.

48

Burton's eyes and nose were red and raw. He held cupped palms over his eyes, waiting, willing his body to stop. His Adam's apple worked up and down.

"We were sick. He gave me his food. He..." Burton's mouth opened and closed, unconsciously simulating what he remembered. "I was getting better. But he couldn't... he couldn't feed me anymore. I tried to feed him." Burton wiped his eyes. "He just laid there."

Zachary licked his dry lips, unable to take his eyes off of Burton. He opened his mouth to prompt Burton for more, but he couldn't.

"He buried him," Burton said in a loud protest, skipping ahead in his story. "He dug a hole and..."

Campbell opened a slim file. He laid it flat on the table before him, looking at Burton. "Allen got sick and died?" he asked, looking down at the white sheaf of papers.

Burton shook his head. "Noooo..."

"What happened?"

Burton sniffled. "*She* did it." He gulped. "Allen wouldn't get up. She wanted him to..." Another sob and gulp. "...to carry the bucket up the stairs. But he wouldn't get up. So she..."

A child too weak to eat, and she had expected him to get up and carry the bucket of filth up the stairs for her. Zachary closed his eyes and shook his head. He thought of his own mother, how she would have reacted to a child she deemed to be oppositional.

It had not only been his father who had beaten him.

Zachary put his arm around Burton's shoulders and hugged him close. "Okay."

Burton leaned into him, sobbing.

Campbell closed the file again, nodding.

"Will you be able to find them?" Zachary asked. He wiped at the corners of his own eyes, which seemed to be leaking.

"We already have. Mr. O'Sullivan, your biker, knew how to reach them. They are in custody now. We wanted to know what Mr. Burton could remember before going any further."

Zachary let out a long breath.

49

Zachary rang the doorbell. He thought about his parting from Burton, driving him to the bus depot to go back home to his adoptive family. Burton was, as usual, on the edge of being drunk. He thanked Zachary for the work he had done and for helping him through the voyage of self-discovery. He slapped him heartily on the back and swore that he was going to go home and go to an AA group. He'd get on the wagon, and he'd get back on track with his life.

Zachary doubted it would be that easy. But he smiled and encouraged Burton and shook his hand warmly one last time before he left.

Maybe now that Sam and Elizabeth Dougherty were in custody facing charges of first degree murder and Burton knew what had happened in that house, he would find the strength inside himself to move on.

And then Zachary got into the car and drove south again. He hadn't made arrangements, but figured she would be home by the time he got there.

But it was taking her a long time to answer the door, and he wondered if he should have called ahead. He hadn't wanted to have to explain.

Eventually, he could hear footsteps, and the door opened.

Zachary looked up at Joss, a few inches above him. He stepped up over the threshold so that he would be at her level. Joss stepped back slightly, her forehead wrinkling.

"Zachary? What are you doing here? What's up?" There was an edge to her voice. She had told him before to set up a time, and not just show up on her doorstep. And, once more, he had disobeyed her instructions.

Zachary put his arms around Jocelyn and squeezed.

Her body went rigid and she tried to pull away. Zachary held on. Not so tightly that she couldn't break his grip, but tightly enough to let her know that he wasn't willing to relinquish his hold so quickly. She was still for a moment and then put her arms uncertainly around him.

"Thank you," Zachary murmured.

"For what?" Joss demanded. "What's wrong?"

"For being my big sister and looking after me. No matter what the consequences."

She didn't move for a minute. Then she squeezed him to her. "Of course, Zachy. You're my brother."

SHE WAS AT RISK

ZACHARY GOLDMAN MYSTERIES #10

To all those who are vulnerable
Which is all of us

1

Zachary gazed out Kenzie's living room window at the pleasant, suburban view. He hadn't realized how much he was missing by living in apartment buildings instead of a nice little house like Kenzie had. When he stared out the window at his apartment, he saw nothing but sky, or looked down at the dirty parking lot, complete with homeless people going through the trash for bottles. He didn't know his neighbors within the apartment building well. They were familiar enough to nod to in the elevator, but that was about it.

What he was missing was the green lawns, the children walking to school, the flower borders and gardens. People smiling pleasantly at each other when they passed on the street or even stopping to talk to each other. It was a postcard picture day and, unlike when he looked at the Vermont trees and hills covered with snow as Christmas approached, Zachary could enjoy the scene.

Maybe he should have moved into a house like Kenzie's. Maybe sometime in the future, he would. Maybe with the way that his relationship was progressing with Kenzie…

He pulled his thoughts away from the possibility. He didn't want to be dependent on anyone's kindness. He had lived with Mario after his previous apartment had burned down, and it was better to be on his own two feet. He got lazy relying on someone else to do the work and keep him on track.

The thought stirred Zachary, and he got up and went into the kitchen. He put in a pod and made himself a cup of coffee and poked his head out of the kitchen for a moment to listen and try to decide whether Kenzie was up yet. He couldn't hear her stirring. No point in making her coffee before she was up; it would just be cold by the time she got to it.

But while he was in the kitchen, he rinsed the dishes that were sitting in the sink, put them into the dishwasher, and wiped the counter, eliminating the rings from his previous cups of coffee. He put the washcloth back in its place and gave himself a mental pat on the back for at least doing something to help keep Kenzie's place tidy.

Fresh coffee in hand, Zachary returned to his place in Kenzie's living room. Since he was there most weeknights now, he had asked Kenzie whether she minded his getting a mobile laptop table that he could use while he was sitting on the couch or in the easy chair, if he kept his space tidy and it didn't detract from the decor of the room.

Kenzie shook her head, bemused. "Sure, of course. You should have some kind of desk instead of sitting hunched over that thing all the time. It's not good for your body."

He was often sore after a couple of hours sitting with it, so he knew she was right. "I just… didn't want to presume."

Kenzie shrugged. "Of course. You're here. I like having you around, having… a few touches that remind me of you when you're out. I don't mind at all."

So he had browsed online until he found one that he liked, and it had been a good purchase. He could sit and type, read documents, or browse databases with better posture, which helped to keep him going for as long as he needed to.

Zachary's phone vibrated in his pocket. He slid it out to look at it, and felt frown lines crease his forehead.

Gordon Drake.

Gordon didn't have any reason to be calling Zachary. Zachary had stayed away from Bridget, his ex-wife. He hadn't been following her or spying on her. They hadn't accidentally run into each other anywhere.

Not lately.

Zachary had cleared everything up at Drake, Chase, Gould after Ashley's death. There was no reason for Gordon to call Zachary back. With the killer behind bars, there shouldn't have been anything else for Gordon to call Zachary about.

Unless there had been another death.

Unless something else untoward had happened.

But even if it had, Zachary would have expected Gordon to go somewhere else to get help. Bridget had not been happy with Zachary looking into Ashley's death, and Zachary didn't think that Gordon would do anything he knew would antagonize her.

Especially not since she was pregnant.

———

Zachary slid his finger across the phone screen to answer the call.

"Gordon? Is everything okay?"

"Zachary, it's been a while since I saw you last. How are things with you?"

Zachary chewed the inside of his cheek. "I'm fine," he said cautiously. "What's going on with you? Everything okay at Chase Gold?"

Gordon chuckled. The nickname for the investment banking firm left out his name, which was a bit of a slap in the face considering he was the principal partner and owner. But he appreciated the appropriateness of the name.

"Yes, everything is fine at Chase Gold," he agreed. "Better than ever. And I have… put some extra controls in place as far as the interns are concerned. We don't want any more… hospitalizations."

"Yeah, that's good." Zachary waited for Gordon to explain why he had called. It wasn't just for a casual chat and to catch up on each other's lives. They didn't have that kind of relationship. Although Gordon had always been very cordial toward Zachary, he knew how much animosity Bridget had toward him. He usually respected her desire to have nothing to do with him anymore.

Unless he needed something.

"I guess you're wondering why I called. I was hoping that the two of us could get together."

"I suppose," Zachary said slowly, feeling his way along. "What did you want to meet about?"

"I would… prefer to leave that for our meeting. It's a rather delicate matter. I prefer to discuss it face to face, somewhere quiet and discreet."

"Okay. If you're sure. Where would you like to meet? Your office?"

"Heavens, no." Gordon was silent for a moment as if considering, though surely he must have known before he called Zachary that they would need an appropriate place to meet. "I can book a private meeting room at my club. Do you know the Ostrich?"

Zachary knew of it. He wasn't a member and had never been there. He wasn't aware of anyone in his circles who was a member. Other than Gordon, clearly.

"I know where it is. What's the dress code?"

"They are fairly relaxed now. No blue jeans or track pants. Clean, neat, and pressed. Collared shirt. No tie required."

Zachary didn't think he even owned a tie. When was the last time he had attended an event where he had needed one? Probably not since he and Bridget had broken up. He had gone to fancy dress parties with her. Lots of places that had required a tie or even a tux with a bow tie. Not the clip-on ones. They had to be proper tie-up bow ties, Bridget had informed him. No shortcuts. People could tell when they looked at you whether you had taken the time or not. They could see right through you.

If that were the case, then he didn't know what point there was in wearing a bow tie of any kind. If people could see through his clothing to what kind of a person he really was, then why try to masquerade as a society man by wearing clothes that didn't suit him?

But he didn't say that to Bridget. He had shaved and dressed up and stood still while Bridget tied his bow tie and made sure that it was straight and everything else was in its proper place.

But he could manage business pants and a polo shirt. He didn't have to go out and rent or buy anything for that. Gordon would be in a three-piece suit if he were coming from work, but he had not told Zachary that he had to be formally dressed. He would probably just stand out more if he tried to look like an upper-class businessman anyway. People paid no attention if he looked like he was working-class or a bum.

"Okay. What time do you want to get together?"

"I have a rather full schedule," Gordon said, a note of apology in his voice. "But I would like to see you as soon as possible. Could you do lunch today? I just had someone cancel on me."

Lunch at Gordon's fancy club.

"Sure. Lunch at the Ostrich Club. Do I… check in with the maitre d' when I get there? I haven't been anywhere like that before."

"There is a reception desk. You can tell Danielle that you are meeting me. She will direct you to which room I have booked or someone will escort you up."

Zachary nodded to himself. He looked at the system clock on his computer. He'd better start getting cleaned up if he were going to look presentable by lunch.

2

The Ostrich was pretty much as Zachary expected it to be. Dark woods, plush carpets, polished waitstaff right there whenever you looked for them. He was escorted to the Roosevelt room by a pleasant young man who didn't try to make conversation or ask him what he was doing there.

Gordon was already seated at the table, his laptop out, working on some document or project. His expression was serious and focused. He didn't look up for a few seconds, but then he closed the lid of the computer and looked into Zachary's eyes, giving him a warm smile of welcome.

"Good to see you, Zachary. Have a seat. What do you want to drink?"

Zachary looked at the young man who stood attentively. "Uh… just a Coke, please."

The man nodded, acting as if that were a perfectly normal drink order. Apparently not everyone at the club was ordering hi-balls or tea. Or if they were, the waiter would never give it away. Gordon ordered some kind of French wine and the waiter nodded and wrote it down, expression not changing. Zachary couldn't tell if it was an expensive vintage or something out of a box. Given the setting, he assumed the former.

"And what would you like to eat?" Gordon asked.

"Uh…" Zachary looked around for a menu. "I don't know…"

"They're equipped to make any popular dish. What do you feel like?"

Zachary cast around for a suitable dish. "I'm not that hungry yet. Maybe just… a sandwich?"

Gordon nodded. "Sure. What do you like? Roast beef? Chicken?"

"Maybe cheese? Grilled cheese?" He felt a little silly ordering something juvenile at such a fancy place. But he didn't have much of an appetite. His meds made him nauseated for a few hours after taking them.

"How about a Monte Cristo?" Gordon suggested. "Grilled cheese and ham?"

"Sure," Zachary agreed. "That sounds good."

"Would you like salad or fries on the side?" the waiter asked.

Zachary shook his head. "Just the sandwich."

He nodded. Gordon ordered some kind of skillet. After the waiter was gone, he turned his attention to Zachary.

"So, things are going well for you?" he asked. "How is business?"

"Going pretty well." A few big cases had padded out his bank account and gotten his name out in the media, so he was doing all right.

"Anything interesting? Haven't captured any serial killers recently?"

"No. I think I'm going to put in all of my listings that I don't do serial killers. Too much time and effort," Zachary deadpanned.

Gordon looked at him uncertainly, then smiled. "Well, you might as well advertise the kind of cases that you actually want to get," he agreed. "I haven't seen much in the news lately. Has there been anything big?"

"I just finished with a man who was looking for his childhood home. Which ended up being where his brother was buried. So that was pretty intense. And the main one before that was a missing girl. Human trafficking. Prostitution."

Gordon shook his head slowly. "You do get around, don't you? Nasty business."

Zachary shrugged. "Yeah. Most people don't come to me because they won the lottery."

"I imagine not. People are coming to you at the worst, most vulnerable times of their lives."

"Yeah. Exactly."

Gordon stared off into space. He looked like a man with something heavy on his mind. Zachary waited for him to spit it out. Since he wanted to meet, Zachary had to assume that there was something he wanted to be investigated. He wouldn't be going to Zachary with personal problems.

Some people were much better qualified than Zachary to sort out relationship problems.

Gordon looked at his watch. A big, highly-polished gold number. "This is rude, but do you mind..." Gordon gestured to his laptop. "There are a couple of things I'd like to put through while I still have the time."

Zachary shrugged. "Sure," he agreed. Gordon wasn't yet ready to present what it was that he wanted. Maybe he was waiting for the food to arrive so they wouldn't be interrupted partway through. Or maybe he would wait until after they were finished eating to turn to the business he'd asked Zachary there for. He hoped it would not take that long for Gordon to get to the point.

While Gordon opened his laptop again, Zachary pulled out his phone. He checked his email, even though there wasn't likely to be anything important that had come in since he'd left Kenzie's house. And he browsed through his social networks. He wasn't big on social networks, but sometimes he did find interesting news stories or something that impacted his work. It was a good way to connect with family or friends, but Zachary wasn't quite ready to put that much of himself on public display. As a private investigator, he didn't want people to be able to track him down too easily. And he knew from experience that people shared way too much on social media. He'd been on the investigating end of a lot of those.

He and Gordon worked independently until the waiter arrived with their dishes. Then they both put the electronics aside and thanked the waiter. Zachary took his first bite of the Monte Cristo sandwich. It was crisp but not greasy, with just the right amount of cheese and ham pocketed inside.

"Mmm. This is very good."

Gordon nodded. "Good kitchen staff. We have world-class chefs. They don't disappoint."

Zachary nodded to Gordon's meal of grilled vegetables and seafood. "That looks good too."

"Yes." Gordon took a few bites, then he pushed the dish a few inches away from him as though he were full. "Zachary, I know I can rely on your discretion. You've proven yourself eminently capable in the past."

Zachary nodded. "Yes. I won't share any company secrets."

"This one isn't for the firm." Gordon was staring off into middle space again, considering. Making his final decision as to whether to proceed or to jettison the whole thing. He swallowed and put his hands palms-down on the table to physically brace himself. “It’s Bridget.”

Zachary had been half-expecting this. He had tried to convince himself that it was about Gordon’s firm, but Gordon was perfectly capable of handling his business without bringing Zachary in. He was the one who knew about investments and financial stuff and all of the ins and outs, not Zachary. Zachary would be hard-pressed to help Gordon with a case of fraud or some other business-related area. Maybe if he wanted to find out if one of his partners were out fooling around where he shouldn’t be, but nothing about the business itself.

Zachary swallowed. He was going to have to tell Gordon no. He couldn’t work on a case that had anything to do with Bridget. He was trying to put Bridget out of his life, out of his thoughts. He didn’t want to be thinking about her when he was with Kenzie. He didn’t want her creeping into his dreams or keeping him up at night. He just wanted to be able to leave that part of his life behind and to move forward.

“What about Bridget?”

Gordon traced a circle on the polished tabletop. He had a quick sip from his glass and poked around at the seafood on his platter. But he wasn’t interested in the food. They weren’t there to eat lunch. He was a man with something far more pressing on his hands than his next meal.

“You know that she’s pregnant.”

Zachary nodded.

“Of course you do,” Gordon said quickly. “Of course. I told you that when she was in the hospital. She’s been quite sick with this pregnancy. It hasn’t been easy on her.”

“Right.” Zachary had, in fact, thought that her cancer had returned. He was relieved that wasn’t the case, but he wished he didn’t have to think about Bridget pregnant either. He had wanted children when they had been married. She had not. She’d had a pregnancy scare before her cancer was diagnosed, and she had no interest in carrying it to term. But she had not been pregnant, so that disaster had been averted.

“What I don’t think I told you is that she is expecting twins,” Gordon said slowly, enunciating his words as carefully as if he were being graded on his diction. “Two girls.”

Zachary nodded again. He swallowed. His mouth and throat were very dry. He irrigated them with a good amount of Coke. "I guessed as much," he agreed.

Gordon looked at him for a moment, then nodded. He didn't ask how Zachary had guessed. That was not the point.

"In the beginning, Bridget agreed to try to get pregnant." Gordon couldn't have any idea the kind of pain that this disclosure caused Zachary. He had failed on so many levels with Bridget. "She was a little reluctant at first, but she agreed to give it a try, see how things worked out. Neither of us knew whether she would even be able to get pregnant and be able to carry the baby to term."

The doctors hadn't expected her to have viable eggs after the cancer treatment. Instead, she had banked them before she started treatment. She had been very sick, and it had taken a lot of coaxing on the part of the doctors. They didn't like leaving a woman with no options. She might change her mind in the future. She might decide, after the crisis was past, that she did want to expand her family or at least to have those choices open to her.

And apparently, she had done just that. They had fertilized a couple of frozen eggs and she had become pregnant with twins.

Gordon fiddled some more, not able to come to the point yet.

"The further along she has gone with the pregnancy, the more difficult things have become. She has had a lot of second thoughts."

But what was she going to do? Terminate the pregnancy? That was what she had threatened Zachary with after she had a positive pregnancy test. She didn't want her body ruined by pregnancy. Didn't want to be burdened by children who depended on her. She didn't think that Zachary would be able to man up and be a good father to them. He could barely take care of himself; how was he going to help with children?

"Has she decided… that she doesn't want to continue?" he prompted.

"She is getting older and we don't know how many chances she will have to get pregnant. How hard it will be to terminate and try again."

"Try again? If she wants to terminate, why would she try again?"

"It changes from day to day," Gordon sighed. "Maybe she's not ready. She could try again in a year or two when she feels more ready, though that will be pushing against her biological clock. Or sometimes she decides that twins will be too much and she should only carry one to term. They can do selective reduction… And other days, she is convinced that there is something wrong with the babies."

It wasn't that surprising that Bridget would be worried about her pregnancy. Many women had anxiety over such a significant change in their lives. It was something so utterly different from anything they had done before. For Bridget, it would mean a big change in the way she lived her life. Being a mother, tied down to two children, instead of being able to go wherever she wanted whenever she wanted to. Things were different for parents, even if she did get a nanny to help.

"What does she think is wrong?"

"Well, up until now, it has just been 'something'—'*What if* there is something wrong with the babies?' 'Something doesn't feel right.' 'I think something is wrong.'—But I'm not willing to operate on 'somethings.' I need answers. Concrete evidence."

And he had found something. But what? Why did Gordon need a private investigator?

"And… you found something?" Zachary ventured.

Gordon tapped his computer. He took a couple more bites of his grill.

"She decided to have prenatal DNA testing done. Just to make sure that everything was okay. It's not just Down Syndrome anymore. They are very sophisticated now. They can do all sorts of testing for genetic problems and predict a lot of developmental issues."

Zachary nodded.

"I went along with it," Gordon said. "I thought this would help her to move on. She would know that everything was okay, so she would feel better about continuing the pregnancy. I thought it was a good solution. Rule out all of those things that she was afraid of."

"But, something came up on the test." Zachary still didn't have a clue why Gordon would want him involved. He couldn't fix genetic issues with his magnifying glass.

Gordon sighed. "Both babies are at high risk for developing Huntington's Disease."

3

Zachary had heard of it before, but knew very little about what Huntington's Disease was. He chewed the bite of sandwich in his mouth slowly.

"What exactly is Huntington's?"

"It's a neurological problem," Gordon said in a flat voice. "Like having Alzheimer's and Parkinson's and Lou Gehrig's all at the same time. Dementia, tremors and movements and, eventually, total loss of control and inability to even swallow." He shook his head grimly. "Not a pleasant thought, both of our little girls ending up with this horrible disease."

"No. That sounds horrible. So… Bridget was right. There is something wrong with them."

"But the thing is, these girls could live normal lives until they are forty or fifty—even sixty or seventy in some cases. A long, fulfilling life before it eventually strikes. We all have a limited time here on earth. None of us knows how long we will be in this mortal sphere. You or I could drop dead tomorrow."

"Yeah, that's true."

"So really, we don't *know* anything. We have no idea *when* they are going to develop Huntington's. Just that someday, sometime along the line, they will."

"So you want to continue with the pregnancy, but she wants to terminate," Zachary summed up. "But she doesn't need your permission to terminate. She can go out and do it at any time."

"Yes. She's agreed to hold off a week or two while I look at some of the possibilities. A lot of people are saying that by the time they reach twenty, we could have a cure. Almost guaranteed, in fact. The research looks very good. They could be gene editing by that time, and be able to prevent them from ever getting Huntington's Disease."

"I don't have much knowledge about medical research." Zachary shifted uncomfortably. "I could talk to Kenzie and see what she knows. Or you could get a genetic counselor who could help you to work through this stuff. A professional."

"I'm willing to believe that we could have a cure in the next few years," Gordon said, making a movement with his hand to brush the comment away. "Especially where we are going with things like stem cells and gene therapy. We've come a very long way in the science, and it won't be long before they can treat this."

Zachary leaned back against his seat. Then what did Gordon want?

Gordon pushed his plate away again. "The genetics of Huntington's Disease are such that a child can only get Huntington's if one of her parents have it."

Zachary considered this. His knowledge of genetics was pretty thin, but he remembered some from high school biology. "But it could be that the parent is just a carrier, right?" he suggested. "Because everybody has two copies of each gene."

"In the case of Huntington's Disease, you can't just be a carrier. You have to have it to give it to a child. Maybe you haven't started having symptoms yet, but it's there, and typically it starts to develop between the ages of forty and fifty."

Which meant that Gordon could develop it at any time.

Things suddenly became more clear. Gordon himself was going to get Huntington's Disease sometime soon. Or perhaps sometime in the next couple of decades. But he would get it, and he wanted Zachary to track someone down for him. An absent parent. A sibling. An old sweetheart. Maybe a child that he'd never been involved with.

Zachary pulled out his notebook and laid it on the table. "Okay, so who are you looking for?"

"Who am I looking for?" Gordon repeated. "Well, I don't know that, do I?"

Zachary stared at him, frowning. "What do you mean?"

"I want to know who the father of the babies is."

It was the second shock of the meeting. Zachary stared at him. Who the father of the twins was? Did he think that Bridget had ended up having an affair with Zachary? That the babies might be Zachary's? Or did he have someone else in mind?

He swallowed and shook his head. "I'm a little lost. Who the father is? It's not you?"

"I just had myself tested for the Huntington's Disease gene. I don't have it."

"Oh."

"I didn't think that I did. It would have to be in my family in the recent past, and I don't have any relatives who have had dementia or Parkinson's or anything else that Huntington's might have been mistaken for."

"Does it have to come from the father?"

"No. It could come from Bridget. But we have the same problem there. There's no hint of Huntington's Disease in her family. No sign at all."

Zachary worked through the combinations and options, his brain whirling away.

"So if it didn't come from you or Bridget, then it came from somewhere else. Obviously, Bridget is the mother, since she's the one who is pregnant."

Gordon raised his finger, shaking his head. "Remember, she probably didn't get pregnant naturally. It was frozen eggs. And that means it could have been someone else's eggs."

"True. Right."

"The clinic might have mixed something up. A vial mislabeled or misfiled. It might *not* have been her eggs or my sperm. It might be someone else's fertilized embryos."

Zachary nodded. "But they must be able to test for that. If they're doing a DNA test for Huntington's, then they must be able to test for parentage at the same time."

Gordon was nodding. "Except that Bridget is against it and the doctors seem to have some sort of ethical dilemma. Or maybe it's legal; they don't want to get sued. Bridget says it shouldn't matter where they got the Huntington's gene from. We should be making a decision based on the risk factors that we know, not on who the biological parents are."

Alarm bells were going off in Zachary's head. *Bridget said it didn't matter who the parents were?* Bridget was the one who had said that she wondered if there was something wrong with the babies and had wanted to terminate before they had even proven it.

"Do you think she had an affair?"

Gordon cleared his throat. He poked at the food still on his plate but didn't eat anything else. He sighed. "What else am I to think? Her reactions and explanations up until now have been… improbable. She had IVF, so the babies should be the implanted embryos. But the other possibility is… the embryos didn't take, but she became pregnant naturally. By… me or someone else."

"She couldn't get pregnant naturally, could she? After the cancer treatment?"

"I've dug into that a little. She was told she *probably* wouldn't be able to. That's why she froze her eggs in the first place."

Zachary nodded. He remembered that part very clearly. How much the doctor had to argue to convince her to at least prepare for the possibility she might change her mind in the future. How she had just glared at the doctor and at Zachary and said that there was no way. But in the end, she had agreed.

"But I guess it wasn't a foregone conclusion that she would become sterile. There is still a slim chance that she would have viable eggs left in the other ovary after the treatments. Slim, but not impossible."

"Okay. So… you want me to investigate whether she had an affair?"

"Or whether she still is having one," Gordon said, his words painfully slow and precise. "I have to wonder… and maybe it doesn't matter. Maybe it makes no difference to anything. But I'm a man who likes to have all of the facts before he makes a decision."

Zachary nodded.

He knew that it was not a good idea.

He should have told Gordon right from the start that he couldn't meet. That he couldn't have anything to do with Gordon or Bridget. And now, he needed to say that he couldn't possibly investigate Bridget. It was a conflict of interest. Or something like that. It wasn't a good idea for him to be following her around, seeing where she went, who she talked to, who she might be meeting on the sly.

His heart raced just thinking about it.

And not the pounding heart he often felt from anxiety and the inherent risks of doing surveillance and possibly being caught.

This racing heart was from excitement and anticipation. His brain was being flooded with all of those feel-good neurotransmitters. He was going to be able to see her again. To follow her. To watch her covertly. And it was okay, because he wasn't doing it for himself. He wasn't doing it for his own kicks, because his OCD brain told him that he needed to follow her and know where she was at all times.

It would be for Gordon.

And for the babies.

4

Zachary told himself more than once that he was not taking the job for himself and that he could have refused if he'd wanted to. He would show Gordon, if no one else, that he was able to deal with his feelings for Bridget calmly and rationally. He could separate his emotions from the investigation and treat it just like any other surveillance job. He would be professional in every way.

That's what he told himself while he was still at the Ostrich Club, and in his car driving home, and throughout the afternoon as he started to put together his plan for the surveillance. It was distracting. He knew from the tightness and heaviness in his gut that he wasn't really fooling himself. He probably hadn't fooled Gordon either. Gordon had a way of seeing right through him. But Zachary's obsession for Bridget was to Gordon's advantage. That was undoubtedly why he had approached Zachary in the first place. He wanted to get the best surveillance possible on his wandering lover? What better choice than to hire the man who was obsessed with her?

Of course, there had been one more bump to get over in his conversation with Gordon.

"This is where thing get tricky," Gordon said, fidgeting with his fork. It wasn't like him to be nervous. Or at any rate, not to show it.

Zachary raised his brows and waited for Gordon to work out what he wanted to say. If it was difficult, Zachary wouldn't help matters by being impatient or pestering him about it.

"I suppose being direct is the only viable option." Gordon cleared his throat. "*You* haven't seen Bridget recently, have you?"

Zachary thought back. "The last time I saw her was at the gas station," he said. "We were both filling up at the same time. That was before I saw you at the hospital."

"I don't mean running into her around town. That's bound to happen from time to time, even if she thinks she can tell you to stay away from her favorite haunts. What I mean is... the two of you have not had any time with just the two of you..."

Zachary shook his head. "No. Why would we—" It suddenly hit him what Gordon was asking, and he let out a laugh of disbelief. "Am *I* having an affair with Bridget? Is that what you're asking?"

Gordon gave an uncomfortable nod. "You and she do have a history. I'm aware, of course, that you still have feelings for her."

"But she doesn't for me. She's made it pretty clear that she doesn't want anything to do with me."

"Yes. But what a person says, and what they feel, and the way they act do not always line up. I have often thought that she is too emotional about you. That she protests *too* much."

Zachary tried to laugh again, but it stuck in his throat. That was what Kenzie said too. That if Bridget really didn't have any feelings for Zachary, she wouldn't care what he did. She wouldn't care if they happened to run into each other somewhere. The fact that she flipped out any time she saw him meant that she still had feelings.

Unless, of course, Bridget wanted something from him, and then she would show up at his apartment and pretend to be sympathetic and friendly.

None of that meant that she still had feelings for him.

"I am not having an affair with her," Zachary told Gordon firmly. He tried to keep his voice completely calm and level and to look Gordon in the eye. To give him all of the nonverbal indicators that he was telling the truth. "I haven't been with Bridget since we broke up. Not once."

"So you are one hundred percent sure that the babies are not yours."

"Yes. One hundred percent. It's been more than two years." Zachary shook his head. "When she found out that she had cancer... I was out the door. That was it. She didn't have time or energy for me in her life anymore. Things had been rocky before that, but we were trying to make it work. Once she knew she was sick, it was a whole different story. She needed to remove everything *toxic* from her life."

Gordon winced. "Understood," he agreed with a quick nod. "I just figured… you were the first one who came to mind when I thought about who she might be… emotionally involved with. The two of you have always had that dynamic. That tension."

"That's just because we used to be together. Not because we're together now."

"Okay. I'm going to trust you on that one. I'd look like a real idiot if I hired you to find out if she was having an affair, when it was you all along."

"It's not. If she's with someone… it's not me."

"I wondered because of some of the early symptoms of Huntington's too. Because the babies' father must have Huntington's, and some of the early symptoms… depression, anxiety, erratic behavior…" He trailed off.

Zachary cleared his throat and shook his head. "I don't have Huntington's Disease. I have PTSD, major depression, other stuff. I've always had it. Or at least, since I was a kid. It isn't from Huntington's."

Gordon nodded. He seemed relieved to have put this part of the conversation behind him. "We should discuss terms, then."

Gordon was a wealthy man, so Zachary had no problem charging him the high end of his usual rates, even though he would have been happy to surveil Bridget for nothing. Gordon agreed without trying to negotiate Zachary's rate.

So he was on the case.

He already knew Bridget's usual schedule and travel patterns. It would be easy for him to start surveillance.

No need to put an electronic tag on her car or to have Gordon install one under the mud mats or some similar out-of-sight location. If Bridget found a tracking device, she would know where it had come from. Zachary had used them in the past, so he couldn't afford to be caught doing it again.

But it was unnecessary. He'd be able to predict where she was going and to see any deviations from her usual practices. It was easy when he already knew her so well.

5

Zachary wasn't sure how to approach the usual dinnertime conversation with Kenzie. He decided right off the bat that he would not disclose who it was he was surveilling. She didn't need to know that. Gordon would expect confidentiality. If Kenzie knew that Zachary was following Bridget again, she might just blow a gasket. Even if it was a paid job.

When they sat down to eat and Kenzie asked him how his day had gone, he had prepared his answer and spoken in his usual voice, giving no sign it was anything other than a usual job. He'd done plenty of surveillance, after all. Couples who fooled around had been his bread and butter for a long time.

"Picked up a new case today," he told Kenzie casually. "Possible extramarital affair. It will involve some surveillance. But from their usual schedules, I don't think there will be anything overnight. Just daytime."

Kenzie nodded. She didn't give him a second look. "Sounds good. Nice of them to keep their dalliances to the daytime for you."

Zachary gave a little laugh. "You'd be surprised. The majority of affairs that I have investigated have been during the day. When one spouse is supposed to be at work or looking after the kids. There aren't that many who are sneaking off to hotels at night. That would be too suspicious."

"If one of them travels a lot, though, they wouldn't have to worry about that."

"Yeah. When one travels a lot, they are usually *both* having affairs."

Kenzie speared a tomato from her salad and looked at him. "Do you get a lot of cases where someone who is having an affair hires you to see if their spouse is having an affair?"

Zachary nodded. "Frequently. People who are unfaithful tend to be more suspicious of their spouses."

"But isn't it sort of hypocritical to investigate your spouse, when you're the one messing around?"

"Sure. But they do it anyway."

Kenzie chuckled and shook her head. "We're a strange species."

"But I don't think, in this case, that the husband is having an affair. Could be, but I don't get that feeling from him."

"So what makes him think that his wife is having an affair?"

"Well… it actually might be a case that interests you. They have just found out that one of their children has Huntington's Disease. And neither parent has it."

Kenzie nodded eagerly. "And Huntington's is autosomal dominant. It doesn't skip generations."

"That's what he said."

"Has *he* been tested?" Kenzie leaned forward. "It tends to come from the father more often than the mother, for some reason. And sometimes it doesn't show up until late in life, so it can be missed if parents and grandparents died before showing any symptoms."

"He was tested. He doesn't have it."

"So then it has to come from the wife or she is having an affair. Has she been tested?"

"Doesn't want to be. She says there is no Huntington's in her family and, from what he knows of her family history, she's right. He's talked to her parents and they don't know of any cases of Huntington's Disease in the family."

"Well, I can see why he would be suspicious, then. I'll have to look up the genetics of Huntington's Disease, see if there can be sporadic cases, but I've never heard of any."

"Sporadic means that it just shows up without either parent having it?"

"Yes. A chance mutation rather than an inherited trait. Sometimes the cells make mistakes during fertilization or division. Something goes wrong in the transcription. We all have mistakes in our genes. It's not quite as clean as what you learn in high school genetics. All kinds of mistakes can happen during those processes. But there are redundancies so that, in most cases, one mistake doesn't cause any problems with your health."

Zachary nodded. "He didn't say anything about that. Just that one of the parents had to have Huntington's."

"It's a nasty disease."

"That's what he said. But they can have a lot of years before they are affected, too, so they could still have a good life."

"Yeah. It's usually a mid-life thing, but I know some cases don't show up until late in life."

"I wouldn't want to be the one making that decision," Zachary said, thinking about what Bridget and Gordon were going through.

Kenzie frowned. "What decision?"

"Oh… terminating the pregnancy."

"This was a prenatal test?"

"Yes."

"That's not usually done. I'm surprised."

"I guess it makes sense… if you can avoid having a child with a medical problem, but…"

"All kinds of ethics involved in eugenics. When is it okay to make decisions based on an embryo's or fetus's genes? At least we are past the point now when it is considered okay to kill or sterilize someone because they are less 'desirable,'"

Zachary shuddered at the thought. "But there are still medical practices where it is okay to decide not to treat someone."

Kenzie gave an uncertain shrug. "End of life care, maybe. Do not resuscitate orders. But other than that, doctors are required to treat people. You can't just decide not to help someone who needs it."

"But some people get prioritized. Triaged."

"In a mass disaster, sure. But again, that's based on who has the best chance of survival. Not personal feelings."

"Never?"

He could see the emotions chase across Kenzie's face. She wanted to say that of course not, doctors never made triage or end of life decisions based on their feelings toward patients. But she had probably seen situations where that was not the case. She was reluctant to share her thoughts on the subject.

"Not consciously, I don't think," she said slowly. "I'm sure that yes, people's prejudices do enter into care decisions sometimes. But doctors go through a lot of training, and there are ethics boards and all kinds of guidelines for making informed decisions."

"I've heard that the mortality rates for women are a lot higher for things like heart attacks."

"Yes. Probably more a function of men being studied more than women, though. Not doctors deciding that they'll just let the women die." Her tone was sarcastic. She knew she was exaggerating what Zachary had said, wanted to show him how ridiculous it was that a doctor would make *that* kind of decision.

"And Blacks have higher death rates with almost any kind of illness or injury."

Kenzie looked for a counter to this statistic. She ended up just shrugging and shaking her head. Zachary didn't believe that Blacks were somehow more medically fragile than whites. And he didn't think that their physiology was any different, unlike the biological differences between men and women. So why were their death rates higher?

"And look at the differences between the way someone with cancer is treated when they are fifty versus when they are eighty. Or the way that someone with autism or Down Syndrome is treated versus someone who is neurotypical. Some classes of people are considered more disposable than others. If you look at the guidelines for the people who decide how to prioritize people for transplants—"

"Don't talk to me about transplants," Kenzie said icily.

Zachary froze, his fork hovering, stopped between his plate and his mouth. He hadn't ever heard that tone from Kenzie before. They'd had their arguments and differences, but he'd never heard that level of controlled fury in her voice before. He just stared at her, not sure how to handle her reaction. He had clearly stepped over some line. He had thought that they were just talking about statistics. They often talked about medical science, especially death, because it was relevant to both of their professions.

"Uh..." Zachary shook his head. "I'm sorry..."

Kenzie stood up. She picked up her plate. She'd only eaten half of her dinner, and Zachary watched in shock as she scraped the rest into the garbage and left the room without another word. Clearly, the discussion was closed. They were done.

Zachary looked down at his plate, unsure what to do. He wasn't hungry. He had only been forcing himself to eat because it was suppertime and he knew that he had to continue to do so to get his weight up to where his doctor would be happy with it. He enjoyed talking with Kenzie and it was one of the things that helped him to get through a meal and to ensure he didn't forget all about eating. He didn't want to eat anymore, but he also didn't want Kenzie to think that he was refusing to eat because of the way she had reacted. He didn't want to make it a power struggle. He wasn't refusing to eat as a way to control her and shame her for what she had done; he just didn't want to eat any more.

He stayed at the table, listening for Kenzie. She went to her room, shut the door, and didn't come back out. She didn't bang around, slamming doors and drawers like Bridget would have done. Or call a friend to do something with her or go out on her own. She was still in the house, close by, but blocking Zachary out.

He sat at the table for another twenty minutes, until he was sure that she wasn't coming back out and wouldn't know how long he had stayed at the table after her. He got up, scraped his own plate, and put it in the sink. Then he changed his mind, rinsed it and put it in the dishwasher, and did the same with hers. It wasn't full enough yet to run the dishwasher, but he did it anyway, just to show that he was being a good partner and not expecting her to do everything for him. He was willing to help with the household. She probably wouldn't care about this while she was so angry with him, but the more he could do to appease her wrath, the better.

He reviewed the argument in his head, trying to find the point at which he had pushed it too far. She usually didn't mind his challenging what she had to say, giving different scenarios and figuring out if there was the possibility that a death had been homicide rather than an accident, or something like that. But there had been times. He had pushed it too far before, but this seemed to be a new line that he hadn't crossed before. Or the line itself had moved.

He went back to his computer, checked his email for anything new, and then returned to his surveillance plan.

He was going to follow Bridget. And not only was it okay, but he was actually being paid to do it.

When Kenzie didn't come out of her room for the rest of the evening, Zachary had to decide whether he would stay or should go back to his own apartment. If he were infringing on Kenzie's space, then he should leave. He wasn't sure if it were because he was in her private space too much, taking advantage of her hospitality. He didn't think he was, because she had given him no signals until then that anything was bothering her. But he should pay attention in case it was.

He couldn't exactly ask her whether she wanted him to stay or not. That would aggravate her further. He should be able to figure it out. He should be able to make a reasonable decision based on what he already knew. They had been together long enough.

Despite all of the criticisms he heard in his head, many of them in Bridget's voice, he wasn't sure how to make everything better. He couldn't read Kenzie's mind and know what he had done wrong or how he could fix it.

Eventually, he decided to sleep on the couch. He wouldn't go to her bedroom and incur her wrath for presuming he could sleep with her after a fight. He wouldn't go home and abandon her and make her think that she didn't matter to him or that the only reason he was there was to share her bed. Sleeping on the couch seemed like a reasonable compromise.

The warm blankets that they had used during the evenings that it got chilly beneath Kenzie's front window had been put away in the linen closet. He grabbed one and a spare pillow. Kenzie had a bedroom made up for guests, but she had never invited him to use it, so he didn't want to presume. He put the pillow down on the couch, lay down, and pulled the blanket over him.

He had slept on other couches plenty of times before. It wouldn't be any harder for him than sleeping on the bed.

Except that his thoughts were chasing around his head in an endless loop, asking what he had done wrong and why he wasn't fixing it.

He didn't know.

He would fix it if he could, but he didn't know what he had done.

6

He had been tossing and turning for a while, trying to convince himself that he could sleep. It would be fine. He would sort things out with Kenzie in the morning when they had both had a chance to sleep.

But he wasn't having any luck in settling down the hamster wheel spinning in his head or the restless, skin-crawling feeling all over his body. He wanted to be with Kenzie, not fighting with her.

He heard her door open and went rigid, listening to see if she were getting up to the bathroom or for a snack to supplement her light dinner. She padded down the hallway toward him. Zachary wasn't sure whether he should pretend to be asleep so she didn't have to talk to him, or to see if she wanted to talk it out.

Which would she want?

Kenzie paused at the mouth of the hallway, looking toward him. She took a few steps toward him. "Hey. Are you still awake?" she whispered.

Zachary sat up. "Yeah."

She closed the distance between them and touched him on the shoulder. "Come on."

He hesitated at first. He'd been asking himself what to do, and now she had told him, but he didn't want to screw things up any worse. He'd had fights with Bridget that had ebbed and restarted several times over the next few days without warning. He remembered his parents having loud arguments and physical fights, subsiding to quiet, and then restarting again later. He didn't want to start talking with her and take the chance of saying the wrong thing.

She grasped his upper arm and gave a little tug. "Come. You don't need to sleep out here. Come cuddle."

"Are you sure?"

"Would I say to if I wasn't sure?"

Would he have asked if he'd known the answer?

"Okay." He followed her back to the bedroom and they got into bed, both moving slowly, unsure of the other's raw feelings, not wanting to upset the fragile truce.

Zachary settled with his arms around her and breathed in the scent of her hair. She was a strong woman. Passionate. She had a mind of her own and used it. They were bound to disagree on some things. And while he spoke from a place of ignorance, knowing only what he had heard and read other places, she was the trained medical professional. She knew how things really worked. She wasn't just going from medical dramas on TV and the screaming twenty-point spam-bait headlines of online news.

He should be more careful of what he said.

"It's okay," Kenzie said. "I was just tired. I overreacted."

"I'm sorry. I didn't mean… to step over the line."

"Shh." She kissed him and cuddled close, her face against his chest. "No more apologies. It's fine. And tomorrow is a new day."

Zachary let out a long, relieved exhale.

Tomorrow was a new day. And he would be more careful not to start any arguments.

The next morning, they both moved around each other carefully and spoke hesitantly, not wanting to renew the discussion of the day before or to challenge each other over their reactions. Zachary felt that he had done the right thing in choosing to stay there but to sleep on the couch. He hadn't deserted Kenzie after a fight, but had given her the space to decide for herself where she wanted him.

They didn't discuss his work, cheating spouses, or transplants. Zachary still wasn't sure what she thought of terminating a pregnancy due to a prenatal Huntington's Disease test. But it wasn't the time to discuss it.

"So, you start your surveillance today?" Kenzie asked.

Zachary nodded. His heart started thumping faster as he thought about it. "Yeah. I don't expect to find anything out the first day, but I'll start today and see what happens."

"You remember you have an appointment with Dr. Boyle today?"

They each kept their own schedules, but Zachary had recently given Kenzie access to his calendar, which she synced to her phone. He had marked any client appointments as private so that she could only see the block of time without seeing any labels or notes that might be confidential. He'd been good about keeping his therapy appointments with Dr. Boyle, so he wasn't sure why she was reminding him. Maybe she was just worried that he was going to get caught up in his surveillance and forget that he had to take a break to go to his appointment.

And the fact was, he didn't want to see Dr. Boyle. Not on a day when he was supposed to be surveilling Bridget. He would feel too guilty after the work that they had put into overcoming his compulsion to follow her. He was supposed to tell Dr. Boyle any time he broke his commitment not to stalk her location, which included just driving by her house and looking for her car or hoping to catch some glimpse of her in the yard. He couldn't very well tell Dr. B. that he had taken a retainer to surveil Bridget.

"I might have to reschedule this week," Zachary told Kenzie, pulling out his phone to look at his appointments. "I can't really pull out of the surveillance halfway through the day to see my therapist. I'll give her a call and see if we can swing a time when I don't need to be on this job."

Kenzie's forehead creased. She didn't like him waffling on an appointment. He'd skipped in the past when things were getting bad, and she probably saw it as a red flag.

"I'm okay," he assured her. "It isn't because I'm having problems. It's just a logistics thing."

"Well… I get that. But you need to make sure… don't let it go too long without seeing her. You don't want to lose the progress you have been making."

"No. Of course not. It's just one appointment. Everybody has to dip out now and then."

"Okay." She touched his arm briefly. "But don't lie to me. It's okay to tell me if you're having problems."

Zachary nodded, feeling even more guilty. He and Kenzie had been doing couples therapy to try to work through his issues with intimacy. They had talked a lot about open communication and role-playing, telling each other about their feelings or how to handle various challenging communication scenarios. And now he was intentionally not telling her something that he knew she would think was important.

But it was because of client confidentiality.

Not because he didn't want to tell Kenzie about Bridget.

7

Zachary knew that Bridget had been dealing with some pretty severe morning sickness during her pregnancy. Enough that it had landed her in the hospital at least once. She had not looked well when he had run into her at the gas station one day.

So he wasn't surprised not to see her leave the house until almost noon. She was a social person, and normally a morning person. She liked to get out early and be involved with her charities and other ventures. But that had probably ceased with her morning sickness.

He saw her exit the house from the back door. She took a few minutes to walk around the grounds, looking at the gardens with their colorful spring flowers. She looked pregnant now. She hadn't the last time he had seen her. She walked with an adorable little side-to-side movement, hand resting on her baby bump when she stopped to consider something, as if she were communing with the babies on what their thoughts were.

He felt a rush of endorphins when he saw her. He had been head over heels in love with Bridget Downy. Smitten with her. And the first little while had been great. She had been encouraging and attentive and had brushed aside his apologies and explanations about the difficulties that he had.

Those things that she had originally thought of as quirks or failings that he could fix had ended up consuming her. She couldn't believe that he couldn't just choose to stop being anxious or depressed, couldn't socialize with her friends without embarrassing her, would forget within five minutes which fork he was supposed to use for the salad course.

Despite her increasing impatience and vitriol, he still held on, loving her as much as ever, until she discovered she had cancer and concluded that Zachary had to go.

Maybe it was because it was cancer that had split him up that he still held out hope that her feelings would change. Cancer had split them up, and now that she was in remission, everything should go back to the way it was.

Even after everything, just seeing her still made his heart skip a beat and made him long for the life they'd had together, especially those early days in the first flush of love.

He watched her waddling slightly around the garden, fantasizing that they were together and the babies were his. He'd been mourning their anticipated children ever since the positive pregnancy test had turned out to be proof of cancer rather than of a child growing inside her. Seeing her obviously pregnant was almost enough to convince him that the past two years had just been a nightmare and their life together was unbroken.

But he knew that it wasn't the case, and pain sliced through his chest at the disappointment and grief.

It would have to be enough just to watch her. He couldn't have her back again, but at least he could see her again. For the time that he had her under surveillance, he could watch her to his heart's content.

He was late getting home for supper, but Kenzie didn't say anything about it. She was looking tired and irritable and hadn't had a chance to start supper yet, so he suspected she had worked late too and just barely beaten him home.

"Kenz. You look beat. Can I take you out to dinner or order in? I'd offer to make you something, but… you probably don't want microwaved dinners."

Her expression softened. "You know what, ordering in would be so great. I don't even know where to start with making dinner tonight."

"What do you want? Pizza? Chinese?"

"Chinese."

Zachary went to the drawer in the kitchen that held takeout menus, and pulled out the one for the Chinese restaurant a few blocks away. They put their heads together and picked out the dishes they wanted to share. He wouldn't eat a lot of the Chinese food, but he enjoyed it.

"So you must have worked late too," Zachary said when the food had arrived and they sat down to eat. "Lots going on at the morgue today?"

She shrugged. "It's not like it's our busy time, but some cases just take longer than others, or are more… emotionally taxing."

Zachary nodded. "Accidents? Murder?"

She wouldn't give him any identifying details, but they had a mutual interest in homicide, something that wasn't usually accepted in polite society. Not the bloody details, anyway.

"Had a tough case today," Kenzie said, staring off into the distance. "A teenager with kidney failure. Those ones are always hard for me."

"Teenagers?"

She hesitated, then nodded. "Yeah. I guess."

Zachary had a feeling he had missed something. He thought back over the conversation and couldn't see anything else that he should have picked up on. But he sometimes let his thoughts wander and might have missed something she had said. Or he might have done something else, like taking the last dumpling when she wanted it. He scanned his plates and the remains of their dinner, but he hadn't taken the last of anything. In fact, he'd barely touched the food on his plate. And maybe that was bothering her. She thought he wasn't enjoying himself or wasn't putting the emotional energy into their time together.

"This was nice," he said, touching her hand for a moment, and then taking a couple more bites of the rice and the noodles.

"Yeah, I'm glad we did something. If you'd left me to make supper, it might just have been toast."

"I could have made *you* toast."

Kenzie smiled. "Yes, you are a pro toast-maker."

"Usually. As long as I remember to take it out and butter it." There had been more than one slice of toast tossed in the garbage after he'd left it to dry out in the toaster.

Kenzie gave a tolerant smile. "I think… I'm going to work on a few things in my office and have a bath. Head to bed early, so I'll be fresh for tomorrow."

Zachary searched her face to see whether she were telling him that she wanted him to go to bed with her, or that she wanted him to clear out so she could have a quiet evening on her own. He frowned, trying to unwind her words and decide what she wanted him to do.

"Should I head out…?" he asked tentatively.

"Head out? Where are you going?" Kenzie shook her head. "I thought this surveillance wasn't going to be night-time."

"No, not the surveillance. I just thought… you might want some space. I can head back to my apartment if you don't want someone else knocking around here tonight…"

"No. Stay." Kenzie put her warm hand on Zachary's thigh, which sent a sudden flush and goosebumps over him. "I didn't mean I'm kicking you out. I'd rather have someone around tonight."

Zachary nodded. His face was burning, wondering if she'd noticed his reaction to her touch. "Okay. You let me know if you need anything. And when you want to go to bed, I can come in for a while even if I'm not going to sleep right away."

"Yeah. That would be nice."

She bent to give him a brief kiss as she got up. "Can you clear up? Put things in the fridge and the plates in the dishwasher? And start the dishwasher?"

Zachary nodded. "Yeah. Of course."

She went down the hall to her home office. He didn't know what kind of work she was doing, whether she had something she needed to log in and finish for work, or she was balancing her bank account, or doing something else that he hadn't thought of. Not that it mattered, of course.

As he carried the takeout containers to the kitchen to put them away, he thought about his physical reaction to Kenzie's touch. It was a positive development.

He'd had such bad flashbacks after he was assaulted a few months back, flashbacks both to the assault and to abuse he'd experienced while in foster care, that he hadn't been able to react naturally to Kenzie. Everything was conscious and forced and, if he wasn't able to push through the flashbacks, he would dissociate, removing himself far from the situation until it was over. Not a great way to improve his relationship with his girlfriend.

So reacting to her touch was good. It was a positive sign. But he couldn't help worrying about the change. What if he was only feeling something because he had spent the day watching Bridget? What if it had been a reaction to being close to Bridget and Kenzie triggering it had just been a coincidence? What if the only person he could have a natural relationship with was Bridget? She was with someone else and would, he knew logically, never get back together with him again, however much he wanted it.

They'd had a good physical relationship, one that had not suffered with the same shortcomings as he had demonstrated in his relationship with Kenzie.

It wasn't fair. It just wasn't fair that he should have so many emotional problems when he was doing everything he was supposed to, going to all of his therapy appointments and doing couples sessions with Kenzie. Things should have been so much better with Kenzie. She was kinder and more understanding with him. She was willing to go at his speed. She was a much better match for him than Bridget had ever been.

So why did he continue to obsess over Bridget? Why was his relationship with Kenzie the one that suffered?

He retired to the living room and opened his laptop on the mobile desk. He took out the clipboard he had used to record Bridget's movements and started to transcribe them into a spreadsheet while they were still fresh in his mind. If he left the logs to pile up over several days, the information would all run together and if he had to decode his messy handwriting, it would be much harder.

Even just the process of transferring Bridget's movements from one medium to the other soothed him and made him feel better.

8

Zachary's phone vibrated. He slid it out of his pocket and put it on the desk beside him, but didn't look at it to see who had messaged him. He needed to stay focused on the job he was doing, or it would take him ages to get back into it. Once he was finished, he would reward himself with the distraction of a message from a friend or family member who was thinking of him.

Or maybe something from Gordon.

Zachary tried to remain focused on the task at hand, his attention starting to drift to Gordon. Was he calling already? Checking to see whether Zachary had been able to find anything out on the very first day of surveillance? It would take longer than that.

It was a struggle to keep himself from being sidetracked by these thoughts, but he got to the end of the log and saved the spreadsheet in a new computer folder set up under Gordon Drake's name. He wondered briefly if he should call it by a code name so that if Kenzie happened to glance at it, she wouldn't be suspicious of his activities. He needed to keep his client information private, especially when it was someone she knew.

He closed the file with relief and picked up his phone.

It was not a message from Gordon.

It was from Rhys, a young man whom Zachary had first encountered when he had investigated the death of his aunt, a woman Bridget had known when she was in treatment for her cancer. Even though Rhys's mother had gone to prison for her part in her sister's death, Rhys had stayed friends with Zachary.

He was selectively mute, saying only a word or two in the course of a day, and did not communicate with conventional language when he messaged Zachary or visited with him face-to-face. The trauma that he had suffered when his grandfather was killed when he was still a little boy had affected him deeply, stealing from him the ability to communicate easily.

Rhys often began a conversation with a GIF, meme, or other picture. His message to Zachary on this occasion was a sad-looking basset hound. It actually reminded Zachary strongly of Rhys's own face. His sad eyes would cheer briefly when he and Zachary were visiting, but would quickly fall back into the same sad, downward gaze as the dog's.

He tapped a message back to Rhys. *Hi. How's it going?*

It was a few minutes before Rhys wrote back again. He sent an emoji with a straight mouth, which Zachary assumed meant he was neither happy nor sad, or was still frustrated by his lack of progress in therapy and dealing with the memories that had recently resurfaced.

Before Zachary had any chance to react to the emoticon, Rhys had sent another picture. One that was becoming very familiar to Zachary.

Luke, the boy he and Rhys had helped to break away from the human trafficking syndicate that he had worked with since he was a teen younger than Rhys.

Zachary had only recently figured out—with Kenzie's help, admittedly—that Rhys was attracted to the older boy. There were plenty of reasons the two of them should not get involved with each other, from Rhys's age to the prejudices against biracial relationships that were still strong in Vermont, to the fact that Luke needed to do a lot more work to overcome his addictions and find his place in the world, unqualified for anything but the prostitution and recruiting that had been his only means of subsistence for the past five years.

But despite his many reservations about Rhys pursuing a relationship with Luke, he couldn't shut Rhys down and refuse to give him any information. Luke was living halfway across the state; it wouldn't be easy for Rhys to see him even if *he* knew where Luke was. And Luke's location was strictly confidential. The cartel thought that he was dead, and he needed to stay out of sight if he were going to have any chance of starting a new life.

Zachary sighed, blowing the air out between pursed lips. He couldn't tell Rhys much more than he had repeated the last few times they had exchanged messages.

Luke is okay. Still working on his recovery. He thought about what else to say. He wished he could give Rhys more. Information that would make Rhys see that Luke was going to be okay without him and that Rhys should be more concerned about his relationships with the kids his own age in his own school and neighborhood. It was so much safer.

But since when had either of them been able to make the safer, more reasoned decision? Rhys was a teenager. At an age when boys were not well-known for making choices that were good for them.

No news is good news, Zachary typed.

As long as Luke was working on his recovery, there was hope. Hope that maybe in a year or two when Rhys was older, Luke would be a safer option.

A thumbs-up graphic from Rhys. A safe reply. Like he was happy to hear what Zachary had told him and not that he would try to pry more information out of Zachary or try to make contact with Luke somehow. Zachary couldn't imagine how Rhys and Luke would connect without Zachary's facilitating it. Unless, of course, Luke decided to look for Rhys. Or gave up on recovery and went back to trafficking. Or both, maybe seeing if he could lure Rhys into the life as well. Zachary's stomach knotted at the thought.

Zachary's oldest sister, Jocelyn, was the one who was providing a home for Luke and trying to help him through the difficult transition period. She had personal experience in what Luke was going through and Zachary couldn't have found anyone better to help Luke. But she had warned Zachary. She had told him that staying away from the life would be difficult or impossible for Luke. It was just too tempting. It was the only life he had known since his grandma had died and, when people were struggling, they went back to what was familiar. Chances were, Luke would not succeed in separating himself from human trafficking. Even if he stayed away from his old organization, he would take up with someone else local and be entrenched again within a few days.

How's Grandma? Zachary typed to Rhys. Vera had been looking after her grandson since his mother had gone to prison. She had been the one constant in his life from the time that he'd been born.

"Zachary!"

Zachary was startled from his conversation with Rhys. He looked up to see Kenzie standing a few feet away from him. There were frown lines between her brows and, by her volume and the tone of irritation in her voice, it wasn't the first time she had tried to get his attention.

"Sorry. Sorry, I was focused on a conversation. With Rhys." Zachary turned the phone toward her, as if to prove what he'd been doing, even though he was sure she didn't really care. "What did you say?"

"You said you would put things away. In the kitchen. The food and the dishes…?"

Zachary pushed himself to his feet. He was pretty sure he had taken care of everything. He remembered putting a couple of cartons of food into the fridge. Maybe he'd just missed one thing—a forgotten soup bowl or condiment cup of sauce.

"I did… didn't I?" Zachary walked past Kenzie into the kitchen.

The dirty plates were still on the table, as were several takeout containers.

He had the illogical thought that someone must have come into the house and taken them back out of the fridge after he had put them away. Or Kenzie was trying to gaslight him. But he knew that wasn't the case. He had just forgotten or gotten distracted.

He grabbed a couple of containers and folded them closed, moving quickly so that he would get it done before Kenzie got too angry or he got distracted by something else.

"I really am sorry. I thought I had done it."

He shoved the containers into the fridge and went back to the table for more. Even after he had cleared all of the food away, Kenzie just stood there watching him, her arms folded in a closed-off gesture.

Zachary looked at her, then back around the kitchen to figure out why she hadn't relaxed yet.

The plates were still on the table. Zachary ran a stream of water over them and put them into the dishwasher.

Kenzie stalked into the kitchen and, before he could shut the dishwasher door, took a moment to rearrange the dishes he had put away. "You know they won't get clean if they are facing away from the spray."

"Yeah. Right. Sorry."

Kenzie pushed the door shut with a bang. She looked around the room and nodded. "Thank you."

Zachary grimaced. He held himself back from apologizing again. "Have you already had your bath?" he asked. "Are you ready for bed?" He turned his phone to look at the face to see what time it was. Sometimes when he was immersed in his work, he lost track of time.

"No." Kenzie pinched the fabric of her shirt between her finger and thumb to draw her attention to it. She was still wearing her work clothes. "You'd think that a detective might notice that I haven't bathed and changed for bed yet."

"Oh, right." Zachary laughed. "Yeah. You'd think, wouldn't you?"

9

After a few days on surveillance, Zachary strongly suspected that Bridget was not having an affair. That didn't mean she hadn't had one, of course. He would poke around iscreetly to see what he could find out about any interests she might have had in the past year but, if she had been seeing someone, Zachary suspected they had broken it off and were no longer involved. It hadn't been long enough to be sure, but Bridget's routine seemed to have changed little since he had last tracked her whereabouts. She slept later and walked more slowly, but still went to the same places as she had previously—no noticeable deviations.

So what did that mean? Zachary brought it up with Kenzie as they got ready for bed. Zachary's thoughts were spinning too fast and he hoped that if he talked it through with her, his brain would settle down and he would be able to get to sleep quickly rather than lying awake for hours. He told her about the IVF, that the couple hadn't thought that they could conceive, and when his client had found out about the Huntington's Disease, he had assumed that his wife had been involved with someone else.

"But if she didn't have an affair, then what does that mean?" he asked Kenzie. "A mix-up at the fertility clinic?"

Kenzie nodded. She climbed into bed and applied cream to her hands and arms, rubbing the moisturizer in to keep her skin from getting chapped. "It does happen sometimes. You hear about a parent ending up with a child of the wrong color, or there's some other genetic red flag and they know the baby could not belong to both parents."

"Like Huntington's Disease."

"Not usually. Maybe a blood type mismatch, the wrong color of eyes, or obvious racial differences. But yes, Huntington's Disease could mean that there was a mix-up with either the eggs or the sperm. Most clinics have lots of controls in place now, so that the parents are shown the labels on the genetic material being used and can be assured that they haven't mixed up files or room numbers."

"But mistakes still happen."

"Yes, they do. Who knows how many have been made over the years that the parents never figured out."

"And it could be the eggs or the sperm. Either one."

"I don't know all of the ins and outs of running a fertility clinic. Maybe one is more likely than the other. But from a purely biological stand-p200oint, then yes. They could have mixed up either the eggs or the sperm. Or they could have implanted the wrong embryos. So, three places they could have made a mistake."

"And if they used the wrong eggs, then the mother's body wouldn't… I don't know… reject the baby?"

"It isn't an organ transplant. It doesn't work the same way. The mother's body will accept an embryo whether it was created from her own genetic material or not."

Zachary nodded. "So I guess I'll talk to the clinic, find out on a no-names basis what their controls are, see where they might have screwed up."

"This client of yours… they haven't done any DNA testing to see if both parents are biologically related to the baby?"

"Is that something they can do before she is born?"

"They can. Most places will wait until after the baby is born, but it is possible to do it prenatally. I figured since they had done the Huntington's Disease test prenatally that they would check everything out before deciding whether to continue with the pregnancy."

"I think… the subject doesn't know that her husband has any doubts. She didn't want to do the Huntington's test herself, and I don't think he told her that he's had his done."

Kenzie nodded her understanding. "There is one other possibility. I hesitate to bring it up, but…"

"What?"

"There have been several recorded cases where… the fertility doctor has been using his own sperm."

Zachary stared at her. "You're kidding." He was repulsed by the thought. It felt like a violation. To fertilize the egg with his own sperm and implant it into a woman felt like an assault.

"Unfortunately, no." Kenzie stopped rubbing the flowery-smelling cream into her hands and looked off into space. She looked back at Zachary, then away again. "I guess it wasn't such a big deal back in the heyday, when they pioneered fertility treatment. Fresh sperm worked better than frozen, so doctors and students generously provided the genetic material in cases where women were using donor sperm anyway. What did it matter whose genetic material they used?"

"Well… I would think it made a difference to the parents. And maybe to the kid who goes through life not knowing his family medical history."

"Yeah. Can you imagine? I guess they didn't see anything unethical about it in the beginning. The science was new. They were setting up their own policies and procedures. There wasn't the regulation that there is now."

"But you think that maybe the doctor in this case could have… used his own stuff."

"It's just one of the possibilities if we are trying to narrow down what happened. It still happens every now and then."

"But now it's been determined to be unethical, right? So why would anyone take the chance?"

"Why does anyone break the law or society's taboos? Because they see a benefit, I guess."

Just like the psychologist Zachary had talked to when he was ten and they were evaluating him for the school and his foster parents. He observed that Zachary would break the rules if he saw it to be to his own advantage. Even though Zachary knew what the rule was, he would break it if he felt like he had a good enough reason.

And so did everyone, to some extent, the doctor assured him.

Some people broke the speed limit only when someone's life was in danger and they needed to get them to the hospital. Others thought it was okay to speed all of the time, as long as they stayed within ten miles per hour of the posted speed limit. Still others sped because of the thrill.

Did the same apply to a doctor using his own sperm to fertilize patients' eggs? Did he do it because he thought it was their best chance at maintaining a pregnancy? Because he wanted to spread his genetic material far and wide? Because it was a thrill?

"These doctors tend to have pretty big egos," Kenzie said. "I honestly think that some of them are doing it just because they think that their progeny will be superior to anyone else's."

"That's pretty… egotistical," Zachary admitted. "They really feel that way?"

Kenzie raised her eyebrows and nodded. "Believe it. Doctors in general are a very arrogant bunch. I've known some doctors…" Her focus drifted. Zachary was starting to wonder what was on her mind. She had seemed to be somewhere else a few times lately, and that was usually his domain.

"Doctors who would do that?" he prompted.

"Doctors who… would do anything they thought they could get away with. Anything to get better results, to exercise their power over death. Or in this case," her eyes focused back on Zachary again, "power over life."

He nodded slowly. He could see how that could be intoxicating. Power over life and death? What could prove their superiority better than that?

Zachary took one last look at his phone screen before putting it on the side table.

"So… how would someone figure that out? How do you know that the doctor has been… providing his own samples?"

Kenzie lay down beside him, her body relaxing. "In the cases that I've heard of, they have done private DNA testing, like for genealogical research, then submitted it to one of the public databases to see who popped up as relatives."

Zachary knew some of the ins and outs of that kind of testing from Heather's case. He nodded. "Okay, sure."

"And before those databases were around, it was a little more difficult. Finding other patients of the same clinic or doctor and seeing if they had the same doubts, or if the children had the same traits. Easier with some traceable trait like celiac disease. They would need to gather all of the data they could before anyone would look at it. Because who would think that one of these eminent doctors could do something like that?"

Zachary shut off the lamp that was still on beside him, then cuddled close to Kenzie, rubbing her back and hoping it would release some of the stress she seemed to be under.

"Is everything okay with you?" he asked in a low voice, nearly whispering. "And between us?"

She snuggled and didn't say anything. Zachary decided just to hold her. If she didn't want to talk about whatever was on her mind, that was fine. As long as she knew he was there and was ready to help or just to sympathize.

His mind wandered to his surveillance of Bridget, picturing her getting in and out of her car, the glimpses he had caught of her as she walked into different business establishments or met with friends to socialize. It still blew his mind that she was pregnant. She, who had said that she would never ruin her body by getting pregnant. He'd always thought that he'd eventually be able to talk her into it, but he hadn't.

Gordon had some real skills.

"Zachary?" Kenzie murmured.

"Mmm-hmm?"

"There's something I want to tell you."

10

Zachary's chest and stomach muscles tightened into hard knots. He tried to ease his breathing. She hadn't said it was something to do with him. But what else could it be?

She had found out about Bridget.

Or she had decided that things just weren't working between them.

She had given it a good long run, but Zachary couldn't shed all of his problems and conform to the person she thought he should be and, like Bridget, she'd decided to stop wasting her time.

"Yeah?"

"Do you remember a long time ago, I told you that I don't have any siblings?"

It was such a tangent from where Zachary thought she was going that he didn't answer at first. He tried to remember when she had told him this. Back at the beginning, when they had just started to see each other? He had probably told her about his five siblings and many foster families, and she had told him that she was an only child. Totally different life experiences.

He couldn't remember it happening, but she clearly did.

"I don't remember specifically," he said cautiously.

"Well, I did… and it's not quite the truth."

How could it be only partially true? A step- or half-sibling? A child who had been adopted out? Been disinherited?

"Okay. Do you want to tell me about it? You don't have to."

"I think I want to." Kenzie squirmed, and Zachary tried to give her room while at the same time keeping her close and letting her know that he was there for her.

He nodded, even though she might not be able to see him in the darkness of the room. He waited, allowing her to take her own time. Kenzie was quiet for a while, and he wondered if she were going to fall asleep without telling him whatever her family secret was.

"The case that we had this week reminded me of my sister," Kenzie said. She sniffled a little. "Amanda."

"Amanda. That's a pretty name. I like it."

"She was quite a bit younger than me, and we were really different in our personalities, but she was like… she was more like my own baby than my sister. I loved to help taking care of her when she was little. She was never my bratty little sister, you know? We never had that dynamic."

"I bet you were a great big sister."

"With Amanda I was. I don't know if I would have been with someone else with a different personality. But with Amanda… she was my baby sister."

She spoke of Amanda in the past tense. She clearly wasn't around anymore. "What happened?"

Kenzie had helped Dr. Wiltshire with a few cases that week; he wasn't sure which one had bothered her and reminded her of her sister.

"It was her kidneys. She had kidney disease. Started when she was really young. She couldn't keep up with her friends, was tired all the time. And then… they figured out that her kidney function was really low."

Zachary remembered the scar on Kenzie's abdomen. He rubbed the spot above her hip gently. She'd told him once it was a surgical scar, but she'd never said what it was for. He'd thought it might have been an appendectomy.

Kenzie nodded. He felt her head moving against his chest. "Yeah… as soon as I was eighteen, I donated a kidney to her. Mom and Dad wouldn't let me do it when I was younger, even though I wanted to. As soon as I could sign the permissions myself, I arranged to give her one of my kidneys."

"That was really generous."

"I would have given her both. Seriously. I loved her so much and wanted her to get better."

"Did the donation… not take?"

"No, it worked. She got better and could do the things she wanted to and not have to sit at the hospital on dialysis. For a while. But a few years later… well, it eventually failed as well. That happens sometimes. Donated organs don't always have the same lifespan as they would normally."

"I'm sorry."

"Yeah." She was quiet, squirming around to tuck her head into the hollow of his neck, breathing warmly on his throat. She smelled and felt so good. If he could just take that moment and stretch it out…

"Anyway. I'm sorry I told you I don't have any siblings. Because I did. I just… haven't shared that with very many people. I'm a private person. Too private, sometimes."

"You're allowed to share or not share, it's up to you."

They had agreed to that in therapy. Mostly in relation to Zachary. If she asked him something and he didn't feel comfortable answering, he was allowed to just tell her instead of trying to find an excuse. And the same applied to Kenzie. It was an equal, two-way relationship.

"And back around when you were working on the Lauren Barclay case, when I got mad at you for asking about that doctor wanting to screen organ donors based on what they said on social media…"

She had blown up at him. Zachary hadn't had any idea why she had been so upset. Except that they were on a break and he had gone to her with a question that he could have asked somewhere else. He'd thought it was because she didn't want to be his go-to for answering all medical questions when they weren't even together.

"That was… because of Amanda? Could she… not get another transplant because of something like that?"

"No, not something quite that close. Just… ethics and organ donations and some of the stuff that I went through with my dad…"

"Sorry. I didn't know."

"Of course not. You couldn't have any idea about it because I hadn't shared it. I can't blame you for something you didn't know."

"Well," Zachary rested his face against her hair, breathing in her scent, "you apologized later and we worked things out."

"It's like Dr. Boyle says, though, if we're open with each other… we don't have to try to read each other's minds."

"Yeah." He wiggled around a little, trying to get more comfortable. "And this girl at the morgue this week…? She reminded you of Amanda?"

"Yeah. So young. It was kidney failure, and something about her… just reminded me of Amanda." Kenzie shook her head a little. "It was such an awful time, Zachary. Losing Amanda and then finding out that my father had arranged for… a gray market medical procedure that contributed to her death."

"Ouch. That's why you're estranged from your parents?"

"I'm not exactly estranged. I'll still talk to them. But… I don't really have anything to do with them most of the time. My mom's personality is so different than mine; I can't really talk to her about anything I'm interested in. Only her fundraisers and social appearances. That gets tedious. My dad and I are more alike, but our opinions, especially on medical stuff…" Kenzie trailed off. Zachary rubbed her back.

He expected her to keep up the conversation, but in a couple of minutes he could tell that she had drifted off to sleep.

11

Zachary had never been to the Westlake Women's Health Center. Bridget had banked her eggs before her cancer treatment, but Zachary had not been welcome to go along with her. At that point, she had already started the break with him. Hints about how she couldn't handle any extra responsibilities or focuses. That he was taking too much of her time and energy. She needed to focus on her treatment and recovery, not on Zachary. But he was not welcome to go to appointments with her. He wasn't allowed to be a part of her medical decisions.

He thought at first that she didn't realize what she was doing, pushing him away but, eventually, she had made it clear. He came home to find his belongings packed into bags at the front door. Bridget had removed her wedding ring. When he had tried to talk to her about it, she just shook her head.

"It's not working out, Zachary. You know it's not. We're not happy together anymore. I need to focus on my treatment. You need to move on with your life."

"We can still make it work," Zachary had objected. "I thought we'd been doing better. I'm not going to abandon you in the middle of cancer treatment. I can help you."

"You can't help me. You can't even help yourself."

Zachary didn't think that being able to address all of his issues was necessary for him to help Bridget, but she was firm. She didn't want him there. She didn't want him anywhere near her.

"Can I help you, sir?" The young woman at the reception desk was looking at him expectantly.

"Oh. I was wondering… my wife and I have been talking about maybe… you know, trying some fertility treatments. Seeing if we can get pregnant that way. But she's nervous about all of this…" Zachary made a motion to indicate the clinic. "She's worried about mistakes, privacy, that kind of thing. I'm wondering if I could get a tour, sort of an orientation of how it all works. So I can help show her there wouldn't be any mistakes."

The receptionist gave him a reassuring smile. "Of course. Can I get your name?"

"Do you get asked this a lot?" Zachary asked. "People must have concerns."

"Yes, people naturally want to know how things are going to be handled when they have a procedure. It's a very personal thing, and our patients want to know that they will be handled with respect and discretion and that their genetic material will be well cared for." She stepped around the desk to shake his hand. "I'm Carole. And I didn't catch your name?"

"John," Zachary told her. "John Smith. And I'm not kidding, it really is. People always think I'm making a joke."

"You wouldn't be the first John Smith we had through here," Carole laughed. "Why don't you come with me to our welcome room. I'll give you some literature to look over while I see who is available to show you around."

Zachary was impressed. It would appear that she'd spoken the truth when she said that people often had similar questions.

"Thanks. That would be great."

He followed her to a small boardroom, where she provided him with a cup of fresh coffee and laid a glossy folder full of brochures and other pages in front of him.

"You don't have to read all of this," Carole gave him a pleasant smile, "It's just for your future reference, and something to get you started. Trust me; nobody reads it all."

Zachary was glad of that. It was an impressive amount of literature. Most of it would have little to do with his investigation. He looked through the various pages as he sipped his coffee and waited for his tour guide to make an appearance. He pulled out his phone and glanced through his mail and his social networks.

He remembered messaging with Rhys, and pulled up the stream to see whether he had left the thread too abruptly and whether Rhys had posted anything after Kenzie had pulled him from the conversation. He tapped out a quick message to let Rhys know that they could talk some more later, so if Rhys was feeling like he'd been brushed off, he would be reassured.

The door opened, and a man in a white lab jacket entered. He had on a collared shirt and dress slacks underneath it. He wore glasses with thin black rims and carried a clipboard. Zachary's overall impression was of a busy, competent doctor.

"Mel Banks," the man introduced himself, holding out a hand to Zachary as he approached the table. "John?"

"Yes. Hi." Zachary shook.

"So how can I help you today?"

Zachary again ran through his patter about his wife, shrugging and motioning at the clinic.

"Of course," Banks agreed. "People are entrusting us with one of their most precious resources. That isn't something we take lightly. I'm happy to give you a tour, but you should come back with your wife so she can see it for herself. That will help to put her mind at ease."

"Yeah, I'm sure she'll come next time. But we live out of town, and she wasn't feeling up to it today. I didn't want to put it off, and had some time today, so..."

"Well, why don't we talk about your journey so far. Do you have any other children?"

"No. We decided to start trying about a year and a half ago, and it was fun at first and we thought that everything would just happen naturally, but... well, it didn't, obviously. By the time a year was up, my wife was getting anxious and had me set up an appointment with a specialist. I forget the name... it's foreign-sounding. Starts with B, or maybe an M? She would be able to tell you."

"Mbatha?" Banks suggested.

Zachary lucked out on that one, beginning with both an M and a B. He had learned that people would go out of their way to provide missing names, especially if you said that they sounded foreign. Throw in a couple of possible starting sounds, and they would throw all the names you could possibly need.

"That must be it," Zachary said with a nod. If challenged on it later, he could say that he had thought that was the right name, but he wasn't very good with names and it was his wife's domain. He could easily have mixed up two foreign-sounding names. It was understandable.

"And what did Dr. Mbatha find? He did a full fertility workup for the two of you?"

Zachary nodded. "Yeah, and he said that probably if we did this...." He indicated his surroundings again. "There was a specific procedure that he recommended. He said we had a good chance of success. I'm afraid... I didn't get all of the medical details." He rolled his eyes toward the ceiling and shrugged his shoulders. "It all makes me a little uncomfortable, you know. All the stuff about women's reproductive systems. I mean... I know my part, but the rest... that's kind of her job. She's the one who knows all of the... female side."

Banks laughed. "You're certainly not the only one who feels that way," he assured Zachary. "We're raised to see women's bodies as something dirty. Messy periods, water breaking, things coming out of orifices. We do our part, like you say, and try to avoid thinking of the rest."

Zachary nodded, his eyes down.

"But you're here. That's a good step. Good initiative, especially since your wife isn't with you. Do you have specific concerns, or is she working...?"

"The timing wasn't good for her, and we live out on a farm. I think... she wanted me to ask the initial questions. She says doctors talk down to women. They're more likely to answer men's questions without treating them like they're ignorant. She's really smart, you understand, but men treat her like she's a child and doesn't know what she's talking about."

Banks sighed. "Well, I hope you will assure her that she won't be treated that way here. I understand it goes on, but... we are very patient-oriented here. We will treat her questions with the same respect as yours."

"I'll tell her. Although... maybe I wasn't supposed to tell you that part. I'll have to think about how to bring it up."

"You take her home those brochures and tell her she can call with any questions. If she prefers to talk to a nurse or a female doctor, of course that can be arranged."

Zachary nodded. "Okay, yeah. I can do that."

"Good. Do you have any questions before we begin the tour? What are your concerns?"

"There was an article we saw, well, several articles, actually, about cases where the wrong sperm was used. Parents ending up with children who they were not both biologically related to. My wife doesn't want to adopt or to have someone else's baby. She is very determined about having a baby that is genetically ours. So… I suppose we want to know what controls are in place to make sure that doesn't happen."

Banks was nodding along seriously. "Of course. It's perfectly understandable she would be concerned about it. Those stories do hit the news every now and then, and we always experience repercussions here. There is an increase in calls from patients; we see a downturn in the number of people signing up for procedures. It's really too bad, because those cases are very few and far between. We have never had a mistake at this clinic. There have been no lawsuits over the wrong genetic material being used. Never, in the two decades this clinic has been open."

"That's great. I'm glad to hear that."

"We are very careful, and of course whenever a story like that comes out, we do an audit of our procedures, try to find any weaknesses. Find out the details of how the mix-up came about at the other clinic and make sure there is no way the same thing can happen here. And it hasn't. We're always doing our best to stay ahead of the game and be absolutely rock-solid on our procedures."

Zachary gave a grateful nod and smile. But of course, he would hear the same thing from any clinic he went to. They would all claim to be rock-solid in their procedures. What doctor or businessperson would admit to being sloppy and frequently trying to recover from or cover up mistakes?

"Let's take a walk around, then," Banks offered, "and we'll talk about procedures and audits that we have in place. I'll show you everything."

Banks led the way. Zachary followed, sometimes keeping up with Banks and sometimes lagging behind to have a second look at something or to see just how good their security procedures were.

12

Samples are collected in vials that are already labeled with patient identification numbers," Banks showed Zachary the cupboard where the collection vials for the day had been set aside for use. "Each donor is asked to verify the number before beginning. Names are not used for privacy reasons."

"And do people check the numbers? What if they can't remember what their number is or would be embarrassed to look it up?"

"Well…" Banks looked troubled at this suggestion. "We find that people are generally concerned enough about avoiding any mix-ups that they will check." He shook his head. "It's impossible for us to know whether someone has really verified it or not. But that's our procedure. It helps to… protect everyone."

Which wasn't true, of course. It was designed to put the onus on the patient. A way for the clinic to cover their butts. It protected them, not patients who were too excited, nervous, or embarrassed to remember their patient number or to look it up.

"We ask the patient to check at the beginning of every procedure," Banks went on. "Every time we collect a sample or remove it from storage, the patient must verify it."

"What about in the lab? They can't verify everything that is done there."

"Good point," Banks admitted. "Of course they are not involved in any of the lab procedures, washing or prepping specimens, fertilization, any of the work done in vitro. We do have procedures in place in the lab as well, to ensure that a worker never has more than one couple's genetic material out at the same time, and there is always a second worker to check the numbers to ensure that they have the right ones."

Good if they wanted to prevent cross-contamination or innocent mistakes. Not something that would help if a doctor were interested in spreading his own seed.

"What kind of security is there for samples while they are in storage?"

"We have excellent security. Nothing is accessible by the public at any time. Someone could not break in here and steal embryos, for example. People are often worried about that. Those embryos are your potential children, and we treat them like your most priceless possession."

"So who does have access to them?"

"Only medical professionals. No couriers or janitors or any non-professional staff would have access to the freezers. Or to fresh specimens."

"But any of the doctors or nurses would be able to access any of the samples."

Banks cocked his head, frowning. "Well, yes, they would be able to. They need to be able to access them for procedures."

"And what procedures are in place to make sure that a doctor couldn't access them for their own purposes?"

"What do you mean? The only reason they would need them is to perform a procedure for you."

"What if he wanted to… sabotage them. Or contaminate them. Swap them. I don't know. It seems like these things could happen."

"Our doctors and staff are professional and very well trained. Something like that… would never happen."

Zachary took a deep breath. He tried to look reassured, but he certainly was not. While they might be protecting themselves from accidental mix-ups, contaminations, or lawsuits, there didn't seem to be any procedures in place to prevent intentional tampering. They just trusted that no one would try.

"We have check-out procedures," Banks said tentatively. "Anyone removing a sample has to put their name on the sign-out sheet."

"Who controls access to it?"

"To...?"

"To the sign-out sheet. Or the freezers or cupboards or wherever stuff is stored."

"Well, there's just a clipboard with a log, so we can keep track of who has accessed what…"

"So it's just voluntary. You expect people to comply."

"Yes. We've had no trouble that way. There wouldn't be any reason for people not to sign the log…"

Zachary could think of a few. The rule-followers would be diligent about always signing the log, but others would be too lazy or distracted, or willfully disobey the rule to avoid detection.

"I guess that's good," he acknowledged. He didn't want to put Banks on the defensive or for him to think that Zachary was anything other than what he claimed, a potential client who just wanted to make sure that the clinic was following some kind of procedure that would help prevent mix-ups.

Banks nodded.

As they continued the tour, Zachary watched for locks and other security measures, counted the number of people he saw back and forth, and assessed what other security measures they had in place. There didn't appear to be any surveillance cameras to monitor the staff. And despite what Banks had said about the janitorial staff not being able to access the freezers, he didn't see any measures that someone with a bump key or set of lock pickers could not get past. The janitorial staff probably had master keys for everything in the clinic anyway. Who else kept the lab and the sample room clean?

After the visit to the clinic, Zachary, as John Smith, promised to come back with his wife when she was available. He returned to his surveillance of Bridget. By this time, he didn't expect to see her doing anything other than her usual meetings and social events. She seemed to have cut back on them, maybe finding the schedule too tiring now that she was pregnant. There did not appear to be another man in her life. Gordon would be happy to hear that.

But he had not answered the question as to who had fathered the babies. Had it been Gordon? A mix-up at the clinic? An intentional switch at the clinic? If it was the result of a mix-up or intentional switch, then which had been swapped? Bridget's eggs or Gordon's sperm?

Which of them was a biological parent to the twins?

And who had Huntington's Disease?

13

While he was watching for Bridget to come back out of the grocery store with her purchases, his phone rang. Zachary didn't generally answer while he was on surveillance, not wanting anything to distract him from the job. But he didn't think there was any danger of his getting distracted from Bridget. And he didn't think she was going to do anything suspicious anyway. Even if she were having an affair, why would she meet her fling at the grocery store?

It was Mr. Peterson, one of Zachary's old foster parents and the only one he had ever kept in touch with. Even though he had only been with the Petersons for a few weeks, their relationship had survived the decades. Mr. and Mrs. Peterson had divorced a few years after Zachary had been with them, and Lorne Peterson had gone on to meet Pat, the younger man who would become his permanent life partner. They had been together for so long that it was hard to remember sometimes that Mr. Peterson had ever been with anyone else. It seemed like something that had happened in a different life entirely.

"Hi, Lorne." Zachary tried to call Mr. Peterson by his first name like he was always told to but, in his mind, he was always going to be Mr. Peterson.

"Zachary. Is this a good time? I should probably have waited until the evening."

"You never know when I might be working in the evening anyway. This is fine, or I wouldn't have answered."

"Good. How are you and Kenzie getting along?"

"We're fine. Maybe even better than usual," Zachary said cautiously. Yes, he still screwed stuff up regularly, but he felt like he and Kenzie were getting closer in their relationship. Something that was evidenced by Kenzie telling him about Amanda and hinting at a few things about her parents. She had always kept those things out of their relationship before.

"That's wonderful to hear. You know how we feel about Kenzie. I think the two of you are a great match."

"Yeah. Things are working out well right now. I hope… they'll continue that way…" Zachary was anxious about putting these thoughts into words. He was always afraid that saying something aloud about his relationship would somehow jinx it. He didn't want to take any chances on messing up anything about his relationship with Kenzie.

The knot in his stomach reminded him that he had already taken a rather large step that he knew could cause a rift between him and Kenzie. She would not be at all happy to hear that he had taken a job from Gordon. Even less so when she discovered it involved him surveilling Bridget.

"Zachary?"

"Oh, what? Sorry, I was just…" he trailed off and left space for Mr. Peterson to just pick the conversation back up again, not wanting to explain or give an excuse.

"It's fine. I'm wondering about next weekend. If you would be able to come for a visit."

"Uh, sure, I think so. Let me just look at the calendar for a minute." Zachary picked up his phone and switched over to the calendar app. "Yeah, that looks fine."

"And how about Kenzie? Could she come too, or is she working on the weekend?"

"Might be working. I'll have to ask her."

Though he had given Kenzie the information she needed to add his calendar to her phone, she hadn't given him hers. That didn't particularly bother Zachary. She might have confidential stuff on her calendar to do with her job. Or they might not allow her to share her calendar with people outside the medical examiner's office as a matter of policy. He hadn't asked. He didn't need someone else's information on his phone; it would only distract him from his own. If he didn't keep his calendar simple and clean, his dyslexia made it impossible to read and comprehend it.

"Well, if she can come, she is invited as well."

"Can they come?" Zachary heard Pat's voice in the background and thought he detected a note of excitement.

"What's going on?"

It had been at Mr. Peterson's house that he'd met Joss, his older sister, a reunion set up by Tyrrell and Heather, the two siblings he'd already met. And he still hadn't met the youngest two siblings, so he wondered whether they were trying to set up yet another reunion. He wasn't opposed to it, but wasn't sure he liked them doing it behind his back. They didn't want him to feel anxious about it ahead of time, but he preferred to have some time to mentally prepare.

"Pat's mother and sister are going to be over," Mr. Peterson explained. "He'd like you to meet them. We talked about that before… Christmas time…?"

Zachary remembered. Pat's father had died the previous year, and he had finally been able to reconcile with his mother and sister, after being shunned by the family for many years for being gay.

"Yeah. Of course. I remember."

"She wants to meet her grandson," Pat called out.

Zachary chuckled. He'd never had a grandparent that he could remember. He didn't know if his parents had been estranged from their own families, or if they were orphans, but he didn't know any blood relations other than his siblings in his biological family. And while Pat had never been one of Zachary's foster fathers, he and Mr. Peterson had both been the only ones in a parental role since Zachary had aged out of care.

"I would be glad to meet them."

"He's up for it," Mr. Peterson relayed to Pat.

"Perfect! I'm going to make ravioli. No one in my family was ever a cook. They haven't had anything but the canned stuff."

"They'll love it," Zachary told Lorne. "Is he making the cheese ones?"

"Is that a request?"

"If he feels like it." Zachary wasn't about to insist. He wouldn't be eating much, and Pat should make something that his family would enjoy, not cater to Zachary.

"Zachary wants the cheese ones," Mr. Peterson reported to his partner.

Zachary laughed and didn't try to correct him. There wasn't any point.

Bridget picked that moment to leave the store with her cart of groceries.

Or rather, one of the grocery store staff was pushing Bridget's cart of groceries.

Zachary studied the store clerk as he and Bridget walked across the parking lot to Bridget's yellow Volkswagen bug. He reached for a camera with a telephoto lens and carefully focused on the man pushing Bridget's cart.

Did he think the man was the father of Bridget's babies? Zachary mentally shook his head at the thought. He did not. But his full report would need to include pictures of anyone he saw Bridget with, especially if it were out of the ordinary.

Bridget walked slowly, and halfway to the car she stopped to rest, pressing her hand against the small of her back. The man pushing the cart stopped and waited, chatting with her. They moved on again, and Bridget climbed awkwardly into the car as the man unloaded the groceries into her car.

Just someone helping her with the physical chore of getting her groceries from one place to the other when she was already carrying a heavy load.

Zachary snapped several pictures, then put the camera back to the side.

"Sorry," he said, realizing that Lorne was still on the line and was probably wondering what was going on. "Needed to get a couple of pictures. I'm sort of on surveillance."

"You told me you could talk," Mr. Peterson reproached. "I don't want to keep you if you're on the job."

"It's fine. She was in the store, so I was just waiting."

"But she's out now, so I'll let you go. I'll email you."

"Okay. But it's a yes to dinner. I'll make it work, whether Kenzie comes or not."

"Excellent. Pat is eager for them to meet you."

14

Zachary waited until after supper to bring up his questions, giving Kenzie all of his attention while they ate. She seemed to have had a better day at work, whether that was because she hadn't had to work any more on the teenager who had died of kidney failure or because she had opened up to talk to Zachary about it. He was glad that she seemed to be less stressed about it.

"I'll be reporting to my client on the surveillance so far," he told Kenzie as they cleared the dishes, uncertain whether it would lead into what he wanted to discuss or not.

"Yeah? How has it been going? Is she having an affair?"

"I don't think so. Haven't seen any sign of it."

"She could have had one a few months back and ended it since," Kenzie suggested.

"Yeah, it's possible. I'll see whether I can find anything out, but I don't know if there is anything there."

"Which means you're back to whether it was a problem at the fertility clinic she had her procedure done by."

"Yeah. Spent some time there this afternoon checking out security procedures."

Kenzie motioned to the couch, and she and Zachary sat down. "What was it like? I haven't ever been to a fertility clinic."

"Nice place. Dark wood and artwork in the waiting room. Looks more like a lawyer's office than a doctor's. Except for the pictures of babies on the walls, of course."

"So that's the outside. That doesn't really tell you what the inside is like."

"No. Good staff. Prepared to answer questions and do an orientation."

"And...?"

"The fellow who gave me a tour… he looked like a doctor, but he didn't introduce himself as one. Just first and last name. When was the last time you heard a doctor do that?"

"Not likely," Kenzie said, shaking her head immediately. "Doctors expect to be addressed as 'doctor' even if they aren't practicing anymore. It's a big deal. You don't 'mister' them. And even if one introduced himself to me with his first name, I would probably still call him doctor. It's just one of those things."

"Yeah. So he must not have been a doctor, right?"

Kenzie considered for a few moments. "Probably not. I don't always introduce myself as a doctor, because I'm not meeting them in that capacity. But at a clinic like that… even if they're trying to make people feel relaxed and at home… people will be more reassured by someone with the title of doctor, even if he says 'Call me Paul' or whatever after introducing himself. If I was getting an orientation—as a patient? Did you say you were a patient?"

"Yes. That my wife and I were trying to get pregnant and had been referred there by our specialist."

"If I was getting an orientation for the fertility clinic, I would want to know that I was in good hands, that the doctor was there to help me and I wasn't just going to be pawned off on the receptionist or a nurse."

"So you agree. He probably was not a doctor."

"No. I wouldn't think so. If he was, he would have told you. So what was he?"

"I'm not sure. He didn't give me a title, just his name. He was dressed like a doctor."

"Scrubs?"

"No. A white jacket over dress shirt and slacks. You don't see lab workers or nurses dressed like that, do you?"

"I wouldn't expect to."

Zachary rubbed his jaw, thinking about the day and everything he had learned at the clinic.

"What was it like?" Kenzie asked. "Do you think it could have been an innocent mistake?"

"They have pretty strict procedures. For the routine stuff. So no… I don't think it was an accidental switch."

"What does that mean, for the routine stuff?"

"Collecting samples, doing implantations, or whatever it is called. They have procedures for all of that stuff, lots of checking ID Numbers on the tubes."

"Okay, but…?"

"But I couldn't see any controls to prevent people from sabotaging samples. Contaminating them, replacing them, that kind of thing. They have a checkout log, but just a paper sign-out sheet. Nothing that tracks it electronically, no person who administers it. Not like the evidence room at the police station, where someone makes sure you are authorized to take out a sample and keeps track of everyone who has touched it."

"Well, I wouldn't expect them to have anything as stringent as the police department. But… I see your point. Preventing intentional sabotage would be different from preventing accidental mix-ups or cross-contamination. But someone like we talked about, a doctor with a god complex, he's not doing it by accident. It doesn't matter what ID Number is on the collection vial."

"Yeah. That's what I thought too. And the security controls to make sure that no one other than the medical staff can access the specimens are pretty lax. A locked door that pretty much any petty burglar or someone watching online videos could get past. It's not secure. They may say that they haven't had any burglaries or any mix-ups in all of the time that they've been in operation, but I can't just take their word for that."

"If there was a burglary, you can at least check that with the police department. They should be able to tell you whether that part is true or not."

"Yeah. But we're not actually interested in whether anyone has stolen anything, but whether they have swapped, replaced, or contaminated anything. And that could be done by someone inside or outside the clinic."

"What are you going to do? Will your clients do DNA testing for paternity and maternity?"

Zachary shrugged. “I think he will. The wife… I don’t know.”

“If she’s not having an affair, then what is the downside? She finds out whether the baby is hers or not. And her husband’s or not. Wouldn’t she rather know before making the decision to terminate or not?”

“I’m not sure. She didn’t want to do the Huntington’s test. I mean, she did DNA testing for the baby, but not herself. The husband went and did his own. But she didn’t want to know. She said it wasn’t from her because it wasn’t in her family. Would she want to find out for sure that the baby isn’t hers?” Zachary shook his head slowly. “I don’t think she does. But I don’t know. Emotions…”

“Emotions aren’t logic,” Kenzie agreed. “Just because something seems logical to us, that doesn’t mean someone would accept our recommendation. There are all kinds of other factors involved. Past experiences, fears, worries about the relationship, how it might affect the child’s life. A lot of sticky emotional issues get involved.”

Zachary nodded. If it were him, he didn’t think he would want to know. He would want to have the child, to raise it as his own whether she were biologically related to him or not.

But he wasn’t like Bridget. Gordon said she had been talking about terminating before she even knew the results of the DNA test. That sounded more like the Bridget he knew. Regretting the decision to get pregnant and looking for a way out. He didn’t know how Gordon had talked her into it in the first place.

It would make sense to him that Bridget would want to have the babies’ parentage tested, even if she hadn’t wanted her own DNA tested for Huntington’s Disease. Maybe Gordon could gently talk her into it.

If the babies weren’t his, then he would concede to Bridget terminating the pregnancy and try a second time.

15

Zachary had been putting off reporting to Gordon. When he reported back that Bridget was probably not having an affair and that his best guess was someone at Westlake was intentionally mixing or swapping samples, that would be the end of his retainer. Zachary would no longer be able to justify following Bridget around and watching her every movement.

Maybe Gordon would want him to make further inquiries about the possibility that she'd been having an affair when the babies were conceived. He could talk to some of her friends and find out whether she was seeing anyone other than Gordon. Or could he? How many of them would know about him? Or would report back to Bridget about the man asking all of the questions. Bridget would immediately recognize the strange man as being Zachary, and he would be outed.

He could involve a subcontractor. Maybe Heather. She hadn't done anything like that in the past, but he had been training her in private detective skills, and perhaps it was time to take it to the next level. She was brilliant on the computer. She had taken immediately to skip-tracing. How would she do on the ground, talking to people face-to-face? Could she find a way to talk to Bridget's girlfriends naturally? So that it seemed to be part of a normal conversation?

Zachary sighed. He had to know that the retainer was going to come to an end sooner or later. And it would probably be sooner. There wasn't any evidence that Bridget was having an affair. It was far more likely she had become pregnant with the implanted embryos than naturally. Not after the cancer treatments. Not coincidentally in the same month that the embryos were implanted. That was just too much of a stretch. He understood that was where Gordon's imagination had immediately taken him, but the truth was probably something much less intimate.

His phone rang. Zachary knew without looking at it that it was going to be Gordon. He swiped the call after verifying that it was, in fact, his latest client.

"Gordon, I was just thinking about you."

"I was expecting a report before this," Gordon reproached.

"Yeah… sorry about that. I was just gathering my thoughts so I could give you a call."

"Gathering your thoughts… that sounds serious. Does that mean that you found something?"

"Well, I made some progress, but I don't have a definite answer for you."

Gordon sighed. "So, you don't know if she is having an affair?"

"Now? I would say not. Nothing in her behavior or daily patterns would indicate that. She's doing the same things that she always did, going where she used to go. Nowhere new, no changes in her routines, other than not getting out until later in the day. Obviously she is still not feeling very well in the morning."

"No," Gordon confirmed. "Not as bad as it was in the beginning, but she's still not herself. Pain and nausea. Mood swings. Irritability."

Zachary didn't tell Gordon that maybe that wasn't because of morning sickness. Bridget's emotional behavior wasn't likely to stop when she was no longer pregnant. Not if Zachary's life with her was any indication.

"So I don't think she's having an affair. I could watch for a few days, just in case it isn't someone she sees very often. And I could dig into her background, her behavior around the time that the twins were conceived."

"No… I think you're probably right. What are the chances that she would become pregnant the same month as we had the embryos implanted?" Gordon didn't know he was echoing exactly what Zachary had been reasoning to himself before Gordon had called.

"Yeah. That's what I'm thinking. And that takes us to the next possibility. That the wrong eggs or sperm were used in Bridget's IVF procedure."

"I hate to think that could be true. I mean, you hear stories, but it can't be very common, can it? That kind of thing must be so rare…"

"It is rare. But not impossible."

Gordon swore flatly. "Have you looked into the clinic? Have there been any other cases where this has happened?"

"I've ordered a courthouse search to see if they've been sued for it in the past. And I'm going to check with the police department to see whether they have had any break-ins or other security breaches there the last little while. But that's a long shot. What are the chances someone broke in to swap samples around or substitute their own genetic material for what was banked? I think that would stretch the bounds of credulity."

"Yes. I've never heard of that happening before. Embryos being stolen, but not… switched."

"Right. What we usually hear about in the media is mix-ups being made by the clinic. Wrong genetic material being used. I had a tour of the clinic and talked with people there, and their controls for making sure that they are using the right specimens for each procedure are reasonable. Did they talk to the two of you about always verifying the identification numbers on the collection vials? About always making sure that everything in every procedure is listed with your file number?"

"Sure. I could even tell you what our number was. But that assumes that they don't make any mistakes in the lab. Unlike during the natural process, we are not present for the fertilization or monitoring of the embryos for the first few days."

"Right. And I talked to them about that. They always have two people verify that the right specimens are being used. Or so they say. They do have internal controls for that."

"So there isn't any chance of an accidental mix-up. That's what you're telling me, right?"

"I wouldn't say no chance, but I think the chances are pretty small. It could happen if someone is sloppy and doesn't follow the proper procedures. But I'm more concerned about the possibility of something happening… on purpose."

"Something goes wrong in the fertilization process, you mean? They use all of the right material, but something is… damaged? I understand that genetic mistakes are more common with fertility technology. The chances of mutations increase every time you touch the genetic materials."

Zachary hadn't looked into that, but it made sense. Mess with Mother Nature, and she would get even with you.

"Maybe… but that's not what I meant. What I mean is, they don't have controls to prevent someone from intentionally contaminating or replacing the samples."

"Intentionally? But who would do that? Do you think I have an enemy who would do that? At the fertility clinic?" His voice dripped with disbelief.

"No. I mean one of the doctors or staff… they sometimes decide to use their own sperm. It's happened a few times. Big lawsuits. Who knows how often it happens without the doctor getting caught."

"Really?" Gordon considered this. "But why would someone risk that? I can understand if there was something to be gained, or they wanted to get back at a rival. But just for the heck of it? People that they'd never even met before? Why would anyone do that?"

"Apparently, some doctors have a god complex. They have huge egos and think that the world would be better populated with their progeny."

"Really? Good grief."

Zachary nodded and waited. There wasn't really anything else for him to investigate. The case was over.

"So, what is your recommendation?" Gordon asked. "I mean… there's no way for us to find out what happened. Who might have mixed up or intentionally switched samples? Is there?"

"Are you willing to do DNA testing to find out? We can do maternity and paternity tests to see which of you, if either, is biologically related to the babies. And who is not."

"Bridget is against doing any testing of her own DNA. I'm not sure, but… I think she's afraid of finding out that she has some bad gene… that breast cancer one, maybe. For someone who has already been through cancer treatment… well, you can see how that could be devastating."

Zachary hadn't even thought about that. And it would be. Bridget was strong, or she wouldn't have survived what she already had. But she didn't need to be told that she was going to develop another kind of cancer. Or one of the other big diseases. Some kind of degenerative disease that they didn't have any cure for. He could understand why she would not want to face something like that.

"Yeah, okay. I can see how she might feel that way."

"Don't say anything to her about it. She hasn't told me that. She's only said that she won't do any kind of DNA testing. I can only surmise."

"I'm not exactly going to be talking to her about it."

Gordon chuckled. "No, I don't imagine you will be."

"You could still test the babies' DNA against yours, see whether or not you are the father. That may not be a full answer, but it could be a beginning. Prove whether you are or are not the father of the babies."

"But to do that prenatally, Bridget has to have another procedure. She would have to know about it. They would have to do either amnio or blood testing. We can't exactly do that covertly."

"No, I guess not. You might have to wait until after the children are born. Then get a cheek swab."

"I don't know whether she is going to carry them to term. She agreed to give us some time to think about it. But I suspect I know what her decision will be. She's going to want to terminate."

A wave of nausea passed over Zachary. How many people in the world would have given anything to be able to raise those babies? Including him. He'd always been more baby-hungry than Bridget. He remembered helping to raise his younger siblings. There was nothing like holding a new baby in his arms. Nothing else in his life had come close.

"What if she carries them to term… and then adopts them out?"

Gordon didn't answer immediately. When he did speak, his tone was bemused. "Why would we do that? If she carries the babies to term, we will raise them. We wouldn't give them to someone else."

"I just meant, if she didn't want them because of Huntington's Disease. I'm sure there would still be couples out there who would want to adopt them."

"Adopt a baby with a fatal disease?"

"A disease that won't kill them until they are middle-aged or older? Sure. I remember hearing about people adopting babies with HIV, back when it was a death sentence."

"No. We're not interested in doing that. I would prefer Bridget carry this pregnancy to term, but if she doesn't want to, then… I guess we'll try again."

Or not.

Bridget might decide that there was no way she was going through it all again. The morning sickness, the weight, all of the aches and pains that she

room as Bridget, he had still violated her. Zachary gulped, trying to keep his anger under control.

He would find out who had done it. All it would take was a little detective work.

17

The next morning, Zachary spent an hour pulling all the names that he could from the brochures and the website for the clinic and then going over them with Heather. They split the names up so that they could get through them more quickly. Zachary explained what he was looking for, and gave Heather some pointers on the searches she would need to have done and the people or organizations that she would have to talk to. How to best get the information they needed from people who might be under a gag order or have signed a confidentiality agreement. While the beginning steps would be ones that Heather was familiar with, she needed a few more pointers on the steps to take after that.

Kenzie called him midway through the morning while he was running one name after another through the databases. Zachary was surprised. Usually, when she was at work, she wouldn't call him, except maybe at noon to see how he was doing while she had her lunch.

It must have been a slower day at the morgue.

"Hey, Kenz. What's up?"

"I was wondering if you were still working on that Huntington's Disease case. Or have you already put that one to bed?"

"Still working on it." Zachary tried to pull his attention away from the list of names. Switching gears could be a problem when he was deep into something. "Did you think of something?"

"Well, I had been doing a little bit of research into whether it could be sporadic, you know, and I've been talking to Dr. Wiltshire about it this morning."

Zachary didn't know how much the medical examiner would know about Huntington's Disease, but he would take what he could get. They would both have more experience than he did about the ins and outs of the genetics.

"Yeah. Did you find anything? Everybody I've talked to says that if one parent has it, the kids each have a fifty percent chance of getting it. If both parents have it, then the kids have a higher chance of getting it, but still not one hundred percent."

"Right."

"But if neither of the parents have it, then there's no way the kids would, right? Or did you find out something different?"

"Well, I discovered it is a little more nuanced than that. You have to change your thinking about how it works."

"Okay." Zachary closed his laptop screen so he wouldn't be distracted by it. He closed his eyes, trying to focus all of his attention on Kenzie's words. "I'm ready."

"When we're talking about genes to the general population, we are usually talking about a binary model. Right? You think of someone as either *having* the gene or *not having* the gene."

"Yes… except I know that you can have different versions. Dominant or recessive. You can have a gene, but if it is recessive, then you don't see it."

"And with something like Huntington's Disease, then it is autosomal dominant, which means that you don't have to inherit two copies of it, like you would for something like cystic fibrosis. You only have to inherit one copy of it."

"Right."

"But I want you to forget the binary model. It is not a matter of having the HD gene or not having the HD gene."

"It isn't?"

"No. It's a matter of how many CAG repeats you have."

Zachary opened his eyes and frowned at the phone. Kenzie wasn't kidding when she said he would have to think about it in a different way. He didn't have any idea what CAG repeats were.

"Stay with me, Zach. I'll get you up to speed."

"Okay. CAG repeats."

"So, everyone has CAG repeats on the Huntington's allele. That's normal."

"Uh-huh."

"Some people have just a few repeats. If they have under twenty-six repeats, then they do not get Huntington's Disease."

"Okay." Zachary could understand that so far.

"Some people have lots of repeats. If they have over forty repeats, they will synthesize a mutated huntingtin protein and develop Huntington's Disease. They start experiencing dementia and other symptoms mid-to-late life."

"Oh. Okay. So a few repeats, they don't get Huntington's, a lot, they do."

"And if they have an extremely high number of repeats, they might even develop Huntington's in childhood. That is very rare."

"I never heard of that."

"It isn't always diagnosed right away, because it is so rare. But in families that have seen multiple cases of Huntington's across every generation, it pops up. These 'super' repeats that cause Huntington's to show up early in life."

"That's really scary. So Br—my couple could have a child that develops Huntington's Disease as a child, not as a fifty- or seventy-year-old."

"If they are one of the few that ends up with this super-expanded gene, yes."

"Sheesh."

"Now, this is where it gets interesting."

Zachary waited.

"You know what happens when they have twenty-six or fewer repeats, and what happens when it is forty or more repeats, but what happens if it is *intermediate*."

"Well… I would guess that you end up with someone who might develop Huntington's, and might not."

"Yes. Exactly. If they have thirty-six to thirty-nine repeats, they have only partial penetrance, and they may or may not develop Huntington's Disease. And there is one final possibility."

Zachary felt an itch, like when he had a word on the tip of his tongue, but couldn't quite reach it. He could almost predict what Kenzie was going to say. Another minute or two to think about it, and he might come up with it.

Kenzie told him. "If you have twenty-seven to thirty-five repeats, you have an intermediate allele. You may end up with a case where the parent *will not* develop Huntington's Disease, but the child *will*."

"How does the child get it, if the parent doesn't?"

"Because the fertilization and division processes are not perfect. The cells may 'mistranscribe' thirty-five CAG repeats as forty CAG repeats. So the parent was too low to get Huntington's Disease, but the child is high enough that they do."

"What are the chances of that? How common is this 'intermediate' gene?"

"A lot more common than you would think. It is rare for it to result in the expanded form in the offspring. That's why it is often left out of the conversation."

"Huh. So it is possible. My couple *could* both be below the range where they will get Huntington's, but still have children who will get it."

"Possible, yes. Not likely, but… possible. I would still pursue the fertility clinic angle as the more likely explanation."

"That's what I'm doing right now. So I'll continue to push in that direction."

"And you should know that sometimes people with this intermediate allele do show some of the Huntington's behaviors. Even though they don't have what would be diagnosed as full-blown Huntington's, they may have some of the behavioral characteristics, movements, and so on. It's like… mild Huntington's. But not diagnosable as Huntington's."

Zachary leaned back, rubbing the center of his forehead. "So there may still be some of these behaviors in the family even if they don't have a family history of Huntington's Disease."

"Yes. Possible."

"So I should watch for some of those behaviors in the doctors I'm doing background on."

"I would. Are your background checks going to be that detailed?"

"Not at first. But I'll delve deeper into the ones that seem suspicious. And sometimes, things are reported in the news or social columns about eccentric family members. Or people act erratically on social media."

Kenzie laughed. "How can you tell?"

"You have a point."

"Yeah. I'd better get back to work, but I thought I'd give you those details while they were still fresh in my mind."

"Thanks! I appreciate it. I'll put them to good use."

18

Zachary decided to meet with Heather face-to-face to collate their research and see where they needed to do more. He enjoyed highway driving, so he went to her house. He sat in the car outside the house for a moment, just looking at the house and remembering the various times he had been there while investigating her cold case. It had been an emotional time and had stirred up a lot of bad memories for both of them.

But that was in the past now. He had helped her to figure out who her attacker had been, and the man was now in jail awaiting trial. For the first time, Heather had been able to shed her fear of running into him again. She started thinking about herself and what she wanted to do with her life. It might seem like it wasn't worth it for a woman her age to just be starting out in a new direction, but how could it ever be too late to start living? She had blossomed since she had freed herself from the chains of the past. She was a new person. Not different from her old self, but better. It was hard to find the words.

The front door opened and Heather stood there looking at him. Zachary pulled the charging cable out of his phone and opened his door. He remembered to grab his messenger bag before getting out. He got his feet a little tangled trying to get out of the car, flustered by her watching him and trying to get out quickly so he wouldn't look so awkward. But he managed to get out without falling on his face. He pressed the switch to lock the doors and slammed his door shut. He tried the handle and it was locked. He looked at it through the window to make sure, and tried the handle of the back door. He pressed the lock button on his key fob a couple of times to make sure that the security system was set, then pressed it once more for good measure. He stood looking at the car.

"Come on, Zachy," Heather invited. "I'm waiting for you."

Zachary turned away from his car and walked up the sidewalk to the front door. "Sorry. Just had one thing to do…"

"Come on in. Let's get right to it."

He was glad that she didn't make a big deal of his delays. He followed her into the house. He could smell fresh coffee and something gingery. He glanced toward the kitchen as they passed the doorway. But Heather led him directly to the dining room table where her laptop sat, surrounded by piles of paper and folders. She had already set out coffee for both of them, and a small plate between the two settings with a circle of ginger snap cookies.

"Those smell good."

Heather nodded. "Help yourself. When my son was on meds for ADHD when he was still at school, I had a terrible time getting him to eat enough. But something like these cookies, they helped. They just smell so good that he wanted them even if he didn't have much appetite."

Zachary sat down and took one from the plate. "I didn't know your son had ADHD. I don't think you mentioned it before."

"They both did. Or do, I guess. But as adults, they're better at managing it. It's so hard when they're in school, supposed to be sitting still in the middle of a whole class full of distractions. It's easier now that they're in the workplace and can adapt their environment. Change things around to make it easier to work. Go for a walk. Take stuff home."

Zachary nodded. It had been a big relief for him to get out of classrooms. Even though he had known that he was jumping into the adult world with no supports, it had been so good to get away from classrooms, from teachers and foster parents or supervisors who thought that he should just be able to turn his attention on and off like a switch.

Even with all of the training that was out there on dealing with students or children with ADHD, they never seemed to have much sympathy or workable solutions. They should have been able to help him with accommodations, but what they offered was always minimal. Or nonexistent. Once he was over fifteen, they thought he should have his brain whipped into shape and be able to do everything that everyone else could.

Even if Zachary had been able to beat the ADHD, to find that miracle pill that would fix his brain or the therapy that would allow him to access that on/off switch that must exist somewhere in his head, he had other learning disabilities on top of it. And PTSD and other mental health issues.

School had been pretty hopeless. It had been good to get out.

Zachary refocused on Heather and looked at the table at the various folders. He delved into his bag to pull out his papers as well.

"Let's get to it, then," he said, knowing that Heather wouldn't mind him skipping over the small talk. They could chat on the phone anytime. He was there to do a job and, if he wasted a lot of time talking, they wouldn't have time to get everything done. "Should we start with… the list, I guess? This will be our master list."

He flipped through his papers, looking for the list of doctors and other staff he had assembled from the brochures and the clinic's website. He probably should have alphabetized it, but he hadn't. He'd just gone with the order he had found them in.

Heather gave a quick nod. "So you want Dr. Weaver first?"

Zachary nodded. Dr. Weaver was one of his names, so he went through the stack again until he found Weaver's various reports, all clipped together with a handwritten cover page summarizing what he had been able to find.

"Looks like Dr. Weaver is one of the owners of the clinic. He was one of the original partners that set it up, so he has been there from the beginning."

"Is he still doing procedures?" Heather asked with a frown.

"No. He's semi-retired, from what I can tell. A figurehead."

"I was going to say; I don't know if I would want an octogenarian doing my procedures. Some people are still razor-sharp at that age, but…"

Zachary nodded. "Yeah, I can understand that. He's also old enough that if he had Huntington's Disease, he should be showing symptoms by now. So I think we can probably eliminate him. If he's been there for twenty years and they've never had a lawsuit over the wrong sperm being used, then it isn't him. And it doesn't look like he has Huntington's, even a mild form."

"Okay. So we can start a pile for 'no' or 'unlikely'?" Heather picked up the sheaf of pages and moved it toward the middle of the desk to start a pile.

Zachary nodded his agreement. He looked back at the master list. He put a checkmark beside Weaver's name. One down.

"Dr. Carrie Ryder is next."

"Man or woman?"

"Man. Not one of the original partners, but he has been at the clinic almost from the start."

"Yeah. I couldn't find very much online for him. He's an older guy. Not an octogenarian, but I don't think he's much into social media or anything to do with computers."

"Any red flags? Anything suspicious?"

"No. And like Weaver, he's been there for a lot of years. If there was a problem, I think it would have shown up before now."

"More than likely. No recent changes in his credit score? Or other changes in behavior?"

"Nope."

"Nothing to indicate that he's had any problem behaviors? Fights with neighbors or the clinic?"

"He seems like a pretty quiet guy. Nothing that makes me think he's been in any trouble."

"Lawsuits?"

"One a few years ago over some kind of property dispute. Nothing professionally."

"I think we can probably put him in the 'no' pile."

Heather agreed. She put her folder on top of the reports on Dr. Weaver.

The first few were easy, but Zachary knew they were going to get harder. The doctors who were listed the most prominently on the website were the ones who had been there the longest, and they were unlikely to be the culprits in any intentional contamination of DNA specimens. If they had been the type to do that, they would likely have started much earlier and it would already have come to light.

He put a checkmark beside Carrie Ryder and they went on to the next person.

19

It was tedious work, but they ended up with most of the files in the 'unlikely' pile, and a handful of names to do further research on.

"So how deep do you want to go?" Heather asked. "Are we just looking for doctors who have been sued or accused of unethical behavior, or are we looking for anything negative? Deep background? Family relationships? Early history?"

"Everything we can get. If there are lawsuits, that's a big red flag. But also things like a change in behavior in the last year or two, someone who is known for unpredictable or inappropriate behavior. And then, whether they have family members who are. I want obituaries wherever we can get them. Start putting together a family tree and marking whether there have been any relatives that might have had Huntington's Disease. Does anyone in the family participate in Huntington's research or post on bulletin boards or discussion groups about it? Are there any legacies or 'please send donations to' Huntington's Disease researchers in the obituaries?"

Heather nodded, scribbling down some notes for herself. "Genealogy sites, obituaries, Huntington's sites. Any runs or sports fundraisers for Huntington's Disease. Any mentions in social media..."

"Someone with Huntington's might also have some strange or erratic social media posts. Overemotional, forgetful or confused, angry, posts showing wide mood swings."

Heather added details to her list. "Marriages? See what behavior has been mentioned in divorce documents?"

"Good idea. Yes."

"What about police files? Can we find out whether any of these people have had assault charges? Or has been the subject of a missing persons report, even for just a short time?"

"Yeah. I'll see what I can get on that front. Mario might be able to do some preliminary searches and point me in the right direction."

They looked at the small pile of files and clipped papers. Heather teased one out of the pile. "I like this guy for it. Forest McLachlan."

Zachary raised his brows. "Why?"

She hadn't known a lot about him when they had done their first run-through of the files.

"I'm not sure I can put my finger on one thing in particular. He hasn't been there for very long, just over a year. Usually, when I am doing a preliminary search, previous employment comes up. Usually, you can trace at least the last three jobs. But there wasn't anything earlier than Westlake Clinic on his LinkedIn profile, or in his social media profiles. Some people just don't have any online media presence." She flicked a finger over to the bottom files in the 'no' pile to indicate the older doctors. "You know, they don't have anything on any of their profiles, if they have a profile in the first place. But Forest has social media profiles. He's filled in things like hobbies, religion, and political affiliations. But he's silent on previous jobs. So, where did he come from? What was he doing before he went to Westlake?"

Zachary took the file from her and looked through what she had already collected on him. "Did he move here from out of state?"

"Yeah. I think I read somewhere he'd been in Minnesota before? Something like that. But no listing of what he did there."

"Okay. Double-check the state, and start getting some searches done. Courthouses especially. Look for a name change, not just lawsuits. See if he's got an ex-wife there who might talk about him. Kids, maybe. Let's do him first. If you've got an instinct about him, let's make sure we do a really good job on him."

"I could be wrong."

"Yeah. But if you have a feeling about him, then there's probably a reason for that, whether he's our guy or not."

Heather shrugged.

"Maybe we'll get him for something else," Zachary said. "I've had it happen more than once. Start doing deep background on someone and realize that it's not the guy, but he's guilty of some other crime. Sometimes worse than what you were initially looking for."

"Yeah?"

Zachary nodded. He grabbed another ginger snap and washed down a bite with coffee that was past being lukewarm.

"Do you want me to get you another coffee?" Heather asked grimacing.

"No. I should be getting back home. Don't want to keep Kenzie waiting. Let's just divide these up…" He went through the 'maybe' pile, handing Heather the files she had already started and balancing them against the ones that he had worked on, taking a couple of her files himself so that she wasn't overloaded. "There we go. Start on McLachlan. Let me know what you find. We'll keep each other apprised."

"Are you going to work on it tonight?"

Zachary hesitated. He tried to make time for Kenzie during the evening, but he was eager to get started on the deeper background on their suspects. If the man who had impregnated Bridget was in that pile, Zachary wanted to find him. He didn't want to wait another day to get started.

"I might do a little tonight," he admitted. "You?"

"Yes." She laughed. "Grant doesn't mind. I do work while I watch TV with him all the time. I won't spend all night on it, but…" She shrugged again. "Some of it."

"You're sure he doesn't mind?"

"He says he likes seeing me working. Engaged in something instead of just… sleeping or vegging in front of the TV."

Zachary nodded. She had a life to catch up on. She had spent too many years inside herself, afraid to move forward. He was glad that Grant understood that on some level too.

"I'm going to be down to Mr. Peterson's on the weekend." He watched for Heather's reaction, still wondering whether they were planning another reunion for him. Mr. Peterson had said it was to meet Pat's mother and sister, but that didn't mean they couldn't have a second meeting up their sleeves. He wouldn't put it past them. "You're not going to be there, are you?"

"No, not this time. Are you doing something special?"

He watched her eyes, but she seemed to be telling him the truth.

"Pat is having his mom and sister over. I just wondered… whether anything else was going on."

"Nothing I know about, sorry. I'm not a part of any plans."

"Okay. Just… checking."

20

Maybe Grant didn't mind Heather doing work in front of the TV as they passed their evening together, but Kenzie definitely noticed Zachary's distraction and commented on it.

"What are you working on? Still the Huntington's case?"

Zachary was correlating names on the page, looking for any sign that the Jacqueline Merrit listed there was the same person as Dr. Jackie Merrit on his list. While he didn't think that they were looking for a woman, it was always possible that someone had just been intent on causing chaos and had mixed sperm samples between clients. There was nothing to say that it had to be a man using his own DNA.

Kenzie prodded Zachary's arm, making him startle. His jump made Kenzie jump as well. Zachary put his hand over his heart, trying to tell himself that there was no need to be freaking out over a love tap from his girlfriend. He wasn't being attacked.

"Sorry," Kenzie laughed. She gave his arm a squeeze and cuddled against his shoulder for a moment. "I didn't mean to scare you."

"No, no, it's fine. I was just focused. What did you ask?" He realized belatedly that he had heard her talking to him, but had tuned her out. He tried to run back the tape in his head, but had been too focused to know what she had said.

"I asked what you're working on. Is it the Huntington's case?"

"Oh. Yes. Background on the doctors and staff that could be our culprit."

"Ah. I guess they're probably in a rush for the information to decide whether to terminate or not. How far along is she?"

"Um, yes. Probably. I think she's probably going to terminate whether we figure out what happened or not. I think she was already looking for a reason to."

"Oh?" Kenzie's eyebrows went up. "Why would she do that? I would think that if she's doing IVF, she's pretty invested in getting pregnant. Why would she want to terminate? Especially before she even knew the baby has Huntington's?"

"I don't know. People can still get cold feet. Decide that they're not ready for it, even though they have been waiting for a long time."

"I guess. I just think if I had decided I was going to spend all of the time and money and mental resources on IVF, I'd make sure it was what I really wanted before going ahead."

Zachary nodded. He looked down at the work he had been doing, rubbing a crick in his neck that he hadn't noticed before.

"How far along?" Kenzie prompted.

"I don't know, exactly. She's… big." Zachary made a movement suggesting a large pregnant belly.

"So, not early."

"No. But I don't know how many weeks or when she is due. Still a few months away."

"Not that it's any of my business," Kenzie admitted. "I'm just curious. It's hard to imagine what they must be feeling like right now. You think that you're going to have that baby you wanted, that everything has worked out and your dream is going to come true… and then you find out that the baby has a potentially fatal disease. A genetic disease that he didn't inherit from either of you. It would be pretty tragic."

"I guess." Zachary fiddled with the keys on his laptop, tapping lightly. "I really can't imagine deciding to terminate, though. I know…" He tried to put the words together in a way that would make sense to her. "I know… what it's like to hold a newborn, and to love her… even though it's the first time you've ever seen her. To decide that you won't let that child be born… I'm not a woman, but once she's felt the baby moving and heard her heart-beat… I don't know how she could make that decision."

"You can't know what you would do if you haven't been there." Kenzie stared off, thinking. "It's funny, you know, that we've both had that experience, with helping to raise a sibling. Not just entertaining the baby or giving her an occasional bottle, but actually being one of her caregivers."

Zachary nodded slowly. "I hadn't thought about that. But yeah. I guess we have. What was it like for you?" He hesitated to ask, but did anyway. "What kind of home did you grow up in? Was it hard on them? Having another baby? Or did they want to?"

Kenzie gave him a quizzical look. "Yeah, of course they wanted Amanda. They had been trying to have another baby. There was at least one miscarriage between me and Amanda. They never intended for me to be an only child, but I almost was. I'm glad they didn't decide that it was too late to have a second baby."

"And your mom… I guess if she didn't have the two of you close together, like with my family, it wasn't so hard on her to be pregnant and to take care of Amanda."

"No. I don't think it was too bad. I don't remember her complaining a bunch about how hard it was to be pregnant. Some women do have a really hard time, feel really bad, but I don't remember her throwing up or being overly tired, or complaining about a lot of pain."

"That's good. So it was easier for her to take care of a baby."

"I don't think it was really very hard for her. I loved helping with everything, even changing diapers. And Dad liked babies too. A lot of men don't get very involved with babies. They figure they'll bring in the bacon and leave that part to Mom. But he was always involved if he was in town."

"He traveled a lot?"

Kenzie nodded. She didn't tell him anything else about what her father did. Zachary assumed he must be a doctor from what Kenzie had said earlier. But doctors didn't usually travel a lot, as far as he knew. Maybe her father had clinics in several different cities that he rotated through. That could be a thing.

Zachary closed the lid of his laptop, deciding that further research could wait until morning. He didn't want to shut Kenzie out. He wanted to have this conversation with her.

"You don't have to do that," Kenzie said immediately. "I didn't mean to interrupt you. If you need to get it done right away…"

"It can wait. I shouldn't have been working on it tonight."

"You can," she repeated.

"No. It's okay." Zachary took a couple of deep breaths and returned to their discussion. "My mom… she didn't do so well with babies. I'm not sure why she kept getting pregnant. I mean, after the first two or three of us, she must have realized how hard it was on her body and that she wasn't cut out to have a big family… but she still did. Six kids. I don't know why she would do that."

"Was she Catholic? Some religions don't believe in birth control. They think it's a sin."

"I don't think so. I don't remember either of my parents being religious. We didn't go to church. I'd never been to church until I was in foster care. Some of the families I was with would drag everyone off to church. But at home… I don't think they were religious."

"Maybe she still thought that it was wrong. What was it like? She just didn't like having kids around? She was overwhelmed?"

"I think… she probably had postpartum depression. I didn't realize that there was anything really wrong at the time. I mean, I was just a kid. Only eight when Mandy was born. But she…" Zachary put his computer aside, shaking his head. "She wouldn't get out of bed. I just thought that's how it was when you had a baby. When you break your leg, you have to have a cast on for six weeks, or a few months, whatever. Or stay in bed if it's really bad. And when you have a baby, you can't get out of bed for weeks."

"Yeah, sounds like she must have had it really bad. Or she might have lost a lot of blood and was anemic. Just having so many children in such a short period of time… she might have had other vitamins and minerals that were really depleted. Essential fatty acids. Deficiencies can cause a lot of psychiatric symptoms."

"Maybe that was it. I just know it was bad… We took care of the babies, me and the older girls. Gave them bottles, changed them, rocked them to sleep and tried to keep them from crying and waking my mom up. She would take them a couple of times during the day when she had to. When we were at school. I always hated going to school, worrying about if they would be okay while we were gone."

"Someone should have involved child services. Gotten her some kind of help. It's pretty dangerous, letting kids so young be in charge of taking care of a newborn."

"I guess so. It was always a relief when she was able to get up again, and I knew that at least the baby wouldn't starve while I was at school."

"How long was it before she could be up and around?"

"I don't know. Seemed like a long time. Weeks."

"Sheesh. She's lucky she had the help she did. If one of you had ever had an accident with the baby because she couldn't take care of it..."

Zachary wasn't thinking about his mother anymore. He was thinking about Bridget. Worrying, as he had many times over the previous weeks, how she was going to take care of a baby.

He worried too much. Bridget wasn't his mother. She wasn't going to have depression that kept her in bed for weeks after the twins were born. If she even went ahead and had the twins.

If she did decide to go ahead, if Gordon somehow managed to talk her into having the twins, she would have help. Not from children who were eight or ten years old, but maids and nannies and whatever else she or Gordon thought she needed to get through. She wouldn't be lying in bed, her babies neglected.

Kenzie cuddled up to Zachary, sliding her arm around behind his back, her touch warm.

"A movie?" she suggested. "I think you could use the distraction. Something light and fun to get your mind off the case."

She knew, of course, that he wasn't just thinking about the case. But he appreciated her putting it that way anyway. He didn't need to be reminded how easily he sank into obsessive thoughts about his past.

Or about Bridget.

But Kenzie didn't know that was what he was thinking about. He at least hadn't given that away.

21

Heather had turned up several facts about Forest McLachlan. She went through what she had discovered point by point over the phone. Zachary made notes in his notepad that he would later expand upon on the computer.

It wasn't an airtight case, but there were plenty of reasons to be suspicious of McLachlan. So far, everything they had discovered was circumstantial, but many cases started that way. Then he gathered the evidence needed to prove his case. Or at least to get the police involved, and they could gather the evidence needed to charge a suspect.

McLachlan had previously worked at another fertility clinic, and it was one that had been in the news for irregularities. It had been under investigation for sloppy or unethical practices. Heather hadn't been able to find any verdict or resolution in the media, but the fertility clinic was no longer in existence. McLachlan had good reason for not wanting that clinic to be on his resume. More than likely, he had lied on his resume, but simply left it off of his social media.

He had left an ex-wife in Minnesota. She would be a good source for them to check in with. Find out what had gone on at the clinic, why she had divorced him, and whether he happened to have Huntington's Disease in his family tree. Heather promised to send him her information via email, so he didn't bother to write it down.

"That's great. Is there anything else?"

"I put in for some courthouse searches, here and in Minnesota. But they will take a few days to get in."

"Right."

"Before the fertility clinic, he was at a hospital. I haven't been able to find any hint of scandal there. So maybe nothing. Or we might need to talk to people he actually worked with to find anything out."

"Sometimes there are non-disclosure agreements," Zachary said. "They promise not to put anything in the media or to talk about what went on, if he'll just go his own way and they don't have to take him to court or deal with the fallout of people knowing what they allowed someone to get away with while he worked for them."

"Why would they do that? Don't they know the same thing is just going to happen at the next place?"

"Yeah," Zachary agreed. "Not exactly protecting the rest of society, are they? They're just getting rid of a problem. Covering their butts. They know that he's going to keep causing problems, but they don't really care as long as it is in someone else's back yard."

"If this sicko has been breaking the rules and doing… disgusting stuff like this for years, then they're partially responsible for that. They can't just say they didn't know. Or that they were gagged. Don't they have a responsibility to do something?"

"You'd have to talk to a lawyer. I couldn't tell you. I'm sure they had lawyers advising them exactly what they could and couldn't do. They probably had to make some kind of report to their professional board, whoever regulates doctors."

"Then why didn't *they* do something?"

"That's why he moved. So he could start fresh in a new state."

"And it didn't follow him? No one checks to see what his status was in Minnesota?"

"Probably not. Or he gave them forged documents. If you see something in black and white, you don't bother to call to find out if it is real or faked. You just assume that what you were given is legit."

"Not me," Heather vowed. "I'm never trusting anything anyone gives me again. It's crazy that he could get away with this."

"So far, we don't know that he has gotten away with anything. All that we know is, he used to work at a clinic that had some issues. We don't know that he did anything. We're just speculating."

"I suppose so," Heather said grudgingly. "But I really think he's the one."

"Probably. But we can't assume that until we find some more evidence. I'll talk to his ex-wife, see if I can talk to anyone who worked with him at the clinic and hospital. Then we'll have a better idea of whether he's done this before. Still not proof of him fathering my client's baby, but maybe enough that the police will investigate."

"Will your client cooperate? Do they want to know? If I had a new baby, I don't know if I'd want them to confirm who fathered the baby. Does it matter?"

"Well, there is always medical history and that kind of thing. They might want to know that." There was a knot tightening in his gut. If Bridget terminated the pregnancy before they caught the biological father, that might prevent them from proving what he had done. Hints and rumors wouldn't get them anywhere in actually prosecuting the guy or preventing him from going on to another clinic in another state and doing the same thing over again. "Uh, listen, Feathers, I have to make a couple of calls. Make sure that we don't lose any vital evidence. Will you send me the info on the ex-wife, and anything you know about who he worked with at the previous clinic and hospital?"

"I don't have much, but I'll send you what I've got. Do you want me to make a few calls and see if I can find out who he was friends with and who else he might have associated with?"

"Yeah, that would be great if you can coax them into giving you any information we can use."

"All right. I'll see what I can wheedle out of them."

Zachary looked up Gordon's numbers on his contact list and tried his direct work line. He wanted to avoid, if at all possible, the chance that Bridget might overhear Gordon on the phone.

He had considered sending Gordon a text to tell him to call back at his earliest convenience—code for when it was safe—but he didn't know whether Gordon had his phone set to show the full details of his text on his lock screen, where there was the possibility that Bridget might see it.

He should have asked Gordon for the best protocol for getting in touch with him when they had first met.

The work line rang a couple of times, and Gordon picked it up. "Zachary. How are you?"

Zachary didn't bother answering the inquiry. It was just a social nicety and Gordon probably wouldn't even hear his answer. "Are you free? Or is this a bad time?"

"Actually, it's a good time. I have a few minutes to myself, for once."

"I wanted to check in with you on… well…" Zachary's face got hot, and he was glad that Gordon couldn't see him. But it didn't make the question any easier to ask. "Whether you and Bridget have made any decision yet on whether to terminate."

"Well, that will be Bridget's choice. I, unfortunately, have no say in the matter. If she doesn't want to talk about it anymore, she can just go ahead and deal with it herself."

Zachary remembered that helpless feeling. When she'd had a positive pregnancy test, the false positive that had been a sign of cancer rather than a pregnancy, she had told him that she was going to terminate, and she wouldn't even talk about it. It was her body, her life, and her decision. He didn't get to have any say in it. She wouldn't consider anything he might have to say about it.

It really didn't make him feel any better that she had told Gordon the same thing. She had at least discussed it with him, allowed him to talk her into waiting while they gathered more information and thought about it but, in the end, it would be her decision, not his.

"I'm worried that if she terminates, we won't have the evidence we need to prove that someone else's genetic material was used to create the embryos. The lab that did the prenatal screen and found the Huntington's Disease, did they do a full genome map? One that could be used for a paternity test?"

"I don't think so. I think it was just for certain anomalies."

"Then if she terminates… we won't have the evidence we need—unless they keep samples. Do they do that? I don't know if you can ask."

Gordon cleared his throat. "I'm not sure how I can suggest that to her unless you've come to a landing on what happened. Do you have something to report?"

"Not yet. I'm still following up. But it occurred to me that if we get enough evidence on this guy—the guy that I think may have sabotaged the samples—to start a police investigation, they're going to need proof of his wrongdoing. If we can establish him as the… uh… sperm donor, then he could be charged with fraud?"

"You have identified someone, then."

"It's preliminary," Zachary cautioned. "I don't have any kind of proof yet. I'm making inquiries; I need to do some interviews, try to find out what I can. Get enough evidence to start a police investigation."

"I'm not sure we want to go to the police."

Zachary hesitated, thinking about that. Someone in the public eye like Gordon would not necessarily want to be known as someone who had been cuckolded by medical technology. Even though there was clearly nothing he could have done to prevent someone from substituting his DNA for Gordon's in the lab, there might still be a stigma attached to not being the father of Bridget's twins.

And what about Bridget? She was all about appearances and reputation. It was very important for her to be seen as someone who was together and as close to perfect as a mortal could be. It had not been an easy decision for her to sacrifice her perfect figure for a pregnancy. Now she was in the position of having to decide whether to terminate that pregnancy. If her friends and worshipers found out that she had been pregnant by someone other than Gordon, that she was at the center of some fertility clinic scandal, what would that do to her?

So what was the goal?

"How far do you want me to go, then?" Zachary asked, feeling his way through the conversation. "If you do not want this guy prosecuted because of the possible fallout for you and Bridget, what is your preferred outcome?"

"I want to know who did this," Gordon said firmly. He cleared his throat, and there was a period of silence as he considered. "I realize that you will not be in a position to be able to prove that this man you are investigating was the culprit, but I want to get as close as possible. And then I want to make sure that he can never do something like this again. I want him fired and blackballed from the industry. I'll do whatever it takes to make sure that happens."

Zachary wasn't sure what exactly that would involve, but he was confident that Gordon could do it. He was a powerful man with plenty of resources. He could talk to prominent doctors and lawyers and somehow find a way to prevent McLachlan from ever getting a job where he had access to genetic materials and embryos again. If Gordon put out the word, Zachary was sure he could make it happen.

"Okay. So here's what I'm going to do. I'm going to talk to McLachlan's ex-wife and previous coworkers in Minnesota. I'm going to find out what I can about what happened at his previous clinic and if there was anything going on at the hospital before that. And I'll do what I can to find out whether he has any Huntington's Disease in his family. I've already got a researcher working on it."

"McLachlan?" Gordon repeated. "Is that his name?"

"Er, yes." Zachary realized he shouldn't have let that detail slip out. He should have kept his mouth shut until he knew more. "But so far, there is no proof that he's done anything illegal or unethical. He's just the best candidate at the moment. If I find out that he was involved in something similar previously, and if he has Huntington's in his family, then I think that's as close as we can come to establishing his guilt, short of a DNA test."

"That sounds reasonable," Gordon agreed. "And if you find there isn't anything there…"

"Then we look elsewhere. He's not the only one on our list. There are several others to look at."

"How long will this take?"

"I'm not sure. A couple of days to do interviews. Everyone I need to see won't be available the same day. Travel time. Maybe wait for some courthouse searches to come in."

Zachary couldn't see that it mattered how long it took. His investigation would not intersect with Bridget's decision to terminate the pregnancy. She would make that decision without knowing who the sperm donor was. He didn't know if she even understood that the positive Huntington's Disease meant that Gordon was not the father of the babies. Or alternatively, that she was not the mother.

"Will you let me know?" Gordon asked. "As soon as you can. I want to know if this guy is the one."

Zachary shifted uncomfortably. Gordon had every right to have animosity toward whoever had perpetrated the fraud, but Zachary had not expected the undercurrent of fury in Gordon's tone.

"Of course," he agreed. "I'll let you know as soon as I know anything."

22

As much as Zachary liked highway driving, he could not drive from Vermont to Minnesota for the investigation. Especially not with Gordon pressing for answers as soon as possible. Gordon had quickly approved his purchase of plane tickets the next day so that Zachary could get right to it.

Zachary picked up his emails from Heather and assembled what information he had on McLachlan's ex-wife, coworkers, and family in Minnesota and started making phone calls. He was as vague as he could be about his purposes for talking to them, trying to make it sound like a routine credit check or something of that nature. Of course, people knew that credit checks didn't involve face-to-face conversations with the lender, but Zachary did his best to make it sound dull and routine, nothing to get alarmed about. He cautioned them against calling McLachlan, making it sound like he wouldn't get whatever financing he was looking for if they contacted him directly.

They waffled and asked questions but, eventually, he managed to get several interviews lined up so he'd be able to get to work as soon as his wheels hit the ground. Others he would drop in on and hope that he could get a few minutes to talk to them.

He had hoped to begin with Forest McLachlan's ex-wife, but she had been harder to pin down than some of his former coworkers, so he would have to catch her later in the day. The fertility clinic McLachlan had worked at before Westlake had new management, and most of the old staff had been turned over, but Heather had managed to track people down at home or their new places of employment. The first person Zachary had an appointment with was Dr. Shane Patton. They met at a coffee shop a block away from Dr. Patton's new job, a large lab that did various kinds of testing that Zachary had never heard of before and would probably never need. He was a young man, his round cheeks giving him a baby-face that probably charmed the girls but also made people doubt whether he could be a real doctor.

"So, what exactly do you do?" Zachary asked him as they sat down with their cups of coffee.

"I do lab tests. There aren't as many openings for physicians as you might think. Yes, people are always complaining that there aren't enough doctors to go around, but there aren't many openings, either. Someone has to pay the doctors. We can't work for free."

Zachary nodded. Dr. Patton was, he thought, starting on the offensive, tired of people asking how good a doctor he could be when he was so young and didn't work at a doctor's office.

"And what do *you* do?" Dr. Patton returned. "I wasn't actually sure when I got off of the phone what it is that you were after. Something about Forest McLachlan, but I couldn't figure out what."

"To tell the truth, I'm a private investigator. I didn't want to say too much on the phone because this is a very confidential matter."

"A private investigator. For Forest?"

"No, for someone that Forest crossed paths with. I'm looking into the possibility that he was involved in an… unethical transaction." Zachary couched his explanation in more vague terms. Dr. Patton might think that it was a pyramid scheme, porn, gambling, or whatever he liked. He didn't need to know that it was something directly related to the work that the two of them had done at the fertility clinic.

"Unethical?" Dr. Patton said it in a hesitant tone. Like he might have misunderstood. He didn't say "Forest?" in a shocked tone, as if he would never believe that McLachlan had been involved in something shady. He was concerned with the word unethical and what it might involve.

"Yes. And I'm just talking to you for background. You used to work with him, didn't you?"

"Yeah, sure. We worked together at Sandhills Clinic. That was a couple of years back. I don't know what it could have to do with anything that's going on now."

"No, I didn't say that it did. But I need to look into Mr. McLachlan's background to satisfy all of the parties involved. It won't take long. A few questions and I'll be done here."

"Dr. McLachlan."

"Oh, sorry. Dr. McLachlan." Zachary noted with interest that Patton had corrected him. Then, as far as Patton was concerned, McLachlan was still a doctor in good standing.

"So." Zachary pulled out his notepad and flipped to a new page. "What can you tell me about him?"

"Well, I don't know what you're looking for. Nice enough guy. Got along with people. Decent at his job."

Pretty uninspiring compliments.

"Were the two of you friends?"

"Friends… no. We were friendly. We talked, you know, exchanged small talk over the coffee. Talked about sports the night before or coming up. Asked after each other's families." He shrugged. "Just… passing acquaintances, really. We wouldn't have been friends if we hadn't worked together. Never would have run into each other anywhere else."

"And he got along with the other doctors and staff that he worked with."

"Sure. Yeah."

"No conflicts there? No one who didn't like him? He didn't make any waves?"

"Conflicts?" Again, Patton repeated Zachary's inquiry and shook his head. "Who would he have conflicts with? I guess it's a high-stress environment in some ways. You have to follow exacting procedures; make sure you do everything right. Don't drop Mrs. Watson's petri dish." He gave a short laugh, inviting Zachary to share the joke with him. "But it wasn't like we were competitors, or fighting over anything. No one knew anyone socially. We just worked together."

"And he was good at what he did? He wasn't the one who dropped Mrs. Watson's petri dish?"

"That was just a joke. There was no Mrs. Watson. It's just a thing. You're dealing with… a very precious commodity. Arguably the most valuable thing in the world to our patients. And it's a very fragile one. You can't make an omelet without breaking some eggs, but when you're working in fertility treatments, you have to be very, very careful not to make any mistakes."

"I would imagine so. Did Mr. McLachlan have a specialty?"

"Dr. McLachlan."

"Right."

"No… none of us specialized. I mean, the younger doctors, we were just there to do the lab work, not to interface with the patients. That was for the gray hairs. They give people a sense of… wisdom and competence. Never mind that not one of them could probably do ICSI themselves. They had the social skills it took to deal with fussy, rich old ladies."

Ouch. Zachary had to school his expression not to give himself away. Dr. Patton was young, but he wasn't that much younger than most of the women who came into the clinic would be. But he made them sound ancient and batty.

"It sounds like you found it a frustrating place to work. You felt like… you were being held back?"

"Yeah. That's exactly it. We could have done so much more than we were doing if they'd just let us. But they only wanted us dealing with the technical stuff, and not to have a personal relationship with the patients. Which really means they didn't want to pay us for the patient-interface work. Keep us doing routine stuff in the lab while they were making the big bucks for consultation."

"Was there a big rift between the older doctors and the younger ones, then? Was it a two-class system? Or were there… a range of skills, and you just felt like yours weren't being utilized?"

"A lot of us younger guys felt like that. You go to school for a billion years, and then you think you're going to make a ton of money and live like a king. And then you find out… you have all of these debts to pay off, and you're basically earning minimum wage. I mean, there is hardly enough left over to eat. And you have to work for another ten years to advance and feel like you're getting anywhere, moving up the ladder. It's a tough economy out there. They don't pay you any more than they have to."

"Yeah. That must be really difficult."

"It is." Patton nodded eagerly, glad Zachary understood. "It's really hard to get ahead."

"And how was Dr. McLachlan handling that? Was he doing any better at advancement than you were?"

"He was trying. You gotta give the guy points for effort. He made coffee for the partners, chatted them up, asked them about their golf scores. Offered to help with procedures. Made a nuisance of himself, but in a good way. Trying to get anyone to take a chance on him."

"And you thought he was just being fake?"

"No. He wasn't fake. Who can blame him for trying to do the same thing as the rest of us? Why shouldn't he?"

"Anything about him ever hit you the wrong way? Like you thought… there was something wrong, or he was doing something he shouldn't?"

"No, nothing like that," Patton cocked his head. "I don't know what you're talking about."

Zachary figured he had elicited all of the up-front information that he was going to get. Bland, inoffensive stuff about McLachlan. It was time to turn the screws and see how Patton reacted.

"There was some trouble when the two of you were at Sandhills Clinic?"

Patton looked away, his eyes hooded. He sipped his coffee, looking like he wasn't surprised by what Zachary had said. He had been hoping, up until then, that it was just an innocent interview. McLachlan needed a mortgage or other kind of loan. A work reference, maybe.

"Trouble? I don't know what you're talking about."

"You really think that I would believe that? Of course you know what I'm talking about. There was a big to-do."

"Nah. Maybe there was a write-up or two in the paper on a slow news day. But it didn't mean anything. It wasn't the big deal that you think it was from reading what the shock-jocks had to write."

"So what was it, then?"

"Just… some procedural stuff. Some women with sour grapes. What you do in a place like that is very emotional. People get overwrought. When things don't work out the way they think they should, they get upset and look for someone to blame. They lay frivolous charges. It's nothing new. Been happening in America for years. You don't like your life? Sue someone. It's not your fault. You don't take responsibility for it."

"What were they suing for?"

Patton studied Zachary. "You know what it was all about. Don't bother trying to snow me. But there was nothing there. And they proved it in the end. There weren't any sanctions. No one got fired. And those women eventually faded into the woodwork. There wasn't any cash prize for suing the clinic. No free money."

"There were claims that mistakes were made. Samples mixed up. Implantations done when there wasn't anything to implant. Sleight of hand."

"And how would they know that?" Patton shook his head in disbelief. "How would any woman know whether we implanted an embryo or just squirted a syringe of growth medium? It isn't like we're transplanting fetuses that have been raised in chambers. It isn't anything you can see. And even if you do everything right, chances are, it still isn't going to take. You implant viable embryos, but for one reason or another, they just don't develop. What's miraculous is that they ever do. That we have this technology where we can make a baby outside the womb, and then put it back in, and it works. Do you know that science like that a hundred years ago would have been considered to be witchcraft? People don't stop and think about what it is that we're really doing."

"It is pretty amazing," Zachary encouraged.

"Women put off having babies until they're forty. They think that because they froze their eggs when they were twenty, that it's just a matter of squirting some sperm over it, and they're going to have a baby. The eggs were frozen, so they're still in perfect condition, right?" Patton shook his head. "No way, Jose. They don't last that long, even in the freezer. You wait ten years, and you're out of luck. They're not going to work. You ever seen freezer-burned meat? You know stuff still gets older and degrades even in a deep freeze."

"I never thought about it. You do hear about women who are just looking at getting pregnant at forty after their careers are firmly established."

"Yeah. And somehow the fact that their eggs have degraded over ten or twenty years is our fault. There must be incompetent people in your lab because my IVF didn't work the first time."

Zachary nodded sympathetically. "And... when it worked? What was this business about mixed-up samples? Do you think that ever happened?"

There hadn't been anything in the newspaper reports about mixed-up samples. That was Zachary's own fiction.

Patton looked at him, trying to decide what to say. He tapped a nail on the table, took a sip of his coffee, fidgeted with his earlobe. "Like I said, these rich old ladies… if anything doesn't go the way they expected, they start throwing around accusations. Do you know how much higher the risks of genetic damage are when you do IVF? People think that because we have this great technology, we can do miracles. Women want the embryos checked for specific problems. We want a baby without BRCA1. We don't want to take the chance that she will have a higher risk of breast cancer. So they want DNA tests done when the embryo has only gone through a few divisions. And we can do it, but there is a risk. Every time you touch that embryo, you could be doing damage. Fertilize it outside the womb, more risk. Do DNA testing to pick the embryo you want, more risk. Then people have a child who is blind or has cerebral palsy, and we're the bad guys. It's our fault. That doesn't run in my family, so how could I have a baby with that?"

"Does that happen?"

"IVF babies have a higher risk of being low birth weight or premature. They have a higher rate of cancer, blindness, cerebral palsy, autism, genitourinary malformations, heart malformations. You name it. There's a huge risk to having babies using technology like this."

"I've never heard that before."

Patton shrugged. "It's not like it's something that we advertise. Go ahead, store your eggs, or come to us if you're having conception problems, or if you want to make sure your child doesn't have a treatable cancer. Let's increase their risks of hepatoblastoma instead. That one kills children incredibly quickly. But who cares? You ask us, we'll give it to you. But don't blame us when things don't turn out the way you wanted."

"So these weren't cases of mixed-up samples. Just… mutations?"

"People don't like what they get, they sue. Your baby is darker or lighter skinned then you are? Must be a mix-up. Baby has blue eyes when both parents had brown? They must have used the wrong sperm. Baby has celiac disease? They couldn't have gotten that from the parents, so there must have been something nefarious going on at that clinic."

"Is that why you're not working there anymore? The lawsuits were just too stressful?"

Patton hesitated. He looked at Zachary, down at his coffee, out the window, thinking through what he wanted to say. "It's under new management now," he offered finally. "None of the old gang are there."

"You were all let go?"

"Eventually, yeah. There were a few waves, you know, a few sets of layoffs, and then once the new management was installed and they knew what they were doing, they brought in their own people and fired the last of the old staff."

"Was McLachlan let go in the first wave of layoffs?"

"Yes. It was one of those things, you know. Last in, first out."

"And you too?"

"Yeah. The younger people are always expendable. Easier for them to find new jobs. Yeah, we both were let go in the first set of layoffs."

"Well, I'm sorry for the rough time you had to go through. You must be a lot happier being out of that business."

"Yeah," Patton said after another pause. "Yeah, of course I am."

23

Not everybody agreed with Patton's litany of complaints. The women especially seemed to have found Sandhills Clinic a warm and nurturing place to work. The focus on babies and motherhood and miracles seemed to touch them in a way that it didn't affect the men. They had found the stories in the news disturbing and stressful, but had nice things to say about the clinic itself.

But they didn't all have nice things to say about McLachlan.

Rose Turner had worked with McLachlan and didn't agree with what Patton had shared about him.

She pushed a few wild red curls back over her ear and scowled at Zachary. "I don't know what this has to do with anything. You need a character reference to give him a loan? Or what is this about?"

"I'm afraid I can't give you details about that. But I appreciate your cooperation."

"I'm not sure you're going to like what I have to say. Maybe you should just go on to the next person on your list."

"If you found Mr. McLachlan difficult to work with, or less than professional, I would like to hear about it."

Zachary noted with interest that unlike Patton, Rose didn't correct Zachary's use of mister instead of doctor.

"Less than professional. Yes, I would say that he was less than professional," Rose snapped. "The guy was always hitting on us. Other doctors, nurses, even patients. He would flirt with the women who came in for procedures. Like they wanted to be hit on by the doctor? That's not what people came to us for. It's just… gross. No one wanted to hear from him. That's why they tried to keep him and some of the others with… social skills problems… in the lab, where they were away from direct patient contact."

"He harassed you? And patients too?"

"Have you ever met a man who just didn't seem to understand when he was being offensive? Like you could tell him right to his face, and he would just laugh it off and say 'I didn't mean it that way.' And then turn around and do it again. He wasn't intentionally offensive. But he was… odious."

Zachary nodded understandingly. He could imagine what it would be like to be in a place like that, so focused on babies and reproduction, and to have a hound dog always making inappropriate comments, hitting on the female staff and patients, and generally making a nuisance of himself. It wouldn't make for a pleasant work atmosphere. They should have made a sexual harassment claim against him. Maybe they had. They could be notoriously difficult for a company to deal with.

"That couldn't have been easy to deal with. How were his skills? If you kept him in the lab, was he productive? Able to do his job?"

She shrugged and scowled. "It doesn't take that much skill. Honestly. If I ran you through it a couple of times, you could do it. Yes, he could do the job… though I wondered, sometimes…"

Zachary waited for her to finish, cocking his head slightly. Rose fussed with her hair some more, making up her mind whether she were going to say anything.

"There was some trouble," she said finally.

"At the clinic? What kind of trouble?"

Since she had brought it up, she didn't assume, as Patton had, that he had already read the news articles about it. She shifted in her seat and looked away from him. Probably reviewing how it would reflect on her, if it would get back to the clinic or someone else in the industry, maybe impact her future opportunities.

"I don't know if I should say anything. I mean… there's no proof."

"Proof of what?"

"There was some trouble," she repeated, starting over and trying to get the momentum to move forward. "There were accusations from a couple of sets of parents that there was something wrong with their babies. They didn't appear to be the right racial profile or had some disease or deformity that hadn't been seen in that family before…"

"So… what was happening? Were they paranoid? Or was there an issue?"

"I don't think they were just paranoid. Not with so many people coming forward and asking questions at the same time."

Zachary noted it was now 'many' instead of 'a couple.' "And was there any kind of investigation? I mean, a clinic like that must have all kinds of procedures in place to make sure that there aren't any mix-ups."

"Yes, of course." She answered a little too quickly and her eyes still avoided his. "There are procedures, security. Of course."

"So… nothing could have been happening? It was just a coincidence?"

"I don't think it was. I think that someone was screwing up fertilizations. Mixing up samples or intentionally sabotaging procedures."

"How could that happen?"

"On the 'accidental' end, maybe someone had dyslexia and was reading numbers wrong. Or was hungover or had poor eyesight. I mean, those numbers are pretty small. A mistake could be made if you were having trouble telling your sixes from your eights, or something like that."

"Was McLachlan dyslexic?"

"I wouldn't know. People get really good at hiding it. But mistakes were made. There were settlements. And then the clinic was sold, started up under new management to shake the reputation. A fresh start."

"So, there was something to it."

She studied the table, biting her lip. "Yes," she finally agreed.

"And you think it might have been McLachlan?"

"Not for sure. There were a few guys at the lab that I would have had questions about, if I was in charge. They were messing around… acting juvenile. You know, just not professional. Forest was just one of the possibilities."

"So you said that it could have been accidental, someone reading a number wrong. And what's the other option? You think that it could have been intentional?"

This was even harder for her. She cleared her throat a few times. Looked like she wanted to get up from her seat and pace around. He could understand the impulse. He didn't like to sit for long, especially when he found himself in the hot seat.

"You want to go outside?" he suggested. "Go for a walk while we talk about it?"

"Oh, no," she dismissed immediately. "I'm good."

He waited to see if she would fill in the details.

"Actually, yes," Rose said finally. "Let's go outside. Get a breath of fresh air."

Zachary nodded. They had already paid for their drinks, so they got up and left, wandering down the sidewalk. It was a beautiful day out. Zachary took in the sun and matched Rose's pace. She was a little taller than he was, her stride a little longer. She was anxious, so she walked fast. Zachary found the speed awkward. His walking pace was usually okay, but he hadn't quite reached the smooth, automatic stride that he had before his accident if he had to speed up. Hopefully, she would settle back to a slower pace once she got talking. Otherwise, he was afraid he was going to trip or have to tell her to slow it down.

"Do you think that someone was intentionally sabotaging samples?" Zachary pressed.

"I… that's one of the options, right? I wasn't in charge, I wasn't part of the investigation, so I couldn't tell you. But I didn't feel like it was something that someone could have been doing accidentally. I just had a gut feeling that… someone was mixing things up intentionally. For kicks? I don't know why someone would do that."

"I don't know why either," Zachary assured her. "I guess since we're not the kind of people who would do that, it's hard for us to understand someone who would. I really don't know. I guess sometimes it's ego. Seeing what they can get away with. Or it could be anger or revenge. Maybe he hit on one of those patients, and she rejected him, so he wanted to get back at her."

"Yeah." Rose nodded slowly. "I hadn't thought about that."

She was slowing to an easier walking pace.

"Did anyone talk to the… whatever you call the owners or managing partners? Someone higher up the food chain. Did anyone ever say that they had concerns about McLachlan or the other guys in the lab?"

"No, not as far as I know. We were all… you know, just trying to keep our jobs. No one threw anyone else under the bus. We hoped that it would just blow over. We didn't think that even if we stuck together, we would lose our jobs anyway."

"But that's what ended up happening when you got new management."

"Yeah. I guess it would have been smarter to make accusations, to try to get the person who was responsible fired. Then maybe the consequences wouldn't have been quite so dire. They'd be able to say 'we found the culprit and everything is good now,' instead of going further and turning over the whole staff."

"Maybe. Maybe enough damage had been done that they would have had to do that anyway. You don't know what would have happened if circumstances had been different."

"Yeah. I guess. Maybe everything would have happened the same way even if we'd all pointed fingers. I thought at the time that I was being loyal to my coworkers, that we were friends and had each other's backs. But now… I'm not friends with any of them anymore. Did I think that I would be? We were never really friends, so why would I protect any of them? Especially jerks like Forest. I'm sure he was probably one of them. Maybe he wasn't the one who messed up the fertilizations. But I bet he knew who did."

Zachary raised his brows. He juggled out his notebook and they stopped for a moment while he made a note to himself to check into that. Even if it hadn't been McLachlan, maybe he could point Zachary in the right direction. Maybe there was evidence somewhere still.

"I haven't been able to get appointments with any of the senior doctors. Did you know any of them?"

"Not well. As well as you know anyone you work with. Which is… pretty much not at all. You learn things like if they're married and have kids, get familiar with the way that they talk and how they like things to be done, but that's about it."

"Do you have any cell numbers that would still be in service? Personal email addresses?"

"No, nothing like that. I got rid of all of those contact details when I left there. I was pretty ticked. Didn't want ever to have to deal with any of those people again."

"I'm sorry. And here I am bringing it all up again."

"It's okay, actually. I feel like… I've never been able to really talk about it before, to process it. I was too busy staying quiet and protecting everyone else. It feels good to talk about it."

"Good. Can you give me the names of the others who worked with McLachlan and might be involved?"

Patton was one of them. Zachary noted a couple of other names that were new to him. Not people who had come up on their previous checks.

"Is there anything else? You said that there were settlements, so you felt that where there was smoke, there was fire?"

"Yeah. I don't think they would have paid anyone off if they'd been able to prove absolutely that there hadn't been any mishandling of genetic materials. Or that if there was, it was entirely accidental."

"Yeah. You're probably right. It wasn't just to make them go away?"

"No. I think they would have taken it to court if they were sure that there hadn't been any wrongdoing by anyone at Sandhills. They would have wanted to protect their good name. But they ended up not being able to do that."

24

Zachary met with McLachlan's ex-wife in her home, not a coffee shop or neutral location like his coworkers. Zachary wanted her to feel at home on her own ground. He wanted to give her a sense of control.

And he wanted to see what kind of place McLachlan had lived in, if they had lived there while they were married. Even if they hadn't, the ex-wife would have mementos. Pictures, maybe things he'd left behind. Things that would give Zachary a better sense of McLachlan and the kind of person he was. He was already getting a pretty good picture of McLachlan.

His wife was pretty. Blond, shoulder-length hair and a thin face. She appeared younger than McLachlan in the pictures Zachary had seen of him. But it was hard to tell sometimes.

She shook Zachary's hand, something that not a lot of women did. Her grip was dry and firm. She gave an image of calm competence. He didn't know what she did for a living, but he imagined that she was good at it and that her clients or customers were happy around her.

"Mrs. McLachlan, it's good to meet you."

"I don't go by McLachlan. I've gone back to Hubble. Don't know why I ever took his name to begin with. I never wanted to be just someone's wife."

"Ms. Hubble. Sorry."

"No, not a problem. You can call me Maureen. Forget about all of the mister and miz stuff."

"Okay. Maureen. And I'm Zachary, always."

"Come on in." She ushered Zachary into her living room. It wasn't a big, fancy house. Not like the mansions that the bigwig surgeons lived in. Instead, it was a little starter house like couples often got as they finished school and launched their careers. Neat, but small. It probably had all of the usual problems of dwellings in their income bracket. Knocking pipes, a leaky roof, windows that were not adequately sealed.

The living room was pleasantly furnished with a couch, loveseat, and easy chair covered with a do-it-yourself upholstery cover to make it match. The chair that Zachary sank into was comfortable enough. The room was clean, with bright sunlight filtering through the opaque blinds, pictures of Maureen and her family or friends on the walls, and some knickknacks here and there. Nothing that was readily identifiable as having belonged to McLachlan.

"This is very nice," Zachary said. "Did you move here after the divorce?"

"No. This is where we were living at the time. We still had another year on the lease, and I said that I would pay the lease and keep the place. Forest didn't want to pay for it, so he didn't object. Though I imagine he came to regret it later. It isn't so easy to get a nice place for a reasonable price these days."

Zachary nodded. "Yes, it's the same in Vermont. Seems like they cost more than they should."

"It's hard to make ends meet if you only have one income. Most people will try to find roommates to split the cost with if they're not half of a working couple. It's a tough economy."

"Very true. Have you seen Forest's place in Vermont?"

"I've seen some interior shots and his view out the window. On social media, you know. Not in person. I wouldn't have any reason to go out there and meet him in person."

"Sure. That makes sense."

"It's nice, but I think it's just a one-bedroom apartment. Not something he'd be able to start a family in."

Zachary glanced around the interior of the house Maureen had kept, estimating the square footage and the number of bedrooms. They had, Zachary figured, intended to start a family at some point.

"Do you have kids?"

"No." Maureen shook her head. "I figured once everything had settled down, we would be able to start. But things never worked out. I don't know if Forest ever intended to have a family, or if it was just convenient to have someone helping to put him through medical school. Pay any extra bills, have someone around to make meals and do the laundry. It was a pretty good deal for him."

"And when he finished school, you figured you would be able to move somewhere nicer and get started on having kids. Let him support you for a while."

She sighed. "It would have been nice, huh? But I don't think that was ever what he intended to do."

"He probably meant to, on some level. But things don't always work out the way we planned. Sometimes they're just… wishes, pie in the sky. Not something that we were ever going to put any effort into."

"Yeah. Maybe. We talked about it once, a long time ago. Seems like a long time ago now."

"You don't keep in contact with him anymore?"

"No. No reason to. Best we just go our separate directions."

"Can you tell me what happened here? When the trouble started at the clinic?"

"Hmm." Maureen settled back into her seat on the sofa. "I didn't know, at first, that anything was going on. He was irritable. Angry, sometimes, for no reason I could tell."

"Did he eventually tell you why?"

"Eventually it was all coming out, and he had to tell me before it hit the news. Or, he wanted to tell me before it hit the news. It was the right thing to do, but I don't think it was very easy for him."

"What did he say was happening?"

"He said it was just sour grapes. People whose pregnancies hadn't worked out the way they expected. When they go to a high-class place like Sandhills, they expect everything to be perfect. And things aren't ever perfect. If they have a miscarriage or the baby has defects, they blame the clinic. Even though that could have happened anywhere. It could happen with a natural pregnancy. But they have to have someone to blame it on."

"I guess that happens. People want to be able to explain why something happened. They want a reason."

"Yeah. I never tried to get pregnant, so I can't say what it would be like not to be able to get pregnant."

Zachary nodded. "So he didn't tell you that anything had actually gone wrong at the clinic? He said it was just people complaining?"

"Yes, to start with. As it went on… it became obvious that something was going on. It didn't just go away, you know?"

"I understand that there were settlements made."

Maureen shrugged. "That doesn't mean anything. It might just be money to keep people quiet, to keep them from saying something in media, ruining the clinic's reputation."

"I'm sure there was some of that as well. But some of the others that worked at the clinic that I have talked to figured that it wasn't just smoke."

"Did you want a drink? I didn't offer you anything." Maureen got up and walked toward the kitchen. "Coffee? Tea? Wine?"

"Just water, if that's okay."

"Sure, yeah."

She returned with a coffee cup and a glass of water. Zachary took the glass from her and sipped the lukewarm tap water.

Maureen sat down. "So what did you need to know about Forest? I'm not really clear on what this is all about."

"I guess you know that when he left Minnesota, he started working at another fertility clinic in Vermont."

"Yes, I know he said that."

"My client's wife is one of the patients at the clinic. There have been some questions."

She pressed her lips together. "What kind of questions?"

"Prenatal testing shows that the baby has a genetic disease that neither of the parents has."

"Some of them can skip a generation or two."

"Apparently, this isn't one of them."

"But that doesn't necessarily mean that someone at the clinic made a mistake." Maureen clamped her mouth shut, then reconsidered. "Okay, it probably does. I don't… I don't like to hear that. I don't like to think about Forest or one of the other doctors at the clinic screwing up samples and making a mistake like that. That's just a parent's worst nightmare, right? Do you have kids?"

"No, not yet."

"I can't imagine finding out something like that about my kid, especially before he was even born. It would be terrifying. And you would be so angry, right? Someone screwing things up like that?"

Zachary nodded. "It's a violation. A betrayal. Especially if…"

She sipped her coffee, looking over the brim at him. She didn't prompt him to continue. As she had said, she didn't like to talk about it or think about it.

"Especially if someone did it intentionally," Zachary told her.

"Intentionally? No one is saying that. Forest wouldn't do that. Who would do something like that?"

"What is Forest like as a person? How did you get along, when the marriage was going well?"

"Oh, I don't know. He was an interesting guy. Very smart, very… self-centered in an attractive way. Confident in himself, you know? That can be very attractive in a man. Women like someone strong and confident in himself."

Zachary wouldn't know. He had never been that kind of person.

"It's nice to know that you can depend on someone," he suggested.

"Yes, it is. I liked it, felt safe with him. He knew he was going to succeed, so I felt like things would go well for us. I believed him."

"But things didn't work out the way you expected."

"No. He kept saying that he was doing great at this or that, that he was the best one in his class, or the clinic, or whatever, and he was going to work himself to the top. He was going to be one of the most prominent fertility doctors in America. I just had to believe that and to wait for that to happen."

"That *is* pretty confident."

"Yeah, and after a while, I got tired of it. He kept bragging himself up, and whenever anything went wrong or didn't turn out the way he expected it to, it was someone else's fault. For not recognizing his genius, or because they were jealous and pulled him down, whatever. The predictions of grandeur grew and grew, but he didn't advance. He was still basically a tech at the clinic. Not even dealing with patients most of the time. Not making enough money to make his loan payments. So here I was, still carrying him, and he was apparently the most brilliant doctor in the country."

Zachary wondered if this was an early warning sign of Huntington's. The literature that he had looked at talked about forgetfulness, mood swings, aggression, and confusion. Were McLachlan's mistakes just a symptom of his disease?

"And after a while, I just couldn't take it anymore. All of the bragging and whining about how everyone else was holding him back. The lack of progress, and worrying about whether he was even going to be able to keep his job."

"Did they fire him, or did he quit and go to Vermont?"

"He was… let go during the management change. They didn't call it firing. So he didn't have that on his employment record."

"He didn't put his Sandhills job on his resume."

"I guess… that makes sense. The way things ended up there, I can see why he wouldn't want people to associate him with it." She looked at Zachary, narrowing her eyes. "It wasn't him, though. No one ever proved that he did anything wrong."

"But that doesn't mean he didn't. Especially where this has happened at his new clinic… it's suspicious, don't you think?"

"I think I would know. If he was making mistakes like that at work, I would have known that there was something wrong. He would act differently. Guilty. Upset. Angry. Something."

"He might. Or he might hide it. Or maybe those things he was saying about everyone else blocking him and what he would do if they would just let him be brilliant *was* talking to you about the mistakes he had made or the things he had done to someone else."

Maureen shook her head. Zachary looked for another segue. He wasn't going to get her to admit that he could have been involved—accidentally or intentionally—in the problems at the clinic. And she didn't need to. He didn't need that to make his case. There were more important things for him to find out.

"What are his family like? Were his parents still living? Did you meet them?"

"Yes. Both were still living, and he has a brother and a sister."

"His parents must be getting on in years," Zachary suggested.

Maureen raised her brows. "No, they're not that old. Fifties, I think."

"And they're in good health?"

"As far as I know. I think his dad has some diabetes, but his mom is doing okay. They're both doing okay, I mean."

"No dementia or anything like that."

"No. They're too young for that."

"Sometimes, it starts younger. What about his grandparents? What's his family history like?"

"I don't know what you're looking for."

"I'm just wondering about these grandiose opinions of himself. Whether they come from his upbringing, or maybe they're cultural or even genetic. You never know, do you? All kinds of things can affect your mood and… stability. Has he ever been treated for bipolar?"

"No, I don't think so. His parents had him in some therapy when he was younger, but I don't know what it was for. He talks about it like it was like, speech therapy or something, but it was when he was older. I don't really know and I never asked. I don't think… not bipolar or anything like that."

"And his dad? Everything has been good with him too?"

"Just diabetes. He was in the hospital a little while back. I didn't know what it was for."

Zachary thought back to the notes he had made about Huntington's Disease. He took out his notepad to refresh his memory.

"How about clumsiness? Problems walking or weird movements?"

She gave him a look. "What are you looking for?"

"Things run in families. If he has grandiose ideas about himself because of bipolar, then his dad might too. Or his mom. Someone else in his extended family."

"No, nothing like that. And what would that have to do with being clumsy? That's not part of bipolar."

"No, but it could be a symptom of another disease. There could be something to explain the behavior you saw. It might not have been by choice."

"I don't know. It got worse, but I think it was just the stress at the clinic. Not being promoted, and then the accusations going around about tampering with people's embryos. It wasn't a disease. He's working at this other clinic in Vermont, isn't he? He couldn't do that if he had some disease that made him quit working here."

"I don't know. Maybe for a while. But this client of mine… it looks like the whole cycle is going to start all over again."

Maureen leaned forward. "Don't do it. It was such a mess, and everyone ended up feeling attacked and unfairly done by. Just… tell your client to let it go. He got his baby and if it wasn't perfect… well, they never are, are they? He's going to have to suck it up and raise it just like anyone. And he can try again. At another clinic, if he thinks there's something wrong at this new Vermont clinic. But don't… don't make it a big thing like Sandhills was. That wasn't good for anyone."

"If you could change the way things had gone down, is that what you would do? Just make everyone look the other way at the clinic?"

"Everyone has to deal with risks when bringing a baby into the world. Whether they use IVF or other technology or just have them the old-fashioned way. There are always risks, and you take what you can get."

"Even if someone else has sabotaged it? If someone other than Forest swapped vials or fertilized the eggs with his own sperm, do you think they should just ignore it?"

"His own sperm?"

Zachary looked at her. "If the baby has a genetic disease that didn't come from either of the assumed parents, then it had to come from somewhere else. Maybe the technician who did the fertilization. Maybe it was just an internal mix-up, but in a lot of these cases—" That was, Zachary knew, an exaggeration, "—then it wasn't an accidental switch, it was the doctor using his own DNA for the fertilization process. When it was supposed to be donor sperm, or even the husband's sperm."

"Forest would never do that. That's horrible."

"You wouldn't like the idea of him fathering babies all over Minnesota and Vermont, would you? Even if he didn't have direct contact with the mothers? It's still not a nice idea."

"No. And he wouldn't do that. I could complain about a lot of things about Forest, but that isn't one of them. He didn't do that."

"He's brilliant. He's egotistical. He thinks that the babies would all turn out to be better if he was the father. They would all be as brilliant and exceptional as he is."

Maureen shook her head slowly, eyes wide.

But Zachary wondered. Forest McLachlan fit the pictures of the egotistical, self-centered doctor that Kenzie had sketched for him. A doctor who thought the world would be a better place if it were filled with more people just like him.

25

Zachary had already promised Mr. Peterson and Pat that he would be at dinner on the weekend when Pat's mother and sister were over for a visit. He finished up his interviews with that appointment in mind, and returned home in enough time that he could drive down Friday night to spend a quiet evening with Pat and Mr. Peterson, knowing that Saturday evening's dinner would be more stressful and he would have to put on his company manners.

Kenzie fussed a bit about whether he was jet-lagged, but it wasn't that long of a flight. He had slept okay at the hotel and he enjoyed the highway driving.

He called Gordon while he was on the road, and outlined to him the discoveries he had made. None of it was proof of wrongdoing on the part of Forest McLachlan. But it was strongly suggestive. He and Heather would delve as deep into McLachlan's family history as they could, looking for early deaths, dementia, aggression, and any unexplained mental impairments. If McLachlan had Huntington's in his family, they would find it.

"What if you don't find anything?" Gordon asked. "Is it back to the drawing board?"

"No, I don't think so. We have other suspects that we can look at, but I think our subject is probably the culprit. I talked to Kenzie about the genetics, and it is possible that someone who is not showing any symptoms or family history of Huntington's Disease could pass the expanded form of the gene on to his child. It's not common, but it is a possibility."

"Then he's the guy. Whether you find it in his family or not, he's the one."

"Probably, but we would need direct proof to have him charged. We can't just go on guesses and circumstances. It is possible that he didn't do anything wrong in Minnesota. Or that he didn't do anything wrong here. Or both. It could be pure coincidence that there were problems in both places. It could happen in the industry all the time, and we just don't hear about it."

"We would hear about it," Gordon insisted.

"They do everything they can to keep it quiet. Just like you did everything you could to keep that business at Chase Gold quiet so it wouldn't affect your bottom line."

There was silence on the line from Gordon.

"Gordon?"

"Yes, okay," Gordon agreed, his tone more clipped than usual, lacking its usual warmth. "They would do everything they could to keep it out of the media. Of course. But if it was happening too often, they wouldn't be able to keep it quiet, would they? It would still get out. You would have parents up in arms all over the country trying to find out who had screwed up and why the clinics couldn't put procedures into place to make sure it didn't happen again."

"Yes. I'm just saying; we don't know how often the clinics have to quash problems like this. It could be far more common than they would have us believe."

"Let me know what your researcher finds out. I want to know as soon as you do."

"I'll keep you updated."

"Thanks, Zachary."

Zachary pulled in front of Mr. Peterson's neat little bungalow and looked at it, feeling warm and happy to be there. He didn't get that feeling from a lot of things. But Mr. Peterson and Pat had been a constant in his life for a lot of years. The only people who had been there for him since he had been a teenager. He'd been through some bad times, and Mr. Peterson was always there, visiting him at the hospital, helping him with a tough problem, working through old memories that were painful to discuss. He'd been there for all of it. And Pat was always warm and welcoming, trying to tempt Zachary with a plate of cookies or the other homemaking hobbies he enjoyed. Neither fell into the stereotypical roles or affectations of gay men popularized by the media. Just two family men devoted to each other and their circle of friends.

Zachary got out of the car with his one packed bag, locked the car, tried the handle, and clicked the key fob a couple more times. He stood there looking at the locks, then up and down the street, looking for anything out of place or anyone watching him. He couldn't help feeling uneasy sometimes, knowing that the couple had previously been targeted because of Zachary's involvement in a case. He wanted them to be safe and needed to know that he wasn't bringing any more danger in their direction.

He clicked the key fob one more time and then forced himself to walk up the sidewalk to the house. He could see lights on in the living room and kitchen. As he got closer, he could see Mr. Peterson on the couch reading. His head went up as he saw the movement outside, and he motioned for Zachary to let himself in.

It made Zachary anxious to know that the door wasn't locked or the burglar alarm armed. He opened the door to let himself in.

"Zachary." Mr. Peterson laid aside his book and stood up, taking a couple of steps over to Zachary to give him a quick hug in greeting. "I wasn't sure what time you'd get here. How was the trip?"

"Good. Dry roads. No traffic problems."

"Glad to hear it. You want to put your bag in your room? Pat will be just a minute. He needed something at the store."

"Okay. Great." Zachary went to the guest room to put his bag down. He guessed that Pat's mother and sister would not be staying overnight. Or if they were, perhaps they would be at a hotel. There was a rollaway in the small bedroom Mr. Peterson used as an office, but that would still leave them one bed short. Zachary could take the rollaway and Pat's mother and sister could share the queen bed in the guest room, but since Lorne had told him to take his usual room, he assumed they had made other arrangements.

He stood in the bedroom for a moment, looking around for anything that had changed or was out of place, but everything seemed to be as it was the last time he had visited. He looked out the window but didn't see any unusual activity in the neighborhood.

Pat wouldn't have gone out and left the door unlocked and burglar alarm unarmed if he had thought that there was anything to be concerned about. And he was probably right. Zachary wasn't there because of a case this time. He wasn't investigating anything in town or anyone who had indicated any interest in Zachary, his background, or his family. It was just a regular visit. And meeting Pat's family.

He returned to the living room and sat down. "How has everything been? No problems?"

Mr. Peterson looked at him for a moment, not understanding. Then he shook his head.

"No, no security issues. Everything has been just fine. We'd let you know if there were any problems."

Zachary looked out the front window, then leaned back, relaxing his muscles. Once he got into the visit, his anxiety would ease. He was safe there. Lorne and Pat were safe.

"How is Pat?"

Since Pat was out, that made it a lot easier to talk about him and get a temperature reading from Mr. Peterson. Pat had been struggling since the murder of Jose. He had gone through a period of depression, but was, as far as Zachary knew, doing fairly well on an antidepressant prescription and occasional therapy sessions.

"He's doing pretty well. Very excited about you meeting his family. It's been a long time, you know, and now he's finally able to merge these two sides of his life together. The family he grew up in and... well, me. And you."

It was hard to believe that Pat's family had refused to have anything to do with him just because of his relationship with Mr. Peterson. Zachary knew there were people out there who were so against gay relationships that they would not associate with anyone who was in one. But Pat was such a warm and giving person that Zachary couldn't imagine him coming from a family like that. And he couldn't imagine how they had held his orientation against him for decades.

But Pat's father had passed away, and his mother and sister had finally decided that they wanted to get to know him again.

"What are they like? What was it like when you met them for the first time?"

"Well, you can imagine that it was awkward. It's one thing to decide that you'll start talking to your son or brother again. But it's another to take that step and meet the person you've hated all of those years. I suppose they thought that I was some kind of…" Mr. Peterson shook his head and searched for the words. "Some sort of devil that managed to tempt Pat away, to twist him into this relationship. It has been difficult for them to accept that he just happens to have a different orientation than they have."

Zachary smiled. He couldn't imagine Pat being anything else. And he couldn't picture Mr. Peterson as being some kind of incubus. In his sixties now, his fringe hair turned white and he had a bit of a paunch. He had always been a father figure to Zachary.

When Mr. Peterson had come out, he had lost his accreditation as a foster parent. Zachary hadn't been told at the time what was going on but, after Lorne was divorced and Zachary's social worker figured out that Zachary had still been visiting him, he had assumed that Mr. Peterson must be a pedophile and a predator. That had led to some interesting conversations.

Zachary had been banned from seeing him anymore. But Zachary had been fifteen or sixteen at the time, and he hadn't listened to anything he was told. It had been only a week later that he had taken his next roll of film over to Mr. Peterson's apartment to develop it in his darkroom. And he had met Pat for the first time.

He'd never felt threatened or uncomfortable around either one of them. If all foster parents could be like Mr. Peterson and Pat… maybe Zachary's teenage years wouldn't have been quite so difficult. He'd had too many issues for the Petersons to handle. Mrs. Peterson had insisted that he be removed from their family. And maybe she was right. Maybe they had not been the right family for Zachary. He hadn't been stable enough to be with any family for long.

"You're far away," Mr. Peterson observed.

Zachary shook off the memories. "I can't imagine anyone thinking about you like that," he said with a little laugh. "You and Pat have always been… well, just you and Pat. You were older than him, but you were never… You didn't force him or lure him into the relationship."

"Of course not," Mr. Peterson agreed. "I could never do anything like that. He's his own person, and if we hadn't been compatible, we would not have stayed together."

Zachary heard the garage door opening and then closing and, in a few minutes, the kitchen door opened and Pat entered carrying a couple of bags of groceries. He saw Zachary through the doorway and smiled.

"Zachary! You made it. I'm so glad you're here."

"Of course. I wouldn't miss it." He had, of course, missed it the first time Pat had asked him to meet them. But that had been Christmas. Zachary was never doing very well around Christmas. He hadn't been up to it then.

"It's so nice to be able to have my family… be part of my family again. My mom is very excited about meeting you."

Zachary's face got warm. He hadn't ever had a grandparent, and the thought of Pat's mom being excited to 'meet her grandchild' felt a little weird. Pat had been more of a father to him the past couple of decades than anyone but Mr. Peterson, and Zachary was happy to call him a foster father or stepfather, but it was strange to think of Pat's extended family being part of Zachary's family.

"I hope she's not disappointed." There was a tightness in his stomach that hadn't been there before. He wasn't exactly the cute baby bundle that most grandparents looked forward to seeing. He was about as different from a cute little baby as he could be.

"Zachary, I've talked so much about you. She's really looking forward to it. You don't need to feel like you have anything to prove or to measure up to. You're just family. I just want my family to meet each other. You're not expecting anything from them, are you?"

Zachary considered. He wasn't. He would take them however they were. Whether they were sharp and acid like Joss or warm and caring like Tyrrell or Mr. Peterson, it didn't really matter. He'd take them as they came. He knew that he wasn't getting a doting grandparent. He was just meeting the woman who had raised Pat. And Pat was a great guy.

"No. It will just be nice to meet them," he agreed.

"I've met some of your siblings now. There wasn't anything awkward about that, was there?"

"No." Pat was always the consummate host. He made everyone feel comfortable. Kenzie and Zachary's siblings had immediately felt at home with him. And Pat would make things comfortable when his family came. "No, it was really nice," he agreed.

"There you go." Pat put his bags on the kitchen counter. "I just have to get these put away. Have you had supper?"

"I grabbed something on the way."

"So, no," Pat discerned. "Granola bars or fries don't count."

Zachary scratched his jaw. "Well then… no, I guess I haven't," he admitted.

"That's what I thought. How are you ever going to put on weight if you don't eat at least three meals a day?"

"I've been gaining weight."

"A little," Pat admitted, looking at him critically. "But not enough. I could fatten you up a lot faster."

Mr. Peterson chuckled. "We're not going to cook him for Easter dinner."

Pat laughed. He moved around the kitchen, putting his groceries away, while at the same time pulling seemingly-random items out of the cupboards and fridge. Zachary watched him through the doorway. Watching Pat pull a meal together was like magic. Nothing like when Zachary put a burrito in the microwave or Kenzie boiled pasta on the stove, adding bottled sauce after it was drained.

"I know you're going to tell me that you're not very hungry…" Pat said.

"No. I don't really need anything."

"Yes, you do. Let me make you something nice."

———

Zachary went to bed with a full stomach despite himself. He felt stuffed. Pat's omelet, toast, and hash browns had been way too much for him. He'd done his best but hadn't made much of a dent in them. Pat was used to that and just laughed good-naturedly.

"You can have it for breakfast tomorrow."

The morning was the worst time for Zachary's nausea. He didn't plan on having a big, eggy breakfast in the morning.

He took a walk through the house to make sure that everything was in place and the burglar alarm was armed. Pat and Lorne headed off to sleep, and Zachary sat on his bed, checking his email and social media and waiting for his eyelids to get heavy enough that he could try to sleep.

26

The next day, he was up before Mr. Peterson and Pat, even though he'd gotten to bed several hours after them. He booted up his computer and worked on what he could until he heard the two men up and around.

He looked at the time on his system clock and decided that it wasn't too early to call Heather and see what she had been able to find out.

Just as his call rang through, his computer dinged and he saw an email come in from her. Heather answered the phone, laughing. "How did you know I was going to send that?"

"I just wanted to know how you were doing. I wasn't sure whether you would have anything yet."

"Well, I worked pretty late the last couple of nights."

Zachary double-clicked the attachment on the email she had sent and looked over the bolded headings. "So he does have some dementia in his family."

"Yes. Nothing that was ever identified as Huntington's Disease, though," Heather summarized. "Usually it says dementia or Alzheimer's. No requests for donations to Huntington's Disease research or anything like that. Sorry."

"That's okay. I didn't expect that we'd be quite that lucky. I'm happy that you managed to find something."

"Yeah. I don't know if it has ever actually been diagnosed."

"In some cases, it isn't, especially if it is later in life, or if they have a few generations where people die young before it hits. I guess some people get it when they're fifty, but some don't get it until they're seventy or eighty. And then… they just call it aging… or maybe Parkinson's."

"Yes. I think there was one in there that they said was Parkinson's."

"Okay. Well, that's really helpful. And you have his contact information in here." Zachary scanned through the information that Heather had sent him. "Okay. I'll talk to the client, and then see whether I can get ahold of McLachlan."

"Do you think you should contact him directly?" Heather asked worriedly. "He's not going to want to talk to a private investigator. He could get violent if you start digging into his family history and what's gone on at these clinics."

"I'll be careful. I'll approach him with some other story. Stroke his ego. Kenzie said that these doctors who have done this kind of thing in the past, you know, substituting their sperm in fertility treatments, they've got big egos, think that they are something special. I'll focus on that. Tell him that I've heard how wonderful he is or something. That my client noticed him at the fertility clinic and wanted me to reach out to him… for something. Advice."

"I don't know. It still seems like… I don't know; I would be worried about it."

"I'll be careful." Zachary had run afoul of enough other bad actors that he knew he needed to be careful. This time, it wouldn't turn out like it had before. And it wasn't like McLachlan was a serial killer. He was a doctor—someone who had sworn the Hippocratic Oath. Do no harm. The danger would not be in his acting violently toward Zachary, but in figuring out that the jig was up and running away.

"Make sure you are," Heather instructed him in her big-sister voice. "Do you need anything else from me?"

"No, I don't think so. I'll let you know if I need something, but I think this wraps it up pretty neatly. He's got to be the guy."

After Zachary was off the phone with Heather, Pat poked his head in.

"Morning, Zachary. Early bird as usual."

"Yeah. You know me. If I get a few hours in, I'm doing well."

Pat knew better than to suggest sleeping pills. He knew what had happened the last time Zachary had taken sleeping pills when he was there and they had interacted with his painkillers. Zachary had nearly ended up back in hospital when Pat and Lorne couldn't wake him up.

"You up for coffee and toast?" Pat inquired.

"Coffee sounds good," Zachary agreed. Toast would be pushing it. A few cups of coffee to get his day going, and he would have something to eat later in the day when he was feeling up to it.

Pat rolled his eyes. "I'll put the coffee on."

Zachary smiled. He listened to Pat clinking mugs and whatever else in the kitchen, and figured he had a few minutes before Pat and Lorne were ready for breakfast. He'd get in another call or two.

He tried Gordon first. The first call went to voicemail. Zachary switched over to his text messaging app and scrolled through to find Gordon's number. He was probably in some big high-powered meeting at Chase Gold. When the markets closed in Japan. Or opened. Or whatever they did.

He shot off a quick text to Gordon, just letting him know that Heather's research seemed to confirm that the employee they suspected might have Huntington's Disease in his family. So Zachary would contact him and, if possible, get the police involved. Zachary wasn't sure what the charges would be. What did you charge someone with who substituted his own sperm for someone else's in an IVF procedure? Wrongful birth? Fraud? Sabotage? He wasn't sure what statute it would fall under.

There was a quick text back from Gordon indicating that he understood and would follow up with Zachary when he was able.

Zachary put his phone down, filed the email from Heather on his client file in cloud storage, then got up off of the bed and stretched. He was dressed for the day, but hadn't spent enough time in the bathroom, not wanting to wake the other men up. He needed to shave if he was going to be shown off to extended family at dinnertime. And probably shower and wash his hair too. He never did much with his hair; just kept it buzz-cut short so that he didn't have to fuss.

When he returned from his shave, he saw that his phone screen was lit up as a call came through. He dove for it and saw Gordon's profile on the screen. He swiped the call.

"Hi, Gordon?" He wasn't sure he had caught it in time. It might have been ringing for a while before he had seen it.

There was silence for a moment. Zachary pulled the phone away from his face and reached out to tap the number to call it back. But he could see that the call was still live.

"Gordon?"

"Not Gordon," came the sharp retort.

Zachary's blood froze in his veins. *Bridget?*

In a split-second, he realized that he must have called Gordon's home number instead of his work number. There was a stabbing pain in his chest. He couldn't breathe.

He had called Gordon's home number, which was also Bridget's number, and she thought that he was stalking her.

A stupid mistake. As a PI, he was supposed to know a thing or two about stealth and not giving the game away when one spouse was investigating the other.

He swallowed, trying to think of what to say. Or should he just hang up and let Gordon try to explain it or to calm her down later? He gasped, finding it hard to breathe.

It was just anxiety. He was used to feeling that way when confronted by Bridget. It would pass. But he didn't know what to say or do.

"Why are you calling me?" Bridget demanded. "You know you aren't supposed to have any contact with me."

"It must have been a pocket dial," Zachary said, his voice strangled, sounding like a thirteen-year-old whose voice hadn't changed yet. "I didn't mean to…"

"I didn't mean to," she mocked. "You shouldn't even have my number in your phone. You shouldn't be able to pocket dial me."

"I didn't have it down as your number; it was on Gordon's… from when I was doing the investigation at Chase Gold. I'm sorry. I'm not even in town; I'm down at Mr. Peterson's. It was unintentional."

"You've always got an excuse. What makes you think I would believe anything that comes out of your mouth?"

"Bridget…"

Zachary could see Mr. Peterson walking down the hallway, past his partly-open doorway. Mr. Peterson stopped where he was and turned toward Zachary. He mouthed the name. *Bridget?*

Zachary made a frustrated motion that tried to express to Mr. Peterson that he hadn't called Bridget and was trying to get off of the phone with her. He didn't want to have to explain why he was on the phone with his ex-wife. Mr. Peterson knew all—or at least most—of the gory details of Zachary's life with Bridget, and all of the ugly stuff that had happened since they had broken up.

Of course, there were still things that Lorne didn't know, but he knew how it had torn Zachary up, how he hadn't been able to let her go, and about all of the ups and downs of trying to get over her since. He knew that Zachary shouldn't be on the phone with Bridget now.

"You know what? Enough is enough. I'm going to get a restraining order. Do you understand me? I'm going to make your life a living hell! You keep calling me. Following me around. Coming into the house when I'm not here! You can spend the rest of your life inside a jail cell. They can keep you there until you finally figure out that I don't want anything else to do with you. You need to leave me alone!"

"Yes, yes. I'm sorry. I didn't mean to call you. Ask Gordon. It was just because of the case at Chase Gold. You know. The girl who died. The intern."

Going to the house when Bridget was not there? He had never done that. Not since she had kicked him out. He'd never fallen that low.

"I know what case you're talking about, but that is over. You don't need to talk to him about that anymore. That's just an excuse to call me and think you can get away with it. But you're not. You're *not getting away with it!*"

Her last words were a shriek of rage. Zachary pulled the phone away from his ear, wincing at the volume and pitch. He tapped the button to end the call. Then he sat there, looking at the blank face of the phone.

He'd hung up on Bridget.

There was nothing else he could have done, of course. But he'd never thought that he would choose to hang up on her. He would always keep her on the phone for as long as he could, just to hear her voice. Even if she were criticizing him, he would rather hear her voice than to think that she was gone from his life for good. That maybe she had forgotten about him altogether. That was what he couldn't handle.

Nothing happened at first. Bridget was probably just as shocked that he would hang up on her as he was. Then his phone lit up again with an incoming call. Again, Gordon's profile. But Zachary couldn't tell whether it was Bridget calling from the house phone or Gordon calling him back from his work phone or cell phone after his meeting ended. Zachary looked at it and didn't answer.

After a long time, the call went to voicemail. Zachary stared down at the dimmed screen, wondering whether Bridget or Gordon would leave him a message.

A text message popped up. Bridget's name. The message didn't come up on his lock screen, but he saw her name and knew that she was the one who had called him back. And now she was texting him. And he probably didn't want to read whatever she had sent him in text. Or maybe she had even sent a voice message or a video message via text. So that she could continue yelling at him.

He swallowed and didn't unlock the screen.

The phone rang again.

He didn't answer it.

Another text notification.

And his text notifications would keep buzzing even if she didn't text him anymore, because he had it set to remind him indefinitely, so that he wouldn't miss it when someone texted him.

Another phone call.

Zachary waited for it to go to voicemail. He swiped to unlock the phone and used his fingerprint to get past the security screen. He went into his notifications and turned off the repeating notifications for text messages.

Without reading the texts from Bridget, he locked the screen again, and put the phone down on the bed, looking at it like it was a live snake. Waiting for it to strike.

It didn't ring again.

Zachary looked up at his door. Mr. Peterson was no longer there. He had moved on, but would certainly want to know why Zachary was talking to Bridget again. Especially in that pleading tone of voice.

27

He tried to breathe until he was calm. It wasn't working. His chest still hurt and he couldn't get enough oxygen. It wasn't a full-blown meltdown, but he still couldn't get his breathing under control.

He left his phone on the bed. If Bridget were going to call or text him any more, he didn't want to see it. He needed to get some distance.

Zachary walked out to the kitchen, knowing that he was going to walk in on Pat and Mr. Peterson discussing him or at least casting glances in his direction while they tried to figure out what was going on. He staggered to the table and sat down heavily.

"You look terrible," Mr. Peterson commented.

Pat said nothing, but slid a mug of coffee across the table to him. Zachary took a couple of sips of the boiling-hot coffee. It probably stripped off the first two layers of skin, but he hoped that it would calm him down and bring him back to the present.

It was a struggle to hold back tears. Not from the hot coffee, but from the memories of Bridget. How close they had been at the beginning. How thoughtful and nurturing she had been. And how that had all dissolved in the two years of their marriage, until none of it remained. But his feelings for her endured, and he didn't know how to wipe them out. Even being in another relationship, he didn't know how to erase his feelings for Bridget.

He took a couple more big gulps of coffee.

"That's going to burn a hole right through your stomach," Pat said, shaking his head. "Slow down. Are you okay?"

Zachary wasn't okay. How could he be okay when Bridget was again on the warpath and he was trying to solve the problem that she didn't even know they had?

He wanted to fix everything, just like she had tried to fix him. He wanted to fix the situation with the babies. But he couldn't. No matter what he did to help bring charges against McLachlan, it wasn't going to change their genes. And Bridget was still going to be in pain over the choice that she had to make. Either bring two babies into the world who were not Gordon's and were going to eventually get Huntington's Disease, or terminate them. It wasn't fair that she should have to make that decision.

The thought that she faced a painful decision like that helped to contain his tears. What was *his* problem? He was upset that she thought he had called her. That didn't compare in any way to the decision that she was going to have to make.

He wouldn't want to be in Bridget's shoes for anything.

He took a deep breath and tried to blow it out slowly. All the way until his lungs were empty. Or as empty as he could make them. He took another breath in. He swallowed and looked at Mr. Peterson.

"Bridget?" Mr. Peterson said.

"Yeah… well… that was a mistake."

"I would guess so. Why were you on the phone with Bridget?" Mr. Peterson put his hands up, stopping Zachary from answering. "Not that it's any of my business. Of course you can call whoever you want. I'm just… concerned. Is there something going on that you want to tell me about?"

Zachary took one more breath, his heart still thumping hard in his chest. "I meant to call her husband. Accidentally called the home number instead of his office."

"Ouch." Mr. Peterson winced.

"Yeah. So she thinks I was trying to call her. I told her I just pocket-dialed, but she doesn't believe me." Zachary shrugged. "Of course not. Why would she?"

"Why would you be calling her? That's not exactly covert stalking behavior."

"No. I don't know. She's just upset to see my number; she's not thinking about whether it is logical for me to call her." Zachary shrugged and shook his head. "And maybe... if I was having problems... maybe I would call her even though I know better."

"Well, there isn't anything you can do other than just telling her what you did," Pat said calmly. "Whether she chooses to believe it, or not believe it, that's her own choice."

"She said she's going to get a restraining order."

"She's threatened that before," Mr. Peterson pointed out. "So far, she hasn't."

"No... but she'll be able to prove that I called her."

"A phone call, especially a pocket dial, doesn't exactly get you a restraining order. It isn't evidence that you are stalking or threatening her."

"She could say it was, though. She knows plenty of the cops at the police station. She could get someone to help her out."

"You have friends there too."

"Who would listen to me over her? I doubt it. I'm the one with emotional problems. People love Bridget."

"You'll get through this, Zachary," Mr. Peterson told him calmly. "You're doing the right thing. You're disengaging from her and not trying to convince her of anything. She's not going to believe it, and you'll just get her more wound up by trying."

Zachary nodded. He took a slower sip of coffee, trying to relax and enjoy it.

Bridget could choose to believe whatever she wanted to. She was going through a very difficult time, so of course she was even more emotional than usual. She had every right to be upset, but that didn't mean he had to be.

It was difficult to go on as though nothing had happened. Zachary finished his coffee with Mr. Peterson and Pat, trying to pace himself by how much was left in their mugs. They had toast too, but he wasn't ready for solid food. When everyone had drained their cups, they went their different directions.

Zachary went back to the guest room and looked at his phone. It was no longer lit up with incoming phone calls. So Bridget had, hopefully, given up. Maybe she had called Gordon to complain about Zachary calling her when he wouldn't take any more of her calls. If that were the case, he might be facing Gordon's anger too, and he was a powerful man. He wouldn't be happy about Zachary calling Bridget and then admitting that he had meant to call Gordon. He would have to tell her what Zachary was investigating or make up a lie. Either way, Bridget wasn't going to be happy about it. She would want to know why Gordon had hired Zachary instead of another investigator. One who didn't have a history with Bridget.

Which was a really good question. Why had Gordon hired him?

It was probably because Gordon knew that Zachary would do whatever he could to help. He would go the extra mile to come up with a solution or to figure out what had happened. Another investigator wouldn't do that. He'd do the basics and, even if Gordon offered to pay extra, they wouldn't go much beyond that. But Zachary would. Because he would do anything for Bridget, even if it were to his detriment.

He picked up his phone and glanced at the lock screen. He didn't really want to know how many times Bridget had called or sent him a text message. Her name and Gordon's were interspersed on the screen, so either she had called him from both her cell phone and the house number that was listed under Gordon's name, or Gordon had tried to reach him as well.

But it was probably best to let the storm blow over. Give Bridget some time to cool down. And the same for Gordon. He was usually even-tempered and patient with Bridget's tantrums. But it would be a good idea to make sure he'd had plenty of time to cool off after learning of Zachary's mistake.

He didn't listen to his voicemails or read his text messages. He touched his computer keyboard to wake up the laptop, and checked the contact details for McLachlan again. He dialed the number that he assumed was a cell phone. There was no answer and he ended up in a voicemail box with the default robotic message. He hesitated whether to leave a message, and then ended up doing it at the last moment, rushing it but hopefully still sounding coherent.

He tried the Westlake clinic number and asked for McLachlan. The receptionist sounded surprised to have someone ask after him. Probably friends would call his cell, and clients wouldn't ask for him at all, since he was a lab worker and not their primary contact.

"May I ask who is calling?"

"It's personal. I just couldn't get him on cell, so I thought I would try him there."

"Well…" The receptionist hesitated. Zachary waited for her to tell him that they weren't allowed to take personal calls or something to that effect. "I actually don't know… Forest isn't in the office today."

"Oh, of course. I suppose it's a weekend, so he wouldn't be, would he?"

"He does work some weekends. We are still open and can be pretty busy on weekends, since that's the only time some patients can get off work."

"But he's not scheduled to be in today?"

"He's not in," the woman told him.

Zachary considered her answer. She hadn't answered whether McLachlan was supposed to be in, just that he wasn't. Was she avoiding the issue?

"Was he supposed to be in today?"

"I really can't tell you about staff schedules. He isn't in the office today. Is there anything else I can help you with?"

"No… that's fine. You don't think there's something wrong, do you?"

She didn't deny it or hang up on him. Zachary sensed she was warring with whether to obey the office policies and keep staff confidentiality or to confide in him as a personal friend of McLachlan's.

"He doesn't normally just not show up for his shift, does he?" Zachary guessed.

"No, I don't think that's ever happened before."

"Have you tried reaching him? I suppose you just keep getting his voicemail, like I do."

"Yes. I've left a message, but I don't know whether to think…"

"That there's something wrong or that he's just hungover or something?"

"He could be sick with the flu and just can't get to the phone. It might be nothing at all."

"But he hasn't done this before."

"No."

Had someone called McLachlan and told him about Zachary's inquiries? He'd tried to ensure that each of the people he had interviewed understood that they were not to call McLachlan to tell him anything about the interviews but, of course, people didn't always listen. If they thought that it was important for McLachlan to hear something, or they wanted to apologize for something they had said that might ruin his chances at getting some kind of financing, they might have called anyway. And if McLachlan knew that someone was investigating both in Vermont and in Minnesota… he would run. He wouldn't wait around to see if he would get put in jail this time. He'd been lucky once, but he couldn't count on Westlake Clinic treating him the same way as Sandhills had.

"I'm a little concerned," Zachary said. "Maybe I should go to his place and just make sure everything is okay."

"Would you?" The woman sounded relieved. Clearly, she could not leave her station to see what was going on. And there wasn't anyone else she could send. Especially if McLachlan had left them short-staffed for the weekend.

"Is this the address that you have?" Zachary asked. "I know he was looking at a new place, but he hasn't moved yet, has he?" He read the address off for her.

"Yes. He's still there. That's right."

"Okay. I'll pop over and see if everything is all right."

She thanked him warmly, and Zachary hung up.

The question was, should he really go see whether McLachlan was all right?

It would mean a two-hour drive to his apartment, just to find out that he had slept in or had rabbited, and then two hours back. He needed to be back in time for dinner. That left him with enough time to spend a couple of hours looking for or talking to McLachlan. It seemed like enough time, but he didn't want to risk being late for dinner.

28

Zachary couldn't spend long deciding what to do, or he would run out of time. He grabbed his notepad and the few things he needed and headed for the door.

"Out for a walk?" Mr. Peterson asked pleasantly.

"Uh… a drive. I need to go check out a suspect. I'll be a while. But I'm going to be back for dinner. You can tell Pat I'll be back for sure."

"What's that?" Pat came out of the kitchen.

"I was just telling Mr.—Lorne that I have to go out. To deal with a case. I'll be back, though. I'll be here for your dinner."

"Okay," Pat agreed, raising his eyebrows. His voice was a little higher than usual, as if he didn't quite believe Zachary.

"I'm not going to miss it. I know it means a lot to you. But I don't want to leave this for another day. If this suspect has run, I can't let the trail go cold."

"Who? Where would he run?"

Zachary looked toward the door. "I'll tell you about it later. It will take some time. I want to get on my way as soon as I can."

Pat nodded. Zachary looked toward Mr. Peterson, seeing what he would say.

"This is important," Mr. Peterson said quietly.

"I know. And I'll be here."

The two of them nodded. Zachary felt a heavy weight in his stomach. They didn't believe him. They thought he was just going to take off and forget about the family dinner. That it wasn't important to him or that he didn't understand it was important to them. Zachary didn't know what else to say. Words weren't going to convince them. He was just going to have to show them with his actions.

But he couldn't leave it another day. If McLachlan had rabbited, Zachary needed to pick up his trail as soon as he could. He could do that and get back in time for the dinner. He wasn't going to forget or take too long. He had the time to deal with it.

He tried to smile at the couple, gave a nod, and went out the door. They would see. He would be back and there wouldn't be any problems.

He *might* have broken the speed limit a little more than usual on his way back to the city. He was usually careful not to pass too many other cars, not to be obviously going any faster than the flow of traffic. Then no police would single him out as being reckless or speeding more than anyone else, and they would not pull him over.

This time, he wasn't as careful. He didn't want to get pulled over for speeding, but he also wanted to get to McLachlan as quickly as possible so that he could be finished and back to Mr. Peterson's in plenty of time to meet Pat's family.

Luckily, he wasn't pulled over. He made it to the apartment he had confirmed was McLachlan's current address without a hitch. In the glassed-in alcove, he pressed the button beside the name McLachlan and waited impatiently.

There was no answering tone. He pushed it again.

Maybe the button wasn't even working. The building was a little run down, there were discarded flyers on the floor of the lobby area. Maybe the buttons didn't even work.

He pushed several other buzzers in a row, hoping that someone would simply ring him in.

There were a couple of irritated answers. Zachary covered his mouth and talked in a muffled voice that would be impossible for them to understand. He repeated the process a couple more times when they asked questions and, eventually, one of them hit the door release, figuring he had a good reason to be there and not wanting to try to figure out who he was or what he was saying. Zachary pulled the door open and took the elevator up to the fourth floor. He found McLachlan's door and knocked. To begin with, just a normal knock. Like any friend or deliveryman might make. When that didn't get a response, he hammered on it more loudly. Maybe McLachlan was sick in his bedroom or the bathroom and couldn't hear very well. Zachary pasted his ear to the door and listened for any activity within the apartment. There was nothing. One of the doors down the hall opened, and Zachary pulled back quickly. He smiled at the wild-haired man who had opened the door.

"Is Forest around?" he asked cheerfully. "He said one o'clock." Zachary pulled out his phone and looked at it pointedly. "He said he was going to be here. Have you seen him around today?"

The man started to pull back from the door, not wanting to be pulled into a conversation. He shook his head, backing up and preparing to close the door.

"He didn't leave, did he?" Zachary pressed. "I know he was thinking about moving, but he didn't yet, right? I mean, I got the right apartment, didn't I?"

The wild-haired man's eyes went back and forth. He shook his head again. "He didn't move. I haven't seen him since last night."

"He was here last night?" Zachary hammered on the door again. "What, is he hung over?"

"He went out. I didn't see or hear him come back." The neighbor hesitated, his hand still on the door to make a quick retreat. "He had a bag with him. I thought maybe… he was going away for the weekend."

Zachary's heart sank. He'd run. McLachlan had run. He swore aloud. "Where did he go? Did he say where he was headed? He wasn't going back to Minnesota to see his family, was he? I'm really screwed if he's gone all the way back home."

"He didn't tell me where he was going. I don't know him. He had a bag, that's all I know. It looked like he was going somewhere."

"You don't know him?" Zachary pressed. "He was a good guy, you never went for drinks? Picked up each other's mail? I thought he was a pretty good neighbor."

"He was okay," the man said, holding his hand up to stop Zachary. "I just didn't know him very well. We didn't talk a lot. Just said hello in the hallways. I don't know anything about his family or where he might have been going."

"Well, if you see him, would you let him know I was by?" Zachary didn't use one of his business cards, but tore a sheet out of his notepad and wrote his name and phone number on it. "I was really hoping to talk to him today. If he shows up… would you…?"

"Why don't you call him?" the man asked suspiciously.

"I have. He's not picking up his phone. It just keeps going to voicemail."

The neighbor's body language shifted slightly, his head tipping in the direction of McLachlan's apartment, a slight frown crossing his face.

Zachary swallowed. He woke up his phone and selected McLachlan's number from his recent calls list. As they both stood there, waiting, a cell phone started to trill from inside the apartment.

"He's home," Zachary pointed out.

The neighbor frowned, nodding slowly and looking at the closed door.

"I haven't heard him, though. He was getting his bags packed. I went out for dinner. I never saw him again after that. Why would he pack his bags if he was just going to stay home?"

"His bags?" Zachary focused on this. "You said he had a bag. Now it's more than one bag? How many?"

"I don't know." The neighbor shook his head. "Maybe… three. A couple of suitcases and a duffel. Just… he looked like he was going on vacation."

"Three pieces for the weekend? He must have planned to be away for longer than that."

"I don't know. I didn't ask where he was going or for how long. I just said 'going on a trip?' And… he said yes. Maybe he's going to Hawaii for a week. I wouldn't know."

"I don't think he's going to Hawaii," Zachary said. The apartment building didn't look like it rented to people who would be able to afford a week in Hawaii. Even with a job as a lab tech, Zachary suspected McLachlan probably barely made the rent. He wouldn't have money to be throwing around on extended vacations. If he was packing three pieces of luggage, he was leaving. For good.

But why was his cell phone in the apartment? Was he still there? Ignoring them and planning to leave covertly once there was no one around? Or maybe he had left his cell phone there so that his new location couldn't be traced. Once he got to his destination, he could pick up a burner phone. There would be nothing to connect him with Westlake or Vermont.

Zachary looked at the closed door again and swore once more. "You don't have the key, do you? Did he give you the key to give back to the super? Or maybe you have his key in case he needed something done while he was on vacation? Take in the newspaper or feed the cat?"

"He doesn't have a cat. And I don't have a copy of his key. We're not supposed to make copies or give them to anyone."

Zachary knocked on the door again. "Forest! Forest, are you in there? I need to talk to you!" He waited for a few beats. "Is everything okay? Do you need help?"

The dread was spreading up from the pit of his stomach to his chest, strangling his breathing. He told himself again that McLachlan had left his phone behind deliberately so that no one could track him. It was too easy for someone to track a phone's location. If he thought that Zachary had figured out what was going on and tried to have him arrested, he wouldn't want the authorities to find him.

Zachary scratched his jaw.

One of those PIs on TV would just pick the lock or kick in the door. It looked pretty flimsy. But Zachary had never kicked down a door in his life, and he wasn't about to try to explain to the police why he had done so.

The call he had made to McLachlan's phone had gone to voicemail. Zachary sighed and dialed the police.

He didn't try 9-1-1. A missing suspect wasn't quite an emergency, even if his place of business were wondering where he had gone. He could still just be out on the town or taking a weekend holiday even though he was supposed to be working. People did that kind of thing all the time. Sometimes even disappeared for several days at a time and then showed up at work as if nothing had happened, expecting to have their jobs still and not understanding why everyone was so pissed off.

He tried Mario's number, but he wasn't at his office, and instead, Zachary got Waverly, who wasn't nearly as easy to deal with as Mario. Mario must have gotten the day off. Or wasn't on until later in the day.

"Waverly. This is Zachary Goldman."

"Goldman," Waverly snorted. "What's your problem this time, Goldman?"

"I need a welfare check."

"And you think we're at your beck and call? Call it in at the non-emergency number like you're supposed to."

"I can do that… I just thought… well, this guy might have had something to do with a fraud perpetrated on Gordon Drake. Do you know Gordon Drake…?"

Gordon was well-known. A wealthy man with good political connections. He probably gave to the police relief fund and all of those other good things. Keeping the wheels greased for when he needed any favors.

"Gordon Drake," Waverly repeated, and this time he had toned down the contempt in his voice. "The investment banker?"

"Yes, that's him. I can have him call it in to the main number if you want. I just thought we could be a little more discreet and send someone over… maybe put a little priority on it."

Waverly cleared his throat. Even knowing who Gordon was, he probably didn't have the discretion to make that decision himself. "Exactly who is this? What's going on?"

"The guy's name is Forest McLachlan. He's a doctor, a lab tech. He didn't show up at work today and his office is worried about him. I'm over at his apartment, and he's not answering, but his phone is ringing inside."

"Well, he's home, then, and just doesn't want to have to deal with you. Can't say I blame the guy. I wouldn't want any private dick looking over my shoulder either. We're not in the habit of using police resources just to go after people who didn't feel like going into work today."

"I think it's more than that. I'm worried that something might have happened to him."

"I thought he was a suspect. Something about a fraud."

"Yes. Gordon isn't going to be happy if we let him slip through our fingers. If McLachlan has left town…"

"But you don't think he's left town. You think he's hiding in his apartment and you want the police to roust him for you."

"Do you want to talk to his neighbor? He's concerned too…" Zachary met the neighbor's eyes. The man shook his head and backed away, but still didn't shut his door, his eyes wide and interested in Zachary's phone call. Clearly, things like this didn't happen every day. It was a spectacle.

"What neighbor?"

"The guy in the apartment next door is worried that something might have happened to him too. He thought that he had left, but with the cell phone ringing in the apartment... Anything could have happened to the guy. He could have slipped and hit his head. You don't know. Don't you think it is a little suspicious that he isn't answering any calls from work or from anyone else? But he hasn't turned off his ringer?"

Waverly considered this for a moment. If someone wasn't going to answer their phone, why would he just let it keep ringing and ringing. Especially when he knew Zachary was right outside his door. He would at least turn off the ringer. Reject the call. Turn off the phone. People didn't like to hear their phones ringing endlessly.

"Fine," Waverly huffed finally. "I'll see if we can spare a couple of officers for a welfare check. But if this is some wild goose chase..."

"I have no idea where McLachlan is. I swear to that. I don't know whether everything is okay or not."

"Give me the information you have."

Zachary gave him the address, McLachlan's phone number, the number of the clinic if he wanted to check in with them, and McLachlan's full name.

"And you want to explain to me how this is connected to Gordon Drake?"

"I don't want to go into details over the phone with people listening in. Gordon wouldn't want his personal business spread all over town."

Waverly grumbled under his breath, but didn't push it. "You might be waiting a while. I don't know how long it will take to free up a unit to send over there."

"I'll hang out here."

29

It didn't take very long for a couple of police officers to arrive. It must have been a quiet day. Or else Waverly had been more concerned about it than he had given Zachary reason to believe. They stopped to talk to Zachary for a moment before knocking on McLachlan's door.

Zachary explained again about McLachlan not showing up for work and about how his phone was ringing inside the apartment but he wasn't answering.

"You want to call it again?" the cop who had introduced himself as Louden suggested.

Zachary nodded and tapped the number again. Once more, they could hear McLachlan's phone ringing on the other side of the door.

The cop banged on the door. "Mr. McLachlan? Police welfare check. If you are there, please come to the door."

There was no answer. Louden banged some more. "If you're in there, you need to answer the door, or we are going to have to force it."

The neighbor was still hanging around watching and a few other doors had opened. People stared, wide-eyed, at the police standing outside of McLachlan's door.

"Does anybody know where he might have gone?" Conners, the other officer, questioned, aimed at the various neighbors. "Did he leave travel plans with anyone? A key?"

They shook their heads, looking at each other.

"Is there an onsite manager? Someone in the building with a master key?"

"Downstairs," a woman offered. "He has an office on the second floor."

"Would you mind seeing if he can come up with a key?"

She looked like she would have preferred to watch him break the door down, but eventually nodded. "Okay, sure."

They waited while she took the elevator down to find the manager. Louden knocked a few more times, just to be doing something. Eventually, the elevator dinged and the neighbor returned with a man with black, greasy hair and stained coveralls.

"I have other work to do," he grumbled as if the police regularly harassed him and forced him to abandon important work projects.

"If you could just open Mr. McLachlan's apartment, it would be very helpful for us. We would like to make sure he's okay."

"Why wouldn't he be?" The manager looked at Zachary, and then back at the police officers while he went to McLachlan's door and jingled through his keychain to find the right key.

No one gave him any explanation as to why McLachlan might not be okay. They just waited for him to open the door and, eventually, he inserted a key and turned it. Louden didn't let him open the door, but motioned him back. He also gave Zachary a stern look.

"You are to stay out here. We are not in the habit of letting civilians into a private residence, whatever you might have seen on TV."

"I'll stay here," Zachary agreed.

He didn't want to contaminate the scene if there were any evidence of McLachlan's wrongdoing or where he had gone. The police would be taking over that part of the investigation. If there were anything to investigate.

The police opened the door far enough to slip into the apartment and closed it again behind them. Zachary could hear them calling ahead to advise McLachlan, if he was still home, that they were coming in. It was a few minutes before they came back to the door.

"No one home," Louden told Zachary.

"Does it look like he's run? I don't know if Waverly told you I've been investigating him for Gordon Drake."

They exchanged looks. "There's one packed bag in here," Louden told

Zachary finally. "And the phone. I don't see why he would leave them behind. If he ran, why wouldn't he take all of his bags?"

"One of the neighbors said that he had several bags packed. The neighbor left while he was getting ready to go, and thought that he had gone away for the weekend because he didn't see any more of him."

"We'll check to see if his car is in the parking lot. But it doesn't make much sense that he would pack his bags and then leave this one here."

Zachary checked the time on his phone to make sure that he was still well within the time he would need to get back to Mr. Peterson's for dinner.

"Maybe… he was interrupted."

"But then he would be here. Wouldn't he?"

"There's no sign… that something happened to him?"

"No blood, no signs of violence. Just looks like he left of his own accord."

Zachary shifted uneasily, thinking about it. His mind went unwillingly to Gordon. He'd had his suspicions about Gordon when he'd investigated Chase Gold. He remembered his worries that Gordon might have been involved in Lauren Barclay's death. Daniel's assertion that Gordon was a psychopath. The little things that had niggled at Zachary, making him wonder if Gordon was all he appeared to be, or if it was all just a mask hiding something far more sinister underneath.

Gordon knew that Zachary had been investigating McLachlan and thought that he was the one who had swapped Gordon's sperm for his own. For a man like Gordon, so powerful and used to having things done his way, it would be a terrible blow to find out that another man had fathered Bridget's children. Had he decided to speed up the timeline and not wait for Zachary to finish his investigation? Had he been sure enough that the culprit was McLachlan that he had gone ahead and taken things into his own hands?

McLachlan had been ready to run. He had been preparing to go. But something had prevented him from taking that last bag and phone. Zachary hoped that he'd just left them behind in error. Maybe he had been distracted or interrupted and decided to just go without them. He was out there on the road somewhere. Maybe they would be able to track him down and maybe not. But he was still okay.

He didn't want to think that McLachlan might be in the trunk of his car at the bottom of a nearby lake.

Eventually, Zachary had to leave. There were no answers to be found at McLachlan's apartment. The manager locked it back up. The officers would report what they had found and would wait to see if McLachlan appeared somewhere or if he was a missing person. There was nothing to be done until they found out more. Maybe he had gone back to Minnesota to see his family. Maybe he had just struck out for Arizona or Mexico or somewhere else he could start over again with a new name and identity.

But it was getting late and Zachary didn't want to take the chance of being tardy for Pat's dinner. He got back into his car and made the journey back to Pat and Lorne's house.

He got a broad grin from Mr. Peterson when he stepped in the door. "You made it!"

Zachary looked at the time on his phone. "Plenty of time for a shower and shave," he suggested.

"Yes. All yours. Thank you, Zachary. I just wanted… I know how much Pat has been looking forward to introducing you to his family. It's important for him to… be able to bring both parts of his life back together into one integrated whole. To… be himself, one hundred percent, and not have to be different things for different people."

Zachary nodded slowly. There had always been that rift in Pat's life. He didn't make a big deal of it. He seemed happy most of the time and rarely referred to his family, but Zachary knew that he had been hoping to reunite with his family one day. And now that he had… to merge the two lives into one.

"I'd better get ready." He touched Mr. Peterson on the arm and walked past him to get himself ready for the dinner.

Zachary paced around the house restlessly, waiting for Pat's family to arrive so that he could get through the initial awkward stages of introduction and conversation. The house was tidier than usual, with reading materials and projects put away, and all decor carefully reviewed and adjusted. Pat was in his glory in the kitchen.

He had made several varieties of ravioli and the sweet and spicy scent filled the air. Some spring potatoes and vegetables rounded the meal out, and there were a couple of bottles of wine to choose from.

On one hand, Zachary was anxious about meeting Pat's family, but the other part of his brain was occupied with trying to unwind the problem of Forest McLachlan. Where had he gone? Had he been warned of the investigation and fled? Or had he been taken against his will? He was comforted by the fact that there was no blood or sign of violence at the man's apartment, but the phone and packed bag were out of place. They didn't fit with the idea that McLachlan had just left of his own accord.

The police would probably reach out to his friends and family, see whether anyone knew where he was or if they had any concerns. But what if no one knew anything and the trail got cold? What if the BOLO on his car never turned anything up?

Was it possible that Gordon had been involved in Forest's disappearance?

As things stood, Zachary wasn't about to call Gordon again. His client had still not returned his text message from that morning but, considering what he might have to say about Zachary's unfortunate call to the house, Zachary figured he could use some time to cool down before they spoke.

There was nothing more Zachary could do for Gordon that evening. The case was, more than likely, closed. Gordon had all of the information that it would be possible to gather for him.

30

"I think they're here," Lorne called out, peering out the window of the living room. "Yes, that's them. Pat!"

Pat hurried out of the kitchen, wiping damp hands on the towel over his shoulder. He smoothed his already-perfect hair and raised eyebrows at Zachary.

"This is it!"

Zachary swallowed and nodded.

"You don't need to look like I'm throwing you to the lions," Pat said with a grin. "Really, they're not going to eat you."

He walked to the door and threw it open to greet his family.

He ushered an older woman into the house. While Zachary knew she must be in at least her seventies, she didn't look it. She had black hair and pink cheeks and not very many wrinkles. She stood up straight, her full height about even with Zachary's.

Patrick's sister was a younger, softer, taller version of her mother. Her hair was a little lighter, but Zachary suspected they probably were both dye jobs. Pat himself was starting to go gray, his appearance at odds with the way Zachary still pictured him when they were apart, as the broad-shouldered, athletic-looking man in his mid-thirties that he had been when they had first met. Not a lot about him had changed in his appearance, aside from the graying temples and some fine lines around his eyes and mouth.

After hugging both women, Pat ushered them over to meet Zachary.

"Zachary, I'd like to introduce Gretta and Suzanne Parker, my mom and sister. Mom, Suzie: Zachary Goldman."

"A pleasure to meet you," Gretta said immediately, holding out a hand to shake Zachary's. He took her firm, dry hand, and hoped that his was not too clammy by comparison. He turned to shake Suzanne's hand as well, but she put her arms around him and pulled him in for a hug.

"No need for formalities!" she insisted. "You're family, right?"

Zachary was startled, but submitted to the hug and stepped back slightly when she released him. He smiled at her.

"Yes. Family," he agreed.

"Let me have a look at my grandson," Gretta said, giving Suzanne a little nudge to the side. She gazed into Zachary's face, her eyes sharp, but not critical. "There's not much of a family resemblance, is there?" she cracked.

Everyone laughed. Zachary shook his head. "Afraid not. It's very nice to meet you."

"Well, it probably should not have taken this long," Gretta admitted. She gave a little sigh and looked up at her son. "We lost a lot of years, and I have no one to blame but myself for that."

"And Dad," Suzanne reminded her.

"I should have stood up to him. Should have said that I just wasn't putting up with that nonsense. But… I thought…" She looked at Pat again, apologetic. "Well, twenty years ago, we had some very different views on homosexuality. There were a lot of proponents for tough love, conversion therapy, keeping gays out of the churches, that kind of thing. We were told that if we made our position clear and refused to associate with Patrick as long as he was 'acting out,' that he would come to see the errors of his ways."

Pat shook his head ruefully. "I did want to see you," he told her firmly. "But… I had to be who I am."

"We heard about families that it had worked for," Gretta said. "They just held out for a few months… or a couple of years… and eventually, their wayward child came back again. Settled down, got married, had babies."

"And were miserable," Pat said. "I knew a lot of gay men and women who died, too. They couldn't bear being cut off from their families, but they couldn't be what society expected them to be. They couldn't live with the pain."

Gretta's mouth turned downward in a deep frown. Zachary didn't know if he would have had the courage to say something like that to her. To point out how much pain their decision had caused Pat over the years.

"Let's sit down," Mr. Peterson suggested, motioning to the living room.

"Actually, if you want to go straight to the table, everything is ready to go," Pat announced. He pulled the towel off of his shoulder, smiling. "Lorne, you get everyone settled and I'll bring out the food."

The painful moment put behind them, everyone cheered up and moved to the table, excited to dig into the ravioli that smelled so heavenly.

"Did you teach him to cook?" Zachary asked Gretta. "He really has a talent for it."

"Only the basics. I wanted my kids to be able to look after themselves. The rest he's taught himself. My mother was an excellent cook. Maybe he got it from her."

"I remember cooking with Bubba," Pat said, bringing a covered dish to the table. "She made such good food!"

"She did," Gretta agreed. Suzanne nodded.

They got settled around the table, Zachary sitting with Mr. Peterson on his right so that he had an anchor among the unfamiliar faces. There was some light chatter as Pat finished bringing the various dishes to the dining room table. They all exclaimed over each dish as it was uncovered and passed around.

"Now, you know you don't have to cook fancy every time we come," Gretta said sternly. "We can eat sandwiches or macaroni or a frozen pizza. It's the company we want; you don't have to spend hours in the kitchen for us."

"Not that we don't like this," Suzanne inserted.

"Of course, we love this. Who wouldn't?" Gretta agreed. "But you don't have to do something special every time. And sometime, you can come home and I will cook for you. Or not cook for you. Depending on how I feel."

Zachary could see where Pat got his down-to-earth nature. He'd always made Zachary feel comfortable and at home, no matter what Zachary threw at him.

"I enjoy cooking. It relaxes me. And this meal is special, because it's the first time that you and Zachary have met."

"Yes," Gretta agreed. "Just don't feel like you've set a precedent that you have to follow every time. So far, we've only had special occasions, but at some point, we'll want to have just casual visits too."

Zachary knew he had put too much of the intoxicating food on his plate. He'd never be able to eat it all. But he didn't want to look like he didn't appreciate it, either. If everybody else had full plates and he only had a couple of spoonfuls of food, they might think that he didn't appreciate the work that Pat had done or that he was a picky eater.

Mr. Peterson glanced at his plate and raised an eyebrow, fully aware that Zachary would never eat that much.

"Patrick said that you're a private detective," Gretta said, looking across the table at Zachary and taking a bite of pasta.

"Yes," Zachary agreed. "But don't think that it's the romanticized job that you see on TV. It isn't anything like that."

"I don't imagine so!" Gretta agreed. "I've always thought those shows were pretty unbelievable. But they are entertaining. So what kind of a private detective are you? What sorts of files do you get?"

"A variety," Zachary said with a shrug. He took a small bite of the cheese ravioli, which melted in his mouth. "Mmm," he looked over at Pat, "this is wonderful." Then back to Gretta. "I don't do a lot of high-profile cases. Mostly small stuff. Surveilling spouses or employees. Doing accident scene reconstruction. Skip tracing. Those are the bread and butter, jobs that will always be around."

"But you have done some murders and others that have made it into the media. I've seen some of the coverage. And you helped with that poor boy that Patrick knew."

"Yes." Zachary glanced over at Pat, not wanting to make him feel bad about what had happened to Jose. "I have done a few of those cases."

"What are you working on right now? Anything interesting?"

Zachary thought about his workload. "Mostly the routine stuff. One of my sisters is helping out now with some of the research and skip tracing. I've been working on one case—just wrapping it up, really—that involves paternity issues."

"A cheating spouse?"

"That's the way that it looked at the start. But it looks like it might have been fraudulently committed by one of the workers at the fertility clinic they used."

"Really!" Gretta shook her head. "That's terrible! How could something like that happen? Don't they have safeguards?"

"Not that will stop men from using their own sperm or mixing their own into a sample. Their security is all against outside parties, and all of their protocols inside are to prevent accidental mix-ups. Not intentional contamination. How would you stop something like that?"

"Well…" Gretta's forehead creased, "there has to be a way."

"If someone is really intent on it, I'm not sure there is anything they could do to stop them."

"They must do the fertilization in a controlled environment. They search people as they come in… keep surveillance cameras on them… film the whole process…"

"Pretty hard to keep eyes on people every second, even with surveillance cameras. What is going on below the tables? What about sleight of hand while fertilizing a sample? You have to assume people are honest and not trying to game the system."

Gretta wrinkled her nose. "How disgusting. Well. I'm never going to one of those places."

Suzanne and Pat burst out laughing. Zachary wasn't sure how to respond to Gretta's declaration. Of course as a seventy-something she had no need for a fertility clinic.

Gretta gave Zachary a small smile, letting him know that she was only joking.

"Well, I agree," Zachary agreed. "I don't think that would be a good idea."

"Would you? With what you know now?"

Zachary considered the question. "Well… if it was the only way to conceive. I guess I would. Bridget—my ex-wife—she had to have her eggs frozen before she had treatment for her cancer. So there wasn't really any other option."

"Then adopt," Suzanne put in. "There are a lot of kids out there who would give anything for a family."

Pat looked over at Zachary for his reaction. The angle he held his head at told Zachary that he was ready to step in and shut down the conversation if he thought it was bothering Zachary.

Zachary swallowed and shrugged. "Most of the kids in foster care are not infants, which is what people want. There are fewer and fewer babies available for adoption all the time, because of improved birth control, abortion being available, and people waiting until they are older to start families."

"How selfish is it to only take an infant when there are so many other kids in care?" Suzanne looked at Mr. Peterson. "You were a foster parent for a while, right? So you saw what it was like. How much love those kids need."

Mr. Peterson looked at Zachary.

Zachary nodded at him.

"I saw kids with very high needs in foster care," Mr. Peterson said. "Most of them were not free for adoption and a regular family would not have been able to deal with their needs."

"But there must still be a lot who could go to forever families. Take the pressure off the system. Give people the children they want but can't have."

Mr. Peterson took a few bites of his dinner, not answering.

"Like Zachary," Gretta said. "You were one of the Petersons' foster kids, and you kept in touch with him all this time. You would have been adopted if you could have, wouldn't you?"

Zachary shook his head. "I wanted to go back to my biological family, I wasn't interested in adoption. I was ten when I went into foster care, too old for adoption. And family groups… you hear about people adopting whole families sometimes on TV, but it's so rare… that's why it's news."

Zachary toyed with his vegetables, looking for something to do with his hands so that he didn't have to look at Gretta or Suzanne.

"Even if everything had lined up… I couldn't have managed in a family. I was in institutional care a lot of the time. Group homes, therapeutic settings, care centers. I was too…" He looked at Lorne, trying to find the words.

"Zachary came to us from a very traumatic background," Mr. Peterson explained. "He had some very difficult issues to work through. We were not able to keep him, and we had all of the necessary training. A couple who didn't have experience dealing with high-needs, traumatized kids… the kind of family who is looking to start a new family together… things would not have turned out well."

Gretta focused on her meal. Suzanne darted glances at Zachary, wondering about him and his background. Zachary didn't know how much

Pat and Mr. Peterson had previously told them about him. Probably not enough for them to understand what he was talking about.

"I still have a lot of issues," he explained. "I'm on medications and regular therapy. And I still have cycles of severe depression, panic attacks, flashbacks. PTSD."

"You look so normal," Suzanne observed.

Zachary rolled his eyes, not sure how to answer that one.

"Having people adopt from the system is not a reasonable replacement for reproductive technology," Pat said. "Some adoptions from foster care turn out great. But it has a very high failure rate. Zachary did well to be able to carve out his niche and find a way to earn a living and stay on the right side of the law. A lot of foster kids end up homeless, addicts, unqualified or unable to find work, or in prison. It's not a perfect system."

"So what is your client going to do now that they know what happened?" Gretta asked, returning to the original topic. "Are they going to sue him? Make him pay child support or something? Is there such as thing as a wrongful birth suit?"

"I suspect they're going to terminate the pregnancy. That was the original suggestion. My client was hoping to avoid it. Not sure she'll ever agree to get pregnant again, and he would like to have a child with her."

"Tough luck for him," Suzanne said unsympathetically.

Zachary tried to swallow the lump in his throat. He hated to think of Bridget terminating her pregnancy. She had never wanted his children, but he had longed for hers. But biology worked against Zachary. He couldn't take on pregnancy, labor, and nursing a baby. He could help to care for a child once it was born, but he couldn't step in and take the rest of the burden away from Bridget. And she hadn't ever considered adoption either.

And now, it was going to be her choice not to have them with Gordon either.

On the one hand, Zachary felt a little vindicated. At least that was one way that Gordon was not better than he was. He had thought that Gordon would step in and become the father that Zachary had always wanted to be. But Gordon couldn't. As successful as he was, as competent in everything, he could not control that.

"How did they find out the baby was not his if it hasn't even been born yet?" Pat asked, cocking his head slightly. "I was thinking it was something in the baby's physical features that had tipped them off. Wrong color of skin or eyes."

Zachary shook his head. "They did prenatal genetic testing to make sure that everything was okay… and found out that the baby had a genetic disease that isn't in either of their families."

"Oh." Pat nodded his understanding. "Yeah, I guess that would do it."

"I have a friend who has that breast cancer gene," Suzanne said. "She's so paranoid about passing it on to her children, she was having IVF and they were testing each embryo for the gene, so that she would only have children without it."

"She had breast cancer?" Gretta asked.

"No. Just the gene that predicts that she has an eighty percent chance of getting it, or something like that. I don't even know the percentages."

"She didn't have any symptoms? They screen for breast cancer so they can catch it right away."

"No, Mom," Suzanne said with exaggerated patience. "She didn't have cancer. She didn't have any symptoms. It probably won't develop until later in life. She won't have symptoms until then."

Zachary remembered what Patton had said about the dangers of reproductive technology, the birth defects and other problems it could cause. He wondered whether Suzanne's friend had been told that. Screen for a known danger like the BRCA1 gene and end up with a child with a hundred times higher chance of getting hepatoblastoma or another fast-growing childhood cancer. Or blindness. Or CP.

If Bridget chose to raise the babies, she would never have to worry about getting Huntington's herself, but she would have to watch her children growing up, knowing that one day they were going to develop it.

She would see one of her daughters starting to develop more erratic, irrational behavior. Maybe get violent. She would know what was happening because they had done the testing. But they wouldn't be able to do anything to stop the progression of the disease.

31

Something suddenly clicked into place.

Zachary's brain clicked into high gear as he suddenly saw everything from a different angle. His ADHD brain started spinning through all the possibilities.

"Zachary?"

He didn't move. He didn't want anything to interrupt the moment of clarity.

They'd been wrong about everything.

Everything.

Zachary heard his fork fall from his hand with a clatter.

He pushed back his chair, murmuring an apology.

"Zachary? Is everything okay? What is it?"

He groped his way to his room and picked up the notepad he'd left on the bed. He started writing it all down. His hand couldn't keep up with his thoughts, and he knew he wasn't getting all of the missing pieces written down, but he persevered, trying to wring it all out of his brain and come up with a clear picture.

He didn't know how much time had passed when Mr. Peterson came into the bedroom.

"Hey, Zach. Are you okay? What's going on?"

Zachary blinked at him. "I just figured it out. I can't believe I didn't see it before."

"See what?"

"We were wrong about everything, start to finish. We started with the wrong premise."

"Uh… we're going to take the ladies out for ice cream. Do you want to come along? Or do you want me to pick something up for you?"

"No. I need to make a plan. Figure out what to do next."

"Ice cream. Do you want some?" Lorne persisted.

Kenzie had found that ice cream was something that Zachary could usually manage, even when he was nauseated and didn't have an appetite. And his doctor approved of a fatty, sugary treat to help him with his weight gain.

"I don't know. I guess if you see something that I would like."

"Chocolate? Maple Walnut? Do you have a favorite?"

"Anything." Zachary flipped through the pages of his notepad. "Cherry Jubilee. Kenzie likes the blue ones. Raspberry. Bubble Gum."

"Kenzie isn't here."

"Right." Zachary stared at the pages. How had he not seen it before?

It seemed like they were only gone for a few minutes and then they were back again. Mr. Peterson brought back a pint of Cherry Jubilee ice cream and put a scoop in a dessert bowl for Zachary but, by the time he paid any attention to it, it was just a puddle of sweet, cherry-spotted goo.

"Do you need anything?" Mr. Peterson asked before heading to bed.

Zachary realized that the house had been quiet for some time. He rubbed his head.

"Did I… did I screw everything up with Pat's family? I left right in the middle of dinner, didn't I? I'm sorry."

"It's fine. They wanted to meet you, and they got their opportunity. They understood that you were working a case. Sometimes inspiration strikes at the most inconvenient moment."

"Thanks. I really didn't mean to leave you all in the lurch like that."

"Do you want something to eat? You didn't finish your supper." Mr. Peterson smiled. "Not that I expected you to eat everything that you dished up! But I think you only had about three bites, and it doesn't look like you made a dent in that ice cream."

"Yeah… I'll have some tomorrow before I leave. Is Pat still up? I should tell him that I enjoyed everything… meeting his family and the dinner…"

"He was pretty wiped out after everything he did the last few days to get ready. He took a pill and headed to bed a while ago."

"Oh. I'll talk to him tomorrow, then. Was he upset?"

"No. It's fine. Talk to him in the morning."

"Okay. Don't let me forget."

"I'll remind you tomorrow, then. Are you going to stay around tomorrow?"

"I might need to go. I have to follow up on this lead."

"Will it wait one more day?"

"I suppose." Zachary considered. Gordon hadn't called him back. The police were not likely to find anything out about McLachlan. If Bridget made her decision that night or the next day, Zachary couldn't do anything about it.

"Then maybe you should take a day off. You worked most of today. Give your body and brain a break. You'll be more productive on Monday."

"Maybe."

"Do you need anything before I hit the sack? You look like you have a headache."

Zachary continued to knead his forehead with his knuckles. "Yeah… I guess I do."

"Your body's way of telling you you've had enough. You want a Tylenol?"

Zachary hesitated. He usually just tried to 'tough out' his headaches. He didn't like to take anything he didn't have to. With the meds he was taking regularly, interactions were always a danger, and he didn't know when his body chemistry might change and he would have a bad reaction he hadn't had before. Or something would stop working. It was best not to mess with the delicately balanced system.

"I guess… just one Tylenol, yeah," he agreed finally.

Mr. Peterson nodded. "I'll get you one."

One precaution that he and Pat had taken was to keep all medications in their bedroom rather than in the bathroom, so that when Zachary was in the darkest depths of depression, it wouldn't be right there in front of him. One less thing to worry about.

Lorne returned with a pill and a glass of water. He watched Zachary take it. "And you've got everything else you need?"

"Yeah. I'm not taking anything else before bed."

The older man nodded. "Good. All right. I'll see you in the morning. Try to get some sleep."

Like Zachary, Mr. Peterson knew that with Zachary's brain spinning through all of the possibilities, he wasn't likely to get more than an hour or two of restless sleep.

It wasn't easy to do as Mr. Peterson had suggested and just take a day off. He wanted to be following up on the new leads. It would wait, but waiting was excruciating.

But Zachary felt like he owed it to Pat to stay and be sociable for another day. To talk to him about his mom and sister and how interesting they had been. He raved about how good the food had been, and had a little of the Cherry Jubilee ice cream for breakfast.

"So… what did you figure out?" Pat asked as he sat back in his chair, sipping his coffee. "Was it on the case that you were talking about?"

"Yeah, it is. I can't talk about any details, but I just realized that I'd been looking at everything the wrong way. I know better than to make assumptions, but you always do… there are always things that you have to assume or take for granted as being true when you start on a case."

"It's pretty hard to challenge every fact," Pat suggested.

"Yes. But I know that clients don't always tell the truth. They keep things back. They have secrets that they don't want you to know about."

"And you think that your client in this case lied to you?"

"They usually do… even if they don't know that they are."

"That sounds very complicated. How are you supposed to solve a case when they lie to you? Especially if *they* don't know they're lying?"

Zachary thought back to his last big case. Ben Burton. He had told Zachary repeatedly that he didn't have any siblings and that he didn't remember what had happened to him as a child. But Zachary had known that those were lies. He had been able to tell by Burton's body language, even if he hadn't known it himself.

"Sometimes you can figure it out by what they say or don't say, by facial expression or body language, the way they react to something. And sometimes… nothing fits until you figure out what the lie was."

Mr. Peterson had been sitting quietly, listening to them. Zachary thought that Pat needed his personal attention, and Mr. Peterson realized that. He was always so perceptive about his partner's emotional state.

"Zachary… this case…"

"Yeah?"

"You're not working for Bridget's husband again, are you?"

Zachary supposed he'd given that away when he called Gordon's home number by mistake and Lorne had overheard him talking with Bridget.

"Well… I can't really tell you who I'm working for."

Mr. Peterson pondered on this, taking another sip of his coffee.

"Do you really think that you should be working this case? Doesn't it… hit a little too close to home?"

Zachary cleared his throat and took another small spoonful of Cherry Jubilee. "It's, uh… had its moments."

"You probably shouldn't have taken it. Don't you have to recuse yourself if you have a personal bias?"

Zachary laughed. "No. I'm not a judge or even a cop. Gordon—if I was working for Gordon—he already knows my… personal bias."

"He shouldn't have come to you. Really. It wasn't a good idea."

"Maybe not," Zachary admitted. "I wasn't sure about taking it. It took some talking me into it. But he knows I'm the best man for the job."

"I'm not sure that's true. You don't have any objectivity."

And that had ended up being his big mistake. Maybe if it hadn't been a case involving Bridget and Gordon, he would have seen what was right in his face all along.

32

Zachary was relieved to finally be making his way back to his apartment. He would go back to Kenzie's Monday night, after he'd had a chance to pursue his investigations. And maybe by that time, he would have everything wrapped up and would be able to tell her a few choice, non-identifying details. She would be curious how the case had turned out.

At his apartment, he showered, shaved, and changed into a neat shirt and pants, looking better than his usual just-short-of-homeless look. It might even be an interview that he should have worn a suit to, but he didn't have a suit, and he was afraid that might be too much.

Despite his certainty that he was right and the urgent need to find out, he was anxious.

It had been years since he had seen or spoken to Bridget's parents.

And she had undoubtedly had plenty to say about him during that time. She would have vented about Zachary and his issues regularly. He was going to be working against a wall of preconceived ideas about him.

Hence the upgraded clothing and clean shave.

Both were now retired. Zachary was sure they were still active in social circles. Like Bridget, they had always been very concerned about appearances and about people knowing how they were serving their community. So there was no guarantee they would be home when Zachary rang the doorbell. But it was still early in the day, and he didn't think they would be gone yet. Most fundraisers didn't start earlier than brunch. Not the ones Bridget had dragged Zachary to, anyway.

Mr. Downy opened the door. After a moment of blankness, his eyes widened when he saw Zachary there and realized who he was. He took a step back as if Zachary were being aggressive. His first reaction to seeing Zachary was that he shouldn't be there. They shouldn't be talking to each other. Mr. Downy hesitated, thinking about this instinctive reaction.

He looked past Zachary, as if he expected to see Bridget there. But when they had been together, Bridget had never stood behind Zachary. She was always out in front, self-confident, wanting to be the first one in.

"Zachary. What are you doing here?"

Zachary cleared his throat. "I'm worried about Bridget."

Mr. Downy considered this. Then he stepped back, opening the door wider to usher Zachary in.

"Honey, who was at the door?" The diminutive woman who was Bridget's mother came out of the living room to see. She stopped short when she saw Zachary, then looked at her husband. He nodded to the living room and they all went in and sat down. Zachary shifted anxiously, wanting to be standing or walking around rather than sitting still. But he needed to look calm and reasonable. He couldn't afford to let them see his wild imaginings and how fast his brain was turning. They would write him off as just being mentally ill and not worth listening to. Any drama or emotion would just be proof that all of the things Bridget said about him were true.

"What's this all about?" Mrs. Downy asked uncertainly. She looked out the window like she too was searching for Bridget's yellow Beetle. If Zachary was there, then Bridget must be too. That was how they had been conditioned.

"I came here because I'm worried about Bridget. I know you probably don't want to see me, with the way that things turned out. But I needed to talk to you… to figure this out."

"Worried about her how?" Mrs. Downy asked. "Bridget is okay. I just talked to her yesterday. She said she's starting to feel better."

"I don't mean about her physical condition… the pregnancy."

"Then what?" As far as Zachary knew, Mr. Downy had never served in the military, but that was always how Zachary pictured him. As a captain or sergeant. Crisp and in control, commanding and demanding exacting behavior from everyone around him.

"Gordon called you before?" Zachary suggested, "To ask you about some family medical history questions?"

"Yes," Mr. Downy agreed. He looked at his wife, then back at Zachary. "What does that have to do with anything?"

"Did you know why he was asking?"

"Because of the pregnancy. He wanted to know what diseases might run in the family. To be prepared for any issues the babies might have." Mr. Downy shrugged. "I don't really see the point. Parents today are so paranoid about the future. But they have to wait and see what happens, just like we did. Nothing has changed."

"A lot has changed as far as medical care and being able to predict problems," Zachary countered. "And a lot of diseases, if you can catch them early, they are much more treatable. The outcomes are much better. Look at Bridget's cancer. A generation ago, it would have been a death sentence. Now she is in remission."

"So the babies might have a predisposition toward ovarian cancer. That's good to know," Mr. Downy admitted. "But you can't predict everything that's going to strike. It's not all genetic."

"But some things are. Some things, they can find in DNA testing."

"If they can find it in DNA testing, then what is the point of a family medical history?" Mrs. Downy put in. She was small and pretty, like a china doll. She always looked perfectly made up and turned out. Zachary supposed that was where Bridget got her good looks.

Zachary rubbed his palms along his pants, trying to dry the sweat and make himself feel more calm and prepared for the conversation.

"Did Gordon tell you that they had done prenatal DNA testing on the babies?"

They both looked shocked at this revelation. They didn't need to tell Zachary 'no' audibly. Their widening eyes and exchanged look told him everything he needed to know.

"How can they do that?" Mrs. Downy asked. "Do they… put a needle into her belly? And into the babies? That sounds very dangerous and unnecessary."

"I'm not sure what method they used," Zachary said. "They can get cells from the amniotic fluid, or from Bridget's bloodstream. They don't have to take it directly from the babies. But I don't know which method they used."

"They should just wait and see," Mr. Downy asserted. "That's how it's always been done. Just enjoy the anticipation of the birth and see what happens after the baby is born. Chances are, everything is going to be just fine. Why spend all of that time worrying?"

Zachary wasn't there to argue the morality of finding out the babies' genetic issues before birth. It had already been done. There was no point in discussing that particular issue any further.

"Bridget had the DNA testing done already. They got the results back, and that was why Gordon was asking you about family medical history."

"We don't have any family history of anything bad," Mrs. Downy said. "Most of our relatives have lived long lives. They die of old age. Heart, I suppose. Eventually, things just wear out."

"You haven't had anyone die young?" Zachary challenged. "Maybe due to accidents?"

"How would that be relevant to family medical history?" Mr. Downy put in, shaking his head. "Accidents aren't genetic. You can't inherit them. You can't get anything from people who died young, before they had a chance to get any diseases."

"But if they died young, you don't know what they might have carried that would develop later in life. If they have a disease that they wouldn't show symptoms of until they were sixty or seventy, and they died when they were fifty, you wouldn't know what they carried."

"And what would it matter?" Mr. Downy asked.

"Because it might mean that there was a predisposition to a disease hidden in your family tree that had never been recognized."

Mr. Downy waved this idea away. "We haven't had a lot of people die young. I don't think that's relevant."

Zachary looked from one to the other. "Does either of you have dementia in your family? Even if it's never been diagnosed. Someone who was experiencing confusion or mood swings before they died? Or having difficulty walking?"

Neither offered any suggestions. No 'Aunt Mary' or 'Great Grandma Downy.' They both just looked at him.

"I don't see how this is an issue," Mr. Downy said. "You said that you came here because you had concerns about Bridget. What business is it of yours what diseases we have in our family?"

Zachary attempted to move the conversation forward. "I am concerned about Bridget right now. That's why I came. I haven't had a lot of contact with her the last couple of years, of course, just chance encounters now and then. But it seems like… she's been getting angrier at me rather than less. I kind of figured that she would start to ease off after we'd been apart for a while. Sometimes she seems… like her old self. But other times… have you noticed more mood swings?"

"That's just the hormones," Mrs. Downy dismissed. "You don't know what it's like. The hormones when you're pregnant are so brutal. I don't think a man can understand it."

"I understand mood swings. I know what it's like to feel out of control. But… I think her behavior was changing before she got pregnant. Don't you?"

Mr. Downy shook his head resolutely. "I don't know what you're talking about."

"Even before we got divorced… she had changed. I thought at the time that she had just decided she couldn't deal with my issues anymore. You don't really know how many problems a person has until you live with them for a while. But now I wonder…"

"Wonder what?" Mrs. Downy demanded. "I think it's just like you said. She didn't know how hard it was going to be until she'd been with you for a while. She knew in her head, but she hadn't experienced it. She didn't know how stressful it was going to be."

"And she was so sick after that," Mr. Downy said. "She was just so sick and weak with cancer and the treatments. She needed to live for herself. Not for someone else. If she hadn't been focused on her own emotional health, she would never have survived it."

"So you don't think that anything has changed, over time. You think she's still the same woman as she was before she and I met."

"People do change," Mrs. Downy pointed out. "They change because of their experiences."

"I don't think that's it," Zachary said slowly. "I'm worried that… she has Huntington's Disease."

33

Mr. and Mrs. Downy's reactions were different. Mr. Downy looked angry, furious that Zachary would suggest such a thing. Mrs. Downy looked terrified. She alternated between looking at Zachary and at her husband, waiting for one of them to speak.

"There is no Huntington's Disease in our family," Mr. Downy finally said in a tight voice, his anger barely controlled.

"There are rare occasions where a child can have it even though the parents didn't. Or there may have been cases in the family that only had a few symptoms, or didn't occur until much later in life, so it was never diagnosed." Zachary swallowed, looking into Mr. Downy's cold, angry eyes. "There are cases where the parents didn't have it," he repeated. "Where it was a first-time mutation."

"You are not a doctor."

"No, I'm not."

"You can't make a diagnosis like that. And even if you were a doctor, you haven't examined her. You haven't run any tests. You can't just know out of the blue that she had something like that."

"No," Zachary agreed. "But it *isn't* out of the blue. Her babies have the gene for Huntington's Disease."

"So it is like you said, they have this mutation, she did not."

"Both babies?"

"If they are identical twins, they would both have it, wouldn't they?"

Zachary wasn't sure. He considered, and nodded slowly. "Yes… maybe. But look at Bridget. Look at the changes over the past few years. Look at how she has become more moody and angry. Her personality has changed."

Mr. Downy shook his head, but Mrs. Downy was not shaking hers. Her eyes were wide with fear, but she didn't deny it like her husband.

"She *has* changed," Zachary said to Mrs. Downy. "You can see that too, can't you? She's different than she was before we got married. And it isn't just bitterness from the marriage. There's been something else going on. Don't you think so?"

Mrs. Downy looked at her husband as if she needed his permission to agree with Zachary, and when he didn't give it to her, she looked down at her folded hands in her lap and didn't agree or disagree with Zachary. He thought he detected a slight tremor in her cheek. She was trying to keep her emotions under control. Staying calm and collected in front of her daughter's ex. Trying not to crack and show any weakness.

"I think it's time for you to leave," Mr. Downy said, rising to his feet.

"You haven't had any concerns about her?" Zachary asked helplessly, sliding forward in his seat to get up. "If she's diagnosed, they might be able to help her, to slow its progression. Give her a normal life for a few years longer…"

Mr. Downy glared down at him. But Zachary could see that his eyes were shiny with tears. He wasn't quite as angry and confident as he pretended to be. Of course he was worried about his daughter. Maybe he had been raised not to show any un-manly emotions, but that didn't mean he didn't have feelings. If Zachary could see Bridget's changed behavior as clearly as he did, Mr. Downy must be able to see it even more clearly. Unless it was one of those things that was harder to notice when you saw the person every day. Maybe he had been too close to her to notice the gradual progression.

But Zachary was sure that Mrs. Downy, at least, recognized the truth of what Zachary said.

He stayed sitting where he was, giving it a few more seconds to see if they were going to send him on his way or whether he could draw out the conversation and get them onside.

"I don't want it to be true either," Zachary said. "And if you really can't see it, if you really haven't seen any changes in her over the past couple of years and it is just me… then so be it. Maybe I'm just more sensitive to her moods after being away from her. But some of the things that she's done in the last little while… have been very out of character." He pushed himself to his feet. "That's what I think, anyway."

Mrs. Downy rose as well. She looked at her husband and put her hand on his arm. Finally, Mr. Downy nodded, giving in.

"Fine," he said with a long sigh. "Maybe there have been changes. But people do change over time. They decide they're not going to put up with being pushed around anymore. They act differently when they're under stress, or when they've had a serious illness or a near-death experience. They even said that some of the cancer treatments could have an effect on her personality. Things can change; that doesn't mean she has Huntington's Disease."

"No. But if she does, it's better she gets diagnosed now, isn't it? So they can treat it and help her."

Mrs. Downy shook her head. "There isn't anything they can do. It's not something they can fix."

"They might be able to slow down its progress. And they say that a cure isn't far away. Maybe not soon enough for Bridget…" He tried to swallow the painful lump that swelled up in his throat. "But what about the babies? There could be a cure in time for them."

"She won't keep them," Mrs. Downy said. "If she thinks there's something wrong with them, she won't risk it."

"Maybe if she knows there will be a cure… or at least that there's a good chance…"

"She won't," Mrs. Downy repeated with certainty. "I know she won't. I'm surprised she hasn't had an abortion already." She sniffled and touched her hand to the end of her nose as if trying to stifle a sneeze. But Zachary knew there was far more behind the gesture than the tickle of a sneeze.

"Sit down," Mr. Downy said, and they all sat again. Zachary rubbed his palms on his knees, thinking.

"She needs to be tested. She needs to go to the doctor and be tested."

"I'd like to see you talk her into that," Mr. Downy said with a sharp bark of laughter.

"I'm probably not the best person to talk to her. But you…"

Mr. Downy shook his head. "*Him*, then. Gordon."

Zachary nodded. "He's a lot better at managing her than I ever was."

"He's nothing like you," Mrs. Downy agreed. She gave a little shake of her head. "I wish that things had worked out between the two of you."

Zachary was surprised. He'd never felt like he had the approval of either of them. Bridget kept trying to mold him into something that would be more acceptable to her family, but hadn't been able to change him like she wanted to. So he'd always known that he didn't fit in with them. That they probably wished every time they saw him that Bridget had picked someone else.

Someone more like them. Someone more like Gordon.

"Gordon is very successful," he said to Mrs. Downy, unable to understand why she would say such a thing. "He's patient and persuasive and wealthy. And handsome. All the things that I am not."

"And you are many things that he is not," she pointed out. "And could never be."

Zachary could think of a lot of his traits that Gordon would never have. Nor would he ever want to have them.

"I can't understand Bridget not wanting to have children," Mrs. Downy said, smoothing wrinkles from her pants as if it were a job that required her close attention. "The pull of motherhood is very strong. It's a woman's natural inclination. I can't understand her attitude about not wanting to have children. She says she doesn't want to ruin her body with pregnancy, but it isn't that. It's much more than that." She shook her head thoughtfully. "I always wanted children. When we got married, I was so excited to become a mother. Every month, I waited for the signs that I was with child. Every time I wasn't, an ache grew in my heart. It became unbearable."

Zachary nodded. That was a feeling he could understand. He longed for children himself, and most women seemed to have an even stronger instinct for nurturing.

"There weren't clinics like this when I was a young woman," Mrs. Downy went on. "All of this technology is new. IVF… it was so new; it wasn't something that you could go to the doctor for. It was brand new."

"That must have been difficult for you."

Mrs. Downy nodded. She continued to look down. The conversation lagged. Zachary looked for a way to carry it forward.

"And it has been scary for you, seeing the changes in Bridget, wondering what was going on. Huntington's Disease is a terrifying prospect. I don't know if you know anything about it…"

She didn't move or answer.

Zachary looked at Mr. Downy. He was staring at a thick book in the bookcase closest to him. Zachary had seen books like that before. He remembered Burton's foster mother pulling a thick volume off of the shelf and leafing through the pages of pictures of all of their foster children.

He had seen pictures of Bridget with her parents. Pregnancy shots of Mrs. Downy. Bridget as a newborn, cuddled in her mother's arms, Mrs. Downy looking at the camera with sparkling eyes and a contented smile.

At their wedding reception, there had been a long picture montage of Bridget growing up, going through all of the different ages and stages, from infancy up through to adulthood, growing lovelier all the time. Her parents were always doting on her. It was the kind of life that Zachary could only imagine. A life where there was plenty to go around, parents who cared for her physically and emotionally, one consistent home from the time she was a baby until she was grown. Even now, as a grown woman, her parents were still there for her, fighting her battles and standing by her side.

Zachary got up and retrieved the photo album. Neither of them stopped him. He paged through it, looking at Bridget's life in reverse, starting at the back and working his way toward the front. There were no ultrasound pictures, but there was that first picture of Mrs. Downy, looking down and her baby bump, two hands wrapped around it as she thought about the baby kicking inside of her.

"We didn't have all of those options they have today," Mrs. Downy said. "Every month that went by…"

Zachary looked at her, blinking. He looked down at the photo album in his lap. Mrs. Downy was there, holding her pregnant tummy. Anticipating the birth. Clearly, something had worked. He looked back up at her. What was it she was afraid to tell him? Had they used a sperm donor? Maybe Mr. Downy hadn't been able to produce children himself, and she had been forced to go through other channels, seeking out someone who was willing to father her child. Maybe *that* was where the Huntington's Disease had come from.

34

What happened?" he asked her softly. "You eventually managed to get pregnant."

She shook her head slowly.

"But you did," Zachary repeated, indicating the picture. "You were pregnant here."

"No. I wasn't."

He stared at the picture, not understanding.

"It was a prop," Mr. Downy said gruffly. "Back then… that's what some people did. Pretended. Then one day… came back from the hospital with a baby." He ducked his head. "But… it wasn't what it looked like. There were private adoptions. It was shameful not to be able to have children of your own. So you did what you had to to convince everyone that you did. That the little blond-haired baby you brought home one day really was your own."

Zachary let his breath out in a whoosh. He stared at Mr. and Mrs. Downy in disbelief. "Bridget is adopted?"

"Things were different back then. They were changing, but… there were still circles… people who would look down their noses if they thought that you had done something like that instead of being able to conceive a child of your own."

"So this whole conversation…" Zachary made a circular gesture to indicate what they had just finished talking about. "About your medical history… none of that matters. Because Bridget isn't your biological child. She doesn't carry your genes."

Mrs. Downy nodded, looking shamefaced. "She doesn't know."

"Bridget doesn't know she's adopted?"

"No."

Zachary took several deep breaths, feeling like he couldn't get enough oxygen. Not a panic attack. He was just so shocked he couldn't seem to work his diaphragm properly anymore. Breathing didn't feel natural.

"Bridget doesn't know that you adopted her. She thinks she is your biological child."

They both nodded this time. Mr. Downy looked studiously out the window. Mrs. Downy was staring at the photo album still in Zachary's lap.

"So Bridget didn't lie about it. She has no idea."

"We have meant to tell her…" Mrs. Downy started, "but it has never worked out. The time has never been right. Just when we get ready to tell her… something will happen. And it doesn't feel right. Now that she's older… it feels like the time has passed. And to tell her while she's pregnant… and struggling with this pregnancy… I just can't do that to her now."

"She needs to know now. She needs to understand the DNA results she got back on the babies and to know what it means for her. And to know that she could have Huntington's Disease herself." Zachary shook his head in disbelief. "Why wouldn't you tell her that when she was going in for her IVF? Explain to her that you don't know her genetic heritage. She could have had counseling and testing before she got pregnant."

"I didn't see what good that would do."

"And when Gordon asked about predispositions to diseases that run in your family? You never thought that maybe it was important for him to know the truth instead of the lies you had been telling all these years?" Zachary knew his words were harsh, but he couldn't understand how they could have gone for decades without ever revealing what they knew about Bridget's heritage. "Why did you lie to him? Why didn't you tell him then?"

"We couldn't tell him and not her. It's our responsibility to tell Bridget…"

"But you didn't. You never told either of them that there was more to it."

"We've tried," Mrs. Downy said.

"You don't know how hard it is," Mr. Downy chimed in. It was strangely incongruous to have this man who Zachary had always seen as a confident, competent man, complain that it was too hard to tell his daughter where she had come from. His protest was strangely childlike.

"I've never had to do it," Zachary agreed. "I can't judge you. I don't know how I would have handled it in the same situation. But you have to tell her now! You have to explain to her that she's the one carrying the Huntington's gene, and she needs to be tested herself."

Neither of them jumped up and volunteered to be the one to break the news to Bridget. Zachary sat, looking at them and looking at the little girl in the pictures.

He had told her about his own tragedies, how he had lost his biological parents and been raised in foster care. And she'd had no idea that their lives were parallels. She thought her life was the complete opposite, having been born as Mr. and Mrs. Downy's natural child and raised by them from birth.

In the end, they agreed to call Gordon. Not Bridget. They couldn't yet find a way to break the news to her. But they would talk to Gordon, explain that they had lied to him. Gordon needed to hear that and to know that it wasn't any wrongdoing on the part of the clinic that had led to the two babies carrying the Huntington's gene. He needed to know that it wasn't Forest McLachlan.

Nor had his wife cheated on him. Instead… a fraud had been perpetrated on all of them. They had been lied to by Bridget's parents right from the start. And then, they would discuss how to best approach Bridget with the revelation.

Bridget was not going to like it.

Zachary was glad that it wasn't going to be up to him to break the news to his ex-wife. If he told her something like that, he would deserve the wrath she poured out upon him. She needed to hear it from the people she loved, not from her ex-husband. He didn't need to be her target anymore.

And after they told her that she was adopted, they needed to tell her the rest.

35

Gordon sat on the Downys' couch like a statue, his face as gray as stone. He could have been a sculpture sitting there. He didn't move. Zachary couldn't even see him breathing. It was like he had been frozen in time.

Zachary couldn't imagine what was going through his head. He had believed that there had been a switch made at the clinic. To hear now that his wife was not only adopted, but that she might have Huntington's Disease must have been devastating.

Not only his babies, but his wife too.

And if she was already having symptoms, then they didn't get to wait until she was seventy years old. They didn't have the luxury of waiting for a cure to the dreadful disease. If she had it now, her days were already numbered.

"Then it wasn't that man," Gordon said finally. "That lab worker at the clinic."

"No," Zachary confirmed. "I guess he got spooked by our investigation and ran, but he wasn't the one who had the Huntington's gene."

"It was Bridget." He looked at Mr. and Mrs. Downy. "It was Bridget all along."

"We don't *know* that," Mr. Downy pointed out. "Not until further tests are done." He shot a look at Zachary. "Just because she's been moody lately, that doesn't mean she has Huntington's Disease. That hasn't been established."

"No," Gordon agreed. He swallowed and looked at Zachary. His eyes said it all. He had seen the changes too. He was more aware than any of them of the emotional changes that Bridget had been going through. And maybe he was aware of other symptoms he had not acknowledged before. The Downys had said that there was no Huntington's Disease in their family, and he had believed what they had said, because it was what he wanted to hear.

Like Bridget's parents, he wanted to believe that there wasn't anything wrong with Bridget. That she was just emotional. Stressed. Hormonal. That it was because of the cancer treatments.

The alternative was too heartbreaking.

"What does that mean to the girls?" Gordon asked bleakly. "If Bridget has symptoms now, what does that mean for them?"

"They've inherited an expanded Huntington's allele," Zachary said. "They'll likely get it around the same age."

"But she'll abort," Mrs. Downy said. "There won't be any babies."

"Can she do that?" Gordon looked at Zachary. "Is she competent to make a choice like that?"

Zachary looked into Gordon's dark brown eyes, feeling like he was drowning in the depths. Could Bridget even make that decision for herself anymore? And if it fell to Gordon to make that decision, what would he decide?

Gordon put his face in his hands and shook his head.

They sat for a long time. Consoling each other and trying to help each other through the terrible news. Zachary wasn't sure what he could do for Gordon to help him keep it together. If Zachary was still Bridget's husband, he had no idea how he would have handled the news. It would have been impossible. And making the medical decisions for everyone would be overwhelming. Even stoic Gordon was shaken to the core.

Eventually, Gordon left. He would pick Bridget up. Inform her that they had been invited to dinner at her parents' house. And when she got there, they would find a way to break the news to her.

Zachary sat there, watching Gordon's car drive away. It was time for him to leave. He didn't want to be there when Gordon and Bridget returned. He wouldn't be a welcome guest at that conversation.

He had been fiddling with his notepad in his pocket, and he pulled it out now. He flipped through the pages, looking at all of the questions and scenarios that he had scribbled down when it occurred to him that Bridget herself was the one with Huntington's Disease. Not just carrying the gene, but showing symptoms. He flipped through the pages slowly.

"What do you know about Bridget's biological parents? Do you have any background information? Their medical history? There are laws that will allow an adoptee to find out important medical information…"

Mr. and Mrs. Downy looked at each other. Mrs. Downy turned back to Zachary. "Her biological parents are dead."

"Both of them? How do you know that? She was an orphan when you adopted her?"

The two of them nodded in unison. Zachary wondered whether it was the truth or just another lie of convenience. It would be easier for them if there were no medical history? They would only have to reveal the absolute minimum—that Bridget had been adopted. They wouldn't have to share anything else about what kind of people her biological family had been.

"What happened to them?" Zachary drilled.

Parents of infants didn't just conveniently drop dead. There had to be some backstory. They had to know something about how they had died.

"I don't see how that is relevant," Mr. Downy said. "There is no way for us to get their family history. It's a dead end."

"You must have been told something about them. What kind of family she came from, if she was born in the United States or overseas. Even if her parents are dead, there could be extended family members. We might be able to find grandparents or cousins and start building a family tree."

"What does that matter?" Mrs. Downy asked, her voice teary. "If she has Huntington's Disease, what else do you need to know? What does it matter how many people in her biological family might have had it?"

She had a point there. "What if Bridget wants to know where she came from? She might want to know more about her biological ancestry. Or to meet blood relations while she still can. You've kept all of that from her."

"She doesn't need to know anything about them."

Zachary knew better. While some adopted children were not interested in knowing where they came from, most of those he had met felt that there was something missing from their lives if they didn't know anything about their biological family. They felt incomplete without it. They longed to meet someone who was related to them by blood, even if it wasn't a parent or sibling.

"She came from somewhere. You've denied her heritage."

"She won't want to know."

"What if she does?" Zachary was thinking about how he could help Bridget. He knew a genealogist who worked with DNA. She could search public ancestry databases, find her relatives, and then start building them into a family tree. Even without Mr. and Mrs. Downy's cooperation or Bridget being able to unseal her records, they could find out something about the people she had come from.

"You can't search," Mrs. Downy said, clearly reading Zachary's expression. "You can't do that to her."

"To her? I would be doing it *for* her. I would be helping her."

"No, you wouldn't. You can't… it would be cruel to do that to her."

Zachary frowned at this. Researching Bridget's heritage would be cruel? How did that make any sense? He would be giving her what she needed. A sense of where she had come from. The comfort of biological family supporting her through her decline. Knowing her whole self.

Mr. Downy shook his head at his wife. "Don't. Don't say anything else."

She rubbed her eyes. Her makeup was getting wiped away. She looked older and more vulnerable. Like a child and an old woman at the same time.

"He's going to look. And you know he can find things. He'll… he'll ruin everything."

Zachary sat forward in his seat. What was she so worried about? Was the adoption not legal? She couldn't just be concerned about the revelation that she was infertile. Not anymore. Society had changed since then.

"You can't hide the truth forever. I can figure it out. If you have a good reason Bridget shouldn't know, then tell me. Because otherwise, I'm going to assume that it's just to cover your own errors."

"What gives you the right?" Mr. Downy demanded, color suffusing his face.

"I want the best for her. Especially… if she has Huntington's Disease like I think she does. I want her to be happy for what time she has."

"She's perfectly happy without knowing anything about what happened before she came to us," Mrs. Downy put in. "She's our daughter now, it's like nothing ever happened. Sometimes I even forget that I didn't give birth to her. When Gordon came and started asking about family medical history, I didn't even remember at first that Bridget doesn't share our genes. It was just so natural to think of her being a part of us."

Zachary shrugged, irritated at their insistence. "Fine. If she asks for my help, you know I will help her. And I can do it. I can find out what family she came from. Help her to meet her extended family. Whatever she wants me to do."

They knew that was true even without his saying anything about it. He had always been devoted to Bridget. He would always do whatever she needed him to.

The two of them looked at each other. Zachary waited, sure they would break. If Bridget really wanted to find out about her biological family, she would. There was no point in their becoming estranged from her because they wouldn't give her the answers she wanted.

Mr. Downy rubbed his forehead slowly. "It was a very tragic story," he said slowly. "I haven't had to think about it for years."

36

Zachary went back home to Kenzie. He felt wrung out. Enervated. It had been an emotional day. On the one hand, he was glad that he didn't have to be there when they told Bridget the truth about her birth. On the other, he was sorry he couldn't see her. Even just a fleeting moment, passing on the street as he left and she arrived. He'd been watching for Gordon and Bridget as he left, hoping to catch a glimpse of her.

Some day in the future, she wouldn't be there anymore. There would be no chance of running into her in town, at the gas station, or her favorite restaurant. No flash of her yellow bug in traffic. No outrage if he pocket-dialed Gordon. She would be gone from his life forever. Something that he had never believed. She had always come back, asking him a favor, checking in to make sure he was still alive, telling Kenzie that she was making a mistake.

"Hey." Kenzie greeted him with a kiss and searched his face, looking concerned. "How are you? What's going on?"

He shook his head. "It's been quite a day."

"Come on in," she ushered him into the living room. He noticed that she did not have anything cooking. Either she had just gotten home, or she'd had something light to eat without him. He sat down and she sat sideways on the couch so her legs were across his lap and she could see his face as they talked.

"So what's been going on?" she asked. "Is it your case, or did something happen at the Petersons?"

"Things went pretty well for dinner with Pat's family. They went home last night; I didn't see them today. But I sort of… missed the latter part of the meal."

She raised an eyebrow.

"I suddenly… had an insight into the case. I had to focus and follow up on it. So I kind of ducked out for the end of dinner."

Kenzie rolled her eyes, grinning. She'd had to deal with him getting distracted like that enough times. At least she knew it wasn't just her. He did it to other people too. "I'm sure Pat and Lorne understood."

Zachary nodded. "Yeah, Lorne said that it was okay… Pat understood. I didn't plan to do that to his family, though. I'm sure they thought I was being really rude."

"Well, they might as well get to know the real Zachary right from the start. No false assumptions."

"I suppose. Pat seemed to be okay the next day… I just wonder if he was covering up how upset he was."

"Like Dr. B says, if you don't tell someone what you're thinking, don't expect them to read your mind."

"Yeah. I don't like to disappoint Pat. He's been through enough lately."

"None of that is your fault either. But that was yesterday. What happened today? It was your investigation, then?"

"Yeah. I had this idea that I needed to follow up on today."

"And how did that turn out?"

"Well… some testing will need to be done, but I think I was right."

"You got your culprit? The fertility clinic employee who contaminated the samples?"

"It turns out… the Huntington's came from the mother."

"I thought she was tested."

"No, she didn't want to be tested. We just had her negative family history. There weren't any cases of Huntington's or possible Huntington's in her family."

"So you think she has the intermediate allele? But how could you know that?"

"No. I think she has Huntington's." Zachary closed his eyes and for a few minutes, just let his mind swim in the darkness behind his lids, trying to come to terms with what he had discovered. The whole process that he had started in motion.

Kenzie bent closer to him and rubbed his shoulder and back. "That's sad. I'm sorry. One of her parents, then, was intermediate. And they passed the expanded gene to her."

"She was adopted."

"Oooh…" Kenzie thought about that. "Wow, okay. She was adopted, so the family history was wrong. Did she not understand that she could have inherited it from her bio family? I know people have disconnects, sometimes, but…"

Zachary pressed his palms to his eyes.

"You need something for your head."

"No. Nothing tonight."

She didn't press. Zachary needed to be in control of his own medications. She had learned that he was better at anticipating what he might need and avoiding interactions than she was, so she needed to leave that to him.

"Do you want to put something on the TV? Chill out for a while?"

He should probably do as she suggested, just put the case out of his mind and relax with her for the rest of the evening. But he couldn't. It was just too upsetting.

"Kenzie… it's Bridget." He pulled his hands away from his eyes and blinked at her.

Kenzie frowned, studying him. "What's Bridget?"

"It was Gordon who came to me. It was her twins that tested positive for Huntington's Disease."

Kenzie's eyes widened. "Bridget's twins?" She started to connect the dots. Her jaw dropped open. "Bridget was adopted? You think *she* has Huntington's Disease?"

Zachary nodded. His chest hurt, like a heavy weight was being pressed down on it. As much as he had wished to be able to get over Bridget and to put his relationship with her behind him, he had never imagined that it would be this way.

He wanted her to be happy. He wanted himself and Kenzie to be happy. He didn't care so much about Gordon. But he had still wanted Bridget to be happy and the thought that she might have Huntington's Disease was a crushing blow.

Kenzie's face was a mosaic of emotions. Shock, anger, sympathy, all fighting for a place.

"Oh, my..." Kenzie trailed off and blew out a puff of air, thinking about it. "Do you really think so?" Her mind was going rapidly through what she knew of Bridget, both what she had experienced and Zachary's history with her. "You think that all of her drama, her anger, that's because of Huntington's?" She pressed her feet against his leg, digging in her toes, wiggling them. "Oh, Zachary."

"What do you think? Am I way off base? I mean... all along, you've been saying that she's the one who is unbalanced, that it wasn't a rational response to my... mistakes. Do you think that she could be... having episodes because of Huntington's Disease?"

"Yeah. She'll have to get in to be tested to confirm it."

Zachary nodded. "Gordon was going to... talk her into getting tested. He knows someone. He wouldn't have to wait; they could get it done right away. I guess they need to do more than just do a DNA test to see if she has this expanded gene. There are other things they need to do to confirm that... she has active Huntington's Disease."

"Yeah. I don't know all of the ins and outs, but of course just having the gene doesn't mean you have the disease yet. But with her behavior... if you're right and all along she's been getting worse because of Huntington's Disease..." Kenzie shook her head. "You know the prognosis is not good. You know how the disease progresses."

"Yeah. I know. Like having dementia and Parkinson's and Lou Gehrig's all at once. And eventually... she won't be able to communicate. Won't be able to swallow. Or to get around."

Kenzie nodded grimly. "I wouldn't wish it on my worst enemy."

"Even Bridget?"

"How can you think that? Of course not. I wouldn't wish it on her or anyone else. Ever."

Zachary massaged his head again, hoping to be able to relieve the headache.

"Have you had anything to eat?" Kenzie asked.

"No. I don't think so."

"Low blood sugar isn't going to help the situation. What do you want?"

"I'll just heat something up. You don't need to make anything special."

"I'm not offering to make anything special. I'll warm you up some left-overs or pull something out of the freezer. Or a sandwich, if you want."

"You're tired too. I can make it."

Kenzie got to her feet. "You're so stubborn sometimes. I'm getting you something to eat. You can speak up now and say what you want, or I'll surprise you."

Zachary thought he should get up and help her, or at least move to the kitchen table where it was easier to talk to her while they waited for the microwave and while Zachary ate. But he didn't have the energy to move from where he sat.

He didn't offer any suggestions. Kenzie opened the fridge and checked the contents of the various bowls of leftovers before selecting one. She put it in the microwave and started it warming.

Zachary closed his eyes and was surprised when she sat down next to him again. He hadn't felt the passage of time. He opened his eyes and looked at Kenzie. She handed him a bowl of leftover frozen lasagna.

"Thanks." Zachary put it onto his portable desk so that he wouldn't spill, and took a couple of bites. He loved lasagna, but he could barely taste it.

"Why would Gordon involve you?" Kenzie asked, her voice betraying anger. "Of all of the private investigators… why did he have to pick you? He knew you would be too close to the issue. That was really rotten of him."

Zachary was surprised by the strength of her words. Was it really that bad? "He knew that I already knew Bridget's schedule, that I would see if there was anything out of the ordinary. Remember that at the beginning, we were looking for evidence that she'd had an affair, thinking maybe the twins had been conceived naturally."

"That was always a long shot. He had to know that it was more likely to be tampering at the clinic."

"I guess. But we thought… at least I thought… there would be safe-guards in place at the clinic to ensure something like that couldn't happen. I just figured… that it wouldn't. That there wasn't any way an employee could swap his own sperm in."

"Gordon didn't suspect that Bridget had Huntington's?"

Zachary thought back to Gordon's shocked expression when they had told him everything. His ashen complexion. The way he sat there, frozen, not wanting to believe what they had told him. Was that the face of a man who had suspected it all along?

"No. From his reaction today… I don't think there's any way he thought she might have it. He was… as white as a sheet. He could barely talk. And Gordon is never in that state. He didn't know. I'm sure of it."

"What a horrible shock. I can't imagine how it must have hit him. This woman that he's been living with for a couple of years… that he was hoping to start a family with…? It's just too tragic. I don't know how she could have hidden it from him. It should have been obvious that something was wrong."

"I didn't pick up on it. Neither did you. We all just thought… that she was overwrought. I thought she had good reason to be as mad as she was. I wasn't a very good husband."

"Not being a very good husband doesn't make a woman completely unhinged. The things that Bridget has been doing—the tantrums over you being someplace by coincidence, acting like she cares and wants to be involved and then dropping you again once she has what she wanted, just the intensity of her anger—that wasn't because of something you did."

Zachary turned that over in his mind, trying to figure out if what Kenzie said made sense. He had already been over it a hundred times in his mind in the past twenty-four hours. He had worked it through in his notebook, thinking about the various scenarios, trying to weigh Bridget's behavior against some kind of standard of normal responses.

It was hard for him to do. He'd faced a lot of anger and emotional behavior in the past. Much of it felt undeserved or like an overreaction to him. To the point that he no longer trusted his own judgment over what was normal.

He poked at his lasagna and mused, "What would I have done if I'd figured it out while we were still married?"

37

She's just here in the hospital as they run the tests," Gordon informed Zachary gravely. "She's had a couple of falls that she hadn't told me about, and they're concerned with the possibility that she could do harm to the twins if she falls again. After the testing… we'll see."

"You didn't know?" Zachary asked.

"I know she's been clumsy lately. Just chalked it up to being pregnant. I've read that a lot of women bump into things, drop things, trip over things. Their bodies go through so many changes; it's only natural. I knew she'd had a couple of accidents. Tripping before sitting on the couch or bed. Catching herself on a wall. She would laugh it off, say that she was getting as big as a house. Even though, of course, she isn't."

"But she told the doctor that she's fallen down?"

"No." Gordon rolled his eyes. "Her assistant. The girl who comes to help her with things she wasn't strong enough to do after the cancer treatments. She knew but hadn't told me. Bridget wouldn't let her."

"Ah." Zachary nodded. Of course Bridget wouldn't want Gordon to know about it. She would keep it quiet. Write it off as just being clumsy because she was pregnant. And when she was no longer pregnant and was still bumping into things and falling down, there would be another excuse. Being tired. Getting up too fast. Having a bit of anemia. Something innocuous to cover up the increasing difficulties she was having.

"How did she... take it? Hearing that she might have Huntington's?" Zachary had problems forming the words, but managed to get them out. He hated that Bridget had to go through this.

"As well as can be expected... she was angry. Said that we were all interfering with her life. Didn't know what we were talking about. That everything is fine and she hasn't been experiencing any difficulties or changes in behavior. But in the end... resigned, I guess. She'll let them run the tests. She says that will prove that she doesn't have Huntington's. I hope to heaven she's right... but I think you and I both know..."

Zachary nodded. He swallowed hard. Since reading that people with Huntington's Disease often had problems swallowing, it seemed like every time he swallowed, he was going to choke. Sympathetic symptoms.

He badly wanted it not to be true. He wanted Bridget to be well.

"The prognosis isn't as bad as all that," Gordon said bracingly. "She could live another twenty years after diagnosis. It's not like it's going to take her in a year, like with cancer."

But what would those years be like? Bridget was already declining. She would need care. Gordon would pay for some sort of care worker at home. For as long as they could make it work. But eventually, it would be too much for home care. Bridget would have to go to a nursing home. She would gradually lose control of all functions. She would be a prisoner in her own body.

"She knows that I'm coming?" he asked Gordon.

Gordon nodded. "She wants to talk to you." He rolled his eyes heavenward and gave a wide shrug. He didn't mention anything about how Bridget had ranted after Zachary had mistakenly called Gordon at home. Bridget didn't want Zachary until she wanted him. She would scream and harangue and tell him that he had to stay away from her or she'd have him put in jail, until she wanted him to do something for her, and then she would be sweet as honey again, talking him into doing something he knew he shouldn't. Just as Gordon himself had done.

Zachary stopped before they got to Bridget's door. "So, Gordon..."

His eyebrows went up.

"We never really had a chance to talk about McLachlan. I know I left you messages, but..."

Gordon shrugged. "He ran. Maybe he wasn't involved in anything to do with Bridget's pregnancy, but he still bolted when you started asking questions. That suggests that he's guilty of something."

"I just wondered… whether you had anything to do with that."

Gordon gazed at him. "I hired you to investigate. So, yes, if asking questions prompted him to run, I guess I'm responsible for that."

"I meant… personally. Did you go over there to talk to him?"

Or to try to get answers out of him another way. Or maybe he hadn't even tried to get any answers. Maybe he figured he knew enough already and just took action. Or hired someone else to do that part.

"Of course not," Gordon said blandly. "You didn't even give me his address."

It would have been easy enough to find. Heather hadn't had any trouble getting it. The receptionist at the clinic had it and verified it over the phone.

"So you didn't do anything when you thought he might have been the one tampering with samples."

Gordon shook his head. His face was smooth. There was no sign that he was lying. There never was.

"The police haven't been able to find any sign of him yet," Zachary told him.

"I suppose he left the state again. Maybe he went somewhere warmer this time. Florida or California. Who knows? He'll ditch his car, take on a new identity, and forge references to get himself a new job. None of us will ever see him again."

His words had the ring of finality. *None of us will ever see him again.*

Zachary couldn't think of anything else to say. If Gordon had anything to do with McLachlan's disappearance, he would never admit it.

He walked with Gordon into Bridget's hospital room.

Bridget was sitting in bed. Zachary's heart gave a tug as he approached her. She was still so beautiful. Cancer and treatment and the early stages of Huntington's Disease had not taken that away from her. She looked more fragile, and yet she glowed with radiance from the pregnancy, as she sat there with one hand over her pregnant belly.

Zachary was reminded of the pictures of Mrs. Downy, pretending to be pregnant, cradling her fake stomach in her hands. But Bridget wasn't faking. The lives of those two babies depended on her decisions.

Her blond hair fell in waves around her face. She was wearing makeup in spite of being in a hospital bed. She wore one of her own nightgowns rather than a hospital johnny. She looked at Gordon, and then at Zachary, a quick movement, analyzing them both.

"Zachary. I didn't know if you would come."

Of course she had known he would come. He would always come when she called.

Bridget smiled sweetly at Gordon. "Could I talk to Zachary alone, Gordon?"

"Of course, sweetheart." He bent to kiss her on the top of the head. "Don't tire yourself out."

"I can talk to him without tiring myself out."

"You don't have a lot of energy with the pregnancy. You need to be careful."

She waved him away. Gordon nodded to Zachary and walked out of the room. There was a man with self-confidence. Zachary couldn't imagine letting an ex-lover sit alone with his wife.

As if anyone could prevent Bridget from doing what she put her mind to. Zachary sat down in a metal and plastic chair near the bed. Not too close to her. Maintaining a respectful distance so that everyone would know that he wasn't doing anything improper.

"So… I guess all of this was your idea," Bridget said, indicating the room around her. "*You* decided that I have Huntington's Disease."

"I don't know," Zachary said. "It was only a thought; I can't prove it. I hope I'm wrong. But if you do… they can give you medications that can help you feel better…"

"Nothing is going to make me feel better right now. Would you feel better if you knew you were going to lose control of your body and your mind and die? Just how would that make you feel?"

"I'm sorry."

Thirty seconds, and he was already apologizing to her. Not for something that he had done wrong, just for generally being in her line of fire. For guessing before anyone else had what was wrong with her.

"They don't know for sure yet, do they?" he asked tentatively.

Gordon had said that she didn't believe she had Huntington's, but she seemed remarkably resigned to having it.

"We'll see what they find out."

Zachary nodded. "I'm sorry. I wanted to help. I never wanted this."

"Gordon should not have involved you in… our mess."

Zachary looked away. He already knew that. Everybody involved knew that. But he felt like it was partly his mess too. He still wanted to be a part of Bridget's life. Even though they were divorced, he still felt like they would be a part of each other's lives forever.

"Zachary." Bridget put her hand on the rail of the bed. Closer to him. Like she was going to take his hand and hold it as they talked intimately about the whole thing.

He swallowed again. His throat felt stretched out and dry. He should have bought a water bottle at the cafeteria. Nothing felt natural. Like it was his own body that was shutting down instead of Bridget's.

"Zachary, I need you to do something for me." Her expression was soft. Her eyes doe-like.

"Anything," Zachary assured her. Though he already knew what it was, and he already knew that he would never do what she wanted him to.

"I need… I need to find out more about my biological parents." She shook her head in wonder. "I can't even believe I'm saying that. I never knew I had any other parents. I never thought that I wasn't a Downy at birth. It's a shock."

"Yeah. I imagine it would be quite disconcerting."

"You're telling me. Anyway… you're good at research and background and hunting down information and missing people. I want you to find out about my parents. Their names, what they did, why they ended up giving me up for adoption. Mom says they are dead, but I don't know if that's true. I need to find out. Soon."

Zachary nodded. "Okay. Let me look into it."

"I want to know while… I'm still myself. I need to know all about who I am."

"Yeah. That makes sense. Well, you know me… how many different places I lived. But I always knew where I came from. I at least knew my biological parents, even if they weren't a part of my life anymore."

"Yes. And I need that. I need that connection to the past."

"Of course."

"I'll give you all of the information I can. Don't talk to Mom and Dad about it. I'm sure they'll just tell you lies. But I want the truth."

38

Zachary would never tell Bridget that he already knew what she was looking for.

He had known that it wouldn't be before-bed reading material, but he couldn't stop himself from a series of internet searches which he had hoped would turn up the tragic story of Bridget's biological parents. She was nearly forty, so he would only be able to find anything about the incident online if someone had digitized the papers it was reported in at the time or someone had used it as a case study for some research project.

He sifted through various stories that had similarities to what Mr. Downy had finally described to Zachary. He discarded them all, searching deeper and deeper. He might have to go to the library or some hall of archives to find hard copy papers from the time. But he would find them. He would get them somehow.

Then he found a medical paper. A student who had done a survey of similar cases. Michael Webber had described it in detail. He had covered their backgrounds, the events that had led up to it, and the incident itself. The bare, cold facts. Zachary sat looking at the screen, oblivious to everything around him, for some indefinite period of time. Until Kenzie was tapping on his leg again, trying to bring him back to a conversation that he had not been a full partner in.

"What are you reading?" she asked, looking at his screen. "Looks like a medical journal from here."

Zachary nodded. "Yes."

"Need some help with it? I can interpret for you."

He adjusted his screen a little, unsure what to tell her. "It's a case I was looking for. Sort of a tragic one…"

Kenzie nodded. She worked in the medical examiner's office. She'd heard more than her share of tragic cases.

"It's an account of a murder-suicide." Zachary let his eyes run down the columns, catching a word here and there. He'd already read it through a couple of times and, in spite of the medical jargon, he understood perfectly what had happened.

"Murder-suicide in a medical journal? Why? What is so interesting about it?"

"Just a few months before the murder-suicide took place… the husband had been diagnosed with Huntington's Disease."

"Oh." Kenzie shook her head. "I know that the suicide rate for Huntington's Disease is pretty high. It's a terrible disease; people don't want to face it, knowing what's going to happen to them. And depression is a big part of Huntington's. They don't know whether the suicidal ideation is because of the prognosis, or because of what's going on in the brain with the neurotransmitters."

"It's pretty bleak. I don't think *I* would want to go on, knowing I was going to face that."

"But murder, I don't think that's as common. I know there is aggression, sometimes assault of caregivers. But that's not the same as murder."

"The medical paper breaks it down. Number of cases, how common it is. Attempted murder is more common than murder itself. Because of the movement disorder, they often don't succeed."

"Still, tragic," Kenzie commented.

"Especially in this case. They left behind an infant child."

"Oh. Poor thing."

"A little blond girl. They didn't have a genetic test for Huntington's back then, so she was never tested to see if she inherited it."

"Whatever happened to her, I wonder."

Zachary looked at Kenzie, surprised that she hadn't picked up on the connections. "She was adopted. Raised without ever knowing what had happened to her biological parents, or even that she had been adopted. So she never knew that she had a fifty percent chance of having inherited Huntington's Disease from her father."

Kenzie's eyes widened. "Bridget?" she asked gently.

Zachary nodded and closed his eyes. "Yes. Bridget."

Did you enjoy this book? Reviews and recommendations are vital to making a book successful.

Please leave a review at your favorite book store or review site and share it with your friends.

Don't miss the following bonus material:
Sign up for mailing list to get a free ebook
Read a sneak preview chapter
Other books by P.D. Workman
Learn more about the author

Sign up for my mailing list at pdworkman.com and get Gluten-Free Murder for free!

PREVIEW OF DOCTORED DEATH

CHAPTER 1

Zachary tried to stay in the zone he was in, just on the border between sleeping and waking, for as long as he could. He felt warm and safe and at peace, and it was such a good feeling he wanted to remain there as long as he could before the anxieties of consciousness started pouring in.

The warm body alongside his shifted and Zachary snuggled in, trying not to leave the cozy pocket of blankets he was in.

Kenzie murmured something that ended in 'some space' and wriggled away from him again. Zachary let her go. She needed her sleep, and if he smothered her, she wouldn't be quick to invite him back.

Kenzie. He was back together with Kenzie and he had stayed the night at her house. It was the first time he'd gone there instead of her joining him in his apartment, which was currently not safe for them to sleep at because the police had busted the door in. It would have to be fixed before he could sleep there.

Kenzie lived in a little house that was a hundred times better than Zachary's apartment, which wasn't difficult since he had started from scratch after the fire that burned down his last apartment. While he was earning more as a private investigator than he ever had before, thanks to a few high profile murder cases, he wasn't going to sink a lot of money into the apartment until he had built up a strong enough reserve to get him through several months of low income.

Zachary had been surprised by some of the high-priced items he had seen around Kenzie's home the night before. He supposed he shouldn't have been surprised, given the cherry-red convertible she drove, but he'd always assumed she was saddled with significant debts from medical school and that she would not be able to afford luxuries.

Maybe that was the reason that she had never invited him into her territory before. She didn't want him to see the huge gap in their financial statuses.

Once Zachary's brain started working, reviewing the night before and considering Kenzie's circumstances as compared to his, he couldn't shut it back off and return to that comfortable, happy place he had been just before waking. His brain was grinding away, assessing how worried he should be. Did any of it change their relationship? Did it mean that Kenzie looked down on him? Considered him inferior? She had never treated him that way, but did she think it, deep down inside?

Once he left her house, would he ever be invited back? He had only been there under exceptional circumstances, and while he hoped that it was a sign that Kenzie was willing to reconcile and work on their relationship again—as long as he was—he was afraid that it might just have been one moment of weakness. One that she would regret when she woke up and had a chance to reconsider.

With his brain cranking away at the problem and finding new things to worry about, Zachary couldn't stay in bed. He shifted around a few times, trying to find a position that was comfortable enough that he would just drift back to sleep, he knew that it was impossible. His body was restless and would not return to sleep again so easily.

He slid out of the bed and squinted, trying to remember the layout of the room and any obstacles. The sky was just starting to lighten, forcing a little gray light around the edges of Kenzie's blinds and curtains. Enough to see dark shapes around him, but not enough to be confident he wouldn't trip over something. Zachary felt for the remainder of his clothes and clutched them to him as he cautiously made his way to the bedroom door and out into the hallway.

He shut the door silently behind him so that he wouldn't wake Kenzie up. There was an orange glow emanating from the bathroom, so he found his way there without knocking over any priceless decor. He shut the door and turned on the main light. It was blinding after the night-light. Zachary squeezed his eyes shut and waited for them to adjust to the light that penetrated his eyelids, and then gradually opened them to look around.

Everything was clean and tidy and smelled fresh. Definitely a woman's domain rather than a bachelor pad like Zachary's. He needed to upgrade if he expected her to spend any time at his apartment. He'd used her ensuite the night before rather than the main bath, and even though it was more cluttered with her makeup and hair and bath products, it was also cleaner and brighter than Zachary's apartment bathroom.

He spent a couple of minutes with his morning routine, splashing water on his face and running a comb over his dark buzz-cut before making his way to the living room, where he'd left his overnight bag when he and Kenzie had adjourned for the night. He pulled out his laptop and set it on the couch while it booted up, wandering into the kitchen and sorting out her single-cup coffee dispenser to make himself breakfast.

CHAPTER 2

It was a few hours before he heard Kenzie stirring in the bedroom, and eventually, she made her way out to the living room. She had an oriental-style dressing gown wrapped around her. She rubbed her eyes, hair mussed from sleep.

Kenzie yawned. "Good morning."

"Hi." Zachary gave her a smile that he hoped expressed the warmth and gratitude he felt toward her for letting him back into her life, even if it was only for one night. "How was your sleep?"

"Good." Kenzie covered another yawn. "How about you? Did you actually get any sleep?"

"I slept great." Zachary wasn't lying. He didn't usually sleep well away from home. For that matter, he didn't sleep that well at home either. But after facing off with Lauren's killer and dealing with the police, he had been exhausted, and the comfort he had found in Kenzie's arms and the luxurious sheets in her bed had quickly lulled him to sleep. There was a slight dip in her mattress, testifying to the fact that she normally slept alone, and that had made it natural for him to gravitate toward her during the night. It had been reassuring to have someone else in bed with him after what seemed like an eon of lonely nights.

It was the best night's sleep he'd had in a long time.

"You couldn't have slept for more than three or four hours," Kenzie countered.

"Yes… but it was still a really good sleep."

"Well, good." She bent down to kiss him on the forehead.

Zachary felt a rush of warmth and goosebumps at the same time. She didn't seem to regret having allowed him to stay over. "Do you want coffee? I figured out the machine."

"Turn it on when you hear me get out of the shower. That should be about right."

"Do you want anything else? Bread in the toaster?"

"The full breakfast treatment? I could get used to this. Yes, a couple of slices of toast would be nice."

Zachary nodded. "Coffee and toast it is," he agreed.

He saw her speculative look, wondering whether he would actually remember or whether he would be distracted by something else.

"I'll do my best," Zachary promised. "But it better be a short shower, because if it's one of those two-hour-long ones, I might forget."

"I have to get to work today, so it had better be a quick one."

He did manage to remember to start both the coffee and the toast when she got out of the shower, and even heard the toast pop and remembered to butter it while it was hot. He had it on the table for Kenzie when she walked in, buttoning up her blouse.

"Nice!" Kenzie approved.

"Do you want jam?"

"There's some marmalade in the fridge."

Zachary retrieved the jar and made a mental note that he should get marmalade the next time he was shopping for groceries. If that was her preferred condiment, then he should make an effort to have it for her when she came to his apartment. He tried to always get things for her when he was shopping, because as Bridget put it, he ate like a Neanderthal. Not one of those fad caveman diets, but like someone who had never learned how to cook even the simplest foods. Most of his food was either ready to eat or just needed to be microwaved for a couple of minutes.

Or he could order in. He could use a phone even if he couldn't use a stove.

"So, your big case is solved," Kenzie said, "what are your plans for the day?"

"I still need to report to the client and issue my bill. Then I've got a bunch of smaller projects I should catch up on, now that I'll have some more time. And I need to get my door fixed. I wouldn't want to impose on you for too long."

Kenzie spread her marmalade carefully to the edge of the toast. "It was nice last night. I'm glad you called."

Zachary's face got warm. All they had done was to talk and cuddle, but he had needed that so badly. He had been concerned that she would be disappointed things had gone no further, so he was reassured that she had enjoyed the quiet time together too. Their relationship had been badly derailed by the abuse Zachary had suffered at Teddy Archuro's hands, which had also brought up a lot of buried memories of his time in foster care. However much he wanted to be with Kenzie, he couldn't help his own visceral reaction when things got too intimate.

"Hey," Kenzie said softly, breaking into his thoughts. "Don't do that. Come back."

Zachary tried to refocus his attention on her, to keep himself anchored to the present and not the attack.

"Five things?" Kenzie suggested, prompting Zachary to use one of the exercises his therapist had given him to help him with dissociation.

Zachary took a slow breath. "I smell… the coffee. The toast." He breathed. "Your shampoo. The marmalade. I… don't know what else."

His own sweat. He should have showered and dressed before Kenzie got up. Greeted her smelling freshly-scrubbed instead of assaulting her with the rank odor of a homeless person.

Kenzie smiled. "Better?" She studied his face.

Zachary nodded. "Yeah. Sorry."

"It's okay. It's not your fault."

He still felt inadequate. He should be able to have a pleasant morning conversation with his girlfriend without dissociating or getting mired in flashbacks. It shouldn't be that hard.

"Are you going to have something to eat? There's enough bread for you to have toast too," Kenzie teased.

"No, not ready yet."

"Well, don't forget. You still need to get your weight back up."

Zachary nodded. "I'll have something in a while."

He still hadn't eaten when he left Kenzie's. She was on her way into work, and he didn't want her to feel like she had to let him stay there in her domain while she was gone, so by the time she was ready for work, he had repacked his overnight bag and was ready to leave as well. She didn't make any comment or offer him the house while she was gone.

"Well, good luck with your report to Lauren's sister today. I know that part of the job is never fun."

Zachary nodded. "Yeah. And then collecting on the bill. Sorry your sister was murdered, but could you please pay me now?" He rolled his eyes.

Kenzie shook her head. "At least I don't have to ask for payment when I give people autopsy results."

They paused outside the door. Zachary didn't know what to say to Kenzie or how to tell her goodbye.

"Call me later," Kenzie advised. "Let me know whether you got your door fixed or not."

Zachary exhaled, relieved. She wasn't regretting having invited him in. She would put up with him for another night if he needed her.

"Thanks, I will."

Kenzie armed the burglar alarm on the keypad next to the door and shut it. Zachary heard the bolt automatically slide into place.

"See you," Kenzie said breezily. She pulled him closer by his coat lapel and gave him a brief peck on the lips. "Have a good day."

Zachary nodded, his face flushing and a lump in his throat preventing him from saying anything. Kenzie opened the garage door. Zachary turned and walked down the sidewalk to his car. He tried hard not to be needy, not to turn around and watch as she backed the car out onto the street, checking to see whether she was still watching him and would give him one more wave before she left. But he couldn't help himself.

She waved in his direction and pulled onto the street.

Late in the afternoon, Zachary headed back to his apartment, hoping to find when he got there that the door had been repaired and he could feel safe there once more. Of course, if the door had been fixed, he would need another reason to go back to Kenzie's. Or he could invite her to join him and they could go back to their usual routines. Just because she had allowed him over to her house once, that didn't mean she would be comfortable with him being there all the time.

But he could see the splintered doorframe as he walked down the hall approaching his apartment. The building manager had promised to make it a priority, but it looked like whatever subcontractor he had called hadn't yet made it there. Zachary pushed the door open and looked around.

Nothing appeared to have been rifled or taken in his absence. Of course, he didn't have much of value. He'd taken all of his electronics with him and didn't exactly have jewelry or wads of cash lying around. Anyone desperate enough to rifle his drawers and steal his shirts probably needed them worse than he did.

Though he hadn't thought about the meds in the cabinet. There were a few things in there that might have some street value.

Zachary started to walk toward the bedroom, but stopped when he heard a noise. He froze and listened, trying to zero in on it. It was probably just a neighbor moving around. Or a pigeon landing on the ledge outside his window. They spooked him sometimes with the loud flapping of their wings when they took off.

He waited, ears pricked, for the sound to be repeated.

Could it have been a person? There in his apartment?

The last time he'd thought that someone was rifling his apartment and had called the police, it had been Bridget. She'd still had a key to the old apartment. She'd checked in on him at Christmas, knowing that it was a bad time for him, and had cleaned out his medicine cabinet to ensure that he didn't overdose.

It wouldn't be Bridget this time.

She didn't have a key to the new apartment, though he would have been happy to give her one if she had wanted it. Bridget was no longer part of his life and he needed to keep his distance from her, both to avoid getting slapped with a restraining order and because he was with Kenzie, and he needed to be fair to her. There was no going back to his ex-wife. She had a new partner and was pregnant. She didn't want anything to do with him.

There was another rustle. He was pretty sure it was someone in his bedroom. But it didn't sound like they were doing anything. Just moving quietly around.

Waiting for him?

He hated to call the police and have it be a false alarm. But he also didn't want to end up with a bullet in his chest because he walked in on a burglary in progress.

Unlike private investigators on TV, Zachary didn't carry a gun. He didn't even own one. With his history of depression and self-harm, it had always been too big a risk.

Zachary eased his phone out of his pocket, moving very slowly, trying to be completely silent. He wasn't sure what he was going to do when he got it out. If he called emergency, he would have to talk to them to let them know what was going on. They wouldn't be able to triangulate his signal to a single apartment.

Just as he looked down at the screen and moved his thumb over the unlock button, it gave a loud squeal and an alert popped up on the screen. Zachary jumped so badly that it flew out of his hand, and he scrambled to catch it before it hit the floor. He wasn't well-coordinated, and he just ended up hitting it in the air and shooting it farther away from him, to smack into the wall and then land on the floor.

———

Doctored Death, Book #2 a Kenzie Kirsch Medical Thriller is coming soon!

ABOUT THE AUTHOR

Award-winning and USA Today bestselling author P.D. (Pamela) Workman writes riveting mystery/suspense and young adult books dealing with mental illness, addiction, abuse, and other real-life issues. For as long as she can remember, the blank page has held an incredible allure and from a very young age she was trying to write her own books.

Workman wrote her first complete novel at the age of twelve and continued to write as a hobby for many years. She started publishing in 2013. She has won several literary awards from Library Services for Youth in Custody for her young adult fiction. She currently has over 50 published titles and can be found at pdworkman.com.

Born and raised in Alberta, Workman has been married for over 25 years and has one son.

Please visit P.D. Workman at pdworkman.com to see what else she is working on, to join her mailing list, and to link to her social networks.

If you enjoyed this book, please take the time to recommend it to other purchasers with a review or star rating and share it with your friends!

facebook.com/pdworkmanauthor
twitter.com/pdworkmanauthor
instagram.com/pdworkmanauthor
amazon.com/author/pdworkman
bookbub.com/authors/p-d-workman
goodreads.com/pdworkman
linkedin.com/in/pdworkman
pinterest.com/pdworkmanauthor
youtube.com/pdworkman